BLOWN COVER

MARK A. HEWITT

ISBN: 978-1-61296-893-3
PUBLISHED BY BLACK ROSE WRITING
www.blackrosewriting.com

Printed in the United States of America
Suggested Retail Price (SRP) $23.95

Blown Cover is printed in Adobe Garamond Pro

For my Mother.

BLOWN COVER

I love the man that can smile in trouble, that can gather strength from distress, and grow brave by reflection.
~Thomas Paine

Prologue

July 22, 1936
Moscow

Two old men, one white the other black, were led from Stalin's Office flanked by jackbooted helmeted police. They were shocked at the proclamation that their next stop would be the Lubyanka. Epaulettes of rank and medals of valor and heroism had been ripped from their uniforms and thrown to the floor, an unmistakable sign that their lives had suddenly become worthless. Those who spoke disparagingly of "The One," the one party in power, were arrested and put in prison for spreading false rumors. Membership in the other party, the prohibited party, would at a minimum, land one in jail. The men had once loyally served the royal family and vigorously switched allegiance to the Communist Party. Their chances of being transferred to a *gulag* to die miserably of starvation or exposure decreased with every step. Breathing the words "cult" and "Bolshevik" in the same sentence in the wrong company was enough for anyone to be tortured or posed before a firing squad. No time for a blindfold. The secret policemen poked at the two septuagenarians with steely bayonets, encouraging their arthritic legs to move faster. The stripping away of their accoutrements of honor and privilege had been their death sentence.

Across the Soviet Union millions of people were being arbitrarily and capriciously labeled "enemies of the Soviet people." They were being imprisoned, exiled, or executed. Many escaped the first wave of the purges and ran to the borders with their families. Those that were caught before reaching freedom were punished as traitors on the spot with a bullet in their heads. Those with education and credentials quickly learned intelligence and loyal service to the government were no longer virtues to be admired or an immediate pass out of the country. Dozens of men, women, and children were condemned to mass graves, killed by a gauntlet of eager young men with automatic rifles.

The latest purge of the party, government, armed forces, and intelligentsia was in full bloom. Major figures in the Communist Party, old Bolsheviks, and most of the Red Army generals were being rounded up, brought before a judge or tribunal, tried, and convicted for plotting to overthrow the government. A lucky few received their charges of treason and guilty verdicts directly from the Secretary General, Joseph Stalin.

As the condemned men filed past, six other men in the antechamber waited for the Secretary General to receive them. One of the men smiled with amusement at the sight of the once famous men being hurried out of the building to their own funerals. Two tried not to tremble at the fact that Comrade Joseph Stalin had sent for them. The other three were merely curious why a group of aircraft designers had been summoned for a meeting with the head of the Communist Party.

After thirty minutes of waiting, the ten-foot tall wooden door to the Secretary General office opened. The superannuated Bolshevik leaders of the Soviet Armed Forces and the young aircraft designers, Alexander Yakovlev, Pavel Sukhoi, and Andrei Tupolev, entered. Trailing them with his hands behind his back and still sporting a pernicious smile, was Nikolai Ivanovich Yazhov, the head of the People's Commissariat for Internal Affairs, the law enforcement agency of the Soviet Union. Few knew that Yazhov directly executed the rule of power of the All Union Communist Party. Fewer still knew he was also the head of the Soviet secret police.

The office was dark and caliginous, an ascetic's cell. Comrade Secretary General Joseph Stalin was hunched over a newspaper. A single Hero of the Soviet Union medal hung from a red tab on an otherwise sterile grey uniform studded by gold buttons and offset with red epaulettes adorned with a large gold star. A thick mustache in the style of Karl Marx hid the end of a half-bent Billiard that hung lazily from the corner of his mouth. Dunhill's *Royal Yacht,* which most pipe and cigar smokers found horrendously offensive, and instantly assaulted the men's noses as they entered the office.

Shuffling feet announced their arrival in the spacious hazy office. Stalin didn't look up from the papers strewn across his desk. The desk was a simple affair of loose parts, a door-sized slab of tiger oak rested atop a pair of red mahogany file cabinets. A brushed steel lamp with a crinoline-blue glass shade and a rotary dial telephone were positioned at opposite ends of the tabletop along with a crystal and bronze inkwell set purloined from the private desk of Tsar Nicolas II. Behind him a wall map of the Soviet Union hung between gold curtains that were more appropriate for a bordello than an office.

Without looking up Stalin barked as if he were speaking from the balcony of the Kremlin. "Comrades, today we celebrate the remarkable achievements of Comrades Chekalov, Baydukov, and Belyakov who flew their airplane across the North Pole to Udd Island in the Sea of Okhotsk. They established another endurance record for the beloved workers of the Soviet Union! This accomplishment again demonstrates that the air forces of the Supreme Soviet are the most powerful on the continent." From under a brush of brows he raised his eyes to each man before he continued more somberly, "But I am deeply troubled. I learned this morning an American woman will attempt to fly around the world." He allowed the news of the aviatrix to waft among the melding of smoke and the uneven breathing of the young men.

There was a hint of malice in his voice. "Don't we have a strong woman pilot to do such things? Don't we have airplanes and women pilots that can race this American around the globe for Soviet Russia, for the Motherland?" The Secretary General sat up and packed his pipe. His pomaded, slicked back hair shone in the dull overhead lamps of the office as he waited impatiently for a response.

The men were well aware of their place in the hierarchy of the Soviet aviation industry. At the top was Joseph Stalin, a Bolshevik with an infatuation for airplanes. He would extol the virtues of the brave heroes who took to the sky when it suited him or when it was politically expedient to do so. They also knew the real story of the Secretary General who, from the moment he saw his first aircraft at the Imperial Russian Air Service, quietly lusted for an opportunity to climb in and strap on one of the rickety flying machines. But because of his susceptibility to severe bouts of motion sickness, Stalin was forced to find other ways to partake of the glory of flying airplanes as any injury or show of weakness risked his position in the party.

To glorify and acclaim the Communist Party's achievements in engineering and aviation, Stalin directed several of the fledgling aircraft designers to build airplanes that would fly higher, faster, and farther. He demanded larger airplanes with more engines and more capacity to challenge the world's aviation records which were repeatedly set and broken by a growing line of British, French, and American aviators and designers. Despite his efforts Soviet aircraft remained outdated, chronically lagging a generation behind each new advance in French, British and American designs.

In the 1920s, Stalin was incensed when the British aviators, Alcock and Brown, entered the record books for the first non-stop transatlantic flight. A year later Stalin spat on the newspaper announcement that Charles Lindbergh had set the flying world alight with the first solo non-stop crossing of the Atlantic. Stalin was enraged that his pilots and Soviet-built aircraft were not only ill-equipped but also incapable of conducting any flying operation of very long duration. Soviet pilots could barely fly a few hundred miles without encountering a seized engine or structural airframe failure leading to a crash.

Soviet aircraft were flying coffins. Dismemberment and death were real possibilities with early Soviet designs, and aerodromes surrounding Moscow were littered with the bent, mangled, and charred carcasses of flying mishaps. Pilots were crashing aircraft faster than the manufacturers could build them; undertakers were burying pilots faster than the Soviet Union Air Forces could train them. Stalin demanded more designs, more pilots, and more records.

Because of their failures several Soviet Air Force generals were hauled before a tribunal and shot for treason. Stalin fumed when manufacturers over-promised and under-delivered on airframe designs. Poor engine production sent him into a tailspin of fury. Several generals dared to point out the obvious, that Soviet aircraft technology was well behind their Anglo counterparts, and that Russian aviators didn't have the right stuff physically and mentally to do well in the international competitions. Soviet engineers, military leaders, and the press concealed the negative aspects of the nascent aviation craze and only reported on the positive.

When Stalin found out the Germans were building airships—huge flying monstrosities—to cross the ocean, he flew into another fit of rage. He became especially volatile when he learned that the Nazis were scheduling commercial zeppelin air services from Germany to South America and the United States. Another group of insolent generals and aircraft designers were rounded up, marched to the Lubyanka Prison, and never heard from again. It was the head of the Soviet secret police, Yazhov, who took great pride and zeal in personally eliminating the weakest of the Communist Party's undesirables; their blood ran in torrents in the drains of the basement of the Lubyanka.

With few achievements and fewer records in the global competition for aviation prizes and races, Stalin's obsession for control turned the Soviet aviation industry upside down. He encouraged several well-placed and trusted members of the Communist Party of America to steal the latest airframe and engine schematics and engineering drawings from a growing number of aircraft, engine, and component manufacturers throughout the United States, Britain, and France. With the purloined designs, he promoted new aircraft designers and generals and demanded greater demonstrations of the USSR's technological progress and prowess. Improvements were rapid in every stage of Soviet manufacturing when the latest plans for engines and airframes came from Washington D.C., London, or Paris on rolls of microfilm.

Stalin established a Soviet-based system of awards and internal challenges to legitimize the socialist system. By flying a complex array of polar routes originating from and returning to the Soviet Union, each establishing a new record, the Secretary General trumpeted the victories for socialism and popularized Soviet aviation culture with the masses. *Pravda* raised the status of pilots and aircraft designers praising them as heroes and turning them into role models for Soviet society. Directed by Stalin, facilitated by Yazhov, and orchestrated by his spies in the Communist Party of America, the Soviet aviation industry began to catch up to their Anglo-Franco-American rivals and became a shining symbol of progress towards the socialist-utopian future.

Stalin chuffed as he glared at the leader of the Soviet Air Force. The thick haze seemed to energize him. The secret police chief, Yazhov, never moved or changed his position. He stood as he awaited the fate of the men before him, like a bored executioner who waited for the next condemned man to walk up to the gallows to be hanged.

General Yakov Ivanovich Alksnis struggled to speak. "Yes, Comrade Stalin. An effort such as this requires much planning. I am aware of a woman, the pride of Kharkiv, Valentina Grizodubova, who has established many flight endurance records. She...is most capable. She is...."

Stalin raised his brows in surprise. The name triggered his memory. The woman had been lionized in a newspaper as the *Soviet Amelia Earhart*. It was the first encouraging thing he had heard all day, but his voice betrayed no hint of friendliness or enthusiasm as he replied, "Comrades Yakovlev, Sukhoi, and Tupolev, I believe Comrade Grizodubova would require a special airplane to fly around the world. Is this something you can do expeditiously?"

There was an unstated sense of urgency to respond, but no one was brave enough to utter a word; no one knew anything of the American woman's plans or route of flight. To answer *nyet* would be a death sentence with Yazhov marching them to the gallows. The aircraft designers swallowed hard. Sukhoi nudged the bravest of the designers. Tupolev reluctantly answered, "Yes, Comrade Secretary General. We have some new designs that could be available for test...flights in a year...or two." Yakovlev and Sukhoi looked at their comrade designer and nodded with enthusiasm. They were engineers, the builders of airplanes, not malevolent saboteurs.

Stalin looked skeptically at the designers as he puffed his pipe. His dark eyes shifted to the Soviet Navy Minister, Admiral Vladimir Orlov. "The Party approved your plan for the construction of battleships, heavy cruisers, and large submarines during the next two five-year plans. We are not in favor of the small submarines with short range that you requested. You may build three times as many of the small submarines for your money as big ones but big submarines are required to further world revolution and achieve supremacy on the seas that circumscribe the Soviet Union. I believe Comrade Grizodubova will require the services of large submarines, especially crossing the Pacific. To refuel. What is your assessment, Comrade Admiral?"

Admiral Orlov wasn't ready to die for his country but was ready to shift the focus off of himself. "Comrade Stalin, you are most generous and correct. A big fleet requires large submarines. Our latest *Pravda*-class submarine, the *Zvezda*, was recently commissioned. She will be ported in Port Arthur where she can be modified to serve Comrade Grizodubova's requirements for a Pacific crossing...*if* she has an aircraft to fly. Do we possess sufficient knowledge when the American will attempt to circumnavigate the globe?"

Not daring to look at Stalin directly, the men focused on the smoke rising from the little pipe. Stalin announced, "In one year."

The military men looked at their feet knowing that timetable was impossible. The aircraft designers shook their heads in defeat. Cookie-cutter short-range warplanes and bombers were being produced in record numbers by the three manufacturers; no one had a commercial, off-the-shelf, ultra-long-range design ready for discussion or production. It had taken two years of modifying basic warplanes to begin the polar flights within the Soviet Union. The typical result from those efforts was several dozen crashes during multiple attempts before a single aircraft was able to make the journey across the vastness of the Soviet Union.

The head of the secret police smiled. Someone in the office was going to die. The question was, "Who?" He rubbed his hands together like a pervert at a peephole waiting for a glimpse of a girl in a bathroom.

Stalin mashed more *Royal Yacht* into a dirty bowl. He relit his pipe and puffed like a steam locomotive between each word. "I would like fresh designs from each of you. I expect you to push the boundaries of airframe and engine technology even further. You have the latest designs from America and England. Improve upon them! In two days' time I will review your designs. I will chose which is best for this remarkable event. We will name Comrade Grizodubova's aircraft—*The Motherland!* You have work to do. *Go!*"

The three designers offered their gratitude and took their leave, grateful to escape the malodorous Dunhill and horrific smoke-filled room. They refused to look at the menacing Yazhov as they departed the office. The heads of the air force and navy lowered their heads in their failure. They could feel the hangman's noose being drawn tightly across their necks by the quiet, evil Yazhov behind them. Stalin asked, *sotto voce,* "You do not think this project is achievable?"

General Alksnis said, "Comrade Stalin, our aircraft engines are not as reliable as they need to be for such a project. These things take time. It's not a simple case of replicating what is found in an engineering drawing. The Americans do not easily give up their trade secrets in castings and forgings; we have to experiment to find the correct temperature range for heat treating. Our latest polar effort took two years to complete and a dozen motors. The engines were destroyed by early crankshaft failures. We lost two dozen men to accidents. And that was flying less than 9,000 kilometers, not an expected 40 or 50,000. We will need a more reliable multi-engine design, like the American's *Electra*, otherwise, we will send Comrade Grizodubova to her death. This will bring much embarrassment to the Soviet Union for poor planning and execution."

The head of the Soviet Navy said, "If the goal is to circumnavigate the earth, we must have places for the aircraft to refuel, to land in the Pacific. Islands have to be accommodated to receive airplanes. We are aware the Americans have been working to build runways, station fuel reserves, and establish radio beacons on some Pacific islands for years." Admiral Orlav added, "We will not have access to the American's runways. We will have to replicate the American's effort. Big submarines will not be enough to provide for the requisite logistics."

There was a tinge of depravity in his voice. Through stained teeth the Secretary General of the Soviet Union said, "What you are also afraid to say, Comrade General, Comrade Admiral, is that our workers cannot accelerate our industrial complex *sufficiently* to overtake the Americans even with plans and drawings provided by our comrades in America. By every sense and measure the Americans have too much of a head start. Is this correct?"

As the military men nodded, their heads created eddies in the smoke-filled room. For their insolence, they expected Yazhov to snap his fingers for Chekan soldiers to come take them away for a one-way trip to the Lubyanka.

Stalin turned livid; his eyes bulged with fury. He yanked the pipe from his mouth and tossed it in an ashtray; glowing embers scattered in and around the amber-glass bowl. "The workers of the Soviet Union will always challenge the capitalists, wherever they are and whatever they do. We will defeat them directly or through subterfuge. This American woman's round-the-world adventure is wholly designed to embarrass the Soviet Union. This is the opening volley of *a...war*. We will fight them in the air, on the land and sea." He calmed for a moment then pounded the newspaper with a balled fist. His pipe bounced about the ashtray from the blows. With wild venomous eyes he growled at the two military men, "*Let me be clear, if we cannot beat this Amelia Earhart, then you find a way to stop her!*" He backhanded his wrist to dismiss the men and gestured for Yazhov to come closer.

Once the military men closed the door behind them, Stalin whispered, "Nikolai, this Earhart woman, she will be on a spy mission;

no?"

Yazhov's steady eyes and a single head nod confirmed what Stalin suspected. "Japan is rising...."

Stalin nodded. "We must stop the Americans, and I believe our designers and military will find a way to do so. They just need the appropriate motivation." Stalin yawned and tapped his desk as he searched for the correct words. He shook his head as he spoke; phlegm rumbled in his throat. "We don't need *Pravda* to know of our...*difficulties*."

"No, Comrade Stalin."

Stalin smiled with stained teeth. "Herr Hitler...also needs *a lesson*. What I want to do is to stop the Nazis. *This Hindenburg*...it's flying to America routinely." Stalin pounded his finger in the middle of his desk searching for the proper phrasing and inflection. "There needs to be...."

"*An accident*, Comrade Stalin?" whispered Yazhov.

Stalin broke out into a huge smile and nodded. "Herr Hitler hasn't been very grateful of our assistance and has proceeded apace developing this monstrosity. Yes. *An accident*. Preferably, on American soil. Foment some distrust. No one will ever get on one of those floating bombs again."

Yazhov smiled and said, "I will make it so, Comrade Stalin. How much time do we have?"

"Less than one year. Our opportunities should present themselves before that American woman's stunt." Stalin pondered for several seconds. Yazhov nervously waited for his leader to finish his train of thought. Stalin added, "If we want to bring America to her knees, we have to undermine three things: their spiritual life, their morality, and their patriotism. For now their patriotism is rooted in their aviation industry. Specifically their aircraft. They are arrogant! They need to be taken down several notches."

The little man responded, "Attack their airplanes and you attack their patriotism. Yes, brilliant, Comrade Stalin."

He nodded. "I would also like to know of all...*transoceanic aircraft*, their destinations...and their flight paths. I'm especially interested in the Pan American airline." His head bounced as he thought. "I am forever interested in...*opportunities*."

As he had done for years, Yazhov would rely on creating mischief or subterfuge, eliminating one enemy with the hands of another. His spies within the Communist Party of America would find a way. They always did. He nodded deferentially. "As you wish, Comrade Stalin."

Stalin grinned broadly and relit his pipe. It fired up quickly with great noxious clouds of stinging smoke. He recalled the great Sun Tzu: *Take advantage of the enemy's unreadiness, make your way by unexpected routes, and attack unguarded spots.* He nodded his assent and raised his eyes as he removed the half-bent Billiard from his lips. He said between puffs, "There is only the fight, Nikolai. Revolution now, revolution tomorrow. Revolution always."

Chapter One

2300 June 3, 2013
Amman

The woman's scream echoing off the apartment building startled him. From his desk of computer monitors and security camera feeds crammed in a bedroom of a multi-story luxury apartment, he had watched her stagger down the access road into the middle of the dimly-lit cul-de-sac as if she were drunk or in distress. Now she screamed, a woeful, distraught, and shrill, "*Waleeed!*" He checked the monitors for other signs of activity before jumping to the window for a cynical yet cautious peek outside. She wailed again, "*Waleeed!*"

He had been on the lookout for any hint of police activity near or around the three-story apartment building. He hadn't expected to see anyone in a *niqab* that night, and he hadn't expected anyone to be screaming hysterically. A jilted woman, most likely. He scoffed at her misery; he'd seen it all before. A husband with his friends smoking shisha, laughing at a promise that he wouldn't beat her if they married. Or more likely, *Waleed* was with other women at the open-air hookah lounge on Prince Faisal bin al-Mohammad Square that U.S. and British embassy personnel and other Western tourists frequented.

Nizar pressed his faced against the window frame to enjoy the spectacle of a woman in despair but jumped when three pistol reports fired in rapid succession. A classic double-tap plus one reverberated sharply in the basement room directly below him. Although quite accustomed to the sound of gunfire, he still flinched. In the nanosecond after the final round's echo faded Nizar knew he'd been tricked. The spike of adrenaline shut down his flight or fight response. In its place, a thousand jumbled thoughts flooded his overloaded mind, as if a grizzly had suddenly stepped into his path and he couldn't immediately resolve whether to flee, play dead, or just piss all over himself.

Only one of the men in the room downstairs had a weapon when

17

Nizar had left them earlier in the evening. The nearly unconscious man he had tasered, stripped, smashed his genitals with a knee, and placed in the wooden stock didn't have a weapon. And the man he'd been assigned to protect with his life didn't need a pistol. There was no need for additional firearms when there was an antiquated Kalashnikov, an early 7.62mm AK-47, resting against a chair or when there were tools of torture and a Panasonic videocamera to film beheadings in the underground room. His hyperactive mind sorted these facts; the gunshots and the woman decoy outside could only mean three things: someone else was in the building; that person had likely killed his master; he had to escape the trap that had been set by an unknown enemy.

Security forces or policemen would arrive soon, if they were not already rolling down the road to the cul-se-sac. He snatched his laptop computer from the desk, grabbed his personal 5.45mm AK-74 and raced downstairs to the basement.

When he reached the landing he peered cautiously around the door, his assault rifle leading the way. He heard the heavy footfalls of someone running up the inclined driveway leading out of the underground garage. He heard a man's voice—an *Amriki*—in the distance yell, "Get in! Get in!" Nizar ran in the opposite direction, to the torture room where he found his master on the floor with the back of his head blown apart. The man's good eye had been obliterated. Two entry wounds in the middle of his forehead could have been covered by a half-dollar; the exit wound was the size of a cantaloupe. There was no need to check to see if the man was alive. The stock was empty; the infidel was gone, along with his clothes, watch, and cell phone. Fresh blood covered the floor beneath the torture stock; a bloody 18th-century Persian-forged, Damascus steel sword lay in the middle of the spreading red pool.

The former CIA Director may have exacted some revenge on his nemesis in the torture room, but there was no time to assess the situation further. From the wall opposite the camera, Nizar pulled down the two black flags of al-Qaeda and lit the ends with a fiery Bunsen burner used to heat piercing instruments of torture. He quickly draped one flag over the body of Bruce Rothwell, the former Director of Central Intelligence. Nizar dragged the remaining burning flag into the garage, opened the door of the nearest vehicle, and tossed it inside. As flames shot out of the room of death and the nearby vehicle, Nizar threw his computer and weapon into the front seat of a BMW, sped up the ramp, and raced out of the compound. He never glanced into the rearview mirror; the mission behind him was complete, although a total failure. Now he had to avoid the Jordanian police and the dreaded Mukhabarat and get out of the country.

·　·　·　·　·

Hiding behind dark sunglasses as the sun arose, Nizar Qasim al-Rimi scanned a fresh copy of *The Jerusalem Post*. He had escaped the manhunt for a suspected terrorist at the border checkpoint. He was at ease as he sipped tea at the little corner Tel Aviv café not far from the army base. His cover as an Israeli Special Operations soldier didn't seem out of place as other military men and women were walking about or entering and leaving the heavily fortified entrance gate of the military installation. His thick neck oozed out of a black polo shirt that hid oversized pectorals and biceps. He looked the part of an elite soldier on a sabbatical in the dirty suede boots and tan cargo pants favored by the Sayeret, the Israeli Special Forces within the Israel Defense Forces.

He was safe for the moment; he finished his tea and focused on the newspaper.

The raid at the Amman Marriott was front-page news, half-panel above the fold. Suspected terrorists had been reported to be occupying the top floor of the hotel, but somehow they were able to escape the dragnet designed to capture them. Jordanian secret police found the suspected get-away vehicle casually parked in a lot at the Dead Sea Resort. It was an armored black BMW 750 with blacked-out windows, identical to the ones driven by the leaders of the Mukhabarat as well as the Jordanian royal family. On the last page of the paper below the fold was a report of a fire that had consumed a suspected al-Qaeda safe house. The remains of a body were found in the debris.

More tea and pastries were served. Nizar thanked the merchant in Hebrew, folded the newspaper, and tossed it on top of the tiny bistro table. He extracted an Israeli passport from a pocket and tapped it on his pants leg as he took in his surroundings. It was getting warm. It was time to leave. He hoisted a camouflaged backpack containing his laptop computer onto his shoulder. He should be able to hitch a ride into town.

Maybe the driver would even drop him off at the airport. The thought of not killing a dozen Israeli soldiers saddened him.

With the principal dead, his masters in the United Arab Emirates had ordered him back to the Persian Gulf state. He had some explaining to do.

CHAPTER TWO

2300 June 6, 2013
Dubai

The effeminate tall man looked down at the heavy cream cardstock with the single digit in the middle: ١. What the Arabic numeral for "one" lacked in substance, it made up for in coded details which were only understood by those in the know. He had received an "extraordinary invitation" from *The One*. The bearer of the invitation was to report to the top floor of the organization no later than one a.m. Standard protocol; if another time was warranted, it would have been specified. The expected dress was the white two-button, high-collar silk *thobe*—those special garments favored by royalty—featuring full sleeves and unadorned with stylish stitching or borders. Standard *agal* and silk keffiyeh. Watches were optional. Nothing more; nothing less.

Extraordinary invitation was also the code phrase that set the logistics and clandestine process into motion. He could expect to depart on the foggiest of nights when the stillness of the city was so absolute as to be both eerie and otherworldly; mere mortals could not see to drive in such conditions, making travel more than unsafe.

The city stood still until the fog dissipated. A driver would fetch the holder of the card and deliver him to the appointed destination in the strictest secrecy and in total silence. The bearer of the card was expected to climb into the middle vehicle and take his assigned seat. No speaking. Redundant black curtains would seal off the windows and separate the driver from the riders. The specially-equipped automobiles would take the most direct route—no deliberate circuitous routes to confuse the passengers. All vehicular and pedestrian movement would come to a halt. *The One* always found ways to overcome all obstacles.

At half past midnight the man, with slight apprehension, climbed into the second of three BMWs lined up in the underground courtyard to be driven to the auspicious meeting with *The One*.

The One. The man took care not to frown or make a face lest there were surveillance cameras in the palace. Surrounded by black curtains, he remembered the feisty imam in his *madrassa* who said, "Allah called himself *The One; Al-Waahid. The One has no second, has no partner, has no peer, and has no rival.*" The man recalled enunciating the numbers from his childhood in Indonesia: *Waahid, ithnaan, thalaatha…*one, two, three…. He could still recite the words faithfully, but that was all the Arabic he could remember. Riding up the elevator and seeing the floors slowly count up, he recalled making the delicate numerical marks, purposefully flicking the ink onto paper that was more vellum than parchment: ١, ٢, ٣…*1, 2, 3.* His teacher was pleased with him that day. The scrawny mulatto boy wasn't especially smart, but he was especially lazy and always had to be cajoled or threatened to perform the most basic recitations or lessons. At the height of his public approval, he would tell the reporters who ardently held onto his every syllable that "there had always been a lazy streak in him." He had rubbed shoulders with kings, presidents, billionaires, celebrities, sheikhs, and the heads of intelligence agencies and science foundations. He was once the most powerful man in the world. Now he was hiding in a well-furnished and well-provisioned palace out of the public eye, and was, by every measure, a consummate failure. The man changed his expression and waited for what seemed like an hour for the elevator door to open.

They had extracted every bit of useful intelligence from him and had allowed him to live. A modicum of fear left his body; he had worried that his life had been placed in extreme jeopardy by the very country he once led. He was both impressed and relieved that his host had kept his word to protect him.

Of course, he had paid handsomely for this hospitality while he was in office. The previous Democrat President had taught him how to become a billionaire in politics. With direct access to the national treasury and through secret accounts that funded special projects, he was able to reward his friends with billions of American taxpayer dollars. He was not alone. Dictators from around the world sent their government's money to the UAE for safekeeping and as payment for keeping them safe when they were forced to abdicate their posts and flee for their lives.

When elected he had promised to shutter the offshore terrorist prison at Guantanamo Bay, but those stinking Republicans in Congress had prevented him from taking unilateral actions to close the facility. Still, he found a way to nearly empty the prison in Cuba as well as fund his emergency billion-dollar golden parachute.

The elevator door finally opened and the man made his way to the conference room and took his assigned seat. He noticed the opulence of his surroundings and mused at the source of the funds, at least for a part of it.

His Secretary of State transferred billions of dollars from one of several secret accounts at the U.S. State Department to the UAE, under the auspices the emirs would take the GITMO prisoners under some benign and publicly disavowed terms and conditions. The White House press secretary insisted that there "was no *quid pro quo*" regarding payments and transfer of prisoners or hostages. The American public and Congress were unaware of the secret accounts at the State Department to facilitate "special projects." The going rate for a single al-Qaeda leader was a hundred million dollars.

American hostages garnered the same rate. Iran indiscriminately took hostages and held them for ransom. The government's intelligence service snatched stupid American men on tourist visas for the most arcane of infractions, declaring they had been captured for spying and would be executed for espionage. If the women were beautiful they would simply disappear. The American press would be outraged only until the next news cycle.

The UAE took in the GITMO terrorists and received their handling fee; Iran took hostages and received similar payments. The man liked round numbers. Everyone got paid. Especially him.

Once the monies were successfully transferred, his only concern was if his friends in Iran and the UAE would hold up their end of the bargain. These kinds of special arrangement had been in place for over a century.

· · · · · ·

In the late 19th century the tiny and crucial Port of Abu Dhabi garnered the notice of the rapacious, post-revolutionary France and the imperious Russian Empire. Suddenly feeling very exposed to becoming an acquired Persian Gulf satellite to the ambitious European countries, the British government established formal relations and closer economic bonds to the Trucial Sheikhdoms in an 1892 treaty. The British government provided a presence and promised to protect the Trucial Coast from all aggression, primarily by sea, and to help in case of land attack. The sheikhs received protection too, but the cost of doing business with the white men of Great Britain included the British provision and prohibition: to be a member of our joint venture, we shall provide protection; you must abandon your slave trade. Signed by the rulers of Abu Dhabi, Dubai, Sharjah, and the other emirs of the emirates, the underlying treaty meant an important source of income—the trading of humans—would be lost to the sheikhs and other merchants. In true Arabic fashion, some sheikhs ignored and violated the British mandate and drove their slavery industry underground.

When the newly independent Government of India imposed heavy taxation on pearls imported from the growing state of Abu Dhabi and other states in the Persian Gulf, one of the Abu Dhabi's most successful pearl merchants drove the previously thriving pearling industry underground and underwater. The Abu Dhabi leaders developed and deployed the first generation of submersibles to harvest pearls and move precious gems and minerals out of the sight of their British overlords. Other trade was acceptable. British magistrates set up a development office, the British-Abu Dhabi Trading Company, to help some small development projects in the emirates.

The seven sheikhs of the emirates formed a separate council innocuously named the Regional Operations Council, or *The ROC*, to coordinate matters between themselves and the British. It became the only operation not run or supervised by the British.

By the mid-1930s, the ruler of Abu Dhabi had created an underworld of proscribed activities. He smuggled everything: precious metals, gemstones, ivory, pearls, treasures and antiques from lost civilizations, rare woods, and of course slaves. The most valuable slaves were women of color; prices were set based on hair and skin color. The Abu Dhabi emir also created an industry to hide the deposed, the former dictators, the deviants, the deported, the deserted, and others who desired or needed to be removed from the public eye. Refugees, sojourners, criminals, thieves, and pilgrims found temporary respite from pirates in Abu Dhabi at great cost.

Abu Dhabi's ruler employed ships of every size. He provided a variety of services for every nation with a navy that visited the growing port of Abu Dhabi, most of which were necessarily clandestine. Forts in the desert, some disguised or doing double-duty as mosques, sprang up and protected the most sensitive clients from being seen. The forts were organized as working communities, not just defensive positions. Thousands of people could be accommodated. They were interconnected through a warren of tunnels; treasure and booty were safeguarded, stored within labyrinthine tunnels where circular stone doors, each weighing thousands of pounds, sealed entrances. Over time, the tunnels, blackened from the soot of oil-soaked torches, were expanded to protect against marauding Arab enemies. Precious metals and minerals were the currency of choice, as were the "expendables," the men and women who were traded daily in the markets along with the offerings of materials, linens, livestock, fruits, wines, and vegetables which came off his ships that travelled the world. As Abu Dhabi grew, so did its fleet of ocean-going boats and dhows.

Ten years later, in the early 1940s, military and commercial airliners with a new crop of deserters and the displaced landed from unpronounceable places and flew off hard-packed desert airstrips for places unknown or unspoken. People brought their personal fortunes and disappeared into the number of forts that dotted the Abu Dhabi landscape and increased exponentially in number every year. Moving through the networks of tunnels and living permanently underground out of sight, like the Morlocks, was encouraged and mandated. If one had come to escape the eyes and ears of a bounty hunter, movement above ground was prohibited. The penalty for violating the movement edicts: public hangings or dismemberment. Consequently, rarely did anyone emerge to frequent cafés or other dens of inequities in the heart of Abu Dhabi. To do so put many lives at risk. If someone was in Abu Dhabi, they likely came to get away from some very bad people or some very mad people.

·   ·   ·   ·   ·

The debrief had gone better than expected. Nizar was convinced he had escaped from a professional assassin but regrettably, his master was not so fortunate. The men around the table had listened to the Jordanian's testimony before dismissing him on the best of terms. The precious laptop that was always with him lay on the table where he once sat. He had testified it contained pictures and video of the man so reviled by his master. It also held hundreds of other correspondences that Rothwell had instructed him to type and send until the injured former CIA Director was able to move a computer mouse without assistance. He had also provided some of the final directives of Dr. Bruce Rothwell, as well as transcripts of everything he said while sleeping or under the influence of pain-killers and sedatives. As a "nurse," he was unequalled.

Nizar's closing statement reflected his complete knowledge of the meetings his master held before escaping to the al-Qaeda safe house. He stated, "My master insisted to the brothers from al-Qaeda and the Muslim Brotherhood that they were to destroy a man, Duncan Hunter. My understanding is that someone from each organization was sent to kill him and capture a woman from the CIA. I have no knowledge if their activities were eventually successful or if the directive to kill the man or capture the woman have been rescinded with the death of Rothwell."

Back in the conference room, the taller and only unmustachioed man of the group of interviewers articulated his narcissistic and paranoid concern that the CIA's Special Activities Division or U.S. Navy SEALs would soon find him. He needed *trusted* bodyguards.

All but one of the seven mustachioed men around the table wore cotton ball-white *thobes* with a starched, two-buttoned, tall collar. Each white pressed silk *keffiyeh* representing their position within the royal family was held in place by a black and gold braided *agal.*

The man at the end of the table was considerably more powerful than the others. The princes—the *emirs*—paid obeisance to the man in black. His black *thobe* was unadorned; a long, diaphanous, black and gold-tissue lamé vest covered his *thobe* like academic regalia. It was outlined in thick gold braided shoulder trim and gave the elder the look of an Ian Fleming villain. A black silk *keffiyeh* was folded forward in such a way as to hide the man's face and protect him from the light. Only the immaculate black spade beard jutted out from the shadows of the material. An ancient jewel-encrusted Arab dagger was slung across his chest. The traditional *khanjar* was filigreed and engraved in silver and gold with a handle of ivory and ebony laminates. His hands rested below the knife. They were long, thin, and white, not like that of an albino but as if he hadn't been in the sun for many years. He was the chief executive officer of many international companies. His brother was president of the country. But he was *The One*, the titular ruler of the United Arab Emirates.

He considered the situation for a few seconds. He barely shook his head as he wondered if the Jordanian's analysis and message were correct. Was the CIA pilot somehow behind the fall of two of the most powerful men in the American government, a president and a CIA director? The woman's involvement seemed to be more infatuation on the part of the dead CIA director than her being a co-conspirator with the infidel pilot; they would deal with her later. The old man's milky white hands formed a teepee underneath a wide wiry mustache, he unconsciously pulled on his superior lip with index fingers as he thought of a plan. The others at the table deferentially indulged his contemplation in silence. He gestured and asked, "Would you consider Nizar? He is one of our most trusted agents. He's fluent in English; he's been trained by the best special operations warriors."

"He failed to protect Rothwell," said the former President of the United States.

The One said, in Arabic, "*You failed to secure America. You were given a second chance.*"

It annoyed Maxim Mohammad Mazibuike to be spoken to in Arabic when *The One* knew it was a significant embarrassment to be in the land of the Prophet and unable to speak the Prophet's tongue.

The One said, in perfect English, "Your Rothwell brought on his own demise by trying to capture and torture the pilot. Nizar would die before he would allow you to fall into the hands of any enemy." He spoke as if he were a well-groomed banker chatting casually to a subordinate.

The former American president bowed and said, "He will be welcome, my lord. Thank you."

Just then the floor moved slightly under them, as if an earthquake had disturbed the foundation of the building. His wide eyed expression questioned the indifferent men across the table. The leader of Abu Dhabi, the largest of the Emirates, gestured with his white hand effeminately. "Just a gust of wind. Very common...at this level. 154 floors. Returning to the situation at hand, I think the least we can do, for now, is to issue a new *fatwa*. That will eliminate entirely any threat coming from that corner of the world. Agreed?"

"Agreed, my lord. Thank you."

"You have done well, Maxim. If not for *that pilot*.... Completely unforeseen. Not your fault. But we have...much to do."

"I will make the arrangements. Vehicles. Bodyguards. A more suitable place for you to live."

The former occupant of the White House replied, "Thank you, my lord. You have been most gracious and generous. The Americans have a saying, payback is a bitch. I would like to pay them back if the opportunity ever presents itself, my lord."

The One uttered, "I believe the Americans also have a saying, 'in spades.' I will seek an appropriate...*response* on your behalf if one is available. Payback, if there is one to be had, I can assure you will be in spades."

"Thank you, my lord. *Allahu Akbar!*" Maxim Mohammad Mazibuike, the former President of the United States of America, bowed deeply, as he always did to show the utmost respect for the royal Arab families.

. . . . .

The sides of the carriage were painted royal blue. The roof was peaked and white, like a royal-creased *keffiyeh*. On the outside there were no markings to suggest the special high-speed electric train car had been created in Germany, or that the coachwork and interior had been handcrafted in Japan by some of the finest craftsmen from several coastal villages.

Mazibuike was debriefed every day. He would depart his underground sanctuary at the same time every day for a ride in the train car to another subterranean facility. No extraordinary invitation was necessary. The curtains were always pulled closed.

The intelligence and information he provided through gentle and participatory interrogation were rewarded with the finest in Islamic accommodations and absolute security. There were no more U.S. Secret Service details to protect him; now he had a small cadre of commandos, the best that money could buy, culled from the best Middle East special operations units from Libya to Israel to Jordan and Kuwait.

He was a willing guest, not a prisoner of war or a captured American in a foreign land. There was no "name, rank, and serial number" as in a survival, escape, resistance, and evasion situation. There was a spirited, and at times, combative exchange between the interrogator and the interrogatee, especially when previous or long-standing information or intelligence was being contradicted or dismissed. The Russians and Chinese only paid for accurate, timely, and relevant intelligence when they could not steal it, or if it miraculously walked through the door. The ROC was the clearing house for actionable intelligence. What drove the price up was the quality of the source. Low-level "tactical" intel was cheap compared to the top-level "strategic" intel, which was categorized by subject and stratified by the ten different levels of government or business source. A was Presidential level, B Ministerial, Cabinet or CEO level. J was at the user-bee or technician level; the virtually worthless stuff.

As the car coasted to a stop, President Mazibuike understood he was a prisoner; a very special type of prisoner. He chuffed at the old axiom that suddenly entered his head: *He who gives up freedom for security deserves neither*. Now he was giving up America's most secret of secrets.

He had work to do.

He hoped he would live to see freedom once again. And his money.

CHAPTER THREE

1100 June 6, 2014
Washington D.C.

"Director Lynche, where is President Mazibuike?"

The Director of Central Intelligence switched on his microphone. No one in the main Committee Hearing Room moved; for the first time in ten minutes, the room was silent. The room was full of people like voyeurs witnessing a public hanging. The question half of America wanted answered had finally been asked.

"Congresswoman Boviary, the CIA does not know where he is." The microphone being switched off was heard by everyone in the room. That wasn't the answer they had been waiting for.

She was as bloated as roadkill on the side of a highway. The termagant Democrat from California asked in her superior shrill voice, "Are you saying you have no knowledge of his whereabouts at this time? Did you lose track of him?"

Unruffled, Lynche again switched on the microphone and left it on. "Congresswoman Boviary, per current law, the CIA has no jurisdiction over the former chief executive. The CIA did not track him after he departed the Oval Office. We have no interest in him." Lynche scanned all of the congressional faces, but no help came from any of them as they sat in their lofty perches. "We would not and did not track him when he left the contiguous 48 states. Press reports indicated that after President Mazibuike resigned, he flew on Air Force One one last time to Hawaii, then immediately boarded a private executive jet for places unknown."

"How could you not track him to ensure his safety? Right wing zealots have continually threatened his life."

"Congresswoman Boviary, President Mazibuike resigned and left the United States over two years ago. I was not the Director at that time; I had been retired from the CIA since 1995. Presidential security is the sole purview of the U.S. Secret Service. I believe they are still responsible for the security of the president and former presidents. Maybe the congresswoman could direct her question to the Secret Service Director?" He sat calmly. He was totally expressionless. The congresswoman was an idiot, and he hoped she would get the hint to move to another subject. She could throw illogical crap at him all day. Nothing she could say was going to faze him.

She scowled at his choice of words and his arrogance. She had two minutes left to embarrass him or try and make him squirm. Through gritted teeth she asked, "What is the status of the FBI's investigation regarding the identity of the person who released the CIA file on the president? Don't you have a problem with a…snitch…a mole?" She wasn't going to give up.

DCI Lynche expected the first question; the second was a red herring. The same question was asked at every Congressional hearing. *Who did it?* More specifically, *who* released the file that proved the Democrat President was not who he claimed to be? With that specific question, Lynche would have to tread lightly. It had the potential to be a minefield, because he knew who had released the file. And he would go to great lengths not to lie to Congress. He would lie if he had to, but today was not that day. He could offer a bit more information to throw off the scent. "I cannot speak for the FBI. My understanding from their progress reports is that there is insufficient evidence to suspect anyone at the CIA of releasing President Mazibuike's file. Those intelligence officers with direct or tangential knowledge of the file have been polygraphed numerous times. No one at the CIA is suspected of releasing the file."

"As for a mole, or what we call a long-term penetration agent, they are a rare breed and a counterintelligence officer's worst nightmare. But that is not what we are dealing with here Congresswoman Boviary. Moles by definition 'work for the other side;' they are generally the agents of the Kremlin or Beijing, the enemies of America. It seems to me whoever released the former president's file did so because President Mazibuike was the real mole, the ultimate mole. Possibly under the direction of the Kremlin, but more likely the Muslim Brotherhood, he succeeded in penetrating the White House. He also penetrated the U.S. Government giving preferential hiring to Muslims for the top government positions, even when they could not pass a background investigation or were qualified for a security clearance. He opened the borders to Muslim refugees at the expense of Christian refugees. The cumulative effect, as we have seen, he did enormous damage to our national security. At every level, President Mazibuike significantly impacted and undermined our intelligence capabilities."

The Congresswoman tried several times to cut off the DCI at his "ultimate mole" and "Muslims" comments, but he ignored her interruptions and talked over her objections. Other Democrat congressmen collectively rebuked the DCI and demanded his censure. The chairman pounded his gavel and called for quiet.

"However, there has been one constant throughout this investigation. The FBI determined the former Near East Division Chief is likely the sole source who compiled the file on the former president. From the time he was a student traveling the Middle East up until he began running for office, the president met with the worst of the world's worst terrorists. For the record, the former Near East Division Chief died suddenly and mysteriously. This was well before the former president's file was released."

The panel and the crowd erupted in a fount of questions and murmurs. The chairman again pounded the gavel a dozen times and demanded silence of his members and the public.

The congresswoman continued, "How did this Near East Division Chief die?" Many of the congressmen on both sides of the aisle expressed heightened interest in the newly divulged news. Even some Democrat congressmen put down their smart phones to listen to the nation's top intelligence officer.

A war correspondent in the public seating area raised his head from his notebook. The previously unreleased information regarding the unexplained death of a CIA intelligence officer was monstrous news. And having the DCI call the former president the ultimate "mole" was breathtaking. He wrote furiously trying to capture the details and agitated mood of the hearing even as he struggled to keep his eyes on the principals and not on a petite redheaded woman with matching eyebrows and lightly freckled face sitting directly behind the Central Intelligence Director. She had an unforgettable face. He had seen her before. Seeing her again in the halls of Congress sitting behind the nation's top spook stunned him.

Lynche took a drink of water. "He was shot with a single round. In

NATO it is euphemistically called a 'terminator round.' It's one shot, one kill ammunition. It's illegal to possess, anywhere. His killer was likely a paid assassin, and I surmise, he will likely never be found."

Eastwood and everyone else in the room watched intently as the redheaded woman passed Lynche a note. He read it and wrote himself a note.

The corpulent congresswoman was both indignant and miffed by the testimony and the note-passing distraction. As if she were threatening him she said sternly, "Director Lynche, I needn't remind you that you are under oath. I want assurances that the CIA has not retaliated against President Mazibuike, that the CIA has not assassinated him with one of these lethal 'terminator rounds.'"

Lynche stifled a yawn. "Congresswoman Boviary, the CIA doesn't engage in assassination. I categorically assert that the CIA does not know the whereabouts of former President Mazibuike, that the CIA has not retaliated against him, and that the CIA has not assassinated him. I reiterate, we have no interest in him." *We have no interest in him.* Lynche regretted saying that line. He had let his guard down in a moment of hubris.

Lynche acknowledged the "ultimate mole" still had secrets in his head that could bring down the United States. *I'd like to know where the bastard is too, but for different reasons.* The congresswoman had time for only one last question. Thank God.

"My final question, Director Lynche. Do you consider the person who released the president's file to be a patriot or a traitor?" She leaned back smugly as if to say, "I got you now, you son of a bitch. Squirm out of that one!"

"Congresswoman Boviary, that is a political question. My opinion on the subject is irrelevant and immaterial." He shut off his microphone, upended a bottle of water, and refused to look at her as she scowled at him.

The mood in the hearing room changed in a snap with a new inquisitor, a Republican from North Carolina. He was a former federal prosecutor with wild spiky hair, a deep knowledge of the law, and a dramatic flair when in front of a camera. When he spoke, he didn't ask Director Lynche a single question. He directed his stinging comments to the other congressmen in the open-door hearing. "My friends on the other side think so poorly of you and your intelligence officers as to suggest the CIA somehow found, tracked down, and assassinated the former president. No rational or reasonable person would think such a thing. For the record, my professional opinion of you and your employees is that you are patriots engaged in some of the most demanding and challenging work on behalf of this nation. I thank you for your service."

Lynche smiled and half nodded at the man's compliment.

The congressman flew into an oratory befitting a Shakespearian character. "They want us to forget quickly how the Democrats in Washington D.C. and the national media foisted an ineligible, an illegal candidate onto the American public. They knew the truth but denied it like the townspeople of Auschwitz. Anyone who tried to point out the obvious, that the man was neither eligible nor properly vetted, was bludgeoned into submission. People were branded in the most vile manner by their high-tech lynching minions in the media. Who authorized Washington Democrats and the media to adjudicate a constitutional issue in public? As those released documents clearly proved, Maxim Mohammad Mazibuike was from birth both a Nigerian citizen and an American citizen, but he was not a naturally born citizen as specified in Article II of the U.S. Constitution, which states: "No person except a natural born citizen... shall be eligible to the Office of President.""

"His eligibility to be president was never a case of where he was born; but rather, how. And the how was very simple—a natural born citizen is a child born of two American citizens. It is a term and condition that is irrespective of location or place of birth. If the Russian Ambassador and his wife have a child at the Georgetown University Medical Center, is that child American? Of course not. The Founders of the U.S. Constitution were clear that America is not in the business of stealing other nation's children when their parents are on business here, going to school here, or being simple sojourners visiting or passing through America. The Founders put that specific clause in the Constitution for one very clear reason; they did not want a split allegiance situation for future presidents."

The Congressman became more intense. There was fire in his eyes as the words sizzled off his tongue. "I guarantee you they never envisioned a scenario of a presidential candidate having an allegiance that was anathema to the Christian values upon which this country was based. Washington Democrats and the media have so distorted the facts regarding the constitutionally-mandated eligibility requirements for president that only adjudication by the Supreme Court could settle the issue of what exactly is meant by the 'natural born citizen' clause. That was and is the job of the courts, not Washington Democrats and their emasculated remora friends in the media."

"The lies surrounding President Mazibuike's ascension to the Office of the President are so deadly, so obvious, and so much a part of the Left's policy to shred the U.S. Constitution and institute one-party rule that we must remind ourselves of them. That we must expose them and the Muslim Brotherhood's *Explanatory Memorandum*. We must expose their lies and their actions at every opportunity. The media and Washington Democrats are solely responsible for 'the ultimate mole,' as you so elegantly put it, Director Lynche, becoming president."

Demetrius Eastwood nearly missed the phrase "... and the Muslim Brotherhood's *Explanatory Memorandum.*" He wrote it in his notebook and wondered, "What the hell is that?"

"It is clear today, that Washington Democrats and the political left of the nation don't want the former president to come out of his little mole hole and be extradited to stand trial for his high crimes and misdemeanors while he was in office. Every day he is alive is another reminder that they were complicit; they were part of the conspiracy to undermine and violate the U.S. Constitution, to bring an ineligible and illegal candidate into office, and in effect, to install a mole—an enemy who is both *foreign and domestic*—with access to the nation's most secret of secrets. And then, knowing the man's true character and goals, they knew that once elected he would execute the most anti-American policies this country has ever seen. For a few years they were successful. He was successful."

He looked around the room and raised his finger in emphasis. "This much we know. No one wanted to listen. A CIA officer is dead for collecting information on the illegal candidate. An unknown whistleblower also knew something was wrong with candidate Mazibuike, and he knew it had something to do with the man's background. Once he acquired the damning information, he released the former president's file. For his success in exposing the ultimate mole, he's considered by some the vilest traitor, the most despicable man the Left has ever encountered. For those on the Right this whistleblower should be considered a patriot for exposing that the Washington Democrats, the political left of the nation, and 99 percent of the mainstream media knew the truth, maintained the fiction and the narrative, and worked hard to cover the truth up. Whatever that is, whatever that was, those actions of the Left were the actions of a criminal enterprise and are not American. They are unpatriotic."

"For the whistleblower, whoever that person is, he or she performed a significant patriotic service to the nation that was every bit as valuable as Paul Revere riding through the night warning that the British were coming. He or she warned America that they had someone in the White House whose allegiance wasn't to Americans or America or our Constitution, that he wasn't on their side, but at the very least, he was on the side of the former Soviet Union and more likely, the side of terrorist extremists. A true patriot blew the cover off of the bogus president—a Manchurian candidate, indeed. Americans now know the truth that one half of their Congress was not only complicit in his bogus candidacy but also in his counterfeit election. I yield the remainder of my time to the Chair."

The men and women in the public seating area were stunned into silence. Demetrius Eastwood finally shut his mouth and annotated in his notebook that the congressman was brave and fearless. He spoke that which could not have been spoken months ago for fear of being tarred and feathered with the stench of ridicule and racism by an unrelenting media, which is buttressed by the most corrupt of the Washington D.C. Democrats. *The media will walk by this story like a dead body in the street; they will want nothing to do with it!* In the marginalia he wrote, *That lad from NC needs a bulletproof vest!*

Eastwood checked his watch and looked up. This time tomorrow he would be heading to the airport for Jakarta, Indonesia for his next assignment investigating the largest known terrorist group in Indonesia, the *Abu Sayyaf.* But first, the bullet train to New York City. Then he had articles to finish. He hoped whatever Islamic extremist group that had targeted him two years ago had given up any thoughts of killing him and collecting the reward of the *fatwa,* like they did Salman Rushdie. It was going to be a long day. Eastwood scanned the hearing room as the chairman pounded his gavel and admonished his members to calm down and "resume order."

He gently shook his head at the proceedings. *The former president sent several billion dollars to the UAE. I know where he went. Ask me! No one will ask me.* The congressman's words *Explanatory Memorandum* still rang in his head. His thoughts were acerbic and caustic, yet all too true. Eastwood was filling in for a friend and this assignment would likely go down as the most opportune and important of his career—that he was there the day the feisty congressman from North Carolina jabbed the opposition party in the eye with a telephone pole-sized spear by exposing the Democrats' own treachery. It was fascinating testimony for an open door hearing.

He was riding high personally and professionally, at least within his own network. His recent exposé on the former president secretly paying billions of U.S. tax dollars, sometimes via planeloads and pallets of cash, to the UAE to take and house some of the al-Qaeda prisoners held at Guantanamo Bay was an explosive bit of investigative journalism. It was too bad none of the mainstream media paid any attention to it. *One of the media's most insidious powers is their power to ignore.* Eastwood privately lamented but wasn't surprised that they snubbed his piece. Only the conservative network he worked for picked up the story and ran with it. It received some airtime in Texas but nowhere else.

There was a momentary break in the action, and Eastwood's focus returned to the Central Intelligence Agency Director who appeared to be enjoying the turmoil and mayhem created by the North Carolina congressman. Eastwood did not know DCI Greg Lynche personally, only professionally and that from a distance. But he could maintain little focus on Lynche. He was continually drawn to the stunning little lady with the flaming red hair sitting behind the DCI. He flipped and flopped in his chair trying to remain circumspect while achieving a better view of her.

When she walked into the hearing room, all eyes had turned toward her and followed her to her seat. Eastwood had watched too, and she took his breath away. Not because of her lithe natural beauty, but because he knew her, had seen her before. For her to be sitting a few rows in front of him was astonishing. He didn't know her name or where she was from or what she was doing in the hearing room. It was obvious that she had closely followed the Director of Central Intelligence into the hearing room, and her proximity to him was purposeful and not accidental. Eastwood concluded that it put her in the rare category of being an intelligence officer for the CIA. She was likely undercover as one of the DCI's personal aides.

A year earlier Eastwood and the redheaded woman had sat on opposite sides of one of the largest airliners ever built, an Airbus A-380. Their Nigerian Airways jet had taken off from New York City and had been hijacked during the flight. Terrorists demanded the aircraft be flown to a runway in Liberia. They landed in the early morning hours.

Almost immediately after landing in Monrovia two commandos miraculously and surprisingly entered the double-deck aircraft and killed all the hijackers. Eastwood was astonished that he knew both rescuers, although they never removed their night vision goggles which helped them to protect their identity. She called out the nickname of one of the rescuers in their black flight suits and black helmets. *Maverick!* Eastwood was agog as *Maverick* raced to her and embraced the redheaded woman as a father comforts his daughter. Seconds later his fellow retired Marine Corps officer, Duncan Hunter, *Maverick*, released her and was gone. Eastwood hadn't suspected it then but knew it now. She was CIA. So was Maverick. That he knew. But were they… *related?*

The story would make good—no—great copy. But he would never and could never report on Maverick from that night except in the most benign terms. He pushed the old thoughts away and let new ones in to percolate in his cranium. Now that he had witnessed the DCI's testimony, he had ideas for letters to the editors of the major liberal newspapers' editorial page. He would dare them to print his work. *Yes, where was the former president? The lunatic fringe of the Democratic Party, those Washington bureaucrats and their facilitators in the media were obviously anti-American. Was the person responsible for releasing the CIA file a national hero or a traitor? According to the questions proffered by the Washington Democrats, the man was not only a traitor but should be shot on sight.*

He chuckled to himself at his next thoughts. *Whoever released that file, if he were ever to become known, would become the most reviled man in America, or the most respected, depending on where one leaned politically.* Whoever that person was, he or she would need more than a little bulletproof vest for protection.

Eastwood had been listening to the little voice in his head and not Congressman Torquemada, the latest in the rotation with a political agenda. The CIA Director answered the same questions as before. Some congressman who didn't understand the basics of island formation, who feared that if too many Marines were allowed on the Island of Guam that it would tip over, offered the latest conspiracy theory: the CIA actually had captured the former president and had him in an orange jump suit in a detention cell in Guantanamo Bay, Cuba. Each Democrat interrogator was filled with more vitriol than the previous one regarding the health and welfare of the former president, who was apparently being held in a secret CIA prison as some espionage thriller writer had suggested from a "close confidential source." Lynche had no answers to satisfy them. The Republicans who asked questions highlighted the CIA's charter, which stated that it wasn't the job of the Agency to find, track, or chase the former POTUS. Lynche concurred and responded, "The CIA is an intelligence agency, not a law enforcement one. Maybe someone should talk to the FBI."

In the hallway, at the end of the hearing, Eastwood pushed through the other reporters striving for a minute of facetime and asked the CIA Director a question. "Director Lynche, what was that like, being asked unreasonable questions that had no answers?"

For the first time that morning Greg Lynche grinned. "I suppose it was a lot like being dragged before the Holy Office of the Inquisition. Seems I escaped… this time." Eastwood, Lynch, and some of the press corps laughed. From the other side of the throng, the redheaded woman in the business suit looked at the DCI impassionately and didn't make eye contact with Eastwood. But it was obvious she had recognized the war correspondent from the Nigerian jet and from his television specials. She was fooled momentarily because he was in a business suit and not his trademark white chambray shirt and tan cargo pants. She would need to avoid him like she had after landing in Lagos.

Eastwood watched CIA Director Lynche, his security team, and the redhead depart the impromptu post-hearing press meeting. He and the media followed them out of the Capitol. A brace of black government Suburbans waited to whisk them away to CIA headquarters through the heaviest of the afternoon traffic. For Eastwood, the trip from Capitol Hill to Union Station was a quick downhill jog. As he entered the train station he unconsciously patted his suit pocket which held a first class ticket for Amtrak's Acela to New York City. Within forty minutes he was aboard and already drafting an article while intermittently wondering what was meant by the Muslim Brotherhood's *Explanatory Memorandum*. The four words would consume his thoughts for miles. When on the train, he fired up his smart telephone to research and read the *Explanatory Memorandum*. Eastwood was stunned into silence as he learned how the document was discovered and its significance.

"In August of 2004, an alert Maryland Transportation Authority Police officer observed a woman wearing traditional Islamic garb videotaping the support structures of the Chesapeake Bay Bridge, and conducted a traffic stop. The driver was Ismail Elbarasse and was detained on an outstanding material witness warrant issued in Chicago in connection with fundraising for Hamas. The FBI's Washington Field Office subsequently executed a search warrant on Elbarasse's residence in Annandale, Virginia. In the basement of his home, a hidden sub-basement was found; it revealed over 80 banker boxes of the archives of the Muslim Brotherhood in North America. One of the closely-held secret documents stood out: The Muslim Brotherhood's strategic plan for North America was entitled, '*An Explanatory Memorandum*: On the General Strategic Goal for the Group.'"

CHAPTER FOUR

2300 June 6, 2014
New York City

The spacious but spartan office halfway up the south face of the 7 World Trade Center appeared to be deserted. No security or cleaning crew worked the hallway outside. No glow or apparent illumination leaked from within the unnamed office space at 2613. The only visible light came from a laptop and a desktop monitor obscured by a man pounding the keyboard. The unremarkable and private office also served as the sometimes residence of the international network journalist and war hero. Demetrius Eastwood's face was recognizable anywhere in America or on Middle Eastern battlefields. That fact sometimes made life problematic and challenging. It was uncommonly difficult to find a conventional and safe location where he wouldn't be the target of the unholy warriors of the radical Islamic jihad. Despite its famous name, the building was a very safe location for someone who could afford the rent and needed a safe house in the center of the city. Having another company lease the office space helped him to establish a modicum of journalistic cover.

The original 7 World Trade Center structure was completed in 1987 and destroyed in the September 11 attacks on the complex in Lower Manhattan. It was rebuilt five years later and was five stories taller. The new building was the second to bear the famous name and address. Appearances mattered. While new businesses filled the floors of the new building, a few individual offices on some floors were intentionally bland and commonplace. If an inquisitive detective attempted to determine the identity of the tenant, they would find the office was the property of QAS, Quiet Aero Systems, an obscure aviation company in Texas.

It had been years since Osama bin Laden slapped a *fatwa* on him. He avoided hotels and restaurants and other crowded situations with natural choke points where a mad jihadi could wait to ambush and kill him just as Sirhan Sirhan killed Bobby Kennedy in a crowded kitchen. No one could have recognized that the threat was imminent or instantaneous, and no one could have made the snap decision to take cover or flee. Too many distractions, too many people, too many opportunities to die. Hotel lobbies scared the crap out of him, so he made a deal with his Marine buddy to use and crash in his New York City office. It even had a shower.

Eastwood largely ignored the podcast discussion coming from the laptop. He was thumbing his smart phone sending a text message to his benefactor. As was his style, it was in bullets with all lower case and no punctuation: *ever heard of an explanatory memorandum?* The answer was nearly instantaneous—surprising him completely, as it was unlike Duncan Hunter to respond so quickly. Eastwood wanted to call him but was transfixed on the response: *MB infiltration of the US.* MB was for Muslim Brotherhood; the US was for United States. In any public discussion Hunter's reply, at least in liberal circles it would have been considered Islamophobic. Then there was more bullets in response. *Why do you think the feds federalized airport screening? They had infiltrated airport security in the 90s. That's how they got wps aboard 4 jets on 911. The 911 rpt was silent.*

Eastwood sat in shock. He said aloud, "I had no idea." Then came more bullets; more surprises. *That's also why 3M placed his guys in top positions in gvt and McLean. Plz tell me you've been paying attention. Read it! Gotta go. S/F.* Semper Fi; always faithful. Shock turned into a grin. He found *An Explanatory Memorandum* on the internet, downloaded the document and an accompanying strategic analysis, and printed both documents. He would read them later. He pushed the Muslim Brotherhood out of his mind. He had things to finish. Eastwood focused on the large monitor in front of him; he nodded absentmindedly. He was satisfied with the pair of articles he had crafted while on the train.

His clothes and hair were always rumpled like a man whose flight had been delayed and he had to sleep in the corner of an airport lounge. He pushed away from the marble-topped desk, walked to the floor-to-ceiling window, and looked down at the masses below who were standing, walking, and driving in the light drizzle, not going anywhere fast. He turned away from the window and checked his watch. It was late; he needed to get some sleep. He had an early flight in the morning. Once again, he slipped into the thick leather desk chair and reread both articles.

No new edits. The first he transmitted directly to the office of the editor of the most virulently anti-Republican newspaper, *The Washington Post*, daring them to publish it.

Submission for the Editorial Page.
By: Demetrius Eastwood.
Title: Where's the Former President?

An hour before midnight on June 30, 2011, President Maxim Mohammad Mazibuike boarded Air Force One for Hawaii. At Hickham AFB in Honolulu, he was seen getting off the presidential jumbo and boarding a private executive jet for an unknown destination. He has not been seen in public since. Three years ago, during a ninety-six hour window, a constitutional crisis erupted in America as hundreds of classified and confidential documents spanning the five decades of President Mazibuike's life were released to several law-enforcement agencies, a hundred members of Congress, and hundreds of newspapers and TV stations across the country. Softbound copies of the documents had been unwittingly printed, bound, and delivered by an overnight printing and delivery service. The documents were also posted on the Internet at several liberal and conservative web sites.

No one claimed responsibility for the release of the former president's CIA file, even the most notorious and likely hackers are abnormally mum. Senior liberal democrats have been in an uproar over the release of the documents, seemingly indifferent to the fact that the head of their party was not only, in the technical sense, an illegal alien, a communist, and a Muslim, but had also consorted with the world's worst terrorists while originally holding a British passport. The DNC Chairwoman has accused the FBI of dragging its feet while investigating the identity of the person who released the file. Documents outlining the president's Muslim roots as well as a comprehensive list of forged or counterfeit documents which had been used to establish his American identity and bona fides were causal in President Mazibuike resigning so suddenly. Since the intelligence services of Great Britain and Israel validated that the documents in the released file were authentic, some liberal democrats have softened their tone.

The Federal Bureau of Investigation has investigated the case aggressively and continues to pursue leads on who could have assembled or released the damaging documents. All those at the Central Intelligence Agency with a tangential relationship with the case file manager were subjected to withering interviews and multiple polygraphs. The only information made available to the press corps was that the late Near East Division Chief, Nicolas Lloyd Dolan, was likely the initiator of the president's case file, which began when the president was a young British national visiting Pakistan. Dolan was likely the sole source contact who assembled the documents. Making the case exponentially more interesting was the knowledge that the NE Division Chief had been suspiciously killed while in the back yard of his house. He was found with a bullet through his chest, his dog howling in despair beside him.

Conversations at the highest levels of the FBI have focused on two interrelated events: the explosive nature and contents of the president's file, and the way the NE Division Chief had been killed. This strongly suggests to the FBI's best criminal profilers that the killer and releaser of the file are likely not the same person.

The level of secrecy and effort to find the perpetrator are reminiscent of when the Agency suspected KGB moles were roaming the halls of the CIA and a phalanx of top-flight FBI investigators were called in to extirpate the spies. The inability of the American intelligence community and the FBI to identify the person who released the file, begs several questions, foremost, could the Russians intelligence community be involved? No one is talking and no one has claimed responsibility for releasing the president's file, and neither has anyone claimed to have seen the former president anywhere on the planet.

Rumors abound that he fled to Indonesia or the Middle East. The former First Lady and their children moved back to their home in Chicago and have refused interviews. The implication is that President Mazibuike has either abandoned his family, or the First Lady refused to accompany him when he departed for Hawaii on Air Force One. Some within the intelligence community have suggested he has gone underground to avoid U.S. Special Operations Forces personnel who would be tasked to return him to the United States to stand trial. Some have suggested the former president is afraid he would be removed from the earth with a missile launched from an unmanned drone. Others have sardonically suggested he has already been apprehended and is secretly occupying an orange jumpsuit in a cell at Guantanamo Bay, Cuba.

A critical review of the released file reveals extensive and unprecedented collaboration between remnants of the former Soviet Union, Islamist terrorist groups operating in the Middle East, and several senior Democratic Party members. The documents also paint a picture of a coordinated effort between senior media executives and rank-and-file journalists. Evidence seems to suggest that they knew the candidate Mazibuike was not the man he claimed to be, and yet they conspired to maintain his cover as an American citizen.

One of the most insidious and abused powers of the media is their power to ignore. The Mazibuike candidacy took full advantage of a complicit press who ignored the truth about their Democratic candidate and conspired to provide "top cover" whenever there were questions about his birth, education, or his international travel history. The Republican candidates suffered under these aggressive media co-conspirators and propagandists. Can I say these journalists' actions were "unpatriotic?"

If at least three intelligence communities and the media knew that former President Mazibuike was an unmitigated fraud yet perpetuated the fiction that he was a constitutionally-eligible candidate can the American people expect to see the media reform into something that resembles journalism? When will they come to view this media as just not another version of Pravda supporting their communist puppet masters in the Democratic Party?

. . . . .

The 2007 Pulitzer Prize winner for national reporting thought the better question might be, "Where is the former president and why hasn't he been brought to justice?"

It was a hard-hitting piece. He purposely avoided any reference to the Muslim Brotherhood's *Explanatory Memorandum* still banging around in his head. There was much more to research on that topic. An analysis of the document had been done by some of the finest minds in the intelligence community. For Eastwood, the first real connections between the former president and the Muslim Brotherhood's strategic plan for America were starting to form in his mind. It was another bit of news the media refused to acknowledge, research or print. More work; another potential article. It would have to wait.

Eastwood was pleased with the tone and pace of the piece. It was anyone's guess if it would be published. The newspaper editor had entertained submissions from conservative or Republican authors before, but had drawn the line on pieces where Democrats were even remotely accused of being or leaning communist. But then he would take every opportunity to revitalize the media's caricature of Conservatives and Republicans as backwoodsmen terrified of commies under their bed.

Eastwood allowed his thoughts to ramble. *Some would say the real identity of the former president was a mystery. I say the behavior of the left and the media was the real scandal. Every bit of personal information on the man was "close hold." They knew who he really was and did nothing; no one sounded the alarm that he wasn't eligible to run for president. See no evil, hear no evil, speak no evil. A complicit press. Criminals.*

The Republicans had their chance to stop him, but that idiot of a senile senator didn't challenge the man's credentials, didn't take him to court. The case against Mazibuike was already a cause of public alarm. But political correctness kept the timid Republicans from visiting the man's church, or demanding his "papers," his academic records, birth certificate, or passport records.

"It was a watershed moment for me," Duncan Hunter had said. *"Lightbulb moment. Some would to say he was the smartest man ever to run for president, but how would we know—no one has ever seen his transcripts! It suddenly occurred to me—they don't want to vet him. The media and the radical Left don't want to investigate him. If they don't want to find out about him, then they already know the answers and Americans will probably not like what they hear. It wouldn't take much to discredit him; it wouldn't take much to wander down Truth Street to see what was really there. But they will never go there."* He was so correct.

Eastwood returned to the case at hand and ripped his second article from the printer. He'd transmit it to the office of the editor of the *New York Times*. They'd likely ignore him too. Their favorite rejection line for something even slightly controversial was *Not what we're looking for.*

He was happy with the second article but the *Times* would never publish it. Writing it made him feel good. It was unlikely any of the conservative news outlets and papers would give it space in their editorial page or discuss it on the air. Editors had the power to approve or spike. That was the nature of the business.

"I'll pack in the morning," he said aloud to his computer monitor as if it were an impatient wife. It didn't talk back and didn't squeal when he shut it down and stumbled to the oversized sofa in the room. It would be another night sleeping in his clothes. It's what the troops in the field have to endure; he could do it too.

He wasn't looking forward to flying to Jakarta and taking the turboprop to Banda Aceh. He and his team were going back into the jungle near Banda Aceh, historically known as the port to *Mecca*. Terrorists and jungles and correspondents do not mix. Journalists had uneven track records of interviewing the leaders of any self-described or government-declared terrorist organization. Some came away with a story, some were able to escape a tragedy, while others lost their lives. Indonesia was a wildcard. The secret to a good trip, pack mosquito netting and take plenty of mosquito repellant and toilet paper. *More bugs trying to kill me.*

With a yawn, Eastwood rolled away from the bright lights of the city outside, buried his face into his shoulder, and fell asleep.

CHAPTER FIVE

2300 June 27, 2014
Peru

The airfield had shut down for the night. The control tower was abandoned. All ramp lights, taxi lights, and runway lights had been extinguished for over an hour. A small roving patrol pickup truck crawled along the inside perimeter of the fifteen-foot high walls looking for any signs of intrusion or interlopers. The special operations forces airport was a fortress protected by a barricade of thick concrete T-slabs topped with triple concertina wire. Infrared thermal systems would pick up the heat signature of any intruder, human or animal.

Any casual observer outside the walls during the day would see the Las Palmas Air Base as a hubbub of activity with helicopters and small armored airplanes flying in and out of the field. At night when it appeared everyone assigned to the facility had gone home for the evening, the tall steel entrance gates and impenetrable concrete walls were foreboding, like the entrance of the Gold Depository at Fort Knox. The level of security at the airfield was intimidating and overwhelming, impervious to attack. Although the airbase seemed to be closed, empty, and still, inside one of several aircraft hangars there was movement.

A pilot in a black flight suit and black helmet climbed onto the wing of a long-winged black airplane and stepped into the cockpit. As he fastened himself into the parachute harness and buckled the seat and shoulder belts, a pair of bottom-rolling hangar doors silently opened in front of him, four sections to a side. The pilot felt the aircraft move as two men in dark coveralls pushed the airplane out of the hangar. Once the aircraft's tail was free of the building, the ground crew raced back inside the hangar and closed the multi-panel doors. The pilot lowered the helmet-mounted ANVIS-9 night vision goggles over his eyes, closed the canopy, and started the engine. The wide six-bladed propeller turned slowly, a product of a reduction gearbox mounted on the output shaft of the reciprocating engine.

The Continental 360's engine exhaust would have shattered the calm and quiet of the night as it came to life and settled at idle power if not for a pair of mufflers and a specially designed exhaust system that ran down the starboard side of the fuselage and over the wing. The noise that came out of the exhaust system was about as loud as an old desk fan.

With no ground or tower controllers on duty to call for clearance, the pilot avoided the lengthy perambulation to the runway and took the most expeditious route to flight, and, once aligned with the centerline, firewalled the throttle. The little airplane took off quickly. Once safely airborne, the pilot wondered if anyone had noticed the late-night departure. If anyone had noticed the noise shadow of the tail-dragger they would not have believed what they saw or heard, or what they didn't see or hear—nothing.

The airplane's radar absorption paint included a nanotube coating that absorbed 99.96% of light. Smooth to touch, the special paint reflected nothing. Neither light nor radio waves. The slow-turning propeller eliminated the supersonic shockwaves that naturally formed across the propeller tips at high revolutions. The oversized propeller was driven by a special belt-driven gearbox and designed to be as quiet as the exhaust system. The aircraft's cumulative noise profile was outside the range of human detection at about fifty feet of altitude. The YO-3A was called *Wraith,* a shadow in the night, like a spirit that cannot be detected by sight or hearing.

Two minutes after takeoff, Duncan Hunter adjusted the throttle to increase the aircraft's climb rate and airspeed and aimed the aircraft toward a mountain range rich with coca plantations, cocaine-producing drug labs, and terrorist camps. But first he had to video a compound which buttressed the mountain chain. With the remote compound on the nose of the airplane, he set up the sensors to take multi-channel video of the target. He deployed the FLIR and low-light television camera and overflew the high walls, guard towers, and buildings. Two orbits of the area didn't register a single thermal hit; no one was home and the compound appeared to be completely abandoned. The FLIR ball silently folded back into the fuselage. *One down.*

The little black airplane sailed north and paralleled the Cordillera Oriental mountain range through clear skies and a still, moonless night.

The lights of the most populous city in the north, Huaraz, became more prominent as he approached its outskirts. Before he passed over the edges of Huaraz he climbed over the Cordillera Occidental Mountains and dove into the valley to kill some plants. He'd hunt for the narco-terrorist group known as the "Sendero Luminoso," or Shining Path after he was done.

Once the aircraft negotiated the range crossing, Hunter slowed the aircraft to eighty knots, put the throttle into the QUIET detent, and maintained three hundred feet above ground level. As he deployed the FLIR and the *Weedbuster* laser, he glanced at the airspeed indicator to watch the additional drag predictably knock another ten knots off his horizontal velocity. He was conscious of the high density altitude and that he was nearing the danger zone of the flying envelope. He had only about ten knots to the onset of stall. The aircraft's flight characteristics at night were silky smooth and stable. Huge shock mounts translated tiny engine vibrations into the airframe. Any hint of buffet was a reliable indicator that would tell him that he needed to add a few RPMs when he started to turn or he would lose a few more precious knots. He'd monitor the angle of attack and the big airspeed indicator and keep the airspeed needle within the green painted arc. The feel of the aircraft was tight, he was level, and with over a hundred such missions under his belt, he was confident tonight would be just another aerial eradication and observation mission. The GPS indicated his target was dead ahead.

He identified the first patch of coca and scanned the area. He didn't find anyone or anything hot in the FLIR. No distinctive thermal images anywhere on the side of the mountain. It wouldn't be prudent to blind someone in the middle of the jungle who would logically wonder why a laser was operating in the area.

Hunter smiled conspiratorially. After he retired from flying the supersonic F-4 Phantom, this was the type of flying he always wanted to do: flying a single-engine spy plane, killing drug crops with a laser, and finding terrorists and drug labs at night. Low-level flying in the mountains of Peru would scare away most pilots. Only the adventurous, like stunt pilots and air racers pushing the boundaries of safe flight and living on the edge, would find the work fascinating and exhilarating.

But above all that, the missions had *a purpose*. There was no other way to find and stop the men who made tons of the proscribed malodorous narcotic compounds for the international black markets. He would forever be challenging himself, operating close to the edge, maintaining total control of the airplane, his body, and his mind.

A few hours of irradiating coca plants effectively took hundreds of millions of dollars' worth of cocaine off the streets. The interference of their business and bottom line infuriated the drug lords. They spent millions of dollars to attack any and all impediments to their enterprise. Anyone involved in the counternarcotics efforts—lawyers, judges, policemen, military leaders and most recently, the aerial eradication men who sprayed the herbicides on the cash crop—were aggressively identified, hunted down, and killed. Cartel leaders wouldn't stop until the offending family members were destroyed as well. That sent a signal that there was no place to hide, and revenge would come when least expected. Cross the drug lords and you and your loved ones would be found, targeted, tortured, and likely killed.

Locating cocaine-producing drug labs, finding the staging points and paths for overland drug shipments, and uncovering the narco-terrorists' hiding spots from the air was incredibly and inherently dangerous. Using a silent airplane paired with an unseen laser was the perfect method to eradicate illicit drug crops. Unlike herbicides, a laser didn't leave any traces or residue or the chemical fingerprints of "being there."

There was a reason the Central Intelligence Agency and the State Department wanted to "take the man out of the cockpit" for the aerial eradication missions. If the pilot or the support crew were discovered, they faced a death sentence. Flying over Peru or Colombia in a single-engine, piston-driven airplane was akin to a suicide mission.

Any problem with the engine and you would go down. The likelihood of surviving a night parachute landing over dense jungle bordered on the impossible. Trying to "dead stick" an airplane into the jungle was a hit and miss proposition. If you hit a tree, the sudden stoppage would kill you. If the landing didn't kill you, then the jungle critters—snakes, spiders, jaguars—the Shining Path, and the men who ran the drug labs would be on your trail in minutes. The silenced black Kimber, Model 1911 .45ACP pistol in his survival vest would only delay the inevitable. This was insane, on–the-edge, almost daredevil flying with no margin for error. The leadership of the CIA had long believed these were jobs for unmanned systems. But even the best unmanned system wasn't a fraction as good as a human in the cockpit. And no one else had an airplane like the one Hunter was in.

The flight into the valley of evil men made him more aware of his environment. His instrument scan became more pronounced, quicker. More things to see, more things to monitor, more things to consider. He took stock of his surroundings before energizing the plant killing system, which increased the noise in the cockpit. A few more RPMs lessened the vibration coming from the reduction gearbox. Who would ever expect an outwardly quiet airplane to be almost deafeningly noisy inside?

As he manipulated the weed-killing laser and FLIR he said to himself, as if he were reading from a checklist and there was someone in the rear seat checking his procedures, "Ok we're here. Setting up an orbit. Laser coming about. Target hot."

He continually checked the area with the FLIR to ensure no human beings were anywhere near the path of the multi-head laser system. His cover would be blown if the laser damaged the eyes of someone on the ground. The drug cartels would become suspicious and would implement countermeasures, likely heat-seeking shoulder-launched, surface–to-air missiles. At least jungle animals, pit vipers, and stinging insects gave you a fighting chance of survival.

The secret to the mission's success was that humans couldn't detect the aircraft visually or aurally, and the *Weedbusters* laser system didn't leave any chemical residue. People didn't normally look up when they were engaged in something on the ground. The powerful four-headed laser was the Goldilocks solution to over-irradiate drug-producing plants. The goal was not to cut the plants, shred them, or set them on fire, but to sicken them with ultraviolet light at "the just right" wavelength and power. The difference between killing a plant and making it sick was calculated in how long the laser beams scanned the targeted plant. Sometimes sick drug-producing plants couldn't immediately be distinguished from healthy plants. Other times, when they were over-irradiated, the leaves of targeted plants would turn as brown as cardboard and curl up like a man slowly balling his fist. The optimum dwell time and power provided the perfect cover. *Weedbusters* was the ideal aerial eradication solution in the war on drugs. And it was Hunter's brainchild.

After four hours and five-hundred acres of drug crops destroyed, Hunter stowed the *Weedbusters* system but left the FLIR deployed. He said aloud for the video and voice recorders, "Four hours of fuel remaining. Everything is in the green. Now I'm going to fly north up the valley. I saw a couple of hot spots during a couple of turns. I'll reacquire them and see what those bad boys are doing at this time of the morning."

Hunter had been virtually silent while targeting and lasing plants from 300 feet above the ground. After a little innocuous climb, he was now in search mode, scanning the jungle for thermal images. Airspeed in the green. Climbing slightly. Sometimes the damn vibration from the engine would make him sleepy if he didn't stay active. Talking to himself helped keep him alert. He fiddled with the FLIR and recalled the story behind his airplane as he drove the aircraft toward the next GPS target.

Only a handful of pilots had ever heard of a YO-3A. Late in the Vietnam War the Army determined they had a requirement for a low-altitude "quiet" surveillance aircraft. Some big brain guys and a brilliant Navy physicist, all with top secret clearances, were pressed to develop an acoustically quiet aircraft. They focused on quieting the airframe, quieting the propeller, and quieting the engine. Several prototypes were built in secret; they called them "quiet thrusters." The first test beds looked like a collision between Frankenstein's monster, a Cessna, and a glider.

Army program managers thought the Navy guy had lost his mind. Under the direction of the Navy physicist, engineers modified a Schweizer glider, installed a heavily muffled engine behind the pilot's seat, ran a long thick driveshaft over the top of the glider's canopy to the front of the airplane, and bolted on a huge multi-blade propeller. The aircraft could take off under its own power. They tested it and validated the concept of low-altitude, virtually silent powered flight. Lockheed was awarded a contract for eleven prototype aircraft, designated YO-3As.

Now there were only three flyable airframes remaining. One was the pretty white and blue-trimmed NASA bird, number 011. The other two were Hunter's and were as black as the belly of a coalmine.

He relaxed a bit and was enjoying the smooth ride after the stressful eradication mission. The lights of Huánuco reflected off of the low-hanging clouds off the starboard wing. A hot spot, the bright white thermal image of a drug lab, came into view. But this was not the night to kill anyone, although it was still early. If they somehow found him in the sky, he would terminate them. No one could get away from a quiet airplane with a FLIR and a gun.

He smiled as he looked out the canopy. In Colombia and Peru he killed coca, and in Afghanistan he killed poppies. Acres and acres of freshly-sprouted poppies. He killed the baby poppies while the Taliban slept in their beds. *Murderous bastard!* Flying the airplane was addictive. There was no way to describe the rush of excitement he got with every mission. The challenge of killing dope or finding and killing a few very bad guys kept him coming back for more.

Duncan Hunter was a former Marine Corps pilot whose nine lives had nearly been used up. He survived a low-level ejection from a crippled F-4 Phantom jet that killed his back seater. That he could eventually resume playing racquetball competitively was a miracle worthy of Lourdes. But he had too much structural damage to his spine from the ejection to ever secure an "up chit," a medical release, to return to the front seat of any high-performance fighter aircraft. The problem was pulling Gs. Too many Gs would likely cripple him forever. He knew he couldn't get into the cockpit of another fighter. Unlike an addict who could be weaned off heroin through synthetics, flying the thundering and amazing fighters was a drug that could not be reproduced by surrogate smaller airplanes. The rush of cheating drug lords out of billions of dollars of drug money was his new flying addiction.

He spoke into the helmet's boom microphone to ensure the voice recorder was operating. "On the nose is a drug lab. Tagged…GPS for the Peruvian National Army. Scanning the opposite mountain where a hot spot is…*it's worth taking a look at.* I'm betting there's a good-sized Shining Path camp up there near the top of the Cordillera Central." He slewed the FLIR to zoom in on the white-hot images directly ahead a couple of miles away.

It was here in this type of environment that the YO-3A showed its unique capabilities. The same capability couldn't begin to be replicated by the boys in the research labs with their noisy little unmanned toys. At least, not yet. The key difference was subtle but vital. If he were to fly directly overhead like a satellite or an unmanned system, the FLIR would find nothing. The trees of the jungle canopy would completely obscure and diffuse the infrared thermal signature. But the combination of critical angle and low altitude allowed him to find and pick out the tiny light sources between the layers of the jungle canopy; glimpses of thermal activity. Flying low-level was the trade secret to success.

"Bingo. Drug lab. Well hid," said Hunter as a pair of white images appeared in the FLIR. The laboratory would have been completely hidden from satellites or a typical ISR platform, but not from the *Wraith*.

Hunter marked the GPS location to be imprinted on the videotape, maintaining heading and altitude for ten seconds. He added a little power and then started a slight climbing left turn. He didn't want to wildly deflect any control surface for fear it would generate a whistle that the guys on the ground could hear.

Next he would head for the mountaintop to check out the camp he had located earlier. Hunter said, "I guarantee you; I'm not going to find a Boy Scout Jamboree up there." The last time he had run across a hideout on top of a mountain he had found two dozen hostages who had been held captive for years by the FARC, the *Fuerzas Armadas Revolucionarias de Colombia*.

Hunter tried to turn the aircraft toward the mountain range, but the controls wouldn't respond to his inputs. They were frozen in place. He couldn't budge them. Even the throttle and rudder pedals were locked.

It was absolutely impossible that an aircraft with direct input cable and pulley control systems could have its stick, rudder, and throttle all unresponsive at the same time. Then he remembered there was one system that tied all of the independent systems together electrically. When the aircraft was in the optionally manned/unmanned mode of flight, computer software controlled the automatic takeoff and landing system (ATLS) servos for all three systems. He surmised that the ATLS had energized and froze the flight controls. He changed hands on the control stick to de-select the ATLS control box on the right side of the aircraft.

The Cordillera Central was beginning to fill up the windscreen and the FLIR. If he wasn't able to regain control of the aircraft immediately, he would fly headlong into the side of the mountain range. At this altitude, bailing out wasn't a viable option. He needed more altitude. He subconsciously pulled back on the control stick with his left hand. It didn't move. He toggled the ATLS power switch with his right. The system did not release. Hunter was afraid he'd snap the stick or his surgically-repaired hand if he applied any more pressure, so he reached for the ATLS circuit breaker on the right hand side circuit breaker panel.

Hunter kept glancing at the big airspeed indicator and at his position in the FLIR, gauging when impact would come. The thought that, "This is going to be bad" crept into his mind.

He glanced up at the mountain growing larger in the windscreen, reached down and found the circuit breaker and pulled it. Even with all power to the automatic takeoff and landing system cut, the flight controls continued to be unresponsive. Hunter reached for the avionics master switch, his last chance to save himself. This action would cut power to all of the aircraft's systems. He pushed the switch to OFF. The power did not go off; Hunter was stunned and shrieked, "*Shit!*" He tried it again, and again, and again. He rocked and ratcheted the switch back and forth, trying to get it to respond. Finally, after multiple tries the cockpit went completely black and the controls were instantly freed.

When Hunter felt the tension in the controls release, he simultaneously dipped the wing, firewalled the throttle, and pulled the control stick hard to get the motorized sailplane turning and climbing. He held his breath; his heart pounded in his chest. The cockpit was as dark as it was outside. Looking outside through his night vision goggles he was astonished to see that the wing didn't hit foliage during the maneuver, even though he was only a few feet over the jungle canopy.

Safe for the moment, Hunter thought about what had occurred. Likely a glitch in the ATLS software had locked the throttle and all the control inputs. He would leave that particular circuit breaker pulled. He would be okay without the ATLS. It was a very good system when there was no moon and a short runway. He really didn't get enough practice landing the YO-3A using NVGs.

Hunter tried to make some sense of it all. He had been flying airplanes for over 30 years and he had never experienced anything like that before. He set a heading for Las Palmas. Something continued to bother him. After a minute he reflected how many times he cycled the Avionics master switch. He was shocked that nothing had happened when he first cycled it. He had toggled it back and forth so many times with increasing desperation, with no effect, that he was startled when the night vision-capable cockpit lights finally extinguished. Normally stoic in the cockpit, he had actually freaked out. How many times had he cycled the switch. Five? Six? A dozen?

Frozen flight controls could not be tolerated under any

circumstances, but having the avionics master switch be completely unresponsive was just as troubling. Under normal circumstances he would return to base and scrub the rest of the mission, but the aircraft's controls were now completely isolated from any spurious electrical input. He knew what he should do—get the hell out of there and find out what caused the malfunction.

Hunter continued the climb and leveled the wings before he turned the avionics master switch back on. As the cockpit instruments reset and the FLIR came back to life after a re-initialization period, he gained confidence the aircraft wouldn't hurt him, that it wouldn't lock up the controls again. He doubled checked the ATLS circuit breaker was still pulled. Then he saw another flash of light in the FLIR. Eleven o'clock on the mountain top. It grew in size as his angle of approach was perfect for intercepting the thermal image. He pushed all thoughts of an immediate return aside and despite any apprehension about the controls locking again, he pointed the little airplane toward the new thermal images. He still had work to do.

"Tally ho. It looks like a campfire," he said to the voice recorder. He double checked the feel of the flight controls. A modular voice and videorecorder ran behind the empty back seat. Any thought of returning to Las Palmas vaporized as Hunter brought the aircraft around to find the best avenue of approach for a closer look. If you get a flash of thermal energy where there shouldn't be any real human activity you have to investigate. He leveled off at 8,000 feet to see if that was a good altitude for optimal viewing and recording angle. Parts of the Cordillera were still higher.

Hunter raised the nose of the aircraft, slowed to seventy-five knots for maximum noise reduction, and eased the YO-3A into the proposed altitude as if he had choreographed the maneuver. While the in-flight emergency was behind him, he knew he was being a bit reckless. His risk/reward consciousness told him to abort and fly back to the base, but his sense of duty and hatred of the cartels and their villainy overwhelmed any trepidation. The thermal image grew in size with every second. He concentrated on flying the aircraft. Airspeed. Altitude. Heading. *Was it worth it? We'll see.* "We're here; let's see if there is anything worth poking our nose into," he muttered.

The *Wraith* again slipped naturally into glider mode. The cockpit video and voice recorders were on and running. The only thing Hunter heard was the suppressed echo of his breathing in the noise-canceling headphones.

"Looks like a Shining Path shindig," he said aloud. "I count about fifteen people. I'm orbiting to get all aspects of the site." After two turns, Hunter ran the throttle up to takeoff power and then quickly back to idle.

The first time Greg Lynche had asked him to purposely perform the noise propagation maneuver was during his first flight in the YO-3A in Colombia. The rapid throttle motion and sudden power change yawed the aircraft significantly before it returned to trimmed flight. The propeller blades accelerated and propagated a low-frequency noise directed toward the ground. "Let's see if they do anything," Lynche, the old man from the CIA, commented. Lynche had changed Duncan Hunter's life with a handshake and had given him the opportunity to fly the YO-3A and do something unique. Find the bad guys; hunt down and find terrorists—those that used the cover of darkness to mask their nefarious actions.

Exactly as it had happened fifteen years earlier, within five seconds the forward-looking infrared's video screen caught the collective surprise of the group of narco-terrorists. Each ghostly image froze in place trying to discern the origin of the low amplitude growl. Then as if given an order, all the men grabbed nearby weapons and ran to a large hidden structure on the hillside. They took defensive positions around the makeshift hut.

Hunter smiled. Just like his first night in Colombia, he was giddy that the quiet aircraft galvanized the men on the ground to move. He controlled them like pieces on the counterterrorism chessboard. *Check!*

The men obviously had something very valuable to protect. Not drugs or weapons. Hunter was certain this was the location where some hostages were likely being held. The thugs wouldn't have responded that way if they were trying to protect a stash of cocaine or a drug lab. And drug men don't store on the mountain tops what they make in the valleys. When narco-terrorists have a sufficient quantity of drugs, they move and transport their loads via the paths and roads leading out of the valley which is the easiest, quickest, and most direct path to their distribution network. Terrorists reserved the jungle-covered hills to hide and protect human hostages, up and away from the prying eyes of satellites and government surveillance airplanes. When they held the high ground, they could protect themselves from invasions from below. Nighttime was when terrorists had most of the advantages. Hunter and the YO-3A neutralized those advantages.

He marked this spot with the GPS, turned, and headed back up the valley. He didn't want them to start looking up at the sky and see how the aircraft masked and unmasked the stars. He had what he wanted. If the men on the mountain held hostages, he didn't want to spook them into moving their captives.

He recalled asking Lynche, "How will we know there were captives up there?"

His answer was prescient. "It will be in the papers. It'll be a big deal. Their military will get awards for rescuing them, and for finding and killing the bad guys." There are some things even a complicit government-controlled press would be forced to report. Terrorist takedowns were especially newsworthy. When Hunter returned from his mission, he would debrief the Chief of Station at the hotel in exquisite detail, with GPS coordinates. When he saw the Director of Central Intelligence, Hunter would give Lynche the downloaded audio and video recordings of the mission on a flash drive.

The near collision with a mountain was a vague memory; the flight control issue was not. He was still flying the mission profile and was at one of two decision points. He checked the Rolex on his wrist for the time and made a few mental calculations. He was ahead of schedule and decided to use the extra time to head to the coast. He didn't like what the flight controls had done to him, but it seemed he had fixed the discrepancy, and the Chief of Station would be pleased if he found a fast boat or a submarine hauling a ton of cocaine heading to Central America.

Fifty minutes later he was over the Pacific. Hunter quickly picked up a small submarine, larger than a simple home-built submersible, in the FLIR. With a pair of snorkels for engine intake and exhaust, its thermal image was unmistakable; it was a cocaine sub. As he closed with the target he depressed a few buttons on one of the multifunction displays on his instrument panel and activated the GUN system. He lowered the weapon into the airstream and engaged the fire control system.

The .70 caliber gun was the product of the CIA's Science and

Technology Directorate. The "black" program developed both a very long-range sniper rifle and a completely new experimental type of ammunition. Hybrid propellants within the ammunition—a combination of black powder and a tiny solid rocket motor—reduced the severity of the G-load on the electronics in the seeker head of the massive bullet. The only drawback of the disruptive technology weapon was that the fire from the tiny chemical rocket motor was visible at night. White streaks. And with each fired round, the FLIR would momentarily "wash out" as hot gasses from the gun barrel and the bullet's rocket motor saturated the sensitive thermal sensor.

He lased the slow moving submarine with a laser designator and fired three rounds into the semi-submerged vessel. The first round hit the rear of the sub, the next bullet hit the makeshift conning tower, and the last round hit just aft of the bow. Thirty seconds later men poured from the top of the submarine as it was apparently taking on more water than a bilge pump could handle. The videorecorder and FLIR captured the interception and the disabling of the submarine.

With his mission fully completed, Hunter said, "Splash one cocaine sub. *Now* it's time to go home."

CHAPTER SIX

1800 July 1, 2014
Omaha, Nebraska

"Can someone tell me why a French boomer is making port in the UAE?" the crusty old white-haired Marine general, the United States Strategic Command Commander, bellowed as he stepped down into the pit of the STRATCOM Global Operations Center. Stunned faces of the Army, Navy, and Air Force officers, and civilians peered over computer monitors in their workstation consoles in the underground two-level, 14,000-square-foot, auditorium-like concrete structure. No one had an immediate answer. Silence was unacceptable.

After a three second pause, a petite, curly blonde-haired U.S. Navy captain who was several layers of workstations away from the seat of power, spoke up from the INTEL section. She couldn't believe the boss would ask such a question. Surely outgoing STRATCOM commanders briefed their replacements. On the off chance he didn't know the particulars of the French-built boat, she said, "Sir, it's the UAE's special boat."

The white-haired general nearly erupted in a fount of invective. "What the hell are you talking about Frappier?" He was curt and dismissive—the four-star general wasn't about to take a flippant answer from the subordinate woman. He kept his eyes directed at the satellite feed as the extra-long submarine with the telltale humpback which housed submarine-launched ballistic missiles slipped into a covered shelter and disappeared from view.

Captain Pamela Frappier was surprised the ancient Marine fighter pilot knew her name. She hadn't done anything since his assignment to merit the level of attention attached to "name recognition." She stifled a frown and responded confidently, "Sir, the UAE bought a Redoubtable-Class French nuclear submarine in the 90s. It's a boomer on the outside but benign on the inside." She used the vernacular to indicate the intercontinental ballistic missile-capable submarine wasn't built to carry missiles.

He stopped himself from shouting, "Are you serious?" The general slipped into his throne-sized, overstuffed, leather, office chair. He waved at the sailor to come to him.

Strategically, the world situation was quiet across the planet. It was one of those brief welcome periods of worldwide calm that occurred very infrequently. The calm was eerily unusual, but in the blink of an eye there could be a new incident on the other side of the big blue marble. For the moment all was quiet, and thankfully so.

The only real abnormality was a known French submarine, a "boomer," which was built to contain a dozen sea-launched, long-range ballistic missiles, was plying the waters of the Persian Gulf. He might have been an old fighter pilot, but he guessed that French subs don't generally play in that part of the world. He scanned the complete Knowledge Wall, dozens of oversized LED screens covering an area the size of a highway billboard that reflected the current global situation. Ten seconds elapsed and the planet was still calm. He knew inactivity wouldn't last for long; the Communists in Russia, China, and North Korea were always pretending to move their nuclear weapons systems out of view from America's satellites, while radical Islamists were always trying to steal someone's nuclear weapons.

Three smaller rectangular monitors were situated at his command desk. He waved a hand and the screens came to life. Motion and biometric sensors detected the general's presence in the technological seat of authority and awoke the sleeping computer screens. The technology was great, when it worked.

The Navy Captain clicked her heels to signal her arrival at his desk. He ignored her for the moment and scanned his monitors for a message of mayhem at any latitude and longitude, but there was nothing. He could get used to days like this before he headed home.

The Global Operations Center (GOC) was the nerve center of United States Strategic Command. The GOC received inputs from various sources and provided global situational awareness for the commander. When the general entered the GOC as the STRATCOM commander, he exercised operational command and control of the nation's global strategic forces—all three legs of the nuclear triad. The

United States' strategic nuclear arsenal consisted of strategic bombers, intercontinental ballistic missiles (ICBMs), and submarine-launched ballistic missiles (SLBMs).

Surrounded by the computer monitors and several colored phones, General Antonio Magnussen looked down at the attractive naval officer. The horn-rims didn't do anything for her; she was a looker who hid her looks for good reason. She could get him into a lot of trouble. Best to get the intel she had and send her away. He remembered her name; he always remembered the pretty ones, the shiny ones. Magnussen was firm. "Frappier, say again."

"Sir, this nuclear submarine was the last one built in France; it was purchased for the president of the United Arab Emirates or some emir there. The boat is not equipped, nor is it capable of launching SLBMs. Like all old French nuclear Redoubtables, it can remain underwater for months. Reportedly, the space behind the conning tower was converted into a living area for the royal family, sir."

He wasn't convinced the discussion was relevant or accurate. "So let me get this straight. It's your contention that we have a French boomer that isn't a boomer, but it happens to be billion-dollar underwater joy ride for an oil sheikh?"

"That sums it up, sir."

"Why?"

Frappier was confused. She contorted her face to send a signal she didn't fully understand the terse three-letter question. He rubbed his hands roughly across his face to gain him some time to reformulate his request for additional information without being abusive. As he sucked air the woman started talking.

"Sir, the UAE has a few diesel boats that operate in the open, and this one nuke which is rarely seen. The diesel boats are used to protect its shores and carry out spying missions against its archenemy, Iran. The nuke typically spends months at pier. When it sails, it enters and departs its pen only at night. Historically, it makes sail to South America, Southeast Asia, and Africa. Specifically, it goes to South America once a year, to Vietnam once a year, to Africa twice a year."

"Why?" His eyes returned to the monitors in front of him. His voice remained calm, but he still didn't get the answer to his question.

"They're not official port calls. The intel evaluation and analysis suggest it's used for smuggling."

Her summation struck a nerve. The general raised his eyes and looked at the woman. He scowled at her in suspicion and disbelief. In a voice that was foreboding and demanding, almost threatening, he said, "Now we're getting somewhere. Out with it, Frappier. I can handle the truth."

Captain Frappier paused to collect her thoughts. She was surprised the four-star wanted specifics on the UAE's special boat program. It was a long-known benign quantity. This one submarine, one of the largest built by a Western power, was purchased with oil money and was operated very infrequently by the UAE's navy. The French president had personally made millions in negotiating the transaction. The submarine was unique—the *Abba Sayeed* wasn't armed in any way. No missiles, no torpedoes, no cannon. The "boat," as it was affectionately referred to within the Navy, was seemingly built for the end-of-the-world wars, but it was purposely demilitarized during manufacture. It was thirty years old—nearing the end of its service life. A civilian-purpose submarine was a total naval warfare anomaly.

The basic situation was simple; America's spy satellites had tracked a submarine from the west coast of France to the UAE. It was immediately hidden away underneath a thousand-foot-long covered pier that was more Quonset hut than awning. Almost a year later the submarine left its covered pier and headed east. It returned months later under cover of darkness. The sub was quiet and was rarely picked up by the ocean's array of sensors. It was stealthy, only being seen by satellites when in shallow waters while leaving or returning to port.

The UAE boat didn't make military sense to her superiors at the Office of Naval Intelligence (ONI) or STRATCOM. Satellite images of the turtleback showed smooth seamless panels in the area and not the expected ballistic missile tube doors with their telltale hinges and circular pressure hatches from which sea-launched ballistic missiles would have normally been launched. Since the submarine was unarmed and therefore civilianized, the STRATCOM Commanders generally ignored it or dismissed it. It was the strategic equivalent of a canoe. No weapons, no threat, no factor. STRATCOM indicated that Navy Intelligence could keep an eye on the civilian boat if they so desired, but neither the Chief of Naval Operations or the STRATCOM Commander were in the business of monitoring civilian-use submarines.

As a career intelligence officer on staff at the ONI, Frappier stumbled upon the unique United Arab Emirates submarine when some lecherous harridan of an admiral tossed her a file and sent her off to do some research and analysis. The lusty lesbian admiral purportedly wanted answers on the mysterious UAE sub, but what she really wanted was a piece of Lieutenant Commander Frappier. Most of the ambitious and competent field-grade officers were familiar with the admiral's tactics and passed along "the gouge" to the more senior officers. "Don't let her get her hands on you, or you're toast." There was a quiet acknowledgement that rebuffing her advances could be a career killer.

The admiral tasked Frappier to find all relevant information particular to the UAE's submarine, the factory that built it, the terms and conditions of purchase, as well as the political reasons why an extremely small Arab nation would purchase a huge nuclear-powered but unarmed submarine. Just as Frappier was getting started on her assignment, a "pop-up" set of orders to the Naval War College in Newport, Rhode Island saved her from the clutches of the rapacious flag officer. On her last day at Suitland the admiral chased Frappier around the four-by-eight-foot desk, promising favorable fitness reports and heavy recommendations for command in exchange for just a little quiet time with her. The gouge was correct. Frappier dashed to the door first and out of the office. She raced out of the building, breaking a heel on the way. Safely in her little red Jeep, she realized the admiral's interest in the UAE boat had all been a ruse. Reporting the incident would tube her career, so she'd have to wait and see if the boss killed her on her appraisal. She drove straight to Newport. She couldn't wait to begin her graduate education in naval warfare and maybe, if there was time, to find some more answers on the "civilian submarine."

No longer a mission requirement but still an unsolved mystery that tickled her professionalism as a naval officer, Frappier had yet to uncover the deepest secrets of the UAE submarine. No country anywhere permitted the acquisition, operation, and use of a nuclear submarine for civilian purposes. A chance meeting with another Naval War College student months later provided a new direction for her infrequent research on her pet project.

She remembered the December 2002 encounter like it was yesterday. She was a Lieutenant Commander in the junior's course then. He wasn't

Navy but an old retired Marine officer. A civil servant. A civilian in the senior's course. Working for the Air Force. No one at the Naval War College believed for a New York minute he was a regular Air Force civilian. Ten uniformed students and the civilian in an expensive black suit gathered for an impromptu lunch in the cafeteria before their departure for the Christmas holidays. Seated across the table from the grey-beard class president, an old Navy SEAL and considered to be "the old wizened one," she blurted, "Captain McGee, do you have any idea what an unarmed submarine would be used for?" Inwardly congratulating herself that she had found the courage to ask the Navy icon, she was stunned when the man in the business suit and expensive Italian tie answered instead. Not even looking up from his soup and salad, he just said, "Smuggling." The huge SEAL snapped his fingers, pointed at the man with the answer, and nodded. "Bingo!" The other students sat stunned in silence. It was the most they had ever seen the two disparate friends collaborate on anything.

Confused, Frappier asked him, "How can you be so sure? What would they possibly smuggle? It's a billion dollar boat?"

The civilian avoided the argument with platitudes. "Never underestimate the treachery of a criminal. Whatever it is, you can take it to the bank that whatever '*service*' they are providing is worth every penny…to them."

Captain McGee said, "It's probably manned by regular military. They'd be trained submariners. They know how to keep a secret, especially if they are appropriately compensated."

The men's statements hung in the air like a noxious gas.

"How would *you* know that?" Frappier asked, even more confused. Their answers weren't really answers. The civilian was being purposely curt and evasive. She wanted a real answer, but as she reflected, she softened; she was more interested in the man's dark voice. It warmed her inside.

"It's what I used to do." No sarcasm, no hyperbole, no hubris; just a matter of fact statement. The man in black finally looked up from his food; their eyes locked.

She didn't look away, but took a deep breath and asked, "What? *Smuggle?*"

"Unofficially, I think we can say Captain McGee finds and kills the enemies of America, I was in the Border Patrol and used to find and stop smugglers. Unlike the methods of my favorite U.S. Navy SEAL, my methods were kinder and gentler." The double entendres were ricocheting off the cafeteria walls. A sly grin swept across his face, belying the fact that he was something other than just a simple Air Force civil servant working at a huge pilot training base in Texas. He bent his cover more than a little.

"Oh." It was her turn to raise her penciled eyebrows to the sky. "What are you doing at the Naval War College?" she asked.

He smiled at her fully and checked her nametag and her rank. "No need to know, Commander Frappier." He and the African-American SEAL stood, as if on cue. The retired Marine had affectionately called her by her next rank and pronounced her name properly; he winked at her as he pushed away from the table, gathered his tray, and without so much as a goodbye, left her last question unanswered. Frappier wanted more than an answer to her question; and she wanted to see more of the man in the tailored suit. Even though she never saw him again, she would never forget his name, Duncan Hunter.

Pam Frappier was energized by this unusual and nearly unbelievable solution. The U.S. Coast Guard dealt with smugglers, rarely did the U.S. Navy. And those were generally domestic interdictions. The scope of international smuggling was not a familiar topic. She researched the history of UAE and their submarine in this possible context. The Naval War College library and SCIF held the keys to the thousands of questions running through her head as she had struggled to resolve the question, "What is that sub used for?" What she discovered among a hundred years of secret naval archives was shocking. Officers within the Office of Naval Intelligence Detachment at Newport had cubby-holed some of the long-lost history of Arab non-military submarine use. The secret to the submarine lay hidden below a level of organized disinformation, much like the round conformal anchors neatly tucked underneath each submarine. It wasn't until she accessed top secret files in another level of the SCIF vault that she finally found some answers.

Deep in the archival history of the world wars there was an old flimsy file on powerful seafaring Arab sheikhs and emirs acquiring and operating submarines, first and second-generation German U-boats as well as rudimentary submersibles. It was truly ancient history. The pages within the file were delicate with age but they were fascinating.

Frappier debated telling the general the full story. It was likely irrelevant considering today's UAE sub didn't carry weapons, which brought a level of indifference concerning the UAE boat. It was assumed it was no threat and no factor to U.S. naval interests. She expected the STATCOM Commander would dismiss her immediately once she told him what she knew, but she had been dying to tell someone. Maybe he wouldn't fire her for wasting his time.

"Sir, some members of the UAE's royal family have had access to submarines going all the way back to the mid-1930s. They operated *dhows* and U-boats by night from the eastern coast of the Arabian Peninsula. They were protected by a small contingent of *Schutzstaffel;* the Nazi Party's 'Protective Squadron.' They smuggled everything from precious gems, pearls, and ivory to spies and fallen dictators and their closest advisors. They integrated submarines into their shipping business. Documents at the ONI and the Naval War College suggest that, before Hitler fell from power Admiral Canaris provided U-boats and crews to second-tier sympathetic countries to be used as escape vehicles for Hitler and senior members of the Nazi party, if and when needed. A U-boat in the Persian Gulf was considered a myth. Released secret documents after the war proved the Germans not only provided one of the newest U-boats but built an extensive dock and pier system as well as a submarine pen and underground maintenance facilities in the Abu Dhabi area of Mina Jebel Ali. A pair of fuel tanks were only a hint of what was installed underground and under cover. German sub crews and the SS protection details were provided women for company and recompense. It is assumed they eventually converted to Islam because the Germans were never heard from again."

"The French were the latest to build a new sub and upgrade the shelter for the UAE. They removed the old above-ground storage tanks and upgraded the exposed pier which is now being used by at least one of the royal family's 300-foot yachts. Ostensibly, the boat is used for the same purpose. When one of the emirates aren't using their yacht, they're likely smuggling high value goods and high profile people looking to become low-profile people."

General Magnussen rolled his tongue in his cheek and brought his hands together as if he were praying. "That is the most gallinaceous and bovine narrative I've ever heard, and damned if I don't believe it. Who else knows this?"

"Just you and me, sir. I haven't been able to get anyone interested in the UAE sub; it's so unusual and interesting it has become something of a hobby to me. But officially, the boat's history and capabilities haven't been a priority."

The general leaned back in his chair for a moment, looking up at the woman. He rubbed his eyes and face again which muffled words. "The previous administration released I-don't-know-how-many terrorists from Guantanamo Bay and turned them over to the UAE. That boat could be used to get those dirtballs back to Iraq or Afghanistan or Pakistan or wherever the hell they came from. Could that sub be used to move HVTs, high-value targets?"

Frappier about fell over from shock. *He gets it!* "Absolutely."

He continued, "Allow them back into the game through surrogates. Who knows what else they're doing? We need to add that boat to the strategic surveillance plan. Does the Agency know? Why didn't the ONI show any interest?"

She started to say something about an unarmed submarine not being "in the ONI's swim lanes" but the general stepped all over her as he continued his verbal stream of consciousness. "I'll take care of that. We need to brief the NCTC...the National Counter Terrorism Center Director. We'll get you on the schedule."

Frappier began to speak but was again cut off. The general wasn't finished. "Work up some slides, flip them to me, and I'll arrange for a meeting. Have you been to the NCTC?"

"No, sir."

"Is there anything else I should know?"

She considered how to answer. He could tell she was hedging a response. "Sir, um, it may be nothing. Maybe circumstantial...."

The general rolled his eyes. "Out with it."

"The *Abba Sayeed* arrived at Subic Bay on 30 June 2011."

"If I am supposed to know why that date is important...I don't." He was more than a little irritated.

"That was the day after the president resigned, took Air Force One, and landed in Hawaii."

From under bushy brows he shot a Frappier a cadaverous look. General Magnussen recalled one of the exposés from the war correspondent Demetrius Eastwood on the former president and the UAE secretly being paid billions, sometimes planeloads of cash were exchanged for the UAE to take some of the al-Qaeda prisoners held at Guantanamo Bay. He recalled the words of the most famous Marine Corps general, Smedley D. Butler, who said, "War is a racket." *A racket is not what it seems to most people. Only a small "inside" group knows what it is all about. It is conducted for the benefit of the very few at the expense of the very many. Out of war, few people make huge fortunes.* Now Magnussen "got it." When liberals aren't killing the rich and famous for their wealth they find other ways of stealing the wealth of a nation. Secretly transferring tax dollars to pay the UAE to take America's enemies was brilliant. Eastwood had found an incident where the former president had negotiated a similar agreement with the Iranians. They took Americans hostage and the president secretly paid the ransom. General Magnussen could hardly believe the pieces of the puzzle that just plopped in his lap.

He recovered his composure and said stoically, "That's likely not a coincidence. Good job, Pam. Send me your numbers and tickets. I will rearrange my schedule, you're going with me to CIA Headquarters. No one would ever think of them using a demilitarized boomer to move contraband and HVTs. It wouldn't take much for one of those skippies to transport suitcase nukes and waltz into Hudson Bay in New York City."

She nodded and answered, "Yes, sir. I'll get right on those slides."

"Frappier, for now, this is just between us girls, okay?"

The old bird can be self-deprecating too? Okay! "Aye, aye, sir." She did an "about face" as best as she could in heels, and walked off with a smile that beamed, *I knew that information would be useful someday!*

General Magnussen enjoyed the view for as long as he dared. Then he blinked and was back to admiring the deceit and treachery of the former president while monitoring the status board to see if anyone on the planet was trying to start a nuclear war. With a wave of his hand, his computers shut down. One last check of the Knowledge Board and he transferred command of the Global Ops Center to the Duty Officer.

CHAPTER SEVEN

0100 July 2, 2014
Dubai

For the second night in a row heavy fog obscured the city below their feet. From the observatory 1,500 feet above sea level the carpet of haze unfurled uniformly and omnidirectionally as warm, moist winds from the Gulf pushed inland before being stopped by the mass of a hundred huddled skyscrapers. With no dry breeze coming from the mountains to roll it back out to sea, the thick miasma sat atop the city, enveloped its high-rise buildings, and extinguished most of the lights below. At ground level, the moisture swirled like the special effects of a bad horror movie. Vehicles were brought to a standstill as the fog made driving treacherous and invited unfettered traffic chaos for those who thought they could navigate by braille. Some people still wandered about in the soupy murkiness which made walking any distance an eerie and frightening experience.

For others, the fog provided the perfect opportunity to move about undetected. High-flying aircraft with infrared sensors that could see in total darkness and look through smoke weren't very effective in penetrating the thick moisture-laden goo, if the thermal imaging companies' marketing materials were to be believed. This was one of the rare times when the government wouldn't be able to find or track some of the seedier elements of society. Street corner cameras only recorded what looked like the inside of a snowball. The unmanned aerial vehicles that were to monitor rooftop crime and the highway traffic between the two major cities were grounded to surveil another night.

Not all transportation was completely susceptible to the weather. Three black, armored BMW 760s, highly-modified self-driving automobiles moved downtown in single file, slowly tunneling through the dense mist. Super computers in the trunks integrated tiny radars embedded in the bumpers and enhanced global positioning system antennas on the roofs enabled precision maneuvering down streets and through intersections in a close convoy operation that was performed better than any human could when the visibility was zero.

Even on a night like this, anyone approaching the faint amber-lighted entrance of the Burj Khalifa looked up to see if they could see the top of the world's tallest building. Tonight raising one's eyes to the heavens was wasted energy. One could barely see three feet ahead. A wide red carpet from the curb to the lobby door ensured anyone who dared to venture out in such soupy weather could find their way inside.

Flanked by muscular security men, the man in dark sunglasses emerged from the middle vehicle and stirred vortices in the thick suspended moisture. He strolled into the building with all of the arrogance of a member of the royal family. At one time he had wielded great power and prestige. But he wasn't a member of any royalty. He was a mongrel, the progeny of a detestable class of foreigners, *Amrikis* and *Afrikaans*. He came by his station in life not through bloodlines or close familial relationships but through an election half-a-globe away. His rise in politics was meteoric, the product of a well-conceived marketing plan, a complicit media which ignored or refused to vet his credentials, and the unmitigating deceit of his political party. He fell from power in a sudden and stunning defeat, an embarrassment of epic proportions. It shattered his psyche and the topic was never far from his thoughts. It floated on the surface like spent oil on pristine water. His escape from public office was successful, yet his quest to determine who had orchestrated his political demise had become an obsession.

A billowy, white silk *keffiyeh* and wraparound sunglasses hid a clean-shaven face and eyes that continued to suffer the crushing blow of discovery and the debacle that followed. Thin, black, kidskin gloves offset the cream-colored *thobe* that draped his broad shoulders.

The collection of mercenaries escorted him through the glass doors of the main lobby and through a bizarre display of polished Zildjian cymbals atop tall brass rods masquerading as a musical water feature. They rode in silence on the world's fastest elevator. The ride took a mere 35 ticks of his gold Cartier, the equivalent of fifty miles per hour. None of the men was interested in the elevator's dreary blue light show of the building's three-hub trademark which was inspired by a local flower, the White Hymenocallis.

The elevator stopped on the 152nd floor, and the security team stepped off. As soon as the door closed again, the man who once graced State dinners and the United Nation dais removed a glove and placed his right hand on a hidden biometric scanner at the top of the information panel which activated a special access control system. He wiped the screen with a kerchief to remove any trace of his fingerprints, returned the glove to his hand, and rode the rest of the way up to the highest occupied floor; a few seconds later he stepped out onto white polished marble of the 154th floor. The topmost suite housed the corporate offices of an obscure international trading company. The elevator doors uncharacteristically remained open as if to telegraph to the occupants that the special elevator would wait until it received the appropriate command to return to the lower floors.

He walked across the Italian Arabesco into the dimly lit conference room where eight men waited. No one stood when he entered. The men did not greet him in the Islamic way; there was no cheek kissing, no embracing, and no words spoken. They had all been reminded that their visitor had become something of a germaphobe since leaving office and insisted on no physical contact, especially not with his hands.

Sitting at the head of the long rectangular table and wearing a black *thobe* and an oversized black *keffiyeh* was the emir. He valued silence, submission, and distance over cultural protocols. There was no tea service and there was no greeting in the Muslim way.

The six other swarthy and bearded men wore white *thobes* with black and gold drapes to indicate their status as princes of the royal family. Their heads were covered with matching white silk *keffiyehs* held in place with black and gold-braided *agals*. The eighth man, wearing a dark suit and an inconspicuous tie, sat nervously near the middle of the table behind a laptop computer. They all watched as the newcomer moved to the opposite end of the gleaming ebony conference table. He did not sit but stopped behind a black leather judge's chair. He gripped the padded stiles with both hands. They all noticed the man's gloved hands. Some wondered if they had been scarred from burns before they remembered that he was pathologically afraid of contamination and bacteria.

At his very first meeting with the emir of emirs, before his battery of debriefings, he had asked for this meeting if a certain "capability" ever presented itself. After a couple of years the emir of emirs had contacted him and indicated that, "We may finally have something for you to consider." They had waited hours for Maxim Mohammad Mazibuike, the former President of the United States of America to arrive. Only the head of the table knew where he lived or how he moved about. The former American president, like so many others, rarely ventured from his palace safe house. But for this special purpose meeting, he had made his appearance without disguise.

He had come only when there was a forecast of heavy fog for the city. He knew the capabilities of the high-flying UAVs and their suite of sensors. He couldn't take the chance that his successor would try to kill him with a missile. He had ordered many air-to-ground missiles to eliminate al-Qaeda's leaders and other radical upstarts., but never the important ones. And no one would ever be so foolish as to fire one of those missiles into such a quintessential Islamic building as the Burj Khalifa.

Tamerlan al-Sarkari adjusted his tie, adjusted his chair, and focused on his laptop computer. He strained not to look at the one they had been waiting for. He recalled an earlier time when Mazibuike was still a candidate and his remarkable soaring rhetoric had made him feel as giddy as a teenage girl with her first crush. *We are the ones we've been waiting for.* Al-Sarkari had been moved by the loftiness of that particular line, the speeches, the promises, and the man's boundless charisma. *He is the messiah!* Al-Sarkari also recalled the latter days of the former president's time in office when his temper turned mercurial, erratic, vitriolic. He fully expected that he had become more angry after his escape from America and his impeachment *in absentia.*

Al-Sarkari was shocked he was still alive. Of course, now he needed to hide his face as well as his movements. His failure within the American Democratic Party was epic, ignominious, and unique. The public release of the former president's secret CIA file had exposed the lie. How many had been elected President of the United States only to be chased from office, not as a criminal, but as a charlatan and a fraud? Only one, and he was standing at the head of the table hiding behind a chair. He allowed an unseemly thought—*Mazibuike should have been the Caliph of America.* Al-Sarkari pushed aside his disappointment. Maybe he could help resurrect the man's destiny. He had work to do. He said with no hint of deference, "As requested, I'm ready to test the system."

Al-Sarkari had been warned about the man in the black keffiyeh, *You must not look into his eyes or speak directly to him. The One's speech is always elegant and above all, courteous.* The American software engineer was potentially endangering himself and the *plan* with a contemptuous and wholly un-Islamic display of haughtiness. American Muslims could be so arrogant.

The former President of the United States asked, "How will we know if we are successful?"

Mazibuike's words came out in fragments of guttural noises that slurred into recognizable words. His voice was soothing but obstreperous. Al-Sarkari caught the unmistakable whiff of *shisha*, thicker, more hashish than marijuana, emanating from the former president. Al-Sarkari snorted. He had heard the Republicans in America say that the man couldn't construct an articulate string of coherent sentences or speak extemporaneously without the aid of a teleprompter. The effect of much drug use as a young man was the apparent culprit. If his nose was correct, Mazibuike was still indulging, at the very least, in *cannabis. At his station in life, he was probably using some of the finest stuff money could buy.* Al-Sarkari didn't look up from the computer screen and said with impassioned indifference, "It will disappear."

The men around the table shuddered in disgust. No one had ever been so flippant. But the software engineer was essential to *the plan.* Former President Mazibuike re-gripped the edges of the chair in aggravation as he glared at the man behind the computer. Al-Sarkari, completely oblivious that his words could be considered rude focused on his computer screen; his fingers raced across the keyboard as fast as an executive secretary typing an immediate termination notice.

Yes, it'll disappear! It was his work, his programming, and he was taking the most incredible chance of his professional life. If even a hint of what he had accomplished was discovered, he would have to get his own dark hole in which to hide. He, too, would only be able to come out when it was safe, like on a night like tonight. A smile crept over al-Sarkari face. He and the former president might have more in common than either realized. The only difference was the President's story had been leaked to the press and members of Congress; al-Sarkari's treachery had yet to be discovered. He would do everything within his power to maintain the charade, maintain his cover, and stay alive. Would the CIA discover him and then send their unmanned airplanes with missiles to kill him too? It was time to show some respect.

"That wasn't the question—how will *we* know?" The former president's eyes bored into the cranium of the man behind the computer.

Al-Sarkari met his gaze and said, "Sir. The press will report the airliner is missing. In a few hours we will know."

The manufactured ire began to melt away. A hint of a smile appeared on the stony dark face. "And it will not be found?"

"Highly unlikely. The candidate aircraft I've chosen will be flying over some of the deepest parts of the Pacific. It will likely be going supersonic when it hits the water. In excess of 700 miles an hour. Vertically. It will disintegrate on impact, as if hitting concrete. The momentum will carry it and all fragments under the surface. Some tiny remnants may float but they will largely be unrecognizable. Irrelevant. Remains will be very difficult to find in an expansive ocean. There will be virtually nothing left. Fragments may wash up on some remote shoreline years from now, but it is unlikely anyone will be able to positively identify the remains as coming from the airliner." His English was pure and crisp with no hint of an Arabic accent.

"That is better. Do it."

The software engineer pinched his lips, nodded, and entered several quick keystrokes. Phase one of the project was complete. As he shut the lid of the thin computer he looked up to the men around the conference table as if to say, "It is done."

Mazibuike pushed away from the chair, turned, and silently walked toward the outer bank of windows. He looked out over the foggy undercast. Some of the lights of Dubai's tallest skyscrapers, those over 500 meters, could be seen dimly twinkling in the thick haze below.

He didn't want to return to the palace below, to hide again in the secret city underneath Dubai, and to be continually on the alert of detection. For once detected, he would be targeted. He feared being hunted down and returned to stand trial like a Nazi war criminal. Adolf Eichmann, one of the major organizers of the Holocaust, had been found by Mossad, Israel's intelligence service, hiding in Argentina. The former president knew special operations forces were likely trying to pick up his trail. If any organization could locate him, it was the CIA. But it would be up to Special Activities Division or SEAL Team Six to corner and capture him. More likely they would be sent to kill him. He had been briefed every time he traveled abroad that a specially trained SEAL sniper team would be in the background in case the presidential security was overwhelmed. Presidents were not to be compromised.

During one of the few Presidential Daily Briefs he had attended, Mazibuike recalled a program called *Broken Lance*. He recalled the CIA Director instructing him of the term *Broken Arrow* for the loss of a nuclear weapon. *Bent Spear, Dull Sword,* and *Empty Quiver* were other coded terms that described the accidental launching, firing, detonating, theft, or loss of a nuclear device. *Broken Lance*, though, was actually a top-secret operational plan to assassinate a sitting president if the president had been captured and held hostage by a hostile group. It was promulgated by a secret executive order and signed by John Fitzgerald Kennedy in 1961. JFK was the original Lance or Lancer living in Lancelot, as the American media romanticized. With rapid international travel becoming the norm, President Kennedy determined the American people didn't want to see their president subjected to torture or paraded around after being captured in a far off land. A president would be, at a minimum, humiliated, but most likely, would be tortured for crimes against an offended people. A captured president was the ultimate horror for America. The country would be at risk, national secrets would be stripped from his brain, and the government would become completely dysfunctional. That is until a new president was installed. *Broken Lance* was the means and the method to eliminate a compromised president.

The CIA, the Navy SEALs, and JFK's special access program terrified Mazibuike. When he became president, he learned there were many things about the American military and the intelligence community that his handlers could not adequately brief him on, and this *Broken Lance* capability terrified him. Americans would do anything to protect their national secrets from the eyes and ears of communists and other enemies of America.

CHAPTER EIGHT

0100 July 2, 2014
Dubai

To the political left, socialists, progressives, and the closet communists, Maxim Mohammad Mazibuike presented himself as a man of the people, of humble heritage and modest means. No one really knew his story, where he came from, how he got his name, what he did for fun, or how he survived. Until Mazibuike's first autobiography was released, no one knew that he had been named after a former African slave and Soviet hero—Maxim Golden. Emancipated and adopted by Tsar Nicholas II, Maxim was educated, raised to nobility, and served in civilian and military capacities until he opened the gate of the Alexander Palace and allowed Vladimir Lenin and his 17 Bolsheviks inside. Golden's treachery facilitated the rapid abdication of the Tsar and set into motion the destruction of the Romanov Dynasty. As Lenin and his friends furiously raped the Romanov women before executing them, Maxim Golden was invited to participate in the gruesome orgiastic festivities. The bloody rite of passage proved Golden was one of them now, a Communist.

Directed by Lenin to work for Felix Dzerzhinsky, a Polish aristocrat turned communist, Golden led one of the growing number of Cheka committees, the new Soviet state security organizations, where dissidents, deserters, Jews, or other undesirables were arrested, interrogated, enslaved, tortured, or executed. After years of faithful and loyal dedication to the Communist Party, a few poorly chosen words in mixed company presaged his fall from the Party elite. Few knew Maxim Golden was personally condemned to death by Comrade Secretary General Joseph Stalin, a closet racist, during the first wave of the 1936 purges. The sometimes executioner, Nikolai Yazhov, the head of the Soviet secret police, took great glee stripping the flesh of the black man in the basement of the Lubyanka Prison. It was a new experience for him. Like most psychopaths, Yazhov bragged about his exploits as well as his most interesting assignments and discoveries.

Maxim grew up as an ignored child in the seedier parts of Pearl City near Honolulu where his mother would rather entertain lusty black sailors on shore leave from Pearl Harbor than tend to her son. To make a little money on the side when the fleet was out, sometimes she'd visit an old friend of the family, a card-carrying communist with money, a bed, and a camera. She'd exchange sexy nude photographs and sex for a few dollars. More often, she would spend her time in communist dives and at the University of Honolulu library meeting like-minded and lusty African students. After dozens of paramours from the socialist and communist coffee shops, Maxim's mother fell in love with a visiting student from Nigeria, Mohammad Mazibuike. Mohammad Mazibuike studied engineering on a student visa and was far more interested in staying in the United States than returning to the African continent with a degree he couldn't possibly use in the tribal areas of Nigeria or in the capital of Abuja. They quickly married only to have the U.S. State Department intervene; the lily white Mary Maxwell and Mohammad Mazibuike were accused of engaging in an obvious case of marriage of convenience for citizenship purposes. The case was quickly adjudicated, and Mazibuike's visa was revoked. He was immediately deported. Mary Maxwell Mazibuike followed her husband to Lagos and then to Abuja.

A few months after setting foot in Africa, Mary Maxwell was ready to leave. Mohammad Mazibuike wasn't much interested in having an American wife if they couldn't live in America. When Mary Maxwell announced she was pregnant with his child and wanted to return to Hawaii to have the baby, Mohammad beat her nearly unconscious. With no money and only her passport, Mary Maxwell Mazibuike dragged herself to the U.S. Embassy for passage back to America. While embassy personnel processed her case she met a ship's captain at a hotel bar. He offered her a job to help prepare food and other services for the ships' crew. A few hours later the *Amira* set sail for Hong Kong and Honolulu with tons of mahogany, tiger stripe, teak and other exotic hardwoods. A hundred miles off the coast of Kawai, she gave birth to a baby boy. Several days after pulling into the commercial port near Pearl Harbor, Mary Maxwell Mazibuike and her mother went into town to register the baby's birth.

When it came time to name the baby on his birth certificate, she named him after the first black communist followed by his father's first name. Maxim Mohammad Mazibuike grew up as a good, handsome, and beautiful boy in spite of inheriting his father's oversized and elongated ears. Throughout his youth and into adulthood, he was oversensitive to perceived slights about his race, his philosophy, and especially his ears. Marijuana, the finest Hawaiian hashish, and cocaine deadened the pain of a father who did not want him and an African heritage he did not understand. It would anger him when he met people.

Maxim was taken in by his grandparents after his mother unexpectedly died of an African parasite. It wasn't a warm embrace of their grandson. They and their friends were rich and upstanding members of the community but were also very pro-Soviet Union, like many in the newspaper and journalism business. The problems of having a mixed-race young man living in the affluent white picket fence neighborhood of Kailua Heights was both ameliorated and lionized by introducing Maxim as a visiting student from Africa. He wasn't thrilled with the arrangement but it provided several advantages as he grew and matured. His grandparents' liberal friends viewed him as something of a science project.

His grandmother explained that his dual-nationality citizenship came with certain advantages. He was entitled to American and British passports, and he should use his British citizenship, granted through his father's country, for his own good whenever he could. He learned to read people and play his race and foreigner status to leverage his future. In the 70s, backed by his communist mentor and closet communist grandparents, his politics evolved into socialism. He was a clandestine communist at a time when anti-communism was still the purview of the hated Republicans and latent Kennedy Democrats. While his teenage politics could be dismissed as the tribal thinking of the immature and uncivilized, they were continually being hardened and radicalized. In most social situations he took his cues from his mentor, a rabid card-carrying communist who hated certain peoples; primarily Jews, Christians and Republicans. But especially white people. As Mazibuike grew, he also learned to detest Jews, Christians, and Republicans. And white people. He demonstrated his disgust for them with the same zeal as the Nazis used against the Jews on Kristallnacht, but without the bloodletting. For something like that he was a thinker, not a doer.

Mazibuike grew to be a loner, more comfortable in the company of men, especially older men, than women. The typical black woman repulsed him while the young white women intrigued him. Intercourse was rough, more to punish the white race and humiliate white women. But somewhere in his complex feelings, effeminate white men were taboo but excited him.

A British passport facilitated entry into the finest schools America could produce. The Ivy League universities that expressed their interest in him, they relished the pleasure of paying his tuition, room, and board. The schools were full of red diaper babies, all grown up into progressive young men and women interested in an interracial fling.

As President, Mazibuike claimed he owned no property other than a modest "fisherman's hut" somewhere along the Hawaiian coast. In truth, the former president was worth hundreds of millions of dollars and owned dozens of properties, including a Maliko Bay cabin on Maui where he would dismiss his Secret Service detail and meet his lover every year when he vacationed with the First Family. Republicans wondered how the president could accumulate such wealth when he had never held a job and had no known investments. His mother died dirt-poor, and he inherited only meager assets when his grandparents died. The press never investigated the source of his wealth or the vague rumors of collegiate homosexual trysts.

As a man of twenty, Mazibuike visited Africa to learn of his paternal heritage. His father was one of nine brothers and sisters. They and their families all lived in or near the slums near Abuja. One third of the family was Arabic Muslims; one third remained pro-colonialists and blamed the Muslims and the communists for the ills of post-colonial Nigeria. The other third was infatuated with the ideals of socialism and communism, of social justice and inequality, and were always at war with Muslim tribes and the colonialists, seeking money and stealing their property whenever they could.

When Maxim visited his father's homeland, courtesy of a student field trip, he was shocked to learn his father wasn't the Harvard PhD candidate his mother described but was the town drunk in the Muslim district. He had degenerated into a vituperative old curmudgeon with five wives with whom he had ten sons and at least three daughters, most of whom were born out of wedlock. The last words his father said to him before he flew back to America were, "You can be many things but remember you were born a Muslim. Be proud of your Islamic heritage. *Allahu Akbar!*"

Mazibuike pushed the old ruminations from his memory and focused on the more compelling thoughts. He had dispatched SEAL Team Six to find and kill Osama bin Laden. If that august group of terrorist hunters could find the master terrorist then they could find him, too. While the CIA likely had weaponized unmanned systems in the area, it was unlikely any one of them would be airborne in this weather. It was doubtful their sensors and cameras could look through the special anti-infrared coated glass protecting the floor; he had likely evaded the killers from the U.S. Navy again. He would live another day.

Even if the weather was worsening, he could not stay at the glass any longer. The Americans were always improving their targeting capabilities. It was time to leave. Every time he moved loose hashish molecules from his *thobe* filled the air.

He turned from the window only to find the men around the conference table. Acknowledging them would show weakness, but he had one more mission to complete. He shuffled past the man with the computer, unbuttoned his *thobe*, and withdrew a business card from his shirt pocket. He flipped it over and over in his fingers, as if it was a talisman. Then, vitriol dripped with every word of his request. Mazibuike looked directly at al-Sarkari, "Can you determine if or when a particular...*Amriki* makes reservations or boards an aircraft?" He caustically used the Arabic word for American.

"Yes, sir. I wrote most of my company's software for the government's frequent flyer and terrorism databases; the so-called no-fly lists. I have all the clearances and have access to those databases when the software needs to be updated." Al-Sarkari was taken aback by the question and was unable to predict what would come next. His eyes fell to the business card in the former president's gloved hand as he thrust it toward him.

"The next time this infidel gets on an airplane swat it out of the sky. He's from Texas, I believe. Can you do that?"

Tamerlan al-Sarkari looked at the unremarkable name inked on the back of the card, nodded, and said, "Yes, sir, I can. I will, for you."

An awkward pause ensued as the men's eyes locked on each other. Al-

Sarkari broke the silent impasse with another incredible display of arrogance. "Will we have a way to stay in contact? I mean, do you want to know when I've located this man and...his schedule?" The men around the table were mortified. He continued, "Do you want...."

Mazibuike finally broke into an arrogant smile, pointed at him, and said, "You do not want to become a burden. You will be given some procedures; Mohaned can you help our new friend?"

The titular head of Abu Dhabi nodded gracefully and said, "As you wish."

"You are most gracious." As men at the table nodded in deference, the former president turned and moved to the elevator, offered a gesture, and said, "Peace be upon you and the Mercy of Allah and His blessings." Then Mazibuike suddenly stopped, turned, and said, "There is only the fight." He heard the chorus of "*Allahu Akbars*" in response.

Before he entered the open elevator, the former president shifted his eyes from the men to the corporate logo of the *ROC* on the wall high above the empty receptionist's desk. A stylized eagle with elongated wings clutched a wreath of palm fronds. It was reminiscent of the traditional Nazi German eagle, standing atop of a swastika inside a wreath of oak leaves. The *Iron Eagle* looked over its left shoulder symbolizing the Nazi Party. The ROC eagle also looked left to symbolize emirate unity. However, inside the wreath of fronds instead of a right-facing swastika lay an elegant and exaggerated Arabic script. Even though he could not read it he knew what it said: "There is only the fight." To him the compressed calligraphy resembled a stylized bug. The eye of the eagle looked back at him. He turned and stepped into the elevator.

As the elevator doors closed multiple thoughts fought for positioning, for resolution, for action. He pondered what would be the outcome of the test, the second phase, and the end. His vision of the future: a world in chaos, America and her president brought to her knees, her enemies able and willing to attack her in her weakened state, her back broken, the end of America. A new *caliph*. The goal of *The One* realized. *Revolution now! Revolution tomorrow! Revolution always!*

The weak have always failed me. An aircraft disappearing.... Like a Las Vegas magic trick. For the second time that evening, he smiled. *Actions have consequences.* He flexed his gloved hands into balls. He was anxious to get it over. He had to be sure it would work. *One jet is the first step.*

There will be consequences for the humiliation I've endured. Breeching America's defenses was so simple, the democrats so gullible, so accommodating, so willing.... But that...pilot...that fucking...pilot....

With funding through the *ROC* organization, a worldwide search was on for the person who had released the president's CIA file. A bounty, a reward, a *fatwa* once he or she was found. But after two years there had been nothing, not even a hint of a clue. Such discipline to keep an explosive secret was extraordinary.

Then, a possible hint of a tip. The former CIA director, another clandestine Muslim, was also chased out of his high-level, ultra-sensitive, government position, was forced to resign and escape America. He suggested there was an exceptional candidate. A CIA contract pilot may have had a hand in the file's discovery through an intimate relationship with a senior intelligence executive. A *Muslima*. A traitor; a *takfiri*. Although multiple polygraphs of the woman failed to shed any light on the dark and murky release, she was the last person known to have had some tangential interaction with the file.

A private nurse had heard the ramblings of the former CIA man as he slept as well as his wretched diatribes in demanding the al-Qaeda and Muslim Brotherhood find the pilot and kill him. It was understood the CIA pilot was unusually gifted in finding the leaders of Islamic movements and exposing them, neutralizing them, or killing them.

The Jordanian nurse could not conceive of a way the infidel was able to be so successful as to give his master, the former Director of Central Intelligence, nightmares. Nizar had said to *The One*, "My master, Doctor Rothwell was convinced that it was the CIA woman who had found the president's file. She must have given it to the infidel who released it to the American public. When he eliminated all other possibilities, he repeated several times, the only possibility remaining must be the truth. For him, this pilot was the only possible solution."

·　·　·　·　·

Mazibuike rode the elevator down to the seventh floor of the Armani Hotel, stepped out, and turned toward a hall lined with suites. He removed his gloves and trembled with anticipation as he arrived at his destination. *No one knows he's here! It's been so long!* He knocked gently;

the door opened immediately, and he stepped inside a room utterly devoid of light.

No words were spoken. The men embraced, kissed passionately, and raced to remove their clothes. They fondled each other with abandon until the man in the shadows pushed the naked Mazibuike to his knees.

. . . . .

As the elevator doors closed in front of the former president, Tamerlan al-Sarkari said under his breath, "Is he always like that?"

The men in white *thobes* caught themselves before berating the American Muslim for his rudeness, demeanor, and actions. Anyone who could make a jet disappear with a computer was not a person to be trifled with, and they demurred an answer. They smiled graciously, shook the man's hand and thanked him for his work. They kissed his cheeks and wished him a good night.

After the *Ameriki* packed his computer and safely departed the conference room, the emir of Sharjah asked the man at the head of the table, "Why are we keeping him?"

The emir of Abu Dhabi shrugged and waved an arm. "We were promised the White House. He delivered. He released countless *mujahidin* into their country. Most importantly, he placed thirty thousands of our *Brothers* in key positions in the government. Thirty thousand. All according to plan. He nearly brought America it its knees. He would have been America's *Caliph*. I think it is still possible."

The old men nodded. They helped craft the strategic plan to infiltrate North America with their *Brothers*.

"And do not forget, he transferred billions of U.S. dollars from their treasury to us. There is still much adoration for him; half of the American people believed he was a prophet and was invincible. They cannot believe what happened to him. Their Democrats and media have convinced the masses that it was a Republican conspiracy. When America falls, we need him to return and seize control of the country to establish the *sharia*. We will have a *caliphate* once we return him to his office. And then we will drain America of its resources. Do we agree there is still much value in the man? I believe he is worth a little more of our time."

Heads again nodded; the emirs folded their hands in front of them to indicate they had nothing more to add or say. They pushed themselves from the table in unison and lined up to pay their respects to the Master. *The One.* One by one, they kissed cheeks, one kiss on the right cheek then three kisses on the left cheek. Once the departure ritual was done, each gripped the other's hands and said, "Peace be upon you and the Mercy of Allah, and His blessings."

.   .   .   .   .

The lift stopped; the two security men entered and wordlessly took up a position on either side of the former president of the United States. With an imperceptible nod, Mazibuike acknowledged only Nizar Qasim al-Rimi, his huge Jordanian bodyguard. The ROC's special security man had been the only one to escape the raid on a safe house used by al-Qaeda and Muslim Brotherhood warriors and leaders passing through Jordan en route to the battlefields. He had returned to his lord and masters of the ROC. His training as a special warfare specialist and his command of English uniquely qualified him to protect the former American leader.

Mazibuike continued to obsess about the past as the old pain returned to dominate his thoughts. *Could this CIA pilot have really done it? Could the Jordanian's information be true? Nonetheless, it will soon be over for him. His next plane ride will be his last.* He turned and glanced at Nizar, sizing him up yet again. For truthfulness. He was one of ROC's finest. Handpicked for the most sensitive positions involving special levels of trust and confidence. *Time may prove the Jordanian was correct and there are consequences for exposing me. Now that we know who you are, you can no longer run...pilot. I would love to kill you with my own hands. But the ROC's many friends will take care of you before you even know we are on to you.*

CHAPTER NINE

0500 July 2, 2014
Jakarta

Demetrius Eastwood sprawled out on the bed of the JW Marriott Jakarta, looked up at the spinning fan blades overhead, and waited for sleep. It wouldn't come. Too many things running through his continually active mind. Even when he slept, his brain would be engaged, as it wrestled with and processed some odd problem that wouldn't go away. He couldn't just put the job away, put the annoyances "on ignore" and hope for the best. He wasn't a typical journalist.

He hadn't even been a typical Marine Corps lieutenant colonel, a leader of Marines, a grunt officer. Infantry. Military Occupational Specialty: 0302. He was tall, short-haired, and strikingly handsome; some colonel at the Basic School said he was the classic Marine Corps "poster boy" and sent him to the Quantico photographer for some "hero shots," color prints. There was little doubt he looked striking in the finely tailored gabardine uniform favored by the general officers, but there was someone else who looked a little better for the inane publicity shots. Being a young, studly, manly Marine was in the eye of the beholder. Second place in the undeclared contest suited him, "just fine," as he would say, and not being chosen as a rear echelon, public relations pogue allowed him to return to school to learn the fine art of leading Marines in combat and killing the enemies of America.

He moved up the Marine Corps ranks as a graduate of the Naval Academy, the Basic Officer's Course, a couple of tours in Vietnam, and a few weeks in a field hospital to recover from injuries sustained during combat operations. Afterwards he would have to wear glasses, bottle-bottom glasses that high schoolers called "brain damaged glasses." Before he transitioned to contact lenses, he told his Texas friends, "I could burn ants up with those things. I could hold them a foot off the sidewalk on a sunny day, and I could roast the little critters. You can never kill enough fire ants."

After a few non-combat tours, he was surprised by his new assignment as a support staffer with the National Security Council. He was given several projects employing aviation assets. He learned what jet and cargo aircraft pilots could and couldn't do, and for his first challenge, he organized a midair interception of an EgyptAir airliner carrying the terrorists responsible for the *Achille Lauro* hijacking. Later he helped plan the aviation "package" for the U.S. invasion of Grenada and the bombing of Libya in response to the 1986 Berlin discotheque bombing.

From his days at the Naval Academy, he had been intrigued with Marine aviation, but with a retired grunt general for a father, there was no question that he would follow in the old man's footsteps. He would troop and stomp in the worst field conditions man could image, even more so after his time on active duty.

As a company-grade officer, he tinkered with the idea of writing a book, his life story. Dialogue and structure issues bounced in his head continuously and affected his sleep. His was a remarkable life, and he wasn't done yet. But he didn't have the training or education to know where to start. As a Marine, he could field strip an M1911 .45 caliber pistol blindfolded, and he could construct the best five-paragraph order in the Corps. But he knew he needed more training to do what he really wanted to do—write. He took a few graduate courses, and he learned to write and write well. He could see his life's career path "out of uniform" directing him toward combat journalism. Since his life story in the Marine Corps was one continuous string of interesting and unique experiences—*he led combat Marines in Vietnam and he worked for the White House!*—he thought he could write a book of his exploits; the good, the bad, and the remarkable and let the royalty checks roll in. Only life wasn't like that. After the CIA Publication Review Board redacted half of his stories, the book opened to mixed reviews. His writing was good, and his editors were also good, but he didn't like going on the road to hawk his book and honk his own horn. His book didn't sell well because he wasn't fully engaged in the marketing and promotion, and he had a mortgage to pay. If he couldn't write for fun and profit on his own terms, he still had a few marketable skills.

He was interested in the counterterrorism arena. There was that little issue of being targeted by the master terrorist himself, Osama bin Laden.

There was plenty of action in the Middle East and Africa—and plenty of journalism work. He sent an unsolicited proposal to the networks suggesting he could investigate terrorist groups and cells, and report on America's warfighters in action. He was hired by a conservative news network and was soon in the fields of Afghanistan, and Iraq, and shithole places in Africa with unpronounceable names and random spellings. His reports were concise and sold many copies. His old photogenic self was pulled onto camera to talk about his latest exploits. Ratings soared when he was on the docket. No longer freelance now, he had a staff when he was in the field.

It was time for him and his team to leave Indonesia where they had witnessed the handiwork of the brutal and deadly terrorist group, Jema'ah Islamiyah. Eastwood had learned who the real terrorists were on the second day in the field, and he yearned to get away from the pit vipers that had no compunction about slithering into the sleeping bag with him and the huge spiders that could catch birds on the fly. When he found one such spider straddling the opening of the makeshift field toilet, he held his bladder for fear the spider might be interested in jumping on and sinking its fangs into another fluttering target.

Safe in Jakarta at the best four-star hotel in town, Eastwood only thought he was too tired to function. With the world's problems caroming about the globe of his cranium, he jumped from his bed, fired up his laptop and connected to the internet. He scribbled notes as he tore through hundreds of emails he hadn't answered while he had been in the field. The preponderance of the emails were requests forwarded through a service that brought him much fame but little fortune. Emails from *Blacklisted News* came straight from journalists on a deadline who needed a source. He answered some of the recent requests—providing source material and information and professional quotes attributed to him for use in the journalists' work. Then he deleted the out-of-date requests and transitioned to another website, *The Reporter's Telegraph*, where journalists, reporters, and bloggers would leave sarcastic or funny titles, snippets of their work, or hyperlinks to their main articles.

Eastwood was particularly interested in the anti-radical Islamic blogs that reported on the individual instances of terrorism the American mainstream media wouldn't touch under a Democrat Party administration. It was better to ignore the unexplained homicides which suggested homegrown radical Islamists were behind the murder and other such mayhem in America. As a member of *Blacklisted News* he would screen the articles that wouldn't or couldn't be approved for publication under any circumstance, or request the use of certain quotes as reference material in his own work. But his real reason to access *The Reporter's Telegraph* was to annotate an event and plot the spread of radical Islam across the globe and America.

As a combat journalist he had seen the aftermath and consequence of the unrestrained growth of radical Islam. In the thirteen years since 9-11, Eastwood and others had documented over 20,000 verified terrorist events. Plotting those occurrences on a map took a little time, but he felt it was well worth the effort. He could see by these events, the march of radical Islamists as they grew and moved across nations and landmasses. One of the unintended circumstances of his data collection was the pictorial representation of the quiet extermination of Jews and Christians in certain parts of the world. The Muslim world. Radical Islamists have been winning the intelligence and information war because many peaceful Muslims fear the terrorists more than they fear the counterterrorism efforts of the United States. Like the Sicilian mafia of the 19th century, criminal Muslim terrorists infested Muslim communities and operated like a gangster protection racket. It was dangerous to stand up to the murderous radicals.

A cohort sent him an email. "Check this out!" the subject line demanded. The articles were from a Texas newspaper.

"The Houston Police Department will strengthen safeguards against illegal surveillance of Muslims in investigations of terror threats and install a civilian representative on an advisory committee that reviews the probes under the terms of a settlement of two high-profile civil rights lawsuits, lawyers said Wednesday."

"The announcement of a deal followed months of negotiations and formally ended litigation over accusations that Texas' largest police department cast a shadow over Muslim communities with a covert campaign of religious profiling and illegal spying."

Eastwood harrumphed, "Typical liberal press," and moved to the next gem.

"Death began with a knock on the door. Hard-heeled boots on wooden floors signaled the approach of the resident. Behind the glass, the ancient peephole darkened as a dull nervous eyeball filled the ocular and scanned the porch. Like the last time, no one was on the landing. Pranksters. Hoodlums. *Scoundrels.*

The three raps on the old weathered door were distinct and directional. Someone *had* knocked. Someone had to be outside this time. However, no one was in the viewfinder. Again. The pupil and iris swirled around the tiny lens seeking a better view.

The peephole was barely adequate, more of an aggravation. Yellowed and streaked with age as if it had cataracts, the aperture didn't provide a wide enough viewing angle to see who was on the other side of the heavy door. It griped his ass that pranksters and unwanted religious people were able to step to the side or duck down below the aperture to hide from sight. This was the third time today that someone knocked, but no one was on the porch. He never heard anyone step onto the creaky landing, and he never glimpsed anyone running away. This time, like the last time, there wasn't anyone there.

He shouted, 'Who's there?' He wouldn't open the door unless he could see who was at the door. Even then, he might not. They had to say something. He wouldn't do it; it wasn't prudent.

A flash of movement from the side of the peephole startled him, made him jump. He jammed his eye closer to the lens, his eyelashes brushing the tiny round glass with every blink of his eye. His demeanor switched from surprised to confused instantly as he tried to discern what dark thing had suddenly and completely obscured the ocular of the peephole.

He asked his wife, 'What the hell is that?' They were his last words and his last conscious thought as a .357 Magnum bullet tore through the peephole, through his eye, and through his cranium. The victim was a retired military man."

Eastwood shrugged and deleted the email. He found a subject line that caught his eye. "Another Missing Girl." He opened the link.

"The distraught family of a 16-year-old Abilene, Texas woman said they remain hopeful she will return safely. Abilene police officials believe Celeste Germaine, who was reported missing June 29, may be in danger. Germaine has brown hair and blue eyes, is about five feet tall, and weighs about 100 pounds. She was last seen wearing Levi jeans, a white polo shirt, and blue Nike tennis shoes.

Abilene Police Department spokesman, Corporal Andy Lewis, said he could not elaborate on what circumstances indicated the danger to the woman. Germaine was last seen about 10:00 p.m. Sunday, June 29th, according to several friends, as she left the skating rink, Skate City. Germaine's parents said they were supposed to pick her up from the skating rink, but she never came out of the building. A search of the skating rink conducted by police revealed no clues regarding her disappearance.

'The last text I received from her was to tell me she was ready for me to pick her up,' Celeste's mother said. Phone calls all went straight to voice mail. No other family members or friends have heard from Celeste, and it has infected the community with anxiety and fear. A neighbor said, 'I'm very scared for her.'

The Police Department's tone changed Wednesday night after officers reviewed security cameras from an adjacent building, according to the Abilene Reporter News."

Other articles tagged and attached to the article by the Abilene author made Eastwood furrow his brow. Three caught his attention: *Secret Sleeper Cell of American Muslim Women Exposed, Encouraged Others to Join Islamic State. Austin "Poster Girl" for the Islamic State Beheaded for Trying to Escape. Lebanese authorities arrested two Beirut airport employees on suspicion of aiding and abetting "terrorist parties."* What the hell? he thought.

He was surprised how the instances appeared to be bunched up, mostly in Texas. The articles were posted, more or less, on the same day; however, no motives were reported. He thumbed through several more and stopped on one from a journalist at the Dallas Morning News who had filed a report that the police were investigating the death of a homeowner who had been shot, apparently while answering the door of his house. Detectives were quick to say there was no known motive for killing the military veteran. There were no known witnesses. There were no suspects. The reporter completed her article with, "The case remains under investigation."

He wondered if he were reading the same article as before. He flipped back and forth from *The Reporter's Telegraph* to his email account. He attached the link and replied to the sender, "Is this the same case?"

Eastwood wandered further down *The Reporter's Telegraph* and stopped when he came across a draft article that had been spiked, or killed by the newspaper editor. The reporter was livid and dumped the draft article on the website, seemingly to protest the editor's decision.

"Surveillance cameras captured a pickup driving along the loading docks of the Dickey's Transportation distribution warehouse. With no fence or roving patrols to chase off the curious and the seedy, the building security managers ensured all access doors and roll-up doors at each loading dock were closed. A master status panel confirmed all one-hundred entrances to the building were locked down.

When a man emerged from the pickup and removed a blanket from something in the truck bed, the security man behind the bank of surveillance monitors isolated the camera feed on the activity behind the building. The security guard was surprised when the man removed a large 'four-rotor helicopter drone' from the truck bed and set the device on the asphalt near the rear of the truck. In seconds, the square contraption lifted into a hover and slowly flew away from the pickup.

The security guard had seen other people fly the small helicopters in the warehouse parking lot. Sometimes there would be children involved in flying the little aircraft in the wide-open spaces of the 200-car parking lot. But never at night and never in the back of the warehouse. He telephoned his supervisor at the security company for assistance to investigate the unusual activity. It appeared that the little helicopter flew on an easterly heading toward the San Antonio International Airport."

Demetrius Eastwood had begun to nod off as he started the next to the last article. "A radical Islamist group has issued a sixty-page handbook for Muslims living in the West. It has been translated into English for those who don't speak Arabic."

"The instruction booklet, called *Safety and Security Guidelines for Lone Wolf Mujahedeen*, provides methods and procedures to blend in with Westerners and how to avoid 'looking like a Muslim.' The first chapter outlines proven methods for jihadis to pretend to be Christians to stay below the radar of the law enforcement and intelligence services. Another chapter outlines how home-grown terrorists can plan for and carry out attacks as they are less likely to be noticed. Nightclubs full of loud music and drunk people are the perfect place to discuss terror plans without being recorded or spied upon."

Now Eastwood was fully awake. He clicked a follow-on report, also reportedly spiked by the correspondent's editor.

"San Antonio International Airport Operations found the approach end of Runway 30 Left littered with the debris of a small flying aircraft. Like the dead eagles and hawks that littered the area around electrical-generating windmills that smashed the raptors into pieces with every cycle of the hundred-foot long *ginsu* blades, no one wanted to talk about the destruction and dismemberment of the mysterious mechanical birds impacting various parts of an aircraft's airframe. It has become a national epidemic at major airports across the United States, and, no one knew the extent of the problem, except the membership of the American Association of Airport Executives and the FAA. Until now, no one had been successful in flying one of the miniature helicopters into an engine of a departing jet.

A Lone Star Airways Boeing 737 crew reported an engine failure shortly after rotation for takeoff. After getting the airplane safely airborne, the crew dumped fuel and made an emergency landing."

The reporter strung his comments together like a daisy chain. Eastwood could sense the frustration in the journalist's incisive but sarcastic remarks. He read on with eyes wide open.

"The security guard on duty had watched the man with the remote control box manipulate the tiny controls for over a minute when the man abruptly tossed the controller into his truck bed and sped off. Hours later as the security crew watched the local news on the television monitor, they learned that there had been an aircraft incident at the airport less than a half-mile from the industrial park and their warehouse."

The next paragraph had Eastwood screaming.

"The catastrophic engine failure of the Lone Star Airways Flight 654 did not make the evening news, but by morning, a local reporter had heard of the incident, raced to the airport, and interviewed several of the passengers. The aircrew would not make remarks. Passengers commented they heard a loud bang followed by a flash of fire coming from the rear of the left engine. The pilot informed the cabin crew and passengers that they had lost an engine on takeoff. They would dump fuel and return to the field. He tried to assuage the passengers' concern by assuring them that pilots practice these types of emergencies in the simulators for hours on end. The actual emergency was handled professionally, by the book. When the airliner landed and taxied back to the terminal, the passengers broke out in applause and cheers. No one was injured, no one felt threatened, and the only inconvenience was having to wait for another aircraft to take them to their destination."

Eastwood looked for a police report, anything that would suggest the apparent attack of a commercial jet was serious and had received the appropriate investigation. There was another aviation related incident in the stack of hotlinks got his attention. "Another Laser Pointed at a Jet." He clicked on the link and found it was another story killed by a local newspaper editor for some inexplicable reason.

"Television correspondent, Dixon Babbitt, reported that as a Southwest pilot was trying to land a Boeing 737 at Houston's Hobby Airport last night, someone shined a laser pointer at the plane. The laser beam reportedly struck the flight deck and the pilot looked right into it. The copilot didn't look into the beam and was able to safely land the aircraft. After the incident, both pilots were transported to the Texas Medical Center for observation. The Air Line Pilots Association says the problem is growing. It is dangerous, and it's against the law.

Babbitt conveyed his concern that shining a laser at an aircraft is only a minor crime under the Federal Aviation Regulations. 'Under current law, it is a misdemeanor offence to interfere with any crew member in the performance of their duties. The airline pilots association is pushing Washington to toughen the laws and make shining a laser at an aircraft a felony.'

He added, 'Some laser pointers can be purchased for as little as one dollar and have a range of up to one mile. Pilots tell us that when they're looking outside to land and see a bright light, the natural tendency is to look at that light for traffic avoidance. There are several dozen pilots across the country who have permanent damage to their eyes because of the lasers. They have all retired from flying.'"

Eastwood rubbed his eyes, he didn't think he could take any more of the stories that didn't make the papers or the network broadcasts. He skimmed over several others in *The Reporter's Telegraph* listing, but nothing caught his attention like the spiked Muslim girls, the jihadi handbook, and aircraft incidents articles. He closed down the webpage and typed in the Washington Post's URL (Uniform Resource Locator), the newspaper's unique address on the Internet. He checked to see if his editorial had made the cut and saw that it had. Relieved at having another successful article published, he felt satisfied and a bit smug. Yawning and pinching tears of fatigue out of the corners of his eyes, he noticed an adjacent article that intrigued him. There would always be just one or two more articles to look at.

He read the first two lines of another terrorism-related article. "Women and Children Abducted by Shining Path Rebels Rescued in Peru." Intrigued, he continued.

"LIMA - Peruvian national police and armed forces rescued 35 people—13 children and 22 women—from a camp in the San Martin de Pangoa municipality in the jungle area of Valle de los Rios Apurimac. Peruvian Deputy Defense Minister Francisco Vasquez reported the women were abducted by the "Sendero Luminoso" or Shining Path rebels 25 years ago from a nunnery in Puerto Ocopa. The Shining Path had set a deadline for payment of the equivalent of $5 million for each of its hostages, but the ransom was never paid and the women were believed to have been lost.

Vasquez told the newspaper, 'The children are between two and 15 years of age. The children were born as a consequence of these women being raped by the rebels.' He explained how some women were used to produce children while others worked in the camps. 'Children born in these camps have been indoctrinated in the Maoist ideology of the terrorist organization. As they matured they would be encouraged to participate in subversive activities. We've seen that with some of the older boys. They do not know any better.' Vasquez added, 'Some of the women rescued were held in underground rooms or huts deep in the jungle. They were held captive for 25 or 30 years and subjected to extreme and repeated sexual violence.'"

Eastwood shook his head. Another incredible story and yet not so unimaginable. He had done a story a few years earlier on the Maoist terrorist group, Shining Path, a collection of militants and splinter groups. It had been weakened by expanded military and police operations over the past decade, but it somehow managed to retain footholds in jungle hideouts used as bases for sporadic attacks and kidnappings. Shining Path had claimed an alliance with al-Qaeda, but it recently publicly proclaimed allegiance to the Islamic State.

He had heard rumors that they held several dozen women in camps. All radical Islamic or Communist-based terror groups engaged in the trade of sex slaves. The latest surveillance equipment on high-flying unmanned platforms rarely found the terror groups' hiding locations. Over his many years in the field, Eastwood had learned terrorist groups across the world sometimes unwittingly dropped their guard on the hostages they took and held for ransom, but the rescue of hostages happened infrequently. He thought he wouldn't track the event or research others that had occurred earlier. But there had to be others. Maybe another time. Definitely another place.

He squinted his eyes, yawned, and made a pitiful sound. Eastwood was tired from his extraction from the Banda Aceh, the commercial flight into Jakarta, and the harassment by the national police once he and his men processed through customs. They had overstayed their visas by a day. Eastwood paid the fine as well as the extra day the hotel charged for the late check in. His bed beckoned but he had one more blog to check before sack-time.

The Blue Line: Ruminations and ramblings from the men and women who proudly wear the badge was operated and maintained by police officers for law enforcement officials. It wasn't a Darwin Award-type of website, one that recognized noteworthy individuals who made significant contributions to human evolution by selecting themselves out of the gene pool by their own actions. No, *The Blue Line* would sometimes reflect on some of the stranger cases to which law enforcement responded. Eastwood would often find little gems, a story that confounded local police departments or impacted federal law enforcement but made perfect sense when taken in a broader context. He yawned again, hard, and squeezed tears from his eyes. The titles jumped out at him. *Two Killed at Evangelical Ministry. White Shooter Kills Eight at a Historically Black Church. FBI Investigating Threat against New Hampshire High Schools. White Supremacist Killed Six at Sikh temple. Los Angeles Mosques Vandalized. Three Killed at Colorado Church. Hackers Hijack Hotel's Smart Locks.*

He clicked to open the next article. "A resort hotel in Kuwait City was the target of a series of hacks, including one that crippled the electronic "smart locks" on guest rooms. Hackers accessed the hotel's IT system and shut down everything, including all the reservation info and the hotel's electronic key system. The attack prevented management from issuing new key cards. Many of the guests were locked in their rooms, while others were locked out of theirs. Lacking other options, the five-star hotel paid the hackers a modest ransom of 1,500 euros in Bitcoin to reactivate their system." Eastwood glanced at his hotel door. That was all he needed. *Now they can hack into hotels and imprison you!*

He shook his head and debated on reading further articles or on hitting the queen with a dozen pillows. But then another subject line caught his attention. *Coincidence? I think not!* Forcing his eyes wide open, Eastwood yawned and read on.

"Shaker Heights Police were summoned to Shaker Square when an SUV jumped the curb, ran over a man, and hit four others who were dining outside the Toffee House Café. One person was killed and four were injured. Surveillance cameras outside the restaurant provided the sequence of events. Witnesses said the driver of the vehicle appeared to target, chase, and run down the victim. Authorities are looking for the dark blue Jeep Cherokee involved in the hit-and-run accident. The manager of the building where the victim lived confirmed the identity of Duncan Hunter, 60. Hunter was a long-time resident of Ohio and former military officer who kept to himself. Funeral services are pending. Police are investigating."

Demetrius Eastwood was stunned. A shot of adrenaline to the heart and brain awoke him fully. *Duncan Hunter? It cannot be!* His eyes raced back to the subject line: *Coincidence? I think not!* What's the coincidence? He read the next draft article, another one spiked by an unknown editor.

"At 11:45 p.m. local time, a beat reporter for the Houston Chronicle received a Daily Crime Report email from the City of Sugar Land Police Department. He had been covering the city's annual Star Spangled Spectacular when the message came across his smart phone: Possible hit-and-run. Sugar Land Police seek information involving automobiles with damage or blood on the front.

This reporter raced out of the parking lot of Constellation Field, watched, and then followed as four police interceptors sped through town to a residential area of the Sugar Creek Country Club. When the police vehicles stopped along Chevy Chase Circle and shut off their flashing lights, this reporter tagged behind as police officers ran to what was once the well-manicured lawn of a multi-million dollar, multi-story home. By flashing my press credentials, this reporter received permission to take pictures of the crime scene. This hit-and-run accident was different, unique in my 20-year experience.

A man's remains and a whimpering dog lay in the resident's yard. The gruesome nature of the dead man's injuries suggested he and his dog had been run down; the dog's leash was shredded as if it had been caught in spinning farm machinery. The man's shattered, bloodied body lay in a twisted mangled mess in the middle of the lawn some 25 feet from the curb. A bloodied springer spaniel lay close to the man and tried and rouse him with its nose. The location of a pair of sandals close to the sidewalk suggested the man had been hit so violently that he had been knocked out of his shoes.

A pair of investigators pointed and gestured with their flashlights as they talked. One said, "It looks like a vehicle chased them down. There is no other explanation for these curving tire tracks that depart the roadbed, drive up onto this lawn, and then drive straight away. The man may have pushed his dog away from the car. I don't see how else you can explain it. A drunk driver would have just plowed into the house." The other detective nodded and then looked around. Curious residents standing on porches could be seen in the light of streetlamps.

This reporter watched one policeman remove the dead man's wallet from the remains of ragged shorts. Another helped a distraught woman walk across the lawn to identify the body. She knew instantly her worst nightmare had occurred and collapsed in the policeman's arms, shrieking hysterically. The dog limped to the woman and put its muzzle in the woman's hand. This reporter didn't think he would be able to get the man's name from the policeman but tried anyway.

The officer may have been shocked by the crime scene and replied, 'Duncan Hunter. Lives at the end of the street. That's unofficial until the report is filed.' This reporter thanked the cop and bid him good night."

A chill coursed through Eastwood's body. His eyes bulged as he reread the two articles in stony silence. Several seconds passed while the spike of adrenaline wore off leaving his skin slightly tingly. He swung his head to the window and reflected how months earlier he and Duncan Hunter had escaped a nasty motorcyclist with a MAC-10 machine pistol. Hunter never said he thought terrorists were targeting him, but it was apparent that day near his ranch in west Texas that someone somewhere had ordered a hit on him.

Eastwood didn't debate on sending his fellow retired Marine an email. Subject line: *Be careful*. In the body of the message he typed: *Do you know some people with your name are getting killed across America? Check Houston and Cleveland blotters. OBTW, is it news to you that lasers and tiny helicopters are taking out pilots and jets? You know who I think is behind these.*

He felt he knew who was behind the mysterious crimes but he had no evidence. The curious 36-page document he had downloaded onto his computer and read on the flight began to burn into his mind. The Muslim Brotherhood's strategic plan for the United States was entitled, *"An Explanatory Memorandum*: On the General Strategic Goal for the Group in North America." It was written in 1991 by a member of the Board of Directors for the Muslim Brotherhood in North America. It had been approved by the Brotherhood's Shura Council and was meant for internal review by the Brothers' leadership in Egypt. It wasn't intended for public consumption. *An Explanatory Memorandum* outlined its goals, modus operandi, and infrastructure in America.

Eastwood recalled an interview with Hunter where he related one of his experiences while working at an airport. Two dozen Muslim men and women had applied for airport security jobs. He warned Eastwood, "If I were running a terrorist cell, what better way to send your acolytes to an airport to find jobs and infiltrate airport security? Probe this question a little deeper—why did the government federalize the passenger screening process after September 11th? Hunter's conspiratorial short answer: some Muslims infiltrated the contracted airport security company." Eastwood shook the thoughts from his brain. *Enough!*

He yawned until tears spilled over unshaven cheeks. A hard shutdown of his computer signaled there would be no more communication with the real world back home. He shuffled to the bed like a zombie from an apocalyptic movie, staggering and dragging a foot. He was tired. He flipped over on his back, closed his eyes, and wondered, "What the hell is going on with Duncan Hunter?"

CHAPTER TEN

0600 July 2, 2014
Jakarta

Several hours after departing Jakarta, Indonesian Sky Link Flight 7070 failed to report its altitude and position with Philippine air traffic controllers. Having the aircraft's flight plan, Manila Area Control Center (ACC) expected radio contact at a certain distance from the radio station. When Manila Area Control didn't hear from Flight 7070 during a communications window of opportunity, air traffic controllers requested another Indonesian Sky Link aircraft inbound to Jakarta attempt to contact their sister aircraft. After several minutes of off-air silence, Indonesian Sky Link Flight 7012 returned to their assigned frequency and reported to Philippine air traffic control that they had failed to raise the aircraft on the airline's operational base or on the emergency frequencies. Unable to establish contact with Flight 7070, Philippine ATC initiated the standard lost-communications procedures and informed the airline's corporate offices of their missing airliner.

Once notified of the unresponsive status of Flight 7070, the Indonesian Sky Link airline operations center attempted to contact the aircraft via the cockpit satellite telephone. To determine if the aircraft suffered engine-related troubles, the Sky Link aircraft maintenance control center retrieved the aircraft's satellite-data-linked cockpit and engine monitoring system data. Airline maintenance managers reported that the cockpit and engine management monitoring system had received trouble-free status reports every quarter-hour. The airline chief executive officer was informed that ten satellite telephone calls to the cockpit crew had gone unanswered. There had been no anomalies experienced in the cockpit. However, several hours into the maintenance history of Flight 7070's engines, the engine status messages had abruptly ceased. That could only mean one thing. The CEO assembled his staff to deal with the crisis of a missing aircraft.

After communication was lost with Flight 7070, the watch supervisor at Manila ACC contacted all air traffic control centers and airport control towers within 1,000 miles of Manila to determine if the missing aircraft had made contact with them or had diverted to another airport. Once the possible divert airports confirmed they didn't have the missing jet or had not received any communication from the lost airliner, he activated the Philippine Aeronautical Rescue Coordination Center.

In Jakarta, Indonesian Sky Link executives issued a media statement one hour after the flight's scheduled arrival time in Honolulu, Hawaii. The extended-range Boeing 777-300ER carried a crew of 16 and 214 passengers. The pilot of Flight 7070 last made voice contact when reporting they were at cruising altitude. The Indonesian Sky Link chief executive officer stated, "Contact with the flight was lost by Philippine ATC, and Indonesian, Philippine, and American governments have initiated search and rescue operations. Data analysis concluded that Indonesian Sky Link Flight 7070 had flown on its assigned flight path between Jakarta and Honolulu. Its last known position, as derived from the aircraft's cockpit and engine monitoring systems, was in a remote location of the Pacific Ocean east of the Philippines. A million square miles. The aircrew did not relay a distress signal. Flight 7070 did not report any bad weather, turbulence, or technical problems before the aircraft vanished. Possible landing sites in the area of the aircraft's last known position confirm the aircraft has not made an emergency landing."

Within seconds of the Indonesian Sky Link press release, American media networks and newspapers learned of the missing Boeing wide-body jet. Journalists descended on airports like a scene from Alfred Hitchcock's "The Birds." Pundits leaped in front of television cameras at networks, breathlessly reporting the correspondents' few known facts. A twin-engine airliner failed to land in Honolulu. There was good weather and no distress call, just a jumbo jet that said goodnight to one air-traffic controller and failed to make contact with the next. Yes, divert landing fields were checked. Some correspondents raised questions about the safety record of twin-engine aircraft flying over oceans. Talking heads were astounded to learn that all-seeing radar technologies did not cover the entire ocean, which made it possible for a 330-ton airplane to simply vanish.

Media networks raced to find aviation experts to comment on Flight 7070. They competed for the best consultants or authorities to give insightful commentary and discriminating analysis. Anyone with a pilot's license and airline passengers with a million frequent flier miles were considered. Networks across America winnowed the expert pool down to a dozen or so candidates. After sorting through hundreds of resumes of airline and military pilots, air traffic controllers, aircraft mechanics, and aviation lawyers, the networks and newspapers offered lucrative personal services contracts and bestowed on their new employees the on-air title of "aviation analyst." Missing from the assemblage of analysts and subject matter experts were experienced aircraft accident investigators. They were dismissed *in toto* for refusing to conjecture reasons for the missing aircraft.

Worldwide media networks flooded international airwaves with sensational video and heart-wrenching interviews of distraught family members who were told the aircraft and all passengers and aircrew were "presumed lost." The shocking images drove television ratings into the stratosphere. The saga of Indonesian Sky Link Flight 7070 became the story *de jour*. Network producers demanded more coverage and analysis. Newspapers and international news networks fielded journalists to Indonesia, Malaysia, the Philippines, and Hawaii to investigate the medical history of the aircrew, the maintenance history of the airplane, and the politics of the pilot, copilot, and their CEO.

With no information other than the airliner failed to arrive at its destination, one "aviation expert" after another announced his or her sources confirmed the aircraft had been hijacked. A retired Air Force general was rushed in front of a camera to report that he "had it on good authority the aircraft was flown at low altitude to avoid radar, and the passengers were taken off the aircraft in Pakistan." A journalist of dubious reputation floated the possibility the missing Indonesian Sky Link aircraft "had been sucked into a black hole." A host of a prime time news journal said, "I would not be surprised if it was taken aboard an alien mothership."

The media's forums attracted a varied assemblage of authorities, from the intelligent and helpful to the deranged and offensive. As some of the technically sophisticated obsessives answered the moderators' infantile questions few of the so-called aviation experts' discussions and judgments focused on villainy. Some pitched wild terrorism ideas.

As the intrigue deepened without a shred of evidence, science fiction writers and espionage novelists flooded cable-news network switchboards begging for airtime to plug their ideas or hawk their books. With no mayday call or plane debris, the consensus of media and their on-air experts was that terrorism was the only reason the ultra-reliable Boeing 777 would disappear without a trace.

The missing Indonesian Sky Link airliner joined a long line of unsolved aviation mysteries in the Pacific, beginning with the 1937 disappearance of Amelia Earhart. When it was learned the Sky Link Boeing 777 went missing on the 77th anniversary of the disappearance of Earhart's Lockheed Electra, Flight 7070 became instant conspiracy-theory material. Networks across America shifted their coverage and speculation into overdrive. Journalists and correspondents attacked the problem of the missing aircraft with willing amateur investigators, enthusiastic crackerjack professional detectives, published priests, and numerologists with advanced degrees in mathematics.

Very few of the cable-news experts cautioned moderators and panel members to face the inconvenient fact that without some tangible wreckage or the all-important "black boxes," the Flight Data Recorder (FDR) and Cockpit Voice Recorder (CVR), it was unlikely anyone was going to solve the mystery of the missing aircraft. Despite all the energy and money thrown at the effort—the broadcasts, the articles, the diverse professionals and rank amateurs, and the incessant expert theorizing—all failed to find or deliver a scrap of the missing Boeing 777.

Experienced accident investigators monitored the telecasts and newspapers covering the air disaster with sickening aversion. They heard or read the anemic analysis and insipid conjecturing. They had seen it all before. They knew the emotions of the families of the passengers and aircrew of the lost aircraft would run the gamut of the universal and well-known stages of mourning—Denial and Isolation, Anger, Bargaining, Depression, and Acceptance. It would take time for them to achieve peaceful acceptance. The focus of the owners and operators of Flight 7070 would be split between the anguish of the grieving families and the continued health and well-being of the company. An aircraft accident had the potential to kill a company. They needed a plan to return the company to normal operations. Family members sought answers to how their family members could have died in such a horrible manner. Airline executives sought answers to the questions stockholders and government executives would surely ask. Was this an accident or was this intentional? All answers must paint the company in the most favorable light.

Savvy accident investigators knew the Sky Link CEO's first and normal reaction would be to deny the reality and pain of the situation. Most likely a set of scurrilous and unsubstantiated charges would be levied against the aircraft and engine manufacturers. Before the sun had set on the first 24-hour news cycle, Sky Link's chief executive officer and Indonesian government air crash investigators lined up in front of a spray of microphones to suggest a catastrophic mechanical failure brought down the 777. Government officials buttressed the CEO's assertions without a hint of proof. Olympic conclusion jumping became the latest reportable sport.

. . . . . .

Demetrius Eastwood awoke to the news of the missing airliner. The American war correspondent raced to the Jakarta airport to cover and develop the story. Eastwood was the only American journalist in the Soekarno–Hatta International Airport, but all reporters were denied access to airport or airline representatives. Eastwood and others were finally allowed into a hastily assembled press pool when the Sky Link CEO stepped to the microphones and made his proclamation that the Boeing Aircraft Company was hiding defects in their airplanes. No questions were allowed from the members of the press. Eastwood shouted at the Sky Link CEO, "What is your proof?"

The question hung in the air like an oversized blimp. The press conference was immediately terminated and every correspondent was ushered out of the airport. Once Eastwood returned to his hotel, government officials buttressed by armed policemen informed him his visa had been revoked and he and his men were being deported. They were led out of the hotel and back to the airport. They were placed on the next aircraft headed for the United States.

. . . . . .

CIA Director Greg Lynche waited on the line for the President. He sat at his desk and sifted through folders with red borders until he found the one from the CIA inspector general that demanded his attention. After ninety seconds, President Hernandez completed the connection and asked, "Yes, Greg?"

"Mr. President, we did not have an intelligence officer aboard the Indonesian flight. For the moment, we can rule out direct or indirect retaliation against the United States."

"Thank you." President Hernandez terminated the call.

Lynche punched a button on his desk telephone to sever the encrypted connection and went back to work.

. . . . .

Professional and private accident investigators disregarded the unsubstantiated charges from the Indonesian airline executive and government investigators. The accident investigators also dismissed the ancient and oblique Earhart coincidences. To find an explanation for the disappearance of Flight 7070 they looked at the historical record of other aircraft accidents. They recognized the government and airlines' comments were eerily similar in depth and scope to those made during another major aircraft mishap, most recently in 1999 when Egyptian airline and government officials were quick to blame Boeing for the loss of their 767-300 ER over the Atlantic Ocean.

Before the flight data and cockpit voice recorders were recovered from the missing airliner, the airline CEO played the diversion well, as the intense pressure and scrutiny of a hysterical media immediately shifted from the airlines to the aircraft manufacturer. However, when the flight data and cockpit voice recorders were recovered from the Boeing 767, media reporting suddenly reversed course. Cockpit audio confirmed that the cause of the crash rested with one of the aircrew. The National Transportation Safety Board (NTSB) found the relief pilot had entered the cockpit, buckled into the pilot seat, pushed the jet's nose over, and held the controls all the way to water impact.

Egyptian government and airline leaders rejected the NTSB findings and followed a completely different line of reasoning: Islam's strong cultural aversion to suicide precluded pilot responsibility, and therefore, the relief pilot wasn't trying to crash the aircraft—he was trying to save it! The Egyptian equivalent of the NTSB reported there was no evidence of deliberate action by the relief first officer. The crash was caused by mechanical failure of the airplane's elevator control system; the relief pilot wasn't able to regain control of the aircraft. The NTSB relented and tested the wild theories surrounding the Boeing 767 elevator control system. No mythical mechanical malfunctions were found.

Correspondents, journalists, and aviation experts walked away from the official government proclamations. Anyone who knew anything about aerodynamics, airplanes, and flight data and cockpit voice recorders knew the airliner had been intentionally flown into the Atlantic. Egyptian authorities took a hard line that the aircraft sustained a mechanical malfunction. A Muslim man could not have been responsible for the death of the crew and passengers. Some investigators working behind the scenes articulated their understanding of the dynamics of the crash to their U.S. counterparts: If airline executives and investigators wished to keep their jobs, they would back the official line.

The case study of the Egyptian airliner demonstrated the political and religious diktats from the highest levels of Islamic governments and kept airlines executives and aircraft accident investigators seeking the truth in check. In the autocratic political structure of Islamic governments, airline executives and aircraft accident investigators were given an unofficial mandate: blame anyone and anything, but never blame Muslim men or Islam. Submit to the unwritten dictum or else.

Numerous professional accident investigators who saw how the trajectory of the Sky Link crash was playing out in the media wanted no part of the discussion. They chose to sit on the sidelines watching the continuing spectacle on television, reading the pabulum articles in newspapers and magazines, and engaging in their own analysis. Knowing too much was a detriment. Suggesting a hint of the truth could be detrimental to their credibility and fatal to their profession. In this case, silence was a much safer choice for them and their families.

CHAPTER ELEVEN

1100 July 4, 2014
Hondo, Texas

A long string of automobiles, pickup trucks, and sport utility vehicles poured through the gated compound. Some had their lights on peering through the dust thrown up by the unending line of vehicles. Some of the younger occupants of the cars and trucks looked toward the heavens for a sign of what was to come. The weather was perfect for a picnic. A gentle breeze cooled sweaty faces in the 100-plus degree weather. There would be fun and excitement on the scorecard as the sun raced to set in the west.

One man glanced continually at the position of the sun. The weather might be conducive for a Fourth of July celebration, but it was also perfect for viewers to witness a rare green flash of our home star at sunset. Unusually warm and moist air from acres of agriculture from the U.S. Highway 90 towns between Hondo and Uvalde created powerful thermals and refracted sunlight toward the earth. The earth's turbulent atmosphere created a path that only higher-energy visible sunlight could traverse, making the last glimpse of the Sun appear to flash green. There was plenty of daylight before that would happen.

Four-wheel drive trucks continued to pour in from the town of Hondo, famous for its welcome sign—This Is God's Country, Please Don't Drive Through It Like Hell. Moms and dads hurried to park and unload their children, steering them toward the inflatable bounce houses and ball pits, providing them a safe place to bounce, slide, and roll. The walls of the rides shuddered with every movement of the fun-satiated children. Parents easily found a spot to spread a blanket or unfold lawn chairs. There was plenty of room to accommodate the hundred employees and their families at the Full Spectrum Training Center (FSTC). Once moms and dads were settled they chatted idly and watched their children running wild and screaming as only unrestrained children can do. But then came a sound, discordant and unusual. Adult heads turned to locate the source. Kids continued to play.

The noise seemed to emanate from behind one of the dozens of white metal buildings that made up the administrative offices of the FSTC. With every second, the sound, whatever it was, increased in amplitude and frequency. There was a harshness to it. The weather was "clear to the moon" with no clouds to be seen so the audible interloper wouldn't be tornadic activity. It was a very unusual sound. It started as a warbling hiss, like the sound a hundred rattlesnakes might make if they were agitated, then it increased greatly and changed tonal qualities. It reminded many of the visitors of high-pressure gas escaping from some trephinated container.

The noise finally caught the attention of the children, and they stopped playing. Some ran to their parents for protection and comfort. Hundreds of curious eyes and ears tried and locate the dissonance. They looked at each other to confirm their tinnitus hadn't suddenly exploded into an unmanageable roar, when the source of the noise appeared in the sky. Everyone stopped what they were doing and shaded their eyes to confirm that they weren't hallucinating.

A man with a jetpack, for that was what it was, of James Bond's *Thunderball* fame, flew into view closing fast from a 1,000 yards away to within a hundred yards of the picnicking masses. Men and women stood up in disbelief as the rocketman flew figure-8s across the field. Out of a hundred jeans pockets a hundred smart phones' cameras were brought to bear and focused to track the sight.

The rocketman shifted his weight constantly to slow down and control his trajectory. Then, with a thundering shot of gas he slowly corkscrewed upwards for several hundred feet before making a gliding coordinated and turning approach over the inflatable playsets. He flew over the parking lots while in a slow coordinated spin before straightening out and sidling and hovering to the administration buildings. He landed and walked on the roofline before another shot of gas rocketed him straight up like a Marine Corps Harrier jump jet taking off from an aircraft carrier. Countless men and women stood still, mouths agape, children clutching legs and necks of their parents as the rocketman shot nearly out of sight. Seconds later the black dot that was the unknown aviator grew in size and returned to earth in middle of the field. He gently landed on his feet in a whirlpool of dust.

The thrusting noise ceased and the dust cleared; the man with the noisemaker on his back walked toward the crowd. They clapped vigorously and hollered like they were at a pig-calling contest. When he came to the first group of picnickers, he removed his gloves and a white motorcycle helmet and shook hands with the people who had rushed to see what the contraption was. What could make such a sound and yet carry a human being around exactly like Buck Rogers from the old black and white movies? Most of the people at the gathering suspected who the man behind the aviator sunglasses and the giant grin was. The Boss.

A big African-American man worked his way through the gathering throng of curious children and adults. He stepped up to the man with a smile and an outstretched hand and said, "You sure know how to make an entrance, Maverick!"

With a speedy twist of a lever in the middle of his chest, the quick disconnect unstrapped the harnessing in a single second. Unencumbered from the straps around his legs and chest, he removed the three-bottle matte-black jetpack and placed it on a table for the curious to see. Every piece of the jetpack was a different shade of black, giving it a wicked and unnatural look. He warned those straining to get a peek to "not touch," for parts of it "were very hot" and "we don't need anybody getting burned."

The training center's full-time medical doctor, a former U.S. Air Force flight surgeon, Geoff Lawson, barked at the pilot, "If I knew you were going to be doing crazy shit like that, I would have never given you an up-chit for your hand." The comment was part seriousness and part admonishment. Lawson had personally overseen Hunter's rehabilitation and had signed the medical releases that help regained his FAA certificates. The men exchanged a quick grin as if to affirm all the flight doc's rehab work hadn't been for naught.

A couple of gentlemen, both pushing eighty and wearing jeans and straw cowboy hats, took over responsibility and helped move the jetpack to a pre-positioned table inside a cordoned off circle—about 25' diameter. The old guys, affectionately known as Bob and Bob, admonished the youngsters, "You can look but do not touch."

Duncan Hunter thanked the well-wishers. Some unseen arm snaked through the throng and offered him some shade for his head. He plopped the black Stetson *El Presidente* on his head, raced to the food line, washed his hands with sanitizer, and jumped into his position on the serving line. He took a quick look back at the latest vertical takeoff and landing research and development product from the Quiet Aero Systems laboratory. Nearly a million and a half dollars had been spent on the latest development of smokeless fuels and solid propulsion technologies, and it was all wrapped up into a human backpack configuration.

Jetting around on a couple of columns of thrust had been a blast but he had a new task to accomplish. So he donned an apron and nitrile gloves, and armed himself with a huge knife and fork. He carved the huge slab of beef brisket and slapped a healthy portion of the juicy meat onto a Styrofoam plate. It belonged to one of his wounded warrior employees, a former Marine who had lost a leg to an improvised explosive device (IED) while conducting combat operations in Fallujah, Iraq. The two men were dressed virtually identically; jeans, white denim shirts, black Stetsons, and matching black Lucchese crocodile cowboy boots. The official Texas barbeque uniform. Their engraved silver belt buckles were substantially different but both approached the size of a 1957 Chevy hubcap. Hunter's shirt was drenched with sweat from his jetpack joyride. It was plastered across his back and was virtually transparent; 1200-thread count Egyptian cotton would do that when it was soaked.

"Thanks, boss." The man with the elephant grey skin was 24 but looked significantly older, like a man with a mortgage heading to the graveyard shift. He had seen war, up-front and personal. Several tours in Afghanistan and Iraq. The experience had the effect of aging the hardiest of athletes and youths. As he sidled away another hungry and severely disabled patron took his place with an empty plate and a full stream of tête-è-tête. Then another and another. His employees.

Hunter chatted with them all. Small talk. The jetpack was the main topic, with cars and airplanes filling out the Chinese menu of discussion options. He knew everyone by name, including the spouses and children. "How's your folks?" "How's little Benjamin, little Breanna?"

The serving line was long, the offerings varied, and it moved with the precision of a Corvette race car at Nürburgring. It was manned with family and the leaders and supervisors of Hunter's businesses. Next to Hunter was his wife, Nazy Cunningham. She was decked out nearly identically as he, with Levi jeans, a billowy white short-sleeved shirt that caressed her full bosom. She wore a tiny strap of leather for a belt and a heavily-engraved silver belt buckle with a shiny fifty dollar gold piece in the middle. A white Stetson, a solid gold Rolex, and strands and strands of turquoise in a twisted torsade necklace completed her colorful ensemble. Like Duncan, Nazy served Brobdingnagian portions of pulled pork with cheer and a smile.

The sight of a former Muslima serving pork would have been, at a minimum, incongruous, but more likely full, hard-on blasphemy had it not been for her renouncement of Islam and conversion to Christianity. She had acquired a taste for dripping-wet pork tenderloin slathered in an award-winning West Texas barbeque sauce. She claimed her first taste of bacon was a near religious experience. Her assimilation from Muslim spy to a full-throated, Constitution-carrying American, in tight, untorn, blue jeans, cowboy boots and hat, and an oversized sterling buckle was complete.

Her long black hair was braided; the ends brushed the no-man's land between her waist and knee. Duncan Hunter playfully bumped her hip with his in a feeble attempt to get her attention and then, when she looked at him, tried to sound sexy with a poor rendition of INXS' favorite, "There's something about you girl…that makes me sweat!" She broke out in a megawatt smile and bumped him back. The playful contact was a reaffirmation that their sensual life was marvelous and wonderful. They worked at restraint, no public displays of affection, but it was virtually impossible. They were obsessed with each other when they were together. Given five seconds of privacy in an elevator or alone in a hall, they would kiss passionately until it was no longer safe for the spontaneous, enthusiastic and scandalous activity. They hadn't seen each other while Duncan prepared for his jetpack flight, and now they were enjoying the moment being back in close proximity with each other, even if it meant they had to keep their eyes on their temporary serving jobs and their hands off each other.

People came and went; some jumped in the serving line for seconds and thirds. It was like rush hour on a Texas turnpike with stop and go traffic at the macaroni and cheese, corn on the cob, and apple pie trays. The end of the line was dominated by a huge antique ice-cream freezer where a tall veteran scooped balls of ice cream onto cones for kids of all ages. There was plenty of "chow," as Hunter would say. If anyone went hungry, it would be their own damn fault.

Toward the end of the serving line, dishing out wedges of carrot cake and apple pie was the daughter, Kelly Horne. She was Hunter's daughter, not Nazy's. Both women took leave from their government jobs in Washington D.C. for what was becoming an annual event in Texas. You just didn't miss some things: the company's 4th of July picnic was one of those things. It was considered a close family affair that spanned all of Hunter's many businesses and employees.

Few knew that Hunter's wife and daughter actually worked at the CIA. Only Hunter and McGee knew Nazy had found the master terrorist, Osama bin Laden, and had interrogated him in Liberia; only Hunter and McGee knew Nazy had also found the CIA file on the former President of the United States. And only McGee and Nazy knew that Duncan Hunter had cleverly released the bogus president's file to Congress and the media, which set the stage for the immediate resignation and departure of the former Commander in Chief. Kelly Horne was just getting started in her career with the Agency as a pilot. No one had a need to know the actions and activities of Hunter, McGee, Nazy Cunningham, or Kelly Horne. No one had a need to know who the beautiful young redheaded woman was. No one had a need to know why she couldn't keep her eyes off of her father and Nazy, bumping their hips like silly kids at a concession stand sharing bits of popcorn. She thought, *You can tell those two are in love.*

At the far end of the serving line covered with red and white checkered tablecloths was the new owner of the Full Spectrum Training Center. A sometimes gruff, take-charge man, William "Bullfrog" McGee was holding court with three very large men who had pistols strapped to their legs. After mumbling a few directions, they dispersed. He scanned the activities along the serving table, all of the inflatables stuffed with squealing children, and the dozens of families returning to their chairs or blankets to sit and eat. With a big fat muscular finger, McGee directed some of the former elite soldiers to presumed trouble spots. The men jumped in to help a family in need of a picnic table, with a recalcitrant lawn chair, or to help a single mother spread a blanket. McGee understood the severely disabled wounded warriors wouldn't ask for help. He nodded his approval that his guys were taking care of everyone, especially the kids. Because it was all about the kids. The louder the squeals of joy and fun, the better. It was a good showing; no one employee appeared to be missing or having less than a great time.

Bill McGee had been one of a very few African-Americans serving in the U.S. Navy as a SEAL—Sea, Air, Land. He was the only African-American officer ever to command the vaunted United States Naval Special Warfare Development Group or DEVGRU, known within the intelligence community as one of the United States' four secretive counterterrorism and Special Mission Units. He didn't suffer fools well and had little time for the teenage boys with their eyes on his daughters. Muscular like a professional bodybuilder, his shoulders were as wide as a Mack dump truck and just as solid. McGee was the most accomplished, the most decorated, and at one time the most successful SEAL in the history of the Naval Special Warfare Command. But he hadn't been able to find Osama bin Laden in the Afghanistan mountains. Now he was the training center's official greeter of dignitaries ranging from the mayor of the local town of Hondo to a congressional staffer from San Antonio. He had deployed his quick reaction force to trouble areas, so now he concentrated on handling out plastic silverware and napkins, and thanking everyone in the serving line for coming. He loved every minute of it.

A country and western band played boot scooting music from a covered pavilion. Women in western wear and cowboy hats line danced with children; teens with thumbs in belt loops and worn cowboy boots of every shape, size, and color pounded the temporary wooden dance floor. Beer bottles were emptied and replaced with regularity. A few of the retired SEALs kept an eye on some of the troops to ensure no one got out of hand.

Three tallish men in dark cowboy hats took turns talking with the attractive redheaded girl with a small gold cross around her neck. They looked the type that could turn a whitetail buck into four quarters in under an hour. An amused Kelly Horne looped her fingers in belt loops and chatted amicably about flying. She was there to help test fly a couple of powered-glider-type airplanes for her father for the international market. The men were more interested in her and her car, a red-on-black 1974 V-12 Jaguar XKE. She didn't say it had been a birthday gift from her father. After an invitation to see the long foreign motor, the foursome walked off as a group to see what was under the bonnet.

Nazy and Hunter had removed their aprons and gloves and slow danced to some slow belly-rubbing music, *The Other Side of Life*, from The Moody Blues. Next he swing-danced with his shocked daughter and sashayed her around the floor as nimbly as Fred Astaire. Countless employees wondered who the young woman could be, but a few of the older matrons thought they could see some family resemblance. Hunter and Kelly cut rugs as he spun her like a top to *Boot Scootin' Boogie*. McGee's daughters took turns with their old man; he worked up a major sweat dancing and pounding his boots on the dancefloor. Nazy and Angela McGee huddled, laughed, and clapped furiously during the father-daughter dance.

Before everyone realized it, it was dark. Hunter cursed himself for getting so distracted that he had missed the sun's last green flash. He turned back to see Nazy's platinum-green eyes sparkling in the floodlights; there was no competition.

Another show was on the schedule. Families and the single men and women swarmed the dessert table and refreshed drinks before the big show began. The band's lead singer offered a final song. "We'd like to close with something that I'm sure this group will enjoy. Apologies to Garth Brooks. This is, 'I've got Friends in Safe Spaces.'"

The adults howled in laughter, picked up the harmony and sang, over and over:
Oh I've got friends in Safe Spaces
If you don't go with us
Then you must be racist
That is our catch phrase
Where is my latte

Come on in and let's get cozy
Showing off participation trophies
Watching CNN
In Safe Spaces

Hunter gestured to the band to stop. He leaned over and kissed Nazy before he left her on their blanket with Kelly. Some young men with sidearms, Resistol hats, and Dan Post boots hovered nearby. He didn't think anything of it, as he had a speaking part and he needed to be somewhere. He wouldn't allow the evening's climax to start until everyone was ready. Bill McGee joined him in front of the assembly. The two honchos wore holsters with matching Colts, Model 1911 .45 ACP with a flat, desert-tan-colored Cerakote finish over the stainless steel slide. Nazy and Kelly didn't remark about every male carrying some sort of firearm. No one else noticed; no one cared. A way of life for men from the combat arms. It was Southwest Texas, after all.

As the employees of Hunter's and McGee's businesses settled into their seats and onto their blankets, the two men exchanged grins. It was the Fourth of July and that meant fireworks. This night was going to be one for the record books. Hunter patted the Motorola hand-held radio clipped to his belt. He was excited to find out what a quarter million dollars of fireworks looked like.

CHAPTER TWELVE

2100 July 4, 2014
Hondo, Texas

The Full Spectrum Training Center had been the brainchild of Hunter's early business partners, the retired Senior Intelligence Service executive Greg Lynche and the retired Colonel Art Yoder, U.S. Army. The old guys thought there was a market for private personal security firms. Security at U.S. Embassies continued to be degraded through the political machine—U.S. Marines charged to protect the embassy and its people were prohibited from engaging invaders scaling the walls of the embassy. The U.S. State Department would never forget when a single Marine Corps private stationed at the American Legation in Peking, China during the Boxer rebellion, had singlehandedly killed over two hundred Chinese as they stormed the bastion. The State Department of today couldn't have teenage Marines getting their hands bloody protecting embassies anymore, but they were open to private security companies providing mature, retired and former men from the special operations community to deter invaders hell-bent on killing or kidnapping Americans.

Other former special operations commanders recognized the new opportunities at the State Department, as well as the CIA, and went into business. Erik Prince, a former U.S. Navy SEAL officer, founded the government services and security company—Blackwater USA—and won billions of dollars in contracts. Prince's Blackwater became the largest of the State Department's private security companies, providing guards for bases, consulates, and embassies abroad. Art Yoder and Greg Lynche quickly determined they were too late to play in that game and couldn't compete with the exponentially growing number of private security companies vying for work with the State Department or the CIA. They also recognized that their inability to get "into the game with the big dogs" was a blessing in disguise. There were many unforeseen problems when building a private security company "too fast," essentially up from the ground floor to the penthouse in one quick motion.

Special Operations guys feel they can do anything, that they can overcome anything. But that growth often comes at the price of unintended consequences. By the time Blackwater and the other private security companies found that they had hired and deployed a significant number of "problem children," more than a smattering of psychopaths and others with personality disorders had been turned loose in very unstable locations and combustible situations, it was too late. Life is cheap in a war zone and some civilians were needlessly killed. Poor vetting of a few psychologically troubled employees had blackened the eyes of Blackwater and others and spelled the exponential decline of that experiment.

Upon hearing of the issues being experienced by the State Department's contracted private security companies, Duncan Hunter asked Lynche and Yoder, "How do guys like that get through the vetting?" Yoder, with his West Virginia drawl explained, "It's easier than you think to hide your past. You should know that."

Hunter nodded and offered, "The Border Patrol was surprised to find they had Border Patrol Agent recruits that were convicted armed robbers and murderers when they showed up at the Federal Law Enforcement Training Center." Under Yoder's and Lynche's leadership, the Full Spectrum Training Center thoroughly vetted their potential employees. A comprehensive background investigation, which included the magic of a polygraph, was conducted before anyone was hired into a sensitive law enforcement and executive protection position. The FSTC never experienced any of the problems that befell Blackwater, *et al.* Yoder and Lynche hired only top-shelf people, a more thoughtful and more professional cadre of specially-trained men in positions requiring special trust of confidence. After demonstrating they were reliable and were not hiding some sordid personal history, they were brought into the family.

As Lynche returned to Washington D.C. to write contract proposals for the lucrative counterterrorism and counterdrug contracts with the CIA, Hunter concentrated on the *Wraith* flying missions and overseeing the continuous improvement of the YO-3A aircraft. While Hunter absorbed a CIA front company and turned it into Quiet Aero Systems; Yoder built the ground business, the Full Spectrum Training Center, as a local niche player in private security and personal protection. At Hunter's suggestion, Yoder focused primarily on protecting domestic and international businessmen, program managers, journalists, and correspondents when they travelled overseas. It was a brilliant scheme and business plan.

Yoder or one of his instructors, former SEALs or U.S. Army Delta, taught students weapons familiarization. Students learned to identify, disassemble, and fire weapons from around the world. If there was a chance that one of the students could come into contact with a foreign weapon in a prisoner or hostage situation, they needed to know how to use that weapon. After the passing of Colonel Yoder, Hunter offered the FSTC to Bill McGee as a reward for saving the life of Nazy Cunningham. Hunter and McGee were family. Brothers from different mothers.

McGee and his handpicked band of former U.S. Navy SEALs refined the hands-on training as well as other aspects and capabilities of the FSTC. His instructors taught primary and refresher courses in defensive driving, anti-carjacking techniques, and the delicate art of driving backward at fifty miles per hour. In a high-speed chase, it took the capabilities of a wildman and a professional driver to spin a car 180° and then continue at the same speed in the same direction to escape the pursuit. The ability to drive as fast as possible in reverse had saved many men in the intelligence community.

While everyone who participated in the defensive driving courses loved to race and spin the cars, some capabilities remained strictly the purview of active and retired Special Forces personnel. Every few months, McGee personally led nighttime, high-altitude, low-opening as well as low-altitude, low-opening recertification parachute jumps for these special operations professionals. Each man wore lightweight, helmet-mounted, combination infrared and night vision binoculars used exclusively by U.S. Special Forces. Hunter sometimes participated in the jumps when his schedule allowed; his parachuting skills were routinely ridiculed by McGee.

Bill McGee returned the FSTC facility to its former glory and added more capabilities in law enforcement and crowd control. For some of the Special Forces operators, their inclusion at the FSTC provided much-desired stability and was their first opportunity to start a family. Wives and children. No more monthly or annual deployments that killed relationships and messed with the heads of spouses, or crushed the fragile developing minds of children who wondered why daddy was always gone or why mommy and daddy were always fighting, and if it was their fault.

· · · · ·

Duncan Hunter and Bill McGee thanked everyone for coming. After a boisterous round of applause, Hunter used his best "command voice" and bellowed, "If we were in any other place in the country, this gathering of patriots would be considered a basket of deplorables. 'Politically incorrect.' We say 'Happy Fourth of July' and 'God Bless America.' Young men open doors and give up their seat for women, young women open doors for old farts like Bill and me and tell us, 'Good morning, gentlemen.'" The crowd easily laughed at his self-deprecating observation.

Hunter waited for the laughter to die down. "This group proudly salutes our flag and give thanks to our troops, police officers, firefighters, and first responders. This group thinks it means something when they stand and face the flag to recite the Pledge of Allegiance—pledging allegiance especially to our country, not just the flag."

Nazy Cunningham and Kelly Horne clapped vigorously with the assembly. When some silence ensued, Hunter provided some context of the work accomplished in the Fredericksburg businesses and at the Hondo Training Center, and congratulated everyone for their hard work in making the businesses profitable. Bill McGee leaned in and put his partner on the spot as he quipped, "That means bonus checks?" Hunter nodded and raised two "thumbs up." The gathering clapped and cheered thunderously. Hunter and McGee shook hands and smiled for the crowd. Excitement and anticipation was in the air.

A man of very few words, McGee waved to the crowd and added, "We thank you for coming, and I hope you enjoy the show. And, oh, by the way, I would appreciate it if ya'll would just delete those photos and videos of that little flight demo. We don't need to see that on YouTube. Thank you!" More polite hooting and hollering from the masses.

Angela McGee and Nazy Cunningham shared a blanket, and admired their men. Pride welled up in them; it looked as if dribbles of tears could flow freely at any second.

Three hundred men, women, and children were ready and had their Annie Oakleys for the best fireworks show in West Texas. McGee winked at Hunter. If it wasn't a signal that he had done well in his unscripted public speaking gig, then it was a signal that it was "Showtime!" The men waved at the crowd as they departed center stage. Hunter unclipped the radio from his hip and spoke into it. Seconds later, fireworks lit up the sky and filled the air with loud reports. The two satisfied men slapped each other on their back as they walked off stage listening to the *ooohs* and *aaahs* behind them.

Hot, burning streaks of light filled the starry night sky. Red, white, and blue balls of bursting trails of light or sparks burst forth overhead, three at a time. Red, white, and blue. Doublets and triplets. The concussions from the mortars swept across the open field, delayed by the speed of sound and distorted by the Doppler Effect. More *ooohs* and *aaahs* erupted from the crowd with every explosion.

When the men stopped at the blanket where their wives were sitting, Hunter leaned into Nazy and explained the difference between the starbursts. "The red ones are chrysanthemums; the white ones with the trails of silver stars produce a weeping willow outline and, surprisingly, are called willows. The blue ones are peonies; no streaks just a spherical break of blue shooting stars with that *crackling* of fireworks afterwards. The chrysanthemums have the thick trail of sparks like a fiber optic ball. Very cool."

Nazy moved into him and said, "They are so beautiful—but they die so quickly. Why can't they stay up there forever?" It sounded like a question that didn't require an answer.

"They are very beautiful," said Angela McGee.

"They're great, Maverick. I like patriotic colors on such a glorious day!" McGee nodded vigorously.

McGee turned and conspiratorially asked, "You ever get to play with M-80s?"

The women ignored their men. "Nah, my favorites were bottle rockets," replied Hunter, shaking his head at old fun memories while new ideas crept inside. More *ooohs* and *aaahs* and the distant thunder of rockets launching the latest barrage of fireworks skyward. He continued, "It would be...*fun* to be able to mount some small rockets on the jetpack. We couldn't get too crazy for weight and balance purposes...." Then reality hit him, "But maybe having a dozen bundled M-80s near my head isn't the best idea I've ever had."

McGee laughed so hard he coughed. After a bout of chuckling he nodded and said, "I think the boys in engineering can work up something for you by the time you get back from Australia."

"That would be wild."

McGee continued through the distant explosions, "After I detonated my first M-80 I *kinda* knew I was going to be a SEAL, because after that, I was always blowing up stuff and wanted to use bigger and more powerful charges. Oh, contrary to urban legend, an M-80 is not equivalent to a quarter-stick of dynamite. Not even close. Now, that C-4 is some good shit." As soon as he finished his sentence, McGee quieted and stared at Hunter, who had moved on to another thought, another episode in their business lives. "Did you get a chance to read that *Explanatory Memorandum* I sent you?"

McGee nodded. "Just confirmed what we suspected. The Muslim Brotherhood has infiltrated America."

"They've dug in—planted roots in the country. And our boy 3M facilitated it all. Put all of his guys in the top government jobs."

"That he did."

"And the world's on fire."

Another quick nod from McGee then, "Thanks to our former president. I read today that in Austin a church was tagged 'Islam or die.'"

Hunter knew "tagged" meant that someone had used spray-paint to leave their message. He nodded. "There are hundreds of new articles everyday on the latest atrocities from these radicals."

"Worldwide. Yeah, he set the world on fire but you got him kicked out of office. He is hiding in a cave so deep I doubt he'll ever come up for air. One out of two isn't bad. Nice job, Maverick!"

"Someone had to do it." The men grinned, stood and walked off toward the administration building.

Hunter offered a last word, "ISIS didn't exist when he took office. It was just three guys in a Syrian hotel with a goat. Now they are everywhere."

McGee laughed. Their ladies just leaned back and enjoyed the show. Hunter sighed heavily and allowed a passing thought: where could that bastard of a former president be?

• • • • •

A year earlier, while Hunter had been completely engaged with Nazy's rehabilitation, McGee offered to fly to Amman, Jordan to eliminate Hunter's growing nemesis. Armed with a half-dozen miniature quadcopters and a pound of C-4, McGee blew the former CIA Director out of the top floor of the Sheraton Hotel. The only problem was that the blast didn't kill Dr. Rothwell; it only wounded him. He lost an arm and an eye in the explosion. The last time McGee and Hunter were in Jordan, Rothwell managed to ambush the master pilot, put Duncan in a torture stock, and cut off his hand. McGee saved Hunter that day, and his hand, and finished the job of killing the former CIA Chief with a few bullets to the cranium. McGee always felt a pang of guilt that he hadn't been able to kill Rothwell the first time, remotely, via C-4 carrying drones. Hunter never said a thing. Unfinished work was like that to a perfectionist.

• • • • •

Hunter raised his hand, the one with the electronic stimulation cast, removed his hat, and wiped his forehead and eyes. He had moved from the unseriousness of arming the jetpack with bottle rockets to the seriousness of how their lives merged into their diverse careers. As he and McGee walked, Hunter said, "I kind of knew I was going to be a fighter pilot. I just didn't know how I would ever get there. I put bottle rockets on everything, even launched them from my bike. I loved to shoot rockets from a jet. They are so cool, but crazy dangerous. Guys get mesmerized when they are launched from under the jet, and their eyes follow them to impact, and sometimes, they forget they're flying a jet and impact the ground themselves." An old related memory popped into his head. Hunter leaned in and said, "I think the best *real bottle rocket* I ever saw was when I was stationed in Yuma, Arizona. An old Gooney Bird, a Super DC-3, was taxiing into its parking spot when it swung around way too wide, way too far from its run-in line—the pilots can't see crap because the nose of the airplane is so high—and the horizontal stabilizer hit one of those five-foot tall firebottles. The stab knocked off the pressure regulator and, I swear, that huge firebottle took off like a bottle rocket right toward the control tower. I stood there frozen, my mouth agape, and watched like a fool the arc of that firebottle as it headed toward the tower. Where I was standing, I had the perfect view—I thought it was going to go through the tower's windows, but at the last second, it drifted off, missing it and the aircraft in the landing pattern. That firebottle blasting off into the sky like a bottle rocket was just an awesome demonstration of the power of compressed gasses instantly released. It still makes me laugh!"

"That's crazy." McGee smiled and nodded. He sucked a lungful of air. They were far enough away from the crowd and the background noise was sufficient to speak openly without being overheard. He changed the subject. What's on your calendar?"

Hunter said, "I'm taking Nazy and Kelly back to DC in the morning, then I'm going to look at a house and an airplane."

"Another jet?"

His head shook gently. "Prop job. Starship."

"Whatever that is. You think you're Hans Solo, or Captain Kirk, or some bullshit?" McGee grinned at his humor. "Just Billy Ray Joe Bob Average trying to do an above average job."

"Nothing average about you!" McGee scrunched his nose and his tiny round eyeglass lenses rode up onto the bridge. The glasses had once given him the air of being incredibly smart, as if he were a scholar. Now they looked out of place on the big man's face.

"That's the pot calling the kettle black."

"Racist!" McGee chuckled so hard he nearly collapsed. It was an old joke between the friends. McGee mocked democratic liberals who called anyone who didn't agree with their views "a racist," or a domestic terrorist, or worse. McGee wouldn't accept the idiotic politically-motivated premise and ridiculed it at every opportunity. He and Hunter were simpatico in their politics.

"I swear, liberals, commies, or whatever they call themselves this week are the scourge of the earth. Life sucks when they are in charge." Hunter smirked.

The band cranked up John Anderson's *Swingin'*. People flooded the dancefloor. *There's a little girl... In our neighborhood....*

"Blood would shoot out of their eyes if they heard you say that." McGee crossed massive hands over massive arms.

"Screw 'em. And, their pet sheep. They should be glad I don't run 'em off the road in their dumb-ass Smart Cars and pansy-ass Priuses with those idiotic 'coexist' bumper stickers."

McGee laughed as he and Hunter embraced as brothers and departed in opposite directions.

After loading the jetpack in the back of the vehicle, Hunter and Nazy drove off in a specially-built, armoured, six-wheeled Hummer6. Kelly Horne drove off in her Jaguar followed by a train of cowboy hat-wearing men in pickups and headed for one of Hondo's honkytonks.

The band stopped playing and the rest of the dancing crowd dispersed to their vehicles. McGee and his former SEALs walked about and checked the area where the 300 guests had enjoyed barbeque and fireworks. Under the flood lights, he stopped, arms akimbo. There wasn't a scrap of paper on the field nor a plastic cup. If anything the field looked as if it had been mowed and trimmed by a squadron of Midshipmen with pinking scissors.

The view made him smile. He could hear Hunter say, "And I bet you when we all leave here, this field won't look like a New Jersey landfill. In other words, there weren't any liberals out there trashing it up!" While Hunter's comments were always in jest, there was always more than a modicum of truth in every observation.

A pair of camouflaged men walked up to McGee. One said, "We got it boss. Go home. We'll close shop."

McGee relented control of the Training Center to some of the single men. He found his family nearby and offered thick arms for his girls, but at that mid-teen age they demurred being hugged or coddled in public. Their actions also telegraphed that there had to be some cute boys within eyeshot. To be seen hanging on a huge protective father was not the signal they wanted to transmit. Angela understood her daughters' shunning their father and allowed them to walk behind, like fawns trailing a mother doe. She took one arm and walked in-step with her husband to their vehicle. McGee opened the door for his bride and ensured she was safely inside before closing her door. The girls opened their own doors.

As the black Suburban ambled down the road toward a couple of men, McGee slowed and rolled down his window. He said, "Good night, and thanks" to the remaining security team at the entrance gate. The men gave the old SEAL an informal salute; McGee touched his brow with his fingers in return.

CHAPTER THIRTEEN

1000 July 12, 2014
Washington D.C.

The Indonesian Boeing airliner, now missing for a week, was the topic of discussion at a closed door hearing of the United States Senate Select Committee on Intelligence. By-name invitations and top secret clearances were required for the panel of distinguished aviation and intelligence community professionals. The Director of the Central Intelligence Agency, the Chief Executive Officer of the Boeing Aircraft Company, a representative from the Interagency Committee for Aviation Policy (ICAP), and a professor of aviation terrorism from Embry-Riddle Aeronautical University offered prepared remarks at the secret hearing and answered questions. The university professor provided a brief history of aviation terrorism and cautioned the senators to never underestimate the tenacity and creativity of the aviation terrorist. "They will take advantage of airlines and airports' security systems and programs, and they will attack unguarded airports, aircraft, the infrastructure and their electronic systems. Wherever they can find a weakness, they will move to exploit those weaknesses for their nefarious goals."

The Boeing CEO and the woman from ICAP suggested a new generation of computer software coupled with artificial intelligence algorithms would do much to preclude future in-flight hijackings of commercial aircraft. Boeing's CEO indicated one of their subcontractors had perfected a "systems of systems" of next-generation, heavily-encrypted software that would preclude a commercial aircraft from ever being hijacked internally or externally, via a hacker, as well as provide real-time cockpit information via a satellite datalink, negating the need for flight data recorders and cockpit voice recorders. The new software would offer pinpoint locations when an aircraft no longer responded to radio calls or crashed.

The CIA Chief acknowledged there had been multiple organizations claiming responsibility for the missing Indonesian Sky Link aircraft. He suggested there had been some highly classified intelligence "chatter" warning Muslim men not to travel by air the day the Indonesian aircraft went missing, but that bit of intelligence was proven to be just disinformation to fuel the harassment of security professionals. "There was nothing specific and nothing was directed at the airline. Such warnings in the past have been linked to explosive devices planted on aircraft. At this moment, we are unaware of any other missing aircraft or an explosion on any aircraft."

Senators demanded to know if anti-hijack software would have saved the Indonesian Sky Link 777. The Boeing CEO replied, "If the method used to bring down the aircraft can be attributed to an explosive device, it is unlikely any software could have saved the aircraft."

The senior Senator from Texas pressed the CEO. "What if someone was able to enter the cockpit and commandeer the aircraft?"

The CEO switched on his microphone and said, "Under those circumstances, then yes, Senator. I believe so. This new heavily-encrypted software coupled with artificial intelligence determines 'hijacking behavior,' such as someone gaining entry into the cockpit and pulling the transponder circuit breakers, or the copilot locking the pilot out of the cockpit. Once the artificial intelligence determines the aircraft cockpit is under siege, it eliminates any further cockpit inputs, severing total control of the aircraft, and reverts to a programmed flight path and autonomous landing profile. It will even open a locked cockpit door in the event the pilot is locked out of the cockpit. The system we've designed is incorporated into our new line of aircraft and can be energized as an automatic software upgrade for some of the older Boeings. A heavily-encrypted patch, if you will, over the aircraft's satellite communication system. It will transmit its own discrete transponder signal for ATC, and the control tower will be able to talk to it and allow it to land safely with the automatic landing system. Yes. We believe it will have a profound effect on the survivability of an in-flight attempt of a hijacked aircraft. Additionally, to achieve real-time CVR and FDR information, a small black box would need to be retrofitted into older aircraft and installed to burst-transmit CVR and FDR information over the data link."

At the conclusion of the hearing, a bipartisan group of senators promised to introduce legislation to mandate counter-hijacking software in all commercial aircraft produced in the United States. Said one senator to the panel, "The aviation industry cannot afford another Indonesian Sky Link Flight 7070."

· · · · ·

The Director of Central Intelligence stepped out of the committee room and into the hall with the man from the aviation university. Greg Lynche turned to Duncan Hunter and said, "I think that went well. Thanks for coming."

"Thanks for asking. Sounds like a *great* plan." The sarcasm was dripping with ridicule.

"Anti-hijack software? That sounds smart." Lynche smiled at his former flying partner. Neither man was a fan of eliminating pilot control and turning airliners into robots, Lynche had once proposed just such a capability twenty-odd years ago when he was the CIA's Chief Air Branch. Lynche wouldn't allow his thoughts to continue in that direction; he was more interested in and anticipated the flurry of epithets and derogatory comments that would surely come from the businessman and part-time college professor. Duncan Hunter was politically a conservative, after all. He couldn't help himself.

"Why are you so nice to them? It's like aiding and abetting an idiot."

Lynche frowned and shook his head. "Says the man who if they ever knew what you did to their leader they would hound you to the ends of the earth to kill you."

Hunter disregarded off the thought. "Those creatures with the small heads and massive bodies think anti-hijack software is the solution? They are a disgrace to human-based life forms—not a lot of brain activity in there. I could feel IQ points being sucked from my body the longer some of those guys spoke, particularly...." From his pocket, Hunter withdrew an innocuous looking memory stick and slipped it to the CIA Director.

"Don't say it!" admonished Lynche as he backed up his reprimand with rumpled brows and a vituperative finger. With his other hand Lynche slipped the computer flash drive into his pocket. No one saw the transfer.

"I think we're screwed. The law of unintended consequences, and all that. Didn't you ever see 2001: A Space Odyssey?" Hunter lowered his voice; there was a new mechanical malevolent quality to his rendition of the spacecraft's computer system that refused to do as it was commanded. "I'd like to fly the airplane now, HAL. I'm sorry, I can't do that Dave...."

Lynche was exasperated with Hunter but broke out in a malicious smile. He nodded in defeat, but took his time before saying, "You might have a point, Maverick" *I hate it when he's right!*

Hunter smiled back, ecstatic that Greg was talking to him again. He always poked at liberals and democrats, and Lynche, a liberal democrat, always ignored him. Lynche loved his protégé and tolerated his politics. It gave the teetotaler and non-smoker some character.

"You're pessimistic. And pathetic."

"Realistic." Hunter's grin was infectious.

Lynche glanced at the arm in the black splint. He knew what the answer would be but asked anyway. "How are you doing?"

"No one's tried to kill me for a couple of weeks. That's a good start." Hunter sighed and glanced around the hall as if a furtive assassin was hiding behind the statuary or the inside of doorways. "I'll always think your predecessor's buddies at the NCS were behind those."

Lynche said, "Now, Duncan...."

"Greg, you know the attempts jumped exponentially after I got out of Algeria, and Rothwell was shocked I was still alive." Hunter had told the newly installed DCI Greg Lynche that during his mission in Algeria he thought the former Director of Central Intelligence, Dr. Bruce Rothwell, had to have had some of his most trusted and loyal guys from the National Clandestine Service on the ground to make sure everyone on the ground was "good and dead," but they were forever pissed to find a hundred Marines from an amphibious assault ship had intervened and had got to the ransom gold first. The only question was, would they be on his ass forever? With the death of the former DCI, the unexplained assassination attempts appeared to have stopped.

Lynche ignored the attack on the most trusted part of his organization. Hunter's ramblings were without merit. "I meant your hand."

Hunter raised the splinted arm a few inches, wiggled his fingers, changed his expression, and nodded. "I'm okay."

Lynche wasn't totally surprised at the outburst and admission. He fumbled with the memory stick in his pocket. "How was Peru?"

"If you read the newspaper, you'd know. I think it was a smashing success. I'm sure we found *the hostages* you were looking for…." Hunter said with a mild grin. "Just like our first time; thank you very much."

Lynche returned the smile at the long faded memory of their first mission together; Hunter's first flight in the YO-3A. But he was more interested in the man's recovery than ancient history in an antique airplane. "Show me."

Hunter touched each finger with his thumb. He said, "My grip sucks but it's coming along. I can fly the jet."

"The FAA and the rules haven't stopped you yet, so why start now? What have you been doing with yourself? I hear there's been unusually high porn activity in that part of Texas."

Hunter half-frowned and ignored the dig. He would wait to tell his boss the latest secret project from Texas. "The Yo-Yo needs some work."

Lynche was suddenly curious. When he and Hunter flew the little spy plane, the YO-3A rarely suffered from maintenance issues. And if it ever did, Hunter would never mention them. "What?"

"Something's wrong with the computer or the software. I'm inclined to believe it's the encrypted software, because we recently got a software update push from the manufacturer that installed the automatic takeoff and landing system. I didn't think anything of it until it almost killed me. Live and learn."

"*What?!* What happened?" Concern was painted across Lynche's sunburned face in shades of brown wrinkles. Lynche had demanded the YO-3A be equipped with an automatic takeoff and landing system and had paid for its installation. *It couldn't be possible!* Lynche waited for the answer he really didn't want to ask: Was it possible the CIA's heavily-encrypted software vendor almost killed their best counterterrorism pilot?

"Flight controls locked up. The automatic takeoff and landing system. Initially, I couldn't override the computer. Even cycling the avionics master didn't work at first; it nearly ruined my day." Lynche's expression of confusion and concern did not register as Hunter looked away for a moment, thinking about the airplane that almost killed him. Then he continued, "We'll figure it out. You haven't had much for me to do. Maybe you were waiting for me to say I'm 100 percent."

"Maybe." Lynche finally grinned. All was back to normal, all discussions of airplanes and encrypted software problems evaporated.

Hunter would tell him eventually why his spy plane "almost killed him." *At least it wasn't a jihadi on a motorcycle.*

"Well, Director Lynche, you know I still have a couple of businesses to run. Teach a little school on the side. But, since you asked, I bought another airplane. And a car. And, I bought a new house. Oh, and the lab came up with a new toy."

These comments raised Lynche's eyebrow, almost to his hairline. First the jets. They were still pilots. It was a natural segue into the other acquisitions. "For someone who has *two* Gulfstreams—I don't think the CEO of Lockheed has two jets—what could you have possibly bought?" His curiosity spiked with a possible new purchase of more rare airplanes in need of a total overhaul. He knew Hunter lusted after a flyable, bent-wing, WWII Corsair. Lynche shrugged his shoulders, waited, and smiled.

"*But she does.* Anyway, a Starship. Something a little smaller. Something a little less subtle than a G-550. It's probably time to give the G-4 back to Uncle Sam or if you don't want it I'll sell it."

It took a great deal to surprise a 35-year senior intelligence executive. Both eyebrows shot up. Lynche crossed his arms, shook his head in amazement, and then forced himself to return to his professional demeanor. He had work to do and so did his former business partner. A check of his Longines chronograph on a brown alligator strap indicated it was almost time to go. He and Hunter looked at the watch for a moment; both men smiled.

"That's quite a watch," said Hunter. The Longines was a very rare 1937 model 13ZN of the large-dial type worn by Amelia Earhart before she attempted her round the world adventure. In the early days of aviation, rather than fitting airplanes with modified table clocks, it was more practical and efficient to use wristwatches. Lynche's was one of only five known surviving examples. It had been a gift from Hunter and Lynche knew Duncan had paid a small fortune for it.

Lynche dropped his arm, nodded, and turned to walk away. His security detail had yet to move; they didn't know he was out of the hearing. He asked before yawning, "Another Aston Martin?"

Hunter nodded. "A double black 1-77."

"Whatever the hell that is. And a house? You finally got a *Safe Space?*" Lynche's subtle dig at Hunter's conservative politics brought a smile to Hunter's face.

"Yeah, that's what it is, a 'safe space.' It's nice, rare and amazing. And the house is more of a log cabin. Maybe *a lodge*. In Wyoming. I don't think they have lodges in the Peoples Republic of Maryland. Rest assured it doesn't have solar panels, wind turbines, unicorn flatulence converters or any other of that green energy farce bullshit stuff."

The DCI shook his head and looked around the hallway and trying not to break out in laughter. "Oh, yeah, you're quite the environmentalist. You have the carbon footprint of Ouagadougou."

"*But I am an environmentalist! Weedbusters* is the perfect green solution for aerial eradication. No herbicides. Just using a little light. What's better than that? Windmills? Solar panels? See, I really am into that green shit. Ouagadougou is unfair. Maybe Bamako or Mako or Bissau. But Ouagadougou?" Lynche recognized the string of African cities where Hunter had killed Islamic radicals before they could massacre Christians.

Lynche grunted. Hunter wanted a reaction but he wasn't going to get much this time. He had work to do too. Hunter thought the conversation was over when Lynche asked, "So what's the new toy? Like the camouflage?"

"No—a jetpack."

"You mean....like Buck Rogers...."

"That's before my time, old man. I think more like James Bond. Or more specifically Bell's test pilot, William Suitor."

Lynche screwed up his face in disbelief. He remembered some of the basic capabilities of the basic system. The CIA was interested, but it didn't seem very useful outside of a four-second scene in a 007 movie. It was more of a parlor trick with exhaust gasses. "Wasn't it only good for...."

"The original, yes, about twenty seconds. Ours is good for over an hour. The secret sauce is in the fuel."

The Director of Central Intelligence registered surprise. He looked as if he had swallowed and was choking on a golf ball. When he recovered he said, "It's not like that flying wing thing with the little jet engines?" Hunter had already started to shake his head. Lynche looked down the hall to ensure their privacy. "We looked into those, too."

"No. A couple of years ago DARPA was looking at innovative solutions to deliver cargo to remote locations. Some smart ass at

Lockheed had already developed an unmanned helicopter to deliver a couple of tons autonomously at high altitude locations. Afghanistan. We looked at developing a small controllable rocket pack capable of hoisting a few hundred pounds of cargo into a remote combat zone. Maybe to the top of a mountain. Strap it on, fire it off, and turn it loose. Quick ammunition resupply; that sort of thing. First, it was too noisy and second, it was too unstable. And there were center of gravity problems. Software engineers couldn't come up with suitable algorithms to maintain stability during flight. We bailed out of their program; one of our engineers suggested they could turn it into a personalized jet pack, like the Bell Aerosystems models from the 1960s, with a human at the controls. It's an E-ticket ride! New proprietary algorithms coupled with my legs hanging down enough to provide the necessary ballast weight—like a kite's tail—keeps it very stable in the air. On one level, trade secret stuff. My manly fat legs naturally provide the necessary stability. It works."

"The secret sauce is in the fuel?" Lynche was enthralled and nearly in a trance. He simply nodded, shook his head, or grunted as Hunter spoke.

"You know solid propellant motors are the simplest of all rocket designs. The problem has always been that, unlike liquid propellant engines, solid propellant motors cannot be shut down. Once ignited they will burn until all the propellant is exhausted. Our scientists perfected a way to compress liquid hydrogen and turn it into a metal. Like diamonds. When you release the pressure it takes to create a solid, it's surprisingly stable at room temperatures. It's the perfect rocket fuel. A digital fuel control injects the pencil-lead-sized pellets of metallic hydrogen into a combustion chamber. It has amazing high performance, and the combustion can be moderated, stopped, or even restarted. Simple, safe, and effective. And it looks remarkably similar to Bell's Number 2 rocket belt design. It's the perfect design for a jetpack; like two wheels, front and back, is the perfect design for a bicycle. I'm sure if we ever show it off, Bell will sue the snot out of us. Think you might be interested?"

Lynche unfolded his arms and said, "You're crazy!"

"No, I'm not. I've flown it. I've gotten pretty good at flying it. Not so crazy."

"With or without a parachute?" the DCI asked incredulously.

"Okay, only a little crazy."

Lynche was jealous again. Hunter was always doing something exciting and fun, while he was always prim and proper as a government executive. Wistfully, he asked, "Weren't we all promised jetpacks by now?"

"Greg, your Democrats promised the moon and never delivered on anything but stealing or killing aviation programs. And you can thank your liberal, cartoon, environmentalist buddies for killing off all the cool ideas. They killed the Concorde, Bell's jetpacks, and *the light bulb*—you know they're not environmentally acceptable." Hunter wagged his finger. "They think free dope, trains, windmills, solar panels, and curly florescent vibrating bulbs they can screw into their ass are the future of America."

"Be nice." He withdrew the memory stick and shook it.

"I always am." By Lynche's body language, Hunter sensed it was time to go. He gestured at the flash drive and asked, "I hope you got what you wanted."

Lynche looked around him one more time. He shrugged and replaced the memory stick in his pocket. "Hitler's compound until he died in 1969. We were just wondering who is in there now." He let the words sink in.

Duncan was surprised. He recalled one of the old rumors that Adolph Hitler had escaped Nazi Germany and made his way to South America. It was one of the CIA's best kept secrets. Hunter smiled and shook his head.

Lynche returned the favor. "So, I'll see you tonight?"

Hunter frowned and played coy. "Of course. There's some things you just don't miss, good sir."

America's head spy said, "You'll have to tell me more about the Starship, and we might just need a jetpack demo. Oh, and do wear a *proper* tie, *Maverick*." He waved a finger at him sternly like an old nun admonishing a teenage heathen. He said over his shoulder as he stepped away to join his security detail, "And no cowboy boots!"

CHAPTER FOURTEEN

1900 July 12, 2014
The White House

President Hernandez and the First Lady received the Lynches, McGees, and Hunters at the White House as they engaged in the obligatory formal introductions in the Blue Room. The President then excused himself to the First Lady and asked the CIA men to come with him "for a few minutes." He led the men into the Oval Office while the First Lady escorted the spouses on a private tour of the East Room. A tea table had been set for four to allow the ladies to sit while awaiting their men's return.

Prior to entering the Oval office, the President's Chief of Staff verbally confirmed with the three guests that none of them were carrying their cell phones or any other electronic device. He then nodded at the President and closed the door.

President Javier Hernandez stepped to the side of the Resolute Desk, stood in front of William McGee, and shook his hand. Standing next to the retired U.S. Navy Captain, Duncan Hunter stood ramrod straight and looked directly across the Oval Office at an imaginary eye-high point on the wall. From 40 years of lifting weights and carrying hundreds of pounds of warfighting equipment during combat operations, McGee was twice the size of the 175-pound Hunter. McGee was one of the finest professional warriors America would ever produce. The men wore tuxedoes, starched white shirts, black bow ties, and shiny patent leather shoes; Lynche had checked to see if Hunter wore his black crocodile Luccheses just to be sure. Lynche also noticed it took about an acre of material to cover McGee's muscles. Only one man wore a smile, the President of the United States. He said, "I'm pretty sure no one has ever received one of these wearing a tux. Are you ready to do this, Director Lynche?"

The old soldiers knew what to do and stood at "Attention," their heads held high, chests out, hands along the satin outseam of their tuxedo trousers. The Director of Central Intelligence replied, "Yes, Mr. President." Greg Lynche took a position perpendicular to the President, held a sheet of parchment up to his face, and read through bifocals, "The President of the United States takes extremely great pleasure in awarding the Distinguished Intelligence Cross to William Randall McGee and Drew Duncan Hunter. As the pilot and copilot team under Special Access Program *Noble Savage*, you demonstrated uncommon and extraordinary acts of heroism and valor, while encountering exceptionally hazardous flying conditions over Northwestern Nigeria. Accepting existing dangers with exemplary courage and determination, you contributed significantly to the destruction of key leaders of the murderous terrorist group Boko Haram and were instrumental in the rescue and recovery of scores of young girls kidnapped by the terrorist organization. Your intrepidity and conspicuous gallantry were again on display as you analyzed a new dangerous and harrowing situation, seized the initiative to intervene, and rescued a hijacked commercial airliner in Monrovia, Liberia. Your actions culminated with the destruction of eight heavily armed hijackers and the freedom of over 700 passengers, aircrew, and the aircraft." Lynche wanted to frown at Hunter, but he was on a timeline.

"Additionally, under the most difficult of circumstances, you were directly instrumental in recovering a cache of tactical weapons of mass destruction before they could fall into the hands of worldwide terrorist groups. Your unilateral actions saved countless lives, both foreign and domestic. And, Mr. McGee, at significant peril to your own safety, you successfully tracked down and rescued your teammate from certain death. Your unwavering courage and steadfast devotion to your country reflects great credit upon yourself and upholds the highest traditions of the Central Intelligence Agency. Given under my hand this twelfth day of July, 2014. Signed Javier Hernandez. President." Lynche looked up, retrieved a wooden box from the corner of the desk, and handed it to the President.

There was no mention of Hunter sending a pair of thermonuclear devices into Iran to destroy one of their major nuclear weapons processing facilities. Everyone in the Oval Office knew he had done it, but some things were best left unsaid, especially during a medal ceremony. Had it been any other person on the planet, the offender would have been sent to the Federal prison at Fort Leavenworth. Lynche knew the President saw Hunter as a hero, and he had other missions for *Maverick* to accomplish.

President Hernandez squeezed McGee's hand and presented him with the heavy presentation case with the other. As the President said a few quiet words, McGee reflected on his life since meeting the man at his side. His squad of SEALs from the vaunted Team Six hadn't found Osama bin Laden in the mountains of Afghanistan after al-Qaeda's 9/11 attack on America. The political realities of not finding the master terrorist was something he didn't immediately comprehend until his spectacular and storied career—the most decorated SEAL in Special Operations Command and the only African American ever to command multiple SEAL Teams—came crashing down. Fired for the botched operation, he was removed from command, and put out to pasture. With no sponsor, no admiral to salvage his career, his punishment for not immediately retiring from the Navy was disgraceful. He was reassigned first as a student, then as an instructor at the Naval War College. Tiny office. Crappy furniture. No window. Total and complete humiliation. He had dedicated over 35 years of his life to the Navy and his brothers who wore the gold Trident. He had nowhere else to go but the gym.

Then someone who didn't care about his career, the gold Trident over his chest full of ribbons, or his skin tone came and sat next to him in the auditorium. They determined they had a mutual acquaintance from the Agency. As friends, they shared their trials and tribulations, and then as partners, they collaborated in and executed one of the most daunting missions ever conceived by the CIA. Here were the accolades he had missed from his failed attempt to capture bin Laden. This mission was equally difficult, daunting, and challenging. He glanced at Hunter, the man who had made it all happen, and smiled broadly.

Bill McGee, the most highly decorated sailor ever in the U.S. Navy, had received countless medals and awards over the course of his service as a SEAL. The others were important—five Navy Crosses, five Legions of Merit, a dozen Purple Hearts—this one was unique and special. It was more normal for clandestine service intelligence agents to receive the DIC posthumously. A contractor had never received this award.

The President sidestepped to face Hunter and presented him with a similar wooden box. He shook Hunter's good hand and said, *sotto voce*, "Captain McGee, Captain Hunter, America will never know of your courage and heroism or your accomplishments contributing to our National Security and Defense. On behalf of a great and grateful Nation, please accept my deepest appreciation and gratitude. We will be forever in your debt. Thank you and congratulations." Hunter accepted the wooden box with a pinched smile.

President Hernandez turned to DCI Lynche and said, "You're next. Captain McGee, would you do the honors?" Greg Lynche exchanged places with Bill McGee; Hunter stepped to the side and held a small presentation case for the President. In his deep rumbling, Barry White, radio-announcer voice, McGee read the citation, "The President of the United States takes extremely great pleasure in awarding the Distinguished Intelligence Cross to Gregory Michael Lynche...." The master spy was recognized for running the simultaneous top-secret operations which culminated in the recovery of thousands of pieces of World War II artwork, tons of Nazi gold, and devising the plan and leading the effort that retrieved man-portable thermonuclear devices stolen from Russian armories after the fall of the Soviet Union. All in the span of a week.

Lynche momentarily glanced at Hunter as he received his medal. For fifteen years they'd been business partners, Hunter piloting and him commanding the suite of sensors from the back seat of an antique spy plane, an aircraft few knew anything about. Everyone who visited the Pima Air Museum in Tucson ogled Lockheed's most famous engineering marvel, the SR-71, and completely ignored Lockheed's other spy plane, the YO-3A dangling over the old Blackbird's back. He had tried to recruit Hunter into the CIA thirty years previously but had lost track of him when he retired from the Agency, only to have Hunter find him a year later. For over 15 years they flew the quiet spy plane for the CIA as contract pilots.

Lynche never expected to become the DCI, the stunning political appointment caught Washington D.C. and the media completely off guard. Hunter made that happen too by planting the seed with the President. To rise to head the CIA was one of Lynche's lifelong ambitions. The other was to fly a high performance jet. Both accomplishments had been orchestrated by Duncan Hunter. Hunter always seemed to make the unthinkable and the impossible happen, like defeating an Iranian surface-to-air missile in the powered glider, and deposing a fraudulent president, as well as celebrating a legitimate president taking the oath of office. Lynche shook his head at the thought, *enemies, foreign and domestic.* Hunter had a knack for finding them and rooting them out of their holes.

At the end of the presentation ceremony, the President shook Lynche's hand, retrieved the citations from McGee, and stuffed the documents into a shredder under the intricately carved desk. Before the assembly broke up, Lynche destroyed the ambience of the emotional event by jumping in front of McGee and Hunter. For a 74-year old he was surprisingly quick on his feet. He made a "give it to me" gesture. He said, "*Gentlemen.* I need those medals back. They'll remain in my safe until…well, maybe one of these days your mission will be declassified. But don't hold your breath. You know the drill. None of this ever happened, and you can't ever talk about it!" Once the grinning McGee and the smirking Hunter surrendered the medals, Lynche gave them an obligatory "Thank you. Well done and congrats."

As Lynche stepped aside, Hunter shook McGee's hand and said, "Easy come, easy go. Good job, good sir." McGee's other giant paw patted Hunter on the shoulder, a sincere demonstration of admiration and respect.

President Hernandez was amused by the antics of the DCI and his two heroes, but only for a moment. He glanced across to the gold curtains that adorned the windows of the Oval Office, down at the rug, the Presidential Seal, and quietly pondered his good fortune. His rise to Speaker of the House had stunned Washington D.C. Just a good old Spanish-speaking Texas boy in black ostrich boots, Javier Hernandez won a congressional seat—as a Republican—that had been safely in Democratic hands for two generations.

He had attended Yale Law School and joined the Young Republicans. Liberal students couldn't comprehend a Republican Hispanic. He had clerked for a Supreme Court Justice and tried hundreds of cases as a city prosecutor in San Antonio. But his real passion was politics, conservative politics. Before he ran for office, he was featured frequently on the local television station as a photogenic news personality. Hernandez turned heads and became an overnight sensation as a no-nonsense guy who was pro-gun, pro-military, and hard on criminals.

As a congressman for the 23rd District, he had reversed decades of democratic malfeasance and political sabotage, and fought for more manpower, facilities and equipment for the U.S. Border Patrol and U.S. Customs. Several re-elections later, Hernandez became the first Latino-American Speaker of the U.S. House of Representatives; less than a year later he was President of the United States of America. He was POTUS with an agenda—protect Americans wherever they were and kill or neutralize terrorists before they could turn into the next Osama bin Laden.

For President Hernandez, killing master terrorists was personal. He lost his baby sister when some unknown terrorist group attacked a TWA 747 off the coast of Long Island. It was obvious the giant airplane was shot down, blown out of the sky. It was just as obvious that the Democratic administration in the White House covered up the surface-to-air missile attack, deflected the terrorist threat to commercial aviation, and thus, provided the spark for him to go into politics. Republican politics.

On his Inauguration Day, President Hernandez vowed he would make amends and take the fight to the terrorists wherever they lurked and hid. He just had to assemble the right team. He had an idea of a special group who could do the work. And, now he had them. The real Fantastic Four. The uncommonly competent and capable Greg Lynche, Bill McGee, and Nazy Cunningham were the support crew for Duncan Hunter and his quiet airplane. The rock star of the program was called *Wraith*, and there were few places on the planet where burgeoning and charismatic leaders of terrorism could hide from the low-flying airplane with the super long wings and the best acoustically stealth technologies American research money could develop. And it had a gun.

One of President Hernandez's first orders of business was to determine what really happened to his sister. He received an Oval Office brief which verified the CIA was operating a black program, a SAP, a special access program, which paid annual ransom payments to an unknown Algerian to prevent another attack on America's commercial airliners. Special access programs (SAP) are the most secret of the secret programs. Unauthorized disclosure of a SAP usually results in the death or capture of a spy.

The unknown murderer became the first entry on a spreadsheet of known and unknown terrorists who would be targeted for elimination. The CIA Director called the list the Disposition Matrix. The program: *Noble Savage*. The name of the SAP was derived from a line in a book telling how early explorers moving west into North America were astonished to see Indians hunting game. In France, the right to hunt was a privilege granted only to the aristocracy and this right to hunt was taken for granted. Since the Indians demonstrated the same carefree right to hunt as the French aristocrats, one of the explorers wrote a book when he returned to France. He entitled one of the chapters, "The Savages are Truly Noble." Hunter was granted the right to hunt for the man who killed the President's sister and hundreds of other Americans whose only crime was boarding an airliner.

Now he was giving the man who made it all possible—the unmasking of a bogus president, his ascension to the presidency, and the payback for the murder of his sister—another medal and his gratitude. When it was impossible to send missiles into terrorist hideouts protected by women and children, he would ask Hunter if he were ready to do more—to fly into the radical Islamic-held territories, to hunt down and kill radical Islamic mass murderers and their leaders. But first, he had a question he had been dying to ask. Only one man in the room could answer the question. The President cleared his throat. He moved to a sideboard and placed his hand atop Sir Jacob Epstein's bust of Sir Winston Churchill. The gesture got everyone's attention. "Duncan?"

"Yes, Mr. President?"

"What's it really like to land aboard an aircraft carrier at night?" Lynche and McGee looked at Hunter; they had often asked the same question only to get some cock and bull story that when you do it right, you live and when you get it wrong, you die.

"Well, sir. The best analogy I've heard is, a day landing on a ship is like sex. It's either good or great. It's truly the most fun you can have with your clothes on. However, landing on the boat at night is like a trip to the dentist for a root canal; you go into it with incredible trepidation, and you may actually get away with only a little pain. But it is never fun, and you don't ever feel comfortable. Once you've trapped, caught the wire, you cannot believe you lived through it. I truly believe hunting tigers in tall grass with a slingshot is less stressful."

As the CIA men and the President all laughed. President Hernandez patted the bronze bust, nodded, changed the subject, and said, "It hasn't been announced, but I'm going to Iran in a week or so. Since their 'incident' and the overthrow of the ayatollahs and mullahs last year, I'm going to re-open our embassy. You may know we're helping to dismantle their nuclear program, and I'll announce all remaining sanctions to their country have been lifted."

The CIA men's eyes ricocheted between them. Their levity was replaced with concern. "Mr. President, is that such a good idea? So soon?" asked Lynche.

"The world is a much better place today than it was a year ago. The moderate Iranians were tired of being a pariah on the international front and they were ready for a change from the tyrannical rule of their ayatollahs and mullahs. We have Duncan to thank for that."

Hunter didn't want any part of this conversation. McGee interjected, "They're worried Duncan will drop another bomb on their ass." McGee grinned when he said it.

President Hernandez suggested, "Maybe that's a trifle indelicate, but maybe it's also spot on. We wouldn't be in this position...*politically*, if Captain Hunter hadn't, umm...."

Before Hunter could meekly offer a half serious reply, Lynche jumped in with, "It was crazy and completely unauthorized. We are very lucky the moderate Iranians...*removed* their radical theocrats." The DCI had only recently forgiven Duncan for his transgressions. But if the President was going to give him a medal for blowing up an Iranian reactor, who was he to think Hunter escaped jail?

"I'll be in and out of Tehran in a few hours. A chance to wave the flag. Tell the locals we are on their side. Tell the Russians to back off." The President was smiling again.

"Maybe sell them some F-16s?" asked Hunter sheepishly. He knew he still wasn't out of the woodshed with Lynche.

"We're talking about it. Like Iraq, they need commercial and military aircraft. They have problems with ISIS and al-Qaeda still. That reminds me...." The President glanced at the black splint on Hunter's arm and continued, "Duncan, did you receive a sufficient reward?"

Lynche and McGee rolled their eyes as Hunter nodded and said, "Thank you, Mr. President. It was perfect." What was perfect was an unknown Rembrandt from an unknown Russian Empire aristocrat that now hung in his office in Texas.

Hunter had found what most treasure hunters considered "the missing Nazi artwork," in a cave in Germany. The missing Nazi artwork was, in fact, the national artwork of Imperial Russia. Before the Bolsheviks removed Tsar Nicolas II from his throne, the last Emperor of Russia gathered the priceless artwork, statuary, gems, gold and silver jewelry, the wealth of the Russian aristocracy and moved the trove to the Louvre Museum in Paris, France. After Hitler invaded France, Nazi soldiers moved the Russian artwork from the Louvre to an underground complex near Kaiserslautern, Germany. One 400-year old piece of artwork recovered from the caves, *Woman near a River*, was a stunning portrait of a woman that looked remarkably like Hunter's wife, Nazy Cunningham.

Hunter changed the subject and nodded at the bust of Churchill. "Somehow, I just knew he would return to the White House when the former president left."

President Hernandez smiled and offered his hand. Hunter accepted it as the President asked, "When will you be ready...for another one?" There was gloomy seriousness in the chief executive's eyes. It was very unusual to see the President's demeanor change so quickly. There was something behind his smile. The President looked at McGee and Hunter several times as if he were searching for a hint in their eyes that they were ambivalent or unsure.

"I'm ready now, Mr. President. I've recently returned from a mission over Peru. No factor." By their expressions it seemed neither the President, Lynche, or McGee were convinced. They all looked at Hunter's hand as he was still wearing the stimulation splint. If he was wearing the splint, it was obvious he wasn't "ready for flight." Hunter found the appropriate words to explain that his capability to perform was greater than his ego "Sir, *I'm airworthy*. Fit for duty. I even have an up-chit from my flight doc! He recommended I wear this for a couple of more weeks; that it wouldn't hurt anything."

Hunter's curiosity was piqued by the President's request. It looked like the protocol to brief a potential target from the Disposition Matrix in the DCI's office at CIA headquarters was being tossed out one of the Oval Office's bulletproof windows.

The President checked his watch and said, "I think we have a couple more minutes. This next mission may change your mind. I want everyone to know what we're dealing with; this one I'm afraid is going to be tough. I know you aware I signed an executive order designating the Muslim Brotherhood as a terrorist organization. And I've issued an executive order which protects the *Noble Savage* team from investigation or prosecution. All for the purposes of national security, naturally. So with that said, I believe it is time to cut off the head of the snake." The men from the CIA were confused and looked at each other with questioning eyes.

The President engaging Duncan directly didn't thrill Director Lynche. He and the President hadn't discussed a next target. Lynche was waiting patiently for Hunter to recover from his injuries and return from his little incursion into Peru. Kelly Horne, Hunter's daughter, and Bill McGee had assumed some of the aerial eradication duties while Hunter recovered. The mission to Peru was largely a test run to see if Hunter and his surgically-reattached hand could again handle the stresses of low-level quiet flight. There must be some sense of urgency for the President to discuss such a sensitive matter with McGee and Hunter directly.

Hunter's heart pounded and his skin tingled from the excitement. He was more than ready. He said, "I'm in Mr. President." Lynche was aghast, McGee shrugged, and the President nodded with a seriousness easily conveyed. Lynche wondered, *This one's important? Who is it that Hunter hasn't killed that could be that important?*

McGee and Lynche were ignored for the moment as the two Texans exchanged serious glances, as if they were sharing data telepathically.

"There's something I want to share with this august group of patriots: the head of the snake and my predecessor."

President Hernandez had everyone's attention. Lynche remained somewhat confused by the President's inarticulate language. Protocol dictated you hold your tongue, let the POTUS speak, and then get the hell out of the office. He was a busy man. Hunter crossed his arms looking like he was enjoying the topic. He heard "my predecessor" and ignored the reference to "the head of the snake." Bill McGee wasn't sure he should be here when this political time bomb went off. Lynche was aghast. Presidents are not supposed to wander off the politically correct reservation. He was sure the intelligence the POTUS was about to spill across the room were too sensitive to discuss with mere CIA contractors.

Hunter tried to interject, politely, "Mr. President...."

But the POTUS held up his hand and continued. He would not be denied in his own office. "We've learned what my predecessor was really up to. As a candidate he used a secret back channel to Tehran to assure the mullahs that he was a friend of the Islamic Republic, and that they would be very happy with his policies. When he was in office his negotiations with the Iranians on their nuclear program, the withdrawal of U.S. forces from the northern part of Iraq, the purge of conservative generals from DOD.... It was a coordinated effort to facilitate the destruction of Israel and then the United States. Remove enough pressure from Iran so they could build a thermonuclear device. They would give their Muslim Brotherhood proxies a nuclear device to detonate in or on Tel Aviv. Then us."

Lynche looked at his shoes and said, "The head of the Muslim Brotherhood visited the White House some 200 times. The Russian ambassador visited the Oval Office half as many times. Those were not social calls."

McGee wasn't surprised and Hunter remained curious. Hunter smiled in smug satisfaction and strained not to shout, *I knew it!*

McGee, ever the professional, smiled and nodded. Lynche returned his eyes to a spot on the wall just above the Frederic Remington bronze *Broncho Buster* and struggled with his collar. He hoped the President wouldn't say anything else they would regret later. The Oval Office wasn't the right place, and tonight wasn't the right time to discuss killing another master terrorist.

President Hernandez said, "He was trying to create the perfect storm to destroy Israel. Since al-Qaeda couldn't get the suitcase devices they wanted, he fostered the conditions for Iran to develop their own bomb, which would have been given to a proxy to do the dirty work. I should say Old Iran."

McGee offered, "Duncan made the case. The key piece of the puzzle for me was that he came from that crazy church that openly hated Israel and Jews. The guy sat in those pews for years. How could democrats elect someone like that?"

Hunter finally got through. "How could anyone not get this? First Israel, then us. It was all according to the Muslim Brotherhood's plan. It was only a matter of time before the Iranian mullahs provided Muslim Brotherhood-affiliated terrorist groups with nukes." He turned to Lynche who suddenly looked like he hadn't slept in a week. Duncan then returned his eyes to the President.

President Hernandez nodded, dropped his eyes to his desk, and slipped a scrap of paper from under the blotter situated atop the most famous desk in the free world. It was made from timbers of the British ship HMS Resolute, the Resolute Desk. The men had heard of the notes former Presidents leave for their successors, and grinned half-heartedly. He unfolded the paper and handed it to Lynche who showed it to Hunter and McGee. It read, "You will pay for your treachery." The President of the United States said, "My predecessor left that for…the next President. Me."

Seriousness replaced the jovial atmosphere in the Oval Office. When the President broke eye contact with Lynche and Hunter, he swung his head toward McGee, he said, "I'm sure, Captain McGee, you're familiar with…*Broken Lance.*"

With those two words, the POTUS announced his next target without naming the next target.

Hunter, Lynche, and McGee had become familiar with the term *Broken* Lance several years earlier when Bill McGee had been targeted by a sniper. The announcement and all the ramifications that came with the two words of the unique special access program were simply stunning. The three CIA men reeled from the information and momentarily closed their eyes from the shock. They sucked all of the air out of the room. Lynche wanted to scream, *"Noooo!"* but there was no air left to breathe and screaming was not allowed in the Oval Office.

One by one, the men opened their eyes to a brave new world. Lynche was dumbfounded. The President of the United States was sanctioning the killing of a former president. It was incredible.

McGee and Hunter stared at each other until McGee nodded. Hunter reciprocated, turned to the President, and breathlessly said, "Bill and I are in with both feet, Mr. President."

McGee nodded, Lynche cringed, and the President said, "He nearly succeeded in establishing a shadow government. Under his administration he ensured that tens of thousands of Muslims were hired in government positions. Hundreds were pushed into the top jobs. What are we up to Greg; 30,000?"

Lynche nodded at his boss. "At a minimum."

"They were likely Muslim Brotherhood supporters. I authorized the CIA Director to polygraph everyone who came in contact with secret information or if they accessed their jobs through some diversity hiring program."

Lynche added, "Or if they exhibited questionable loyalties."

Hunter glanced at Lynche. Along with other CIA contractors, new hires, and civil servants at the State Department, CIA, and congressional staffers he and McGee had been subjected to a no-notice, unusually comprehensive polygraph. He didn't know there had been a breech in the government's security defenses which had been assumed to be facilitated and orchestrated by the former president. The new president had demanded a purge; if those federal employees and contractors who came into contact with sensitive information and they couldn't pass the new expansive polygraph, they were removed from their government position or government contract. Hunter now knew why. He couldn't believe Lynche had kept the rationale for the enhanced polygraphs from him. He pushed aside the thoughts and said, "You could tell from satellite photos that he wasn't on our side."

The President continued, "If there is an opportunity to cut off the head of the snake—I know he takes his orders from someone—I want it done, too. This is a good start. Any problems, Greg?'" inquired the Chief Executive as he turned to Lynche.

It was crazy. A madman could not have conceived such an idea. The DCI would have to support the mission or resign. But he couldn't do that. This was too explosive. If they failed, they would all go to jail. Or get killed. *But if the man was legally considered a legitimate terrorist and not an American citizen....*

Lynche couldn't stop the flow of conflicting information entering his head. Having the President plant the thought of assassinating a former president was like driving a spike through the middle of his skull. His head pounded as his blood pressure spiked. He feared his next overstimulated heartbeat would send a rush of blood and burst any hint of an aneurism. Lynche couldn't believe he was still standing, still conscious. He reeled from the proposed assignment, shook his head, and mewled, "After dinner, I hope?"

CHAPTER FIFTEEN

1930 July12, 2014
The White House

After the premeditated secret medal ceremony, the President, Lynche, McGee, and Hunter strolled into the East Room two by two, the President and McGee, Lynche and Hunter. They joined their spouses in front of the Gilbert Stuart portrait of George Washington. First Lady Mrs. Hernandez had just finished describing the circumstances of the painting that Dolley Madison had rescued when British troops sacked Washington and burned the White House. It was a poignant juxtaposition; the old British Empire raiding and ransacking the White House and the current evening's festivities where some members of the British Royal Family would be honored and feted. Nazy Cunningham was still new to U.S. history and did not know all the details of the War of 1812 so she soaked up every word the First Lady said.

The women giggled when, with a wink and a chuckle, Mrs. Hernandez said, "Of course we won't discuss that tonight."

The President thanked "the ladies for their indulgence" and offered his arm to the First Lady. The other men offered their arms to their wives and followed the First Couple to the State Dining Room.

The President and his wife sauntered through Cross Hall to receive the royal family. The Lynches, McGees, and the Hunters queued for the formal reception. Angela McGee, wearing a brilliant deep blue Oscar De La Renta evening gown that emphasized her hips, tiny waist, and natural coloring stepped on tippy-toes to whisper into the ear of her massive husband, "I cannot believe this. Meeting the President. Dinner at the White House." McGee winked and smiled at her.

Although he had been retired from the Navy for ten years, he was still a fit and indefatigable athlete, at least from outward appearances. Underneath the tuxedo were the marks of a man who had lived through much combat and had the scars and the heavily damaged feet to prove it.

148

For over 35 years, he had always run to the sound of gunfire while engaging the enemies of America. Like most senior SEALS, he was quiet but thoughtful and carried himself with the unmistakable poise and confidence of a former commander of the vaunted SEAL Team Six. Tiny round eyeglass lenses gave him the air of a scholar with PhDs in weapons, special operations, and assassination methods. His physique was achieved from several lifetimes in the weight room and was manifest of his athletic prowess. He was as equally comfortable in scuba gear or a parachute harness as he was in formal wear. And now it looked like he would participate in another very special mission. An evening like this could hardly get any better.

A very confused Connie Lynche, the DCI's silver-haired statuesque wife, immediately got to her point. She hissed in Greg's ear, "What are we doing here?" She had been to many formal dinners while Greg served at U.S. Embassies abroad as Chief of Station. She had the personality, sophisticated good looks, and a wicked tennis backhand to complement the tall, ruddy CIA Chief of Station at posts around the world. Although equal partners in the marriage, his third, her second, she would do as she was told to help in the execution of his duties. She could keep a secret and knew it was futile to discuss work with the senior-most intelligence officer and master spy. But when Greg had directed her to take Nazy Cunningham and Angela McGee to the hairdressers and to shop for "something appropriate for a State Dinner," she had been taken aback. *State Dinner? The White House?*

Greg Lynche hadn't immediately understood the silence and long pause at the other end of the telephone line during that conversation. His brain was always racing a thousand miles a minute. He quickly added, "And you'll need something as well." There was nothing comparable to the elegance and formality of dinner at the White House, and the husbands would surely gasp at the cost of appropriately furnishing their brides for their once-in-a-lifetime outing. But Nazy had brandished Duncan's American Express credit card at every store and salon they encountered, knowing her husband wouldn't say a thing about dresses, manicures, pedicures, and hairdos. Hunter would say, "It was a business expense." That the evening was all for him anyway; medals don't come cheap and neither do perfectly coiffed, beautiful wives.

Connie had selected a black Dior evening gown that showed off her bosom and her naturally silver-tinged red hair. A thigh-high slit flashed her tanned tennis legs as she walked. She was miffed that her husband hadn't seemed to notice that she was positively stunning for a 70-year old.

His mind had been elsewhere, left in a puddle in the Oval Office with the mention of *Broken Lance,* and he barely noticed she was on his arm until he sensed the unmistakable heat of an icy stare. He turned to her and responded by leaning into her ear, "I don't know. British royalty? Prince somebody? The Duchess of ummm, I don't know. It doesn't matter. Duncan's getting an award. We won't get introduced. We're here to have a good time. The food should be good."

The couples entered the State Dining Room and exchanged glances of disbelief, amusement, and awe at their surroundings. They were surprised how small the room actually was. Gold lace curtains adorned with heavy cords, tassels, and damask draperies framed each window. Bohemian cut-glass chandeliers hung in a row over an intricate parquet floor. Mirrors and paintings adorned the empty spaces between classical fluted pilasters on white painted paneling. Each linen-covered table was set for six, the Presidential Seal on every piece of china, crystal, and gold flatware. Swollen centerpieces of yellow roses and red carnations towered between crystal candlesticks with two-foot tall candles. Folded blue napkins, extravagant menus, and bold calligraphic announcements rested at each place setting. It was a typical set up for a State Dinner for a visiting monarch. The rent-a-crowd were all State Department and British Embassy VIPs, with the exception of the McGees, Lynches, Nazy Cunningham, and Hunter. The notecard on their table stated they were the personal guests of the President.

At her first formal Presidential evening event, Nazy was the least animated of the women but the most striking. Arched brows, lined eyes, subtle orchid lips, and a gown that accentuated her every curve, caused all heads to turn as she walked in on Duncan's arm. Her cinnamon-scented perfume followed, exotic and ambrosial. She was a wife's worst nightmare, a cultured exotic beauty who was smart, well-spoken, poised, and who exuded a sense of innocence and virtue that could completely bewitch and captivate a trophy husband. But she only had eyes for Duncan. She was a worried mess and didn't want to look as if she didn't know what she was doing. Not that anyone would have noticed. She cut a devastating and dazzling figure with her light olive skin, platinum-green eyes, and her yards of hair that was clipped up and wrapped in a tight bun. The sophisticated shimmering white silk Versace ball gown with a hip bone-high leg slit, hugged her curves to perfection and was set off by a bodice which barely contained each large, taut breast. Starburst diamond earrings and a scintillating, thick diamond choker coruscated in syncopation with the spotlights and her steps. It was the only distraction to her ample billowy cleavage which seemed to have its own gravitational pull on the eyes and heads of those in the room.

Duncan had never seen Nazy's hair up like Audrey Hepburn's character in *Breakfast at Tiffany's*. She was dazzling. His bride was more than merely striking; she electrified the room. He grappled to find the right adjectives and superlatives; he gave up and asked playfully, "I'm not going to ask how you got all your hair up there. Am I going to be shocked at what all this cost?"

His comment was answered when Nazy seductively stuck a nude leg through the slit of her dress. Hunter's eyes followed the movement of the taught line of flesh below her bosom. Trying to maintain his composure he swallowed hard and grinned; his brown eyes locked with her platinum green ones. He pulled her close and said, "Yep, definitely worth every penny." Then they stepped off together as if the movement was choreographed. She was momentarily abashed at flaunting her nude leg and coquettishly hung her head low, but her response was more a function of her conservative Muslim upbringing than shame. She got over it within her next heartbeat and mildly upbraided herself. *I'm not even wearing underwear; God I can be so backward on such an exciting evening.* Her eyes scanned her friends with their husbands, and she hoped no one could read her mind.

All of the other women used their right hand to take their husband's offered left arm; so did Nazy, reluctantly. She wanted to be on the other side of Duncan but took her cues from the women ahead. She was reluctant to hold onto his damaged arm with any pressure; her grip was hesitant and uneasy.

He was still in an electronic stimulation splint while recovering from a series of surgeries to reattach his hand. The injury had been considered an "occupational mishap" in the service of the CIA. Lynche's predecessor, Dr. Bruce Rothwell, the previous Director of Central Intelligence, had cut it off with a sword. Hunter had regained the movement in his fingers and thumb, and he worked to improve what little grip he had. He had come such a long way, and she was worried that if she tripped on her evening gown or broke a heel, she would pull on the fragile arm and irreparably damage the delicate connection of titanium plates and screws that held together the once severed radius and ulna. She also worried about straining the tiny sutures which held together the repaired tendons in his hand.

Nazy hadn't asked why the President spirited the men away after arriving. She knew of the awards—she and Lynche had crafted the language for the certificates—but she sought confirmation that there had been no discussion of extracurricular work. Previous visits to the Oval Office had sometimes resulted in another dangerous mission, usually to Africa. Worried that Duncan had already done too much, too soon with the repaired hand in Peru, she leaned hard against him. Kohl-rimmed eyes and a splash of make-up could not disguise her concern and sorrow. Proud to have his ravishing wife on his arm at such an event, Hunter was unaware of her anxiety. She tugged gently at his elbow to slow him down. Pain and fear oozed through her words as she whispered, "Does he want you for another...?" She couldn't say "event." It wasn't the time or place to ask such a question. But her eyes pleaded with him for an answer. The right answer. He stopped and she followed.

Killing charismatic terrorists was a nasty and dangerous business. He had the only adequate and precision tool to conduct such an exclusive objective. After fifteen years of safely executing clandestine surveillance and eradication missions, his two previous assignments had nearly killed him.

Her words distracted him. He followed the vector of the icy strap of diamonds around her neck as his oculars got lost in the game of bouncing around in the décolletage of her gown. When he turned his head toward her, his eyes confirmed her worst fears and told her everything that she needed to know.

She pinched her lips tight, then reached up, and gently kissed him on the lips. Hunter loved kissing those lips but realized that making out in the White House was probably frowned upon, even though they were newlyweds and spontaneous indecorous displays of affection might be forgiven. But being with Nazy at that moment took his breath away; he was sweaty, almost panting, in anticipation of abandoned passion. He took her hand with his good one and brought it to his chest; he nuzzled her ear and whispered in his best sexy husky voice, "Baby, you're the most beautiful woman in the room and I cannot keep my eyes off you. That is a stunning dress. What I really want to do is to blow this popsicle stand, take you back to the hotel, and kiss every square centimeter of your body." The words instantly made her smile and forget about work. She crushed a rippling tanned breast into his chest. He inhaled her perfume, his lips just millimeters from her ear. "Let's not talk about work. Okay?"

The words from her husband melted her heart. She nodded, a bit embarrassed of her insecurities and being unnaturally indiscretious. She composed herself and whispered, "I love you, Baby."

He extracted his face from her hair as her smile lit up the room. After being formally introduced to the President, his wife, and some British prince and princess, Hunter escorted Nazy to her seat. As he helped Nazy slide her chair up to the table, he leaned over, stole a peek down her dress, and said into her ear, "We'll probably never get invited back, so let's have some fun and enjoy this night."

As Hunter took his seat, he met the eyes of Lynche and McGee. He had the greatest friends a man could possibly ask for and a wife that was his smoking-hot soulmate. He'd just been awarded one of the highest awards the CIA could present to its employees. His businesses were booming. The President would award him another medal for his work hiring disabled war veterans to work in his garages and aircraft manufacturing facilities in Texas. He was going to take his smoking hot wife to bed after the White House soirée and not leave until the sun came up. He knew he was the luckiest man alive.

Greg Lynche watched the two lovers; the couple could not turn off the heat even while visiting the White House. He thought the medals and the night would be a way to start weaning Hunter off the black programs. *He's just relentless, slightly unhinged, and bordered on the hysterical a lot of the time. In other words, Hunter's the perfect guy for this stuff. It would be a crime to remove him from the special access programs. He wants to succeed badly. He doesn't give a damn about the stardom. You won't find him on Twitter, Facebook or Instagram. If it hadn't been for the presidential medal and this awards ceremony, we'd never catch him on a red carpet even if he was the guest of honor. Check that—especially if he is the guest of honor. While he loves the game and ignores the rest of it, I'm afraid his time is up.*

He and President Hernandez had looked at the dwindling number of potential targets on the Disposition Matrix. With the exception of one unknown, un-named terrorist at the top of the list, the known leaders of the Islamic State of Iraq and Syria were the only remaining targets. The ISIS leaders were very difficult to find and target. They had learned from the mistakes of Saddam Hussein and Osama bin Laden to be aware of America's airborne systems of eyes and ears, and to be on the move always. American *Predator* unmanned aircraft armed with Hellfire missiles would strike when they least expected it or if they let their guard down. With virtually no reasonable targets for the CIA to pin down for Hunter to find and eliminate, the special access program had run its course.

Every day that passed the unmanned technologies were progressing to the point where Hunter's quiet airplane could be replaced, theoretically. It could already land and takeoff without a pilot. The new automatic takeoff and landing (ATLS) software had already turned Hunter's YO-3As into an optionally-manned platform, when it was working properly. A full-mission unmanned version had been tested but the targeting algorithms were complex. Hunter's daughter could continue to fly the *Weedbusters* aerial eradication missions until the unmanned systems came on line. The surveillance missions could be moved onto the ATLS-equipped YO-3A but not the armed aircraft. Kelly Horne would never be tasked to conduct aerial assassinations. That meant if the CIA had a requirement, Hunter could do a few more of the manned kinetic missions.

Hunter's *Noble Savage* mission in Algeria had almost killed him. With the President possibly in office for only one more year, Hunter's next assassination mission could be his last. Lynche rattled the President's words around in his head and shook his own. Then other ugly thoughts crept in, *It will martyr him! We cannot allow that to happen.* For now, martyrdom and politics were the least of his worries.

There was still the growing concern that Duncan's and Nazy's covers had been blown by the former DCI, a jealous and vindictive man. At the thought of his predecessor, Lynche looked across the table at Bill McGee.

It did not bother him that the killer of the traitorous Dr. Rothwell and other enemies of the United States was sitting a few feet away, engaging his bride in tennis talk and replacement knees. Another look and grin at Hunter brought him back to the realities he would face when he returned to CIA headquarters in the morning. He didn't want to believe the President was serious, but he knew he was. The new mission would likely kill them all before it was over. It was best to think of something less lethal than "cutting off the head of the snake."

Why had the President used that specific term separate from the context of the former President? Were there two targets to consider? He'd have to get clarification when he and the President were alone.

The spike in aviation terrorism was a topic Lynche just could not adequately address. He didn't have the background, experience, or education to fully grasp the enormity of the situation. But Duncan did. Hunter painted a grim picture, that now anyone with a few hundred dollars could be a *jihadi* and cause untold mayhem on commercial and even military aircraft. Homegrown *jihadis* could blind commercial pilots with laser pens or send quadrotors, small, unmanned aerial vehicles—*drones* in the civilian vernacular—into the huge engine intakes of jets taking off at airports across the country and around the globe. Hunter warned Lynche about them; there was little defense for the small drones in the wrong hands. Companies like Amazon, Wal-Mart, and others wanted to offer same-day delivery services, using a multi-rotor unmanned aircraft to deliver small items like a book, a music CD, or a stick of deodorant to a residence in an hour. Such a service had great appeal for merchants. But for Hunter, the little aircraft were the latest innocuous toys for terrorists to exploit. He saw the potential of death and destruction where many others could not or would not.

On September 11, 2001, it was Duncan Hunter who clued the FBI to check out the x-ray screeners, the men and women sitting behind the x-ray machines at the security checkpoints in some of the major airports. The FBI's investigation found there was indeed, a widespread conspiracy to interject Islamic sympathizers into the airport security function. The top secret volume of the 9-11 Commission Report highlighted the scope of the infiltration at the nation's major airports and recommended the removal of the easy-to-penetrate contracted screening process which culminated with the federalization of the nation's airport security. It was a highly confidential matter that the radical Islamists could still find creative ways to get weapons and bombs onto an aircraft. Infiltrating America's airport security was one of their greatest achievements. The nightmare scenario of *jihadis* leaving their sleeper-cell mosques to attack aircraft operations and the aviation industry was approaching faster than anyone could have imagined, with the exception of Professor Duncan Hunter. He predicted that the day was soon approaching when commercial aircraft fell from the skies without a trace of evidence as to what caused the crash, such as the missing Indonesian Sky Link aircraft. Hunter had called it. Again.

Lynche shook his head at the thought. His wife looked at him suspiciously, as if he were dreaming about a place far away. It was in times like this that he was easily distracted. Connie nudged him and the pressure brought him back to the present. He winked at her as if to say *Sorry!*

Duncan, the man of the hour, waved his hands politely to quiet the table. He spoke briefly and softly, thanking everyone at the table for their love and support, and Nazy for making him a better man. As he raised a glass to toast his tablemates, he caught the eye of a man staring at him from across the State Dining Room. The man immediately broke eye contact; Hunter completed his toast, and the other man returned his gaze to his tablemates. Hunter would not look across the room again; he was completely involved with his friends and his wife. The man across the room struggled to keep his eyes off the man and his ravishing pluperfect woman in white silk. So did many others in the room. Even the President and the prince occasionally sneaked a peek at the remarkable Nazy Cunningham.

At the head table, the President and his family chatted amicably and politely with the British royalty. Talk of cowboy boots, busts of Churchill, and knights in shining armor skipped along the linen covered table; laughter and smiles abounded. Wine was poured and dinner was served. Speeches were to follow dinner, along with award presentations to innovators and entrepreneurs, and some companies that worked very closely with the intelligence communities of America and Great Britain.

Hunter took a moment to scan the room for anyone interesting. Finding no one more interesting than his wife and friends, he returned his full attention to them.

Chapter Sixteen

1900 July 12, 2014
Washington D.C.

On the 14th floor of the National Press Club building, most of the members of the White House press corps were fuming, cussing, and slamming down beers and gin and tonics at a long conference table stuck along the wall in a far corner. The oxymoronically-named Reliable Source Bar and Grill was the rallying point for the disaffected media royalty who had gotten their panties in a wad when the news came across the wire. The press corps were no longer invited or allowed at the White House for the evening at what looked to be a simple state dinner for members of the British Royal Family. A dozen elite Washington bureau reporters, journalists, and network correspondents were working up the beginnings of a good hangover after having been disinvited at the last moment, ostensibly on orders from the President himself. Tuxedos and ball gowns were stuffed back into closets to await the next White House gala. The topic of conversation: Why didn't the President want the press there? All they were told was the White House spokeswoman would provide an official statement in the morning along with an official guest list. What was the likelihood the guest list would be full and accurate?

As men and women of the White House press corps bitched about being excluded from the state dinner, Demetrius Eastwood thrummed his fingers on the table, indifferent to the carping on either side of him. When he had been informed of the change in dinner plans, he had gone straight to the top floor of his Washington bureau's office and staked out the entrance to the White House's North Portico. He hadn't been behind the telephoto lens very long before he spotted Duncan Hunter, Bill McGee, and Nazy Cunningham, all dressed to the nines, step from a government limousine with two other women in gowns in tow. Then, much to his surprise, the Director of Central Intelligence stepped from the vehicle. Now he had a better idea why the press had been barred from the state dinner shindig, but he couldn't begin to conceive of a reason why the nation's top intelligence official, the Director of the National Counter Terrorism Center, and a couple of CIA contractors were attending a state dinner. As the men and women disappeared from view, Eastwood was certain that no one in the State Dining Room would ever be able to forget Nazy Cunningham in that titillating white ball gown.

Eastwood dawdled his way out of the network office. He walked to the National Press Club mumbling to himself. He thought he might have heard something from the hyperactive Duncan Hunter, but *Maverick* hadn't responded to his email asking if he knew Duncan Hunters were being killed. He double-checked again just to make sure. Eastwood determined Hunter was likely too busy to take time to read his ubiquitous BlackBerry. Sometimes Hunter would reply in a few seconds or at most a few hours, if there were a stated sense of urgency. *Maybe he thought I was joking*, thought Eastwood. He stopped suddenly; then it hit him as if he had walked into the side of a lamp pole while fingering his smart phone. *Maybe the email was intercepted and spiked by the Indonesian government. Hell, I was persona non grata after the plane crash!* He remembered governments, especially foreign governments, were in full control of their nations' internet; they controlled what came in and what went out of their countries.

He and his team had been arbitrarily fined, and then unceremoniously evicted from the country. It would have been nothing for Indonesia to find, track, and intercept his and his teams' smart phone calls and email, and then kill them before they could leave their country. The technology to intercept, screen, assess, and determine intent or substance of email traffic had long been a staple capability of the local intelligence community and secret police. Islamic nations were notorious for monitoring cell phone and email traffic, especially those from the international smart phones of journalists and diplomats. Hunter would have replied had he received an email like that. It had been ten days; Eastwood castigated himself for not thinking it through and for not following up. He should have just asked Captain McGee when he returned Stateside. McGee was much more reliable answering email than Hunter.

He started walking again, oblivious to any potential danger. The National Press Club just wasn't that far and Eastwood doubted the

Islamists who had targeted him a year ago were still on the job responding to a *fatwa*. In New York City maybe, but no one would be trying to hunt him down and kill him in Washington, DC. He hoped.

Eastwood knew of Greg Lynche. Was it odd the Director of Central Intelligence was with his Texas friends? He knew Nazy and Hunter were both Agency-types. McGee was the oddity. He would love to find out, but knowing that Hunter, McGee, and Nazy were likely going to the State Dining Room was not only newsworthy—whatever it meant—it was also likely related to their work. He could not report on them. He would not report on them. Not tonight. Not ever.

It was obvious Hunter was well; the last time he had seen him, Hunter was recovering from a significant hand wound. Even through the telephoto lens Nazy Cunningham was still as breathtaking as he remembered. Two years earlier, Eastwood had helped Bill McGee rescue Nazy from a group of Muslim savages. This was the first time he had seen her since McGee had worked furiously to reattach her breast after some troglodytes tried to dissect and dismember her. Apparently, she too had fully recovered from the trauma of Algeria. And she must have had her lengthy tresses cut for there was no possible way all her hair was balled up and pinned so simply. There was little doubt in his mind she would be the most devastatingly beautiful woman in the room.

When he entered the Reliable Source Bar and Grill, he turned toward his fellow rejected journalists and scanned the crowd to see whom else he knew. Several correspondents called him, "Colonel." He waved with a saluting gesture; a touch of his fingertips to his brow. A longneck beer was pressed into his hands. All thoughts of the White House were replaced with jumping into the conversations surrounding *The Reporter's Telegraph*. News is news. Work is work.

● ● ● ● ●

Across the State Dining Room, opposite the men and women from the CIA, a table of men talked quietly among themselves. They were an eclectic and a diverse group of scientists and engineers from Chimera Avro-Software Technologies, a small company in Santa Clara, California. They specialized in developing special-purpose, heavily-encrypted software for unmanned aircraft, primarily for automatic takeoff and landing systems, but also for integrated anti-hijacking systems for commercial aircraft. Chimera Avro was notorious for its secrecy, and for good reason. Its encrypted software allowed their aviation customers, the manufacturers of commercial airliners, to guarantee to the operators—the airlines—that their aircraft could never be hijacked "electronically" by a rogue programmer or a "hacker." The proprietary software was specifically designed and encrypted to prevent those experts, in hacking or "cracking" from operating anonymously in the computer underground seeking to exploit weaknesses in an airliner's computer system.

The awards program also suggested the company's research and development of their proprietary "hack-proof" software for unmanned aerial vehicles. But the evening's festivities did not mention that Chimera was a highly secretive developer of specialized aviation software for the CIA. In-Q-Tel, the CIA's commercial venture arm, was an early investor in the company. The company and its chief software designer would receive medals tonight for developing the encrypted software that prevented the hijacking of an Airbus and a Boeing aircraft after Islamic extremists entered the cockpit and killed the crew. Artificial intelligence determined the cockpits were under assault. Sensors and microphones in the cockpit picked up the sounds of death, the lack of the crew's heartbeats though the pressure sensors in their seats triggered the anti-hijacking software. The proprietary software determined the crew had been incapacitated, and it removed all further inputs from the cockpit, turned the aircraft to the nearest airport and landed them safely. In was the best possible scenario. Hijackers had been thwarted from taking control of the aircraft and many of the passengers were saved along with the aircraft.

While there was much to be joyful about tonight, the missing Indonesian airliner was not far from the thoughts of most of the people sitting around the table. They were confident that if their computer software had been activated in the Boeing aircraft, Sky Link Flight 7070 would not have gone missing but would have landed safely, somewhere. Like the others.

One of the scientists at the Chimera Avro-Software Technologies table continually referred to a brochure listing the events and the names of the awardees to be recognized by the President of the United States. He had been shocked to see the name, Duncan Hunter, on the guest list;

the man's short biography consumed his thoughts. He searched the room to see if he could find Hunter among the twenty or so tables. A week ago, Duncan Hunter had simply been a disembodied name on the backside of a business card, like the name of a species of roach to be stepped on without further thought.

Dr. Tamerlan al-Sarkari was visibly stunned when the man named Hunter took the podium to receive his award. With a gold medal for developing the anti-hijacking software that stopped two in-flight hijacking attempts suspended from his own neck, al-Sarkari watched the President present Hunter with a medal. His eyes followed Hunter off the dais to a raucous reception when he rejoined his friends at their table. Al-Sarkari didn't recognize anyone at Hunter's table. But he evaluated the people sitting around that table, an older couple, and African-American couple, the *Muslima* in white silk had to be Hunter's wife. She was a strikingly good-looking woman, but the way she carried on and hung on the man's shoulder, she was likely a *takfiri*, an apostate. A devout Islamic woman would not dress so provocatively or conduct herself so brazenly. The thought of inflicting pain and harm to the woman who left Islam for an infidel brought a thin smile to his face. A little taboo. He grew more infatuated with her, knowing he was going to kill her infidel husband. Al-Sarkari would like nothing more than to inflict even more pain on her. And he knew just the way to do that, too.

As he did every morning, that morning he had checked the classified national passenger database to verify a Duncan Hunter was still scheduled to fly to Sydney, Australia. He had found it curious that the man's name wasn't found on the domestic traveler's list. He had looked not once, but twice. He always checked. *How odd.... How did he get here? By train?* His eyes flitted back to the woman with her face in profile. He thought, *"In about a week, she'll be mourning the loss of that bastard infidel. Insha'allah."* God Willing.

· · · · ·

The CIA Director's armored limousine and security escort pulled up to the entrance of the JW Marriott in downtown Washington, D.C. Connie and Greg Lynche said goodnight to the McGees and the Hunters and thanked them for a wonderful and memorable evening. As the black vehicles drove away, Bill and Angela McGee, and Duncan and Nazy awkwardly waved goodbye before strolling inside the hotel. Not one of them was even tipsy. Doormen opened the doors for the couples. Everyone inside the hotel's first floor surreptitiously turned to watch the stunning brunette in white. Salacious thoughts rose as her heels clicked on the marble floors as the group made their way to the elevators.

Bill and Angela McGee were raucously welcomed by their two teenage daughters when they entered their hotel suite. Once inside their bedroom, in an impromptu-choreographed move, McGee quickly unzipped his wife's gown before racing to get out of his "monkey suit." Inside two minutes, the McGee siblings were spread out on the floor near their parents who were now comfortable in sweat pants and long-sleeve T-shirts, curled up on a sofa to watch a pay-per-view movie. The smell of microwave popcorn filled the room.

As their room door closed behind them, Hunter unzipped Nazy's gown and let it fall to the floor. She stood there for a few seconds in nothing but black heels. She coquettishly turned her back, unpinned the compressed ball of hair and gently shook her head. Her hair cascaded down her back and covered her sensual backside. She looked over her shoulder and gave him one of those looks that turned his knees to jelly and gave him an erection like a Saturn V rocket launching from Cape Canaveral. She stood still, letting him admire the view. He kicked off his shoes and socks and spun her around. He nearly stepped on her toes. She ripped the buttons from his shirt and unbuckled his belt. As Duncan ripped the Velcro from the splint on his arm and dropped it to the floor, Nazy removed her diamond choker necklace. As her hands went behind her head to undo the complicated clasp, her pendulous breasts were thrust into the air as if she were in a photo-shoot for a men's magazine. Her nipples brushed his chest, discharging a spark of static electricity.

Nazy never had the chance to remove her shoes as Hunter folded her in his arms, then took her by the hand and led her to bed.

•　•　•　•　•

He awoke with an erection but didn't want to get out of bed. He played with himself for a while. He had no place to go to and didn't expect any visitors. He didn't want to know what time it was. Living underground for extended periods would do that to anyone.

Maxim Mohammad Mazibuike shuffled to the opulent bathroom, pissed, and used the bidet. Instead of accessing the gymnasium and workout room, he turned on the shower. Hot steamy water and scented soap softened his beard as he shaved, first his face and then his pubic area. Scraping off the stubble below his belly button, the familiar slickness aroused him again. In the middle of the long soapy shower, he slowly masturbated to thoughts of his lover. Then he bounced between sauna and the steam room, finishing with a cold shower to close his pores and cool him off.

He dressed in casual black slacks, a cashmere white turtleneck, and a black Nehru jacket. The ensemble gave him the look of a 1960 New Delhi politician at a press conference.

He took his breakfast in the computer room. Televisions piped in news from around the planet. Al-Jazeera, Moscow 24, and CNN were his favorites. He used to be able to control the media, the narrative, the content, but now he could only control the channels. The situation was depressing. He had traded his freedom and liberty for a measure of safety. So far, the safety aspect was working, and he was appreciative, but he yearned for more freedom, a little temporary liberty. The televisions were a blur, he was focused on something else, far away.

From the moment he arose, the thoughts running through his head had centered on another break from the safety protocols that kept him out of the public eye.

Take the elevator to the hotel. I did it the last time. I can do it again.

Thoughts of "the last time" made him smile. He stiffened in his trousers. Maybe he could see him again. Maybe he could get away. *Maybe he needs me as much as I need him?*

Mazibuike swung around to face the computer monitor. He logged on to the world's largest on-line auctions and typed in the title of the book, *Witness*, with the bizarre starting bid price of $10,000. He had a query from a buyer.

It was from *him!* He would reserve his jubilation until he received a response.

He typed, "Can you pick up in ten days? Same place?" It was code of course, but the National Security Agency didn't have the capacity or bandwidth to track or decode an occasional on-line auction request from the billions of on-line auctions. The subtle counter-surveillance measure was the perfect foil to use as an innocuous means of communicating over an unsecure line with someone anywhere in the world. He wouldn't wait for an answer. Mazibuike knew what the answer would be; he just needed a window. A timetable.

And the best part, no one would even suspect or follow him.

CHAPTER SEVENTEEN

0700 July 15, 2014
Santa Clara, California

The newspaper headlines jumped off the folded page, the heavy font stressed its importance and eye appeal: *Secret Cell of Muslim Women Encouraging Others to Join Islamic State Exposed* and *Saudi Engineer Charged with Espionage.* Tamerlan al-Sarkari could not finish his breakfast; his stomach suddenly churned with bile, and his hands shook. The articles hit too close to home. A Muslim engineer charged with espionage was most disturbing. He swiped his mouth with a napkin as he read the case involving a Saudi Arabia-born engineer with a top-secret clearance and his attempt to steal classified plans for the Air Force's newest unmanned aircraft. Search warrants and court documents indicated the case against a 35-year-old naturalized citizen, Ahmed Mostafa al-Hamdani, of Victorville, California was one of the most serious cases of espionage against the United States. The Saudi engineer had admitted he was guilty of attempted espionage and would face a sentencing judge later in the year.

Al-Sarkari closed his eyes after reading, "Prosecutors recommended a sentence of at least 20 years." He thought he would throw up. He tried to control his breathing to calm himself. He began to visualize his name in place of the accused. After three minutes of staring blithely across his patio, unfocused and unhearing, he returned to the article.

"Al-Hamdani had thought he was selling plans and schematics for the state-of-the-art unmanned quiet aircraft to an Egyptian spy. Following a lengthy covert investigation conducted by the FBI, he was arrested. Al-Hamdani had told an FBI agent that he had pursued an engineering job at Northrop Grumman specifically to steal the aircraft's plans and schematics. The Saudi engineer was born in Riyadh, married a U.S. citizen in 2001, and became a U.S. citizen in 2005. The incident marked the tenth espionage case of the year involving insider threats to America's national security by targeting air and sea-based platforms under development."

He reread *Secret Cell of Muslim Women Encouraging Others*. Al-Sarkari hadn't anticipated or fully understood American law enforcement's responses to espionage and terrorism. At the very beginning of his journey he hadn't thought that what he was doing was espionage and murder. He hadn't viewed himself as a terrorist, in a cell; a sleeper cell. And while he never thought he would be caught or stopped, the articles gave him pause, if only for a few moments. He was now convinced of the sense of urgency to return the caliphate to its rightful place in the world; that was the goal. If the former president wished to eliminate an insignificant pilot, it would be his pleasure. Embracing Islam means surrender, submit, comply. That's how he would look at it; it wasn't murder but the elimination of a pest, an infidel. He looked at his plate. *A few eggs have to be broken in order to make an omelet.* He reminded himself that a mere handful of Bolsheviks brought down the haughty Romanovs to create the Soviet Union, and a handful of Nazis overthrew Bismarck to create the Third Reich. He nodded at the thought of a few Muslims bringing down the United States, the west, and helping establish the caliphate across the world. Killing the pilot would be as easy and as insignificant as stepping on a dung beetle.

He got up from the table to head to his office. It wasn't only the jetlag after the international conference in Dubai that made it difficult for him to return to his daily routine. He had tried to focus on his mission but was thwarted by his boss, the company chief executive officer. Al-Sarkari hadn't wanted to go to Washington D.C. for fear of missing the window of opportunity to kill the infidel. But after checking the international passenger reservation database and determining Duncan Hunter was still on schedule for a later departure to Australia, he had ultimately relented.

Al-Sarkari knew and his CEO acknowledged that he was the reason for the company's recent string of billion-dollar successes. Receiving an award at a prestigious event at the White House would only enhance the reputation, prestige, and value of the company—as well as the size of his bonus. At the White House, he had seen the man he was to destroy in his special way. It was an incredible bit of luck! *Praise Allah!* Ultimately it was a good thing to see the infidel up close. And his woman. He couldn't comprehend chopping off the head of a man for crimes against Islam. But he could send him to his death *remotely*, encapsulated in the pressure tube of a commercial jet, trapped like a rat and unable to get out. With a simple command from his laptop. The thought of Hunter dying in his sleep wasn't sufficient; but the thought of him banging on the cockpit door made him laugh aloud. *Cockpit doors are now impenetrable. You are so toast!* The thought made him grin like an idiot on a psychiatry ward. It would have been perfectly fine for Al-Sarkari to kill all of the unbelievers for Allah. Too bad Al-Jazeera wouldn't have a camera on board the aircraft to transmit to its subscribers how an Islamic genius could eliminate boorish infidels and their majestic airplanes.

What was the term being used to describe lone wolf super terrorists? Super-empowered individuals. Al-Sarkari rifled through his copy of *An Explanatory Memorandum* pausing at the heading, Understanding the Role of the Muslim Brother in North America. He read for the tenth time: *America is a kind of grand jihad in eliminating and destroying the Western civilization from within and "sabotaging" its miserable house by their hands and the hands of the believers so that it is eliminated and God's religion is made victorious over all other religions. It is a Muslim's destiny to perform Jihad and work wherever he is and wherever he lands until the final hour comes, and there is no escape from that destiny except for those who chose to slack.*

He was no slacker. He smiled at his success. He was now a secret agent for the caliphate. He had found a way to avoid the FBI by traveling to the UAE. But it was much too soon to gloat; he still had to maintain some semblance of cover until he severed all ties and turned his back on America.

His parents named him Tamerlan at his birth on February 18, 1975, on the date of the death of Tamerlane, the "Sword of Islam." "Timur the Lame" defeated the Mamelukes of Egypt and Syria, subjugated the emerging Ottoman Empire, and before his death, worked to restore the Mongol Empire of Genghis Khan. There was another reason to name their baby after the most powerful ruler in the Muslim world. Tamerlan al-Sarkari was born with a shortened leg and a clubfoot; Tamerlane the Great walked with a significant limp. His father insisted it was not a coincidence but a sign. They had to give the baby a strong name to offset his congenital weakness.

During a growth spurt at the age of eight, Tamerlan's leg abnormalities worsened caused by a critically insufficient blood supply in the deformed extremity. Gangrene invaded his bad leg and foot. Tamerlan's parents were faced with another tragic situation. Doctors had to amputate the decaying leg below the knee, or their son would die. Weeks after the surgery, he was fitted with a prosthesis that allowed him to walk with only a faltering step. He would never be able to run; he learned he would have to stand and fight in school. And with a name like Tamerlan, he was bullied.

Growing into a Muslim hero's name was more challenging than his parents had imagined. They had their careers to worry about, so they didn't spend much time or effort encouraging him. While Tamerlan's deformity created ridicule among his peers, it also scared off women. To hide from their eyes and torment, he turned to the Spartan and disciplined world of computer science. He could hide his leg under a computer table. Always.

All through graduate school, he had been a non-practicing Muslim, like his parents. On September 11, 2001, he was shocked by the attacks on the World Trade Center and the Pentagon. His feelings about the news that Muslims had perpetrated the attacks weren't totally patriotic but not unpatriotic either. He was confused by the dynamics of the attacks and of America's response. The President was quick to point out that Islam was a religion of peace. People that knew him, knew that he had a famous Muslim name and was likely a Muslim. But they also knew he was the farthest thing from being a radical, an Islamist; he wasn't even a "practicing" Muslim. Some tried to seek answers to the apparent dichotomy. They would ask, "What kind of religion could inspire people do that? Muslims killed people on those airplanes and then killed thousands more by flying those jets into those buildings. When they're screaming, '*Allahu Akbar*,' that's not the work of a religion of peace. That's evil in action." Al-Sarkari could only agree, but at the same time, he felt conflicted for some unknown reason.

After the 9/11 attacks, several people around al-Sarkari openly mocked Muslims and cursed Islam. At first, he dismissed the surreptitious digs at his assumed religion. However, he wasn't going to mosque or praying five times a day. Americans could be so stupid, so judgmental. He wasn't involved in Islam, and he was embarrassed to admit he didn't know anything about the Qur'an. He knew nothing of the master terrorist Osama bin Laden and knew little of the man for whom he was named.

His parents had left Egypt in the 1960s. They had turned their backs on the clamoring religious busybodies of the Muslim Brotherhood who demanded that she wear more modest Islamic clothing and that his father reject the Western styles of dress—no suits; *thobes.* They immigrated to America, finished their doctoral studies, and became American citizens.

Al-Sarkari grew up on McDonalds hamburgers, drive-in theaters, and was encouraged to become an engineer or a scientist like his parents. He learned about other religions but never took time to read the Qur'an or understand Islam. He was afraid of women, especially American women who were brash, forward, loose, and even intimidating, he only understood computers and software. If he articulated any interest at all, it was in docile, compliant women, the opposite of his workaholic and driven mother. No Oedipus complex for him. Once he became rich, he preferred the company of prostitutes who would do what he demanded and leave. He was interested in female genitalia and fellatio, but rarely intercourse, for that meant getting naked and exposing his stump of a leg.

While he was still in college, al-Sarkari was recruited by the biggest and most prestigious information technology companies, but he took an offer from a small firm in California. Once hired, al-Sarkari's professional life took off with one invention after another, one patent after another. One wall of his office was covered with the bronze plaques from his thirty-plus patents. Working with the sensitive government programs, he received Top Secret security clearance with Sensitive Compartmented Information access. He created what was called in scientific terms, "double embedded software." Within the company, it was known as "double-helix programming." Secret coding twisted around lines of hidden code embedded within the regular operating lines of code. And then it was subjected to the proprietary encryption technology he had developed. Like three-dimensional chess with different levels of chessboards, his invention was described as three-dimensional programming, with three levels of code and three discrete encryption strategies. Totally reliable, completely unbreakable, and with an appropriate triggering command, it could not be hacked into or overridden.

The new encrypted software was the perfect and only reliable solution for countering hijacking and hacking situations in unmanned aircraft. The U.S. government didn't want the Russians or the Chinese to hack the computers on armed Predators and have them suddenly attack the men who had just launched them. Software engineering made al-Sarkari a millionaire virtually overnight.

As a logical extension of his triple-embedded software, he proposed a way to protect commercial airliners from hostile agents gaining unauthorized access to the flight computers aboard an airliner. The specialized software would prevent the aircraft's computer operating systems from being hacked by a hostile organization or country, such as China. He proposed to the Boeing Aircraft Company that he could modify the encrypted anti-hacking software developed for and used on unmanned aircraft, and expand its capabilities to prevent their newly manufactured aircraft from ever being hijacked. Boeing's executives quickly saw the value of developing the software package and awarded an initial eight-digit contract to Chimera Avro.

After five years of work, led by al-Sarkari, the programming was complete. A dozen certification flights proved the software was an excellent and foolproof tool against an inflight hijacking or an external hacking, and that the aircraft operator or airline could even control the aircraft remotely once the embedded software was activated. Boeing installed the Chimera Avro software and a small artificial intelligence interface box in every new aircraft that rolled out of Everett's assembly plant, but they didn't activate the program. Airlines would have to pay extra for the anti-hacking and anti-hijacking capability. Someone had to pay for all that security.

When a member of the Chimera Avro anti-hijacking software development team jokingly admitted to the Boeing implementation team, "The only person that could now hack into a Boeing aircraft was Tammy," Boeing demanded the company install a safeguard to interrupt the program. Al-Sarkari immediately demonstrated that he had included the safeguard; five cycles of the avionics master switch would disable the software and return the aircraft to its original operational settings. Every aircraft was built with an avionics master switch, and pilots could regain control of the aircraft if the emergency passed. He recommended only the captain of the aircraft be given the secret override command. Boeing engineers were ecstatic, and the Chimera Avro-Software Technologies board of directors awarded al-Sarkari a percentage of the company.

Al-Sarkari's interest in Islam spiked after the horrific scenes of the Boston Marathon bombing. He couldn't run or jog but always admired those that could, and he would cheer for the disabled contestants as they crossed the finish line on crutches or tiny racing tricycles. Three days after the bombing the FBI named their prime suspects. Tamerlan Al-Sarkari nearly fainted when it was announced one of the bombers shared his name. He expected the FBI would be banging on his door any minute.

When the FBI didn't knock down the door to his house, he cracked open the green leather-and-gold embossed cover of the *Qur'an*. The Arabic calligraphy on the cover had always intrigued him and the intricately woven lines of Arabic reminded him of his double-helix programming, how the lines of code were woven through and around the base line of code. When he came to the first chapter with its seven-line message about seeking guidance from a merciful creator, he looked up and wondered how anyone could find fault with that. Al-Sarkari's mind was like software running in the background. He put the book away and returned to his programming.

He couldn't push all of his thoughts out of the way. As his interest in his namesake and Islam grew, so did his curiosity about the terrorist groups al-Qaeda and the Muslim Brotherhood. He hadn't heard of them before September 11, 2001. Al-Qaeda had achieved what had been considered impossible; they had somehow smuggled weapons through airport security, hijacked four Boeing aircraft, and turned three of them into flying bombs. Newspaper and television reporters indicated passengers overpowered the hijackers of the other airplane.

This episode in aviation history was noteworthy, and he read as much as he could on the dynamics of hijacking an aircraft. He came up with one startling fact: when given the opportunity, pilots and hijackers and even passengers would fight for control of an aircraft. When he began to storyboard his software's mission and goal, he subscribed to Occam's Razor; the simplest solution is usually the best. He would remove all external inputs to the airplane's controls. All controls, mechanical and electronic. The challenge was Herculean.

Using artificial intelligence and a few simple algorithms, al-Sarkari wrote parallel programs. One system would remove all electrical control of the aircraft, rendering the cockpit useless to an unauthorized person. Hijackers wouldn't be able to move control surfaces or the engines' throttles. Nor could they shut down the engines or make radio calls from the cockpit. Hijackers would not be able to shut off the electrical systems or kill the program controls by pulling individual circuit breakers or fuses. Switches and buttons on the autopilot or transponder would cease to respond to manual inputs. To freeze every system, switch, knob, indicator, instrument, and control box from a potential hijacker required thousands of lines of code for each function or indication. And in the case of interrupting electrical power to crucial systems by mechanical means, such as pulling circuit breakers, special tiny relays were installed in the circuit breaker panels to prevent the critical electrical systems from being disabled by hijackers. Only a total electrical failure could shut down the mainframe computer and reset the anti-hijack software to its default settings.

By using Chimera Avro's proprietary automatic takeoff and landing system software that was originally designed for unmanned aircraft, al-Sarkari assembled a prototype system for commercial aircraft that would remove all internal controls from the cockpit. The program would land an airliner, either at a predetermined location or allow the artificial intelligence system to find or choose the closest location. Or, if desired, the airline's managers could use their special activation codes to take control of the aircraft and have it fly to a chosen destination, such as a military airbase. Hijackers could break into the cockpit and kill the crew, but they could no longer control the aircraft and turn it into a flying bomb or a weapon of mass destruction.

The other system al-Sarkari developed was the backbone of the first. It would provide virtually real-time flight data and cockpit voice recordings. It was the perfect solution for the instantaneous tracking of long-range, overwater flights in the normal operating spectrum, in the unlikely event of an aircraft hijacking or midair explosion. Burst transmissions from aircraft to a satellite would continually track the aircraft's position, the cockpit's voice recordings, engine operational data, and other systems monitored by the installed mainframe aircraft computer system and as recorded by the FDR and CVR.

The data was transmitted every few minutes to the Boeing Cloud where it would be stored in logic pools, by an airline or a government agency, across multiple servers and locations. Boeing would be responsible for keeping the data available and accessible whenever there was a need to retrieve it. And, in the case of an accident, Boeing information technology specialists could retrieve the aircraft's FDR, CVR, and engine monitoring data virtually instantaneously from the Boeing Cloud, providing performance and positional data, and cockpit voice recordings.

No longer could an airline or government official blame the manufacturer for the loss of a hull due to unknown or external factors beyond their control, such as a pilot pushing the nose of the airplane into the ocean. Boeing could immediately recall all cockpit voice recordings and FDR data. But more importantly, Al-Sarkari could hide his tracks by interrupting the scheduled satellite updates and terminated the satellite datalink. Investigators would never know how the aircraft suffered a failure if al-Sarkari sent it wildly off course. It would be virtually impossible to find its remains in the open ocean.

Al-Sarkari was well aware of the potential of the monster he had created. Boeing was wise to demand an override protocol. Al-Sarkari installed a few more lines of code which allowed Boeing Operations Center to override the autonomous anti-hijack software and fly the aircraft remotely. The company wanted to be sure the aircraft computers couldn't be electronically hacked into by an external source. Al-Sarkari explained that was the purpose of the triple embedded lines of code and the levels of encryption. When purchasing the software, Boeing would provide the airline leaders the discrete "key code" for every one of their aircraft. It was the responsibility of the airline to ensure only an authorized user could activate the override system. Boeing would maintain the original key codes under lock and key in case of emergencies.

As the system administrator, al-Sarkari had developed all of the key-codes and maintained a copy of each. He named the real-time, satellite-based FDR and CVR system, "Virtual Flight Following." He named the anti-hijacking, anti-hacking program, "Impenetrable Cockpit." His fellow programmers affectionately called the monitoring and anti-intrusion systems "HAL 9000," after the movie 2001: A Space Odyssey. Virtual Flight Following and Impenetrable Cockpit, like the HAL 9000 mainframe computer, could monitor and control every system on the aircraft once it was activated. And it would take an extraordinary act, a trade secret, to disable the system once it was energized.

Tamerlan was proud of his accomplishments. The company CEO and al-Sarkari flew to Paris to market the Virtual Flight Following and Impenetrable Cockpit to Boeing's competitors, Airbus, at first, to little avail. After learning of the theory and concept of operations of the Virtual Flight Following and Impenetrable Cockpit systems, Airbus contracted a European firm to assess the American software and estimate the costs to develop similar capabilities for the European aircraft manufacturer. After a month of software evaluations in a simulator, the assessment company determined the R&D costs to develop such a suite of programs and the patent licensing expenses would drive the cost of a European-developed software package into the stratosphere. The Chimera Avro-Software Technologies' CEO and al-Sarkari flew to Paris to sign the billion-dollar contract.

The Airbus CEO informed the Chimera Avro Team that Russian and Chinese intelligence communities had gotten wind of the American company's software from a disgruntled socialist at Airbus. They would likely develop software for their indigenous-manufactured aircraft. On the return flight, while the over-celebrated CEO snored loudly next to him, al-Sarkari pondered the unimaginable.

As the Impenetrable Cockpit solution architect and software designer, al-Sarkari suddenly realized he could be in real danger. If the Russians and Chinese could steal the concept, then it was feasible that al-Qaeda or the Muslim Brotherhood would soon know he was the chief software designer. He had been the face of the company as the chief designer. He had developed all of the slide presentations, given all of the speeches, conducted all of the demonstration inside the simulator. It would be obvious to the communist countries what he had done and what he was personally capable of doing. They could kidnap him and force him to hijack any flying Boeing or Airbus aircraft. No longer would a terrorist group need a bevy of men to hijack an airliner and turn them into bombs, he could do it electronically. From his laptop. With a gun to his head and only a few key strokes and mouse clicks, he could send an Alaskan Airlines 737 off course to the North Pole. He could make FedEx cargo A330 aircraft disappear over any ocean. He could already override the programming of unmanned Predators to do as he saw fit. As he rattled off all the mayhem he could be forced to create, it came to him—he could even hijack the aircraft he was on. From his laptop. One of the largest aircraft in the world, the commuter train of the global village, the Boeing 747.

Of course, he knew he had such power, but he had no desire or reason to do anything so drastic, so extreme, so out-of-character. It was a technicality. He was a millionaire and had achieved riches beyond anything his parents could imagine. It was possible the quality assurance inspectors would find the special embedded software and alert the company leadership their system administrator had gone rogue. Finding the specially hidden code and recognizing the crucial few clues that lay in the embedded software, like a hungry leopard in the bush, awaiting for a gazelle, would require a bit of luck. But the fact was, few people other than the Chimera programmers could legitimately and effectively scrutinize the company's proprietary billion lines of code. Tamerlan was the master at hiding the secret commands and triggering software. It was a personal challenge for him to be able to hide the devilish lines of code, like DNA, in plain sight. Like he hid his leg, under a computer table.

He was acutely aware of the importance of what he had done in the context of preventing aviation terrorism. The FAA's Administrator was astounded that the systems worked. Certification flights proved the virtual FDR, CVR, and engine monitoring tracking systems worked as designed. Additional validation and verification flights proved the anti-hijacking, anti-hacking programs worked better than expected. The automatic takeoff and landing system landed the aircraft as well as any pilot. Always on the runway's centerline, and always bringing the aircraft to a full stop. What airline wouldn't want this capability?

Surrounded by patents, certificates and awards, and multiple computer screens in his corner office, al-Sarkari leaned back in his chair and gently shook his head at all he had accomplished. The *Explanatory Memorandum*, from cover to end, rattled around his head. Doing jihad in order to achieve it in the real world. The idea of becoming a jihadi, *the new Sword of Islam*, as was his namesake, grew in appeal.

"Who do I talk to?" he pondered. He couldn't trust anyone in America because, like in the newspaper article, the FBI was everywhere. Their job was to find and trap spies. If he was going to do something, he wouldn't be so stupid as to do it in America.

The software architect's conference in Dubai had put him out of reach of the tentacles of the FBI and its nest of spies. It had taken all day for al-Sarkari to observe the men at the conference before he felt confident enough to single out three to approach.

He had a capability and could demonstrate it. The first man looked at him strangely; the second man just walked away thinking he was mad. With great trepidation, the third man he approached said he might be able to help him or at least point him in the right direction. Al-Sarkari had said, "I have something to say to your master, the ultimate decision maker." No one immediately trusted the spontaneous and clumsy wannabe *jihadi*.

On the last day of the conference, he was summoned to the Armani Hotel in the Burj Khalifa. There he met a man, an unusual man. An Emirate sheikh. The CEO of an airline based out of Sharjah. His private coach was a new Boeing 747-400. What made the sheikh memorable was that it was rumored he wanted to purchase the remaining Aerospatiale Concordes for his airline and make one his private supersonic coach. Airbus scoffed and refused. Then a Concorde crashed in 2000 under curious circumstances. The Emirate sheikh approached the CEO of Airbus again wishing to engage in additional Concorde talks. Then, after the 11 September terrorist attacks in 2001, Airbus took all of the Concordes out of service and scattered them to museums. The sheikh was furious and publically vowed he would never buy another Airbus for his airline.

After al-Sarkari was searched and interrogated, the sheikh entered the conference room. They didn't greet each other in the Islamic way, no cheek kissing. No tea was served in the quiet way of a host. He was an American and wasn't even afforded a handshake. "You have one minute." The sheikh looked away, bored, indifferent.

"I can hijack any Boeing or Airbus aircraft. Even multiple aircraft. I can remove the pilots from the controls and communication systems *electronically*. Is this something that would be of interest…to the *caliphate*?"

The sheikh raised his chin and turned to look at Tamerlan al-Sarkari with sanguinary eyes. He tapped his fingers on the sofa chair for several seconds until he suddenly stood and walked toward the door. Al-Sarkari's heart pounded in his chest; adrenaline spiked his circulatory system by the buckets and set his skin on fire.

The sheikh refused to face al-Sarkari directly as he addressed him. "You will return to Dubai in two months. You will demonstrate this…*capability*." His English was a product of the finest American schools. Then he left the room.

Tamerlan recalled that the sheikh left his business card on the conference table that day. Two months later, he demonstrated his capacity to send selected Boeing aircraft into mountains or oceans. The former President of the United States slipped him another business card and ordered him to dispatch a man named Duncan Hunter, for reasons only known to him. A Google search of the man was inconclusive. There were dozens of Duncan Hunters in America. All but one in Texas were irrelevant. Al-Sarkari wondered what he had gotten himself into and if he would live to tell about it. He reasoned and said aloud, to no one in particular, "Not likely."

CHAPTER EIGHTEEN

1700 July 15, 2014
McLean, Virginia

The Director of Central Intelligence's special project team filed into his office. They encompassed the Director of Operations, the Director of the National Clandestine Service, the Director of the National Counter Terrorism Center, and the Director of the Intelligence Directorate. With the exception of Nazy Cunningham, each had been with the Agency for over thirty years. They settled into chairs around the DCI's personal conference table; each was curious about being summoned to the seventh floor. They all had received a simple email from Lynche, "Do you know where the former president is? Be prepared to discuss what info you do have regarding the location of the former POTUS."

The Director of Operations, the DO, Quint Miklos, was bumping fifty and was all business. He was cordial but avoided small talk. Grey hair, dark eyes, and shallow cheeks, he looked like he had been ridden hard for his thirty some-odd years at the Agency. He looked forward to the day he attained the mandatory retirement age; he shook his head and wondered where this conversation would lead. He recalled an article in *The Washington Post* which specifically asked the very same question.

Jeff Mustin, the DI, the Director of the Intelligence Directorate, was everything Quint Miklos was not. He was a tall muscular man with a shaved head, like a Marine Corps drill instructor, with a neck as thick as a tree trunk. Penetrating blue eyes like Frank Sinatra's gave him an air of intensity. Everyone called him Moose. He made eye contact with the DCI and shook his head. The topic had been discussed several times with his team of spies. The whereabouts of the disgraced former president was important and should be discussed at their level. The problem within the Intelligence Directorate was that no one cared.

The Director of the National Clandestine Service, Steve Castaño, was a smallish man, early fifties, close to five-six with lifts in his shoes. He didn't have a single grey hair within his thick black hair or bushy mustache, courtesy of routine visits at a hairstylist. His hands were severely scarred from a childhood accident and he subconsciously kept them hidden in gatherings. He was thoughtfully quiet and rarely said anything in meetings unless one of his guys was getting screwed. Then he would erupt like a dozen volcanoes. He also wore dark glasses to hide his eyes, even in well-illuminated rooms. It was his turn to look at the DCI and shake his head. The best spies kept their mouths shut and listened, and Castaño listened very intently. The topic was incredible.

Lastly was Nazy Cunningham, the Director of the NCTC. Her meteoric rise through the ranks to secure the top counterterrorism job made her a target for derision and innuendo from some of the less-senior intelligence executives. She had interrogated al-Qaeda and Taliban leaders, and she single-handedly located the Osama bin Laden compound in Pakistan simply by having the man's wives followed from Saudi Arabia. Hours after landing in Islamabad, several intelligence officers from the U.S. Embassy were led to a remarkable compound in Abbottabad. Nazy was a breathtaking beauty in her mid-forties, and was the fantasy of nearly every male at the CIA, especially when she wore a skirt. Which was often but not today. She said, "No, Director Lynche."

Greg Lynche brought a huge coffee cup to the table and started the meeting with a "thank you" and a nod to Moose to start the presentation.

"This is what we know—if anyone has something new, chime in. This briefing is TS/SCI. *Slide!* At 2330 on June 30, 2011, President Mazibuike boarded Air Force One at Andrews Air Force Base bound for Honolulu. The effective date of his resignation occurred the following morning, at 0800 Eastern on July first. Immediately upon landing at Hickam, former President Mazibuike dismissed his Secret Service detail and boarded a private jet, which was registered in the Philippines, with a flight plan to Clark International Airport, the former Clark Air Force Base forty miles north of Manila. Dispatches from the Chief of Station state that former President Mazibuike did not get off the aircraft at the Clark Airport when it landed. Conjecture is he got off that jet somewhere enroute. Possibly Fiji or another airport within the Philippine Islands, maybe at Subic Bay International Airport. No one knows for sure, is that correct?" Heads nodded around the table.

Nazy said, "There is a shipyard across from the new Subic Bay

International Airport, the old Subic Bay Naval Base."

Lynche turned his head for a second to consider what Nazy had said. He didn't dismiss the observation outright and offered, "It could have been a decoy. He was the president; he knows about decoys and the value of decoys. He had ample time to arrange one."

The DO Miklos said, "Bottom line, he was the POTUS. No one ever thought anything about him needing to be followed. He was the most famous man in the world; he had been humiliated and had resigned. He left the country to escape impeachment. Hell, supposedly, he even left his family in the U.S."

The National Clandestine Service Director said, "So, he is out there. Has anyone heard of a sighting? We haven't been told to be on the lookout for him. No BOLOs. I know if he had popped his head out of whatever hole he's hiding in, my guys would have said something." Castaño's eyes begged for an answer. No one had one to give him because of his silly dark glasses.

Mustin said, "I don't think anyone has been really looking for him. No one is talking. There has been nothing. No chatter. Nothing."

Lynche asked Mustin to continue.

"Can we speculate where he is most likely to be hiding? In consultation with Director Cunningham, I submit he was closely aligned with the Saudi Prince Azzam Mohammad Bakaar Bashir, who mysteriously disappeared from his yacht 150 miles off the coast of Liberia."

Castaño asked, "What do we know of the dearly departed prince?"

Nazy interjected, waving a thick mahogany-colored folder. "This is his file. He had a greater relationship with the former DCI, Frank Carey, than President Mazibuike."

Only slightly agitated, the DO Miklos asked, "Why are we doing this now? I mean, the man is gone, out of our lives. A stain on the country, granted. Why now?"

Lynche replied, "POTUS request. Is that sufficient?"

"Why?" asked DO Miklos. He shrugged his shoulders almost in an act of defiance.

Lynche turned to the DO, both men grew more irritated by the second. Lynche controlled his temper. The other executives watched the dynamics between the top two men at the Agency. Lynche spat, "Maybe he wants to talk with him. Invite him over to the White House for tea. I don't know, nor is it my role to question the President. President Hernandez wants to know of his whereabouts, and our job is to find him."

Mustin suggested, "Maybe send a Hellfire up his ass?" intimating the current president would authorize a missile strike on the former president.

Lynche frowned at the comment. He was losing control of the meeting. "Listen up. I know nearly everyone in this room, me included, voted for the man. His treachery hit us very hard. How could the intelligence community's senior executives be taken in by that fraud? *I know.* I have a friend that asks me that all the time, all too often. How he could know Mazibuike was bad when we didn't is another story for another day. But we have to push that aside for now, for the good of the country. Learn from it."

DO Miklos added, "We've taken the appropriate countermeasures to the Muslim Brotherhood's successful infiltration of the government. I have some numbers ...."

Lynche waved away the offer for the moment. "Now we need to find him, for whatever the reason; the ultimate decision maker asked us to locate him. It may be President Hernandez wishes to bring him to stand trial. You can't send the FBI to do it—this is our bailiwick. If the goal is something like that, I think the President is committing political suicide, although it would be the right thing to do." There were clenched jaws, furrowed eyebrows, and nodding heads around the table.

Castaño kept his damaged hands out of sight. He asked, "Is there anything in the man's file, the one that was released to God and country?"

DO Miklos spit, "His handling of the OBL mission should have given us a clue he was bad."

"Quint, what do you mean?" asked Nazy. It was a simple question, not one of sarcasm. The DO had been in the Agency a long time. He had seen things the other senior executives hadn't. By the tone of her voice, she really wanted to know what he was thinking. And if it wasn't simple frustration, then what he was feeling.

"I mean we planned and scheduled every aspect of the mission to capture bin Laden. For months, he wouldn't let us go. Then there was a document release and Mazibuike was basically forced to authorize the raid. But then, in debrief, we learn he directed the SEAL Team commander to ensure OBL was dead before they left the compound." Tight jaws rippled around the conference table. It was all true. The public may have been indifferent to the disgraced and discredited former president, but for some in the CIA, the man was a traitor and had escaped every bit of justice he deserved. Others, including half of the senior intelligence officers around the DCI's conference table, agreed Mazibuike was a traitor. The other half weren't so sure.

Nazy Cunningham and Greg Lynche never flinched or looked at each other. They knew the truth. Before the SEAL team commander took off from their base in Afghanistan, he announced to his team that he would not obey the presidential order. Instead, the Team tasered, captured, and drugged the old terrorist, before they spirited him away. One of bin Laden's relatives was shot in the face and was buried at sea; a bit of nighttime prestidigitation to fully execute the conspiracy. Lynche and Duncan Hunter flew halfway across the globe to pick up the head of al-Qaeda, and then Nazy Cunningham flew into Monrovia, Liberia and interrogated him. Hunter got rid of the body in the most gruesome way. Any time Osama bin Laden's name was mentioned, Greg Lynche would shudder as he envisioned OBL strapped to the pilot's chair of an old Yakovlev commuter jet while being eaten alive by rats.

Lynche wanted out of this line of the conversation and changed the subject. "That's all water under the bridge. Where would he go? Nazy, have you given this some thought? This is your area." All the men turned their eyes to her.

"Middle East. He's a Muslim male and will return to the ME."

Lynche said, "I asked Nazy to work up a psychological analysis on the former president. I thought it might be useful in fully understanding the man. The press lionized him, and if we didn't have that file, many of us would still be thinking he was the second coming. Nazy?" Lynche bit his lower lip unconsciously. He too once celebrated the election of the Democratic President. But not Duncan Hunter. He had the man pegged as a closet-communist, closet-Muslim, and an illegitimate president from the moment he first saw him on television.

Nazy passed out red-bordered manila files to the men around the table. After they scanned the documents with TOP SECRET headers and footers contained therein, she began. "Citing national security concerns, President Mazibuike used an executive order (EO) to have all of his records expunged in the United States. President Hernandez countermanded Mazibuike's EO and signed an executive order for the CIA and FBI to access all pertinent medical and collateral information, scholastic and immigration records, including psychiatric and medical records, and psychological testing of President Mazibuike. This investigation was conducted both domestic and abroad. Agency psychologists conducted an examination of the documents. They included the president's known history and present syndromes, a description of the tests employed and the results, the examiners' findings and opinions as to diagnosis and whether the former president suffered from a mental disease or defect."

Nazy spoke from memory. "The examiners also reviewed all writings and academic examinations obtained from the universities he attended, as well as his health and medical records. Elementary, junior, and high school records describe his childhood as relatively uneventful. He denied any history of physical abuse in his family although his mother obsessed over his negro dialect. He confided specific verbal and emotional abuse during his upbringing to a counselor. Unsealed immigration records revealed the father was denied citizenship after immigration officials charged his parents with marriage for convenience to secure citizenship. The father was deported, and the mother followed him to Africa. His mother returned to the United States to give birth, and the president was raised by his maternal grandmother. There was a man referred to as an uncle, not a blood relation, but an actual card-carrying communist who mentored the young Mazibuike until he left for college. Mazibuike was not accepted well by the neighborhood children or his peers at school."

Nazy addressed the group. "Maxim Mohammad Mazibuike is a 55 year old male of African and American heritage. Testing showed him to have a slightly below-average IQ. However, he claimed that his IQ was over 170, a genius. Teachers annotated that he did not fit in with the other children and was the subject of considerable verbal abuse and teasing from them. Counselors suspected substance abuse attributed to his frequent absences and moodiness. He had little involvement in sports or interest in group activities, other than basketball, because he was tallish."

"There were no periods of service in the military, British or American. In his autobiographies, Mr. Mazibuike acknowledges a significant history of illicit substance use—primarily cannabis and cocaine—as well as alcohol and nicotine. This is confirmed by other sources of collateral information. Mr. Mazibuike described his religious affiliation as Christian and he attended the United Church of Christ as a senator. This church was largely a front for the Nation of Islamic Brothers. No other church affiliation was known up until his file was released. Now we know he was a non-practicing Muslim, with a Muslim father, a Muslim step-father, and with madrassas training."

Mustin interjected, "Funny for a Christian to say the sweetest sound he knew was the Muslim call to prayer and the future must not belong to those who slander the prophet of Islam."

Lynche's irritation was palpable and gestured for Nazy to continue.

"No history of inpatient psychiatric hospitalizations or ongoing treatment, although from records sequestered and sealed during his administration, he had experienced several weeks of intense and persistent sexual excitement involving fantasies of being a female. During university, he reportedly became involved with men. Subsequent to those episodes, he investigated sex change surgery."

The men around the table now understood the report was no longer a formality to establish an understanding of the former president. It was disturbing that the president's psychosis steered off into mental illness. It was very difficult to profile and predict the actions of a mental defective. They returned their eyes to Nazy Cunningham and listened intently.

"The attending university physician annotated that the president was aware that such ideations would require a psychiatric referral; he referred Mazibuike to the university health center for evaluation. Health records described that while seated in the waiting room, he became anxious and humiliated over the prospect of talking about this to another doctor. When he was actually seen, he at first did not discuss these concerns with the doctor, but rather claimed he was feeling some depression and anxiety from the possibility of being drafted into the military. The psychiatrist viewed his anxiety and depression as not atypical for a college student. Mr. Mazibuike eventually confided his real reason for the office visit. There was no follow-through or additional appointments, and no further medical records were found during the document search."

Lynche offered, "With this new information, I don't think we can rule out a sex change operation. If he tumbled down that path, he could vanish completely."

The Director of Operations said, "Agreed. Makes the search more complicated. A closet Muslim seeking a sex change operation? Approaches impossible."

The NCS Director asked, "Are there any other documents that suggest he began the sex change protocol?"

As Nazy shook her head, she was focusing on another line of reasoning. She jotted down a note that she would discuss with Lynche privately. She looked up to find the men staring at her. She continued, "It was widely known in the universities that the military would not accept those with a sexual identity disorder. They were immediately disqualified. His interest in sex change may have been a ruse to guarantee he would not be considered for the military."

Lynche said, "Good point."

The other men around the conference table sat in silence. Not bemused but bewildered. The former president's life was a closed book despite two autobiographies, as were the rumors of his sexual proclivities. They recalled the taunts from conservative pundits and talk radio that Mazibuike had spent over three million dollars to seal all of his records for a Presidential run. This material, had it been reported in the media and the press, would have changed the election. Any hint of sexual identity affiliation or disturbances would have been killed by every left-leaning managing editor.

She continued, "But, there is an interesting turn. His psychiatrist reported the president's experiences at Harvard. In essence it was described as a very isolated existence with only infrequent interactions with other students. His law professors found him unremarkable and unreliable, often missing classes with frequent visits to the health center. Noteworthy, the psychiatrist with whom he discussed his sexual difficulties and orientation, died mysteriously after his nomination to president. No witnesses, and no one was ever charged with a crime. Two men, who were found to be Muslim, were suspected and interviewed but released."

The men all lifted their heads. "*What?*"

"Gentlemen, that's a brief summation of thousands of documents.

Conclusion, after analyzing psychological tests and studying the former President's autobiographies and his Agency file, which document over 40 years of his life, Mr. Mazibuike's was a man whose early potential was ruined by a life of drugs, gender psychosis, and paranoid schizophrenia. Although he later married and had children, his history was one of almost total absence of interpersonal relationships. His Agency file demonstrated that he was a sympathetic and romantic communist, that he was authoritative and totalitarian, and a non-practicing Muslim. His is a complex history of delusion of grandeur; that he could stop the oceans from rising and that he could bend the will of the public to bring about a fundamental change in America. Questions?"

Lynche said, "Nice job, Nazy. Let's find him. Her. Him. Draft a dispatch for all station chiefs to report any hint of the man. I don't want to say be on the lookout for a woman, just yet. If we get a hint he may have acted on his old ideations and taken up a *burqa*, we'll deal with it then. For now, any sightings, rumors, unusual activities which could be associated with him, we want to know about it. He's overseas and is no longer under the FBI's purview. You know the drill. We'll meet this time every day for a recap, a how goes it meeting. This topic is for our ears only. No email notes or sidebars. Meeting adjourned."

Mustin still had slides to display. Lynche dismissed him with a wave of his hand. All left—all but Nazy Cunningham.

When it was just the two of them, she asked, "Is this what the President wanted Duncan for?"

Lynche nodded. "And Bill McGee," he absentmindedly added. Then he said, "Nazy, what's your real take on where he is? You've been perfect finding bin Laden and al-Zawahiri and others." He didn't want to ask her what she thought about sex reassignment surgery. "You have a sense. What do you think?"

"Director Lynche, my sense is this one is a little different. If he truly had ideations of being a woman, I cannot believe he'd head for the Middle East. You go to Europe. As a woman he could disappear. If such ideations were ever acted upon or articulated, no Muslim leader would take him seriously. We're talking about smart and incredibly powerful Muslim men. OBL and his ilk were warriors part-time, Muslims full time. For Mazibuike and his billionaire friends, Islam is only an affectation. Islam isn't what brought them their wealth and power. OBL just wanted to fight, first the Russians then Americans, from his house if he could. Then he wanted to be surrounded by his wives and children. He killed a few infidels for show, to impress his followers. The princes of Saudi Arabia and the emirs of the UAE are of a different type. They can buy new wives and children anytime. They're...."

Lynche finished the sentence for her. "For show; irrelevant. I don't see those guys banging their heads on the floor three, four, five times a day."

Nazy was momentarily distracted by the spurious thought and said, "Yes, sir. Irrelevant. With them, the only thing that matters is their wealth and power, and their position, and they are solely focused on how they can improve their wealth and power, and position. Their *status*. I don't think he'd go feminine or go to Saudi Arabia."

"The Saudis absolutely hated him. I cannot get over the image of his deep-waisted bow to King Abdullah, like he was going to kiss his shoes." Lynche allowed an indelicate thought, *Maybe they knew he wanted to be a girl.... Maybe we should be looking for size 13s under a burqa.* Nazy again interrupted his train of thought.

"Yes, sir. We determined there was much bad blood between the former President and the Saudi royals; the Saudis were not impressed with him. It was apparent Mazibuike didn't have a direct association with al-Qaeda and the Muslim Brotherhood. They seemed to be knowledgeable, quiet supporters. But there's another group that rises above the rest, and we don't know much about them. I think that's where he would go and that's where I'm going to look first."

"Where's that?"

"I don't think the usual suspects would be much help. He needs a great deal of help to stay off the grid for so long. Ever hear of a company called ROC? In Arabic it sounds like 'rook,' the chess piece."

As he was prone to do when he didn't want to articulate a response, Lynche shook his head.

Nazy continued, "I know a little. The former Near East Chief had reason to believe it was some kind of a shady organization, like the Chicago Weather Underground. I understand that group's goal was to create a clandestine revolutionary party for the overthrow of the U.S. government. The NE Chief was convinced that when they weren't acting like some sort of Arabic mafia, one of the assumed goals of the ROC was to create a clandestine revolutionary movement for the return of the *caliphate*. They financially supported AQ and the Brotherhood and other terrorist organizations when it suited them."

"Where does the *Explanatory Memorandum* fit into this?"

"The Muslim Brotherhood's roadmap to infiltrate America? Information and analysis is not complete. However, anything that moved them closer to establishing a *caliphate* in North America they were all for it. Anyway, I first heard of ROC when I was stationed at Riyadh. I knew of the mythical bird, *Roc*, that carried away *al-Addin*; Aladdin in English, but not the organization. I started a file, but that was the only mention of ROC for the time I was there. As my team and I were going over some new intel, basically, the new occupants of the newly opened Burj Dubai, the initials ROC popped up again. They occupied something like the top three floors of the building. The Burj Dubai."

"It's called something else now." Lynche had seen it in several briefs but couldn't remember what it was. Intelligence services across the globe always tried to acquire the top floors of any remarkable building before another intelligence service beat them to it. The race would be on, not to occupy the top floor but to control the roof, to conduct surveillance. When you held the highest point in the area, you could surveil the area and be king of intelligence.

"It was the Burj Dubai. They renamed it the Burj Khalifa. The Khalifa Tower. I asked my head analyst to look into the ROC. It's not much, but what she has is fascinating stuff."

"Yeah?"

"Yes, sir. What do you know of Captain Nemo?"

"Jules Verne? *Twenty Thousand Leagues under the Sea?* Nazy, I don't have time for fiction." He crossed his arms to show his displeasure.

"She thought there may be a connection."

Exasperated, Lynche waved his fingers to encourage Nazy to continue. He checked his watch to see how long it would take before his head exploded.

"Originally, Captain Nemo was a Polish scientist, but Verne's publisher demanded that Nemo be made an enemy of the slave trade. As a compromise in the book, Nemo becomes the son of an Indian Raja and a descendant of the Muslim Sultan Fateh Ali Tipu of the Kingdom of Mysore in southern India." The Arabic names rolled off her tongue like a native-born Arab, which she was. "Some researchers claimed Verne's Nemo was actually based on the little known Muslim sailor, Abbasayeed. He sailed east to Japan and China, and even to South America, bringing back silks, pearls, ivories, silver and gold, and slaves from his travels. His journeys to and from Abu Dhabi made him rich."

"Nazy, where are you going with this?"

"I received a brief from STRATCOM. They have knowledge of a nuclear submarine operated by the UAE."

"I sense a connection." He crossed his arms, intrigued.

"The UAE have been operating submarines from the days when they weren't so united. They have a history of harboring political refugees, dictators that need to disappear. They even provided U-boats by Hitler for the evacuation of Nazi leaders."

Lynche was incredulous. "That's documented?"

"Yes, there were entries in Admiral Canaris' diary. He positioned U-boats in Spain, Western Africa, and the Arabian Peninsula. The emir's U-boats were used to smuggle contraband, gems, ivory, spies, and people. They even engaged in occasional banditry."

"What's the rest of the story?"

"Like the fictional Nemo, Abbasayeed was fascinated with sailing underwater and traveling to secret cities on remote islands. He built a submersible, not quite like the deep-diving submarine of Nemo, and he hid it when he visited these secret cities to avoid pirates and bandits. He also used a sea eagle he called *Roc* to find land. And, he named his ship after the little armored mollusk that floated under the water, the Nautilus. After his death, we learned a Prince Azzam was very closely associated with the underground organization ROC, which had built or bought or stole a submarine, possibly Soviet or French, for the Emirates to operate. STRATCOM indicated that the submarine is a French Redoubtable and named *Abba Sayeed*."

"Ok, that's interesting."

She said, "It gets better. The *Abba Sayeed* arrived at Subic Bay on the 30th of June."

Lynche knew that date was important, but could not make the connection. His face showed that he did not understand the significance of the date.

"Sir, that was the day before President Mazibuike resigned. He flew

Air Force One and landed in Hawaii."

Lynche's eyebrows were getting a workout. He grinned at Nazy conspiratorially. "Shit."

"Prince Azzam was so rich he could have paid off the national debt of France. What we didn't know until recently was that he had acquired his own private submarine under the guise of another submarine for the UAE Navy. Maybe our former president stepped off a jet and boarded the *Abba Sayeed,* at one of the Philippines islands with an airstrip with a shipyard or submarine pen nearby? Aren't there radar records of that part of the Pacific?"

Lynche frowned then said, "First, there is no real radar coverage over the oceans. So that's a dead end. But the rest of it. That would make sense; explain much. You know at that level there are no coincidences. Check with the NRO. See if they tracked a business jet to an island on that night. And let's get some more information on this ROC. Ask the Israelis first. Good job, Nazy."

"I'm on it." Nazy turned and walked out of the office with Lynche's eyes trailing her delicate ankles and bright blue heels with every step. She had forgotten to tell him what had been on her mind: information on "the rumor." She would work on it by herself.

CHAPTER NINETEEN

1900 July 15, 2014
Del Rio, Texas

It had been a long, warm, and almost windless summer day. The kind of day that set record highs in locations normally known for their bouts of cloud-free skies and triple digit temperatures. The sun set behind the Sleeping Lady, the distant Mexican mountain formation west of town, inviting a gentle intermittent breeze from the Chihuahuan Desert to spill across the border, like a blast of heat when opening an oven door. East of the San Felipe Creek, U.S. Border Patrol Agents departed their USBP Station compound in their four-wheel drive trucks. Teams would spread out to the four cardinal headings to patrol the known thoroughfares and Rio Grande crossings, as well as the well-established "lay up" areas where human smugglers—*coyotes*—would have their illegal border crossers wait in the brush with their gallon jugs of water for their ride to the big cities to the north and east.

East of the border town of Del Rio, the Queen City of the Rio Grande, lay the sprawling Laughlin Air Force Base complex. Once the secret airbase for U-2 spy planes that took high-altitude photographs of Russian missiles in Cuba during the height of the Cold War, Laughlin traded its mission of high-altitude reconnaissance with space suit-wearing pilots for a high-tempo, undergraduate pilot training operation. U.S. Air Force and international student pilots would crawl into turboprop, cargo, and supersonic training aircraft, thunder down one of three runways, and fill the skies with the sounds of jets turning jet fuel into jet noise—the Sounds of Freedom. At the end of flight operations, when all of the available daylight was exhausted and the sun finally slipped behind the supine silhouette of Dolly Parton, maintenance and logistics technicians worked through the night to repair, inspect, and prepare aircraft for the next day's flight schedule.

After a very long day flying with youngsters that were just beginning to learn which end of an airplane could hurt them, most of the instructor pilots were physically and emotionally spent. Some dragged tired butts home to eat a real sit down meal and to unwind with the spouse and kids. A handful would remain in the Operations building, the sprawling complex of flying training squadron offices. Anderson Hall, as it was called, named after the U-2 pilot shot down over Cuba, Major Rudolph Anderson, contained within its walls a warren of briefing rooms, an auditorium, and a covey of classrooms where a group of diehard instructors attended an occasional graduate school class.

A new course was beginning, and the professor greeted each student entering the windowless classroom. He expected a full house, with lieutenants, captains, and majors arriving from the local squadrons as well as from other military bases in the greater San Antonio area. Occasionally, a Border Patrol pilot found time to work on a master's degree. Border Patrol helicopter pilots relished the idea of attending classes. It was a break from the routine of twelve-hour days being shot at by drug smugglers and apprehending scores of tuberculosis-infected illegal aliens already on U.S. soil.

The instructor could smell them, the salty redolence of a dozen men and women in flight suits bearing a white arc of dried sweat across their shoulder blades—a badge of honor from training the newest generation of Air Force student pilots. It was a familiar scent. It reminded him of his time flying high performance jets, flipping the aircraft around in high-G dogfights, making high-dive angle bombing runs, or operating off an aircraft carrier. During his time in a jet, he'd lose gallons of water to sweat, drenching his skull cap, flight suit, and his socks. He could tell which students flew the modified corporate jets, the air-conditioned cargo aircraft trainers, by their neat, perfectly combed hair and dry flight suits. And he could tell who flew the turboprops and supersonic trainers. They looked as if they had been put through a 1913 Sears wringer washing machine, and in most cases, they had.

Some student pilots were just "difficult." Students pilots pulled form-fitted helmets over grey skull caps, clipped oxygen masks to their helmets, zipped up the compression anti-G-suits, and crawled into torso parachute harnesses all in an effort to impress or scare the hell out of their instructors as they learned "proper pilot technique." Air-conditioning in the aircraft was inadequate when the temperature rose above 90°F. Wet hair, wet flight suits, and sweaty drenched socks were the trademarks of the high performance flight instructor as their students worked tirelessly to learn the fine art of aviating, navigating, and communicating in the three-dimensional tumultuous world of the military pilot.

Some of the instructor pilots (IPs) who survived their student's adventures became students in the evening by taking graduate-level college classes at night. These IPs were the brightest and most motivated of airmen, even if they stank. And the professor loved it; he loved them like they were his own children. He shared that special bond with his students which transcended his role as classroom professor. The deep mutual understanding and affinity among flyers made each academic gathering a near family occasion.

The confined space of green boards and desks warmed significantly as the class grew to twenty students on its way to thirty. When the building's air handling unit finally kicked on, it blew a continuous torrent of cool air into the room and pushed the fetid odors out the door. The stench that had permeated the air quickly dissipated, and an agreeable atmosphere, courtesy of the lowest cost, technically acceptable air handling unit, became the norm. Surrounded by some of the finest operational pilots America could produce, the old fighter pilot at the lectern was energized, ready to go. If you can't fly—teach! And he loved teaching almost as much as he loved flying. Almost.

He bantered with some of his "studs" as the classroom filled before class officially started. Some asked political questions while others commented on his previous class, an accident investigation course, and the revelations that a TWA jumbo jet had been shot out of the sky in contravention to the official findings. He was about to give up hope that there was a courageous soul among them who was brave enough to ask a personal question, when a new student, Captain Andy Grindel, asked why he was wearing a shiny black cast on his arm. Another long-time student, Major Matt Minor, also jumped in and fiendishly asked, "Did I see you coming out of the pressure chamber building today?"

Duncan Hunter held up the splinted forearm and hand and said, "A minor industrial accident. As for the pressure chamber…*Major Minor*," Hunter softly scolded, "Yes, sir, you certainly did. *You were there!*"

The major turned in his seat and clued in the class. "Professor Hunter is getting a ride with the Thunderbirds." The Air Force Flight

Demonstration Team was the keynote act when the airbase hosted its upcoming airshow. Sometimes a few well-deserved individuals in the community were offered incentive or orientation rides when the military's flight demonstration teams came to town.

"That's not for public dissemination," cautioned Hunter with a playfully raised index finger. He knew no one in his classroom could keep a secret like that. Any conversation regarding his splint was dead and buried, and that was fine with him.

"Well, how'd it go?" asked another captain, almost impishly. It was typical pilot-ese, that good-natured ribbing when an opportunity arose to poke at the aviation professor. Clearly some of the students were interested in learning at what point in the pressure chamber their instructor ceased to function and lost consciousness. All military jet pilots were trained to recognize the signs of hypoxia. Before an Air Force student pilot set foot in an airplane they were going to fly, they had to experience the sensation of working in a low-pressure, low-oxygen environment learning to recognize the symptoms of the onset of hypoxia. Getting knocked out was a rite of passage. A little non-attribution schadenfreude was in order for the old guy who seemed to be on top of the aviation world as a former fighter pilot and semi-famous college professor who lectured on all things aviation, especially aviation terrorism. Some were simply jealous he drove to class in the ultimate fighter pilot's car, a rare Aston Martin.

Hunter grinned as Major Minor intervened. "I can report he was un-frickin' believable. So everyone knows there's hardly any O2 at 30,000 feet. The rubber glove ballooned to the size of a medicine ball. His hands and lips were blue but he didn't miss a beat, subtracting 7 from 1,000. At 33K he finally said, 'I probably should go on oxygen.' Everyone else in the chamber had been on oxygen at 18,000 feet of pressure altitude. The new students didn't know why Professor Hunter was in the chamber, but they were waiting for the old guy to turn black, pass out, blow up like a balloon and explode. Only he didn't. Three techs waited, ready to get a mask on him."

"33K?" asked several incredulous students simultaneously. The pressure chamber training was designed to remove air and replicate the high-altitude environment of a high-performance jet flying in the jet route structure. Except for pilots in poorly scripted Hollywood movies, fighter pilots always wore their O2 mask and were force-fed aviator's breathing oxygen from a positive-pressure regulator. If they didn't get a mask on, within seconds they'd be hypoxic, unconscious, and unable to fly a jet.

Everyone in the class had been through the training and seen the demonstration where a latex examination glove was tied off at the wrist and suspended by a string from the ceiling of the pressure tube. Then air pressure was gradually reduced in the chamber. At sea level, the white powdered glove was deflated and limp. As air was pumped out of the chamber, the pressure inside the glove, which was greater than the pressure surrounding it, caused the latex glove to expand. Greatly. It was an image that never left pilots for it also demonstrated that the gasses in their bloodstream and intestines were also expanding making them flatulent, their fingers swell, and their skin tingle as microscopic gas bubbles escaped from the pores in their skin. The whole purpose of the training was to demonstrate to the pilots that they cannot tell when they're about to pass out unless they quickly recognize the symptoms of decompression and are able to take immediate corrective action.

Major Minor nodded. "Some people can climb Mt. Everest naturally without O2. Professor Hunter is one of those, apparently."

Hunter tried to move the conversation along with a bit of humor and humility. "I know Major Minor was just trying to see when I would flip and jerk around like a fish out of water. I may be old, but I remember that a lot of folks can last at 250 for a while and the chamber operators usually quit the demonstration after about 10 minutes at 250. I know you were just screwing with me and took me up to 330. I hope you know, Major Minor, your conduct will be reflected on your course grade." Hunter pointed at the Air Force office mischievously, then grinned and the class laughed heartily.

Hunter continued, "It's not every day an old F-4 jock gets to fly with the Thunderbirds. That's going to be very special. I thank the Wing Commander for nominating me, and Major Minor as project officer for running me through all the wickets. That's one flight I'm not going to miss." He paused for effect, pushed aside the old joys and fears of flying a fighter again. "And on the off chance that I'm not able to take the United States Air Force up on their invitation, Major Minor, you have to promise me that a suitable substitute will be able to take my seat. I know one. He is the most highly decorated Navy SEAL, and he's never been in a fighter."

"Done!" said the Major Minor.

Hunter grinned at the beaming major and said, "*Now* can we start class?"

After waiting a few seconds as the students settled in their seats, Hunter gripped the edges of the lectern in one sleek powerful movement and dove into his opening lecture. "Welcome to the Aviation Terrorism course of instruction. You know who I am; you all know each other; I'll get to know you soon. Let's get this show on the road." The overhead projector came to life with pictures of crashed or burned out aircraft. "Why are terrorists infatuated with airplanes? When they're not hijacking them, they're trying to blow them up. What's going on here? Thoughts?"

The unexpected introduction and barrage of questions caught them off guard. No one was brave enough to interrupt the monologue. Most had been with the instructor through other classes. They knew to listen and take notes. Hunter had their attention.

"There are certain moments in history, if you're interested and paying attention, that might provide some understanding of the twisted and changing mind of an aviation terrorist." Hunter energized a hand-held clicker and a photograph was projected on the wall behind him. "Take the iconic image of the crushed cockpit of Flight 103, a PanAm 747, lying in a field in Lockerbie, Scotland. Take the dozens of jets flown to Cuba. Take Flight 800, the TWA 747 that, officially, fell from the sky due to a fuel cell problem." Hunter smiled as he delivered a line of rodomontade; his class didn't know he was silently bragging. "Last year, a Nigerian Airbus 380 was hijacked before Navy SEALs got aboard and rescued the aircrew and passengers. Dozens of examples, year over year. Why do they do it?"

From a voice at the rear of the classroom, "To make a political statement."

Another said, "Those that went to Cuba, I think, sought asylum. But that's political, I guess." Hunter shrugged more than nodded.

From the front row Lieutenant Flynn suggested, "At Entebbe, didn't Palestinians want to get back at, to punish Israel and the Jews?"

A hand shot up before the young woman answered, "D.B. Cooper did it for ransom."

"All good. All good. We have numerous examples of groups or individuals committing acts of aviation terrorism for politics or pesos, or to punish a group like the Jews, or a government or a country, such as Israel. When we frame a statement like that, it begs the question, the groups that commit these acts, are they criminals or are they terrorists? So to get started on understanding this very complex subject, what I'd like you to do is think about the difference between terrorists and criminals, and then we'll discuss the difference between motive and method."

Hunter waved his unsplinted hand in the air for imaginary emphasis. He ran through another series of slides, photographs of famous aircraft hijackings and bombings. "There's been some research by some academic *pinheads* noting the similarities in the behavioral and operational methods of both terrorists and organized criminals. While it is true terrorists and criminals often use the same methods to achieve their goals, the two are more likely to do so for divergent motives. What separates and distinguishes the two is this—*personal profit drives the hijacking criminals while political upheaval drives terrorists.* D.B. Cooper was in it for the money; he hijacked an aircraft and held it for ransom. He was a criminal. And he was a dumb ass criminal—he should have brought his own parachute."

The class laughed aloud as they scribbled notes.

"Many of the first generation hijackers felt compelled to hijack their way to Cuba. Why Cuba? Let's talk about this a little bit."

The students were being driven into an area of thought they hadn't considered before, and it hadn't been discussed in their textbook. Their demeanor shifted to confusion and embarrassment. They didn't know much about Cuba or the dynamics that saw numerous criminals get aboard aircraft, make terroristic threats, and demand the airline pilots head straight for Havana. Few were aware of the reason the building they were in was named after an Air Force officer shot down on a mission to Cuba. Hunter knew the "Cuba Connection," as he called it, was key to understanding the politics and nuances of the birthplace of aviation terrorism.

"Fidel Castro was a young lawyer when he and his comrades overthrew the thuggish Batista in January 1959. How many of you know that Castro appeared on "The Ed Sullivan Show just a few days later?"

The look on every student's face was shock. Hunter flipped to the next slide to show a picture of Castro and Sullivan embracing warmly.

"Castro promised to improve his country's democratic institutions," Hunter said as he waved his hand, "He also promised Cuba would never again fall prey to a dictator. I think this is why Shakespeare said we should kill all the lawyers." The classroom erupted in laughter. He continued, "And then one very star-struck Ed Sullivan compared Castro to George Washington."

Every student shook their heads in amazement, as if the professor was lecturing in his underwear. Their eyes never left Hunter's.

With a hint of sarcasm, Hunter said, "After Castro was swept into power, there was a substantial number of Americans who earnestly believed that the little strip of land 90 miles off the coast of Key West had become a more diverse, equitable, and more *wonderful* place than the United States. It shouldn't be a surprise that these people were lefties, and they were so eager to experience the promised utopia of Havana that they committed this string of spectacular hijackings in order to reach Cuba. Muslims make the trek to Mecca; lefties make the trip to Moscow or Havana—it's closer! For the atheistic left, I think you can say Havana is still viewed as something of the promised land."

Hunter selected another slide. Some of the students vaguely recognized the man in the photograph. "One of those who was so bewitched by Castro was...*Lee Harvey Oswald*, the assassinator of President Kennedy. Here he is in New Orleans handing out pro-Castro literature—what does that pamphlet say? 'Hands Off Cuba.' Those leaflets weren't directed to the Kremlin. Let's say that over time all but the most hardened liberals would come to rue their naiveté with respect to Castro and Cuba. In this very special case, some who were enthralled with the communist experience, defied the moratorium on flying to Havana and hijacked airplanes to Cuba, thinking they would be welcomed with open arms. Commie birds of a feather and all that. These were not terrorists but cheap lazy bastards; they were real criminals who hijacked airplanes to get to Havana or get away from the police. They didn't want to blow up the airplane or kill those inside; they just wanted a free ride to the island's socialist paradise. Granted, some had political motivations, but they were largely non-violent; they just wanted to get away from America and go to Cuba. They claimed asylum, a political term, but they too were just too dumb to realize Castro would be suspicious of any American who showed up at the airport without a good reason, and asylum wasn't a good enough reason. Why was that?"

A student from the rear of the classroom offered, "Castro was afraid the hijackers were CIA plants sent to kill him?"

Hunter nodded. "Or to destabilize the new Cuban society. He didn't know if they were simply malcontents, the mentally ill that Kennedy wanted to get rid of, or just hardened criminals. So it should be no surprise Castro treated the vast majority of the hijackers as security risks. Only a few people were celebrated as political fugitives. The hi-profile and communist Angela Davis didn't hijack an aircraft but was a celebrated visitor in Cuba."

"Let me finish this dogleg of the discussion; I think it is relevant. I think it is safe to say most of the hijackers assumed that amazing things awaited them in Cuba, that the Cubans would embrace them, hail them as comrades-in-arms, and train them to spread the communist revolution to every corner of the globe. Imagine their surprise when they were strip-searched and interrogated by Castro's secret police. Instead of being free of a decadent society obsessed with money, war, and race, they were trucked to south Havana and tossed into isolation rooms in something that was less of a political prison and more of a squalid dormitory. It wasn't as bad as the Hanoi Hilton. The hijackers were bullied and tortured by armed guards, forced to witness the executions of political dissidents, and found the food less than edible. It wasn't the paradise they had envisioned. It didn't take long for the majority of these hijackers, especially the African-American hijackers, to realize that Castro and his communism weren't the promised land."

"However, the murderous bastards of September 11th—from bin Laden to Mohamed Atta—were in it for other political reasons. Upheaval. Political punishment and payback. Bolsheviks interested in bringing down America. They were terrorists who embraced premeditated murder and mass civilian casualties to achieve their political goals. They took hijacking to a new art form; they didn't bomb airplanes out of the sky like Flight 103, the PanAm jet over Lockerbie, they turned airplanes into bombs and changed the complete dynamic of aviation terrorism. Can we agree on that?"

Heads nodded throughout the class. Hunter continued, "So what is terrorism but intimidation or violence to achieve political gain? We are going to look at terrorism in the aviation industry through the eyes of politics, not organized or transnational crime. We will not conflate the previously discussed criminal activity with terrorism. But we will talk about methods and motives."

Hunter shook a computer mouse and loaded a new set of slides. Once a picture of the 9/11 mastermind filled the screen, he said, "I said terrorism is intimidation or violence to achieve political gain. In the world of aviation terrorism, you'll be hard pressed to find an example of terrorism that is not ascribed to a category of political types—*radicals.* There are a couple hundred examples of aviation terrorism and virtually every one of them is attributed to radicals. Specifically, Islamic radicals. What is a radical? Allow me to define a radical as those people who relate to or advocate for fundamental, transformative, or revolutionary changes in current practices, conditions, or institutions. Ergo, radical Islamists use political Islam to achieve revolutionary change or political gains. And unlike the clowns that ran to communist Cuba thinking they would be warmly embraced, these bastards kill on an unprecedented scale. Instead of following the money—as in Dan Cooper—and instead of following the path to leftist utopia, when dealing with terrorists, follow the blood."

The other major in the class raised her hand and asked, "Are you saying all intimidation and violence is terrorism when it's committed by a radical Islamic jihadi yelling *Allahu Akbar*?"

"When they're mowing down kids at a movie theater while screaming *Allahu Akbar*, it's not workplace violence, no matter what the former democratic administration would like you to believe. It's mass murder of civilians. You have to get the nuances and distinctions *correct*. There you go, *talking politics*. Trying to get me into trouble." Hunter finished with a grin. "So let me be clear, your average Jordanian, Kuwaiti or Saudi Air Force F-16 pilot may be a follower of Mohammad, but they are not lunatics or radicals. They are not the problem. They are like you and me; they'll drop a bomb on al-Qaeda's ass or any of the ISIS' heads any day of the week and not think anything of it as long as they are serving their emir, king, or president. They know they have terrorists and that that Islam needs a reformation, like the Protestant Reformation in 16th century Europe. They are fighting a religious war within. They are fighting their indigenous terrorists more than we are. And to a lesser degree, we have the same problem in this country; we have our own radicals who bomb police stations, ambush policemen, assassinate presidents, and would drop a bomb on our heads without any *Allahu Akbar* if they could. But we call them... *Liberals. Democrats.* But that's another story for another day. The bottom line, these...these people are...how about, *they're just not on our side?*"

Hunter didn't want to say Democrats and Liberals so early in the class to describe the American radicals committed to violence. His students would either handle it or complain and have him booted from the school. He surmised these students wouldn't issue a formal complaint against him. But they had just started class. There'd be plenty of time for that.

The class was confused by Hunter's last statement, but he wouldn't let them dwell on actual or hidden meanings. He continued, "That was a good question, we're trying to make a distinction. I dare say your typical Islamic terrorist is the most aggrieved namby-pamby, pantywaist on the planet, much like the *liberals* in our country. They blame anyone and everyone for their troubles, real or imaginary. You can spin a wheel of fortune and come up with a new reason why Americans are to be blamed for something egregious, or need to be killed, or why Western aircraft need to be attacked. Many incidents of Muslim malfeasance are ascribed to infidels, in keeping with the general tendency of Islamic supremacists to blame everyone but themselves for their own wrongdoing."

The room was silent, perfectly silent. No demonstrable yawning. No rustling of papers on desks. No shuffling of flying boots under tables. Hunter had their attention.

"Bin Laden blamed America because U.S. forces were in Saudi Arabia, the land of the holy shrines, and he sent 19 jihadis to our country to kill 3,000 of our compatriots. Civilians. The photogenic Islamic rage boy screamed 'Death to America' in front of every camera ever pointed at him. What is our problem? The answer—whatever grievance was the flavor of the week. The point here is that if you are looking for motive on why the U.S and our allies are targeted and attacked, we're now going to have to get down and dirty and dive into the cesspool of world politics. Remember, what is terrorism but intimidation or violence to achieve political gain?"

Professor Hunter took his students down several paths of discussion. Beginning with the most recent aircraft incident—the Indonesian Sky Link Flight 7070—he compared and contrasted other Islamic air carriers that had an airliner that unexpectedly "fell from the sky" and how the Sky Link flight was similar to the early stages of the EgyptAir Flight 990 accident. A check of the time and Hunter said, "I think it's time to call it an evening. When we come back next week, we'll discuss coincidences and maybe use this little exercise to talk about the Concorde mishap."

From the back of the room, "Wasn't that an accident?"

"That's what the NTSB said about Flight 800 too. Do you really think a strip of metal from a Continental jet knocked down Flight 4590?"

The images of the Air France Concorde on fire as it lifted off from the Charles de Gaulle Airport had been seared into every pilot's cerebral cortex. It was the only fatal Concorde accident during its 27-year operational history. An extensive investigation concluded a titanium strip from the previous departing jet likely punctured a tire and sent a pressure shockwave rupturing the Concorde's number five fuel tank. The case was open and shut, until Hunter suggested otherwise.

"Muslims, er, terrorists were responsible for that too?" It was an awkwardly phrased and politically incorrect question, but Major Minor was intrigued. The other two dozen students were also. Some students believed the instructor wouldn't re-engage the subject and began to stand up. It was time to go.

Hunter threw up his hands in feigned exasperation and said, "This is the aviation terrorism course. Why else would we talk about it?" Then as an afterthought he added, wagging his finger, "And, don't get me started on the Hindenburg!" He looked around the class and saw that no one was moving. He'd have to kick them out.

"I was thinking of giving you some homework, but if you want to stay and talk Concorde or the Hindenburg, I suppose we can stay a few more hours and you can turn in a ten-page report on my lecture." Hunter's students took the threat seriously and vanished in a flash, leaving stale air and the echoes of flight boots pounding the floor tile on their way out the door.

CHAPTER TWENTY

2000 July 15, 2014
Clarksburg, West Virginia

Special Agent in Charge Hunter Louise Papp stood at the window of her office at the National Crime Information Center. She rubbed her eyes and yawned like a lioness satiated after a kill and ready for a nap. It had been a very long day. She was ready to go home, kick off her heels, fix a glass of wine, and throw something frozen in the microwave for dinner. Her tummy rumbled for it was empty and needed filling. She'd didn't want to think about being back in the office in ten hours just to start all over again. Maybe tomorrow she'd be able to go to the gym. Slip into the spa and enjoy the sauna. Maybe. More likely, it would be another evening that she would miss her favorite show on television. A glance at her Seiko indicated *he was late*, but she'd give the Watch Supervisor a few more minutes before she gave up, shut off the lights, and went home. Reflected in the picture window, she shook her head again in utter disbelief at what she had found in the database. *I was just thinking of him!* What did it mean? Probably nothing, but this one was different.

The possibility that it was all a coincidence just didn't measure up. Not all coincidences are created equal. This coincidence was not a simple coincidence. *I was thinking of him!* Carl Jung called it "synchronicity." She saw her name in the database, as if some unknown hand had masked the other names on the spreadsheet, and her eyes were immediately drawn to the lone name. *Her name.* Hunter. Several times. Hunter wasn't that common for a first or last name. The first entry didn't even elicit a smile, but the second and third entries brought concern to her face.

They had been students at the Naval War College. He was in the senior class, she in the junior. From time to time, she would get a glimpse of him between classes or during gatherings in the auditorium—the name of which escaped her but it would come. The Air Force, Navy, and the FBI named buildings and rooms after their heroes. Then she remembered. She would sit in the back of the McCarty Little Hall Auditorium, safely ensconced in the middle third with hundreds of other students all around her for some kind of protection, just like fifth graders at assembly trying to avoid the teacher's pets with cooties in the front row. But he would sit in the corner seat on the front row with the class president, a huge and muscular African American. A Navy SEAL. Always just the two of them. Side by side. Kind of a salt and pepper pair, only reverse. He would usually wear a black suit, the SEAL in a sparkling white uniform. It always struck her that the two men were an odd couple. So different by their outward appearance. But there was something that bonded the two men. Everyone knew it; they could see it. At every assembly or mass lecture, hundreds of eyes were naturally drawn to the two men on the front row. No one knew why or what it could be, and no one had the temerity to ask.

Duncan Hunter. He was frequently the topic of discussion of some group. It was well known that he was an Air Force civilian as well as an adjunct college professor, and now he was a student. That made little sense. The CIA, NRO, NIMA, and NSA students in the junior class remarked that there was something extremely odd about him; no one believed he was just a civil servant like his student ID indicated. It wasn't because he dragged an old Corvette racecar on a trailer behind his truck. And it wasn't because he lived in one of the few suites on the Navy base set aside for visiting admirals. One of the civilian students had a friend run a background check on him. It was mind-blowing. Hunter had *all* the top *CIA* tickets, Top Secret clearances, even Cat One Yankee White access—direct access to the President. Why and how could an *Air Force civilian*—at *the Naval War College*—have those? He always met with the SEAL, in the library, in the SCIF. It didn't make any sense then. More questions than answers, even ten years later.

Then there were the women. Hunter was the fantasy of most of the female student population at the Naval War College, at least those that weren't lesbians. Papp jumped in the race trying to chase him a little, throw him a smile, or toss a comment at him when in the cafeteria, like the other military officers and government civilians in skirts. He intimidated her a little. Maybe a lot. Stories circulated he might have dined with some of the women, but no one would admit anything, not even a movie or a group dinner. Tongues would have wagged. But he played some sport, racquetball. She would never forget his great, chiseled legs under short nylon black shorts that accentuated his thighs.

She also remembered the night he broke her heart. He walked into the Red Parrot restaurant in downtown Newport with a striking dark haired woman on his arm. He hadn't even noticed her standing there outside in the cold without reservations, waiting to get in. They drove up in an elegant old white car. With a chauffeur. The woman wore a skin-tight white dress that underscored her every curve; she was the most stunning creature the people inside and outside the restaurant had ever seen. And she had his complete attention. Hunter Louise Papp, a farm girl from Iowa in jeans and trainers couldn't compete with that. *Why was I thinking of him and why is his name on this spreadsheet multiple times?*

On the document before her listed three dead Duncan Hunters, all killed within the last week. One murder could be considered odd—a random occurrence. Two was a coincidence, maybe the beginning of a correlation. But, three...*three was a trend*. How could three Duncan Hunters die in three different cities? Inside of a week? The odds were one to infinity. Houston, Cleveland, Dallas. White males, 50-60 years of age, former military men. Suspicious deaths. She recalled he was from Texas. Big black four-wheel drive truck with Texas tags. Ran around the base in little black shorts and without a shirt during the summer. Played racquetball. Her chest heaved a little at the old thought. He wore black suits with red power ties. Now she remembered. A young congressman with the same name was on television from time to time. How could she forget?

She asked for photographs. Autopsy reports. Passport pictures. In a moment of inspiration, she asked the Watch Supervisor for a readout of all Duncan Hunters in JPAS, the Joint Personnel Adjudication System, to determine addresses and clearances. Even though he had crushed her dreams, she hoped the information would point to another Hunter, and that it was all a simple coincidence. No synchronicity. She hoped he wasn't dead.

Ten more minutes passed. It was too late; the confirmations would wait until tomorrow. Special Agent in Charge Papp decided the information wasn't coming, pulled keys out of her purse, and headed out of the office. Before she could take more than two steps, Special Agent Ray Nail, the evening Watch Supervisor, lightly knocked on the doorframe and entered.

The spry, thin man with thinning hair said, "We've got vitals on the three men you requested. I made copies as some new information came across the wire—sorry it took so long." He handed over a half a ream of paper separated by four colored cards.

She slipped her keys back into her purse. "Anything interesting?" She thumbed through the stack of photographs, hoping to find strangers looking back at her. Dallas case file was first, then Houston, and finally Cleveland. Chronological order. She didn't want to see what was behind the card. Fear and curiosity temporarily paralyzed her. She could hardly believe she was acting this way.

"Nothing. No priors on any of them. No connections to organized crime. First blush—they are random. Besides the name, the only commonality is there are no suspects. Other than that, no discernable pattern." He paused as his boss struggled to lift the red card of the autopsy photograph of the man from Dallas. Her facial emotion transitioned from fear to concern to indifference to relief. He waited for her next missive.

She returned the photograph to the stack. "Anything in JPAS?" she asked.

He knew where this would lead; the new head of the National Criminal Information Center was like all of the other supervisors he had had. When it came to jumping into a sea of crime data, there was a logical, thoughtful process and jumping over several steps would rarely yield the desired results. The program didn't work that way. It wasn't their job to troubleshoot crime data. His job was to see she didn't do something silly or unprofessional, like jump on a speeding train with no tracks. He leaned over the stack of papers and pulled out a single sheet of paper. He read, "The only Duncan Hunters in that particular database are two congressmen from California, the dad's retired, and one in, umm, Fredericksburg, Texas. Now, *that lad* has clearances and accesses out the wazoo. Navy Intel. CIA. TS/SCI. Staff Approvals. Polygraphs. Plus an active Level One Yankee White; that's direct access to the White House. I had no idea what that was. *I had to look it up!*" Nail handed her another document. "I also retrieved his passport."

The new Duncan Hunter file had created the most excitement the National Crime Information Center (NCIC) had seen in years. It was a boring place that good agents tried to avoid like the plague. Worn out agents were sent there to finish out their careers, like the unwanted dolls and games that were sent to the Island of Misfit Toys. They were on the ROAD—Retired on Active Duty. Special Agent Papp had been hand-selected for the posting and had been charged to turn the problematic NCIC program around. Only a transfusion of fresh blood would bring the NCIC back from the dead. The new Hunter file breathed life into some of the old warhorses. There was *interest*. Some began to look at criminal data history. They queried the database for Duncans and Hunters, and then for the miscued Hunter Duncan. Found two more. Detroit and Los Angeles.

Using national criminal data reports, Papp had found the first threads of evidence and the connective tissue to determine if Islamic terrorists were targeting some men with the same name or some combination thereof. A man named Duncan Hunter was someone special inside the Intelligence Community and it was more than likely that he was in great danger. In seconds, she had transitioned from information analysis to running an interdiction operation. Maybe she wasn't sent to West Virginia as punishment after all.

A smile crossed her face as she accepted the enlarged facsimile of a tourist passport photograph. She didn't want to be caught looking at his picture too long. He was still very good looking. And his full name was Drew Duncan Hunter. She learned something new.

Now the information made sense. The group at the war college was right; he was different. Probably the reason he wouldn't let anyone get too close to him. He held one of the very special top-level clearances at the Agency. Higher than top secret. Every access on the planet. Access to the White House. But it still didn't answer the question why Duncan Hunters across America were getting killed.

Ray Nail could see it was time to provide the additional information, hot off the presses. "Ma'am, there's been two others. Duncan Hunters. A couple of minutes ago. Chicago and New York. Same MO. Apparently random but suspicious. NYPD has a suspect in custody. Apparently, the perp reacted to social media posts specifically demanding an attack against the man."

Her eyes widened and her brows begged for more information. He handed her another sheet of paper. He summarized as she read the perpetrator's statistics. "Male. Muslim. 35. Claimed there is a million dollar *fatwa* on Duncan Hunter. *Allahu Akbar* and all that crap." Her jaw dropped in disbelief. He pointed to the stack of papers. "I think those congressmen may not be the target; my money is on the guy with the clearances. It's probably a case the bad guys don't know exactly, where he is, so they're trying to take out all of potential candidates. I think it is more likely that the Texan is somehow on the ayatollah's shit list."

She looked up in disbelief. It was all clear to her now. Her mind raced to another idea. After several seconds of coming to grips with the different loci of the problem, she said, "His cover's been blown."

Nail said, "That's a big 10-4." Polite police lingo for "No shit, Sherlock."

She asked, "Does the CIA know?"

"Director Papp, we're the national clearinghouse for criminal information. We push info to the law enforcement agencies when they request it. The FBI deals with the domestic criminal, the CIA deals with foreign enemies." He smiled in newfound respect for his boss. "And, I don't know how you did it. That was pretty impressive ma'am. We're on new ground here. I've been here a long time, but I personally don't know anyone over there and wouldn't know who to call if I did. Anytime we had something weird, previous directors would call the Director of Operations at Quantico. Maybe he has a hot line to Headquarters or Langley or a contact. We have to have a liaison officer over there. I read somewhere there's at least a dozen of our guys at the National Counter Terrorism Center."

"Thanks, Nail. I'll make a few calls."

"In case you plan on being here for a while, I put on a fresh pot of coffee. I also ordered a couple of pizzas." Ray Nail smiled at her and looked at her in a new light. She was a good-looking woman with a body she took care of and a face that didn't require makeup in order to be easy on the eyes. Papp was all business; she wasn't the type who might be interested in extracurricular activities. No beers at the college bars. No lunches at the Appleby's. She kept her distance from the male agents and didn't socialize after hours, which only fostered rumors of her sexual preferences.

Special Agent in Charge Papp said, "You're a god, Ray. That was simply fantastic. This has just gotten interesting. Thanks for all your help. Ray, since this is likely a CIA issue, this information doesn't need to be disseminated any further. Our eyes only, for now. And I can get my own coffee."

"No, no. I'll bring it." He nodded, pushed away from her desk, and left the room.

She forgot about going home. She pulled the passport photograph from the stack of papers. Like years earlier, thoughts of him again excited her, but this time it was to warn him that he was in mortal danger. If he wasn't already dead. She wouldn't leave until she was convinced someone somewhere would sound the alarm. She had emails to send and calls to make to FBI Headquarters. If Islamic terrorists were indeed after him, maybe she could warn him.

She picked up his passport photograph. It had been a long time ago. Maybe it was silly, but if she were able to warn him or save his life, maybe he'd finally look at her the way he did that tart, that woman in white. If he hadn't already married her.

· · · · ·

The Marine "white top" helicopter landed atop the Secret Service Headquarters building. Nazy Cunningham stepped out and was greeted by a posse of Secret Service Special Agents, the Deputy Director, and the Director of Secret Service. As the Director led her off the roof, the helicopter lifted off and followed the "course rules," the approved flight plan for negotiating in and around the restricted space of the White House as it returned to Anacostia.

Tall and quite thin, the Director stood out from the other Special Agents who were shorter and more muscular. He towered over the National Counter Terrorism Director even now in her stiletto heels. The walk to his office was short. He dismissed the others, leaving him alone with the CIA executive.

Nazy thanked him for seeing her on short notice. He invited her to sit, but she articulated that she knew he was busy and she wouldn't take up much of his time. She had a question and hoped he would be able to help her.

"I cannot imagine what you need from me."

She told him. Five words.

He pursed his lips; they contorted as if he had taken bite out of a lemon. Momentarily, he was at a loss for words. An hour ago he had finished his workout in the gym. He had remarked to his deputy who was running on the treadmill next to him that "It's unusually quiet. It's times like this when you know the shit is about to hit the fan." And then she came into his life, flying to the rooftop of his building like a new age leggier and sexier Mary Poppins. He had known about her, had seen her several times coming from the Oval Office after delivering the President's Daily Brief (PDB). There was a running joke within the Secret Service about the former president's reluctance to meet with any CIA intelligence officer to receive the PDB. And now, the new president and the new CIA Director had chosen Miss Cunningham to brief the PDB, and they thought it likely wasn't for her speaking skills. The Secret Service Director had never spoken to her, had never met her. He had clandestinely ogled her from afar. But now that he heard that British accent of hers, he was also charmed.

She wanted him to divulge a secret entrusted to the Secret Service. He strained to keep his eyes off her bosom so he stared at her face. She wanted him to violate the special trust and confidence of the Secret Service? He was conflicted.

After the assassination of President William McKinley, Congress directed the Secret Service to protect the President of the United States. Like the CIA, the Secret Service was entrusted with safeguarding the most secret of secrets. Special Agents swore to uphold their oath not to divulge any of the information they may come in contact with in the service of protecting the President, his family, and certain other political executives. No exceptions.

A classified CIA file had been released to the public. It outlined the case that the former president was a fraud, a criminal. A likely terrorist mole. Articles of Impeachment were drawn up in Congress. But the Department of Justice was filled to the rafters with leftist and radical civil liberties lawyers who refused to investigate the released documents. They were more interested in the traitorous leaker.

The new Republican President fired them all.

Mazibuike resigned from office and returned to his home state. He had dismissed his personal security detail immediately upon landing in Hawaii. No Special Agent countermanded the order that wherever the President, current or former, may go they were there to ensure his safety. The Secret Service allowed the disgraced President to disembark from Air Force One and board a business jet by himself. Although President Mazibuike had resigned from office, the Secret Service still had an obligation, an oath to never disclose any information on any president, current or former. It was what put the "special" in special trust and confidence.

Maxim Mohammad Mazibuike was an illegitimate president. I never took an oath to protect an illegitimate president. He crossed the Rubicon and told her what she wanted. "Miss Cunningham, if you like I can provide his file. I can send it over to your office later today."

Nazy Cunningham shook the Director's hand and thanked him for his help.

He escorted her out of his office to the basement where a Secret Service driver would take her to CIA Headquarters. He leaned in and admonished the driver, "Hey Sport, try and keep your eyes on the friggin' road."

CHAPTER TWENTY-ONE

0430 July 16, 2014
Fredericksburg, Texas

Three miles north of town on Country Road 965, an old Chevy pickup slowed, left the two-lane asphalt, and pulled onto the shoulder. Headlights illuminated yucca and mesquite and an ancient barbed wire fence strung across a dry creek bed, but no coyote or whitetail. The driver killed the engine and the lights, and slipped out of the truck. As he scanned his surroundings and listened to the sounds of the night and a cooling engine, he donned a faded desert camouflage jacket and a hat. He removed a hunting rifle from a canvas gun case from behind the seat. He loaded the Winchester with a single cartridge and put a handful of bullets in a pocket. He scanned the road north and south. Nothing. He cut three double-twist galvanized barbed wires, starting with the top wire and working his way down, and then pushed the drooping wires to the back of the fencepost.

He lowered the tailgate and withdrew two heavy boards from under a four-wheeler. A minute later, he drove the off-road vehicle out of the pickup and onto the gravel of the shoulder. In one motion he slipped the rifle into a leather gun case between the handlebars, steered the ATV through the opening in the fence, and headed for a rocky outcropping several hundred yards away.

After an hour of slow crawling over rocks and avoiding a dozen varieties of cactus, he located the perfect blind. He shut off the machine, shouldered the rifle, and climbed to the top of the hill. Three buildings lay five hundred yards away. The Milky Way filled the clear sky as he waited for his quarry.

Before the sun rose, the houses came alive as a shadow of a man jogged away from the largest of the three structures. The kitchen lights burned bright in the riflescope as a plump woman with long dark hair worked over a stovetop, handling skillets and a coffee pot before setting a table on the back patio of the largest of the houses. A husky, black haired, bow-legged man entered a barn made of corrugated steel situated between the two houses. He placed crosshairs on the woman's chest to gauge the distance. She was not the one he was waiting for.

•   •   •   •   •

After her morning workout and shower, Nazy Cunningham entered her office and fired up her computer. She had received a cryptic email from the FBI's deputy director of operations on her government-issued BlackBerry. He had broadcast to her and others in the CIA only the unclassified subject line: One of yours may be targeted. The FBI hadn't called the CIA operations center. There was no sense of urgency. They sent an email. She was infuriated that she would have to wait until she came to work to read the classified message. What did Duncan always say about the FBI? *They're not on our side.*

She found and opened the message and read the bullet sentences: Multiple individuals with the same name have been killed across the U.S. in the last week. NYPD has a suspect in custody claiming the individual is the subject of a nationwide $1M *fatwa.* Apparently, a member of your organization has the same name.

When she read the name at the bottom of the email Nazy howled in horror and immediately dialed his number.

•   •   •   •   •

The man in camouflage flicked off the safety and checked the wind direction and speed by the movement of the American flag flying in the compound. He steadied the Winchester 300 Magnum but couldn't sight in on his target as the sun first peeked over the horizon. The man was moving too fast, too sporadically to draw a bead.

The man, in running shorts and jogging shoes entered the kitchen, conversed with the woman, then meandered out onto the patio through the French doors. He held a large bottle of water and a towel in one hand, and a cellphone and a tiny dark device in the other. The target took a seat and toweled his face

The man pulled away from the riflescope to check his surroundings one last time. Sensing he was clear he regained the sight picture of the man on the patio and placed his finger on the trigger.

· · · · ·

Duncan Hunter spilled chilled water down his throat as Theresa Yazzie served him *huevos rancheros*, juice, and coffee. As she left, he noticed he had several missed calls from Nazy. He squeezed the earpiece into his wet ear and pushed the number 1 speed dial to call his number one girl.

· · · · ·

The wind had freshened and deflected the barrel slightly. The man held his eye away from the riflescope just enough to see the target settle in for some breakfast and make some motions to indicate he was going to make a cell phone call. Within a few seconds, he achieved the perfect sight picture. The crosshairs remained rock-solid on the target's glabella, the area between the eyebrows and above the nose. He squeezed the trigger.

· · · · ·

Immediately after wedging the Bluetooth accessory into his ear, Hunter felt the earpiece start to shoot out of his sweaty ear. He turned quickly to grab the arcing earpiece with one hand while holding the BlackBerry with the other as the unmistakable supersonic crack of a bullet snapped by his ear.

· · · · ·

The recoil of the Magnum disturbed the view in the scope. When the rifle returned to its natural aiming point, the chair of the patio table was empty, and his quarry was nowhere to be seen. He searched for the body on the deck and for secondary indications of an impact—blood and brain matter should have covered the glass and logs behind the tiny table. But there wasn't human debris splattered against the house. When he saw the bullet hole on one of the glass panels of the French doors, he knew he had missed. He chambered another round and scanned the house for any sign of the target. He cursed himself and resolved he could still shoot through the windows if the target showed himself. He didn't have much time to wait. The police would likely be on the way.

. . . . .

Nazy Cunningham burst into the Director of Central Intelligence's office with the news from the FBI. As she dashed through the door, she yelled "Duncan's the target of a *fatwa!* The FBI identified eight Duncan Hunters—*dead*—across the country. Greg, I cannot get him on his BlackBerry! He's usually running this time of the morning." She stopped and placed her hands on the front of his desk and leaned over. Her body language and her eyes pleaded for help. Her ruby-red zipper-dress strained every stitch.

At the first sight of her, he unconsciously turned away to shield his eyes from her beauty. She had one of those faces that could make a man forget what he was doing. When Duncan Hunter first saw her he was instantly mesmerized, forgot what he was doing on a racquetball court, flipped over and landed on his back. Lynche knew he mustn't look into the valley of cleavage hovering over his desk lest he do something equally stupid. His eyes opened to meet hers as he tried to process what she had said.

He was used to dead monkeys being thrown in the middle of his desk. This was the first time he didn't throw it back into the face of a subordinate and tell them they needed to fix the problem themselves or give him a couple of options in order to make an informed decision. But this one was cut and dry. He waved at Nazy to sit down, to relax, as he called his former business partner.

. . . . .

On all fours Hunter raced away from the table and ran like a greyhound along the deck that surrounded the house until he got to the front of the building. He burst through the front door and screamed at Theresa to get on the floor and come to him in the living room. Hunter was certain he was the target and not his hired help but she couldn't remain in the line of fire. He was careful not to put any daylight between him and the suspected location of the sniper as he went back out to the corner of the house. He stood up, jammed fingers in his mouth, and whistled. When Carlos Yazzie moved to the doorway of the barn-like garage, Duncan yelled at him to bring the Hummer to the front steps.

Theresa's arms and legs flailed about; she wasn't used to crawling on her belly. She moved more like a turtle chasing a worm than a women trying to escape a house fire. Back on hands and knees, he scurried to her, gripped her hand, and pulled her toward the hallway like a lifeguard struggling to rescue a person against a murderous rip current. Once the shaken woman had made it to the safety of the log-lined hallway, he helped her up and pushed her into his bedroom. He entered his closet, opened the latch to an underground safe room, and led her down the stairs. He handed her his BlackBerry and told her not to open the hatch unless she heard either his or Carlos' voice.

Inside the safe room along a bank of tables, sat two large computer monitors with 24-hour closed circuit television camera feeds that were so sensitive a person could at 200 yards tell the difference between a dog and a coyote, a cat and a raccoon. Surrounding the ranch house were thermal-imaging cameras that could detect heat sources in the distance and in the undergrowth near the compound. Body heat was the one thing an intruder couldn't hide. Hunter glanced at the two monitors, found the tiny humanoid heat source climbing from the distant rock outcropping, and slammed his fist on the table. He cursed and spun around.

The safe room was bullet, gas and bombproof and had its own food and water, medical supplies and communications, and an impregnable supply of fresh air. And then there were the weapons safes. Hunter opened a pair of gun safes and removed several weapons, magazines and binoculars. Then he raced up the stairs, lowered the trapdoor, and ran out of the house. The hunt was on.

·   ·   ·   ·   ·

The ambush he had carefully set had been for naught. He had failed. Now he had to escape. He extricated himself from the hide, climbed down from boulders, and quickly got onto the four-wheeler. He tossed the rifle in the scabbard, started the ATV, and drove off as fast as he could.

. . . . .

Hunter exchanged places with his ranch foreman and drove the six-wheeled black vehicle around the ranch house and down an old rutted path which paralleled a lengthy stretch of hills and rock outcroppings. The three-axle, off-road Hummer6 was an updated version of the Mercedes-Benz W31staff car, extended and covered, but protected against armor-piercing ammunition.

Using his binoculars, Carlos Yazzie had difficulty locating a human in the rocks as their vehicle bumped and bounced over the uneven and rough terrain. The effect was like riding a pogo stick in a swaying boxcar. When Yazzie noticed a dust cloud off in the distance, he glassed the source of the mini dust storm between bumps and found a man atop a small all-terrain vehicle. "Tally ho, Captain!" he shouted over the roaring of the big block motor. "One man. Dead ahead," as he pointed to the billowing dust cloud.

. . . . .

Early morning noise carried easily over the flats, even over the muffled engine of the ATV. When the man in camouflage heard another vehicle behind him, he stopped to see if he was actually being pursued. He turned in the saddle to see a dark truck coming his way, about two football fields away. It wasn't supposed to be like this. Who in their right mind would confront a man with a rifle? Maybe he would have another chance to redeem himself if the target was coming to him. Such an arrogant infidel. Now he got anxious. He unsheathed the rifle and took aim at the driver side windshield. He trembled slightly and the crosshairs of the scope wandered across the bouncing windscreen. He tried to time his trigger squeeze to send a round to the target in the truck.

. . . . .

The sound was deafening when the bullet smacked the two-inch thick polycarbonate windshield. The bullet hit left of center but did not pass through the layers of anti-ballistic materials. The unintended consequence of the bullet-proof glass absorbing the energy of the round was that when the bullet hit the glass, the point of impact turned opaque. Hunter was thankful the windshield stopped the rifle bullet. It motivated him to mash the gas pedal to close the distance between him and the shooter. With his part of the windshield unusable, he leaned heavily across the console to look out of Carlos' clear windscreen. Then they heard another bullet slam into the front of the truck. Hunter didn't let up on the gas pedal as he aimed the Hummer at the man shooting at him.

· · · · ·

Theresa Yazzie walked in circles in the spacious underground room, unable to comprehend what was happening to her as she worried about her Carlos and Duncan. She stopped at the CCTV monitors as Hunter had done, then jumped and nearly tossed the little black device into the air when Duncan's BlackBerry rang and vibrated in her hand. When she regained control of the apparatus, she pushed a green button and answered.

Nazy and Lynche were surprised to hear the housekeeper answer Duncan's cell phone. That had never happened before. Nazy felt a chill course through her body. She could think of only one reason Duncan's housekeeper would be answering his phone, and that was he was dead. Nazy nearly fainted. Lynche snapped his fingers at Nazy to get her attention. He immediately spoke through the speakerphone. "Theresa, this is Greg—where's Duncan?"

"Mr. Duncan is with my Carlos, I think someone…someone try to shoot at Mr. Duncan." Nazy was immediately beside herself with grief and anxiety. She slapped her mouth closed with her hand.

"Theresa, where are you?" asked Lynche.

"I'm in the safe room, Mister Greg. Mr. Duncan told me not to let anyone in unless it is him or my Carlos."

Lynched punched a button to mute the caller and said, "See, he's ok. He'll be fine. I'll bet you he's after the guy that tried to shoot at him. There's nothing worse than having a pissed off Marine on your ass."

Nazy wasn't amused, but she recovered her composure, reached across the desk, and unmuted the telephone. "Theresa, you stay there until Duncan returns, and please have him call me at my office. Can you do that?"

"I'm so worried, Miss Nazy."

"I know you are Theresa, but Duncan and Carlos know how to take care of themselves. They'll be ok and should be back soon. Please have him call me."

"Ok, Miss Nazy." Theresa Yazzie didn't want to terminate the conversation. Just having someone to talk to, even 2,000 miles away was comforting. She was very afraid but did as she was asked. "Ok, Miss Nazy. I will."

Lynche and Nazy took turns. "Bye, Theresa. We'll talk with you later." Lynched lifted the receiver to break the connection and returned it to its cradle. Lynche had solved the dead monkey problem. He had determined Hunter was ok, and he hadn't peeked down Nazy's dress, but he had more pressing work to do. Yet, Nazy wasn't leaving. She had something else on her mind.

She said, "What are we going to do? There's a *fatwa* on Duncan. His cover is blown." Nazy pleaded for some direction, some guidance. Greg was supposed to be concerned.

He unconsciously scratched his chin as she spoke, keeping his eyes out of trouble and allowing his brain to start functioning again on Duncan Hunter's problem. He tapped his fingers on the desk. He looked down at the confusion of files, memoranda, papers, files, and reports. After several uneasy seconds, he said, "How does a terrorist know to go after Duncan at his house when he is off the grid? This is worse than I thought. We'll have to kill him."

Nazy's emotions were being flipped and jerked around like dog thrashing a bone. She was horrified. *"Who? What?"* Was he advocating killing her husband as if he were an irritation, a bug?

Lynche realized from her mortified facial expression that he was speaking figuratively and she was thinking literally. "Nazy, we need to kill off the Duncan Hunter *persona*, give him a new identity. Take the pressure off him. Like we did when you entered this place. I have an idea."

Visibly relieved, she asked, "What are you thinking?" She nervously fingered the zipper at the top of her dress.

Lynche smiled conspiratorially.

CHAPTER TWENTY-TWO

0600 July 16, 2014
Fredericksburg, Texas

The man on the ATV couldn't outrun the big black truck but began to swerve away to avoid being run over. Hunter ignored the feint and timed the intercept perfectly. The collision was sudden, rapid, and noisy as the man and machine crumpled against the bumper and disappeared under the Hummer. The sounds of metal and man being pulverized under the heavy vehicle were abrupt and turbulent. As soon as the racket ceased underneath, Hunter crushed the brake pedal with both feet until the six-wheeled vehicle came to a stop. He and Yazzie jumped out of the Hummer with pistols ready to fire and were immediately enveloped in a swirling cloud of dust and dirt. They ran through the haze until they came upon the scattered remains of the man and the little metal machine. The man in shredded camouflage had been decapitated, and most of his limbs looked as if they had been through a meat grinder. It was the most gruesome thing Yazzie had ever seen.

Hunter's adrenaline had peaked from seeing the dead man's parts scattered along the path. He nervously scanned the rocks and the landscape for other threats. After a few seconds, he said, "Carlos, I think this guy was a lone wolf. I'm gonna bury his ass right here. Could you drive back to the garage and get a shovel; I'm going to see where he came from." Hunter kicked a dismembered leg closer to the headless torso and began to search the man's shredded and bloodied pockets.

"Boss, I'll bury him. You cannot do that kind of work yet with your arm. We need to find his vehicle. It has to be close."

"Thanks, Carlos. I find his tracks." Then almost as an afterthought, he said, "You need to let Theresa know it's safe to come out of the safe room. You tell her to start packing. It's not safe here. Hell, it's not safe for any of us anymore. We're leaving."

Yazzie was as shocked as if Hunter had kicked his loyal dog. He nodded and turned toward the Hummer to retrieve a shovel.

Hunter ran down the old path until he found and followed the incoming tracks of the ATV. He located the dead man's pickup on the other side of the rock outcropping, near the county road.

· · · · ·

"They want him dead so we'll kill him. Draft something up for a Memorial Wall ceremony. We'll acknowledge Duncan Hunter died in the service of his country. Give him a star. Get with public affairs for a press release. Schedule a burial at Arlington. Also, we'll need a rent a crowd. I'd like to do this today. I know burial at Arlington may take some time but just having Duncan on the docket...." DCI Lynche let the thought dissolve and then asked Nazy, "Did I miss anything?"

She was stunned. "I don't believe so Director Lynche."

"Nazy, when he calls you please have him call me. I want to tell him what we're doing. I have to tell the President what we're doing, but that can wait."

Nazy nodded once and waited for more direction.

"This may not stop it but it should make the terrorist organizations believe their *fatwa* was successful. Call off the dogs. Then all the other Duncan Hunters of the world can go on their merry way and live life without thinking al-Qaeda or some other nutjob from their local mosque is trying to kill them. And, if we play this correctly, Duncan may be able to retain his identity. Otherwise, we'll have to give him a new one, like Buck Naked or Stanislaw Styvendorvitch; something appropriate."

Nazy beamed at his assessment, plan, and outlook but frowned at his spontaneous humor. Her husband was still in trouble. She turned away and headed out the door.

Embarrassed by his thoughts of how her hips wrestled around in her tight pencil skirt, he said, "God, that woman is going to give me a stroke." He threw his arms up and glanced around his desk. "Okay. No more hypothetical dead monkeys to deal with. Now, what is it that I'm supposed to be doing?"

· · · · ·

Hunter moved the shooter's truck and set it on fire. He repaired the loose barbed wire fence. He and Carlos revisited the burial site of the dead man and his wrecked ATV. They checked the area to determine if the unmarked grave and disturbed earth would withstand the scrutiny of the sheriff's deputy who would surely come to investigate. The old Apache, Carlos Yazzie, knew how to trail game as well as cover his tracks. Hunter couldn't tell where the collision occurred or where Yazzie had buried the shooter.

Theresa and Carlos returned to their home behind the main house. She was grief-stricken and cried like a baby as she slowly packed their belongings. Hunter entered the little house and embraced Theresa. He held her hands as he told her they needed to get away from Texas; that it was no longer safe to stay with him. He apologized for putting their lives in danger but knew it was best they go somewhere where no one knew who they were, a place where they would feel safe and comfortable. He told her if she and Carlos were interested, he had a new house in Wyoming. "It's like the ranch house but much bigger. And it's much colder than here, but the penalty for moving is you can see the Great Tetons whenever you wake up. You don't need to tell me right now. But you and Carlos do need to leave as soon as possible. Whatever you leave behind, I'll have your stuff packed and sent to you."

Theresa dabbed wet eyes. "Are you in trouble, Mister Duncan?"

Hunter smiled, more to assure Theresa the effort to leave was a simple precaution and not the opening salvo of an undeclared war with unnamed terrorists. "Theresa, I don't know if I'm in trouble or not, but I've been expecting something like this, although I never really thought they would find me and attack my house. Us. I cannot take any chances that you and Carlos could be hurt when someone is trying to get to me."

"Where will we go?"

He squeezed her hands and said, "If you don't have a place in mind, I'd say go home to Arizona for a little while. I'll call you later to see if you want to come to Wyoming. There is no way I can run the new house by myself. It's too big. Okay?"

She sobbed, and he reached out to comfort her. She said, "You'll starve without my breakfast every morning." Carlos was amused. Hunter looked at him with empathy and compassion, and winked at him. No one treated his wife the way Duncan treated Theresa; she was more sister than his housekeeper before his accident. They would play their silly games. After he finished several repetitions on the pull-up bar, Theresa would walk out of the house and demanded to know what was wrong with her cooking. "You no like my breakfast? I make *huevos rancheros* just for you! With Julio's salsa!" And he would respond, "Theresa, of course I love your *huevos rancheros*. I'll eat when I get back from my run." She would wait for him to return and serve him a plate right out of the oven. Their relationship could have been an idiotic Seinfeld episode.

After kissing Theresa on the cheek he let her finish packing. Hunter and Carlos returned to the ranch house. They removed several heavy black containers from a vault in the underground safe room. Twenty-four of the smooth black containers remained. They carried two to the dirty and scuffed-up Hummer and one went to the bed of Yazzie's truck. Carlos knew what was inside each case: fifty rolls of fifty $50 American Gold Eagles. 2,500 gold coins; market value about $3,000,000. Carlos tried to refuse the largess but Hunter wouldn't have any of it.

As the men returned to the ranch house, Hunter knew he was forgetting something, something else important that also needed to go. The sense of urgency to get the Yazzies off the property and on the road was clouding his judgment, but he wasn't giving up. With Carlos following, he dashed into each bedroom, the kitchen, and his office hoping something would trigger his memory or he would recognize it when he saw it.

Between rooms he said, "Carlos, you need to go somewhere safe and lay low. I don't think you'll be followed or threatened but you can't take any chances. If something does happen to me, you'll need what's in the box. If I survive this, I'll call you in a week or two when I get settled. I'm blowing out of town for a week. Australia. If you don't hear from me in a month you need to really disappear. New identities and the whole lot. Take care of Theresa and take care of yourself."

When the men returned to the living room, Hunter glanced around and found it. Not the newly acquired Rembrandt. Not the LeRoy Neiman painting Hunter had commissioned after he won a Vintage Grand Touring race in his old yellow Corvette race car, but a six-foot long Apache trailer warbonnet. Carlos had presented the 19th century warrior headdress, with double rows of foot-long white-tipped eagle feathers, ermine trim, and intricate beadwork to Hunter shortly after he came to work for his old boss.

Hunter pointed to the most obvious and dramatic item in the room. "And don't forget to take your warbonnet. I'd hate to come back here, find the house burned down, and then remember we left it."

Yazzie nodded. "Are you going to be okay, Captain?" He still addressed his boss by his Marine Corps rank. Yazzie was emotional, and Hunter thought the old jarhead was going to cry. The emotional ups and down of the morning was taking its toll on both retired Marines. He had been Hunter's right hand man for fifteen years; they took care of each other as brothers. And Carlos could keep a secret. He didn't exactly know what Hunter did for the government, and it didn't matter. In his eyes, Hunter would always be his hero. Theresa credited Duncan for saving Carlos from becoming a washed up drunk and making sure he stayed in the Marine Corps. When Hunter built the ranch, he needed someone he could trust to help him run it. He called Carlos, and the Yazzies left Carrizo Junction and the White Mountain Apache Reservation the same day. They never looked back.

Duncan was too stressed to be emotional, so he saluted Carlos and patted his shoulder. "I can take care of myself, even with this bum hand. Now get that warbonnet off the wall, and you and Theresa get the hell out of here!"

"Aye, aye sir."

. . . . .

With the Yazzies gone and Bill McGee and a crew inbound to the ranch house, Hunter called Nazy in her office. She was out. He then called the Director of Central Intelligence. Lynche answered and kicked everyone but Nazy out of his the office.

Lynche was direct. "I had to kill you to save you. Let's hope it works, at least until we can sort out what the hell is going on."

"I appreciate that, I think. What is going on? Being dead, I'm always the last to know."

"Maverick, at least eight *Duncan Hunters* have been killed across the country. There's a *fatwa* on your ass. An FBI agent from the National Crime Information Center identified the trend, determined that it was someone with tickets who was the likely target, and not some

Congressman or Billy Ray Joe Bob car salesman from Hoboken. It was hard to warn you when you don't carry your phone...."

"You'll have to forgive me. I was being shot at."

"What did you do with the body?"

"No need to know, Director Lynche. My problem, not yours. Sir. What's this you had to kill me to save me?"

Lynche momentarily frowned at Hunter's lack of cooperation but then explained the CIA would be publically announcing one of their undercover intelligence officers had been killed in the line of duty in New York City the previous night. "I'm installing a star on the Memorial Wall in about an hour in the name of Duncan Hunter. You're scheduled to be buried in Arlington National Cemetery to make it official. That should ensure Al-Jazeera and the usual terrorist suspects get the word out to their minions and mosques that someone got lucky so the little bastards can collect their bounty. Since they are randomly killing anyone with your name, it seems to suggest they don't know who's the real target."

"I don't know what to say. 'Thanks for killing me' just doesn't seem appropriate."

"This shit isn't going to work until...unless...you go underground. I need some time to fully change your name and identity. You need to be careful and stay out of sight. This situation needs a little time to run its course. It would be best if you disappeared for a while."

"I know I'm going to regret asking this but please give me some cool name and not some asshole name."

Lynched searched on his desk for the scrap of paper with a proposed list of Hunter's new names: Carter Braxton. Conrad Rucker. Serge Larko. Michael Hostage. He circled "Dante Locke." It was just perfect. Named after the Italian poet of the late Middle Ages and the author of the *Divine Comedy*, widely considered one of the greatest literary works and a masterpiece of world literature. Lynche often thought that dealing with the conservative Duncan was at times, like getting pushed into one of the seven levels of Hell. As for Locke, some random name generator from the bowels of the Old Headquarters Building was responsible for that.

He nodded and laughed heartily. "I was leaning toward Ernesto Guevara, but since you have a little blood of *the Prophet* running in your veins, maybe something like *Saddam Ahmadinejad* would be more appropriate. Or maybe Buck Naked. You'll get it soon enough." It was rare for Lynche to have the upper hand on Hunter and when it happened, he would take advantage of it for as long as he could. "Where are you going again?"

"Australia; I'm giving an aviation terrorism lecture in a few days. I told you I bought a house in Wyoming. Jackson Hole. You know, Greg, it wouldn't look good if a dude named Torabinejad or Marx went to the local Safeway for a gallon of milk." Hunter dismissed the DCI's argument as silly, Lynche wouldn't do that to him. He got serious. "I sent Carlos and Theresa away. When that bullet whizzed by my ear, I knew my cover had been blown, but by what you're saying, it's not completely shot. You're doing one of those liberal Jedi mind tricks and blaming someone else. Why the guy in New York?"

"Duncan your cover's blown. Regarding the dead guy, no extended family. He was an easy target. Doubtful anyone will investigate him. We and the FBI can manage it. It was smart to get the Yazzies out of there. I know we discussed this, oh, a year ago. You know it would only be a matter of time."

"I know. Greg, I have classes to teach; I have the business. That's the cover. That cover's not blown." Hunter was fighting for his life.

"No, Duncan, let me repeat, your cover *is* blown; that life is over!"

"Greg, no disrespect, but Rushdie's been able to do it. Live normally."

"An obscure cleric issues an eight-dollar fatwa because of a book he hadn't read. No one really took notice. Rushdie's got a bodyguard. You have every drug cartel, all of al-Qaeda, the Muslim Brotherhood, the Taliban, Shining Path, the FARC, Jema'ah Islamiyah, Boko Haram— and let's not forget the full House and Senate Democrats *and the KGB*— all after you and want you dead. You don't need Bill McGee as a bodyguard; you need the whole damn Marine Corps! All of this…diversion is to give you some time to disappear. If you don't go to ground immediately, you're going to be fully exposed. Rothwell's buddies will try to ensure you are really dead and buried."

"Some of those dudes are at your place. NCS. And you know I'm right."

"In your dreams. Listen, someone will get lucky, find you at a moment where you're unprotected, and you'll be done. Rothwell got lucky catching you. It's going to happen again if you are not smart. I'm saying this because it's true and you know I'm right. If you're not going to be serious, you'll regret it. Maybe not today. Maybe not tomorrow, but soon. And you have to start thinking of Nazy and not just of yourself. And for God's sake, don't go anywhere without your body armor."

"Of which I have the latest genetically-modified spider silk vest to protect me. But what you're trying to say is the commies and the Islamists at the State Department will learn from your guys that they never even heard of an intelligence officer named Duncan Hunter, that you nailed a star on the wall and buried an empty box because you're playing chess while everyone else is playing checkers? That the word will get out to their spies, and then everyone will know the real McCoy might still be out there, and now they have to find me with a new name."

"That's it. If you were a government employee, it would be different. I'd yank your ass out of there and stuff you in a dark and remote place where no one would ever look. You have a few days to get your affairs in order before you're officially off the grid. But know this; you're going to be in grave danger the whole time. Remember, body armor."

"I suppose I can leave early for Australia. Spend some time on the beach. Snorkel the Great Barrier Reef or something. Where's Nazy; what about her?" His mind raced. What did he need to do immediately, and what needed to be done before he flew to Hawaii to catch his flight? He barely heard Lynche.

"Meetings. There *is* a terror war going on. She's busy. Mass murders going on every day on the planet in the name of jihad. Maybe looking at some old documents from a defector. What about her? Oh, she's next. My predecessor didn't do you two any favors. She'll have a protective detail; she's a government employee. That's the easy part. The inescapable fact is I may have to put both of you in a witness protection program. When that officially occurs, you're through playing spy. I don't see any way around it, we're going to change both of your names. I don't know if you can work, if you can even work again for us. I think this shit is bad, Duncan. Here, I can take care of Nazy. But you have to leave. Leave Texas. The sooner the better.... Belay that! Now!"

Hunter reflected on what the new world order was going to look like with Islamists continually hunting for him to kill him, whatever his name happened to be. A bullet had just missed his head. Would al-Qaeda death threats compel him to cancel trips, would he need a bodyguard? Lynche continued to talk. "….and before you return from Australia, I'll have a new passport for you. You cannot grow a beard overnight, but I'll have a technician meet you and teach you how to change and maintain your looks. I'm thinking *Duck Dynasty* is in your future."

Hunter scoffed and doubted the Ivy League Greg Lynche even knew who was on or what the reality television show, *Duck Dynasty*, even was. He ignored Lynche; he had an idea. He asked, "Can you make me disappear in Australia? Kill me after my speech? Maybe some policeman can find a body in an alley or something? Maybe wash up on the beech?"

Lynche considered the notion. "Let me work on it. Can you leave early?"

"For Sydney? I was leaving for Hawaii in three days, lecture the following. I'm out of here in an hour. I'm packing the bus. Moving the essentials to the new place." Hunter was scanning the living room windows waiting for Bill McGee and the crew to arrive, when a Texas State Trooper's Crown Victoria entered the circular driveway of the ranch house. "Greg, I have to go. I have a trooper coming to my door. He's probably investigating a burned out vehicle and a missing man."

"You better make sure it's a real cop and not a trap."

Hunter scrutinized the trooper and ignored the caution. "Can you make some time for me? I need to come to Washington."

"Haven't you been paying attention? Why here? Why now?"

"I don't know if I'll ever see Nazy again. Air travel today is so unpredictable, unless you have your own jet."

Lynche said, "Fly into to Manassas. Let me know when you're getting close. I'll have someone to pick you up."

"Thanks, Greg."

"Hey, and be safe. And, wear your body armor! I'm serious!"

"I will. Cheers."

• • • • •

Hunter invited the Texas State Trooper inside for coffee or iced water, but the man refused both. He stood in the doorway and explained he was investigating a vehicle fire off the roadbed a few miles north of the ranch. He wondered if Hunter had seen or heard anything. Duncan admitted with a grin, "Well, Carlos, my foreman, swore he saw a *chupacabra* yesterday."

The trooper thinly smiled at the mention of the local legend and allowed Hunter to continue. "I thought I heard a couple of shots well off in the distance a few hours ago. My ears are not that good from being around jet engines in a previous lifetime. I'm always concerned about illegal aliens and drug smugglers passing through the property—they favor a crossing north of here, between my ranch and General Donovan's place. Most of the time they just climb over the fence. Poachers are another story. They will cut the fence. I'm more concerned about a stray bullet hitting the house. If that was gunfire, it had to be a mile away or so, maybe it came from the highway, up north."

Hunter explained he had heard the distinctive report of weapons but he didn't find anyone or anything suspicious after a cursory inspection of the fence line. "I routinely check for illegal aliens crossing the property when I'm out for a jog, but this morning I turned toward town, and I didn't see anything suspicious." He related that he found some old tracks, obviously illegal aliens, but since it seemed like they were very old, he didn't call the Border Patrol.

The trooper never removed his stiff grey cowboy hat. He took a few notes, shook Hunter's hand, and departed the ranch. Less than five minutes after the trooper departed, a half-dozen vehicles, and a motor coach pulling a lengthy enclosed trailer entered the compound led by Bill McGee in a standard up-armored Hummer 2. He and Hunter discussed the situation and Lynche's plan to kill him. Duncan expressed his concern for the safety of everyone at the shop and for McGee. "I understand I have a *fatwa* on my ass. But I think they are just after me. A bunch of unlucky Duncan Hunters are dead, and someone almost got lucky."

The men stood there for several seconds when Hunter announced he remembered Eastwood's email. "Dory had sent me an email. About Duncan Hunters being killed and…lasers at airports…I blew it off. OBE, now."

"Shit happens." *Overcome by events. That's for sure!* McGee nodded in the direction of the rock outcropping. He said, "If I could, I'd go after the usual suspects. Whoever came out here had to have come from a mosque, likely San Antonio or Austin. Definitely not a local from the YMCA. Do you know what he looked like?"

Hunter shook his head. "Bloody. Mangled. I was thinking a true Middle East believer, though. He wasn't a white or black convert." ·

"You need to get moving, Maverick. We'll take care of the place and the shop. I'll get someone over here to pack yours and Carlos' trash. What do I tell everyone?"

"For those that are interested, they know I'm going to Australia for a lecture. Let's say, I plan to take some time off afterwards. Dive the Great Barrier Reef or something. I'm on sabbatical or some such BS. Then I'll disappear. I think that's the plan so far." Hunter broke lock with McGee's eyes, reached over and stripped the Velcro straps from the black splint. He tossed it on the sofa. When he looked back into the dark eyes of Bill McGee, there was more concern.

Unshackling the arm from the electronic stimulation splint didn't seem to be a necessary action. McGee nodded at the splint in the sofa. "Is that a good idea?"

Hunter smiled. "It'll have to be. I'll be ok." Then he unclasped his Rolex Submariner from his right wrist and transferred the watch to his left. It was the first time he dared wear his prized Rolex on his left wrist, where it belonged. The chronograph was loose and barely covered the hideous scar that circumscribed his wrist.

McGee watched Hunter with delectation. "I suppose our next job has been cancelled."

Hunter looked at the watch with approval. "I don't think so. I think I just have to get away from this place and take the pressure off everyone in this area. We have to wait for Greg to tell us if the game is off." A curious thought entered his head and the momentarily vacuous stare from Hunter concerned the energetic former Navy SEAL. When Hunter shook the corrosive thought from his head, he was back, grinning like a fool who didn't know he had been centimeters from being killed. He added a request, "Bill, can you get in touch with Dory Eastwood and let him know I got his messages and I'm out of town? I'll be in touch soon?"

McGee nodded and shook his partner's hand. He could see the fire in Hunter's eyes. All over the world fighter pilots were the same. They would never stand for an enemy attacking their nest and there would be hell to pay. McGee said, "I will do that. We were supposed to get together when he passed through town. Take great care, my friend. And, wear body armor. I'm not shitting you."

"You too, Bullfrog. I'll let you know how it goes."

An hour later, a convoy composed of a black, armored, Hummer 2 and a maroon bus pulling a trailer left the ranch house for the last time and headed north. McGee drove the damaged Hummer6 into town for repairs. Hunter raced the Aston Martin to the airport.

Outside of Fredericksburg, a white and blue-trimmed Gulfstream G-550 departed the Gillespie County Airport on an easterly heading.

CHAPTER TWENTY-THREE

1630 July 16, 2014
McLean, Virginia

A Marine Corps Color Guard marched through the Original Headquarters Building lobby toward the Memorial Wall. The outboard Marines carried hand-polished M-1 Garand rifles on opposite shoulders. They stopped, marked time, and pivoted 180°. The Marines with weapons silently moved to Present Arms while the flag bearer rendered Honors by lowering the light blue flag with the Seal of the Central Intelligence Agency. The American Flag remained ramrod straight. The National Anthem played over the loudspeaker system. Those present for the ceremony faced the National Ensign. Onlookers stood up straight and remained standing when the music ceased and the color guard retired the colors and marched out of the lobby.

A well-dressed woman in a navy suit stepped behind a lectern off to the side of the Memorial Wall and read from a script. Her voice was strong and unwavering, and the acoustics of the space carried her words clearly. "Good afternoon, ladies and gentlemen. Today we gather to honor the sacrifice of another intelligence officer who has died while in the performance of duty. Behind me there are 130 stars mounted on white Alabama marble. Each star represents a fallen hero of the Central Intelligence Agency. On this day, we shall add another star to the Memorial Wall. The identities of some who lost their lives while serving their country in the field of intelligence will remain known. Their names will live in memoriam within the Book of Honor." The woman gestured to the black Moroccan goatskin-bound book in a steel frame beneath the stars of the Memorial Wall. She continued, "For others like today's honoree, the identity of this newest star will remain secret, even in death."

Approximately 100 people filled the lobby and each was silent for the somber occasion. Several paramilitary officers from the Special Activities

Division (SAD) of the National Clandestine Service were on hand to witness "one of theirs" being honored. The vast majority of those on the Memorial Wall were killed in the line of duty while on assignment with the SAD, usually in a remote or hostile location.

NCS Director Castaño and several others from NCS and Special Activities Division were shell-shocked. They stood with their arms across their chests, a clear sign that they were distraught. Castaño was confused and livid behind his dark glasses.

A pause in the ceremony allowed onlookers to reflect on the simple yet dramatic display. Each three-dimensional star measured 2¼ inches tall by 2¼ inches wide and was a half an inch deep. Every star was spaced six inches apart from the others. Every row was also six inches apart from the other rows. The newer stars were black, while some of the older stars had faded to grey.

The woman at the lectern stepped away as Greg Lynche, the Director of Central Intelligence, took up a position behind the lectern, opened a notebook, and delivered a few words. "Our honoree was cut down in the prime of his life, in the service of our nation. He was awarded the Distinguished Intelligence Cross for uncommon and extraordinary acts of heroism and valor. He accepted existing dangers with exemplary courage and determination and contributed significantly to the destruction of key leaders of several terrorist groups. Most recently, under the most difficult of circumstances, he was instrumental in intercepting special weapons before they could fall into the hands of worldwide terrorist groups. Enroute to headquarters, he was ambushed, cornered and killed by a member of those terrorist groups. His unwavering courage and steadfast devotion to country reflected great credit upon himself. Like those before him, he has upheld the highest traditions of the Central Intelligence Agency. Signed this sixteenth day of July, 2014." Lynche turned as a pair of Marines approached the Memorial Wall with a black star resting upon a light blue pillow. An intelligence officer stepped forward, lifted the star from the pillow, and pressed it onto the marble face. Lynche continued, "America will never know of the courage and heroism or the accomplishments of our honoree as he gave his life to our National Security and Defense. On behalf of a great Nation, please accept our deepest appreciation and gratitude. We will forever be in your debt."

Lynche raised his eyes and his voice. "Our fallen intelligence officer will be laid to rest at Arlington National Cemetery soon. Ladies and gentlemen, that concludes our ceremony. Thank you for coming."

Lynche joined Nazy Cunningham, and they walked to the elevators. Once inside, he asked, "I couldn't tell if we were successful. Did we leak his name?"

Nazy nodded and added, "There were some busybodies from State that asked. I didn't have to spell it out. But Director Castaño and several others from NCS were nearly apoplectic."

"He'll be pissy."

Lynche had likely violated some obscure protocol created by the National Clandestine Service leaders. Lynche said, "Just about everyone on the Wall are NCS, and yeah, this one isn't. I'll talk with him. Or maybe I won't. He'll just have to get over it."

Lynche glanced at her before returning his eyes to his shoes. "That should do it. You're next. But I have no idea what I'm going to do with you."

"Director Lynche, I think my days under cover are gone. I don't want to go back to the ME. But I don't think I'm ready to be just an analyst or a housewife."

The doors opened on the seventh floor. Lynche stepped out, Nazy remained inside. He jammed his hands in his pockets and tried to smile as the doors began to close. He held them open as she crossed her arms and sighed heavily.

He needed to say something other than, "You're through Cunningham. Time's up. Pack your trash. You need to go." He found a way out. She would only take a few seconds to summarize anything noteworthy. "What's your assessment of the Yazhov archive your guys are working on? Did we get our money's worth?"

"There's about another 1,000 pages we haven't analyzed yet. When I left, we were going through a single submarine reference. It was a little odd in the context of the archive—there is nothing like it so far. Out of our purview. One of our Navy SEALs looked at it after it was transcribed, of course, and he did a little research. He suggests the document references an unusual operation, a single submarine on a secret mission...."

"Nazy, subs are always on secret missions."

He embarrassed her with his interruption but she continued, "He suggested the submarine was operating in the South Pacific. His analysis was that at that time, Soviet submarines had never been known to travel so far south, so far from port. But that wasn't what he found that was so remarkable."

Lynche was confused. He mashed his eyebrows together like a hairy car crash. "What was it?"

"The date. The location. July 1937. Three hundred miles from—I think this was translated correctly—a Howland Island."

The DCI was struck mute with the date and those two words. The intelligence that came into the Agency sometimes had a way of doing that to the most seasoned professional spy. Pieces of a puzzle would neatly fit, but often there remained one critical piece that was missing, and without it, the puzzle would remain unsolved, incomplete. Sometimes forever. And sometimes when one least expected it, someone would find or drop an innocuous scrap of information which illuminated an old case, showed it a new light.

Lynche was a master spy first, but he was an experienced pilot second, and he knew his aviation history. July 1937. This was five years before there was an official Office of Strategic Services, the predecessor of the Central Intelligence Agency. "A Soviet Sub? In the area....where *Amelia Earhart* was last heard?" He tried to make questioning gestures with his hands but failed spectacularly as the elevator door sensed an easing of pressure. He caught himself and put a hip into the door and repositioned his foot to hold the doors open.

Lynche's eyes bulged out of his sockets. That was a combination of words he didn't expect to hear. Maybe they were some state secrets from torturing those who were processed through the Soviet Union's most dreaded prison, the Lubyanka. His hands flew in and out of his pockets and finally wrapped around his shoulders in excitement. This was the best part of being the top spy. Secrets no one else would ever know, were his to enjoy or suffer. "*Amelia Earhart?* What are you talking about, Miss Cunningham?"

Nazy said, "Our Navy SEAL said the same thing. I had to look her up and read about her. Our analysts haven't gone any further, but the trajectory of the story is that the Soviets may have been in the general area where she disappeared. Thousands of miles from port. It had to be at sea for months. Those two intersecting events...it cannot be a coincidence."

Lynche shook his head to erase the thought of Russians being in the area or even remotely responsible for America's darling aviatrix going missing over the Pacific Ocean. "How?" Another thought tried to burrow its way into his consciousness. He was forgetting something or a string of somethings. Distractions like information on long lost aviation heroes could disrupt the thinking of any rational person. He was stunned by all of the intangibles and variables now running through his head. The implications could be earthshattering. *Now the circumstances of her disappearance could finally make some sense!*

"Don't know yet, fully. Maybe later this week we'll have the analysis done in that area. Of all the documents in the archive we've reviewed so far, that one is the most interesting. I know Duncan would think it was interesting."

"If we find any evidence or hint the old Soviet Union was responsible for Amelia Earhart—directly or tangentially—you make sure it is boxed POTUS, DCI, Eyes Only. Double-wrapped. Need to Know." He nodded and waved his hand as if he were pushing aside that distraction for another. Information on the dead aviatrix was interesting, but he had other more pressing business. Like Duncan Hunter. "Nazy, we also need to sweep up the loose bits."

"Pardon?" Her British accent was especially strong when she asked a question. She missed the DCI's change of direction of thought. Confusion tinged her question.

"Someone at the FBI figured it out. Someone luckily determined the threat on Duncan. We need to find out who that person is and see how many others may know we have attributed the death of a Duncan Hunter to cover our boy. We probably need to get them on a non-disclosure agreement, an NDA. Say it's an ongoing investigation. Whatever. It needs to happen quickly. Whatever it takes."

Nazy crossed her arms over her chest and nodded. "I'll handle it personally. I'll let you know what I find out."

Lynche removed his foot to allow the elevator doors to close. Before they did, he said, "Thank you." In a second, she was gone but the thoughts of her and the spontaneous mission lingered in his mind. How many more fictions would be necessary to bury the history of Duncan Hunter?

How could this have happened? roiled in the DCI's mind. *Russians, likely. Islamists, maybe. Never saw it coming. We were so focused on the Middle East element of terrorism that it was inevitable we ignored the system operating in the background. We overestimate our security while we underestimate the brainpower of our old Soviet counterparts. In fact, even with the Wall falling and the coup, they haven't ever stopped their intelligence collection and disinformation activities. We tried to buy what was in the heads of several senior KGB and intelligence officers. The Agency offered them millions of dollars for their memoirs.* Lynche stared ahead and harrumphed. *When they were approached, several retorted, rather bluntly, "Not interested." One even yelled, "You haven't read what's in my file! If you had done your homework, you'd know it says, "Not to be pitched!" Radicals and old KGB types are never off the job, even when they're retired or unemployed. They cannot be bought off. Ever!*

I go back to my question—how did it happen? I must be losing my mind; I've been out of Operations too long. Forgot more than most will ever know. We are creatures of habit. How did Nazy find bin Laden? As a former Muslima, she was intimately acquainted with Muslim men, how they think, and how their terrorist bureaucracies function. They were sexually deprived when in battle, and once they found shelter, they would send for their families. Follow the wives!

It's in the repetitions, as any cryptoanalyst knows. Find the repetitions. Break the adversary's cipher. Find the repetitions. Then you have the keys to the kingdom.

Duncan always stayed at the five star hotels under his own name as a businessman. The old KGB officers at the Russian embassies likely started a file on him, just like we would do when we try to identify Russian intelligence officers in the field. He flies a corporate jet during the day. That put him in rare company. How could he not be noticed? We assumed too much during the early days. There were probably several dozen more trivial indicators which were likely used to ID Duncan and sift him from the regular crowd of our IOs. Lynche sucked a lungful of air and shook his head. It was worse than he wanted to believe.

In the case of Weedbusters, it wouldn't be too hard to connect an episode of plant killing with his presence in the country. How many times did he go to Afghanistan—thirty? If they were on their game they would have collected some data. The repetitions of the carrier aircraft. Starting with me, being retired, I see where I was lackadaisical on Wraith and the Noble Savage missions. I knew better. It was inevitable his cover would be blown. I cannot believe I was that blind.

Rothwell knew full well what Duncan did, where and when he flew. He had the numbers. The data. He knew all of the structural defects in our security and he sent al-Qaeda and the Muslim Brotherhood to take advantage of them. Nazy was part of the problem too. She is so good but so much of a distraction that it clouds the male mind. She must have driven Rothwell insane because he couldn't have her. I know she doesn't want to leave the CIA, or her work. It's obvious their cover is irretrievably blown. Duncan's been shattered.

Firing them will kill them both. But what good will that do? He and Nazy will always have to worry about Rothwell's cohorts finding them and killing them. I think the offended Islamists apparently gave up on killing Rushdie. Even if that's true, there's no way they will ever let Duncan and Nazy live. They know too much and have hurt too many radicals to let them go and live in peace.

Lynche returned to his desk, removed his suit coat, and plopped in his chair. The inbox was full of files, stacked a foot-high, with nothing in his outbox. A number of files were piled in the middle of his blotter where he had left them before delivering Hunter's fake eulogy. He closed his eyes and said aloud, "Now, where the hell was I?"

CHAPTER TWENTY-FOUR

0830 July 17, 2014
Clarksburg, West Virginia

The unscheduled visit from the head of the CIA's National Counter Terrorism Center had the FBI Special Agents at the National Crime Information Center in a twitter. They rarely received anyone other than an occasional Department of Justice or FBI senior executive passing through the area on a boondoggle.

Special Agent in Charge Papp checked her watch every few minutes as she waited for the appointed time. Since making the calls to FBI HQ to inform the Agency that one of their intelligence officers may be in trouble, she hadn't heard anything. She didn't know if the silence from FBI HQ was odd or not. She didn't really think the CIA would back-brief the FBI to let them know if anything happened to their precious spy. She couldn't imagine anyone from McLean coming to personally thank the NCIC for their help and analysis, so a visit from them had to be for something else. She couldn't concentrate on anything but then she heard it. She looked through the window of her office and located the black dot against a partially clouded sky. It grew larger with every second.

The small dark green helicopter with a white painted top slowly approached the NCIC parking lot. Papp moved away from the window and headed downstairs to meet the visitor at the dedicated helicopter landing area on the far side of the parking lot. Rotorwash whipped an orange windsock around as the helicopter touched down.

The male FBI Special Agents were disappointed the woman in the helicopter wore slacks. She obviously knew not to wear a flimsy dress which would fly up into the swirling winds generated by the overhead rotor blades. She slipped out of the helicopter with the feline grace of a leopard dismounting a tree after a meal. Long legs led the way followed by long black hair held firmly in a tight ponytail. The woman bent over and ran like a sprinter out of the starting gate so as to not give the spinning rotor blades a chance to hit her head. When she was clear of the spinning wings she slowed and stood erect. She carried a belting leather folder in her hand but no purse.

Louise Papp stopped in her tracks. Visions of a white clingy dress gracefully stepping out of a white Rolls Royce flooded her mind. No one had a head of hair like that. *"That's her!"*

Nazy Cunningham approached the other woman with a genuine combination of friendship and enthusiasm and a kilowatt smile. She was glad to be off the helicopter and back on terra firma. The ride with the Marines was fun, but not that much fun. She had work to do.

Papp struggled to make sense of what she was witnessing. The last time she had seen this woman was twelve years ago on the arm of Duncan Hunter in Newport, Rhode Island. Naval War College. *Damn, she's a spook! Now it's beginning to makes sense!* She regained some sense of composure as the CIA officer held out her hand with a palpable display of affection.

"Nazy Cunningham. So good to finally meet you, Director Papp."

"Please call me Louise. You know how to make an entrance, Director Cunningham. Nothing subtle about arriving by helicopter." Papp nodded toward the aircraft which had begun to spool up its main rotor.

"Please call me Nazy. They were on a training mission. I was more of a stowaway than passenger." The women laughed as they left the noise and commotion behind them. The helicopter's engine noise and rotor speed increased, and it lifted off of the landing pad just as they entered the NCIC.

Both women had infectious smiles. They sized up each other gently with a sincere twinkle in their eyes. Papp went to her office, followed by Cunningham who was glad they hadn't gone to the conference room. What she had to say was private.

Nazy waited patiently for an opportunity to discuss her visit. Papp was still mildly stupefied by the person sitting across from her in her office. With a thousand questions still running through her head, Papp turned on her down-home, Iowa farm-girl charm and asked, "Director Cunningham, what brings you to our little backwater?"

Nazy tried not to frown from the probable interagency rivalry. This could be more difficult that she thought. She continued with the formality. "Director Papp, what I have to say needs to be covered by an

NDA. This is very sensitive."

"Duncan Hunter." It was a statement, not a question.

Nazy sensed something supercilious in her voice. Not proud or vainglorious, but not humble either. She nodded as she opened her notebook. She extracted a sheet of paper and handed it to Papp.

The Director of the NCIC ignored the document for the moment. She knew what was in it. She argued with herself what to say, what to ask, what to release. "Is Duncan....*safe?*"

The question struck Nazy a little odd, almost as if the woman knew who Duncan Hunter was. *How was that even possible?* She paused and said, "Please sign the NDA, Louise. I'll tell you what I can. This has significant national security implications."

She should have expected it. Papp took a pen and placed it on the paper. The pen didn't quiver. She said, "Nazy, you don't know me, but I know you. More accurately, I've seen you before. Red Parrot Inn. White dress. Old white car. You were with Duncan Hunter that night in Newport."

It was Nazy's turn to be shocked. That was the day, the place, the dress, the car. Duncan had told her she was a lousy spy. That was the day she left Islam. That was the place where Duncan offered to help her escape the men who had sent her to meet him, befriend him, to spy on him. Duncan had extricated her from the men who were controlling her, threatening to return her to Jordan. He enlisted the help of Greg Lynche to remove her from Newport. The only thing he didn't do that night was remove her dress. She did that by herself. *She knows more than I could have assumed. This could be trouble.* Nazy nodded absentmindedly.

Papp frowned, signed the nondisclosure agreement, and waited. She hadn't seen it before, but the huge diamond on the woman's ring finger suddenly appeared when Nazy moved her binder as if on cue to indicate that there was more to the story. Papp wanted it all.

"Duncan's fine. Your discovery was prescient. As my boss and I were trying to contact him, someone was trying to kill him. Duncan's not an easy man to kill."

"Thank you, Nazy."

"Louise, you have me at a disadvantage. I can tell you some things. I'm curious how you know Duncan."

She told her. Hunter Louise Papp didn't elaborate. Just the high points. He was in school in the senior class; she was in the junior class. He was very handsome. Everyone thought he was a spy. It wasn't anything he did or said, but just the way he carried himself and the interesting people he associated with. The official story was he worked for the Air Force. It had to be cover story. Her eyes flashed to the diamond solitaire. Nazy caught her looking at it. No one at CIA with the exception of the DCI, knew she and Duncan were married. Papp sensed the woman's line of thinking. "Are you married?"

Nazy nodded. Embarrassed.

"To Duncan?"

"I can't say."

"You already did. Congratulations, Nazy. Let's wrap this up. You need me to keep my mouth shut. I will do that." Papp wanted the CIA officer out of her office. She wanted to get away from her own building. Go for a long walk or something. She wasn't hurt; she didn't know exactly what she was feeling.

"Louise, I need your help. I need to know how you uncovered the conspiracy that is playing out before our eyes. As you determined, Duncan is subject to a *fatwa*. An Islamic death sentence."

"But you know why. And who issued it."

"That's in the need to know arena, Louise. Between us girls, of course."

The women's relationship shifted to business. "How did you discover...that several Duncan Hunters had been killed? Can you walk me through that process? We're concerned how the other side is targeting these men apparently just to get to Duncan. We haven't picked up anything from our international sources. Absolutely no chatter anywhere."

"Nazy, it was a fluke. I saw my name on a spreadsheet and then there was another. My full name is Hunter Louise Papp. Hunter is not that common. I saw that there were three deaths attributed to Duncan Hunter, and I immediately thought of Duncan from the war college. We ran some other databases, filtered out the combinations, Duncan and Hunter, and found several more. The NYPD picked up a perp who claimed to have killed a Duncan Hunter as suggested in the *fatwa* and demanded the bounty. I asked for passport photographs of the deceased. We checked the JPAS for your Duncan's clearances and determined he was Agency. I called our Ops who was supposed to call your Ops. Now you're here."

Nazy asked, "What kind of project were you working on when Duncan's name popped up?"

"I'm trying to find missing women. Males were supposed to have been filtered out of the database, but for some reason they weren't. I saw my name three times but quickly ascertained the names were men, deceased men."

Nazy was quiet for a few seconds. She wouldn't let her mind race ahead of her mission. She offered an olive branch, "We have a human trafficking office in the NCTC. Maybe we can help if there are international connections?" Nazy thought she was genuinely trying to be helpful. But the words *missing women* rang loud in her head. On the night she wore the white dress and was spirited away by a man named Duncan Hunter, she had been a missing woman and bad men were looking for her.

Papp shook her head. "Nazy, we're domestic; you're international. You probably have a Special Agent in that office as a liaison. It's fairly sensitive. Under this President, we are charged to see if we can find these women, these girls that have disappeared under a variety of circumstances. The Cleveland case, horrific to say the least, is likely not the only one. For that one we got a break. One girl, held for ten years, escaped. Police rescued the others. National news." She tapped her finger on a pad of paper. "There are hundreds of girls snatched off the streets every year, and no one knows what happens to them or where they are. Few escape. Most don't ever turn up. We're trying to analyze the data to see if we can find these girls and bring them home. Human trafficking and sex tourism in countries such as Cambodia, the Philippines and Thailand, and the Middle East—the problem is huge. Targeting low-level recruiters and pimps doesn't dismantle the leadership of sophisticated trafficking networks. That is our real goal."

Nazy Cunningham's first job at the Agency was as an intelligence analyst. She also had poured over databases to find clues to locate weapons of mass destruction or terrorists that didn't want to be found. Her training as an attorney, with an eye for detail during document reviews, proved invaluable during targeted analysis. She was good. She found the weapons and the terrorists when the men could not.

Armed with her analysis and findings, the clandestine service and some of the special operations command warriors would conduct "snatch and grab" missions. Invariably, they'd come home with a bad guy bundled up and ready for interrogation. Al-Qaeda and the Taliban had a problem similar to what Louise was investigating. Some of their finest soldiers were snatched off the streets across the Middle East, and no one in al-Qaeda or the Taliban circles knew how it happened or where they were. When captured and spirited out of the town or the country, by U.S. Special Forces, no one escaped. Nazy saw the commonality. The process were likely the same; the targets were different.

"Any clues who is doing this? I mean, is this organized?"

Papp nodded and paused before speaking. It wasn't going to hurt to discuss the mission. Her sense of urgency to get Nazy out of her office had passed. After those thoughts she said rather meekly, "Mosques?" as if it was a word not to be discussed "outside of family." The CIA was definitely outside the FBI family.

Nazy was slightly taken aback but fully understood the implications. Some Muslim men and clerics had strange ideas regarding women. She remembered part of the *sura* that they would cite, *"The good women are therefore obedient, guarding the unseen as Allah has guarded; and those on whose part you fear desertion, admonish them, and leave them alone in the sleeping-places and beat them."* Old men would buy and marry children. The Islamic fringe group, Boko Haram, after killing their parents and brothers would kidnap hundreds of Christian girls and either sell them as sex slaves or "marry" them to forcibly convert them to Islam. She relived her own horror at being coerced to spy on Duncan. If she had refused she would have either been killed or returned to Jordan and the vicious husband she had run away from. Her punishment for embarrassing him would likely have been death.

Nazy's attention returned to the conversation when Papp said, "I can't even call it a trend. It's just a collection of disparate things. We're using some new investigative tools such as Automatic Number Plate Recognition (ANPR), essentially license plate readers. They use closed-circuit television or speed enforcement cameras to catalog the movements of cars or individuals. When there is an event, a missing woman, the local police department downloads the data from their cameras, runs them through a processor, and looks for trends. We are seeing an inordinate number of recurrences of certain vehicle license plates in the proximity of the last known location of a missing woman. More often than not, the vehicles' tags are traced back to entering or leaving a local mosque."

"Seriously?" Nazy was now intrigued.

"There are amazing activities going on, in or near mosques. The former president pulled our Agents out of known anti-American and pro-terrorism mosques, and the courts have all but prohibited us from any form of surveillance. But there's some, uh, analysis still going on. Very thin, very low profile. I'll probably get fired for telling you."

"I'll never tell. Like what?"

"Since we've been crunching data there's been an escalation in other unexplained events. In the vacuum of surveillance, more strange things are occurring. Inexplicable things."

Nazy's raised her eyebrows in surprise as Louise continued.

"We are seeing is an increase in those little helicopters; like you see at the malls, crashing around airports. Airports are keeping the information from the public and reporting it to us. We have a few instances of a suspicious vehicle leaving from or returning to a mosque after a report of one of these things flying into the airport, flying down the runway, or even hitting an airplane. Then there are the reports of laser pointers aimed at the aircraft cockpits. Even the Pope's airliner was hit by a laser."

"Are these originating from mosques?" Nazy was not convinced—she had to be missing a piece of the puzzle.

"We don't know exactly. We take some of that license plate data, plot the occurrences, trace the vehicles, and where do you think these vehicles are found after the event?"

"Mosques."

"That's right. Oftentimes. Before and after the fact. At or very near certain mosques. But we cannot say for certain that they all originate from there. And it is above my paygrade to investigate any further. Before I came to West Virginia, our leadership was told to stand down if a mosque was involved or even suspected to be involved in anything like this. Of course, that was under the former president. The official word is the new president has negated the former's executive orders. But our director is reluctant to return our field teams loose on these Islamic centers."

"So you can't directly surveil them, at least not yet?" asked Nazy. She checked her watch. Her ride would be arriving soon. While the FBI's mission was interesting, she had to finish up.

Papp shook her head.

"Louise, this doesn't leave here. Duncan has been targeted, *repeatedly*, for assassination. This—I don't know what to call it—saturation effort for lack of a better term, nearly succeeded. You deduced his cover had been blown, and your actions here are helping us understand the extent of the conspiracy, their commitment to kill him. It's not local. It sounds like it's organized. I can say that there is a funeral scheduled at Arlington National Cemetery for a Captain Duncan Hunter later in the month—there are some things even we cannot do fast. We leaked some information that the bad guys succeeded in killing the prime target of their *fatwa*. We're sure everyone after Duncan is a radical member of some organization. Maybe they too, are operating under the cover of a mosque, but we hope these actions will eliminate the pressure on him and the other men with that name. I want to say 'thank you' for all you have done to expose the conspiracy against…him." Nazy wanted to say, "My husband," but thought it better to leave that issue alone.

The windows began to rattle signaling an approaching helicopter. Hunter Louise Papp glanced at the wedding ring again. She no longer viewed the woman sitting across from her as an adversary. Nazy Cunningham, if that was her real name, had long ago won the heart and mind of Duncan Hunter. Maybe she could be helpful in the FBI's mission to find missing women. Maybe not. It would likely be forgotten when she left. Government promises are like that. Whatever the outcome, there would be few hard feelings.

At the landing pad, as the Marine helicopter idled with rotor blades swishing in the background Papp said, "I'd like to keep in contact, Nazy."

"Me too." The women easily exchanged business cards, handshakes, and goodbyes. No hugs. Purely professional for the onlookers.

As the intelligence officer walked to the helicopter, Louise Papp stood her ground and waved. Her skirt freshened in the helicopter winds. The noise level increased exponentially as the engines and rotors increased in velocity. When the dark green helicopter lifted off, Papp turned away and said into the diminishing background noise, "That Nazy is the luckiest woman on the planet."

CHAPTER TWENTY-FIVE

0830 July 17, 2014
Dubai

Flashing lights and a ringing bell signaled the arrival of the train car. Mazibuike jumped at the sound, dropped his hookah, and arose from the gilded and ornate chair. The thick, sticky smoke of hashish swirled around him. His security man, Nizar, also sprang up from his room and ran to the door while he pulled an automatic pistol from a backside holster. Whether it was indifference to the potential threat or the haze of the cannabis, the former president stood his ground and did not seek shelter in the safe room in the food preparation area. Neither man had called for a lift, and unannounced visitors were never received. No one ever stopped at the palace without being invited, without the visit being coordinated beforehand, and properly received in the Islamic fashion.

Mazibuike frowned at the intrusion while Nizar went through the motions of protecting him. He recalled his childhood Islamic lessons which were beaten into him at the fundamentalist madrassa in Jakarta, as he wasn't the best Muslim student: "*The one who comes, greets the Muslims that are present. The one who rides, greets the ones who are walking. The smaller group greets the bigger group. The one who is walking greets the one who is sitting. The younger greets the elder. When a guest arrives at the home, they should be served food and drink. Whatever provision is available, it should be served to the guests without any haste or being anxious whether it will suffice them or not. Allah blesses the provisions and the provision becomes sufficient enough for everyone. The guests should be made comfortable and at ease in every way possible.*" The armed Nizar would not allow unannounced guests to enter; he would send them away.

The two men exchanged glances. Then the former president nodded, abandoned his water pipe, and sought shelter in another part of the palace. Other men of the security detail raced to the palatial French doors. Nizar engaged the peephole and saw a barefooted woman step from the regal train car. She was covered from head to ankle in a royal blue diaphanous frock and a matching colored hijab. She walked to within a few feet of the door, stopped and bowed, and presented an envelope with both hands. She maintained her position as if she were a mannequin.

Nizar threw open the door, snatched the envelope, and walked back to his master. Mazibuike was shocked to learn a woman was on the landing. He took the proffered envelope and opened it.

My dear Maxim,

On the occasion of our successful venture, please accept a token of my gratitude and appreciation. Ani will bring you great pleasure.

The card was signed with the Arabic number one. *The One.*

Nizar waited for a response. Mazibuike considered the offer carefully. He wasn't prepared to blithely reject his benefactor's gift, he wasn't interested in a woman. He hadn't been interested in sex since his arrival at…what he called the Enchanted City. His palace's opulence was beyond comprehension. He had been in the company of several Saudi royals as president, with the finest rugs, drapes, furniture that craftsmen could assemble or that money could buy. Oil money could buy much when the price per barrel was high.

His current residence was a sprawling palace on the order of the Taj Mahal; its floor area was 20,000 square feet. A single story. A single French door. The intricate herringbone cut tile and the extra white Thassos and Arabesque mosaic work that spanned the domed ceilings were in the style of the grand mosques all across the Islamic world, although, none contained the typical stylized calligraphic flourishes and creative lines of Arab poetry that decorated mosques. The floors were polished white Arabiscato marbles from Italy. The main columns were smooth Kashmir gneiss from India. Detailed paintings of blue-domed mosques, intricate masonry, and tall gold-topped minarets filled recesses masquerading as windows. Columns, arches, and flying buttresses revealed the devilishly intricate and beautiful stone, tile, and mosaic work.

Every room was stunning in its beauty and perfection. No two rooms were alike, but each room was illuminated by hidden lamps in the ceiling which were easily adjusted by a hidden light control panel from total darkness to full illumination.

Mazibuike had received countless classified briefings of significant, completed, ongoing and proposed projects around the globe. However, he had never received a presentation on the underground city of Dubai. He heard of one billionaire sheikh who wanted to build a full-sized mountain, while another wanted to build a replica Niagara Falls. Then there were the buildings in Abu Dhabi and Dubai. Multi-billion dollar, multi-year projects. Over half of the world's tall cranes were employed. He was surprised American intelligence services had little clue what lay beneath the expressways which connected the two great cities.

The first tranche of twenty of the programmed one hundred underground palaces tripped through Dubai's subconscious, paralleling the E10, E11, and E12 highways between Abu Dhabi and Dubai with a spur to Sharjah, which served as the train station and wheelhouse for the dozens of private coaches that ran through one of the four major aqueducts.

He understood there were some 20 miles of abandoned subway, an earlier project which ran from Abu Dhabi to some unknown terminus. He learned that a contingent of Chinese workers several thousand strong had dug the channel, cast the eighty-foot long, twenty-foot-high, ten-foot thick interlocking concrete pieces, and assembled the pieces like Lego blocks to make one long continuous string of connected sections. Unlike most subways, there were four ten-foot diameter tubes arranged side-by-side like the four-across exhaust pipes of a Ferrari racecar. They served as the conduits for a mélange of elegant and personal railway cars which connected the underground palaces.

It took ten years to complete the palaces, the subway, and the highway that ran above it. Then very well-paid Muslim artisans from around the world descended on Abu Dhabi to create the artwork for the palaces and to furnish each room. When the work was complete the craftsmen and artisans disappeared. Their families never heard from them again.

Previous mega-construction projects had been concentrated along the coast, expanding the boundaries of Dubai and Abu Dhabi. Some in the intelligence community had expressed interest in what was being built in the desert. It was a little curious that all the construction work was hidden under huge tents that spanned an area as big as two football fields. One nosy KGB intelligence officer was taken to an abandoned subway station outside of Abu Dhabi. The implication was the Emiratis were replacing their old decrepit subway station with a more modern version and connecting it with Dubai. U.S. intelligence officials intercepted the Soviet's assessment and immediately disregarded their rationale. Agency analysts dismissed the project as a nuclear fallout shelter for protection against the Iranian nuclear threat.

The emirs of the Emirates spent their money on a host of outlandish multi-billion dollar, multi-year projects, such as constructing the Palm Jumeirah and the Burj Khalifa. Satellites saw a pristine six-lane, superhighway emerging from under the tents and intelligence analysts thought nothing of it. Or more accurately, the Near East Division Chief chuffed at the idea of a bomb shelter and decided it wasn't worth opening a case to determine what those crazy Arabs were spending their oil money on.

The arrangement and configuration of the underground complex reminded Mazibuike of the community of Shaker Heights, Ohio, where the rich and famous lived outside the heavily industrialized city of Cleveland. Two brothers had envisioned a planned community as a suburban retreat from the manufacturing complex surrounding Cleveland. The brothers built some of the most spectacular homes for the magnates of industry, and they connected the properties with their very own private railroad. The steel and rubber mill moguls walked a few paces from their mansions and boarded a waiting and lavishly appointed railroad coach for an unencumbered and opulent ride through the countryside to their lofty offices in downtown Cleveland.

Mazibuike had many more thoughts of the secret city, for that was what it was. And now it was home, or at least shelter. Hiding in the underground complex was a nerve-wracking experience. The owners of the palaces strived to maintain the secrecy and uniqueness, as well as the comfort of homes. There were few servants and they rode in special cars that ran from another building in Sharjah to the servants' entrance and quarters. Foodstuffs magically appeared in specially constructed refrigerated vehicles at the servant's stoop at scheduled times.

Everyone associated with the complex suffered from a deficiency of vitamin D_3 because of the lack of sunlight. This had been explained to him by the emir, as he waved a colorless hand and provided a brief outline of what the palace was and what it was not. "It is primarily a safe haven, a place to get away from the eyes and ears that exist everywhere in high-traffic areas like our above ground buildings," he said with a smile as if he were only telling a partial truth and dared Mazibuike to call him on it. "The city…we have a little bit of everything, if and when you want it. We even have…*a zoo.*" His smile was tinged with conspiracy and intrigue.

The former president dismissed the idea of an underground zoo as hyperbole as he took the daily vitamin supplement. But as intended by the designers, his comfort was complete. Anything he desired could be provided in minutes, if not seconds. In the early days he had challenged the emir's braggadocio and asked for a Häagen-Dazs ice cream bar; Nizar returned with three chocolate varieties within a minute.

The air was always pure and clean, as if all of the automobile and diesel truck exhaust which often permeated the air over the highway of the Dubai-Abu Dhabi corridor had been scrubbed from it. Every other day a five-foot high silver robot, a taller and more streamlined version of the Star Wars' R2D2, would enter each room and flood the area with ultraviolet radiation. The unmanned system was identical to those used at high-end Western hospitals to kill all of the bacteria and sterilize operating rooms.

He felt secure, not exposed, within the structure. The prince claimed that few knew of the complex and bragged that it had special defenses to protect it from outside forces. Oil money could buy security and deflect outside interest in ways threats could not.

Mazibuike believed that there were enough safeguards in the underground warren of palaces that he would not get caught like a rat in a box. He heard a few rumors about the palace and learned more truths. Conversations were likely recorded by microphones and cameras hidden in the fluorescent and ultraviolet lamps in the ceiling. All of the rooms were outfitted with the latest electronics systems and the finest audio equipment Europe and Japan could produce. They avoided American-made goods for fear the National Security Agency had planted communications software or tracking hardware in the devices. He learned while president that CIA and NSA geniuses with computers could turn virtually anything electronic into a camera or a microphone, and he also learned a few tricks of the counter-surveillance trade. He always placed a strip of electrical tape over his computer's built-in camera as a precaution.

And now the man who provided the palace had offered a present. Something he could not refuse. The woman who waited on the white polished marble landing had all of the beauty and charm of a *houri*.

He felt like a chess piece being moved on the board by a master. He would use her and abuse her in the Islamic way. If she didn't die from the experience, Nizar would hand her off to the security detail. She wouldn't be allowed to leave the complex. She was to serve and please. Whatever her origins, she was now irrelevant and disposable.

Mazibuike said to Nizar, "Bring her to me."

CHAPTER TWENTY-SIX

1700 July 19, 2014
Honolulu, Hawaii

Some people in the security line made small talk. Some shuffled baggage and pushed roll-aboards through the rat maze of stanchions and barrier tape. Others stood quietly waiting. An apathetic Transportation Security Administration officer waved the next passenger to her lectern and checked to see if the name on the ID and boarding pass matched. She scrutinized his documents.

The international terminal warranted additional scrutiny. He had been through it all countless times. He wore sunglasses with his dark business suit. While the shades were a common sight in Hawaii, they would undoubtedly catch the eye the TSA behavioral specialist who monitored the actions of passengers from a strategically placed camera in the ceiling. A scan of the man's passport and boarding pass gave the behavioral specialist sitting in an office half a city block away the information she needed to profile the traveler. Computer software at the Terrorist Screening Center automatically compared the name scanned from the embedded chip in his passport to several databases, primarily the No-Fly List and Terrorist Watch List. Names of all airline and shipboard passengers were fed to the FBI's secret Domestic Passenger Tracking and Movement Database as well as the CIA's International Passenger Tracking Database.

By the time the TSA agent had compared the traveler's passport photograph with his actual face, a red or green light would illuminate on the lectern. A red light would require another TSA agent to conduct a more intensive screening of the passenger. A green light signaled the traveler cleared all of the law enforcement and terrorist databases. When a green light illuminated, the TSA screener returned the documents to the traveler and motioned the man to the processing lines on his right. Duncan Hunter said, "Thank you," and moved to the processing line under the watchful eyes of more surveillance cameras, airport security, and law enforcement personnel.

Now Hunter studied the man sitting behind an X-ray machine. Aviation terrorists learned from one another and chose "soft targets," easy marks. As the September 11th terrorist event proved, the x-ray screener position was the weakest link in the passenger screening process, but the young tanned male TSA officer with his head focused intently on the computer monitor didn't elicit any warnings. Hunter divested himself of his two-tone Rolex Submariner, belt, suit jacket, and oxfords, and queued for mandatory irradiation. He passed through the magnetometer in stockinged feet. He couldn't wait to pick up his belongings and get away from the uniformed men and women with their rubber gloves.

As he departed the security checkpoint, Hunter recalled the day Osama bin Laden struck America. He remembered calling Greg Lynche to inform him that he knew how the hijackers got on the 9-11 jets with weapons: the contract screeners at the X-ray machine ignored the images of weapons on the monitor and allowed knives and utility knives or "box cutters" to pass into the "sterile" area of the airport. That the screeners reportedly wore hijabs completely surprised the FBI agents—and the retired CIA intelligence officer Greg Lynche—but not Duncan Hunter. He said, "I guarantee you there were no federal air marshals on those flights and there was probably no electronic surveillance of the security checkpoint, and if there were, then the FBI needs to review the security surveillance tapes and look specifically for female X-ray screeners wearing a hijab. The hijackers with weapons in their baggage would look for and guide onto her and her head cover." Once the FBI composed themselves and asked the right questions the concourse checkpoint surveillance tape proved Hunter's thesis. There were no federal air marshals on any of the flights, and a Muslim woman wearing a hijab was at the x-ray machine. And according to the 9-11 Commission Report, only one of the three departure airports had electronic surveillance at the security checkpoint. But that was a long time ago, and America had federalized airport security screening for only one reason: Osama bin Laden's al-Qaeda found and exploited the weakest link in the passenger screening process: the X-ray screener.

The FBI was astonished that over 50 Muslims, working for the contracted security firms, disappeared from a half dozen airports when the FAA shut down the airspace. It was a network that had not been on the FBI's radar. FBI Special Agents began aggressively surveilling mosques and stopping terrorist attacks until President Mazibuike stopped and prohibited the practice.

. . . . .

Tamerlan al-Sarkari typed his user name and password to access the FBI's Domestic Passenger Tracking and Movement Database; a certain passenger was again on the move. The man al-Sarkari had seen at the White House had just passed through the international terminal of the Honolulu airport. He smiled and said to himself, "*There you are!* Time to get to work."

. . . . .

Duncan Hunter checked into the Admiral's Club Lounge to wait for his boarding call to Sydney. Qantas Airlines Boeing 747-400, *The Spirit of Australia*, was delayed. New takeoff time: TBA, to be announced. With ice water in hand, he found a remote, overstuffed chair that overlooked the airport ramp. He parked his bag and plopped into the chair. He checked his surroundings, taking minimal notice of his fellow travelers in the half-full lounge. He wondered if one of them was there to kill him. No one looked out of place except two men who were obvious federal air marshals; it was difficult to hide a weapon on your body without covering it with a sport coat. They wore the nastiest and cheapest tweed jackets available at the local K-Mart.

No one behaved as if they had seen him before or noticed him at all. He doubted anyone could have followed him to Hawaii. He was good at disappearing, covering his tracks, and then reappearing when least expected. The CIA's training for clandestine officers was superb.

He sighed heavily and reflected on what he had been through the last few days. On the top of the list was that he had been shot at; a bullet missed his head by a fraction of an inch. Then the ghastly memory of the dismembered man he ran over flashed through his brain before he recalled that he had uprooted Carlos and Theresa from their home, banished them to seek shelter on their reservation in Arizona. He had missed Theresa's *huevos rancheros* breakfast. It saddened him that he might never see the Yazzies again.

Even before Lynche's telephone call he knew that the assassin and his rifle could only mean one thing, his cover had been completely blown. He had planned for the possibility years earlier when he and Lynche were just starting out as surveillance pilots for the Agency. He had been forced to leave Texas before when a band of Muslim men overran his ranch house outside of Del Rio. A basement safe room had saved him that night. The next morning, by direction of the Director of Central Intelligence, Hunter was on his way to Newport, Rhode Island to hide out for a year at the Naval War College. There he had met and befriended the greatest U.S. Navy SEAL ever to wear the uniform. There he had been targeted again, this time by a stunning Muslim goddess. The vision of Nazy stepping out of an ancient white Rolls Royce into the cold of an approaching snow storm still made him smile. She had taken his breath away, and the Roll's chauffeur's, with the little white dress she wore that night.

Hunter had expected that someday he would have to evacuate his base of operations. But he never expected that he would be forced to run because a dozen men had lost their lives simply because they shared his name.

Should I have seen this coming? Was I so preoccupied with Nazy, and Kelly, and the business that I became complacent with this enemy? Am I burning out? You cannot burn out if you're not on fire. Was I too arrogant? Lynche would say, "Oh, hell yes!"

A child of about five or six years old bounced into the lounge followed by scolding and overloaded parents. She tossed a stuffed toy, a pink zebra with a small blue balloon tethered around the critter's neck, into the seat next to Hunter, then raced to the large picture window and stared out at the enormous aircraft just yards from her. Hunter smiled at the little blonde girl with her hands and face pressed against the window as her apologetic mother in a bright red muumuu, obviously purchased from a Waikiki market, rushed to corral the frisky moppet. The father wore an ostentatious flowery Tommy Bahama shirt and parked rolling suitcases and shopping bags near the seat occupied by the bizarrely colored furry ungulate and announced rather loudly that he was heading to the men's room.

The scene struck Hunter. He also had a daughter, now a grown woman. He hadn't known she existed until she divulged her secret in his classroom. He read her mother's diary and knew it was true. His old flame with the flaming red hair from 25 years ago. The daughter he didn't know anything about was in the Air Force, was a pilot like her mother...and father. And now Kelly Horne was in the CIA flying Hunter's other YO-3A on surveillance and *Weedbusters* missions. Ideations of having missed raising his little girl and being a doting father were dashed with thoughts he almost vocalized: *I've probably ruined her life getting her involved in this business.* The boarding call for his flight helped Hunter disengage from the spectacle of the kid and her parents with a simple thought that *Kids should have parents to take care of them; and I haven't been taking care of my own little girl.* Hunter sighed as he gathered his roller bag; his last vision was the goofy pink and black zebra looking at him as it was being strangled by a red ribbon attached to a small balloon with the stylized Qantas kangaroo emblazoned on it.

* * * * *

Tamerlan al-Sarkari snorted at the data. He received approval to "exercise the system" via the on-line auction website. The contact solution was solid. He found the registration number of the Qantas aircraft through an on-line search engine, Instant Flight Tracker. Qantas Flight 1144. Armed with the aircraft's flight number, Instant Flight tracker provided type, make, and model of the scheduled aircraft as well as its registration number. Using the registration number beginning with the letters VH, al-Sarkari searched the FAA's on-line database for the aircraft's serial number. He already had every Boeing aircraft's access code. Now he had the two most important pieces of information needed to assume control of the aircraft and override the autonomous anti-hijack software. He looked around his room and cackled like a giddy teenage girl on her way to prom.

* * * * *

Hunter settled into his first class seat near the front of the aircraft. He kicked off his shoes and took water and juice from a tray offered by an attractive long-legged, dark-haired flight attendant. Her Aussie accent was as silky and sexy as Nazy's British accent, and it made him smile. He felt the mammoth aircraft sway slightly as hundreds of people boarded and found their seats for the ten and a half-hour trip. Meanwhile the catering service filled the stores for the upstairs, fore and aft kitchens.

As he waited he vaguely recalled the President awarding the benign-looking software engineer who designed the systems that prevented aircraft full of passengers from falling out of the sky or being driven into the side of a mountain. Maybe he had been wrong about the anti-hijack software when he testified before Congress. Greg Lynche had poked at him to drive the point home that he had been wrong. *So I was wrong!* The admission stung. *I was wrong.* Duncan sighed heavily and pushed the thoughts out of his head. He tried to be perfect and was rarely, if ever, wrong about anything. With the possible exception of Nazy.

Over the intercom system, another sultry-speaking flight attendant ran through her pre-takeoff checklists, informing the passengers that the main door was closed and asking them to pay attention to the safety demonstration. Being on the Boeing made him feel safe for the first time in a few days. He ignored the flight attendant's safety brief. A frequent flyer, he knew the script as well as they did. Before he snapped a noise-cancelling headset over his ears he heard, "In the event of a decompression, an oxygen mask will automatically appear in front of you. To start the flow of oxygen, pull the mask towards you. Place it firmly over your nose and mouth, secure the elastic band behind your head, and breathe normally." Instructions on life vests, the operation of electronic devices, and smoking in the lavatories were lost to the quietness of the headphones.

Hunter checked his email and text messages one last time before takeoff. Bill McGee had packed the ranch house furnishings and moved them from Texas to Custer, South Dakota. In a few days they would be taken out of storage and delivered to Wyoming. The motorcoach, the trailer, and a Hummer2 were in the Jackson Hole Airport hangar with the Gulfstream G-550, along with his paintings, the Rembrandt, and everything else from his ranch office. Under the watchful eye of a frowning flight attendant, he powered down the BlackBerry.

His mind turned to the white and blue Gulfstream G-550 and what to do with it. It wasn't like he could afford to continue to operate the jet;

he was doing well financially but not on the level of Sylvester Stallone or Floyd Mayweather. President Hernandez rewarded Hunter with the Gulfstream after he successfully completed his mission to Algeria by finding and eliminating the terrorist who shot down commercial aircraft. President Hernandez was probably not aware of the unused ransom was still aboard the aircraft, some $100 million dollars in American gold eagles. Hunter looked to spend some of the bounty. He had looked for some mountain property that was near a jet-capable airport. Jackson Hole was perfect for the skiing, for the isolation, and for an emergency residence in case the gossamer connections between the CIA's cover and his professional business cover were ever broken.

He had stumbled upon the newly built and vacant hangar during a cross-country flight when he needed a place out of the weather for mechanics to perform maintenance on his old red-trimmed Gulfstream G-IVSP. Surprised that the hangar was available, he secured the title to the hangar, rented a car, and started looking for a house in the area. He had visions of skiing or ice skating with Nazy, hanging out at a lodge afterwards, and nursing hot chocolates. Some of his best memories of her were from their first date. He had exposed her as a spy, turned her to work for the CIA, and showed her how to French kiss. But with their current schedules, they could rarely coordinate their time off so they could get away from Washington D.C. Maybe when he acquired a new identity and recused himself from the counter-terrorism business, maybe then there'd be time to teach Nazy how to snow plow or ski. Then they could return to Jackson Hole and settle down in the place where they married late one night two years ago.

He tapped his fingers on the glass in his hand, scanned the first class section, and again ran through the meat of Lynche's hastily thrown together plan. After he and McGee said their goodbyes at the ranch house, Hunter ignored the older Gulfstream in the hangar and flew the G-550 to Manassas, Virginia. He cashiered any notion there would be a "tail watcher" at the large general aviation airport south of Washington D.C. If any group had a chance of getting a bead on him while he was on the run and using one of the Gulfstreams, it was the tail watchers. They concerned him the most.

He viewed tail watchers as a loathsome group, an international den of rats run by an unknown headmaster. Hunter was convinced they were organized and managed by an old KGB colonel; Lynche disabused the notion, claiming Hunter was forever finding the dusty fingerprints of the former Soviet Union on anything remotely related to the business of determining or monitoring the movement of CIA intelligence officers or their contractors. But Hunter's intuition was more correct than the DCI would give him credit for, as the tail watchers were found to be a loose confederation of eyes and ears dedicated to unmasking members of the West's intelligence communities. The main business was run out of a tiny office in a nondescript building three blocks from the Lubyanka Prison in Moscow, and those in the franchise who filled their computers with information were well paid for their services.

These liberal busybodies, who were recruited from socialist groups, hung out at or near major airports and made it their goal in life to identify and report on aircraft suspected of transporting the rich and famous, mavens of commerce, members of Congress or Parliament, and senior members of the British Ministry of Defence and the U.S. Department of Defense. But their prime directive was to identify and track the executives as well as the spies of the intelligence community. Professional tail watchers primarily focused on business and corporate aircraft transiting near the major international airports, such as Dulles, Heathrow, and Charles de Gaulle, and virtually every major international airport in Europe, the Middle East, Southeast Asia, South America, and Australia.

Tail watchers would rent apartments or hotel rooms and employ telescopes to read an aircraft's registration number, its "N number." The letter N signified the aircraft was registered in the United States, the letter C marked aircraft registered to Canada, D for Germany, VH for Australia and so on, in accordance with the Convention on International Civil Aviation. Once a tail watcher identified that a particular tail number had landed or taken off, the information—video, photographic, or data—was dumped into a computer and transmitted to chat rooms and other liberal, communist, environmental, or terrorist websites across the globe. American N numbers with vague or questionable histories were deemed to be "probable covert aircraft" or, most likely, those used in the transport of CIA executives or members of the National Clandestine Service on a covert mission. Tail watchers made a name for themselves by identifying suspected "rendition aircraft" which transported high-value al-Qaeda or senior Taliban terrorists to other countries to be interrogated or detained. Guantanamo Bay, Cuba was a frequent destination of the marginally marked business aircraft. Hunter had said to Lynche more than once, "Tail watchers are not on the side of the good guys—and you'll never convince me they're not KGB."

He glanced out the cabin window and returned to his thoughts. He would bet that whoever had put the hit out on him likely didn't know his company possessed two Gulfstream business jets; the red-trimmed jet had much history and bona fides operating out of the Texas airport, while the blue-trimmed and virtually new G-550 was rarely used, then it only came out at night. CIA analysts confirmed the G-550's N-number had never been entered into the tail watcher's database. He ensured the spotlights on the G-550's tail were extinguished anytime they were on the ground by adding a landing checklist item—pull the tail floodlight circuit breaker. Hunter wanted to keep the jet out of their database for the foreseeable future.

DCI Lynche had arranged for Hunter to be picked up by an armored Agency staff car when he arrived in Virginia. The driver was on time and never said a word to his passenger. He quietly deposited him at the CIA's remote mountaintop conference center complex. It was an especially secure facility with floodlights, heavily armed guards, and an entrance gate that was impenetrable to everything including an Abrams tank. A heavy, ten-foot tall fence enveloped the complex with signage declaring "The Use of Deadly Force is Authorized," which likely precluded many jihadi wannabees from making a run at the checkpoint or pole vaulting over the barrier. Triple-strand concertina inside, outside and atop the chain link even dissuaded field mice and lizards from entering. No one would be looking for him there, and no one would be waiting to ambush him when he checked into his room. No one except Nazy Cunningham. She attacked him before he was completely inside the door. Somewhere between the doorway and the bed, she said breathlessly, *"I missed you so."* He was barely able to pry her lips off his.

Nazy made love to him as if she would never see him again. Afterwards she snored on his shoulder while Hunter lay awake. Her perfume, redolent of ruddy cinnamon, still tickled his nostrils while an overhead fan dispersed the smells of lust and cooled the overheated couple.

In the morning, he and Nazy showered together in the impossibly small stall before meeting with the Director of Central Intelligence who arrived unapologetically by a Marine Corps white-top helicopter. Nazy wore a black skirt that accentuated her legs. Hunter wore a suit without a tie. Lynche wouldn't be caught dead without a tie or a business suit.

Over breakfast at a table in a corner of the complex's cafeteria, Lynche laid out his assessment of the threats his favorite couple faced. It wasn't just the food that was bleak and depressing; their collective expressions showed nothing but resignation. You can only be a spy for so long.

It had been good during the early days of his CIA career under the leadership and guidance of Greg Lynche, the spymaster extraordinaire. But Duncan Hunter's long-term cover as a high profile Texas businessman and scholar had also become his undoing. He was too well known to live a normal life, and he was too well known in university and the business worlds to capriciously die from freak causes like James Dean crashing his Porsche sports car in a head-on accident, or Buddy Holly dying in a plane crash shortly after take-off. DCI Lynche had come to understand that if he had to kill the Duncan Hunter persona, there could be no body over which to mourn.

Trying to disentangle Hunter from the real world he had created in the aviation industry and academia in order to get him into what was essentially a witness protection program looked to be too hard, too little, and too late to do properly. Changing the identities of defecting politicians and generals was so much easier than changing the aviation maven Hunter persona. The only good news was that Hunter did not like microphones or cameras and had kept out of the limelight of network broadcast features. Unrecorded academic settings, lecturing on aviation terrorism, were small enough for him to fly under the radars of the cartels and terrorist networks.

Defecting politicians and generals were usually set free once they were debriefed. They were given some help to resettle in obscure locations often with meaningless low-visibility jobs and a government stipend to help them keep quiet. It had been a good idea to initially credit the terrorist group responsible for issuing the *fatwa* with the killing of a man named Duncan Hunter. Now after a few days of critical thinking, Lynche was convinced it wasn't a sufficient distraction or legerdemain to allow the real Duncan Hunter to live, to manage his business, to teach and lecture, or be the occasional consultant. Lynche had thought it through and was convinced that awarding a star on the CIA's Memorial Wall and burial at Arlington National Cemetery was only the opening gambit of a much larger contest. Hunter was reluctant to concur with the DCI's guidance on the subject. Like a man who had just been told he had cancer, Hunter was in denial.

Old training was hard to break and he scoured the 747's cabin absentmindedly for threats. Hunter shook his head in defeat and disgust. *It may really be over. Illegitimi non carborundum! It's hard to accept defeat. I cannot believe the bastards have won.*

CHAPTER TWENTY-SEVEN

1700 July 19, 2014
Honolulu, Hawaii

"It'll be over soon," cooed al-Sarkari smugly as he stared into the widescreen touchscreen monitor. Effeminate delicate fingers raced over a computer keyboard. During a previous visit to the targeted remote computer he had cracked the Windows password, performed man-in-the-middle attacks, and captured network passwords. Then he had used a bevy of exploit codes, the ultimate hacking tools, to attack a specific web server to get to the root access of the remote computer and planted backdoors. In essence, he had set up a dummy account on a remote computer within a business in Frankfurt, Germany from which to break and enter several U.S. government databases. Now he scanned the ports of the remote computer to find out which ones were open and found the FBI's Domestic Passenger Tracking and Movement Database. Confident fingers pounded the keyboard as he quickly found the flight number of Hunter's flight. With his index finger he touched the monitor to expand the flight number's data and properties, and destination. Two taps on the screen brought up the aircraft's registration number and Boeing's 747-production serial number.

A smile cracked his stoic face. Tamerlan reviewed the database to determine the proper key code to override the aircraft's computer software. Copied and saved. Then he closed the connection of the remote computer, virtually wiping his fingerprints off the layers of computer security software he had just breached. It was a good day to be a software engineer. Al-Sarkari could do anything, and if he was a little lucky, no security administrator would even bother to run the security analytics since he hadn't changed or saved any data from the government system. He'd be home free.

He nibbled on a pistachio pastry and sipped orange juice as he logged on to the world's largest on-line auction website. Al-Sarkari found the auction he was looking for, the one given to him by the ROC chieftain, and selected the option to "Ask Seller a Question." When the appropriate page loaded on the screen he typed, "after payment, dispatch parcel immediately." He repeated the process with other on-line auctions in the U.S.

.   .   .   .   .   .

Frustration prevented him from relaxing; his mind continued to wander around past memories. He couldn't focus on the book in his lap, so he gave up on it and put it away. He remained detached from the events around him; he dismissed the extraneous background noise in the first class cabin.

We have enough money to disappear but how naïve is that? They never give up; we will always have to worry about being discovered, followed or ambushed. The house in Wyoming is a good start, and it's a fortress. Safe rooms. Not many mosques in Jackson or Wyoming to be concerned about. In his television special, Demetrius Eastwood had interviewed several former imams who had renounced Islam and warned him that, "A devout Muslim is at war with infidels always. Every devout Muslim is an Islamist. The truth is that there isn't a single mosque in Norway or Sweden or in all of Europe that isn't run by or isn't under the control of what you in the West call Islamists. I fully expect this interview will lead to my death. I know because I would've been one of the first to send true believers out to find and kill those who turned their back on Islam. And you must kill the defectors in the most gruesome manner to send a signal: submit and never think about leaving Islam." After exposing their god-like president, I became the unexpected target of democrats and liberals. Now I'm in the crosshairs of a billion pissed off Muslims who want me dead. Both groups want my head on a pike. Hunter pinched his lips and deliberately changed the thoughts bouncing back-and-forth between his ears.

McGee, again, saved the day! Saved me; saved Nazy. Just an amazing man. Thank God for SEALs and their ability to think outside the box and be creative in coming up with ways to win in any situation. Maybe like the "old me" on the racquetball court? Old thoughts of playing racquetball with his gang of former old national champions brought a wry grin. *Ingenuity becomes an invaluable weapon when faced with limited resources and every action has to be a zero failure mission.*

Hunter moistened his lips in the dry aircraft air. He yawned and took several deep breaths. He was becoming more uncomfortable, which was unusual for him for a long-duration flight. He had a little pressure in his head and his heartbeat was clearly elevated. He had thought he'd be able to relax and sleep in his lie-flat seat once they were airborne, but there were too many unresolved issues that needed attention.

His mind wandered all over his life and settled into the arena of the armed YO-3A and its software problems. *I was just beginning to get more comfortable with that damned automatic takeoff and landing system; it was more accurate than I ever could be with the radar altimeter, GPS, and flight computer in flying a precision approach to any spot on the globe. But it acted up! No! It tried to kill me.* The old electronics technician in him wondered, *Why and what did I do to make it go stupid? Was it something I did? No. No. No! Having the flight controls lock up isn't normal. It wasn't me; it was the airplane. Had to be. I definitely cannot let Kelly in the airplane without a working and reliable ATLS. Yes, I had done it hundreds of times, but now with all of the sensors on the aircraft, it was heavy and squirrely, especially in crosswinds. Yeah, the damn thing tried to kill me.*

His head rolled from side to side like the last ball in a tilted pinball machine. His neck was stiff. Hunter turned his head to alleviate the pressure but only heard his vertebrae creak. He val salvaed to try and equalize the pressure in his ears.

I'm not ready to give up or give in. I don't want to walk away from it! But I need to face it—it's over. I cannot play racquetball anymore—am too afraid of reinjuring my repaired Achilles or my hand, I cannot drive my racecar anymore—no time with all of the businesses and Nazy. Why am I going to Australia—one last lecture to stroke my ego? I could have cancelled it. Someone else could have filled in. Too late now; I'm committed—I'm going to Australia! Hunter closed his eyes for a second, but no more. As his temples pounded, his eyes shot open and his racing mind was on to a new topic.

I need to take the gold and find a new place to hide out. Take the money and run away with Nazy.

Nazy. She didn't tease me like she usually does. There was a sense of urgency. Did she think it would be the last time? Go back to a place where we ached to go to again? She held me so close, I wondered if she was afraid that I wouldn't come back to her. Hunter smiled at this train of thought and encouraged his mind to relive the last morning he and Nazy were together. *You couldn't get a nanotube between us.* He remembered. *Her scent was heavy in the air even with the fan blowing.*

He labored a bit to breathe deeply, almost straining to fill his lungs, but the thoughts of Nazy filled him with fire and energy. *She took my hand and dragged me to the shower. Oh, she had... that... look. Not bedroom eyes, but that coy, sexy, peek-under-her-brow-look that screamed, "You know what I want and I want it now!" I don't even remember how the water was turned on. Hot, steamy. I went for the soap but she pushed me onto the floor. Urgent! I banged my head as she moved to straddle my face, nearly smothering me.*

Hunter was breathing rapidly; he didn't recognize that he straining a bit to fill his lungs. *She didn't know I couldn't breathe. She was killing me, but she was completely oblivious immersed in her own immediate ecstasy.* Hunter nearly smirked as his chest heaved. *If I'm going to die from a lack of O2....*

His thoughts took a radical shift. Some other old memory was screaming in his head. A warning. *Nazy's not trying to kill me—they're trying to kill me....* Then the vision of the naked Nazy hovering over him, dissipated in an instant, replaced by the hiss of the wind racing over the aircraft's fuselage. His noise-cancelling headphones had slipped off. His chest heaved; his lungs clawed for more air. *Danger, danger!* Now his head really hurt. *What the hell?*

A glance out the cabin window proved it was still nighttime. Hunter looked up at a large computer monitor on the forward bulkhead. The aircraft was halfway to Australia over the most remote part of the Pacific Ocean. He yawned hard; his legs were stiff and tingly from hours in the seat. He casually scanned the darkened cabin. No one moved nor could he hear anyone snoring. *The men always snored.* His head bobbed; his chest rose and fell as his lungs screamed for more oxygen. He wanted to close his eyes and sleep. *Working too hard.... So tired.... Can't focus....*

Breathing is a natural bodily function, one that is usually ignored even when the brain craved more oxygen and sent the commands to the lungs to work harder. It is nearly impossible for anyone to recognize the onset of hypoxia, and many pilots across the globe have been caught unawares when their aircraft slowly depressurized and rendered them unconscious. People who faint rarely recognize the warning signs that they are about to pass out, and when they wake up they are clueless why they are on the floor. Duncan Hunter, distracted by memories of his bride in the shower, failed to recognize the warning signs that he was a mere sixty seconds away from unconsciousness.

. . . . .

Al-Sarkari keyed several commands into the computer and moved the mouse to find the location of the second aircraft, the second target as suggested by the on-line auction communication system. "Post at your earliest convenience." He stared at the monitor. He recognized the numbers. 26000. 27000. Both aircraft were fully mission capable and ready for flight. However, the flight schedule: TBD. To be determined.

He'd have to wait until one of the aircraft was dispatched and airborne before programing it like he had the Qantas jumbo. The newspaper indicated the president would be traveling soon to a meeting of leaders. In Iran.

He copied and saved the two key codes to override the aircraft's computer software. It was time for bed.

As he slept, al-Sarkari dreamed of the green-eyed Muslima in the white ball gown he had seen at the awards ceremony. She was where she should be, on her knees between his.

. . . . .

There weren't that many passengers in the first class section and only Hunter had his reading light illuminated; all of the other passengers were down for the evening. Some would say it was smart to sleep away the distance. Hunter's mind was no longer bouncing between a fuzzy vision of a rapacious and satiated Nazy and the turmoil of a career being compelled to end. He was exhausted; his chest was heaving as if he were hyperventilating. *What's going on…am I having a heart attack?*

He balled his hands into fists; they felt overly stiff and puffy and ached as they were swollen. Again he yawned and strained to fill his lungs. He needed to check his hands so he brought them into the reading light over his shoulder. Between deep gulps of air, he noted his fingers were a medium shade of blue. His ring finger was swollen around his wedding band. Very unusual. *That's weird.* He stared at them as he again struggled to breathe, struggled to make sense of his surroundings. Somewhere in his subconscious, Hunter asked a question, something dull and indistinct. Something that he wasn't able to immediately put into words. He was confused and growing more so with every second.

Between heaves of his chest he turned his head to scan the area for threats, a habit long ingrained into his psyche. He saw the little kid's balloon had escaped and was stuck onto the ceiling. It was many times bigger than the last time he had seen it. The little white kangaroo was now the size of a dog. He remembered something vaguely about balloons and swollen fingers and...air. Some old training tried to kick in, alert him; to smack him in the back of his throbbing head to wake him up and make him pay attention. He hazily remembered the last time he felt this way, but the thoughts would barely come: *I probably should go on oxygen.* But, there wasn't anyone with an oxygen mask to rescue him; to save him. *Where's the oxygen?* He looked up as if the thought would be sufficient for those silly round yellow oxygen masks to hear him and drop down from the overhead panel. When they didn't drop onto his face, between eyelids opening and closing like a camera shutter driven by a power winder, something in the back of his brain shrieked, *Find a mask!*

Hunter realized he was about to die. He lifted the seat belt buckle and tried to escape, jump out of his seat, and run. *Find a mask!*

He struggled to walk toward the galley, toward the cockpit. Hunter staggered and wobbled; his head was splitting with pain. No oxygen in his lungs. No O2 getting to his brain. When he saw two flight attendants spread out on the floor of the galley kitchen with their arms and legs askew at odd angles, it didn't register that they were unconscious. He searched frantically for the flight attendant's gear locker. His vision began to tunnel. *Find a mask! Find a mask!* He dropped to his knees and tore open doors as fast as his fat fingers could. He threw the flight attendants' carry-ons across the kitchen, and he finally found what he was looking for—the cabin crew's portable oxygen bottles and masks. He fell to his elbows and raced against time and unconsciousness to turn the valve and start the flow of O2. His vision narrowed and darkened as if he were pulling Gs in his old fighter jet; his eyelids slammed shut as he brought the mask to his face. He collapsed onto the floor as oxygen hissed from the center of the grey silicone rubber, his nose and mouth mashed into the oxygen mask.

The few remaining functional synapses he had left in his cranium sent the strangulated commands: *Breathe. Breathe, you big dummy. Breathe!!*

Oxygen escaping from the mask filled his lungs with the life-saving element. Number eight on the periodic table. Between nitrogen and fluorine. The most essential element for life. His eyelids fluttered open. He jerked several times as he lay on the floor of the aircraft, his head at an awkward angle. After ten deep gulps from the bottled oxygen his vison began to return to normal. No more tunnel vision. The fresh O2 did nothing to alleviate the pain in the back of his skull or the pounding in his temples. It still felt as if they were being attacked by a jackass riding a jackhammer.

He couldn't remember why he was on the floor or how he got there, so he didn't move. A precaution. Hunter had no idea how long he had been out. Having an O2 mask crushed onto his face was a signal he understood: *I'm alive!* He labored groggily to an upright position with one hand while he held the O2 mask to his face with the other. Full consciousness swept over him as the auxiliary oxygen streamed into his lungs; he took stock at his predicament. He strapped the portable O2 system onto his chest with the Velcro tabs.

The cabin was cold; the flight attendants were unconscious; his fingers were still shades of blue, and the kid's balloon was the size of a medicine ball. All signs that the cabin had become depressurized and everyone aboard was hypoxic. Comatose, maybe even dead. Heart failures for many if he didn't get moving. No time to grieve. It was time to live. His head snapped to the cockpit door. *I have to get in! Find out why the airplane is killing us.*

He pulled out more oxygen bottles from the storage bin and strapped O2 masks over the noses and mouths of the flight attendants. Maybe they could help if they weren't dead, he reasoned. He spun the valves to start the oxygen flowing to their lungs and hoped they would recover. He didn't have time to wait to awaken them. Then he stood up and banged on the cabin door. It was wasted energy, the door was locked. Cockpit doors are always locked. And, as he had taught in his graduate school classes, they were impossible to breach. He mouthed into the mask, *I have to get in!*

Hunter pounded the door several times before assuming the flight crew was also incapacitated. He found the interphone system near the flight attendant jump seats and tried to make contact with the cockpit. No one answered. No surprise. Hunter felt the aircraft under his feet. It wasn't climbing or descending, but it was turning. He assessed his predicament: The airplane had to be flying on autopilot; the cabin had become depressurized; the crew were incapacitated, and there was no way to get into the cockpit. He scrutinized the door to see if it was a pre-9/11 door or if it was a post-9/11 door. Of course, it was a post-9/11 door with all of the reinforced, armor-plated safeguards. A sophisticated lock extended pins into the frame, and a bracing bar on the inside would even keep King Kong from breaking down the door.

He recalled ridiculing the failsafe design when a mentally defective copilot locked his pilot out of the cockpit and flew the aircraft into the side of the mountain in the Alps. Hunter had challenged his students with the scenario of how a pilot could penetrate the cockpit if his copilot had locked him out? And their answer was simply: firepower. *Firepower! Shoot your way into the cockpit; go after the weakest link—the deadbolt latch. And I know where some weapons might be found!* He crossed his arms over the O2 bottle strapped to his chest and raced out of the first class section, down the stairs, and nearly stumbled onto the first deck. His legs were still not functioning 100 percent but his brain, flushed with 100 percent aviator's breathing oxygen, was becoming more razor sharp. His adrenaline levels again spiked. They were all going to die if he didn't do something. That drove him to action. *The pressure chamber training helped to keep me alive and recognize the decompression; now if I can just get into the damn cockpit!*

He looked for the red emergency exits signs near the middle of the aircraft and ran to them. He looked for men wearing sports coats. When he found an unconscious man with a tweed blazer, he reached inside the jacket and pulled out the semiautomatic weapon of an air marshal. He released the magazine to check the number of bullets, then racked the slide to chamber a round. He ran back upstairs to the cockpit of the Boeing 747 sucking O2 out of the bottle on his chest like an infant slurping the last drop of milk from a bottle.

CHAPTER TWENTY-EIGHT

0700 July 20, 2014
The White House

As the CIA executives entered the Oval Office, President Hernandez gestured to a sofa and said, "Good Morning, Miss Cunningham, Director Lynche." They positioned themselves side by side as the President pushed himself from behind the Resolute Desk and came to greet them. Any early morning meeting at the White House with key leaders of the CIA was usually attended by others members of the President's inner circle; the Vice President, the Chairman of the Joint Chiefs. But not today.

For this occasion, President Hernandez, DCI Lynche and the National Counter Terrorism Center Director Nazy Cunningham were all dressed by Brooks Brothers; dark suits, white shirts, white blouse. The men wore the prototypical government business shoe, brown Johnston Murphy's, and she wore a classic black pump with an ankle strap. Her pencil skirt flattered her figure, and the men sported innocuous blue ties. The men noticed Nazy's uppermost button was fastened over the mound of cleavage which lay below. They ignored her thin black Zero Halliburton.

Handshakes preceded the somber greetings; there was no small talk. Before taking her seat, Nazy handed the President a red folder from her slim briefcase. She smoothed her hands over her buttocks before she touched the sofa to ensure her skirt wouldn't get unnecessarily wrinkled. As she sat down she began, 'Good morning, Mr. President. This is the President's Daily Brief."

The President's Daily Brief (PDB) is a Top Secret document produced each morning by the Director of National Intelligence for the President of the United States. The DNI's office is responsible for gathering, fusing, and summarizing intelligence from all collecting agencies, the CIA, the Defense Intelligence Agency, the National Security

Agency, and the Federal Bureau of Investigation. The PDB is considered the most highly sensitized classified document in the government and has historically been briefed in the company of other high officials, generally the Secretaries of State and Defense, and the National Security Advisor. Rare, special editions of the PDB have been "for the President's eyes only." Today was one of those days.

Nazy Cunningham began her presentation with an overview of the threats to the security of the United States. The President asked questions regarding the clandestine introduction of weapons of mass destruction into the U.S., and the Russian Federation's support for international terrorism and revolutionary violence. An FBI addendum highlighted the prospects for a resurgence of the international communist movement into the U.S., as well as conditions and trends of Islamic State fighters posing as Libyan and Syrian refugees affecting the security of Europe and the United States. Director Lynche discussed Syria's role in international terrorism and the ongoing insurgency and instability in Libya, Nigeria, Central and South America. Venezuela was providing passports to Middle East terrorists. He highlighted the roles and effectiveness of some leaders of the former Soviet Union and the Islamic State in attacks on certain segments of America's industrial base, primarily commercial aviation and nuclear power plants.

President Hernandez waited for the real debrief; Director Lynche and Nazy Cunningham exchanged no looks. Lynche said, "We think we have an idea of where he is." An almost undetectable Presidential nod suggested that Lynche was to continue. "There is one singularity, someone who believed they recognized his build, broad shoulders, and height. He wore gloves, a *thobe* and a *keffiyeh,* and entered the Burj Khalifa. That was on the morning of July second. The source did not see his face."

Nazy added, "There has been absolutely no chatter; nothing regarding his whereabouts, his death, or any movements.

President Hernandez remained focused, quiet, and nodded for more.

"The NRO records a Gulfstream jet flew from Honolulu to an airport outside of Manila, the old Cubi Point Naval Air Station." Nazy looked at her boss. "They landed at night. Within an hour of landing, STRATCOM reported an Emirates submarine departed from the old Subic Bay naval base. It was next seen pulling into a submarine pen in the UAE."

For the first time since they began, the President smiled. "UAE? I wouldn't have guessed that."

"Mr. President, the former president had exceptionally good relations with UAE. I don't know exactly how many Guantanamo detainees he released into their custody. The real question is where is he...*living*." Lynche didn't want to say, "hiding."

Nazy Cunningham spoke up. "Mr. President, the destination of the submarine is the source of much speculation. Our overheads, ah, satellites, tracked the submarine to a location between Abu Dhabi and Dubai. An area called Ghantoot. A sheltered peninsula with a covered dock which is sufficiently large to handle an extremely large submarine. Before the UAE became a confederate of emirates, the area had been a lay-up area for smugglers. And that particular location was rumored to be the base station and a hiding place for a little known ancient Muslim sailor, Abbasayeed."

Lynche blurted out, "The original Captain Nemo."

"Of Jules Verne fame?" asked the Chief Executive.

Nazy nodded and continued, "Sort of. Abbasayeed sailed to Africa, Indonesia, the Philippines, Japan, and China, and South America. He traded in silk, pearls, ivory, gold. His ships out of Ghantoot made him very rich. At one time he had a fleet of a hundred *dhows*. Traditional sailing vessels and a few steamers."

Lynche interjected, "But the best part...."

Nazy nodded imperceptibly. "Like the fictional Captain Nemo, Abbasayeed built one of the first ocean-going submarines—more of a semi-submersible with aerodynamic snorkels. A steamship. He used it, reportedly, exclusively for special cargo such as weapons and slaves."

"And he used it when he visited secret cities and to avoid pirates and bandits," offered Lynche.

President Hernandez was amused but unconvinced. "Ok, what I'm hearing is there may be a case for Mazibuike to have taken a submarine to the UAE, but you don't have any proof. I need...."

Lynche cut him off. Nazy handed the President a photograph. "We believe the submarine took him to Banda Aceh. We may have his picture in Sharjah coming off a business jet from Banda Aceh. Courtesy of the NRO."

The President of the United States broke out into a broad conspiratorial smile. *She wouldn't say they know it's him because of his ears.* "Well, now, that's a start. What else do you have, or are you going to string me along?" His smile belied his attempt at friendly sarcasm.

Both Lynche and Nazy returned his smile. Nazy handed President Hernandez another red file marked "EYES ONLY." She spoke from memory. "Mr. President, first, we do not know where your predecessor is, specifically. He could be anywhere in the UAE or even somewhere else. But we do have a few ideas that we have been trying to flesh out. Israeli intelligence and British MI6 provided much of the information I'm about to share. The British have a greater presence in the UAE than we do and have operated in the area since the 1900s. Both intelligence services reported they were very interested in the activities of a large cadre of workers in and around the area of the covered pier. In the late 1990s the British Navy was able to get a scuba diver inside." Nazy handed the President several glossy black and white photographs of a two-boat underground submarine pen. "That is a Redoubtable-Class French nuclear submarine. The *Abba Sayeed.* It is not equipped with submarine-launched ballistic missiles. It features a hundred-foot long palace-like living area for the royal family behind the conning tower. The submarine was built in secret for the first *Ra'is* or president of the United Arab Emirates, Zayed bin Sultan Al Nahyan." The Arabic names and words rolled naturally off her tongue.

"Why would the French sell a *nuclear* submarine to UAE?"

Lynche answered, "Dismissing the fact the French would sell the rope to hang themselves if they could make a profit, this was an off-the-grid boat. Many politicians benefited from that transaction. The French president pocketed much of the money. You may know the French supplied Iraq and Iran with weapons, ordnance, and aircraft during the embargo years. This is nothing new, except we didn't know about the submarine. STRATCOM keeps an inventory of boats, and they had the unnamed UAE submarine in their databank. But it hadn't received much interest until recently."

Nazy Cunningham chimed in. "The U.S. Navy reports that the Redoubtable-Class sub doesn't get much activity. However, the boat left its underground pen on the day your predecessor's file was released to Congress and the media. It headed east. NSA confirmed a telephone call was made from the Oval Office to a State Department Trade and Development Agency office in Hawaii. That office then made contact with an aircraft charter company in Sharjah, UAE, and a law firm in Honolulu."

"Do we know who received the call?" President Hernandez had been briefed Mazibuike supporters within the NSA were monitoring the calls from the Hernandez White House. Transcripts of his calls to foreign leaders were continually being leaked to the media. The only question was did Mazibuike's loyal supporters monitor the telephone and cellphone calls from the White House when Mazibuike was in office? Was there another source? There had to be a paper trail.

"The Secret Service has investigated the associations between your predecessor and those in that law office." Nazy stopped short again, not allowing her woman's intuition to take over her tongue. It wasn't the right time, and it definitely wasn't the right place. *There had to be a paper trail.* She hadn't even shared her thoughts with Lynche. When Lynche began speaking she heard her name and returned her attention to the conversation.

"Based on the proximity of the telephone call and some of the history surrounding the submarines, Nazy thinks there may be a link with an office within the Burj Khalifa. We believe it is called ROC." Lynche looked to Nazy to continue the brief.

"Isn't that some kind of mythical bird?" asked the President.

She said, "Yes, sir. We believe Zayed bin Sultan also led the ROC from his ascension to the UAE presidency. We discovered he had been a member of the Abu Dhabi emirate which specialized in ocean trade, just as Sharjah specializes in aircraft maintenance and manufacturing, and Dubai has positioned itself as an aviation hub for commercial aviation." Nazy looked to Lynche as if passing a torch.

Lynche said, "The UAE's oil reserves are the seventh-largest in the world. They have spent their money wisely on building infrastructure, healthcare, education and, um, other projects."

"Greg, when you say, 'other projects' I know there's more to it. Is this going somewhere?"

"I think we have arrived at our destination Mr. President. We believe Zayed bin Sultan also built a secret underground city."

The President mashed his eyebrows together as if two wooly

caterpillars were colliding. "What?"

"A secret city. Underground. Between Abu Dhabi and Dubai. And they did it right under our noses. The NRO and NGA can confirm. We believe that is the location where your predecessor is likely hiding." Nazy handed the President more photographs and diagrams. President Hernandez scrutinized them thoroughly.

Then he lifted his eyes and shook his head in wonder. Nazy Cunningham finished her brief with a little history on how the UAE came into being and how the old president of the UAE managed to construct an underground city. "Mr. President, oil was discovered in 1958 and oil exports began in 1962, primarily with British petroleum engineering assistance. In the late 1960s, Sheikh Zayed bin Sultan hired a Japanese architect to design and plan the city of Dubai. When he was elected as President of the UAE in the early 1970s, he turned again to this Japanese architect to design and plan for an underground city whose purpose remains a mystery. The scope of the project is, as you can see, breathtaking. It could be nearly seventy miles in length and a thousand yards wide. Adding to the enigma of the construction in the desert, several hundred craftsmen from across the Islamic world and thousands of laborers traveled to Abu Dhabi and were never heard from again. This may or may not be a coincidence or even relevant, but at the same time of the secret city's construction, hundreds of women started to vanish from nearly every country around the world, every year; several thousand in all. They were also never heard from again. The trajectory of the coincidence is that some of them were likely used as sex slaves for the craftsmen and construction workers."

Lynche added, "And if the royals were still into harems…."

President Hernandez nodded the inference.

Nazy was nearly finished. She handed the President more pages marked TOP SECRET. "Architectural drawings of a subterranean submarine pen and schematics of the French submarine raised more questions than answers. The submarine was apparently constructed to serve as the private underwater sailing vessel for the royal family. The submarine pen was hardened against thermonuclear attacks. In the case of a nuclear attack, it could have been used to escape the region. We believe that particular sub was used to transport President Mazibuike from the

Philippines to Banda Aceh. The submarine could also be used to transport cargo as well as…humans. Possibly as many as a hundred."

"Smuggling?" asked the President incredulously. "But they have all the money in the world."

"Possibly," offered Lynche. "Probably." It was a difficult assessment to confirm. The meeting was coming to a close and his eyes had drifted across Nazy's bare legs several times. A harmless normal reaction. He lifted his head and his voice. "They have a long history of harboring political refugees. Admiral Canaris provided U-boats to the Abu Dhabi emir in the late 1930s for emergency evacuation of Nazi leaders…."

"Or Hitler," offered the President.

"Yes, Mr. President. Canaris set up a network of U-boats stretching from Spain to Western Africa to the Arabian Peninsula. They were positioned for the extraction of the Nazi leadership and their treasure. When the crews weren't hiding, they took to banditry. The emir's boats were used to smuggle anything and everything that was profitable. African or Islamic dictators ousted from office found their way to the UAE with their families and likely with the treasure of their nation. With the revelation that there may be a secret city under the desert, these overthrown dictators and political refugees may literally have gone underground. That is also the Israeli assessment."

Nazy handed the President more maps of a superhighway against a backdrop of nothingness and sand. Nothing obvious to hint there was a warren of tunnels and structures under the miles of concrete.

"The only report, now taken in this context, is that he may have entered the Burj Khalifa. The night he was seen entering the building was one of the city's foggiest nights. The fog was so dense the UAE's fleet of unmanned aircraft was grounded, and commercial flights into and out of Dubai and Abu Dhabi were delayed." Lynche looked up at the President who was still fiddling with photographs marked TOP SECRET.

"Would he be afraid of drones?" asked the President. "Were there any in the area to confirm he was there?"

"Mr. President, like you, he knows of their capabilities and limitations. On a night like that, to the best of our knowledge, all unmanned assets were grounded. Reportedly it was so foggy that night that there was nothing to see. If he was going to emerge he'd want to do it when there was no chance of him being detected, tracked, or targeted." Lynche was concerned where the conversation was leading.

"Why would he expose himself? In a public place?"

Nazy answered, "Sir, men like him are not masters of the tradecraft, but they know enough to be effective staying out of sight. We think he attended a meeting. Our analysts think there may have been someone he needed to meet. Most likely, the masters of the secret city wouldn't allow that person or persons to learn of their underground facility. It was likely a business meeting. They chose the right time to move without worry of being spotted by cameras either fixed or airborne. They know enough to use countermeasures to mask their movements. Mazibuike used the weather; OBL had a huge overhang to prevent satellites and unmanned systems from being able to take a look."

The President asked, "When was this again?"

"July second," answered Nazy.

"Why is that date familiar?"

Lynche swallowed hard. "Mr. President, that was the same night the Indonesian Sky Link jet disappeared over the Pacific."

The President, the CIA Director, and the Director of the National Counter Terrorism Center exchanged conspiratorial glances. *How is that even possible?*

"Greg, you said my predecessor knows enough to mask his movements. He also knows of our strategic assets and capabilities. This is where Duncan's airplane comes in handy, I take it."

"Yes, sir, it does. But we probably wouldn't have been able to see anything on the ground either. However, if your predecessor went to the top floors of the Burj Khalifa, Duncan would have been able to fly above the fog and look inside the windows. Our next step is to put some boots on the ground, special activities division, to see if we can locate an entrance to the secret city."

Nazy gathered the files and photographs and returned them into the black metal briefcase. The President rubbed his hands together as if they were wet and clammy, knowing he would have to shake hands and didn't want his guests to shake a hand that was dripping wet. Meeting over.

Everyone stood as if on cue. The President shook Nazy's hand and kept his eyes on hers as he spoke. He was the perfect gentleman.

"What's Duncan doing?" He held her hand until he got his answer.

Nazy looked to defer the answer to her director. Lynche shrugged, "On his way to Sydney for a lecture. Probably asleep; I think they're halfway across the Pacific. If he's behind a stick and flying, he cannot sleep. However, you put him on a jet or a C-130 as a passenger, and that lad is out like a light."

Nazy smiled. The President grinned and patted her delicate hand before releasing it. Lynche took the President's offered one.

"Good brief. Thank you for coming. We'll try this again in 48 hours?"

Lynche nodded as Nazy opened the Oval Office door and stepped out. Their time with the President had ended, and it wasn't time yet to discuss the interesting Soviet submarine link with the lost aviatrix, Amelia Earhart. A line of people were waiting to march into the office they had just vacated. Nazy saw and made eye contact with the Director of the Secret Service, but neither acknowledged the other. The CIA executives departed the White House in silence.

Once in the DCI's limo Nazy turned and asked her boss, "Do we know what Duncan is really going to do? Going to Australia was not the smartest thing in my book."

Lynche pointed at her playfully, "He's your husband!"

Her smile lit up the inside of the dark limo. "Well, he usually knows what to do. And if he doesn't, at least he's very resourceful." She looked out the window toward the Washington Monument.

The car lurched forward. Lynche let the remark air out. His eyes scraped her bare knees and ankles, then he concurred. "That he is."

CHAPTER TWENTY-NINE

0700 July 20, 2014
Dubai

Maxim Mohammad Mazibuike spun away from his computer monitor and shut down the Sony PlayStation video game console. He stood and stretched. He mumbled, "Killing three hundred to get the one...." He allowed his thoughts to wander. He had received the encrypted message through the game console; *It is done.* It defied logic how the National Security Agency couldn't break the game console's encrypted communications, but the Agency's limitations in cracking the code had been briefed during one of the few President's Daily Briefs he had attended. All that mattered was that the infidel who had orchestrated his fall from power was finally dead. Now he had another immediate target for the American computer man. Then one more and his revenge would be complete.

He ran his hand over the video game console. *Who would have thought that communications on a device like this could be more difficult for the NSA to monitor than all the other encrypted messaging applications?* Mazibuike vaguely recalled the brief on how terrorist groups had employed the inexpensive encrypted messaging services of Japanese and American-manufactured game consoles and inadvertently circumvented and completely thwarted the government's heavily funded decryption and data collection efforts. While the NSA was capable of intercepting and decrypting individual messages, there were gaps in capabilities and limitations to the effectiveness of their surveillance regimens. Al-Qaeda discovered they could use certain code words or coded terms which would limit their exposure and decrease the chances that an intercepted message, run through the NSA's data crunching monster would be sufficient to tip off authorities to their plans.

For most communications between the ROC office and Mazibuike's palace, they used the Japanese game consoles and its relatively direct method of sending messages between players. For more elaborate methods of encoding communications, players used their avatar's weapons to send a spray of bullets onto a wall spelling out whole sentences to each other. The shared screens method was completely undetectable and untraceable by the NSA's computers. The ability to "get one over" on the Americans was enough for a thin smile to form on his otherwise granite stoic face.

How terrorist groups learned of such parallel encryption techniques was the subject of a billion-dollar special access program. The spy agency was very adept at using data to analyze telephone-calling patterns in an effort to detect terrorist activity, but those capabilities were negated when terrorists began using the "email draft workaround." Instead of sending a message through a routine email service which was susceptible to government surveillance, terrorists would write out an email and save it as a draft. Other terrorist groups would later log in to the same email account and check the Drafts folder for the hidden message. Another multi-million dollar program was funded to find a solution to this terrorist workaround. As soon as al-Qaeda suspected their method had been compromised, terrorists across the globe ran to the nearest electronic store for a Japanese game console. In a few days the al-Qaeda and their affiliates were back in business. The game console was a quantum leap for terrorist encrypted communications. And although he didn't communicate directly with the *Amriki,* he could.

The head of ROC had established a protocol from which no deviation was permitted. Mazibuike knew if he defied the old man's instructions, he would be bounced out of the palace and might even be eliminated; terminated. He would simply disappear. So an underling took care of and managed the ROC's communications. The head of ROC was a very cautious man. Very rich, very smart, and very cautious.

Of all of the ROC chieftains, only the elder Nabil bin Mohaned had the moxie to speak to the former President of the United States with disdain and contemptuousness. And there wasn't a damned thing Mazibuike could do about it. Mazibuike was a guest, and as such, was afforded all of the appropriate Islamic customs, but Mohaned could make him disappear with a flick of his wrist. Mazibuike's mercurial temper was always held in check when in the presence of the mighty Mohaned. And Mohaned, *The One,* brought the *Amriki* to Mazibuike. Revenge is also an

Islamic custom. In their own time.

Sheikh Nabil bin Mohaned al Khalifa, former emir of Sharjah, current Chief Executive Officer of Air Sharjah, had taken revenge on the Airbus conglomerate. It was reported in *Aviation News and Space Technology* that Nabil bin Mohaned, one of wealthiest men in the world, had offered to purchase all remaining Aerospatiale Concordes for his airline. British Airways and Air France had fourteen supersonic transports. France and England hadn't been able to make the aircraft profitable for thirty years; Mohaned was certain he could. And if he couldn't, so what? The Airbus CEO scoffed at the offer and nearly spit in Mohaned's face. The Frenchman couldn't and wouldn't explain why he would not approve the sale. It was more than a simple matter of pride; he would never allow the transfer of what was considered a national treasure, on the same level as the *Arc de Triomphe* or the *Mona Lisa*, to what was tantamount to a nomadic camel driver. The Concordes were not for sale at any price.

Three months later a Concorde crashed under mysterious circumstances. Accident investigators claimed a strip of metal on the runway punctured a tire. The French General Intelligence Directorate (GID) secretly suspected the last people to touch the aircraft, a pair of Muslim maintenance men, had planted a bomb on the aircraft. A mosque was raided, but the chief culprits had already left the country. The suspects were reportedly located in the UAE. They had visited their families for several days before they disappeared. With the prime suspects in the UAE, French aviation authorities sought a scapegoat. While the GID strongly suspected an Islamic connection, government aircraft accident investigators blamed an American air carrier that had taken off just prior to the Concorde's fatal flight. The French aviation authorities had torn a page from the EgyptAir Flight 990 accident and blamed everyone but the Muslim men last at the scene.

The weather conditions were again conspiring to make a trip to the surface possible. Mazibuike would have to wait for the signal and the conveyance. Until then, he returned to his room and listened to infidel music, some light jazz. He read American newspapers daily and, when he was really bored, he read scraps of books loaded onto an electronic book reader. Phase 1 was complete, the elimination of the infidel. Phase 2 was initiated. What he had in mind for Phase 3 was too incredible even to share with his benefactor. Mazibuike would have a new task for the *Amriki* computer man the next time he saw him

The next significant weather event expected for Dubai was over a week away. He would have a visitor, and that made him smile. By that time, he'd be the most revered man in the Muslim world. After a glowing Al-Jazeera interview, the Islamic world would know who had brought the Americans to their knees.

. . . . .

Hunter bounded down the first class aisle to the cockpit door, an arm around his oxygen bottle strapped across his chest to prevent it from dislodging the mask and falling off his body. He braced himself, and with both hands on the Model 1911 Colt ACP, took aim at the lock and handle mechanism of the cockpit door. He pulled the trigger. Again and again. The sound of the pistol was deafening in the enclosed cabin. Bullets slammed into the aluminum with the force of a butter knife. The lock was superficially damaged but wasn't blown apart as he had hoped. He looked at the futility of his work and shrieked into his mask in frustration. He looked at the weapon incredulously as if it was purposely being recalcitrant and not providing the necessary firepower to blow the door lock apart. Then he remembered what was essentially a trivial pursuit question; the air marshals carried special ammunition designed to incapacitate or knock down a terrorist. The ammo wasn't designed to be able to puncture a hole in the aircraft's aluminum skin. Apparently, the ammo was useless on the new armored doors. He dropped the spent weapon and stared at the door. *What is it going to take to get in?!*

Undeterred, Hunter spun around like a dervish and scanned his surroundings again, looking for something that could be used to cut into or break down the door. The ineffectual and incompetent bullets had done little damage; they were too small and didn't have enough velocity. The clock was running out. *Need more firepower!* A flight attendant stirred at his feet as he realized they both had big giant bullets strapped to their faces. The solution was staring at him. Oxygen bottles contained high-pressure gas, and if released suddenly, could make for a significant projectile. Like a fire bottle. Like a bottle rocket.

Like a madman possessed, Hunter pulled a serving cart from under the kitchen's counter storage and aligned it with the cockpit door. He ensured the wheels were perpendicular to the direction of travel. He didn't want the cart going anywhere; just the bottle. He removed the emergency O2 bottle from the inert flight attendant's face, and tossed it on top of the serving cart. The valve and hand-wheel protruded sufficiently toward the back of the jet for him to swing at it with something hard. *I need something heavy and hard! Look, look, look!* His head jerked around almost spasmodically as adrenaline and fear galvanized him to move faster. He jumped around the serving cart, retrieved the Colt, took stock of his makeshift silver bullet, and aimed it at the cockpit door.

Hunter's mind raced as he computed the chances of success. He knew the regulator reduced the air from the oxygen tank in stages as it traveled from the tank to the user. The first stage of the regulator accomplished the first stage of pressure reduction by reducing the high-pressure air in the tank to an intermediate pressure. He placed his damaged hand over the silver bottle to hold it steady, used some Kentucky windage to fine-tune the expected direction of flight, re-gripped the barrel of the weapon, then viciously swung the handle of the Colt at the weakest link, the junction of the regulator and the oxygen tank.

The regulator snapped off cleanly, and before Hunter could complete his follow-through with the Colt, the sudden release of a 1000 psi of O2 escaping out of a hole the size of a number 2 pencil eraser rocketed the tank out from under his hand and slammed into the cockpit door. The deafening sound of the six-inch wide projectile smacking into the upper left of the reinforced aluminum panel was offset by the instantaneous buckling of the cockpit door. The armored door folded like a taco shell and was torn from its mounting. The O2 bottle fell to the floor and spun around as escaping gas screamed to a higher pitch as its energy was spent.

Duncan Hunter blinked several times as his cerebrum processed his success. Dust and debris swirled around the cockpit's puncture wound as the O2 bottle spun around on the floor as it emptied its life saving gas. He reached inside the cockpit and lifted a door brace he had expected to be there. He tore aside the crumpled door as best he could and then stepped inside the cockpit. He found both pilots unconscious with their chins on their chests. Hunter removed the aircrew's emergency oxygen masks from the bulkhead behind their seats and placed them over their faces. Oxygen flowed to the aircrew.

He took stock of the cockpit with the eye of an experienced corporate jet pilot—same set-up just more of everything. He was stunned to find the instrument panel quiet, no warning or caution lights. He found the cabin pressure indicator off to his right and was bewildered by its reading—8,000 feet. Normal pressure altitude for a commercial airliner at cruising altitude. *That's impossible!* Hunter located the autopilot, and well versed in emergency action procedures, programmed the aircraft for a lower altitude. If anyone was going to live through this, they needed to be at a lower altitude, and they needed to be there quickly.

The autopilot did not respond to his input. It didn't accept a lower altitude setting nor would it respond to a new heading. Hunter tried to shut it off, to reprogram it with a flick of a switch, but it was as if the electronic control box refused the simplest linear mechanical command—OFF. He screamed in frustration and looked around the cockpit one more time. What was he missing? He recalled what he had to do in the YO-3A; recycle the avionics master switch. *Reset the aircraft's computer?*

He looked above his head at the overhead panel and located the auxiliary power unit control panel and the avionics master switch. When Hunter cycled the toggle switch to OFF he nearly suffered a stroke. Absolutely nothing happened in the cockpit. The lights and all instruments, communications, and navigation equipment should have shut off with the single throw of the switch. But nothing happened. He was so pissed off that he ratcheted the avionics master switch back and forth multiple times while screaming, *"Come on, asshole!"* If he couldn't shut off the aircraft's electrical system they were going to die. A glance at the aircrew confirmed they were still unconscious. He cycled the switch again and screamed into his mask, *"Shut down, you bastard!"*

After five cycles of the avionics master switch the cockpit went completely dark. Pitch black as if he had been dropped into the middle of Carlsbad Caverns. One more cycle of the switch and the lights illuminated in the cockpit. As did multiple caution lights, as did many warning lights and corresponding aural warnings and tones. Hunter jumped in shock and relief as the electricity returned to the airplane. He heard noises behind him as dozens of oxygen masks fell from the overhead compartments.

Cabin pressure valves slammed shut to steadily increase the pressure inside the cabin. Hunter immediately felt his ears pop as the cabin pressure increased as the system struggled to return to its factory setting. He was overjoyed as the pressure altitude indicator needle swung from its accurate reading above 30,000 feet to 20,000 and then to 15,000 feet of pressure altitude. It was moving in the right direction. Hunter knew some people, if they were still alive, would get cramps from the wildly swinging difference in atmospheric pressure. Hunter also felt the aircraft move under his feet as the jumbo jet dipped a wing and dropped the nose. *Shit! No autopilot, no altitude control. Be careful what you wish for, you just may get it!* He located and engaged the autopilot immediately, and with confirmation the system was operating normally, he programmed it to maintain current cruising altitude. He held his breath as the aircraft regained straight and level flight then watched as the auto-throttle system worked the jet's throttles automatically as the airliner leveled off its assigned altitude.

He was physically and emotionally spent as he turned around in the cockpit still with the O2 bottle strapped to his chest and face. He slipped to the floor and rested between the pilot and copilot's seats. His chest was still heaving from the extraordinary exertion; his head continued to pound as if an air marshal was beating on his head with a pistol.

He looked at the mayhem in front of him, at the twisted and folded cockpit door at his feet, and at the first class cabin with the yellow spider webs of O2 masks hanging down. He had been too late to save them, and the emotional swing overtook him. When a flight attendant with an O2 bottle pressed against her face, stumbled into view he nearly wept. Immediately afterwards the pilot behind him began to stir. *At least I'm not going to have to try and land this damn thing.*

Duncan and countless other pilots had found it amusing when fellow aviators had lost consciousness during a hard G-turn and began the long and disconcerted path to recovery. Now watching the flight attendant struggle regaining the use of her faculties, Hunter was not amused. He recalled the time he had knocked out his squadron executive officer (XO) during a hard-G break over the airfield. The XO's G-suit fitting had popped out during the snap-turn and pull, and the onset of over six Gs was too much for the old guy in back seat to strain and grunt away the blood rushing from his brain and pooling into his lower extremities. He did not to remain conscious. Duncan had looked in his canopy mirrors as the major did "the funky chicken," the uncontrollable jerking and torqueing of the body's extremities until sufficient blood or oxygen returned to the brain, and normal brain functions were restored. After flopping around the back seat uncontrollably for what seemed to be an inordinate amount of time, the XO slowly recovered and assured Hunter that he would kill him for the stunt once they got out of the jet. But the XO's embarrassment was too great—he was in a fighter after all—and he never said a word. The event became his and Hunter's little secret.

The flight attendant looked at Hunter incredulously. He was spread eagle in the cockpit with an O2 bottle velcroed on his chest. Hunter found some spare energy to nod at her. He was too distracted to notice the pilot's flipping, flopping, jerking, and spastic gyrations behind him; he just wanted to go back to his seat and sleep. A dozen aspirins to kill his headache would be nice. But he was too tired to move and there would be so many questions from the pilots when they awoke to find oxygen masks on their faces, their door broken down, and their aircraft commandeered by a Yankee sitting at the base of their center console. Not to mention that there would be one pissed off federal air marshal who had lost his weapon while he was unconscious.

The pilot, now fully conscious with his own splitting headache, looked around the cockpit and performed the essential immediate-action pilot duty—aviate. As he scanned the instrument panel for attitude information—the aircraft appeared to be in straight and level flight—he was surprised to find himself on the emergency oxygen system; he didn't remember donning the mask and headgear, and he didn't remember what set of emergencies precipitated such actions. The cockpit was awash in warning lights, tones, chimes, and female voices urgently announcing, "Pressure altitude! Pressure altitude!" He glanced across to the far right of the instrument panel to find the analog aircraft pressure altitude instrument. The red needle was unwinding into the green arc range toward 8,000 feet. He reached across the console to push his copilot to wake up. That's when he nearly jumped out of his uniform. He blinked wildly in shock at finding a man sitting at the base of the center console. The man's eyes locked with his. Finding an intruder in his cockpit, the pilot gulped aviator's breathing oxygen by the liter. An interloper *in the cockpit* meant the aircraft had likely been hijacked. He turned his head over his shoulder to find the impenetrable cockpit door was buckled, folded in half like a long silver napkin. He and the man on the floor again locked eyes. Not knowing if he was in danger, the Australian pilot waited for the man to make the first move.

Hunter removed the oxygen mask from his face and pushed the O2 bottle off his chest. Breathing the thin but increasing oxygen levels in the cockpit wasn't a smooth transition from the forced-fed oxygen from the emergency O2 bottle, and he took several breaths in order to fill his lungs with the life-giving breathing oxygen. He offered a puffy red hand for the pilot to shake. Hunter's voice croaked with emotion as the words came out, "Good day, mate! I think someone tried to kill us."

The Qantas pilot just stared at him. Both men jumped when alarms and an electronic-generated woman's sultry voice shattered the silence in the cockpit; a sense of urgency was conveyed with every piercing tone and syllable. "Emergency! Low fuel! Emergency! Low fuel!"

CHAPTER THIRTY

0700 July 20, 2014
Pacific Ocean

The Qantas pilot turned toward the instrument panel; the sense of urgency registered on his face as his eyes bulged with panic and consternation. Master Caution lights flashed yellow under the glare shield and across the instrument panel. Whatever pain and fatigue had suppressed Duncan Hunter's instincts were instantly gone when he heard the words, "Emergency! Low fuel!" He spring-boarded off the cockpit floor and spun around seeking the source of the in-flight emergency. His knees straddled the center console. The two pilots eyes' converged on the fuel quantity indicators on the instrument panel. The lady's electronic voice was correct; they were nearly out of fuel.

Their eyes moved to the global positioning system to find that they were well off course from the aircraft's programmed route of flight. It was over a hundred miles to the nearest 747-capable runway, Clark International Airport. The Qantas pilot freaked out, pointing at the moving map display. "Why are we out of gas? We don't have enough fuel to get to Clark!"

The muzzle of a .357 Sig Sauer P250 slid behind Duncan Hunter's ear. He felt the pressure immediately and all of the fight left him. A deep voice said, "Don't...fucking...move."

Hunter closed his eyes. Urine nearly dribbled into his trousers. He didn't see the pilot look over his shoulder at the federal air marshal with his weapon drawn, both hands on the pistol's grip and with a focus-filled and angry look on his face. After a couple of interminable anxiety-filled seconds, Hunter heard the calm voice of the pilot demand, "Stand down; stand down, now! He's one of the good guys."

Federal Air Marshal Njord Cota wasn't convinced the man at the base of the center console was a good guy. The so-called impenetrable cockpit door was smashed and folded like a cheap antique dressing

290

screen. His partner was unconscious and missing his weapon. And there was a man, obviously not part of the aircrew, inside the cockpit. It would take more than a simple command to make him break off his position. Cota redoubled his grip on his weapon and barked, "Code word!"

Hunter stood frozen like a springer spaniel on point on a ring-necked pheasant awaiting the next command. And he kept his eyes closed. His mind raced. There wasn't a trick in the trade that could get him out of this precarious predicament of having a gun mashed behind his ear. Only the truth and a code word. A drop of piss seeped into his pants.

The pilot sucked a lungful of air, remembered the code word, and provided the "all clear" signal. The pistol was removed from Hunter's ear; Duncan heard it slam into a leather holster. He opened his eyes. He was still alive; the instrument panel was still awash in yellow caution slights. And the jet was still almost out of gas. "Thank you." He didn't turn to look at the air marshal who had almost shot him. Hunter ignored him, as he had other emergencies to contend with.

The pilot uttered, suddenly defeated, "I recycled the fuel dump valve and it is closed. But we cannot make it to Clark. We'll run out of fuel during the decent."

"Do we have enough gas to fly over the airfield at this altitude?" Hunter used the informal term for jet fuel, a familiar code word among aviators. The expression conveyed to the pilot in command that Hunter was also a pilot. The copilot hadn't recovered. Even with the supplemental oxygen, his chest didn't rise and fall. He was dead.

The pilot twisted his head to the interloper. They hadn't met formally. There might not be any time for that. He said, "I believe so. We're doing ten miles a minute with these winds. I think we have fifteen minutes of fuel aboard. The GPS indicates we can make it overhead but we cannot descend. We're still out of gas."

Hunter spontaneously offered, "Dirty penetration," while scanning the instrument panel trying to find some additional fuel or new solution to their predicament. Hunter stopped his scan and turned to the pilot who was furiously turning screws in his own head.

The man blinked wildly and then nodded his agreement.

Hunter suggested, "Throw everything out. Flaps, gear, hold the nose up right at stall. She'll drop like a rock. Like riding a runaway elevator. Maybe shut down the outboards. Two minutes or less to get down. We might make the field."

More nodding. The solution was brilliantly wonderful in theory. It was a maneuver he had rarely heard of and never practiced in a simulator, but it was all he had. "Aye. I'm going to need help. I've never done anything like that before. Non-standard approach." He nodded at his comatose partner. "Pull him out and you strap in. What's your name?"

"Duncan Hunter." He smiled through his concentration.

"Kim Gentry. Move it, Hunter. I don't know what this ship will do." The captain said over his shoulder to the air marshal, "Thank you for your service. You need to return to your seat." All Hunter ever saw of the marshal was a glimpse of a nasty old sports jacket with cheap leather patches at the elbows as he left the cockpit.

As Captain Gentry radioed Clark International Airport and declared an emergency, Hunter unbuckled the copilot and dragged him out of his seat and onto the floor of the cockpit area. He was careful not to let the man's head drop. Once he had climbed over the copilot's body and strapped in, Captain Gentry asked, "What do you fly?"

"I'm an old F-4 pilot. Occasionally I fly a G-five fifty."

"Ever do a dirty penetration in a G-five?"

"G-four, over Africa."

"That must have been something. We're going to have to override the computer—I'm certain it won't allow such a maneuver." His hands were a blur as he switched knobs and pressed buttons. Autopilot on, automatic flight control systems on; he checked the instruments and ensured the aircraft was heading to Clark International. Pilot stuff.

"Still here."

"What happened to us?" Gentry had come to the point in his recovery from hypoxia that he was fully functional; all of his faculties had returned to normal. As aviator's breathing oxygen continued to flood his lungs and heart, his senses improved with every second. It was weird to have an unknown person in his cockpit, an uninvited guest who was not a terrorist, an angel instead of a devil. Somehow the Lord sent a pilot to help him through the travails to come. He would have been more emotional, as victims of crimes and trauma usually are, but there was little time for melancholy or celebration. There was a jumbo jet to fly. There might still be hundreds of passengers alive and counting on him to use all of his years of training to save them, to save himself.

As the two pilots prepared the jet for an emergency descent, Hunter flooded Gentry's internal database. Hunter's assessment was brief. His conclusion was terse. And it was unbelievable. "I think someone hacked into the aircraft's computer. I believe someone tried to kill us."

Gentry dismissed the pedestrian questions of How and Why, and leaped straight to another more interesting question. He blurted out, "Do you think what happened to us is also what happened to the Sky Link triple seven?"

Hunter nodded before he spoke. "I do now." The radio came to life in their headsets as the Clark control tower cleared them to land. Altimeter and heading information was relayed. There was radar contact. They were cleared for a straight in approach.

"Fifty DME. Fifty miles, five minutes out. What are we doing again?"

Hunter was calm and direct, as if he was ordering coffee and a piece of pie. He spoke in a mixture of English and Aviator. "This is what I did with the Gulfstream. As we approached the field at ten DME, I pulled the throttles to idle until gear speed. With the gear down, I held the nose up to let it decelerate, then I dropped the flaps. I flew it with the nose, with the yoke all the way in my lap; fully stalled but wings level. Fighter pilot stuff. Just enough pressure on the yoke to manage the buffet. The jet always wanted to fall off to one side. When I needed to, I lowered the nose a bit or mashed opposite rudder to keep the wings level."

"I flew it like a fighter pilot flies a rolling scissors in aerial combat; near stall, inside buffet, and I controlled it where I wanted to go with the nose. If it gets a little too unstable, lower the nose. When I needed to turn, I mashed the rudder. I found it required full deflection for a couple of seconds, so once the jet starts to move release the pressure on the pedals to see how we're doing. Easy to over-correct. I had to corkscrew in; we're set up for a straight in. Much easier. With the engines at idle my fuel flow was negligible but increased significantly as we descended, obviously. As the ground rushed up, I used elevators and power to break the decent—flared it like an Air Force pilot with three miles of runway— to set up for ten seconds of groove to flare and touchdown. At that point, we should have a normal configured airplane, set up for the middle of the runway, and you'll have it in the proper landing attitude. I know you can do it, too. Easy."

The men looked at the fuel quantity indicators then at each other.

Over the glare shield they could make out the microscopic runway lights and the strobes of the approach lighting system of the former Clark Air Base in the distance. Hunter had been there several times but not in the front seat of a 747. Clark Air Force Base had always been a great place to get a little wild and crazy. Now it was Clark International Airport, and it was on high alert. The control tower wanted answers. Gentry and Hunter ignored them. They had one shot at making history. Crash Fire and Rescue trucks stood at the ready for the impending crash.

The old Clark Air Base was located about forty miles northwest of Manila. It had been a stronghold for Filipino and American forces since the end of World War II. Americans abandoned the U.S. Air Force Base as well as several Naval facilities near the small hamlet of Olongapo after the eruption of Mount Pinatubo in 1991, which substantially damaged the airfield. The Filipino government assumed control of the old base, developed the infrastructure with new passenger terminals and parking lots, and re-dedicated the facility as Clark International Airport. Everything was new except the runways.

Captain Gentry wasn't convinced Hunter's plan would work. Hunter could hear it in his voice. "The 747 isn't as nimble as a Gulfstream. Or an F-4. These planes have a personality like no other. They are slow behemoths."

Hunter acknowledged and said, "I know they are all different. But it is still a jet and you're a great captain. You can do this. It's all feel. It's just a steep straight-in. I'll talk to you on the way down. No factor."

"Clark on the nose. Fifteen miles." He shook his head as if he was convinced that what he was about to do wouldn't work. "We're going to die."

Hunter shook his head and barked, "Captain Gentry, it isn't our day to die. And I am pissed someone tried to take us out. I promise you, I will find the son-of-a-bitch who did this and I will personally kill him."

The Qantas Captain stiffened and looked at the American and nodded. He now believed every word of the man sitting in the copilot seat. Professional pilots are uncomplicated, exceptionally well-trained men and women. They must be unemotional in a crisis, and their thinking must remain straightforward, otherwise people die. Usually, violently. Clark International Airport control tower broke in and provided updated runway wind information.

Hunter said, "It's time, sir."

Duncan Hunter theorized that when the aircraft computer took over the aircraft and its systems, all of the indicating systems froze while some unseen hand manipulated some life support systems while leaving others alone. Artificial Intelligence had likely been injected into the computer or its software. It was the only thing that made any sense. Somehow the cabin pressurization system was systematically and gradually shut down, subjecting the crew and passengers to the insidious and gradual effects of hypoxia while maintaining cockpit indications that the system was operating normally. *Freezing the indicator. That is something you see only in simulators!* The autopilot also didn't function properly, as it hadn't maintained the aircraft's programmed heading but had arbitrarily turned ninety degrees to port. And somehow, the computer overrode the fuel dump valves to run the fuel out of the tanks. *That is something else you only see in simulators! See if the aircrew is paying attention!* Hunter expected the engine monitoring system had also likely been shut down.

That was when it hit him fully. *The aircraft's computer acted like it was being selective...as if a simulator instructor was programming an aircraft simulator for which systems would fail or degrade to see if the crew could detect the discrepancies. An unseen hand was controlling it. It wasn't an accident or an electrical malfunction, but it was programmed to kill us, take us off course, and dump fuel so a large fuel spill couldn't be seen by search and rescue aircraft. Not only did someone want to kill us, they didn't want anyone to find us.*

When the aircraft ran out of fuel it would fall from the skies, accelerate to supersonic speed, and disintegrate when it hit the water. At that speed, hitting the incompressible water would be like smacking concrete at 1,000 MPH. Any remnants of the aircraft would be far from its programmed track.

Once the avionics master switch rebooted the aircraft's main computer, the aircraft functioned normally. Hunter was unable to believe it was an accident. His mind continued to work the tangibles and the intangibles of his findings. The old accident investigator in him screamed, *The jet was hacked. This was done on purpose!*

Captain Gentry flew the aircraft at maximum range to save every drop of Jet A remaining in the tanks. At the expected fuel flow rates, the 747's four engines should flame out in five minutes. There is no such thing as dead-sticking a jumbo jet. With the runway lights seven miles below them and ten miles away, Captain Gentry looked out the windscreen and said, "I have the jet. AFCS and autopilot off. God, help us." He reached for the throttle quadrant and pulled the four engine throttles to idle.

$$. \quad . \quad . \quad . \quad .$$

At the sound of the emergency klaxon, airport employees poured out of their offices and stepped outside to witness the excitement. Panic erupted inside the Terminal Radar Approach Control; controllers indicated the aircraft's route of flight at cruising altitudes made it virtually impossible to land safely, the Qantas 747 could not possibly make it to runway. With every sweep of the ASR-9 airport surveillance radar antenna, air traffic controllers sought a radar blip that indicated there was an airplane they could talk to. However, the aircraft flew above the airport's surveillance radar systems. The primary radar provided long range information, while the flat antenna on top of the radar dish provided secondary or short-range radar coverage area. But since the Boeing 747 was flying from directly overhead out of the belt of radar coverage, air traffic controllers were useless. Some of the radar approach controllers (RAPCON) believed the emergency was a prank. They left their radar positions to go outside.

Outside of their RAPCON bunker, controllers tried to visually acquire any wayward aircraft. Several men challenged the decision from the Control Tower to accept the aircraft's declaration of an emergency. Did anyone know if the jet was a hijacked aircraft? Did anyone really know if there was a jet?

After confirming the aircraft emergency, Crash Fire Rescue firefighters donned their fireproof uniforms and boarded every available fire truck. Once in their assigned positions, they also waited for a visual on the aircraft. Most firefighters and air traffic controllers looked for the landing lights of the emergency jumbo where they expected to see them—on the assigned heading for a ten-mile straight-in, a few thousand feet over the water and continuously descending.

Then someone shouted from one of the fire trucks. The man-made light was directly overhead among the countless stars in the clear night sky. People bent their head as far back as they could until the third through seventh cervical vertebrae reached their rearward limits. The angle was uncomfortable, but no one could tear their eyes away from the mayhem coming their way.

Second by second the light got larger and lower, which eased the pressure on their spines. The men and women of the CFR questioned each other with looks and gestures. They sensed the aircraft would crash; they had never seen such an approach, and therefore, the only outcome would be tragic. The jumbo jets required a long, steady, systematic, straight-in approach. No one could fathom why the aircraft was so close to the airport but still so high in the sky.

Movement ceased on the ramp at Clark International Airport. It was eerily quiet; they sensed death was approaching from on high. CFR trucks backed up slowly in case the aircraft crashed at the approach end of the airport and splattered when it hit the ground. No one knew what to do, but the watch commander suggested they should all pull back until the aircraft touched down. So they moved cautiously but quickly, like mice retreating from the cat who had suddenly stepped into view.

Those on the ground couldn't hear the aircraft as it approached. It was like a ghost. They followed the landing lights, mesmerized by the verticality of the aircraft's positioning. It was impossible to arrest the decent from such a vertical approach. It looked to them that the jet's trajectory would be short of the field, and it would crash well short of the runway. Then the lights changed position in the sky. An old firefighter muttered, "The nose is too high. They won't make the field."

The ground crews could make out the outline of the jet when it was a mile high and a mile from the approach end of the runway. By the number of engines they knew it was a 747. For several long seconds the bulbous nose of the Boeing rotated upwards and held impossibly high, momentarily reaching 60 degrees angle of attack which arrested its rapid descent. Wide-eyed spectators thought the jet would plant its tail in the ground when the nose of the aircraft gently lowered to the expected angle for landing, as if a premier danseur gently lowered his ballet partner after a fish dive of a *pas de deux*. Now the runway approach light system illuminated the underside of the jet and gave witness that the aircraft had slowed its descent and was, incredibly, in the appropriate landing configuration—gear down and flaps fully extended—as it passed over the remaining approach lighting and navigational aids. The landing gear softly touched down a thousand feet from the beginning of the runway; small puffs of smoke came from the 32 landing gear wheels as they touched down. The jet's engines hummed surreally quietly in the night. No sounds of thrust reversers.

The Qantas jet was safe on the ground. Everyone watching screamed and clapped in joy, while the CFR trucks raced after the jet as it barreled down the runway, spoilers deployed, landing gear trucks neatly centered astride the runway centerline. The jet slowed, turned off the runway to the last high-speed taxiway, and stopped. There would be no taxiing to the terminal building; the fuel tanks were dry. Starved for fuel, first the outboard engines and then a few seconds later, the inboard motors shut down. A dozen firetrucks chased after the jet like a troupe of unweaned puppies following their lactating mother. Only the turbine of the auxiliary power unit near the tail wailed on the ramp. It would run for a few more minutes keeping the lights and the air conditioning on inside the jet, before it too drained its tiny fuel tank dry.

Three stories up in the cockpit of the Boeing 747, Hunter smiled at the ashen profile of Qantas Captain Kim Gentry. Hunter quickly unbuckled from his seat, crawled out of the heavily padded chair, and patted the pilot on the shoulder. When Gentry didn't respond, Hunter thought the pilot might be in a state of shock. The possibilities and reasons were endless. The wild descent to touchdown, the near crash, or the guilt that he may have lost hundreds of passengers when their brains had ceased to function from the lack of oxygen. Hunter shook the older man's shoulder to get his attention. He said, "You did great, Captain Gentry. You saved the day, and you're a hero. Now, sir, *I* need a favor."

The pilot looked as if he had aged a hundred years in the last two minutes. Beginning with his hands, he began to shake in reaction to the stress of the steep approach and the long-duration flare to break their rate of descent from 30,000 feet per minute rate of descent to the approach standard of 500. It was an incredible display of piloting by the seasoned pilot. As his hands trembled Gentry became emotional. He had never been so close to dying or losing his passengers. So when Duncan Hunter asked him for a favor, he was confused and then incredulous. Exhausted and mentally crushed, he would agree to anything at that point. He watched with a cool singularity, a morbid unnaturalness as Hunter removed the dead copilot's uniform.

·　·　·　·　·

With emergency crews and law enforcement spilling into the aircraft, getting off the aircraft was nearly impossible. Some flight attendants and passengers had survived the decompression, continued oxygen deprivation, and long-term loss of consciousness. They suffered a range of maladies from fainting to seizures, some remained comatose in their seats. Half of the aircraft was a morgue. For those with chronic medical or breathing issues, the decompression set into motion conditions that were right for the onset of cerebral hypoxia resulting in brain death. The fuzzy demarcation between those who lived and those who perished was simply a matter of genetics and depended on how well the body dealt with the reduced oxygen content in their blood. Everyone's body was different; everyone responded to the lack of oxygen differently.

One person recognized the symptoms of the onset of hypoxia and was able to acquire an external source of breathing oxygen. And at the end of the day, Hunter saved the lives of half of the passengers aboard. Timing and luck won out when the captain of the 747 recovered from hypoxia and was able to function as a pilot. Hunter knew he wouldn't have been able to safely fly the jet if both pilots had been totally incapacitated. Maybe he would have been able to engage an automatic landing system but the captain's knowledge of the Boeing 747's emergency procedures, switchology, and immediate corrective actions saved enough fuel for the successful near-vertical approach.

CHAPTER THIRTY-ONE

0700 July 20, 2014
Manila

The three-striped copilot in uniform jacket and cap directed law enforcement and medical personnel pouring through the aircraft door. Some ran upstairs to the cockpit. Others ran to the nose or to the back of the aircraft. With a break in the action, the copilot stepped through the door and off the aircraft. Hunter raced down the passenger stairs, leaving the pilot and aircrew to deal with the living and the dead. He was ushered inside the terminal building by nameless people all too willing to help. Once inside the terminal building he was directed to the awaiting arms of Philippine Customs agents. Usually there was no way to get out of the airport except through the gauntlet of extremely curious and serious Customs agents. But to Hunter's surprise, every member of the Customs service was focused on a smart phone. To a person, they typed and sent messages with flailing thumbs.

Hunter queued in the CREW ONLY line and presented the passport of the copilot. He picked the line of the most distracted customs agent who quickly processed him through. The agent barely checked the photograph in the passport against Hunter's harried face. He was CREW in uniform. No real scrutiny. He was no doppelganger, but he was a reasonable passport match at a glance. Having a jet nearly crash on the airport property was extremely unusual, and Hunter expected some questions from the government agent. But the customs man dismissed the peculiarity of the single flight crewmember and went back to playing with his smart phone.

Hunter avoided the onrush of media, journalists, and photographers on his way out of baggage claim area and followed the signage to "Ground Transportation." He found the taxi stand usurped by arriving satellite television trucks. He was largely ignored by the Manila taxi hawks who normally were vociferous when vying for a pocketful of pesos.

Flight crews generally took the hotel shuttle buses that were neatly prepositioned in front of the terminal. The airlines always take care of lodging and transportation. No out of pocket expenses. A few cameramen swung a videorecorder his way, but Hunter covered his face with his arm and the copilot's hat and made his way to the head of the displaced line of taxis. Once he was safe inside a stinky and dirty taxi, they drove away from the main terminal unmolested.

Well away from the terminal and on the highway to Manila, Hunter removed the undersized cap and ran his hand through his hair. He took in the sights and sounds of the old American air base. When he was on active duty he had flown into Clark Air Base. It had been a wild and crazy place with pretty, petite, Filipino girls vying for his attention, ready to serve him an overpriced beer or themselves in an upstairs room for an obscene amount of money. Quarters or pesos stacked a foot-high, they took them all. But this stop at the Clark Airport redefined insane. He was shocked to be alive and stunned that he had gotten safely away from the airport amid all the confusion. He regretted that people had died on the jet. In the face of incomplete, dubious, and erroneous information and with high levels of excitement, Clausewitz's "fog of war" had enabled him to escape the normal scrutiny of customs and law enforcement, at least for the moment. As the taxi approached the outskirts of Manila, Hunter directed the driver to take him to U.S. Embassy.

．　．　．　．　．

Demetrius Eastwood's cell phone ringtone bleated a poor rendition of The 1812 Overture through a diminutive and inadequate speaker. He recognized the number, the Network Security News Desk. Something important had occurred somewhere and had to be disseminated immediately to the appropriate correspondents. He answered the call while jamming a hands-free device into his ear. "Eastwood." He listened intently while some woman read the breaking news. "A Qantas Boeing 747, Flight 1144, enroute from Hawaii to Australia has landed in the Philippines with almost half of its passengers dead or severely incapacitated. Mechanical malfunction possible. Also possible terrorism. The FBI and the CIA are enroute to Manila. No further information at this time. Questions?"

Eastwood had none and said so; the connection was terminated. He called his contacts with the Federal Aviation Administration. They knew nothing more than the initial flash message. He switched on the television. The Communist News Network, as his friend Duncan Hunter called the competing cable network, had reporters and a feed truck on site and was reporting the incident as BREAKING NEWS. His cell phone rang again. Another woman stated he needed to come to the network immediately for a panel discussion on the Qantas aircraft. He would be the terrorism expert on the panel.

Without thinking Eastwood blurted, "You need Duncan Hunter. He's the best damned aviation terrorism subject matter expert on the planet. In my humble opinion."

"If you can get him to the office in an hour, I'll boot you off and put him on. If he's not available, I need you. Clock's ticking. What's it gonna be, Dory?"

Eastwood looked as if he had shaved from a razor pulled from a trash can. Hunter hadn't responded to his calls or messages; Bill McGee responded that Hunter would be "out of pocket" for several days. Eastwood has assumed Hunter was ensconced at his ranch in Texas. But with the McGee message, now he knew Hunter was likely and completely off the grid. Hunter could be assertive and outspoken, but he tended to be allergic to attention, and not just at press conferences or network panels, but all attention. Maybe it wasn't such a great idea after all. Eastwood said, "See you in an hour."

With the missing Indonesian Sky Link Flight 7070 still fresh in the minds of reporters and the traveling public, news of another large aircraft mishap from the same region of the world was going to be newsworthy. The continuous telecast was dominated with minute-by-minute updates from the on-scene reporters broadcasting via a satellite data link from the incident airport, Clark International. Another reporter in Seattle provided information on the Boeing 747 with file footage of the aircraft, as she discussed its enviable international safety record. A correspondent in Washington D.C. reported on the airport, how it had once been an American military airport, how it had been abandoned after a local volcano erupted, and how it had been converted from a military facility into a civilian airport.

The suspicion that terrorism had struck another airliner sent the newspapers and networks into a frenzy. Like the previous incident with the missing Indonesian jumbo jet, newspaper journalists and network anchors were convinced that they could solve the mystery of why half of the passengers and crew on the Qantas aircraft died, and why half of them lived. Espionage novelists flooded the networks with resumes hoping to get a little airtime to hawk their theories and their books.

When Eastwood arrived at his network in his signature white chambray shirt, cargo pants, and Merrill hiking boots, he found a team of experts—from the military, from the Federal Aviation Administration, from self-described terrorism experts, but no accident investigators—waiting to go on the air. A petite black woman with glasses too big for her face and an iPad in front of her nose looked at Eastwood and consulted her electronic device for the schedule and agenda. She looked confused. Eastwood asked, "Your boss had me come down for an expert panel?"

The woman shook her head, "You're not on my list of experts, nor are you anywhere on the schedule, and you're not on the agenda. These things are volatile and fast moving, and the experts change from minute to minute. You know the drill."

"So you booted me from the panel? You don't need me?" *Every establishment pundit, aviation consultant, and bathroom attendant in New York City is running through the Green Room, and there isn't time for me? Seriously!?* He was getting more fired up by the second and detested his producer for wasting his time with this last minute change.

"Not now—but, stick around, I'll let the producer know you're in the building in case they need a little color commentary."

It wouldn't do any good to complain. *Don't even sigh* he thought; *The pretty witch from the East with the electronic clipboard could make life good or miserable. If not her, then the producer. Smile and be polite and thank her for her time.* Eastwood heeded the little voice in his head and headed upstairs to the main newsroom and crisis action center for the latest streams of information from the disparate reporting centers.

He found a chair and sat to watch the anchors at work. Eastwood pulled out his smart phone and tried to contact Duncan Hunter again with a text message: *Where are you? I could use your help on the Qantas airplane.*

. . . . .

Tamerlan al-Sarkari screamed at the computer monitor. He had been waiting for the first news reports to come across the wire. He expected the expected, the sublime; an aircraft hadn't checked in from its route of flight or hadn't reported its position to a major airport in the region. But that wasn't what was being reported. An aircraft had made an unscheduled landing near Manila. Every major news service from Al-Jazeera to ZeeTV was covering the mystery of Qantas Flight 1144. Details were sketchy. The aircraft declared an emergency. Half of the passengers were dead. The captain of the aircraft, a 30-year veteran, saved the remainder of the passengers and the aircraft. The first questions about terrorism were asked; the first answers were, "It cannot be ruled out. More details when they become available."

"Noooo!" he shrieked like a high school girl at a hair-pulling contest. He rubbed his hands across his face leaving red marks from the pressure. His temples pounded, and his blood pressure rocketed to new highs. He battered the keyboard, typed in the URL for Al-Jazeera news. A couple of clicks of the mouse and he was receiving the latest news in real time. *There has to be more than one Qantas aircraft in that area! It cannot be mine!*

From another monitor he logged into the Boeing engine monitoring system database to determine if "his" Qantas aircraft was resting near the bottom of the Marianas Trench. He prayed it wasn't at the Clark International Airport. He shuddered when the satellite "pinged" the aircraft and received positional data consistent with an airport in the Pampanga province of Luzon region of the Philippines. His aircraft *was* high and dry. He wailed like an old Muslim woman who had learned her son had blown himself up with a suicide vest.

What could have gone wrong? It was a perfect plan; executed to perfection. But it failed! What failed?

Al-Sarkari's urge to access the aircraft's digital cockpit voice recorder was strong, but he was afraid to leave any more electronic fingerprints, afraid of even accessing the on-line auctions. Afraid of what lay in the hidden messages. Failure would not to be tolerated.

He stared at the television images of the gold-colored emblem of Al-Jazeera and the people on stretchers. The trademark of Al-Jazeera looked more like a poorly drawn stylized insect than Arabic calligraphy. He was unmoved, unfeeling. *They are expendable, irrelevant. The caliphate is all that matters. And The One.* More images of reporters interviewing passengers, airport workers.

Then the Al-Jazeera crawler across the bottom of the screen spelled out breaking information. The flight crew was sequestered pending an investigation. American and Australian safety board investigators were enroute to Manila. The Qantas CEO would be making a statement soon. A list of the deceased would be released pending notification of next of kin.

The passenger list! Need the passenger list. It could be hours before he knew the fate of the man he was tasked to eliminate. If he had been successful in at least that, they might allow him to live. He delayed logging into the on-line auctions to communicate with "the seller." He needed answers to the questions that would surely come. The last thing he wanted to see was a coded message to return to Dubai as quickly as possible.

Again, he stared at the monitor and thought *if I go to Dubai, I'll never return.* He thought about running. *But where ?* Al-Sarkari shook with fear and nearly wept.

· · · · ·

At a table for four, Greg Lynche and Nazy Cunningham sat with the head of the National Clandestine Service as well as the Director of Operations. Their location in the cafeteria of CIA Headquarters wasn't conductive for swapping the latest national secret, but it was a good place for discussing open-source news as well as "waving the flag" to let the *hoi palloi*, the CIA employees and contractors, see their leaders in an informal setting out of their corner offices. The ambience of the cafeteria was as good as any three-star restaurant in the Washington, DC area but without the candlelight and slavish wait staff.

They had read of the Qantas aircraft's troubles in the Philippines from their in-house news service, *The Early Bird.* The Director of the National Counter Terrorism Center, Nazy Cunningham, asked the Director of Operations if he had heard anything new on the Australian jet.

Nazy had a pit of churning vipers in her stomach. Duncan was travelling to Australia, and she hadn't heard from him other than his usual text messages. Some announced he was boarding the aircraft, some were simple, lusty, *billet-douxs*. His penultimate text message informed her his jet had been delayed, and he would call or text when he was safe "on-deck" or in his hotel room.

To get her mind off Hunter and on to something more interesting, Lynche had invited the other CIA executives for coffees and crumbs in the cafeteria. Nazy had some old intelligence that was worth sharing. Older than dirt. Possibly explosive but it would never see the light of day. It would never leave the Old Headquarters Building. The only ears were the one-hundred tiny ponytail palms that lined the cafeteria windows.

Lynche nodded at the men and said to Nazy Cunningham, "Tell 'em what you told me."

She smiled demurely and said coquettishly, "The Hindenburg may have been brought down by a drone. Courtesy of the Communist Party of America."

The National Clandestine Service Director fired questions at her. So did the Director of Operations, Quint Miklos. "How is that possible?"

Behind dark glasses, NCS Director Castaño asked, "That technology was mature in...1937?"

Lynche asked the best question, "Why?"

Nazy brightened, nodded, and glanced to the ceiling for the right words to answer his question. Then her eyes met his. "Nikolai Ivanovich Yazhov, the head of the Soviet secret police, met with a group of Communist Party of America members visiting Moscow. One of them apparently worked at a military testing field for aviation experiments in Dayton, Ohio and apparently stole the plans for a secret remote control airplane."

The men around the table knew the basics of the Hindenburg disaster from books and movies. They had seen the video archives but couldn't remember ever seeing another aircraft, however small, in the vicinity of the zeppelin. Unexpectedly strong headwinds had put the airship hours behind schedule, and its landing at the U.S. Navy's largest airship facility in Lakehurst, New Jersey was expected to be further delayed because of afternoon thunderstorms in the area. Advised of the poor weather conditions at Lakehurst, the airship's captain diverted the

Hindenburg over Manhattan Island to demonstrate the power and glory of the Nazi Party while waiting for the passing weather to clear.

"A Communist Party cell in New Jersey received a copy of the remote controlled airplane plans. They built a working model and apparently Comrade Yazhov reported to Stalin that the tiny aircraft had flown into the Hindenburg when it attempted to land."

The NCS Director's face questioned the validity of the woman's assessment and stated the obvious, "I didn't know remote control airplanes were operational in 1937."

Lynche shook his head in disbelief, even though he knew the intelligence to be sound. "Um…I didn't know that either."

Nazy shrugged and said, "One of our analysts couldn't believe it either. She found several sources that reported the first remote control airplane flew in the early 1930s. They were carrying cameras three years later. The army put explosives on some. There were hobby groups all along the Eastern seaboard, just like today. A copy of the little red aircraft that was used to bring down the Hindenburg is on display at the Air Force Museum. Some were used during the early days of the war." Nazy uncrossed her arms and gestured as she talked. "It's fascinating these unexpected gems and bluebirds—something no one would ever consider and it comes out of nowhere." The men recoiled at the information, nearly upsetting their flimsy restaurant chairs.

Lynche grinned like a Cheshire cat. *"Red aircraft?"* he stuttered.

Nazy offered, "Apparently. I haven't seen it."

The NCS Director Steve Castaño asked, "Where did you get this?"

"The first source was the new Yazhov papers. A secondary source came from the FBI; they were about to post new versions of its Communist Party of America (CPA) files on Whittaker Chambers and Alger Hiss to its online 'FBI Vault.' But not everything. One of the files contained information on the Communist Party's sleeper cell attack on the Hindenburg airship. My contact at the FBI knew we were looking into some old CPA connections and thought its discovery was worth sharing. That's two sources for a single event. That information will never be declassified or released to the public."

"It's not an airship, it's a zeppelin," corrected the NCS Director.

"Seriously?" asked the DO and the DCI in unison. They would not give the NCS Director a break for being an ass. *What is his problem? Was it Nazy?* He may have problems with women, but he should be professional enough to keep his mouth shut about something so minor.

Nazy refused to be annoyed by the petty corrections. "One of the many spies who had a tangential relationship with the convicted spy, Alger Hiss, also had an interest in remote controlled aircraft. A Communist named Axlerod, a descendant of Pavel Axlerod of Menshevik fame, built and flew radio control model airplanes in New Jersey from the early 1930s. The researchers say they used a standard telephone dial to send commands to the airplane via shortwave frequencies. It was mounted on a square steel box and you dialed 6 to turn left, 5 to turn right, 4 to go down, 3 to go up. I think dialing 1 and 2 controlled the engine. Isn't that amazing? I had no idea."

Lynche was surprised at Nazy's thorough understanding of the ancient system. He had never heard of such a set-up.

"I bet Axelrod disappeared after the Hindenburg went down," said the DO.

Nazy nodded. "Reportedly, he moved to Chicago. Never to be heard from again."

The NCS Director asked, "Wasn't there a guy in the previous White House by that name?"

"They're all related," said Lynche, smirking disgustingly. "All little closet commies. And they all come out of Chicago. Can we know 'why' now?"

Nazy's British accent was strong. There was a hint of malevolence to the answer. "Apparently, Stalin...ordered...it."

Silence fell at the table as a nondescript man with thick black glasses approached and walked directly to the CIA Director. He knelt and whispered into his ear, "Director Lynche, you have a call from the Manila Chief in your office."

Lynche and Nazy Cunningham immediately took their leave of the other senior intelligence service officers at the table and walked silently abreast to the elevators to the seventh floor. All thoughts of a drone downing a dirigible were left on the cafeteria floor for the janitor to sweep up. The foremost thought for Lynche and Nazy was that the Manila Chief of Station would report the death of one Duncan Hunter.

The National Clandestine Service Director never took his eyes off of the legs of Nazy Cunningham as she left and he asked the Director of

Operations, "What is it with those two? They are up to something."

Annoyed, the DO Miklos asked, "What are you trying to say?"

"Have you seen her house? If she didn't wear a skirt she'd be investigated."

The DO asked incredulously, "You know where she lives?"

Castaño's eyes left the backside of Nazy Cunningham and turned to Miklos. "One of my guys stumbled on…it's a four million dollar mansion overlooking the Potomac. It's not even in her name. She could be another Aldrich Ames. Who would ever suspect her?"

Miklos dismissed the treasonous charge with a look of frustration. He wanted out of the ridiculous conversation. "You know she's married…. That's quite a rock on her finger. Maybe it's the husband's."

Castaño dismissed him and shook his head. "She's so far up his ass…."

"I don't know…. *You* didn't find bin Laden."

The NCS Director turned to the DO; he didn't appreciate the dig at his directorate's failures in the mountains of the Tora Bora. That was a long time ago. His Special Activities Division's intelligence officers thought they had located the master terrorist several times in Afghanistan and Pakistan but were forever thwarted until a no-name analyst named Nazy Cunningham suggested the Agency should analyze and monitor the movements of bin Laden's family, especially his wives.

Her initiative and concept of operations led the CIA to an odd compound in the hamlet of Abbottabad. A couple of Osama bin Laden's wives made their way to the small fortress under the cover of darkness. It was obvious the analyst had found and exploited the weakest link in bin Laden's security, his libido.

The NCS Director contained his aggravation. He stood and walked away from the DO without so much as a goodbye.

The Director of Operations said to himself, "What the hell is his problem?"

· · · · ·

Maxim Mohammad Mazibuike's eyes rolled back in his head. His fury was unchecked as he demolished everything atop the desk where he was sitting. The sounds of destruction reverberated in the underground palace.

Nizar came running. The other guards took defensive positions at the entrances. Upon finding a furious former president, Nizar turned and departed. Attacks he could fix; anger he could not. As he left the bedroom he noticed the only piece of electronics equipment still undamaged was the large television monitor on the wall. The Jordanian bodyguard retreated to the electronics room and scanned the channels to see what could have gotten his boss all worked up.

As expected, the Al-Jazeera network reported on the missing aircraft. The former President of the United States had looked forward to this little success of killing the man who he had suspected was responsible for releasing his CIA file. He had such high expectations of this mission. Now it looked like a failure. An aircraft landed in the Philippines. An emergency. Mechanical malfunction suspected. Possible terrorism. Over a hundred people dead.

He flew out of his chair as his brain screamed, *How did this happen? This has to be the aircraft the Amriki was supposed to crash.*

Mazibuike rushed past Nizar as he entered the electronics room full of computers, televisions, and computer games. His personal security guard jumped up from his seat and left the room closing the door behind him. Mazibuike jumped when the telephone rang. No one ever called. He debated whether to answer it or not. He picked up the receiver but didn't utter a word.

"Have you heard?" The familiar voice was Mohaned. *The One.*

"Yes. I'm unsure if it is…ours."

"Of course it's ours. We need to discuss this at your earliest convenience."

"We need to have…*him* explain the failure." Mazibuike shook his head.

"I've sent for him."

"I have more work for him."

"My friend, I'm not sure if this process is…*reliable.*"

"When do you wish to meet, my Lord?" It irked Mazibuike to grovel.

"I return to Dubai in three days. The weather will cooperate. I will send the car for you."

"You are most gracious. Safe travels. Peace be upon you and the Mercy of Allah and His blessings." Mazibuike replaced the receiver and turned up the volume on the television. More information on the incident aircraft was coming from multiple sources. He called Nizar and sent him to the kitchen for food. He sensed it would be hours before he learned if the infidel Hunter had been eliminated.

He believed in the plan, the process to bring America to her knees. *Americans love their airplanes. You will pay for your treachery.* He wiggled the mouse to awaken the computer. He drew heavily on the hookah and exhaled filling his lungs and the room with smoke.

Mazibuike would move up his timetable for revenge.

CHAPTER THIRTY-TWO

0200 July 21, 2014
Manila, Philippines

The cloud cover and the humidity steadily increased in advance of a frontal system. A two-day torrential rain was forecast. Residents looked forward to the monsoon. It would wash the city's polluted Jovian atmosphere down drains and give relief from the heat. At frontal passage, the temperature would drop a couple of degrees while spiking the humidity from 80 to 99 percent. They had seen it all before. The rainfall would be one-to-two inches per hour; in other words, no sane person would be caught dead trying to fly in such a storm system. The deteriorating weather was a signal for airlines and pilots to act if they didn't want to be grounded for days.

Duncan Hunter could smell the approaching storm and knew it was going to be a nasty one. They always were in the PI. His entry to the U.S. Embassy in Manila was expedited when he surrendered his DIP, his black-cover diplomatic passport, and stood still for a retina scan. A laser scanned the picture, bar code, and embedded chip in the passport. The unexpected night visitor wasn't on any VIP matrix, and he wasn't just any American citizen or diplomat passing through the area. That meant he wasn't State Department but CIA, running in the black, under cover. He had *access*. Within seconds of the passport scan, the Ambassador and the senior CIA intelligence officer assigned to the embassy were notified of the distinguished visitor.

The Marine Security Guard returned Hunter's DIP and gave the former Marine a badge and lanyard that allowed unescorted entry and access within the embassy.

"Thanks, Devil Dog," said Hunter appreciatively while evoking the motivational nickname for U.S. Marines given by World War I German soldiers to describe the Marines' rabid dog-like fighting spirit. The Marine Security Guard stiffened and snapped to attention; Hunter rendered and returned the salute and then walked off in the direction of the Chancery.

The Deputy Chief of Station met Hunter in the reception area and informed him the Ambassador refused to meet him at such an odd hour. The COS was "…in town, likely banging one of the locals."

"I would have thought it would have been the other way around," said Hunter sarcastically. It was just as well. All he needed was a SCIF, an encrypted telephone, and a hot line to CIA Headquarters. The Deputy COS provided. Hunter shed all of his electronic devices before entering the secure communications facility.

The heavily encrypted telephone call to the CIA switchboard bounced off a couple of geostationary satellites before reentering the atmosphere south of Bogota, Colombia and landing atop the New Headquarters Building. Hunter recognized the voice of Lynche's secretary, Penny Mayo. She would usually flirt with him, but today there was no small talk; he told her it was important he speak to the Director. She informed him that Director Lynche hadn't responded to an earlier page, but she would send someone to find him. She put Hunter on hold; he waited five minutes before he heard the heavily encrypted, gravelly, and out-of-breath voice of Greg Lynche.

"This better be good."

Hunter told an abbreviated version of what happened to him on the Qantas 747. Nazy Cunningham and Lynche listened intently to Hunter's brief, and Lynche had dozens of questions for Hunter. Lynche was well aware of the dangers of a loss of pressurization at altitude but had never experienced it in all of his flying. When Hunter's rapid monotone voice got to the issue of breaking down the cockpit door, Lynche was incredulous. Cockpit doors are impenetrable. *How is that possible?* Lynche screwed his eyes shut, jammed his chin into his chest, and asked, "How did you get in the cockpit?"

Hunter ripped an answer. "I took the air marshal's gun and knocked the regulator off an emergency air bottle. Aimed it at the door—it was just enough to rip the lugs from the frame." He finished by saying he worked with the captain to regain command of the aircraft, execute a dirty penetration, and make a perfect landing at the Clark Airport.

Lynche asked, "Come again?" Nazy didn't understand the pilot talk but wasn't going to ask questions. She slithered off the desk, took a seat, crossed her legs like a normal visitor, and listened. Duncan was safe.

"Greg, I think the jet's computer was hacked. Or more troubling, there is something wrong with the computer software. When I entered the cockpit I found all of the controls and systems locked and unresponsive. I tried to regain control. The captain was out; I got the crew on O2. I recycled the avionics master—but nothing happened! Just like the YoYo over Peru. I had to cycle the switch about a half dozen times before power was finally cut. The pressurization returned, and I was able to program the autopilot to maintain altitude. By that time the captain was coming back to life, and he took over and landed the airplane. And the jet dumped fuel."

Lynche's head shot up. He blinked wildly. He was missing something. "Okay, the jet dumped fuel, but I'm not getting the significance...."

"An uncommanded fuel dump isn't a normal electronics malfunction. Someone programmed that airplane to kill us."

Lynche locked eyes with Nazy. She asked, "Duncan, what are you thinking?" The encryption technology ruined her sultry British accent during transmission.

"Hey, good looking." That sexy voice usually made her toes curl, but not this time.

She asked, "Are you really okay?"

"I am." He knew he wasn't very convincing, but he wouldn't go into how close to death he had come. Nothing good would be served by it.

"I think we need to find out who makes the software for that 747." The he added as an afterthought, "Maybe 777s also."

"The Indonesian jet?" asked Lynche.

"Yes, sir."

Nazy recalled an event where something similar was... awarded...and then offered for discussion, "Didn't the President award a medal to a software company that made an aircraft...hijack-proof? There cannot be that many companies doing that kind of work."

Lynche said, "That's one and done work." Sole source contracts that no one else could perform.

The delay in transmission masked Hunter's ratiocination. For a moment Lynche thought the connection had been severed, then Hunter's voice bubbled up through algorithms and scramblers. "Unmanned systems too. The computer software in the YO-3A is configured for the optionally-manned or unmanned automatic takeoff and landing system. Good catch, Miss Cunningham. Director Lynche, I remember something like that too, but not the company's name. I think I was distracted by a goddess in white."

Nazy smiled at the offhanded compliment. She knew Hunter was smiling at her on the other side of the world.

The Director of Central Intelligence finally came up to speed. "That we can find. If we can determine that the software in the YoYo is from the same company as the software used in the Qantas 747 and that triple seven, I think we'll be on track to solve this. Maybe someone has breached all of the security firewalls."

Hunter blurted, "No, no, *no*! I'm thinking that is unlikely. The only thing that makes sense is that it was programmed. It wasn't hacked. It's…it's…it was *an inside job.*"

Nazy shot out of her seat, leaned over the desk phone and said, "You're saying the software company was able to take over control of the jet? Why would they want to do that? I don't get it."

The DCI kept his eyes on Nazy's and shook his head; he was just as confused as she was.

Hunter talked over their silence. He was thinking several steps ahead of the CIA executives. "It would be brilliant to slowly bleed off the pressurization—the pressure altitude gage was frozen at 8,000 feet when I entered the cockpit. Hypoxia is insidious, and you almost have to be on the lookout for it. I cannot get over the sight of that indicator at eight-K when I was sucking oxygen like I was on top of K2. That was the first clue the indicator was purposely locked to read a given altitude.… Normal aircrew scan would see it was normal and blow right past it. If it's the same company, I think we're talking premeditation and programming. If not, we're in trouble. Someone has to tear that jet apart to find what caused it to go off the program. As Nazy said, there cannot be that many companies doing this kind of work. Must be sole source stuff. The culprit must have all kinds of levels of access."

Lynche said quickly, "Agreed."

Nazy asked, "Duncan, you've talked about the dangers of airplanes and unmanned systems getting hacked. You don't think yours could have been hacked?" She sank back into her chair and crossed her legs.

Lynche caught himself breathing hard and this time it had nothing to do with Nazy sitting across the desk, one leg gently bouncing, thinking intently. She was staring off into space, fixated on a spot on the wall. She understood the ramifications of Duncan's analysis but found the conclusion totally unbelievable. Chilling. Someone tried to kill everyone aboard the aircraft? When Lynche started talking again, she snapped out of her reverie.

Lynche asked, "How'd you get off the jet?"

Hunter was curt. "Long story—I'll tell you later." He wanted to hear Nazy's voice again, squelched underwater British accent and all.

"Tell me now."

Lynche and Nazy could hear Hunter take a deep breath before speaking. "I took the dead copilot's ID and uniform to get off the plane. I put my tourist passport on him to exchange places. So your vision of killing me occurred, just not on your schedule."

"You know I'm going to have to fix that mess."

Nazy nodded. Fixing the circumstances of the death of an unknown civilian half a world away was out of her purview.

Lynche spat, "Okay, we can intercept the courier and redirect her to the PI. You'll get a new set of passports and she'll change your appearance. Don't shave."

"Negatory. There's bad storms heading this way. At least two days' worth of bad. Typhoon season."

Lynche turned to his computer and began typing furiously.

Hunter leaned back in his chair, an irritating and tortuous seat designed for the smaller frames of the Philippine people, lost in other thoughts. There was a very long and uncomfortable pause between the two men when Hunter asked a spurious question. "Do you have any idea where the old POTUS may be?"

Nazy raised her eyebrows. Why would he ask such a strange question in the context of the rescued jet and Hunter's escapades?

Lynche grunted, "Nazy thinks UAE. But before we dive into that question, I just received an update email. Do you know almost half of the passengers died? But you saved the other half. And the jet. The captain has probably been removed from flying duties while an investigation is conducted."

"He's a hero. I wouldn't have been able to land it without him."

316

"That's another thing you want me to fix?"

"He could have said something, that some Yankee broke into the cockpit, saved the day, and then ran off. I think he's a patriot for keeping his mouth shut. Someone will screw him if you don't intervene and plug that hole."

"Ten-four. I'll fix it." Lynche shook his head with disgust. Hunter was always breaking something that he had to fix.

"Master plumber Lynche. Thank you, sir." Nazy flashed perfect white teeth and gently nodded.

"Okay, Maverick. Hunker down at the chancery, don't leave, don't eat the fish or drink the water."

"You know I don't eat fish, and I'd never drink the local water." Nazy frowned and nodded her agreement. Hunter hated seafood.

Lynche admonished, suddenly playful, "You're getting up there in age—just don't know if your memory is all that sharp anymore...." It was a dig with no malice. He knew Hunter was the smartest man he'd ever met and his mind was as sharp as ever. Duncan Hunter had been one of a hundred million Americans to take a simple aptitude test designed by the CIA's Science & Technology Directorate. The cleverly disguised examination sought to determine how quickly a subject could balance 16 penny nails on the head of another. The timed outcome predicated genius and unique complex-problem solving skills. The intelligence specialists had found that a solving time under three minutes was noteworthy, under two was exceptional; anything under 60 seconds and the CIA wanted to discuss immediate recruitment. Hunter was the first person in five years to break the code and solved the puzzle in 58 seconds. The man who had found the uniquely gifted Duncan Hunter had been assigned to identify unusually capable and talented people across America for intelligence officer training was now the Director of Central Intelligence.

Then Hunter said, "And Greg, you need to get with the White House...." Lynche's brows crushed together as he turned away as if in great pain. He didn't want to hear anymore from Hunter. As soon as he said *White House*, he knew where his best friend was going. It was all too fantastic, too unbelievable.

"...and have the aircrew fly with emergency oxygen at all times. They need to put an external pressure altimeter indicator in the cockpit. If the jet secretly starts dumping pressure or becomes unresponsive, they need to cycle the avionics master continuously until the program breaks lock."

"*Shit!*" Lynche spat and shuddered at the thought Hunter planted six feet deep into his skull. The delicate hairs on Nazy's arms stood up as gooseflesh coursed over her body. The fear was palpable a dozen time zones away. "You don't really think...."

"*Oh, yes I do.* You cannot discount it. Remember that note 3M left for the President. If they can reach out and touch a random 747 over the Pacific, they can touch anyone's 747s, anywhere. Even the President's."

Lynche knew Hunter was right and pounded on his keyboard harder than ever. He mumbled, "The White House will have a conniption."

Hunter's voice was becoming watery as if the connection had taken a detour under the Wilson Bridge and travelled up the Potomac River to the CIA. "Not my problem. Tell me what we know about our guy."

Nazy was confused. She didn't know to whom Hunter was referring.

Lynche spoke over the sounds of the keys clicking from the keyboard. "Maybe we'll have something tomorrow. Meet me same time tomorrow. Better yet, I'll call you."

"Wilco." Hunter was agreeable and tired. Another rough patch of dead time on the line ensued.

A poisoned thought crept into Lynche's mind. Something he should have asked earlier. "I have to know you didn't kill the copilot." Nazy's head shot up and turned like a robotic mannequin during a power surge. If she could have growled at the DCI she would have. *Maybe he knows a side of Duncan I don't.*

His voice was full of melancholy. "Greg, I tried everything I knew to get into that cockpit. It took too long for me to find a solution, break the code, and because of that, because I didn't figure it out fast enough the copilot never recovered. Once I got in, I immediately got ABO on the pilot and the copilot. I hear over a hundred people died. I couldn't do anything for them and I'm not going to relish those memories." And then the husky watery voice was quiet.

Lynche was ashamed. Nazy was heartbroken. The DCI sucked a ton of air and said, "I had to ask."

"I know, boss. No factor, no issues. It would have been more difficult for you to fix if I broke his neck or something just so I could escape. I should have been clearer."

Lynche let him off the hook. He had moved on to prepare for another discussion he didn't want to have. "You'll have a new ID soon, when the weather cooperates. We'll have to figure when we can get something to you. As I recall, there's not many Air Force planes going to the PI."

"That I don't know. Thank you, Greg. Just so you know, I would have called on my BlackBerry but for the local electronic surveillance."

"No, you did the right thing." Lynche tapped his fingers on the desk. "*You always do the right thing.*" He nodded and was reminded of the line in a Milosz book: *I have too much admiration for those who fight evil, whether their choice of ends and means be right or wrong.* Hunter always pushed the boundaries of right and wrong.

"Even Iran?" Hunter grinned, eyes closed. He had programmed one of his YO-3As to fly an impromptu kamikaze mission to deliver a pair of stolen suitcase nuclear devices into the side of an Iranian nuclear reactor. President Hernandez gave him a medal; Lynche continued to give him shit.

"Don't push your luck, Maverick."

Nazy exhaled in relief and re-crossed her legs. All was okay in the world again.

Lynche said, "Talk with you tomorrow." Before Hunter could tell Nazy he loved her, Lynche severed the connection. He spun around in his chair turning his back to her, fingers in a teepee. He needed some undistracted time to think, to confirm he would need some help. A division of labor.

Nazy frowned and waited for the DCI to issue guidance or tell her to go back to work. It wasn't his style to cut Hunter off or to turn his back on her. She dismissed one affront, as the two men really didn't have anything more to say. As for the other, she waited.

Lynche sighed audibly. "Nazy?"

"Yes?"

He spun the judge's chair around 180° and asked, "What do you know about *Broken Lance*?"

CHAPTER THIRTY-THREE

0800 July 22, 2014
Fredericksburg, Texas

The men and women around the conference table hushed when Bill McGee's BlackBerry rang to signal an incoming call. He checked the number on the screen. It was the boss. He held up a finger and answered, "Yes, sir?"

McGee listened with an intensity they hadn't seen before. He picked up a pen and began to scribble notes. For three minutes he listed one item after another. Suddenly McGee's call was terminated without so much as a "bye."

He looked at the notes he had made and pounded his pen in rhythm with his thoughts. After another silent minute he aimed his pen at an employee at the same time he issued a directive. Ten employees, ten directives. The last person to receive the icy pen pointing at him was told, "You need to determine what company wrote and installed the ATLS software. Do not contact the company." McGee dropped the pen on his pad of paper. "Everyone, this is vitally important. Do not use your computer to send me an email that you have complied with these taskings. Find me and tell me in person."

Bob Jones, one of the YO-3A's septuagenarian aircraft mechanics and the last person to receive the malevolent end of the vertex pen asked, "Have we heard anything from Duncan?" There was a significant delay in McGee's response which began to upset the superannuated, bald and bearded mechanic. When McGee shook his massive head and winked, Bob Jones didn't believe him but understood him. The directive to "make her ready" was more than a command to prepare the YO-3A, the *Wraith*, for a mission. It was a tacit acknowledgment that Duncan Hunter needed him and the other Bob on the team, and that McGee was going to do whatever he could to help.

For fifteen years, Bob Jones and Bob Smith had maintained the company's miniscule fleet of YO-3As in better than new condition. Adventures with Hunter were more than secretive exploits of the brave and daring; they were professional, patriotic, and profitable. They had also become personal. Bob and Bob would make the *Wraith* ready for flight and transportation, and they would wait patiently for the warning order to load the airplane onto a CIA cargo aircraft or some other military aircraft like the C-17 Globemaster III.

Seemingly in deep thought, Bill McGee tapped his pen on the tablet in front of him. He nodded to himself and scribbled a note, tore off the sheet and handed it to Bob Jones.

Bob Jones read the paper, nodded, and said, "We can do that."

McGee dismissed the old guy with, "If I missed anything Bob, you just do your thing. You don't need to tell me. Prepare for the worst."

Bob responded with a single "thumbs up."

.   .   .   .   .

The vibration of the cellphone in his pocket was enough to startle him. He had been hyper-focused on the panel discussion on the main sound stage. Learning from it, critiquing it, and becoming nauseated by it. Four men and a woman were ostentatiously and wildly conjecturing on the troubles of the Qantas aircraft in the Philippine Islands. A pretty blonde lawyer-turned obstreperous correspondent encouraged a rancorous dialogue between an airline pilot, a retired U.S. Navy SEAL, and a novelist. The stunning display of journalistic incompetence in front of a horde of cameras and a standing-room crowd of morbid observers had saturated his senses as well as his sense of propriety, and he had zoned out like an epileptic who had wandered in front of a strobe light and couldn't tear his eyes away. Then the cell phone buzzed and Demetrius Eastwood had returned to the present. One check of the tiny screen and he dashed out of the media congregation, ran down a hall, and ducked into a space called the "Green Room," where performers waited. He mashed the "connect" button.

"Maverick! Thanks for getting back to me so quickly...."

"Dory, I don't have much time. I'm in the PI. I was on that jet."

Eastwood was very nearly unbalanced and wobbled with the news. After a second to regain his composure, he asked, "What is it about you and jumbo jets in trouble?" He was immediately teleported to a front-row seat of a murderous hijacking when the cabin lights went out and he heard the unmistakable sound of a silenced weapon being fired with the "pinging" of spent cartridges being ejected near where he was sitting. When the lights came back on Duncan Hunter was standing in the aisle in a black flight suit, brandishing a .45 with a silencer, and wearing a night vision goggle helmet—and he had his arms around an attractive redheaded woman. A dead terrorist lay in the aisle.

Hunter ignored the question. "I need a favor."

He goes weeks without so much as a text message and now he calls from the Philippines asking for a favor? When Eastwood found his tongue he said, "Sure, anything for you, Devil Dog."

"Dory, you need to tell your network that the jet simply experienced a significant electrical malfunction. Not terrorism. That you heard it directly from…the copilot of the flight."

Eastwood mumbled, "Um, um, ummm." *You're not the copilot!* "Duncan, I don't know…."

"Say it's the pilot. We need some time to find out who did this, and if the networks start jumping up and down saying it was terrorism then I'm afraid more of these will occur. May occur."

"You know what really happened?" That Hunter was a spook employed by the CIA wasn't a secret between them. But having Hunter ask him to be part of a conspiracy was surprising, even astounding. As a member of the press, he had always held Hunter at arms' length. Whatever had happened to the Qantas aircraft had to be of strategic importance. If Hunter was involved that meant three-letter agencies. Intelligence Community. Stuff above top secret. Stories he would never be able to tell or write about.

"Yes." Hunter provided Eastwood the basic narrative and enough of an alibi to be credible.

"And…and you can't say?" Eastwood felt he was being drawn in to another far-off conspiracy. Somehow he had survived an earlier conspiracy that resulted in the staged suicide of a Marine Corps colonel at a Marine Corps Air Station. The colonel had his head caved in from behind, an assailant stuffed a shotgun in his mouth. The "suicide" had been a signal for everyone on the program to keep their mouths shut. If not some rogue CIA types would sneak up from behind, bash their heads in, stuff a shotgun in their mouths, and pull the trigger. Eastwood closed his eyes and shook his head at how close he had come to being terminated. Having al-Qaeda always riding his ass was one thing. But having former Agency-trained assassins on his trail was a road he never wanted to travel again.

Hunter responded. "Yes. One day soon I'll tell you the full story. But at this point, no one has a need to know."

Damn! "Okay. I'll do it. One day you'll tell me the whole story?"

"I will, and I *will* make it up to you. By the way, yes I know mosques are behind lasers being shone into cockpits and small UAVs being flown into the intakes of jets. You need to write something on how wannabe jihadists are flooding airports with potential employees for security and maintenance positions; preparing themselves for attacks on aircraft and airports. European airports will be the first to find out the hard way. They have been completely infiltrated. We created the TSA because American airport security had been completely compromised by al-Qaeda. I hope that answers your questions. Thanks, Dory. Gotta go. I'll be in touch."

He snapped, "Wait!" to a dead line. He looked around the Green Room to ensure no one had heard his conversation. No one had.

Eastwood staggered out of the Green Room as if he had too much wine instead of a bottled water. He wandered back into the sound studio and pushed through the throng of suits and skirts waiting for their turn at the table under the bright lights and big cameras. He found the woman with the electronic clipboard standing next to the producer and made his way over to them. He leaned over and said to the stoic women, "I just heard from the pilot of the Qantas aircraft that it was a severe electronic malfunction. It wasn't terrorism."

The producer shook her head violently. She glared at Eastwood and panned her eyes to the awaiting subject matter experts, pundits, and authors of thrillers lined up for their moment of glory in front of the network's cameras. "I didn't hear that. Dory, I'm not going to need you today. You can go home."

Eastwood paused for seconds to consider what he was going to do next. *Fish or cut bait!* He brushed between the clipboard goddess and the termagant of a producer and strode out into the studio toward the moderator and table of "experts." The producer was apoplectic but unable to move or utter a syllable. No one stopped him. Other than Don Rickles, no sane person would ever interrupt a broadcast. The former attorney, now lay correspondent, saw Dory Eastwood approach her.

"Apologies for the interruption, but I just got off the phone with the copilot of the Qantas jet and he assured me what they experienced was a major electrical malfunction. It wasn't in any way terrorism."

"But the cockpit door?" asked the airline pilot at the thick Plexiglas table.

"A brave air marshal did what he had to, to ensure the aircrew was alive. He found them hypoxic, and he put their emergency oxygen masks over their faces."

"So an air marshal saved their lives?" asked the author of thrillers.

Eastwood didn't respond to the question but apologized for the disruption and walked off the stage. The petite producer harnessed her fury and ran to him, pointing her finger up at his face as she hissed, spittle flying across his shirt and chin. *"You don't know what you've done Eastwood! You...You're fired! I'll see to it you'll never work here again. Get out before I have security haul your ass out of here!"*

He jutted his jaw, flecked expectorate from his chin, turned, and left the studio.

At the elevators he said to himself. "Another day of winning friends and influencing people."

He flagged a taxi. It stank. The driver was a stinky African man with only half a mouth of teeth. He rolled down the window for fresh air. The ride to 7 World Trade Center was made in silence, which suited him under the circumstances. A half-hour later he was back inside his unnamed office and fixed a steaming cup of coffee from a well-provisioned Keurig machine. He glanced at the coffee mug and smirked at the image of an infamous cartoon of Mohammed with a bomb in his turban lacquered on the outside of the cup. He needed something to distract him. The Drudge Report. Michael Ramirez cartoons. Then he would move to *The Reporter's Telegraph* and *Blacklisted News* to hopefully find a clue to what he had gotten himself into. Maybe it was time to update his resume and look for work.

Eastwood reached for his smart phone. He deliberated for a minute what to say, if anything. *What the hell?* He composed a text message for the Marine in the Philippines: *Mission Accomplished.* He was stunned when he received a reply in a few seconds. *Still employed?* He laughed, buoyed and heartened by the simplicity of the question. Eastwood said aloud, "I don't hear from you in weeks, and now we're texting like high school girls in homeroom. So, what the hell are you doing, Maverick?" His question was answered with another question. The exchange of text messages was no longer amusing. *Do you know where the former POTUS might be?*

Demetrius Eastwood first thought, "*That is an interesting question.*" He texted a response: *I asked the same question in a WaPo article a couple of weeks ago.* His brain went into overdrive—why would Hunter want to know where President Mazibuike might be? *Why would he want to know that information sitting in the PI?*

The immediate response from Hunter made him laugh. *I don't read that liberal tripe. Sorry I missed it. I stay away from the media—you know, those low-IQ people that photograph well and can only speak with a teleprompter. So you don't know either?*

Maybe he was projecting; maybe he was assuming too much. Eastwood suddenly realized Hunter was truly hunting the man. He had a very general idea what Duncan Hunter did for the CIA. He, Bill McGee, and a very injured Nazy Cunningham had been evacuated from the U.S. Embassy in Algeria to one of the U.S. Navy's newest aircraft carriers. One of the most incredible sights Eastwood had ever seen and filmed was a WWII biplane landing on *U.S.S. Eisenhower.* The pilot emerged from the airplane only to be scrubbed from head to toe by a decontamination team. It was Duncan Hunter who stepped out of the Beechcraft Staggerwing, walked to the fantail of the carrier, stripped, and was hosed down with the decontamination solution. In thirty-five mile an hour winds they scrubbed every inch of his skin with a yard-long brush. Only an elite member of the CIA could warrant such service on an aircraft carrier in the middle of the night. Hunter said he killed the guy that shot him out of the sky, and he stole his ancient airplane to escape the African continent. *The last of a Marine's Marine.*

Then there was the bullet. More rocket ship than ammunition. He had dug the unique projectile out of the dirt in Nigeria after the Boko Haram leaders had kidnapped a few dozen Christian girls and taken them into the brush to be raped or killed. But someone intervened, and the girls got away. The thumb-sized bullet sat upright on his desk as a reminder; a souvenir of what he knew to be another Duncan Hunter event.

And then there was Hunter and McGee rescuing a hijacked aircraft. At night, in the middle of Africa, within a couple of hours of landing. Eastwood would never be able to comprehend how Hunter was able to get aboard the airplane, shut off the lights, kill the hijackers, and get off the aircraft before the pilots returned to the cockpit to fly the jet to their final destination. The man was amazing, and he had been there to witness some of Hunter's finest work.

Hunter had also been in the Border Patrol. They track and hunt humans who have infiltrated our borders. You have an interesting skill set, Mr. Hunter.

The computer screen illuminated his face. Eastwood surveyed the room. He responded to the text message. *Rumor mill says the ME. All deposed dictators find refuge in the UAE. Except Idi Amin, of course. I think the food and room service must be better there than Riyadh.*

"Maverick, what the hell are you up to this time?" he said to himself. He was saddened no other text messages came through. The chain was broken. He hoped Hunter got what he was looking for.

· · · · ·

The thick passport full of stamps and visas was handed back to him along with his boarding documents. He knew the drill. Normal people pass through the magnetometer without setting it off, but with a prosthetic leg, he knew that at a bare minimum he would be shunted to a cordoned area for additional screening, frisking, and humiliation. It was an international flight; they might even force him to remove the prosthesis. Then a TSA agent would carry his artificial leg like a dismembered trophy for all to see before plopping it into a grey tub and running it through the X-ray machine. The horror stories of the TSA's asinine and imbecilic rules and regulations for children, the elderly, and the handicapped were legendary and true. He placed his smart phone, watch, and belt on top of his shoes and jacket in one of the industrial grey tubs. Computer in another. His carry-on bag went to the head of the line on the conveyor belt.

As a frequent international traveler, he didn't acknowledge the TSA agent who initially handled his documents. He fully expected the highly sensitive magnetometer would sound an alarm that some proscribed indeterminate amount of metal had passed through its arches disrupting the magnetic field, exceeding the detection parameters. Bells accompanied flashing lights. On the other side of the disturbed magnetic field device with his passport in one hand and his boarding pass in another, he quietly informed the obese TSA agent that he had an artificial leg. She rolled her brown eyes as if they were subject to the Coriolis and directed him to another line, directing a supervisor to conduct a physical inspection.

A harried, thin man in a dark blue uniform snatched up a flat, black wand metal detector with the letters GARRETT emblazoned on its paddle. Tamerlan al-Sarkari lifted his trouser leg for a visual and physical inspection. The wand squealed and vibrated with every pass along the front, back, and sides of the prosthetic. With a flick of his hand, the TSA allowed him through to collect his belongings from the X-ray machine. He was visibly relieved to have escaped the shame and degradation of having to remove his prosthetic lower leg and have it run through the X-ray machine to ensure it didn't have a knife or a derringer or fingernail clippers contained within. Instead of being subject to the latest TSA indignity and disgrace, he panicked and lost his composure for a second as he could not locate his computer. As fast as his heart had spiked with adrenalin, believing his computer had been stolen, he saw the silly grey tubs and his roll-aboard located at the end of the X-ray machine's conveyor belt. He donned his shoes, watch, and jacket, and placed his computer inside his bag.

Two hours later, al-Sarkari boarded a Qatar Airlines Boeing 777 for the thirteen-hour flight to Doha. The thought that he was leaving America for the last time didn't trouble him greatly. He was thinking of ways to extend his life.

●　　●　　●　　●　　●

The Director of Central Intelligence spun his chair from his computer monitor to face the woman sitting across his desk. He said, "Nazy, I'm going to read you in on a Special Access Program called *Broken Lance*. The *raison d'etre* for this unique SAP is an Executive Order signed by JFK in 1962. President Kennedy was the original Lance or Lancer."

Nazy Cunningham's face showed concern and confusion. Her brain was working overtime, and he had her full attention.

Lynche continued, "You've probably heard of the term 'Broken Arrow' for the loss of a nuclear weapon."

The Director of the National Counter Terrorism Center nodded, a little confused. She had watched the movie with the same name with Duncan. She was unsure of any other terms associated with nuclear weapons. They weren't standard Agency terms or more appropriately, they were not typical counterterrorism terms.

"Bent Spear, Dull Sword, and Empty Quiver are the Pentagon programs that result from the accidental launching, firing, detonating, theft, or loss of a thermonuclear weapon. All these programs came from strategic plans to deal with the loss of a nuke, or in the case of *Broken Lance*, the loss of a president. *Broken Lance* is a special operation to rescue or ...*remove* a president in the event he was ever kidnapped or taken hostage. Or if he fell into enemy hands."

Now she was very confused. She articulated her confusion. "We haven't...lost a president, Director Lynche...."

"Oh, but we have." A somber Greg Lynche didn't smile. He was dead serious. "Only 15 people in the US government are read-in on *Broken Lance*. Ten SEALs, the President, the Secretary of Defense, the DCI, the Attorney General and the Secret Service Director. And now you. Number sixteen. *Broken Lance* could only be authorized if at least three of the principals agreed."

Her ears started to buzz as if a spontaneous burst of tinnitus had struck without warning. The DCI's words were being drowned out. It slowly dawned on her what Director Lynche was intimating. *Broken Lance removes a president?* "Hold it—*Broken Lance* is Presidential authority to assassinate a sitting president?"

"In this case we're not talking about a *sitting* president." He allowed her impressive logical mind to fill in the blanks.

When she finally understood, she unconsciously covered her mouth with her hand. *President Mazibuike is not a sitting President.* From behind her fingers she asked, "Why tell me?"

Nazy lowered her head. She knew where her boss was going. She recalled asking her husband, "Does the President want you for another event?" Another name on the President's Disposition Matrix, the spreadsheet of a special group of charismatic terrorists targeted for elimination. The elimination program was called *Noble Savage*; the DCI and the President identified and Duncan targeted high value targets in the Middle East and Africa. Now she knew. Now it was clear what her husband had been asked to do. Duncan just didn't eradicate drug crops; he was a terminator. The Agency had used very few assassins, and those that they did use were, as far as she understood, one-trick ponies for international targets. Top terrorists. One man, one target; the contract assassin was never to be heard from or used again. And they were never an American citizen. *Broken Lance* changed everything.

Nazy trembled as the words bounced out of her mouth. She whispered, "Is it a suicide mission?"

"The Navy SEALs who volunteered knew it was. They were prepared to go behind enemy lines to execute their mission."

"Thank you, Greg. That had to be difficult. Telling me."

"I love you guys as if you were my own flesh and blood. I don't like it but…there really isn't anyone else that can do something like this as well as and as quietly as Duncan. Now we can take targets out with a missile. We expect to leverage the capabilities of Duncan's airplane to find him. It's not necessarily a suicide mission."

"How did the SEALs do it?"

"Worst case scenario. Two-man sniper teams would parachute into an area. Find the target and execute the mission. Then get away if they could. Duncan has an airplane as a getaway vehicle."

She shook her head. What she heard in her ears was her blood racing through her temples and carotids. Her blood pressure rose and darkened her lips.

Lynche continued to discuss some of the particulars of the special access program and the executive order. "In the case of a President being caught or captured, President Kennedy determined the American people didn't want to see their President subject to torture, paraded, or humiliated. Any U.S. President would be tortured for information and the country would be at risk; the government would be completely dysfunctional. And as you have ascertained, for the U.S. Navy SEALs it was considered a suicide mission. Once they were in country there was no expectation they would be able to get out alive. It was a volunteer assignment. Bill McGee was a Lancer."

Nazy nodded slightly at the revelation that Duncan's close friend was involved in what had to be the most closely guarded secret assignment within the intelligence community. She said, "This is virtually an impossible mission. They are going to need a great deal of help. I've anticipated something like this. We've been working to find the former president. With the new information I received from the Secret Service, I think I know how to find...*him*."

Lynche finally smiled. Nazy said "him" in such a way that Lynche wondered if it was meant to be a *double entendre*. He looked into her eyes and said, "I knew you would. You're our secret weapon. You've always been our secret weapon. That's where you come in."

CHAPTER THIRTY-FOUR

1300 July 22, 2014
McLean, Virginia

The Director of Central Intelligence was the thin man among the heavyweights in the Intelligence Community who were seated around the conference table. Of the newcomers, General Richard Hilburn, National Security Agency Director was the fittest of the group. He had never been one to carry extra pounds even though he rarely had time for the gymnasium or a jog. He was the former Commander of U.S. Cyber Command and a career U.S. Army intelligence officer. Dr. Scott Hernon, Director of the National Reconnaissance Office, was dour, fleshy and colorless. He was an electronics genius who had been self-confined to a windowless existence for forty years, a captive of his research and his work inside a SCIF. No one knew more about designing, building, and operating the reconnaissance satellites of the United States government. The National Geospatial-Intelligence Agency (NGA) Director, Gerald Neighbors, was tall and beefy and a trivial pursuit buff. The first flecks of grey had invaded Neighbor's beard and the temples of his short cropped hair. A gym rat of the first order, he used muscles and an acerbic wit to get what he wanted.

Greg Lynche welcomed the directors of the various agencies along with the Deputy Director National Counter Terrorism Center Ted Rainbow, sitting in for Nazy Cunningham, the NCS Director without his dark glasses, Steve Castaño, and the Director of Operations (DO), Quint Miklos. Castaño and Miklos ignored each other; a case of residual hard feelings from their earlier meeting with Lynche and Cunningham. Once the DCI's salutations and greetings were finished, the DO took over the conduct of the assembly. He reiterated the purpose of the meeting—to discuss the findings of the investigation into the Indonesian Sky Link and Qantas flights, as well as update the DCI on the task to determine the location of the former president. As he ran through several slides, the men listened but did not take notes.

"Regarding the Qantas aircraft, last night the FBI raided the corporate offices of a software company, Chimera Avro-Software Technologies. The CEO was interviewed and he fingered the chief scientist, Dr. Tamerlan al-Sarkari. Dr. al-Sarkari arrived in Doha, Qatar about ten hours ago. His whereabouts are unknown at this time. A 'Be on the Lookout' dispatch was issued at Middle East embassies with the caveat to observe and report, but do not detain or arrest."

"What's his story?" asked NSA Director Hilburn.

Quint Miklos responded, "Only child of Egyptian immigrants. PhDs, no active religious affiliation. They left Egypt to escape the Muslim Brotherhood. Their graduate work isn't classified and is not relevant. Tamerlan is a software prodigy. Invented several cutting-edge aviation programs designed to eliminate the so called 'black boxes' found on all commercial aircraft. Dozens of patents. One invention replaced black boxes with a satellite-based Flight Data Recorder and Cockpit Voice Recorder system called, 'Virtual Flight Following.' Earlier this month he won the Presidential Medal of Innovation for his anti-hijacking, anti-hacking program called 'Impenetrable Cockpit.' The proprietary heavily-encrypted software is on all Boeing and Airbus commercial aircraft, as well as most of the unmanned systems in the U.S. inventory. Now you want to know the bad news? The CEO indicated that when the Sky Link aircraft was lost and the Qantas aircraft was mysteriously stricken, he wondered if their software could have been responsible. Al-Sarkari had been acting a little strangely after the Sky Link airplane went missing. Their quality assurance engineers had run several in-house checks to determine if their software could have played a part in the aircraft's disappearance. The QA shop found some irregularities. The CEO was insistent that al-Sarkari still had the codes. He still had access to all Boeing, Airbus and unmanned aircraft."

"What does that mean, access," asked NGA Director Neighbors.

The DO continued, "As I understand it, the system is set up so that the aircraft computers are linked to several sensors and all of the instruments and control boxes in the cockpit. A command, control, and a monitoring system. If the aircraft computer determines 'unusual activity' in the cockpit, such as more than two people in the cockpit, the Identify Friend or Foe system gets shut off, or the autopilot circuit breaker is pulled. Anything the artificial intelligence deems inappropriate to the conduct of the flight or any unscheduled deviation of the flight plan triggers al-Sarkari's anti-hijack program to take control of the aircraft. The computer removes any input from the cockpit, say, someone tries to steer it off course or push it into the ocean. The computer overrides all inputs and safely flies the aircraft to the nearest runway and lands the aircraft."

"How does it do that?" asked NRO Director Hernon.

Lynche responded, "The aircraft's computer is not only coupled to the Virtual Flight Following and the Impenetrable Cockpit anti-hijacking programs, but also to the automatic takeoff and landing systems. Another patented al-Sarkari program."

The DO screwed up his face when he said, "Sounds sort of *benign*."

"That doesn't sound too bad," said the NCS Director Castaño, shaking his head. Everyone in the room but Castaño had their hands on the conference table.

"That is normal operation," asserted DO Miklos. "The CEO thinks al-Sarkari, like the airlines, can query the status of a particular aircraft."

"What difference does that make?" asked the NRO Director. He wasn't trying to be a pest with his questions, but his demeanor and tone suggested he was growing more irritated with information that had nothing to do with him. He had other more important business he could be doing, and he didn't want to be in the room. Lynche noticed the man's aggravation. If he had to be there, then he wanted answers.

The DCI said, "Let me answer that by saying the FBI and NSA computer scientists have checked the software and the company-provided encryption technology, the keys and the lines of code. They said they haven't seen anything like it before. Unusually complex. NSA thought they were dealing with a commercial-grade electronic Enigma machine. What we know is that only the airlines and the aircraft manufacturers are supposed to have the activation codes to initiate, program, and execute the anti-hijacking software *externally*."

Lynche let the information sink in and then continued, "The software CEO insisted his company only set up the activation codes for each aircraft and then provided Boeing and Airbus those codes. Just to be clear, the airlines received the activation codes from Boeing and Airbus when they purchased their airplanes. The airlines are responsible for programming their aircraft on how to respond in the event of an in-flight hijack. The computer would sense the hijacking and either fly the airlines' preprogrammed route or return the airplane to the departure airport or fly to the nearest airport. The crew could be dead in the cockpit, the hijackers could try to steer the aircraft, but it would land via the preprogrammed automatic takeoff and landing system. The computer and software do everything—land, stop, shut down the engines—but they cannot open the passenger doors."

Miklos flipped to another slide. Hernon shifted positions. "The airlines also have the option to alter the programming in flight. They can do that by accessing the aircraft's main computer through the satellite data link and the aircraft's Virtual Flight Following program. The software company was supposed to be completely removed from the access process when the programs and the activation codes were delivered to Boeing. And Airbus."

"So he thinks al-Sarkari may still have the codes?" asked the NGA Director. "So he really could get inside?"

DO Miklos nodded. "He created them. Yes. Copies."

"For all Boeing and Airbus aircraft?" again asked NGA Director Neighbors.

DO Miklos answered, "All commercial aircraft. No military aircraft were affected that we know of, but the CEO was unsure if the commercial derivatives were modified with their systems. It was all under al-Sarkari's purview. Supposedly, the military never received the anti-hacking or anti-hijacking software package. No need. But the Gulfstreams and Air Force One; we don't know. That is another question."

Greg Lynche watched the other intelligence executives' faces for signs of concern. He knew what they were thinking. "This al-Sarkari fits the profile of a super-empowered individual. Lone wolf. Kaczynski on steroids. But we cannot be certain. I informed the White House that Air Force One crews must wear external oxygen for the duration of their flights."

"Seriously?" demanded the Director of the NRO.

"The guy who saved the Qantas jet was one of ours," replied Lynche.

"The press reported it was an air marshal," impishly offered the NRO Director.

Lynche said, "Don't believe everything you hear or see on television."

"So he was one of ours?" asked NCS Director Castaño, looking around and gesturing with one scarred hand as if he had been napping and missed the end of a magic trick. As soon as the words left his lips, he regretted asking such an obviously dumb question.

All the men muttering around the table could spot an ongoing special access program without the DCI uttering a word. It wasn't their first rodeo; they understood the DCI's reluctance to acknowledge a SAP and all of its special handling and reporting, even among friends and peers.

But now with Castaño's confusion, they knew it wasn't being run by the National Clandestine Service. That peculiarity was well past the realm of strange—it was unique. Collectively, there were hundreds of years of intelligence service sitting around the table, and this was a first. The DCI was privately running an operation. A special access program like no other. They also knew the rules. Disclosure could put a human resource in jeopardy; disclosure of the individual would likely result in death.

Still, they looked at each other. Hernon calmed down a visibly upset Castaño. He suppressed his anger and thought, *If it isn't one of my guys who the hell is it!?*

Previous conversations between the DO and the principal deputies had revolved around how strangely the boss had been acting lately. There was the spontaneous Memorial Wall Dedication. Then, there was the fact that the DCI hadn't left the office; he was spending nights at his desk. And then there was the constant huddling with Cunningham. There wasn't a single person among them who thought there could be something sexual between them, but their actions were bordering on indecent. It wasn't time to press the Director for more information. The brief had just gotten started. They weren't bored, although they wished that Nazy Cunningham was there to entertain them with her voice, legs, and cleavage. She could huddle with them anytime.

DCI Lynche ignored his NCS Director. He wasn't going to provide any more intel on the subject and was ready to move to the next subject. The real purpose of the meeting. Lynche said tersely, "Next question."

The NSA Director, something of a computer genius himself, believed there was something more ominous in the DO's report. General Hilburn said, "What you are intimating is that al-Sarkari can take over virtually any airborne commercial aircraft. Are we to understand that accessing the aircraft can be done from anywhere?"

Lynche said, "Yes."

"How would he do that?"

Miklos turned to the NSA Director and replied, "The software CEO said al-Sarkari was the system administrator. He alone developed all of the key codes, the activation codes. They ran it like a SAP, very limited knowledge of the work, a program manager, eyes-only, and it was done in a commercial SCIF. The CEO suggested al-Sarkari could have been the one who accessed the aircraft since he maintained a copy of the activation codes. He could have taken control of the aircraft remotely."

"But all he could do is initiate a return home program or tell it to fly to the closest airport," countered the NRO Director.

"Not if he embedded additional code, additional commands," said Director Lynche.

Every man turned from the slide show and stared at the DCI.

Lynche continued, "Classic super empowered individual. We have to expect the worst. We've essentially lost two aircraft in the same part of the world. Near some of the deepest parts of the Pacific."

DO Miklos interjected, "It's obvious he has to have the codes. That part is not rocket science—they're the same as the Microsoft upgrade codes. You know, five sets of five letters and numbers. All of the codes were developed by al-Sarkari personally. Boeing or Airbus classified material security specialists installed the software and programmed each aircraft on their assembly lines. Boeing and Airbus also sent out teams of security specialists to install the software and program the airlines' aircraft that were already in their fleet. The CEO initially insisted al-Sarkari turned over all the codes after contract completion. But as we have seen with any computer program, there are system upgrades from time to time. Apparently, Al-Sarkari pushed system upgrades to Boeing and Airbus to be installed in their flying aircraft, without the knowledge of the manufacturers or the airlines."

The NSA Director blurted out, "It's a Trojan. Crap, I'm never getting on another jet."

Miklos continued, "The CEO is sure every Boeing and Airbus aircraft in operation also received these software upgrades. He said, 'The result, technically, is that al-Sarkari could access any flying commercial airliner in the world and make it disappear.'"

This chilling thought was not lost on the intelligence executives. The NRO Director asked, "How many aircraft are impacted by this software?"

DO Miklos said, "Three years ago, Chimera pushed updates for all Boeing and Airbus airliners manufactured after 2000. The CEO estimates a minimum of 10,000 aircraft received updates. Today, there could be as many as 15,000 airliners that are affected."

The NSA Director repeated, "It's a Trojan horse."

"There's more," said Miklos, flipping to another slide. "The FBI determined there were two external requests for information on two airborne aircraft. Care to venture which two?"

"Sky Link and Qantas," replied three of the men.

The DCI nodded. "Boeing and the airlines claim they did not remotely access the jets. That only leaves al-Sarkari. The question is, 'Why?'"

Lynche interjected his positional power into the discussion. He didn't want to discuss the possibility that Duncan Hunter had been the target of a *fatwa*, that several other Duncan Hunters had died, and that the man at the heart of a very special executive special access program had nearly been assassinated—multiple times. It was a possible explanation for the latter aircraft but what about the first? Finding a rationale for its demise was troubling. No answers. Lynche allowed an embarrassing thought, *Where was Hunter when you need him?* The circumstantial case was building that the software scientist, al-Sarkari, had targeted Duncan Hunter, and if that was a true statement, he must have been able to determine Hunter's flight plan. Could the man be so cold that he would kill everyone on the airliner to eliminate the CIA's best contract pilot? Planning for that required a monumental effort and would likely require a foray into another set of classified programs. Lynche realized this was much worse than he had initially thought. He uttered, "Shit!"

The four-letter word raised the eyebrows of the four men around the table. The DCI continued, "Quint, is the FBI cooperating?"

"They are. So is the CEO."

"Did he say why did al-Sarkari went to Qatar?" asked Lynche.

"He said he needed to make a customer call."

"Was that normal?" asked the NRO Director.

"He indicated it was very unusual for the chief scientist to go on a customer call, but he is one of the senior executives and his travel never needs to be approved. They pride themselves on providing the finest customer service."

NSA's General Hilburn interrupted. "This is what we've been able to do. At your request Director Lynche, in the last twelve hours, we traced his movements over the last year, to England, Germany, and France, and most recently to Dubai and Abu Dhabi. Company credit card, company cell phone, company laptop. Stayed at the best hotels. Five stars. His last trip he stayed at the Armani Hotel Dubai. Miss Cunningham has the specifics."

The first written note taken at the table was by Greg Lynche at the mention of Armani Hotel. Everyone noticed.

"He's not very good at covering his tracks. There's been no further activity on his card, cell, or computer." The NSA Director continued, "We determined he arrived in Doha via passport tracking systems. No further activity. Now he is gone. Off the grid."

The Deputy Director NCTC, Ted Rainbow said, "He knows his cover is blown. He's running." Heads nodded around the table.

After being silent for much of the brief, the NCS Director popped up, "Okay, he's already Muslim. Was he active or activated?"

DO Miklos said, "The CEO said no to both. However, the CEO said al-Sarkari had started to read the Qur'an recently. Until just recently he had been a wine drinking, non-practicing Muslim."

Lynche encouraged, "However...."

Miklos got the hint. "However, the FBI said they found a shredded copy of the Muslim Brotherhood's *Explanatory Memorandum* at his residence."

Lynche hung his head and talked to the table. "This intel is very bad."

The group knew the *Explanatory Memorandum* described aspects of the global jihad's strategic information warfare campaign as well as its structure, reach, and activities. For a self-radicalized jihadist, it was a guidebook. Like finding a lost missing piece of a puzzle, the book on Tamerlan al-Sarkari was complete.

"We have a winner," interjected the NSA Director, tossing a pen on a closed notebook. The other men mashed their lips into frowns.

Lynche looked up and asked the NSA General. "Rich, can we get to his computer?"

"We have the serial numbers. The CEO had their IT shop push them to the FBI, and their liaison forwarded us that data. If he is as smart as everyone thinks he is, he'll swap machines soon. Dump his old one for a new one. But if he is stupid, we'll find it and kill it, if and when he connects to a system." He snapped his fingers for emphasis. "And we'll know where he is, if anyone is interested."

"You can do that?" asked the NGA Director.

General Hilburn offered, "As soon as a computer attempts to access the internet, the internet interrogates the computer, in essence asking 'Who am I talking to?'" He snapped his fingers again. "When his computer 'checks in,' he'll get an answer that he will not like. Instant blue screen of death as we kill his DOS and suck out every bit of info on his hard drive. We do to his computer what he did to those aircraft— remove all control."

"Sounds like you would like to be the one sending the spike to kill it," said Lynche, almost laughing.

"You bet I would." All the men laughed including Greg Lynche.

CHAPTER THIRTY-FIVE

1300 July 22, 2014
McLean, Virginia

"I don't know; the mere fact he appears to be off the grid now tells me we're too late," interjected NGA Director Neighbors.

"The computer data information is at NSA; they're working it," said the Director of Operations. Agreement orbited the conference table.

"Break, Break. New subject," announced Lynche. "Rich, I think we need to see if the FBI can determine if al-Sarkari was able to access their Domestic Passenger Tracking and Movement Database. Quint, we need to see if he was able to access the International Passenger Tracking Database. If that shithead...."

NCS Director Castaño finished the Director's thought. "The bastard would be able to determine if a certain person made reservations or boarded an aircraft, and he could...."

Lynche finished the gruesome thought. "...kill everyone aboard the aircraft." The CIA had been able to go for years hiding the identities of their spies as they moved through train stations and airports. Terrorist organizations were known to have planted bombs on airplanes or shot aircraft out of the sky if an American or British intelligence officer was suspected of being aboard. The old Soviet Union organized the loose confederation of liberals and radicals dedicated to finding and destroying the CIA, one intelligence officer at a time. In the intelligence business they were called Tail Watchers.

"This is unbelievable power in the hands of one man. Now that we know this, I know where you are going. I doubt the Chimera CEO would be able to answer this question. If he can do one, can he do multiples? Or all?"

The data geek, NGA Director Neighbors said, "There are, at any given time, between 500,000 and 700,000 people airborne, worldwide."

Lynche thrummed his fingers and nodded in rhythm.

Neighbors continued. "150,000 people in Hiroshima and 80,000 in Nagasaki died from two bombs. That's a third of what is possible with that man's laptop."

"With a single key-stroke?" asked NCS Director Castaño. Hidden scarred hands were lifted momentarily above the table top. Everyone took notice.

General Hilburn of the NSA said, "Possible. Probable. Likely."

"So we have work to do there. I want to talk about the real reason we're here. POTUS whereabouts. Let's go around the table."

The general from NSA said, "Within five minutes of the release of his file, he used his BlackBerry to call Oahu. He said he required transportation from Hickham Air Force Base. The reply was, 'We will be there.' That is all."

The doctor from the NRO said, "We have imagery of a Gulfstream business jet at the commercial side of Oahu International. Another at the Subic Bay Airport."

Lynche asked, "Was there a sub in the shipyards?" He knew the answer already. He just wanted to know if there were sufficient satellite imagery.

"Two, actually. A Philippine sub and a French Redoubtable. STRATCOM has been interested in the French-made sub. Thinks it's UAE."

Lynche nodded, and the NGA director took his turn. "Director Cunningham requested imagery and analysis of the suspected submarine pen near Abu Dhabi. NGA programmed a new ground penetrating radar satellite (GPRS)—what do you call it, *geepers?* For frame of reference, they flew GPRS over the Valley of the Kings in Egypt and found a dozen more potential burial sites. It is very effective. We weren't prepared for what we saw between Dubai and Abu Dhabi, with spurs to Sharjah and the submarine pen."

The men's curiosity were piqued. Lynche said, "Surprise me."

"Slide! As you can see there is a network of underground structures. Very well defined. Uniform squares radiating out from their highway system. There are 77 of them. Unsure if there is any significance to that number. We believe there is, at a minimum, a dual-track, probably high-speed subway system running underneath the freeway. Major utilities run between the lanes, much like they do here."

"Entrances?" queried General Hilburn.

"Yes and no. Slide. They're evenly-spaced; what we thought were drainage grates are much larger and, upon closer look, they are consistent with standard subway air duct grating and ventilation shafts. I would expect these shafts also serve as emergency exits. Someone might be able to get out, but it's very unlikely anyone could get in…easily."

Most of the men at the table were unfamiliar with subway grating, and the NGA Director could see it. He continued, "Everyone is familiar with the video of Marilyn Monroe standing over a subway grate when an approaching car pushed the air in the tunnel up the ventilation shaft and blew her skirt up. Standard press-locked steel bar grating. Runs the length of the freeway. And yes, there are almost a hundred miles of mains and service pipes. With the number of ventilation shafts, it could be a very high speed system."

"I'm curious, what's the technology to detect underground structures?" asked the National Clandestine Service Director Castaño.

The NGA Director answered, "Years ago, DARPA and IARPA asked industry to solve the problem of how to detect tunnels and submerged submarines. Through experimentation using deep UV lasers as LIDARs, light detection and ranging, industry found a discrete wavelength that picked up and reflected subtle hollows or cavities. Submarine propellers cavitate the water behind the prop, and the UV LIDAR could detect those cavities to a depth of a couple of hundred feet. We had similar success with ground-penetrating, three-dimensional LIDARs finding tunnels which were not too deep and an impressive network of ancient Roman roads and ramparts that had been stripped of their stones or obscured by development and farmland."

"One wavelength for subs, another for tunnels—more of an industry trade secret. There are many false positives with the ground penetrating radars unless there is a discernable pattern, like those squares along the highway. Like I said, we used the Valley of the Kings to help refine and calibrate the system. Straight-line tunnels like smugglers are known to build are very difficult to find in the clutter of a space-based reflection. Mountains give us fits." The NGA Director was grinning as he was bragging. "But boxes radiating on either side of the freeway, it's not just unusual, it's unique. Those squares are huge, possible twelve to 15,000 square feet each, assuming a single story. I've never seen anything like it before. There is no other place like it in the world."

"Like the Dubai's Palm Islands, Palm Jumeirah and Palm Jebel Ali," offered Lynche. "They have a thing for mega-structures."

"Wasn't the submarine pen near Jebel Ali?" asked NCS Director Castaño.

Without looking at Castaño, DO Miklos responded, "Yes."

"They're not hiding oil in those *containers*," said the NSA Director.

The Director's intercom buzzed interrupting the men's preoccupation with the presumed underground city. Lynche returned to his desk and answered the page. "Yes?"

The secretary said, "Miss Cunningham."

"I'll come get her when we're done." The words sank the hearts of the men around the table. No Nazy Cunningham to look at.

NCS Director Castaño was intrigued by Nazy's unknown activities with DCI Lynche. They might not be sexual, but they were certainly interesting, and if they were interesting, he should be in on the discussion. He turned his head and focused to get back into the conversation.

Lynche returned to the table and said, "We know this is only a start. Thank you for all of your help. I'd like to reconvene the day after tomorrow; I'll send out a meet-me notice. While I have you here, I am going to need a few people. A comm guy, a guy who can get in and control the elevators of a building, as well as a guy who can control all the security systems of a mega-building. If any of those guys can be doubled up, that would be good. I want the smallest possible footprint."

NCS Director Castaño twisted in his seat like a man getting teeth extracted without anesthesia. He had been trained to control his emotions, but there was obviously something that bothered him. He stopped fidgeting in his chair and uttered, "Since those are probably all my guys, I have a right to know what they are getting into and where they are going."

The other men around the table were stunned. You don't challenge the Director on a simple request for people, whatever special access program they would be read-in on. His tone was overly demanding and brusque. *He really didn't say that! Has he lost his mind?*

Greg Lynche turned to Castaño. The outburst wasn't expected. He ignored the statement for a moment, to allow the man to retract his unprofessional demand. When Castaño didn't see the error of his ways immediately, Lynche cut him to shreds. "Sounds like what I really need is someone who can just provide me with the support I need when I need it."

NCS Director Castaño was motivated to backtrack. Scarred hands were raised as if he were being held up at gunpoint. "I'm sorry, Greg, that came out all wrong. Of course, whatever you need we will provide. No questions."

Lynche lowered his eyes and continued. He didn't call him by his name. All was not forgiven. "Has that pilot, uh, Kelly Horne returned to your place? She was an intern up here until a couple of days ago."

"Yes, sir. She's one of mine." Castaño was as docile as a kitten. Gone was the demonstration of power and status. His hands remained hidden in his lap.

"I think she's pretty good. I can use her."

"She's a rock star."

Lynche tapped his vertex pen on the table. The sound was deafening in the enclosed office full of tension. "I'd like her back. No email. I don't want any lowlife contractor at NSA grabbing any part of this discussion. Need to know only. Eyes only. Questions?"

There were none.

"Then, that's all I have. General Hilburn, can you stay for a minute?"

When the other men were gone Lynche asked, "Somewhere there must be some plans for an engineering effort that size."

He smiled wide. If the DCI hadn't suggested it, he would have. It was better coming from him. "Got it. I'll get my safecrackers on it."

"Thanks, Rich."

"For whatever it is worth, I don't envy you. This shit is bad."

Lynche nodded, shook the man's hand, and walked him to the door. The NSA Director left quickly. Nazy followed Lynche into his office and closed the door. She waved a file in her hand.

With no preamble she said, "There's a boyfriend and *he* just went on vacation. Guess where?"

"Dubai."

"You're very good, sir," cooed Nazy. It wasn't suggestive, just meant as a compliment. But there was something else in the pragmatic solution, both unstated and undefined. She would get this way when she was missing something obvious.

Lynche ignored the line. He took a large gulp of air, yawned, and said, "Well, that'll probably be one airplane that will arrive at its destination."

Nazy was confused. A flat-lined frown marred her unlined and remarkable face. *What did he mean by that?* She didn't ask for clarification as Lynche had his way of getting to the point of a subject, however obscure or tangential. She had known him a long time. An explanation would come. Probably something from the meeting.

"What's his name?"

Nazy opened the Secret Service file in anticipation the DCI wanted specifics. She said, "Zavian Vonnah."

It meant nothing to him. "A bit exotic. What's his story?"

"The Secret Service believes they, he and 3M, met in Chicago at a socialist conference before he ran for office. Attorney and Counselor at Law. Hawaiian law firm then U.S. State Department. U.S. Trade and Development Agency in Hawaii. Speaks Russian. Russian trade. Stayed in the Lincoln Bedroom some twenty-times. When attending several State dinners at the White House he was always a special guest of the president." She continued, "They are both tall, but this Vonnah is taller, almost skeletal compared to the president. And lighter skinned. Reportedly, he is abstemious and prone to intestinal ills. I understand his friend looks just like him. Could be a double. And we know he had a room at the Armani Dubai for a week. He departed on the third of July."

"Why does that date sound familiar?" Lynche knew before he asked.

"That was the day after the Indonesian Sky Link aircraft disappeared."

"Oh." He wasn't surprised at all.

"You're supposed to ask, '*And…?*'"

Lynche frowned and telegraphed a scolding. He was too old for such bullshit games but she was smiling and leaning over. "*And?*"

Nazy said, "That is also the exact same day al-Sarkari checked out of the Armani Dubai Hotel and returned to the U.S."

Lynche pondered the ramifications of the data point for a moment and said, "Why do all roads lead to Dubai?" He bent over his desk and thrummed his fingers.

"All we have to do is find him." Nazy started to apologize for being obtuse. Then it hit her. *Which* him *are we talking about?*

He said, "That's Duncan's job."

"Isn't that more of an NCS job, sir?" She was becoming more confused. *Of course, Broken Lance. Duncan to find and terminate the former president.*

Lynche believed Nazy had changed topics; that she must be talking about al-Sarkari. "Finding al-Sarkari isn't Duncan's job."

She said, "Yes, sir. I thought finding Mazibuike was more of a Duncan and Bill McGee job." She thought, *Isn't it more of NCS Castaño's job to find this Zavian Vonnah? Find and track him?*

He nodded. "That's what I really meant to say. We have a possible window of opportunity; it's time sensitive, and we have no one in position to make the intercept. It normally takes days and weeks of planning to get a surveillance team in country. I'll have—*we'll have* some help by the end of the day." The NCTC Director's mashed lips conveyed that she couldn't help him, that she was powerless to help him further.

The National Counter Terrorism Center is the primary organization for integrating and analyzing all intelligence collection efforts pertaining to international terrorism. The NCTC is the terrorism intelligence fusion center and serves as the central and shared knowledge bank on terrorism information. It provides all-source intelligence support to government-wide counterterrorism activities. Nazy and her intelligence officers integrated, disseminated, and used terrorism-related information for other members of the intelligence community; the NSA, the NRO, the NGA, and others. But the NCS, the National Clandestine Service, had the spies—the spies necessary for an immediate action operation. Lynche had asked NCS Director Castaño for the necessary bodies, the technical support to execute the *Broken Lance* operation.

She provided the crucial intelligence to her boss. It was up to Lynche to assign the IC taskings. He was a master of designing concepts of operations for a mission. For thirty-five years he had learned from the best. Dulles, Helms, Schlesinger, Colby, Bush, Webster; the old guard. But they never had a problem like this one. More powerful than a bomb, with the click of a computer mouse thousands of aircraft could fall out of the sky killing a half million people or more.

Finally, the words came to her. She needed affirmation. "Who are we talking about?"

It was Lynche's turn to be confused. Several times he tried to answer. Then it dawned on him. "Are these...really *connected*?"

Nazy nodded and said, "They must be. We don't know who al-Sarkari has met or is meeting. We assume there is a ROC connection. Now I'm certain Mazibuike sent for his lover, and he is on the way to Dubai. Muslim men exist solely to gratify their sexual urges. Bin Laden, al-Zawahiri, all sent for their wives and they led us to their hiding place. So will Vonnah."

"It could be a coincidence...."

"Both men were at the Armani Hotel during the same timeframe. 3M looks to have been in the building the same day. The Secret Service found Mazibuike has an affinity for this Zavian Vonnah. They carried on an affair whenever Mazibuike vacationed in Hawaii or visited the White House. The CEO of that software company thinks al-Sarkari had a thing for...submissive women, and as far as we know, he has never been in the same state at the same time as the former president. But if Vonnah, al-Sarkari, and Mazibuike were in the Armani Hotel at the same time....*as it appears*...." The connections were not there to include a direct link between the president and al-Sarkari. She gave up in frustration and settled with, "There are no coincidences in espionage. Tradecraft 101. If we don't believe it isn't a coincidence, the question is how are they *not* connected?"

Lynche paused, nodded, and the two intelligence executives shared the same thoughts. How it is possible that they could be connected? Under what conditions? *Simple logic conclusion, Mazibuike knows both men. How and why?* They needed more information, more intelligence. Lynche looked up at Nazy and asked, "You're trying to intimate Mazibuike knows both men. *How are they connected?*"

She batted her eyes and stumbled through something she had said earlier. She reached back into her prodigious memory and found it. "It must be a bluebird—something that no one ever considered, something that comes out of nowhere. A third party. 3M was horny and sent for him. I don't know."

His eyes met hers. She nodded and said, "Duncan could figure it out."

Lynche nodded. "I think we just did. The Armani is in the Burj Khalifa; Mazibuike, this Vonnah and al-Sarkari will rendezvous again.

Maybe after their meeting, Mazibuike and Vonnah get together in the hotel."

Nazy and Lynche stared at each other for several seconds. One nodded, then the other. Each trying to determine if their logic was faulty. He broke the silence with, "It's going to be a rough evening, Nazy. Have Penny order us some food; we have some calls to make."

"Yes, sir."

For the first time in his life, Lynche didn't lift his eyes to watch Nazy Cunningham walk out of his office. He was going to need help killing the former President of the United States.

His first call went to the Australian Prime Minister. Duncan Hunter had broken several chains of custody that could expose him, the missions to find al-Sarkari, and the missions to kill the former president, and his little pet goat. Lynche had little time to repair the links.

CHAPTER THIRTY-SIX

0700 July 23, 2014
Dubai

There it was. Duncan Hunter. The names of the deceased from the passenger list of Qantas Flight 1144 had been released and were printed in newspapers across the globe. Maxim Mohammad Mazibuike folded *The New York Times* and tossed it on top of a pile of other newspapers. He smirked and muttered, *"About fucking time."*

Al-Jazeera and CNN played on competing television monitors, volume off, closed captioning on. He liked the quiet of the palace but not the confinement. The security team was off in some corner of the structure; only Nizar was seen before and after meals or within seconds after being called.

With the Hunter character disposed of he turned to war-gaming the next phase of the plan. He had run phase two through his head for days and weeks in anticipation of the *Amriki's* successful interdiction. But it wasn't as…*perfect* as they had expected. Somehow the Australian aircraft survived. Was that a function of the software, or was it a function of the size of the aircraft? Or something else? For him to attack his successor, Mazibuike had to be certain the *Amriki's* computer program operated flawlessly. But it didn't matter if the software hadn't operated as expected, there was absolutely no chance an attack on the American President could be traced back to him. All he did was provide the target. The slavishly willing *Amriki* did all of the heavy lifting; he did all of the work. *Praise Allah!*

He returned to his computer terminal to express his gratitude to the Abu Dhabi emir for the *fatwa* and the expediency with which it was successfully carried out. He signed off with, "Peace be upon you and the Mercy of Allah and His blessings." Mazibuike turned to find a response on one of his on-line auctions. A three-digit number that wouldn't mean anything to anyone. As a number, it was completely anonymous and harmless, completely obscure and devoid of meaning. That is, unless one knew the code. Mazibuike smiled broadly knowing he'd be with *him* again soon.

. . . . .

Tamerlan al-Sarkari paced the floor of his hotel room. Newsprint was scattered across the king sized bed. He had succeeded in part of the mission, the infidel was dead, but the aircraft still survived. Part of the program worked as he had programmed it. The gradual loss of pressurization to cause the slow onset of hypoxia of the pilots and passengers. Dumping fuel and turning the aircraft away from its programmed route should have sent the 747 into the ocean with an infinitesimal chance of its remains ever being discovered. *But it landed!*

He hadn't slept on the flight and even with the jet lag, he was so worked up that he still couldn't sleep once safe inside his hotel room. He was running on shots of adrenaline every time he asked himself, *How could I have failed? How could I have been outsmarted?* That was an impossibility. He was transfixed by the situation. He had checked and double-checked the programming in the simulator before the first operational test of the Indonesian Sky Link 777. What was he missing? What had he overlooked? What assumptions were made that were true in the initial planning and execution, only to be found to be false with an intact aircraft on the tarmac in the Philippines? He pounded his bad leg with his fist and excoriated himself. *I missed something. I missed something. I missed something!* He strained not to scream, *"What is it?"*

The expanse and furnishings of the hotel suite suddenly weren't sufficient for the ramblings and ruminations of the distraught scientist. He needed fresh air and food to help him think. But the driver from the airport had encouraged him to remain in his hotel room. Was that a request from a subordinate or a command from one of the emirs? He recalled the words explicitly. "It is requested...you remain in your room. Until you are called. You may order room service for anything, or if you desire something other than food...newspapers or books. For a woman, you must ask for '*the cappuccino special.*'"

He settled down for a few moments contemplating the final words of his loquacious driver. "For a woman, ask for '*the cappuccino special.*'" *Is it really that simple? Whatever I desire will be provided? Discretely?* He shook his head at the diversionary thoughts and returned to worrying about his programming. He slipped on loafers and stared at the door, debating whether to defy the implicit command or assume it was merely a request.

He pocketed his plastic key and stepped into the hallway. Al-Sarkari looked forward to taking a walk around the massive structure. He wanted to look up at the spectacle of the Burj Khalifa. After some dinner and after the sun had set he would call the front desk and ask for "*the cappuccino special.*"

.   .   .   .   .

The Australian Prime Minister was astonished to receive a telephone call from the head of the American intelligence apparatus. He didn't know what to make of the contact. The Director-General of the Australian Secret Intelligence Service served as the liaison between the national foreign intelligence agency of America and the head of Australia. To the best of his knowledge, the PM had never before met or spoken with the gentleman from McLean, Virginia. He approached the telephone with caution.

Greg Lynche apologized for the drama; it was not his intention to circumvent the established communication protocols between senior members of one government and the head of state of another. Lynche quickly outlined the reason for his unorthodox call. He explained that an American intelligence officer had intervened and had actually rescued the Australian Qantas jumbo jet. He had survived a gradual decompression at altitude and found the crew incapacitated. The American broke down the cockpit door, resuscitated the captain of the 747, and helped him land the aircraft at the Philippine airport. His actions were necessary and timely. The airliner was literally minutes away from running out of fuel.

The DCI didn't embellish the narrative. He also shared that what the Qantas aircraft had experienced was, in all likelihood, not an accident. "My assessment is that we must maintain the narrative that Flight 1144 experienced an inflight malfunction. I don't think it is in our best interests to convey this was a terrorist attack, that the aircraft's computer was hacked. My man is investigating the incident."

The PM thanked the DCI and assured him that Australia would

officially maintain the fiction as the investigation was conducted.

Lynche continued, "Mister Prime Minister, there is more. My intelligence officer switched places with the dead copilot to get off the aircraft. Sir, while my man is investigating the aircraft's mishap, it makes good sense for my officer to maintain the fiction for a little while longer. I'd like him to travel immediately to Dubai under the copilot's name.

"Director Lynche, I thank you for your candor and concern. Please know I shall take care of the copilot's family and arrange for your man to freely travel under cover to Dubai. Once he is there, I surmise, he will no longer require the use of the copilot's identity?"

"I will say my man will not sully the copilot's good name. His passport is only to facilitate entry into the country. Once he no longer requires the use of the copilot's identity, I shall ensure the passport is returned to Canberra via the most expeditious means possible. Our embassies will handle the transaction."

"I will make it so from my end. Your man deserves a medal for saving the lives of so many Australians and the aircraft. Whatever you need from Australia, please do not hesitate to ask."

"Thank you, Mister Prime Minister. I'll work with your Director-General."

"You've made for an interesting evening, Director Lynche. I half expected you to say something like, 'We never had this conversation.'"

Lynche laughed on the other side of the world. "That would be a benefit, sir."

"Consider it done. I hope your man is successful. Thank you and goodnight."

"Mister Prime Minister, you've been most accommodating. Thank you, sir and good night."

．　．　．　．　．

The Secretary of Defense called an early-morning press conference at the Pentagon. Mary Katherine Wentworth called in a panic. The impromptu presser conflicted with a family event. She was terse and direct. *"Something's up! I can't make the presser at that time and I was hoping you'd be able to sit in for me. You know what questions to ask."*

Demetrius Eastwood smiled at the thought. Of course, he would sit in for her. He barely had enough time to pack a bag and jump on the Acela Express to Washington D.C.

Both were cleared and badged Pentagon correspondents. He hadn't been invited to sit through the painful Pentagon press briefings recently. He'd rather be embedded with combat units than sit in the cheap plastic seats and be ignored. Mary Katherine Wentworth was an award-winning chief intelligence and Pentagon correspondent. She would normally attend every Pentagon press conference regardless of the day or time. It was her job. She sat in her designated chair in the front row. She would always be called on to ask an important—but not too direct—question. If you pressed too hard, you'd be relegated to the second or third row, where you would rarely get an opportunity to ask a question.

She was ecstatic that Eastwood would attend in her place. He promised to take great notes. Her accounting on the intelligence community and the Pentagon were regular features on the conservative network's prime time talk shows, exclusively reporting from the Nation's capital. Her star was steadily rising, and she had her own hour-long Saturday show. Mary Katherine Wentworth was floored when Eastwood told her he had been fired. But since he didn't have anything on his dance card, he would be glad to help her out. If she fully understood, being fired meant Eastwood was unemployed. She couldn't pay him for his time. He knew what she was thinking. Pay was important for journalists. He said, "No factor, it'll be worth the trip."

She said, "Maybe I can make it up to you over dinner."

"Maybe next time," he said through a smile. There was no potential romance involved in the transaction. None implied, none expected. She was just a friend in need of a hand, and he had the bandwidth to help. She was a happily married wife with a half dozen children. There was always room at the family table. He'd been to dinner several times and regaled the husband and boys with stories from the Marines on the front lines in Iraq and Afghanistan and Africa. The girls were always bored.

Mary Katherine Wentworth had helped him countless times, especially with sharing press conference information from the intelligence community. He found her seat in the middle of the first row. It seemed as if everyone at the presser had the largest possible Starbucks cup in their hands. He wondered if there was more brandy in the cups than Arabica or Colombian.

The Defense Secretary entered the visitor's center with general officers trailing him like remora following a shark on the prowl. After a few opening remarks the SECDEF cited credible terrorist threats and stated the president had ordered the U.S.S. George H.W. Bush and its battle group from the northern Arabian Sea into the Persian Gulf. He said the move would give the President additional flexibility if military action were required to protect American citizens and interests from Jordan to Oman. At the end of his very brief comments, the Secretary of Defense took no questions, turned away from the lectern and walked away with all of the little fish who had rows of big shiny stars on their epaulettes following in his wake.

"Damn, what was that all about?" asked Eastwood to no one in particular. He wasn't the only person in the room who was confused. It was proving to be an expensive trip for the paucity of the information disseminated. Mary Katherine would not be happy.

The press corps was atwitter; no one had any idea what was to be served by such an egregious and curious display of perfunctory duties. In minutes, the room was cleared, leaving him alone with his thoughts. It could mean only one thing. *Something was up! Why did DOD announce the movement of the aircraft carrier in such a truncated manner? Carrier battle groups movements are....* A squirrel had been let loose in his head. *What am I missing? What am I forgetting?*

Eastwood made his way to the National Press Club. Half of the correspondents he had seen at the Pentagon press conference congregated on the 14th floor for breakfast still clutching *venti*-sized coffees and Frappuccinos. After consuming half of a hearty ham and cheese omelet, Eastwood dropped his fork and broke out in a grin. *Carrier battle groups are constituted of an aircraft carrier and a large number of escorts that define the group; destroyers, supply ships, and...submarines. What made the Bush battle group special? It was adapted to be a support base for special operations. Helicopters. Marines. U.S. Navy SEALs!* He whipped out his smartphone and texted his contact at Special Operations Command.

· · · · ·

Profiles of some of the deceased were highlighted on local network new reports. In the San Antonio area, networks and newspapers ran short stories of the retired Marine, fighter pilot, educator, and businessman. Small concise tributes from old Marine Corps aviators and Hunter's graduate students peppered the articles and newscasts. His aviation company in Fredericksburg, Texas released a statement. "It is with extreme sadness that we hear our beloved leader, Duncan Hunter, passed away last night aboard Qantas Flight 1144. For those of you who knew Duncan and were touched by his intelligence, compassion, and generosity, we ask that you join us and celebrate his life and his contributions to his country and to his community. Please join us in offering our heartfelt sympathies and condolences to his family and friends. Funeral arrangements are pending."

. . . . . .

A wood fire crackled in the fireplace. The bungalow was overly warm, but Theresa and Carlos Yazzie ignored the temperature, finished their coffee, and focused on the early morning television news channel. An aircraft had landed in the Philippines with half of its passengers dead. The coverage was extensive with panels of experts speculating on the causal factors which likely contributed to the Australian airline's aircraft problems. They exchanged impassioned glances with each other.

Carlos doused the fire in the fireplace with cold coffee. Theresa finished packing their vehicle. Before the sun rose they drove out of Apache Junction. Jackson Hole, Wyoming was loaded in the GPS.

. . . . . .

The U.S. Air Force C-17 Globemaster III landed at the Sharjah International Airport and taxied to the maintenance ramp. Aircraft of every size from every manufacturer were parked in scores of rows adjacent to maintenance hangars. After taxiing past three Russian Ilyushin Il-76s, a DC-10, and a pair of Boeing 747s, the pilot of the Globemaster found a place to park in an overflow area that was devoid of other aircraft.

The aircrew performed after landing checklists and started the auxiliary power unit as the crew chief lowered the crew door and stepped out of the aircraft. He walked to the front of the C-17 and signaled "cut engines" with his hand. As the engines wound down, the loudest noise on the ramp emanated from the small turbine of the auxiliary power unit. After a few minutes the APU was also shut off and all was quiet at Sharjah, with the exception of the movement of commercial airline traffic at the terminal and on the runways.

A 30-passenger bus drove up to the Globemaster III. A man in a white uniform offered to transport the C-17 crew to the airport terminal or the maintenance office's Customs facility. Bill McGee and three former U.S. Navy SEALs, as well as the old guys Bob and Bob rode in the rear seats while the U.S. Air Force pilots and the enlisted aircrew rode in the front. Every man and woman from the Air Force supersized cargo jet surrendered passports and processed through the Customs kiosk without any issues.

After their baggage had been X-rayed and checked for contraband, the crew boarded a slick, high-rise luxury tour bus for the JW Marriott Marquis Hotel in Dubai. Located twenty minutes from Dubai International Airport in the heart of the city on the buzzing Sheikh Zayed Road, the Marriott Marquis was very close to the Burj Khalifa. Everyone moved to the left side of the bus to witness the spectacle of the Burj, *the Tower*. For the aircrew, it was simply a tourist sight, something to be experienced and photographed. With every mile closer to the unique structure, they held up their smartphones and snapped pictures. Of themselves and of each other. *Selfies*.

For the other men on the bus, the building was a fortress to be breached. Once on the highway linking the cities of Sharjah and Dubai, Bill McGee nudged one of the retired SEALs sitting next to him and silently pointed to the newest wonder of the world, fifteen miles ahead in the hazy distance. At 2,722 feet, the Burj Khalifa was the tallest building in the world and the most dramatic. The gleaming elegant spire and stacked columns reaching to the heavens defied a mere mortal's sense of proportion. It was easy to be awestruck in the UAE. It seemed every structure was new and fresh, either *overly* tall or *overly* wide or *overly* long, and either aesthetically exciting or captivating. But there was nothing like the Burj Khalifa, more of a silver stiletto that pierced the sky than a simple tower.

McGee muttered to his seatmate, "It's amazing what a little oil money can do." No pictures for him or the other former SEALs or for the old maintenance men. As he gazed upon the Burj, McGee realized that

Hunter's quiet airplane was probably the only tool for the mission.

He wondered how they were ever going to find Mazibuike in something as large and expansive as the Burj Khalifa. If the intelligence was wrong it, would mean another humiliating defeat for the intelligence community, and for him. McGee closed his eyes and lowered his head.

Ten days after the Twin Towers fell twenty-five U.S. Navy SEALs from SEAL Team Six, led by thirty-five-year veteran Captain William "Bullfrog" McGee, parachuted into Afghanistan's Tora Bora region. The mission: to find and kill Osama bin Laden, the architect of the September 11th attacks on America. For three months McGee and his SEAL snipers killed Taliban and al-Qaeda in great numbers. Few of the top leaders were captured in the near-impassable Hindu Kush Mountains. When the last cave complex had been taken, searched, and all defenders overrun, Osama bin Laden and Ayman al-Zawahiri were nowhere to be found, they were still at large. The human intelligence was bad; the signals intelligence had been "spoofed." The CIA had chased a low-level al-Qaeda man with a radio and a recording of Osama bin Laden giving directions. Special Operations Command and the CIA needed a scapegoat for this failure. McGee was removed as commander of SEAL Team Six. The storied career of the Navy's most-decorated SEAL was over.

Returning to the present he thought to himself, *History has a way of repeating itself.* Don't want it to happen again. *Maybe we'll all get luckier if Hunter is able to find him.*

Halfway to the hotel the Burj Khalifa filled up the bus windows. McGee grew less confident of success the closer they approached the magnificent tower. It was impossibly massive. He shook his head in defeat. Four guys and a pilot were not going to be successful. They needed reinforcements. Lots of reinforcements, like a brigade of Marines.

· · · · ·

Nizar Qasim al-Rimi closed his laptop computer. He received the warning order to prepare the security team for a "lift." The clock started; thirty hours. Under the cover of darkness when the coastal fog was expected to be at its greatest, he and the personal security detail would escort the former U.S. President from the palace to the central station for above-ground transportation. At the twenty-nine hour mark they would enter the subway car for the forty-minute ride. Then later they would leave the confines of the luxurious subway car, enter armored vehicles, and depart the underground garage.

It did not surprise him. The command center directed him to use the same procedures as on the previous lift. The threat assessment was also the same: No known threats. In the four-block message, he was encouraged to maintain his vigilance, report anything suspicious, and expect a new status report in six hours.

Nizar would check on his American charge and prepare his meal. Then he would eat with the security detail.

• • • • •

Twenty-two flight attendants and the five aircrew filed out of the Qantas Airbus 380 after all passengers had deplaned. The flight attendants were less chatty and less energetic walking down the arrival concourse than they were when they first boarded the aircraft. The fifteen and a half-hour flight from Sydney to Dubai had drained the energy of every one of the men and women dragging the special roll-aboards and flight bags of AIRCREW. They looked forward to getting through UAE Customs, taking the bus to the hotel, and sleeping for a few hours.

The Sheraton Deira Hotel sent a luxury coach to retrieve the Qantas flight crew; the ride to the hotel took a few minutes. The flight attendants and aircrew stepped off the vehicle like a lazy and exhausted swarm of uniformed bees as they followed the captain into the hotel. But a three-stripe copilot with dark sunglasses who was sitting in the rear-most seat stayed aboard. He asked the driver, a man with the facial features, complexion, and personality of an armadillo, to return to the airport. After an exasperating few seconds, the driver slowly closed the door and wordlessly complied.

At the airport the copilot took his time getting off the motor coach. When he finally stepped from the bus the driver closed the door behind him, preventing him from changing his mind. From the curb he returned to the inside of the terminal building and went to the men's toilet before spilling outside to the taxi stand. Within twenty minutes he entered the JW Marriott Marquis Hotel and bypassed the concierge's and reservation desk for one of the restaurants. He was ushered to a table and after a glass of water and a menu were provided, he pulled out his BlackBerry and began punching buttons.

· · · · ·

Two women and three men stepped from the British-registered Gulfstream 650 and into a small van for the ride to the Sharjah International Airport terminal building. The women wore dark shades and pastel dresses in the diaphanous style made famous by the Princess of Cambridge. They cleared customs through the VIP executive building. A silver Rolls Royce carted the women, while the men rode behind them in a black Suburban.

Along the way a member of the royal family pulled up alongside the Rolls in a fire engine red Ferrari; a cheetah with a gold spiked collar rode in the passenger seat. The man in the *thobe* and white *keffiyeh* tried to get a better look at the women in the limousine, but the darkened windows precluded the rubbernecking.

The taller of the women in the Rolls said to the other, "There's no telling what you'll see in Dubai."

A pair of enthusiastic doormen rushed to open doors for the leggy women, however the security detail waved them off and performed the reception duties. The men and women joined up at the limo and walked from the curb to the Armani Hotel as a group. The tall woman stopped, hooded her eyes, and looked up, straight up to the wavy face of the Burj Khalifia. She found it garish, overpowering, and a bit dizzying. The bodyguards waited until the principal had finished gazing at the structure before entering the hotel.

Every head turned when she entered the hotel lobby. The personal security team lead watched as a man, presumably focused—head down— on a smartphone, altered his initial direction and assumed a trajectory to approach his female clients. The man continued his pace until he suddenly looked up as if a movement from the corner of his eye had startled him into breaking eye contact with the electronic device. He noticed the long-haired woman in dark shades vectoring to the reception desk. He took two more steps and collided with a building column. He crumpled to the floor and lost the grip on his smartphone. It arced high in the air and came down into a smashing crash of broken glass and metal pieces. The security man momentarily turned to the man on the floor, now being assisted to his feet by doormen, baggage handlers, and the concierge, and monitored the distraction. Through subtle hand signals, he cleared the area and dismissed the potential threat.

The shorter woman checked the group in. She handed the clerk five passports. The clerk returned the passports along with five electronic keys. A minute later, they were whisked to the top floor of the hotel where all of the oversized suites with oversized balconies were.

. . . . .

He wasn't just distracted by the stunning dark haired woman; Tamerlan al-Sarkari was struck mute at seeing *her, the infidel's woman*. The goddess from the White House had walked across the lobby floor to the reception desk. With his smartphone destroyed and the hotel employees efficiently cleaning up the mess, he turned his eyes to the woman at the reception desk. He scanned her body before coming to rest on her uncovered nude legs. He completely ignored the other woman with her and the three beefy men in suits. *Was it really her? How could that woman be in Dubai? She should be in mourning! I killed her husband! Of course, it's not her. It cannot be her. I'm just obsessed with that woman.* He ran for the elevators. He tried to convince himself, *It cannot be her! But what if it is? Why does she need... bodyguards...in Dubai?*

More questions ran through his mind as he reached the elevators and found the men and women gone. He returned to the reception desk and inquired as to the woman's identity. The clerk wouldn't divulge any information citing privacy concerns of all of their guests. He asked if the woman's name was Hunter; the clerk assured him "no one by that name" was a member of that party.

Al-Sarkari nodded at the clerk and turned away from the counter. Maybe he had made a mistake. After all, she wore very dark sunglasses. Possibly it was a simple case of mistaken identity. The longer he thought about it, he convinced himself that that was exactly what he had experienced. He felt like a fool. He had lost his appetite with the loss of his smartphone. Al-Sarkari dejectedly returned to his room and ordered food. The front desk was very courteous when he ordered "*the cappuccino special.*"

· · · · ·

The Swimmer Delivery Vehicle (SDV) lifted off the back of the U.S.S. Dallas with a compliment of a pilot, copilot, and a four- member combat swimmer team. Once away from the submarine the copilot, a U.S. Navy SEAL, deployed the SDV's surface antenna for UHF communications and GPS navigation. He also deployed an electronic periscope which was essentially several tiny cellphone cameras that would provide some visual markers, depending on sea state. The dark nickel-diameter periscope barely made any wake and was invisible at night. The sea state was calm and the shore of the United Arab Emirates was easily seen on the dashboard screen. The other SEALS' job was to hold on, remain calm, and conserve the oxygen in their SCUBA tanks. A thousand yards out, the electrically-driven, submersible SDV was making ten knots.

The Mark 8 Mod 1 Swimmer Delivery Vehicle had been developed to deliver SEALs and their equipment for covert or clandestine missions in denied access areas. The primary modification of the Mark 8 SDV was the incorporation of a specially-treated aluminum alloy shell covered with sound deadening and radar absorption materials, the same as those found on the U.S. Air Force's stealthiest aircraft. The SDV also had compressed air to extend the range of a swimmer's own air tanks.

Tonight's mission was proceeding as planned. The SDV would intercept the target submarine from abeam, turn, and follow it to its underground pier. An encrypted signal from the aircraft carrier U.S.S. George H.W. Bush announced the 420-foot long Redoubtable-class submarine had crossed the inner marker and had slowed to minimum maneuvering speed. The waters of the Persian Gulf were polluted and visibility was nil. But the copilot had plotted the position and course of the submarine on his dashboard computer screen, as well as their own position. The periscope optics ensured they were on course. They hadn't been hit with a sonar ping which suggested the submarine's sonar had been shut down for docking.

The pilot nodded and accelerated the SDV to its maximum dash speed. The little black submersible fell in line and followed behind the sub in its propeller wash. The SEALs held on tightly as the SDV bounced up and down like a bucking brahma bull trying to throw off its unwanted rider. As the submarine's prop stopped the big boat glided into its slip. The copilot reeled in the trailing antenna and lowered the periscope as the pilot set the SDV on the floor of the submarine pen. The SEALs in the back of the SDV watched a huge chain link fence rise up behind them from the bottom of the underground submarine pen, trapping the SDV inside.

CHAPTER THIRTY-SEVEN

1500 July 23, 2014
Dubai

Nazy Cunningham professionally welcomed Bill McGee into her suite. They embraced politely in the company of the CIA men and Duncan Hunter's daughter. He walked across the room and, similarly, gently hugged Kelly Horne then shook the hands of the three men sitting at a small conference table, laptop computers in front of each. A light-neon green rubberized device with flashing green lights sat in the middle of the table. The "Growler" generated a bubble of electronic noise and prevented anyone and anything from electronically eavesdropping on their conversation. The last man to shake hands with the former SEAL said, "It's clean." It was his way of saying the room had been swept for electronic eavesdropping equipment, and as a backup, they had not one but two Growlers. They could speak without concern that their words were being recorded or that they were being monitored or photographed by tiny cameras. McGee nodded and said, "He's on his way."

The news brought smiles to the women. They'd all be together again. Hunter would likely be pissed that his wife and daughter were on the forward edge of this battlefield. McGee was concerned too. This wasn't a place for women, especially these women. But he had to believe that the old man, the head spook, Greg Lynche, knew what he was doing. He wasn't sure what Nazy and Kelly were doing in Dubai or how their presence would add to the core competency of his men. Nor did he have an idea what the other men were doing. He'd find out soon enough. The Growler's light flashed every few seconds.

A knock on the door startled everyone in the room. The CIA man in the middle pulled a silenced Beretta 9mm pistol from behind his back. Nazy opened the door, and in stepped Duncan Hunter wearing a commercial pilot's uniform complete with a billed hat. As he removed his cover he saw McGee, his daughter, and the three obviously CIA men in the room. His first thought was about kissing his bride, who was now wearing a designer sweatshirt and matching teal sweatpants. Her cinnamon-based perfume was strong and he wanted to give her a kiss that would make her knees weak. But he wanted to throttle Greg Lynche for putting his girls in harm's way. This operation could be over before it ever got started. These were the people he expected to be at his funeral, not at the front end of a black operation. Confusion and fury raged a war on his face, and everyone in the room could see it. The last guy in the room was the last to know what was going on. He couldn't articulate the words, "Why are you here?" to Nazy. She saw the pain in his eyes and smiled.

He hadn't expected to find her in Dubai. She had vowed never to return to the Middle East. Now she had broken that vow twice. The last time had resulted in his hand being severed. Just the thought of that injury made his scar itch.

Hunter struggled to maintain her cover and his. He reached out and shook Nazy's hand. He searched her eyes for any hint of fear or trepidation. Finding none, he turned and offered his hand to Kelly. "A pleasure to work with you." He released her hand and then shook hands with a very smiling Bill McGee. Hunter worked his way around the table and introduced himself to the guys behind the computers without giving his name. "I'm the pilot." He wore a pilot's uniform. It was obvious. Hunter noticed the green Growler's light flashing and one of the CIA assured him that, "The room is clean. There were six fiber optic cameras. Bedrooms and bathrooms. Cannot trust these bastards. Everything has been neutralized."

"Now that you're here we can get started," said Nazy leading Hunter to the table. To the men and Kelly Horne she asked, "Can I have a few minutes?" The CIA men had anticipated the request. They stood and walked to an adjoining room with Kelly on their tail.

She wasn't distraught or conflicted, but her knuckles were white under tension. After Duncan and McGee took a seat, Nazy remained standing and said, "This op has gotten more complicated. Your assessment that there was something wrong with the Qantas aircraft's software was validated by the manufacturer. We think it's very bad, and we don't have a lot of time."

"This isn't about...*Broken Lance?*" Hunter inquired meekly. He thought, *The original mission was to find the former president and eliminate him. Why is she talking about software? Did the DCI change the mission? Did he call an audible at the line?*

Nazy both shook her head and nodded. *Yes and no!* Now it was McGee's turn to be confused. She relayed what she knew about Chimera Avro-Software Technologies. "They specialize in special-purpose, encrypted software for commercial airlines which essentially ensures an airliner could never be hijacked or commandeered by a hacker. They also developed and integrated anti-hijacking systems into their automatic takeoff and landing systems for unmanned aircraft. This software package is what the CIA required for the YO-3."

"But it had a glitch...."

"We believe you experienced an anomaly in the *Wraith* over Peru. Yes. We still don't know how or why a control problem manifested itself in your airplane. But in the Qantas aircraft, we think, and the software company's CEO thinks their chief scientist is behind it."

"Don't tell me he found Allah," offered McGee.

"That is what it looks like, 10,000-foot view. He's here in the hotel."

Hunter was startled but not shocked. "That's why you're here?"

"Partially. Greg thinks this al-Sarkari can disrupt a thousand or more airplanes in flight. Simultaneously."

Hunter closed his eyes to absorb the full impact of Nazy's statement. He took a deep breath. She continued, "We don't have a lot to go on, but we believe the vectors of three men somehow intersect here at the Armani. They did on the second of July."

"What third man?" McGee and Hunter asked the question simultaneously. They turned to the other and said, "Great minds think alike." They weren't prepared for what they heard.

"The former president has a boyfriend."

"You're tracking him like you did OBL," said Hunter.

Nazy nodded. She had once shared with Duncan how she had found the master terrorist Osama bin Laden and his compound by finding and trailing his wives from Saudi Arabia to Pakistan. She recalled he had commented, "It's all about sex with these guys."

Hunter said, "So the software jihadi and the boyfriend were in the hotel at the same time three weeks ago. Now they're here again. The target has been 3M. I don't see a common vector that links the three of them." McGee nodded.

Nazy said, "We're very certain President Mazibuike was also in the hotel on the second of July."

Hunter leaned back in his chair and crossed his arms. "He's in on it." McGee's head snapped to Hunter.

Nazy continued, "You are free to assume that. But we don't know that, emphatically. We don't know how this al-Sarkari and Mazibuike were able to get together."

McGee chimed in. "That's more than a coincidence."

Nazy said, "Al-Sarkari was at the White House with us."

Both men were incredulous. Hunter uttered, "What, what, what…" as if he were a motorboat put-putting across a lake. Then he got serious. "Of course Mazibuike's in on it. The ability to send a thousand aircraft crashing at once would be the ultimate terrorist success story. That's incredible. Think of it as payback. Payback for uncovering him. Payback for chasing him from the White House. It's about payback." Nazy and McGee reluctantly concurred.

"We think since the scientist and the boyfriend are in the hotel, he will likely come to them. From wherever he is hiding. And that may be underground, figuratively and literally. Also, on the second of July, Dubai had one of its legendary summer fogs roll in off the coast. Another fog event is expected tonight and tomorrow." While Hunter and McGee stewed in the ramifications of the challenges ahead of them Nazy explained what the other men and Kelly were doing on the mission. "The one with the thinning hair is Duane House. He's NCS. He accessed the hotel's registry to find where the two men's rooms are. Bob Marsh, the chunky one, is also NCS. He has accessed the building's elevator controls and the security cameras. He told me their system is top notch, but he can open any or all doors, or he can shut down any or all security cameras. Greg thought we needed someone like them if you are going to assault the corporate headquarters on the top-most floors."

"The other guy has to be CIA," said McGee.

"Freddy Saldaná is a comm expert. Checks the rooms for bugs, kills electronic surveillance, taps phone lines. Monitors all of the building's security cameras. He has toys. He'll talk to you while you're airborne. He has the codes and the frequencies. The DCI said he is the best."

"What about Kelly?" asked Hunter with a grin.

"Greg didn't know what kind of shape you'd be in after your adventure on the Qantas aircraft or if you'd be able to fly the Wraith. So she is your backup pilot, if you need her. My personal assistant, otherwise."

"Who are you supposed to be?" Hunter's question was tinged with the aromatics of their sex life, of role play and such.

Striking a pose she said, "British supermodel. Photo shoot. Actually flew in from London, burgundy British tourist passport—that reminds me, I have new ones for you. New name. I need your cover passport." Hunter unbuttoned a shirt pocket and switched passports with Nazy. Touching her hand was electric.

"You have the accent and you are definitely a supermodel in my book." A look from Nazy told him to behave.

"I still don't understand why we're here."

Nazy retrieved a black Zero Halliburton and sat down at the small table. "We looked at possible places of exile. Eliminated those that were obviously incompatible for a man of his stature." For the next ten minutes, Nazy explained Mazibuike's escape, the corporate jet that conveyed him from Hawaii to the Philippines. The submarine from the PI to Banda Aceh. Another jet to the UAE. And the Secret Service file on the President's lover. She handed out photographs of each man and enunciated each man's name, "Tamerlan al-Sarkai and Zavian Vonnah."

"Definitely not local boys," offered Bill McGee.

"Do you have any ideas how 3M got together with this al-Sarkari? Are they lovers too?

Nazy shook her head. "No reason to think so. Not when the Secret Service only knows about Vonnah. They were not too keen in providing information on him."

McGee said, "I can only imagine." Hunter guffawed.

Nazy smiled and said, "You know how the Libyan ambassador died, but you probably don't know why."

McGee's interest suddenly perked up, as he had been on the ground in Benghazi the night of the attack on the U.S. Consulate. He raised his eyebrows to encourage Nazy to continue.

"In Hawaii, under the pretext this Vonnah was an important businessman, emissary, or diplomat, the Secret Service detail first cleared the area so the president could be with his lover, and then the detail moved to a location to give them some privacy. The Libyan ambassador had his security detail bring his gay lover to the consulate, and then they moved to another building at the rear of the compound so they could also be alone."

McGee said, "So the State Department and the Secret Service run cover for the president's and ambassador's lovers? Is this… *normal?*"

Hunter asked incredulously, "These guys running a security detail or an escort service? *Are you kidding me?*"

Nazy frowned and nodded as Hunter shook his head in disgust. He asked, "So Greg thinks everyone will somehow meet, I'm assuming, here in the hotel…."

She interrupted, "We war-gamed the options. We think 3M will have a meeting on the top floors of the building. Late tonight, early morning. When the fog is the thickest. Like the last time. Or tomorrow. Of course, it's all speculation."

Something started to bother Hunter. Something was amiss with their plan. He let the undefined thoughts roll around lazily in his head. He took a quick look at his wife and shook his head in amazement. "If he isn't already in the building, how does he get inside?" asked McGee.

"The embassy reports that it gets so foggy that all vehicle traffic stops out of necessity. The building is locked down and there is only one way into the building after hours. Through the hotel lobby. We have a semi-confirmed report he may have walked through the lobby zero-one-ish. On the night of July second."

"Probably during the height of the fog. Can we take him before he enters the hotel?" McGee asked.

"We don't think that is prudent. We'd like to ensure he meets the scientist. You neutralize both. But the priority is to stop the man who can make a half-million people fall from the sky. That suggests we need to ensure they meet." Nazy conveyed seriousness when she spoke. Her eyes confirmed her conviction for the plan.

She relayed the basic CONOPS and the retrograde plan. "When you're briefed and ready to go in, Kelly and I leave. Before the fog gets too bad. I don't want to, but Greg thought it was best. Supermodel cover. Photoshoot. In and out."

Hunter smirked and said, "My timing always sucks. So what did you wear?"

Nazy was embarrassed but said conspiratorially, "The crochet number with the sea shells." She seemed to derive some sort of twisted pleasure with the announcement.

Now she had Hunter's attention. He had bought her a few bikinis for a trip to Bora Bora but they never made it to the airplane. Three days in the Gaylord Texan instead. No pool. The seashell bikini was his favorite. "Hopefully, I get to see those pictures," said Hunter through a grin, but Nazy's smile said, "No."

"I'm just teasing. It was just a one-piece with cutouts on the side. I'm saving the bikinis for you—when you take me somewhere." Hunter smiled at the thought.

McGee brought the two lovers back to earth. "I assume the Agency guys leave when the work is done?" He was always thinking of work and the troops.

Nazy turned her eyes from Hunter and nodded. "When you no longer need them. You give them the word. They move to their rooms and then to the embassy."

Hunter said, "When the fog lifts. Got it." He nodded almost imperceptibly, thinking. McGee had seen the look before. Something complex or obscure had been turned loose in Hunter's head. Nazy had seen him wrestle with a challenging topic before, and she sat down to allow him to finish.

"Was I targeted?" he asked. The question caught McGee and Nazy unawares.

Nazy recovered and said, "It's possible. There's the *fatwa,* after all. We have nothing definitive."

"Do you think this Sarkari would single you out and try to kill you and everyone else on that airplane? You're not serious?" McGee rarely talked to his friend that way. Ridicule wasn't his bailiwick, and the line came out much more caustic than he intended. He retreated as Hunter looked at him nonplussed. McGee pointed and added, "You're the one with the big brain. Figure it out. Consider all the possibilities—eliminate those that are wrong—what do you have left?"

Hunter sucked air by the gallons. "Terrorists have targeted Agency guys across the planet. Killed them by bombing their airplane or shooting a plane down with a missile. You can never put anything past them."

McGee was embarrassed. He knew that.

"I…think…our former president…." Hunter paused to let his mind catch up with his mouth, "…somehow knows I released his file. He's livid." After a few seconds, he continued, "…and this al-Sarkari…he is the instrument of revenge. They must be working together. It's the only thing that makes any sense why a megalomaniac like 3M and a computer turd are here. I said it before, it's payback. Revenge. Those two colluded to kill me. 3M gave the order, the code red; the computer dude did the dirty deed because he could." He thrummed his fingers on the table. Nazy and McGee appeared to be in a mild state of shock. Nazy covered her mouth. McGee, not a mouth breather, was momentarily agape.

Hunter continued, "Rothwell had that nurse-bodyguard that was with him until the very end. That sucker beat the shit out of me, softened me up for Rothwell's little fantasy." Hunter held up his hand that had been reattached, the thick, wicked, raised, red scar circumscribed his wrist above the two-tone Rolex. "I told Lynche he needed to find that bastard. I have not heard whether he escaped or was caught. That dude had to be full of intel; on you and me."

Nazy and McGee concurred, nodding. Nazy said, "We were so focused on getting you out of the hospital and back to the U.S. that we dropped the ball. I remember you telling Greg to find the nurse, but I thought you might have been…."

McGee recalled the event in Amman, Jordan. He finished her sentence. "…hallucinating. You were barely conscious and drugged." McGee shook his head. "I admit I forgot all about that turd too. I know we saw him. I don't know what you remember of that night. You were leaving the Marriott. He was likely that big assed Arab that helped the *burqa* into the big black BMW parked in front of the Amman Marriott. I'm certain it was Rothwell under that black bag. I remember when he passed me I caught a glimpse of large tennis shoes—not diminutive girly feet—under the *burqa*. When I shot him he was wearing those shoes. I assumed Greg and the Agency worked to find the nurse."

Hunter said, "We need to ask him." He pulled out his Blackberry, crafted a text message, and sent it.

Nazy said, "Until then, we must assume the nurse disappeared after Bill killed Rothwell and rescued you." The men agreed with tiny nods. "The question is, if he got away, where did he go?"

Hunter let her question go unanswered. He turned to McGee and continued, "Rothwell checked our personnel files. Nazy gave him a flash drive of Osama bin Laden's last words. When I was in that stock, Rothwell blamed Nazy. He said she had found the former president's file and he accused me of releasing it. What if the nurse knew all of this too and sold or gave that information to his superiors, and that information reached…Mazibuike?"

"The nurse," said McGee. "He was almost bigger than me. If I hadn't stumbled upon you…. It could have been fatal."

The discussion surrounding Hunter's facetime with Rothwell's henchman brought back the horrors of that night when the huge man in the red and white checkered *keffiyeh*—the colors of the tribe of Jordanians—had pummeled him after repeated bouts of Tazering. It was a miracle Hunter's heart had continued to beat. When he was exhausted and nearly unconscious, the big Arab had stripped him and inserted his limp arms into an ancient torture device. The pillory trapped Hunter's arms and exposed his hands and wrists for individual dismemberment. He had kicked Hunter viciously between the legs, the additional pain and trauma had caused him to fade in and out of consciousness. Hunter remembered the man all too well. If he ever had the opportunity to reciprocate and deliver a commensurate dose of pain, he would do it in a microsecond. Hunter smiled as he remembered threatening Osama bin Laden with a Die Hard car battery and hooking his testicles up with jumper cables. There was always an appropriate payback. Now it had apparently come full circle. He might actually get his chance.

Nazy bounced in her seat, waiting for another insight. "All roads lead to Dubai. Greg said it. He has to be here, too. And I'll wager that nurse is either UAE intel or part of a private security detail. If not for al-Sarkari then maybe 3M." She let her analysis simmer between the men.

McGee offered, "It's probably what he does. In retrospect, he was a dude. Special Operations for somebody's Islamic army. We have to be doubly careful if we think he's in the building. That dude will remember me. It's hard to hide a black man in a white man's world."

"Probably the three of us," said Nazy, glancing at the Growler, still flashing; hopefully, still working, then she changed direction. "I have something else that may be very important." Nazy got up, went to a bedroom, and returned with a roll of paper. Hunter was intrigued; McGee was just curious. She unrolled the curled papers as she spoke. The men looked at the schematics and shrugged. Nazy crossed her arms over the documents.

Hunter took a minute before asking, "So what's the plan?"

Nazy said almost sheepishly, "Al-Sarkari and Vonnah are in the hotel. There's heavy fog forecast tonight. Greg said it was likely 3M would make an appearance; we thought at some point he would enter the hotel and meet his lover. I'm more inclined to think he's meeting both men. Separately. Not simultaneously. Likely business first, pleasure second. Greg was sure you'd figure out the challenge, develop a plan, and execute."

McGee shook his head in disbelief, looked at Hunter and said, "We've been given our marching orders. Better get planning, Maverick."

"Who is in what room?" asked Hunter.

"Al-Sarkari is in 509 and Vonnah is in 707. Top floor of the hotel." Hunter would remember the former number as an Air Force bomber wing and the latter number as a Boeing jetliner. Jets, jets, jets, all the time.

Nazy just smiled at the two irreverent men. She lifted her arms from the engineering drawings and said, "Greg said it is your call. It may not be wise to ambush him as he enters the hotel."

Hunter and McGee were left to ponder the possibilities.

Nazy continued, "I submit Mazibuike is meeting al-Sarkari in this building. Our guys can track 3M into the building, monitor what floor he gets off. Same for al-Sarkari. Same for Vannah. You want to ask why I'm so sure."

Hunter and McGee smiled and nodded. They knew they were about to be steamrolled.

"We've recently uncovered evidence that there is an underground city between Dubai and Abu Dhabi. 3M and countless other deposed dictators could be hiding in there. We think he's living in there. The men could meet him wherever he is hiding. However, I think 3M doesn't want to meet them in his hiding place. Information like that could easily be extracted out of someone as untrained as al-Sarkari and Vonnah."

"Good point." Hunter and McGee agreed.

Bill McGee said, "All you'd have to do is give them the Perrier spritz and they'll talk. He can't let them know where he's hiding."

Hunter concurred. "Any meeting has to be here."

Nazy said, "The Saudi's brought some acquaintances of Idi Amin not to his palace in the desert, but to a business office. This may be something like that. I think it's the only real option."

Then McGee stressed the obvious challenge. "So there are seventy miles of underground buildings and passages where someone can hide?"

"Seventy-miles?" asked Hunter wide-eyed. It was beyond belief. "Anyone that goes inside the subterranean city would be safe. Untouchable. It's too big to mount a hunt for a single person." Hunter allowed his mind to freewheel; *How would you get in, get out?* "Do we have schematics of this city? The worst thing about tunnels and caves is that you have to have exits. I would think the architects of that project would have to have built in emergency exits."

Nazy didn't look at the men. She pushed away from the table and walked across the room. She returned with a roll of engineering drawings. "We acquired most of the layout. There are exits presumably associated with each space. Probably emergency exits or control points. We really didn't have time to have some engineers go over these."

Hunter and McGee leaned over the plans and exchanged concerned glances. After thirty seconds of quiet perusal, they found a centralized transportation hub at one end of the system. There was a multiple-car subway system in the middle with basic structures radiating outward from the subway. Several structures remained unmarked and undefined. A terminus near Abu Dhabi branched out near the Palm Jumeirah and apparently connected to another structure that accessed the sea. There were few entry and exit points. The men knew the existence of the underground complex changed the dynamic of the operation. Hunter asked for a satellite view, which Nazy provided. The only thing of interest was a lagoon near the end of the subway system.

With the mention of the lagoon, Nazy was apologetic. "There's also an underground submarine facility. We believe one of the UAE's emirs, probably Abu Dhabi's, has unfettered access to the submarine and maybe has used to it to move...."

Hunter said, "...a former president."

"Yes, we believe 3M was picked up in the Philippines by their submarine. He was offloaded at Banda Aceh and flown to the UAE."

McGee pointed to another ship in the lagoon.

Nazy said, "The royal family yacht. About four hundred feet long, if I remember correctly."

The men's hands left the satellite photographs and returned to the schematics of the Burj Khalifa and all of the surrounding structures. Nazy interrupted their train of thought. "You can see there is no apparent underground link or connection with the Tower. It hadn't been conceived until well after the Valley of the Kings was completed. There may have been one that was built during its construction. We do not have sufficient schematics on the basements or underground passages of the Burj or anything that resembles a separate branch to this building. But the fact that the Burj's basement and this underground structure is separated by just over a mile...."

"Probably suggests they are connected. Valley of the Kings?" asked Hunter.

"Greg thought this is where unwelcome kings and deposed dictators go to live out their lives, out of the eye of anarchists and assassins." Nazy almost said, "...guys like you" but didn't allow the spurious thought to slow her down. "It's likely the home for some of the world's worst terrorist chieftains. And maybe 3M. He gave it the name since it resembles Egypt's Valley of the Kings."

McGee wasn't amused, but nodded and summed up the challenges succinctly, "If 3M pops his head out of his hole we cannot allow him to get away and slither back inside."

"Basically, we have one chance," said Hunter. "If he doesn't somehow use the underground parking lot to get inside, then he has to come through the front door."

"We still have to get the computer man," said McGee. "If he is going to unleash hell and have airplanes rain from the sky...." The thought of aircraft falling and hundreds of thousands of people dying was too enormous to contemplate.

Nazy leaned forward over the drawings and spoke to them, giving a running comprehensive dialogue that the men didn't interrupt. She briefed them on the ROC, its history and leaders, and their new base of operations, the top three floors of the Burj Khalifa. "One of the elevators is dedicated to serve the ROC floors. It's the single longest continuous elevator in the world as well as the fastest. When there are people on the floor, the elevator remains on the floor until it is dispatched to pick up someone from a lower floor."

"Daunting," offered McGee. "Can our guy control that elevator?"

Nazy shrugged her shoulders; "That's why I brought him. We'll see."

Hunter said, "He'll figure it out." He didn't believe a word he said.

"Greg was afraid you'd say 'no'," Nazy whispered. She and the old CIA spook knew it was an impossible mission. If it wasn't impossible, then it was suicidal.

Hunter said, "I don't think I said we can't do this."

Bill McGee returned to his seat and said, "I think we'll have to charge Greg double! We have much work to do. And you have to get to the airplane before the weather rolls in."

Hunter smiled at his wife and his friend and nodded.

"We do," said Nazy. She finally realized Duncan was wearing a commercial pilot's uniform. A thousand questions banged around her head like a ball in a Chinese ping pong match. *How did he get out of the Philippines? How did he get to Dubai? How do I get him alone? No time for any of it.*

But Hunter and McGee were deep in thought and conversation, huddling over the labyrinthine drawings. The Growler still flashed its assurance that anything that was said could not be recorded. When her man began to make motions to leave, to head for Sharjah and the *Wraith*, Nazy realized this might be the last time she would ever see her husband alive. She grabbed his shirt, drew him to her, and kissed him passionately.

"You two need to get a room," said McGee, looking away, smiling at the thought.

Nazy shook her head and freed her lips from Duncan's. She could barely speak. Breathlessly she uttered, "There's no time. You have to go. And…and so do I."

Before Hunter and McGee left the room, they found and thanked the men from the CIA and NCS. Kelly Horne came to the doorway and hugged and kissed her father out of the sight of the CIA men. Nazy joined the trio by the door for one final group embrace. Tears ran down the faces of the women.

Only Nazy knew her husband might not return. Kelly Horne was not briefed or read-on to the program that stood a significant chance of killing her father. But she surmised something was afoot with Nazy's response to them leaving. McGee tried to comfort the women as he patted their backs.

As quickly as they assembled, Hunter and McGee were gone. They headed to Sharjah where the quiet airplane rested in its shipping container in the cavernous C-17. Twenty minutes later Nazy and Kelly Horne departed the hotel for the airport. The CIA man monitored the communications while the men from NCS continued to monitor the elevators and the security cameras for their targets, the former president and two other men.

The man from the CIA glanced over at one of the sofas at a long duffle bag. It was full of weapons courtesy of the U.S. Embassy. He had expected the former SEALs to take and use them as necessary. He had been surprised the other man in the pilot's uniform hadn't stopped to see what the embassy's armory had provided. He patted his shoulder holster unconsciously. *Working without a weapon is nuts.*

CHAPTER THIRTY-EIGHT

2000 July 23, 2014
Sharjah

The five hundred foot tall rolling wall of water advanced toward the coast; silently, gradually, completely. Long term residents were all too familiar with the occasional sandstorms which came up from the south, explosions of grit and dust followed by blasts of heat off the desert floor. They had seen the same rollers of golden sand cover every square millimeter of the city and turn the buildings a dingy brown. This time it was moisture. Every exposed surface accumulated the water vapor which grew into macroscopic droplets before accelerating the accretion to saturation. Accumulated water ran off architectural angles and surfaces, and spilled like rainfall on a dense canopy of a tropical jungle.

Duncan Hunter stood under the dripping wing of the massive U.S. Air Force jet with his support crew, Bob and Bob. He was in a panic, and they were no help. Hunter scrunched his shoulders and said, "I cannot take off in this crap—too dangerous." The words of defeat hung in the over-moist air. For the first time in over a hundred counterterrorism missions, Hunter had to cancel a flight. Never for maintenance, not once when the mother ship had maintenance problems, and he definitely never cancelled for weather. It was suicidal and ridiculous to try to taxi the *Wraith* when he couldn't see. Visibility was nonexistent, and he could collide with one of the other aircraft parked on the Sharjah transient ramps. Then he would have to blow up or set fire to the *Wraith*. With an hour of daylight remaining, Hunter couldn't take the chance that someone would see the black airplane in the twilight of the evening as they off-loaded the YO-3A from its container. He wouldn't be able to taxi in the fog with any measure of safety. He was screwed.

He wouldn't be able to fly above the fog. He wouldn't be able to find the former POTUS on the top-most floor of the Burj Khalifa. He wouldn't be able to target the computer scientist and kill him with the

YO-3A's gun. All possibilities to find, intercept, and kill the men were squashed by the worst weather phenomena Hunter had ever experienced. He had assumed it wouldn't, couldn't be so bad. The fog was so think Hunter thought it would leave a mark if he took a bite of it.

Standing in the stifling fog, he was reminded of another time when it had been as bad or worse. He lived through it, although just barely. It shook him to his core; his arrogance had again gotten in the way of his judgment. He was the wingman of a flight of a pair of F-4 Phantoms—he was Dash Two—with the by-the-book, ten feet of step-down and his eyes lined up on the leading edge of the flight lead's right wing. He was in position, solid and stable, nose down in a shallow dive, flying together "in formation" at 350 knots when they penetrated a thick cloud deck. Lead said, "Try to get in a little closer" just before the gray jet disappeared in the thick gray cloud. The back-seaters of the two aircraft exchanged radio calls. "Ya got me, Goof?" Hunter's RIO, call sign "Goofball," asked him if he had "sight of the aircraft?" The proper procedures for a "lost sight" event would be to call over the radio, "Lost sight," and the two pilots would take the appropriate action to achieve safe separation—lead would pull up on the nose and speed up and the wingman would retard the throttles and push the nose slightly lower. Hunter did neither but responded to his back-seater, "I'm flying off a shade differential." Seconds later the two jets poked out of the bottom of the cloud just as they had entered, with ten feet of step-down and Hunter's eyes still bore-sighted down the leading edge of lead's wing. The two back-seaters bounced in their seats at the unbelievable display of airmanship. Hunter realized his mistake—he should have called "lost sight" when the jet first disappeared. He was furious at himself for his lack of judgment as well as his sheer stupidity. He might have been a flight student, but only a moron could think he could fly formation off "a shade differential."

Now he was faced with a similar situation. The fog checkmated the *Noble Savage* team. The game was over.

Bob Jones leaned into his boss and said almost as an afterthought, "You know, Boss, Bullfrog thought it might be a good idea to bring your...*little black toy*. Just in case...."

Hunter's first thought was that McGee had brought the silenced black Colt M-4 or Hunter's favorite revolver, his matte-black, match-grade, .357 magnum Colt Python. Black guns mattered in special operations. But Hunter could see that Bob Jones was referring to something else. The two men smiled at each other for a long New York second until Hunter finally deciphered the nuance of his quip. He patted the old man's shoulder; they turned and ran inside the C-17 Globemaster III.

·   ·   ·   ·   ·

The CIA men monitoring the hotel's cameras floor-by-floor, announced that they had "movement." The secondary target, al-Sarkari, had entered his room hours earlier followed by a voluptuous African woman with big hair. After twenty minutes the woman departed al-Sarkari's room. At midnight he stepped from his room, in a suit, with a computer bag over his shoulder and proceeded to the elevator stack. He rode the elevator to the hotel lobby, changed elevators, and stepped into the express elevator.

The next announcement from the CIA man was that "number two" had stopped on the 151st floor. When the elevator doors opened the NCS technician shared the image from inside the elevator; a man wearing a *thobe* and a *keffiyeh* had stepped inside with al-Sarkari. The man in traditional Arab clothing frisked the computer scientist, then placed his hand on a screen above the columns of numbered floor buttons. The elevator doors closed automatically, and the lights in the wall panels changed to an eerie new color. The men rode the rocket to the 154th floor. McGee and his two SEALs took notice of the men. The game was afoot.

"Two's landed. 154."

Duncan Hunter keyed his microphone switch twice to acknowledge he had received the encrypted radio transmission.

·   ·   ·   ·   ·

Visibility outside the C-17 was nil. Inside it was clear. And loud. The aircraft's auxiliary power unit provided cabin lights and air conditioning. Hunter had changed into a black Nomex flight suit, black tactical boots, and a dull black helmet with the four-tube panoramic night vision goggles and thermal optics. His helmet and all of the metallic parts of the jetpack had been treated with an experimental nanotechnology coating that absorbed over 99.95% of the light that hit it. The coating played tricks on the eyes of anyone who looked upon it. It erased any three-dimensional features—it was just black, like the inside of the belly of a whale—and devoid of any depth perception. One had to flip over the strange black void to determine that it was a pilot's flying helmet.

Hunter threaded his arms through a black shoulder harness and slipped his six-inch Colt Python inside. Speedloaders in one pocket. A black Kimber, Model 1911 .45ACP pistol with hollow-point ammunition, fixed silencer and Crimson Trace conformal-grip, laser sight into the lowest of his flight suit pockets. The black M-4 with night vision was slung across his body armor and flight suit. A short loop of rappelling rope hung from the jetpack's belt. The jetpack had proven to be sensitive to uneven weight distribution, so he lashed a long, huge fighting Bowie knife to the leg opposite the .45ACP automatic. The curvy scimitar-blade with thick serrated teeth across the spine was more machete than K-Bar and would have given Crocodile Dundee a terminal case of knife envy.

Bob Smith approached and offered a stick of white *plastique* the size of a Fort Know gold brick and encased in a zip-lock bag. Hunter slipped it and a handful of detonators into an open pocket. Bob asked, "Expecting trouble?" A pound of C-4 was always carried in a vault in case the *Wraith* crew needed to destroy the YO-3A spy plane if it crashed or was so disabled it couldn't have been recovered by the *Noble Savage* or U.S. Air Force crews.

Hunter answered by raising and lowering his eyebrows in rapid succession, a la Charlie Chaplin. "My old scoutmaster said to always 'Be Prepared.'"

Bob Smith said, "My mama always said, 'There's nothing like a little protection.'"

Hunter retorted, "My mama said, 'Don't leave home without it.'"

Bob winked and mouthed, "Be safe."

. . . . .

Bill McGee and his former SEALs couldn't see the Burj Khalifa or the doors of the Armani Hotel even though they were only a few feet away from the structure. Tiny radio buds in their ears were alive with bullet phrases from wrist microphones: "Can't see."

"No joy!"

"This is a bad idea."

"No one could possibly drive through this shit."

"Ten-four. Even if someone was able to find this place we would have to be standing on the red carpet when they drive up. But no one can drive through this stuff. This is a no go. Abort to the OP," said McGee, referring to the makeshift "observation post," the set of rooms occupied by the CIA men on Nazy Cunningham's floor. His frustration grew exponentially with the deteriorating weather. No one could possibly travel in the fog. While the weather guessers got the fog right, the intelligence had been wrong again.

The retired SEALs slipped their weapons back into their clothes and reentered the hotel.

. . . . .

Former President Maxim Mohammad Mazibuike and his personal security team led by Nizar Qasim al-Rimi stepped from the palace to an awaiting subway car. Mazibuike was visibly impressed every time he left the confines of his underground home to travel to one end of the subway system. Its beauty was spectacular as only a billionaire oil sheikh could make it. Unlike other grungy subway systems, the conduit between Abu Dhabi and Dubai wasn't industrialized or claustrophobic, it was spacious and adorned with highly stylized tiled and mosaic artwork. The same as those found inside the underground palaces as well as in the world's most photogenic mosques. In some ways it reminded him of the elegance and grandeur of the Moscow subway system. Any and all electrical cables, plumbing lines, conduits, tubing and lighting fixtures were strategically hidden from view, giving the subway rider an undistracted, thoroughly comfortable, and eye-pleasing trip.

The "lift" to the transportation center was made in under a half an hour. The men exited the subway and moved to awaiting BMWs, the same self-driving and optionally-manned cars they had used before. A security man slipped behind the steering wheel of each of the three black cars and guided the vehicles out of the transportation center into the fogbank. They stopped to allow the GPS system to synchronize and then selected the auto-drive feature of the car before taking their hands and feet off the controls. Sensors in the cars determined the driver was no longer in an "override" situation and began accelerating. The second and third cars synchronized their position and speed with the vehicle in front of them through GPS and miniscule radars embedded in the car's bumpers. The drive was made in utter silence.

Riding in an autonomous vehicle in thick fog normally induced severe cases of vertigo. Passengers who were not trained to keep their heads still quickly felt the sensation of spinning, tilting, swaying, or just being unbalanced. The human brain could not adequately resolve what the eye saw—nothing but white—and what the ear felt—linear horizontal movement. Under normal circumstances the eye provided feedback and equilibrium as the brain adapted to the inner ear changes or relied on other mechanisms to maintain balance. Pilots flying through thick clouds focused on their cockpit instruments, avoided moving their heads, and didn't try to look outside. Some of the men in the cars avoided vertigo by pulling dark curtains over the windows. They kept their heads down and played some game on their smartphones. Nizar appeared to sleep during the trip.

Mazibuike's first drive through the fog to the Burj Khalifa had been spooky. He had struggled not to show his fear, and he had trembled inside from thinking the American Special Operations men would burst out of the fog and take him back to America to stand trial. Tonight was no different. His nightmares were a continuous loop. He feared being found, captured, and brought before a billion hate-filled eyes that wanted nothing more than to see him publically tried and executed. He had lived the lie until someone had released his *file*. But now he wouldn't allow the suicidal thoughts to find purchase in his mind for very long. Martyrs of his stature do not commit suicide.

The electronic voice from the GPS announced, "Your destination is on your right." The security team put away their miniature computers and prepared for the next phase of the lift.

Nizar was especially aware that the upcoming transfer from car to building was most critical. That was where the former president was most vulnerable. Two men would walk ahead and astride the red carpet. No sounds meant the coast was clear; that it was safe to proceed. The weather, as before, precluded any worries of high-flying unmanned aircraft with missiles. Neither the U.S. nor the Emirates would ever allow any airborne harbingers of death to be so close to the world's tallest structure. It was another reason to have the ROC's meetings inside.

When the doors opened, Mazibuike followed Nizar. He would not be rushed. Thirty steps and they were inside. The men scanned the lobby, found no threats, and proceeded *en masse* to the elevator. The door opened as Mazibuike, Nizar, and one other bodyguard drew near. They immediately stepped inside.

·   ·   ·   ·   ·

The NCS man monitoring the elevators was shocked at who he saw enter the lobby and proceed to the elevators. An equally stunned Bill McGee raced to one of the laptop computers and said, "He's in. They must have comms because the top floor dispatched the elevator to the lobby." McGee and the other CIA and NCS men leaned over the man's shoulders to see the video image of the man who had disappeared, who was once the President of the United States, who was now in a *thobe* and *keffiyeh* in an elevator flanked by two of the biggest Arab men they had ever seen.

McGee broke out a thin smile and shook his head. *There's the guy who beat the shit out of Hunter! How did they get inside?*

The Americans watched the men in the elevator stand nonchalantly as the lift shot them to the 151st floor. One bodyguard got out. The remaining men rode the elevator to the 154th floor. McGee shook his head. *Wow! Lynche and Nazy called it!*

McGee turned to the CIA man and slapped him on the shoulder. "Let him know number one is on the floor. 154. With the computer guy." *Game on!*

·   ·   ·   ·   ·

Duncan Hunter stepped out of the gray C-17 into white goo. He kept the fuselage in sight and walked to the aircraft's nose. Bob and Bob and the Air Force aircrew followed. They had an idea what the man with the strange black George Jetson backpack was going to do, and it was going to be fascinating to watch.

Hunter gripped the handles of the jetpack, twisted the throttle twice to start the flow of pelletized rocket propellant into the combustion chamber, and then twisted it a third time to set the thrust sufficient for a one-foot hover.

One more twist of the throttle and he shot straight up into a snowball of hell. He kept his head as still as possible as he accelerated for fear of inducing a case of vertigo. With no attitude or drift instruments, he wouldn't be able to discern if he was turning or drifting. He had to trust his senses and could not allow any spurious inputs from his eyes or ears as they tried to make sense of what they were experiencing. This was a time when Hunter needed to trick his brain into thinking he was just in an elevator instead of being a human rocket ship flying through a snowball.

When he popped out of the fog he screamed at his success. Beneath him a white fluffy carpet of clouds stretched as far as he could see. He was nearly vertical as he came out of the fog; his feet had acted as an appropriate counterweight. He slowed his ascent to a hover. Differential thrust slowly spun him around to see the upper half of the Burj Khalifa lit up like a shiny steel dagger off in the distance. No other tops of buildings could be seen poking through the carpet of fog below him.

His radio came to life in his helmet. He had almost forgotten he was wearing it; the adrenaline spike was causing him to breathe hard and making his skin tingle. Hunter heard, "Numbers one and two on one five four." White strobes and red anti-collision lights marked the tallest point of the building. He was alone with no other structures or lights at his altitude. He estimated he was between 1,500 and 1,800 feet above ground level.

More manipulations of the throttle shot him across the gray woolly blanket that covered the UAE. Hunter set a course for the tallest building in the world and hoped he could find the men he was sent to kill. As the lighted tower got bigger, he tried to figure out a way to do that. If he had the YO-3A he would just shoot them with the aircraft's gun. Now he had to improvise. On the fly.

. . . . .

In the conference room, al-Sarkari dared not to look at Mazibuike's eyes. The former president was livid as he peppered him with questions and directives. "What went wrong and why?" How did…how could the aircraft land? We want to know what you have done!"

The man in the malevolent black *thobe* and matching *keffiyeh* at the end of the table lowered his chin and hid his face. He crossed his white hands and placed them gently atop the traditional Arabic dagger which adorned the middle of his chest. The other six emirs placed their hands on the table and lowered their eyes. They wanted answers too.

Tamerlan al-Sarkari explained, "In addition to bleeding off the pressurization—which should have killed everyone aboard the plane—I programmed the fuel dump valve to open as the jet turned ninety degrees from its route of flight. I chose the Pacific corridor because there is no radar over that part of the ocean. No one could track the jet. When the jet turned and ran out of fuel hundreds of miles off course, the jet crashes…."

Mazibuike yelled at him. "But it didn't crash! It landed!"

The old wizard at the head of the table asked, "How do you think it survived?" He didn't look up from the table; his dull deep voice bounced off the ebony table and reverberated in the otherwise quiet room.

"There must have been a mechanical malfunction with the pressurization system." Al-Sarkari provided a brief overview of the effects of hypoxia and how the previous jet met its demise. "I've given this much thought. The only thing that makes sense to me is that the pilot was already on supplemental oxygen, like when the copilot visits the lavatory. That is a regulation. One of the aircrew must be on oxygen if the other leaves the cockpit. I believe that the pilot realized the jet wasn't responding as programed, that he was able to reset the flight computers, stop the fuel dumping, and fly it to the nearest airport. I understand from the press reports the jet's engines flamed out when it landed. There is still much from the official narrative that doesn't make sense."

Mazibuike calmed down. "The infidel was on the plane?" He already knew the answer. The newspaper had confirmed.

"The infidel was on the plane; yes, sir. His name was on the list of the deceased passengers." The former President nodded as did the old man in black. *At last, something positive!*

Maxim Mohammad Mazibuike paced the floor tugging on his chin with a gloved hand. Something was bothering him.

The others in the room could see it. The old emirs were ready for the meeting to be over; they were getting antsy and shuffled in their seats. They had many concubines to visit before the sun rose. They considered the tiny blue pills to be the greatest invention in the world, especially since their bodies could no longer respond without chemical assistance, and there were many new women to bring them pleasure. While the former *Amriki* president was deep in thought, the elders turned to the head of the table to be dismissed. They had fun and adventure in mind, and were not concerned about an aircraft that should have crashed on the other side of the globe. But to leave would have been impolite.

The emir at the head of the table thrummed his fingers across his knife and looked over Mazibuike's shoulder. He winced as if in pain. He sought validation from the other men, but they had descended into their own thoughts and were not paying attention to their surroundings.

A *shadow* passed across one of the building's floor-to-ceiling glass panels. Mohaned almost missed it. He looked at Mazibuike who was still pacing with a thought he could not articulate. His mind screamed, "It is impossible!" His eyes flitted back and forth from Mazibuike to the window and back again, something was very wrong but words would not form.

CHAPTER THIRTY-NINE

2000 July 23, 2014
Dubai

Duncan Hunter rocketed to the topmost occupied floors. Two of the three were completely illuminated; the middle one was dark. Only a man sprawled out on a sofa could be seen on the lower floor. Bored, napping. *Not the target.* He twisted the jetpack's throttle imperceptibly and rose to the next illuminated floor. He flew around to the other side of the building, searching the outside offices until he saw men around a conference table. A man in a Western business suit sat a conference table. He was talking and making gestures of emphasis. An open laptop lay in front of him. The man with his back to him acted as if he was one very pissed off former American president.

"Tally Ho!" Hunter said into his boom microphone. He used the nearly one hundred year old radio call for, "I see him," the cry of a fighter pilot at the sight of a bogey, his target. Hunter encouraged the jetpack to climb slightly and backed away to get a better view. Then he shot straight up and found what he was looking for. A balcony; a platform. The little black jetpack again responded to his deft touch of throttle inputs and landed two stories up, directly above the conference room window.

A hundred and fifty floors below, Bill McGee and the CIA men heard Hunter's radio transmission, and their jaws dropped in awe. McGee had no idea that Hunter had taken the jetpack with all of its limitations and squirrely handling characteristics instead of the YO-3A. The weather had to be as bad in Sharjah as it was in Dubai. Somehow Hunter wouldn't let a little fog get in the way of completing the mission.

Hunter assessed the situation. He had burned a prodigious amount of fuel flying the thirty miles from the Sharjah Airport to the Burj. He had burned more on the long climb to the 154th floor. With no gauge to indicate fuel quantity, he checked his Rolex to determine how long he had been flying. He calculated that, at best, he still had about ten minutes of fuel remaining. He should have enough fuel to get down to the ground, but he didn't have enough to return to Sharjah. He wouldn't be able to find the ground until the fog rolled out and that meant sometime well after noon when the sun burned it off. He had to act now while the two targets were in the same room. That was going to be an issue. The sense of urgency demanded immediate action. His mind raced with the possibilities.

He decided he wouldn't chance trying to crash through the glass; it was likely made of some high-strength polycarbonate. Even if it wasn't bulletproof, he'd still bounce off like a bird smacking a window and breaking its neck. A .70 caliber bullet from the quiet airplane would likely go through the window and still make a mess of a human on the other side, but he wasn't in his spy plane. Flying the jetpack through the window pane was out of the question.

No, his only option was the nuclear one. *More firepower!* He reached into his flight suit pocket and brought out the stick of C-4. *Plastique.* He unclipped the rappelling rope and played out enough length to reach the middle of the illuminated window below him. He fixed the limit of the rope with his teeth and molded half of the *plastique* into a ball around the end of the rope with his bare hands. Then he retrieved two impact detonators from his pocket and pushed them inside the easily malleable explosive ball. C-4 always reminded him of fresh white Play-Doh. *There's nothing like a little C-4. Don't leave home without it!*

He had to get in and out! He repeated the words for motivation. He had ten minutes of fuel. Just like playing competition racquetball. *In and out!* He spoke into his microphone, "Shut down all cameras on one five four. Copy?"

After an interminable pause his earphones crackled, "Cameras off, one five four."

He returned the other half of the C-4 to his pocket and stuffed his hands back into his flying gloves. *Now or never!* Hunter again played out the length of rope with the plasticized explosive at the end and began to swing it away from the illuminated window directly below. He had one shot and he didn't know how it would end. *In and out!*

·   ·   ·   ·   ·

The shadow had disappeared; the head emir was now transfixed on a rope that dropped from above the window. It had a ball of white at the end like the clapper of a bell. He stepped to the side of his chair and leaned forward, disbelieving what he was seeing. He opened his mouth as if to speak, but nothing came out. An old thought that bubbled up from the depths of long dead memories told him to run. He started to move to the elevator.

The men at the table were ignoring the former President's diatribe at the computer man as they concentrated on their leader. They wondered why he stood and acted so strangely. Their eyes moved to follow his focus.

Maxim Mohammad Mazibuike stopped railing at the *Amriki* when he noticed the old man's mouth was agape and his eyes were fixated over his shoulder. As he began to turn to see what was mesmerizing the man, the glass panel behind him exploded. The concussion rocked the floor, and the impact also collapsed and shattered the adjacent glass panels. Shards of glass flew into the conference room eviscerating everything in the room.

. . . . .

In and out! Hunter nearly jumped off the balcony but arrested his descent with a twist of the throttle on the jetpack. He pirouetted 180° to face the building and descended to the impact point. He flew into the room— transitioning from an out-of-ground-effect hover to an in-ground-effect hover—which kicked up loose debris, ceiling tiles, and glass. He landed on his feet, shut down the jetpack's nozzles, hit the harness' quick release in the middle of his chest, and lowered the black jetpack to the floor. Motion at the corner of his eye caught his attention—a threat—and he drew the M-4 up from his chest. He pointed at the peripheral motion.

A very old, near-albino man in a bloody black *thobe* reached the elevator; the man in a business suit—likely the computer scientist— trailed him by a fraction of a second. The elevator doors closed behind them before Hunter could bring his weapon to bear and aim. Hunter couldn't go after them; he had to clear the room first.

Before he could say into his microphone, "Number two was on the loose," shots rang out from across the room; the report of a bullet cracking over his head was muffled by his helmet. He dropped to his belly and returned fire; he was officially in a firefight and that wasn't where he wanted to be. *Shit! Shit! Shit!* Tiny tufts of debris and trash still floated in the space as the wind whistled through the gaping holes in the glass panels. He had to find the shooter and get off the floor. He had to hurry.

Hunter's eyes ricocheted around the room. Surprisingly, some of the ceiling lights still worked. He found men—*no threat*—moaning in heaps, on either side of upended chairs. The laptop computer still rested atop the conference table, open and ready for business. He wondered if he had gotten there, before the computer man could send the commands to thousands of airliners to kill their crew and passengers.

Then Hunter saw him. The former president had been blown across part of the conference table, he was trying to run away but his legs were not working. Blood covered his legs which suggested flying glass had severed both Achilles tendons and shredded the backs of his legs. Hunter ascertained, *He's not going anywhere.* Another three shots cracked over his head aimlessly. Hunter presumed that the shooter was on the other side of the conference room wall behind a desk that had been overturned, and that he was firing without aiming. He estimated where the shooter was and fired twenty rounds through the length of the desk. He dropped the magazine, turned it 180°, and reloaded. Then he rolled closer to the conference table and the whimpering, sobbing, injured men. Hunter could see their faces had been shredded by flying glass; most of the men no longer had corneas, irises, or sclera, as if razor blades had raced across the men's faces and decimated their eyeballs. Vitreous media spilled from their ruined eyeballs and wetted the men's cheeks, clear fluid mixed with blood.

Mazibuike looked to be relatively intact from the waist up. The back of his *thobe* was drenched with blood from the flying shrapnel. He strained to crawl toward the elevators, trying to get away from the madman who flew through the window.

Before dealing with Mazibuike, Hunter had to ensure the shooter had been neutralized. He tried to creep around an outer wall but the detritus on the floor was too much for concealed or silent movement. He picked up a good-sized shard of glass and threw it toward the other end of the conference room. No shots rang out. *Do or die!* Hunter sprinted to the edge of the desk, rolled and shot the body of a man in the middle of his chest. He was already dead; he had fallen over in a hump. A giant man. Hunter poked his M-4 carbine at the man's head. Vacant eyes returned the death stare from the still recognizable face of "the nurse." Rothwell's nurse. The man who had captured Hunter, the man who had beat him viciously and locked him in the torture stock. Hunter's rage welled within him, and he shot the dead nurse twice in the head for good measure. Brains and bone spurted from the exit wound and splattered onto the floor.

Then Hunter spun around to take care of the living. He walked around the conference table and popped each man with two shots to their *keffiyeh*-covered skulls. *Now for the president.* Hunter walked over broken glass and office debris to get to him. He ripped off the man's *keffiyeh*. Mazibuike turned to look into the face of death; his words slurred slightly, "I knew... you'd come...for me."

"I don't think so, asshole. You think I'm dead."

The former president was confused. Through great pain he struggled to answer. "Who...*who are you?*" His eyes pleaded for assistance and mercy.

Hunter released his grip on the carbine and allowed the slung M-4 to drop and hang from his chest. He raised the visor of his helmet then reached down and withdrew the wicked Bowie from the leg scabbard.

The sight of the shiny serrated knife sliding out of the leather sheath struck Maxim Mohammad Mazibuike mute; his fear turned to horror and his bladder emptied.

His voice had a gravelly Vincent Price quality as he took one final look around the conference room. "Duncan Hunter."

He shuddered as fear changed to fury. *That's impossible!* He spat at the man in black; disbelief tinged every shrieking syllable. "*You're dead!*"

"You tried to kill me with your little computer friend, crash the jet I was in. Nice try, mother fucker."

"You...you...you don't have to do this...I can make you rich. You can...*name your price!*"

Hunter twisted the knife in his hand to see if it would be sufficient for the work at hand. The edge had been finely honed and was razor-sharp. There was an unnatural evil in his eyes.

Mazibuike's eyes bulged. He screamed, "*Allahu Akbar!*"

Hunter said, "Whatever," and swung the Bowie with all of his might.

• • • • •

A single severed head rested atop the conference table still oozing blood and blood-tinged fluids. Its eyes closed, as if to black out the bloody remains of friends. Hunter quickly captured a picture of the gruesome scene with his BlackBerry then snatched the head off the table and ran across the damaged room. He slowed to a walk as he reached the hole in the side of the skyscraper. Building momentum like a *jai alai* player slinging a ball from the *cesta* as fast and as hard as humanly possible, he threw the head out of the blown out window. It immediately disappeared into the night. Freefalling, it would reach terminal velocity in seconds and when it hit concrete below, almost a half-mile below, it would splatter into a pulverized mash of blood, bone, and brains. Then he dragged the remains of the former president to the window and kicked the body over the side. Once he recovered his balance, Hunter calmly strapped on the jetpack and slipped the laptop computer inside his flight suit. He called into the microphone for an IR beacon to be placed outside of the hotel room. He sucked a lungful of air and hoped he had enough fuel for a landing.

• • • • •

Pandemonium erupted in the hotel room; the NCS man in charge of monitoring the Burj's elevators, Bob Marsh, tried in vain to stop the falling elevator carrying the old man and al-Sarkari. He clicked icons and typed commands—nothing worked. He was frustrated beyond comprehension and shouted between gritted teeth to emphasize his predicament, "It must be in some kind of emergency mode; I cannot find the program to override it!"

"Are you sure?" asked McGee disbelievingly. He could see the man's futile attempts to manage the express elevator; the computer mouse was unresponsive. When the man's fingers flew over the keyboard he was still unable to slow down or stop the escape pod.

McGee was momentarily buoyed when the NCS man said, "It looks to be slowing!" Then joy turned to disappointment. "No, it bypassed the lobby and is heading…for the sub-basement. It has to stop. *Level three!*"

The CIA's communication technician, Freddie Saldanã, jumped when he heard the request for an infrared beacon from the man referred to as, "the pilot." He said to McGee, "He asked for an IR beacon. I don't have one!"

McGee pointed to a backpack. Saldaná dashed to the bag, pulled out a small alarm clock-looking device, McGee took it from him and flicked a switch which caused a tiny red light to illuminate. Saldaná ran and placed it outside on the balcony. *How could a pilot…. Could he parachute? It was impossible, no one could find or land on the balcony in the fog!*

Bill McGee and his SEALs were out the door heading for the stairwell. Ten stories down. *No telling what we'll find when we get there!*

Bob Marsh announced another group had entered an elevator. Ground floor. The communications expert raced back to Marsh's monitor to find a group of people ascending. The equipment inside the elevator showed a three-man cleaning crew lackadaisically leaning against the three walls of the car for the long trip up. Saldaná ignored the workers and shifted his focus on the old man in the other elevator.

The three men watched the ancient man remove a dagger from his chest scabbard and cut the throat of the man in the suit, nearly decapitating him. The murderous scene froze Saldaná's voice, but he was able to make gurgling sounds and flailing gestures to the NCS technicians. Marsh and House could not believe what they saw.

As the elevator doors opened the body of al-Sarkari fell out. The old man stepped over the body; Saldaná tried to contain the grotesque feeling in his gut and run for the bathroom, but he could not move, save to turn his face away as he vomited. When he recovered sufficiently to talk, he wiped his mouth with the back of his sleeve and said, "I think it's time leave." Marsh nodded; House shook his head and said, "We have to wait for the pilot."

Collectively, they asked themselves, *"How is a pilot going to get here?"*

． ． ． ． ．

The Burj Khalifa was constructed of ever increasing heights of three cylindrical vertical columns. Some would say the differential columns radiated outward and upward in a spiral like the tubular columns of lava found at Devil's Tower in Wyoming or the columns at Reynisfjara Beach in Iceland. Duncan Hunter flew out of the hole in the side of the Burj Khalifa and pivoted so he could see one of the three faces of the main building. He looked down but could not locate the flash of an IR beacon in his night vison goggles, so he flew sideways in a descending spiral around the three main columns in the hope he would see the infrared pulse below him. He counted on the image intensification qualities of the NVGs. Even obscured by fog, some of the IR radiating from the beacon would be captured, intensified, and displayed in his NVGs. His luck had run out. Either the IR beacon wasn't working or he was on the wrong part of the building. With no other choice he descended with the hope he would soon pick up the flash of the beacon.

Into the fog he flew. The jetpack continued to function perfectly, but his fuel situation had to be critical. The jetpack was a demonstrator, not an operational unit with instrumentation and gauges. He descended straight down the face of the sparkling wet steel columns of the Burj Khalifa. The fog was still extremely thick, but Hunter's steady and controlled descent was aided by the lighting on the floors he passed. Where the lights were off, he tried to maintain his interval with the building based on a shade differential; the darker the background was the closer he ostensibly was to the building. Going down was easier than going up, but the fog made the descent hellishly nerve-wracking. He didn't want to slam into one of the other columns or run out of fuel. Dante Alighieri would have understood and sympathized with Hunter's plight as he continued to slip further into the abyss.

Then he saw the flash of IR light in his NVGs off to his right side; he leaned in the direction of the energy source and drifted toward it. He was on the wrong side of the main column so he deftly skirted around the building until he could see the flash clearly beneath him. The tiny success buoyed him. He nearly yelped. Hunter hoped it was free sailing to the balcony, with no wires or antennas to disrupt his vertical descent.

As the balcony came into view, the high-energy IR pulses were now blinding him. He reached out with his toes to touch the tiled platform when one of the jetpack's nozzles sputtered and quit. The other nozzle momentarily provided some thrust. Hunter instinctively chopped the throttle but wasn't quite quick enough and the sudden loss of thrust on one side tipped him over. He could have slammed into the balcony floor or even been shot over the side, but instead he fell from about two feet as the residual thrust spun him around and slammed him into a corner of the balcony. Old gymnastics training enabled him to land without breaking his neck. When the jetpack burned its last pellet of rocket fuel, Hunter found himself on his back, flailing about like an upended turtle on top of the jetpack. He collected his thoughts and took inventory of his extremities. He was intact and celebrated the unconventional landing by filling his lungs with air. *Luckiest guy on the planet.*

He hit the quick disconnect and climbed out of the harness. He rolled off the jetpack, sat up, and removed his helmet.

The three CIA men heard a noise outside on the patio. They went to the slider. They were unable to immediately comprehend what lay at their feet. One part was "the pilot." Their eyes were drawn to his flight suit which was covered in blood. The other part was a mystery as the special black coating of the jetpack shocked their eyes and brain into believing that nothing they could recognize was there.

Hunter asked, "SITREP!" He stepped past them into the room, pulling out a laptop computer from his flight suit. The men snapped out of their shock and began to explain what they had seen.

The puker from the CIA, Freddie Saldanã, was handed the laptop computer. He said, "The scientist is dead. He and some old man entered the elevator...."

The elevator control technician Marsh finished the sentence, "and activated an emergency descent. I couldn't stop or slow it down."

A stunned Duane House offered, "The old man had a dagger on his chest—he...he...he cut the man's throat right before they landed on the sub-basement floor." Hunter frowned and nodded as if that was a good thing. He had promised to kill the computer scientist, and now someone else had done it for him.

Pointing to the laptop, Hunter said, "Make sure this thing gets to the DCI. No one else. Where's the SEALs?" Hunter removed the M-4 slung over his shoulders, and without looking, tapped the Colt Python with his fingers to ensure it was still tight in its shoulder holster.

"They went after the old guy. We don't know who he is."

Hunter donned his helmet again, found the microphone switch and keyed the mike. "Bullfrog, what's your twenty?" It was cop lingo for "What's your location."

Hunter pointed at Marsh, the security specialist, as he waited for a response from McGee. "Shut down the cameras on all floors of the hotel and open the door to 707." He pointed at the communications agent and said, "Freddie, inform the boss you have the goods, mission complete. Say I was unable to discern if I succeeded in stopping the computer geek. You guys, get out of here—head to your safe rooms as briefed, and when the weather clears, get to the embassy. I won't be coming back." He tossed a thumb in the direction of the balcony, "And get my backpack out there to the embassy also. It folds up; so don't break it; *capiche*?" He broke out in a broad conspiratorial smile. Three heads nodded. Hunter shook their hands

A grainy response came through the computer's and helmet's speakers. "Sub-basement three." Hunter asked the men, "How do I get there?"

The NCS man said, "Stairs at the far end of this floor."

"Did you get that door open?"

"I did." Marsh nodded excitedly; he was eager to comply and waited for the next set of commands.

"Kill the lights and cameras on this and the seventh floor. When you get to your rooms disable all the lights and the cameras in the hotel. Smoke the security system. Kill the elevators for thirty minutes. Can you do that?"

Marsh was still nodding as he said, "I will: I can."

Hunter looked from under his brows as he racked the charging handle of the M-4 to chamber a fresh round. "Thanks and good luck."

• • • • •

The M-4 led the way as Hunter raced out of the room and headed for the stairs. He put his helmet on and flipped his NVGs over his eyes just as the lights went dark in the hallway. He took the stairs two at a time until he reached the next landing and threw open the firedoor. He hurried down the hall to room number 707. A "DO NOT DISTURB" tag hung from the handle. He opened the door with one hand and brought the silenced Kimber to bear with the other. Laser sight on.

Hunter saw a man sitting on the bed with a telephone to his head. As the man began to turn toward the sound of the opening door, Hunter put two shots into the back of the man's head right where the laser dot stopped. He retraced his steps and raced down the stairs as fast as his legs could go.

The first thing Hunter saw when he stepped from the stairwell were cars. He looked left to where the elevators were and ran to them. There were bloody shoeprints on the landing. What was left of al-Sarkari lay wedged between the doors of an elevator. A prosthetic leg with a shoe matching the computer geek's other foot lay in the cab of the elevator. Hunter tip-toed around the pool of blood and the red footprints. He scanned the area, an underground parking lot, and found McGee and the three SEALs at the far end waving their hands to get his attention. He ran with the energy of a sprinter still hopped up on adrenaline. His boots "chirped" with every footfall. When he joined up with McGee and company, the old SEAL gave him the once-over, saw blood on Hunter's flight suit, and asked, "Yours?"

"His."

"You're not subtle. Boyfriend?"

Nodding once, Hunter asked, "What do we have?" The SEALs listened as McGee brought Hunter up to speed.

"I think we are at a crossroads. You saw what the old guy did in the elevator. I don't know who he is."

"Me either. I'm assuming he's the head guy. From what I could see our 'buddy' wasn't the head guy either, and neither were any of his friends. I didn't recognize any of them. They must be bastard brothers of the royal family."

McGee and the other SEALs nodded.

Hunter continued, "If he's not on the boss' *matrix*, he probably should be. Where'd he go?" Hunter's eyes shot over to an open steel door.

"He left a trail." McGee and the SEALs pointed to the heavy steel door. Hints of blood left by bloody shoes pointed the direction—into the dark.

Hunter scanned the area for other clues. *Could it be as simple as following him down this tunnel? Or was this a trap?* A huge brass combination lock about thirty feet away looked to have been used to secure the door. By all appearances the lock had been discarded when the old man unlocked the door and ran inside. Hunter jumped over a rail like a gymnast and retrieved the lock. He recognized the sequence of the number wheels—0-9-1-1. No one in America would ever forget the day al-Qaeda attacked America with airplanes. No one in the Arab world would forget the joy and pride they felt the day al-Qaeda attacked America. Seeing the numbers and being reminded of that day pissed him off. He said, "I see that." Then he showed McGee the underside of the combination lock and the old SEAL gritted his teeth.

McGee offered, "I say we go after him. He might be, 'The One.'"

Hunter said, "Head of the snake." He was reminded what the former president once said while campaigning for the White House: *We are the Ones we've been waiting for.* Everything spoken by the man had to be taken in its appropriate context.

"Where does this lead?"

"We think it's an emergency conduit to the underground city's transportation center. Where they manage the subway. This conduit had to have been laid at the very beginning of the project. Someone knew what they were doing."

"There's seventy miles of underground buildings, he's long gone. We'll never find him," uttered one of the SEALs. McGee and Hunter heard but did not listen. They exchanged glances; unblinking.

Hunter said, "I say we try." He tossed the lock in his gloved hand. "If it gets hairy we should be able to find one of the escape chutes and get back above ground."

Bill McGee raised his fist and stuck his arm in the air, as a "Black Power" salute reminiscent of the 1968 Olympics; the other SEALs followed and pressed their fists together. Hunter's fist completed the five spoke hub. McGee growled, *"Let's roll!"* After a second they broke away.

CHAPTER FORTY

0200 July 24, 2014
Dubai

Bill McGee led the three former SEALs and Duncan Hunter through the tunnel from the basement garage of the Burj Khalifa. The smell of old gasoline exhaust hung in the air suggesting a small motor vehicle had been used to travel from one end of the tunnel to the other. After a few moments of jumbled footsteps the men fell into McGee's cadence, a nice jogging pace for a retired SEAL, eight-minute miles. Twenty minutes later McGee raised his fist to signal a stop. Everyone but Hunter had broken out in a major sweat. An abandoned Vespa scooter lay outside another large steel door. McGee cautiously looked around the door and his heart sank. He stepped back and told the men what he had seen.

"There's a hundred cars and Land Rovers, a couple of small subway cars that look like they came out of a circus, and an elevated booth suspended from the ceiling—maybe a dispatch office—with one 'technical' visible." McGee used the term "technical" to refer to a likely armed enemy not wearing a conventional uniform. "I didn't see any obvious garage door, but he could have gotten in a car and is probably long gone."

Hunter said in his best gravelly Claude Rains, "We need to visit the dispatch guy and see if he took the subway.... The weather is still shitty. I don't think a getaway vehicle is the answer."

McGee questioned Hunter's logic at first—he liked his own assessment of the futility of continuing the chase—but then saw that there was no harm in investigating a bit more. They appeared to be out of immediate danger, and he didn't really want to go back through that tunnel. He agreed, "Yeah, see if he took the subway. I agree. The weather is too crappy to get away in a car. Nazy said there's a sub pen at the other end. Would he make a run for one of the underground hideaways or go for the submarine? There's also a yacht."

Hunter and the men nodded.

McGee was directive. "I'm not the right guy to waltz in there, just a shade too dark I'm afraid. Maverick, you look like you've been hosting a chainsaw massacre. Compere, you look more like a local than any of us. Take a walk; see if you can get in, but don't hesitate to shoot the turd if he gives you any lip."

The former SEAL Dave Compere nodded, slipped his pistol into the small of the back, inside the waist of his cargo pants, and walked out of the tunnel like he owned the whole inventory of the garage. He walked by Ferraris, Bentleys, Rolls Royces, BMWs, and Mercedes limousines and continued on a vector to intercept the middle of the gondola. His eyes never left the man standing in the picture window of the two-story-high booth. With no apparent door on the main floor in sight, Compere walked around the structure until he found a wide set of metal stairs leading up to the elevated compartment. He didn't knock, just walked in like he was a pissed off Arab sheikh and that the man upstairs had lost the keys to his McLaren Grand Touring car.

The man in the room was courteous, well-heeled but suspicious. Compere tried English since his Arabic was so bad he could only adequately enunciate *Allahu Akbar!* but after that, he couldn't even order *shisha* at a *hookah* bar. "Speak English?" *Don't lie, don't die.*

The man froze; in one fluid motion Compere pulled the .45 from behind his back and shot him. The report of the silenced pistol in the enclosed space barely registered in Compere's eardrums. He waved from the window. The two former SEALs established a defensive posture under the gondola as McGee and Hunter raced up the stairs.

The room looked more like the operations center at the Burlington Northern Railroad than the cozy room for the night watchman of a parking garage. Electronic situation and status boards were laid out ergonomically so a single person could manage multiple events. Lights on a painted line illuminated methodically and sequentially to simulate movement and indicated there was one subway car moving through the system in the direction of Abu Dhabi. In the direction of the getaway sub. A computer touch screen was likely the source to select and dispatch a subway car, but every icon button was labeled in Arabic. No one on the team read Arabic.

Time was wasting.

Hunter jumped behind the triptych of computer monitors and pressed icons until he found one that magically sent an unmanned subway car outside the dispatch room into motion. After some trial and error, he determined the layout was a simple logic circuit, and the old aeronautical engineer in him quickly figured out the control boards. He scribbled notes on a pad of sticky notes as McGee directed Compere to listen intently, stand guard, and operate the board. McGee pointed to the other SEAL, Tommy Thompson, and said, "Stay here and don't let anyone sneak up on or molest Campy up here."

In less than a minute Hunter, McGee and the former SEAL, Mike Boroff, entered a heavily gilded and frocked subway car that Compere dispatched to follow the other car on the tracks to Abu Dhabi.

· · · · · ·

The fog covered the buildings of Dubai like an old man who pulled a blanket over his head. Uneven waves of condensate rapidly filled in the spaces around every structure from Abu Dhabi to Dubai, except the upper third of the Burj Khalifa. At ground level it saturated everything it enveloped with a fine mist. The roads were wet, and water dribbled into the gutters. In the underground submarine pen the wall of fog was momentarily held at bay by the trapped and uncirculated air inside, which kept the space free of clouds.

The U.S. Navy SEALs had waited while the UAE submariners left their boat and were replaced by a smaller maintenance crew, a skeleton crew who would probably continuously monitor the health of the reactor and the general integrity of the boat. Nuclear submarines were unlike other boats that could be locked up until it was needed again. Even when docked, they required a watch crew to monitor the nuclear reactor. Once the SEAL Team leader determined the activity in and around the submarine had run its course, they swam the length of the sub underwater and emerged from the water via a rebar ladder, and climbed onto the pier near the submarine's bow.

Maintenance and administrative shops paralleled the twenty-foot wide pier. All the windows were dark, the submarine and maintenance crews appeared to have gone home. None of the SEALs could locate closed-circuit surveillance cameras, but that didn't mean there were none.

With hand and arm signals, the six Navy SEALs spread out to investigate the work spaces. They took pictures in the diffused red light, the same red lighting systems used aboard naval vessels during "lights out."

The pier was long enough to easily handle two similarly-sized submarines. And an airplane. Hidden in the shadows at the very front of the underground dock, an ancient, black, dusty floatplane of WWII vintage floated on huge pontoons. There were no discernable markings on the empennage or the tail. It was a complete mystery. Cobwebs that hung from the wings and bracing were thick with moisture, suggesting the aircraft hadn't been touched in many years.

A klaxon rang, giving the U.S. Navy SEALs a start. Adrenaline ran high as they slipped back over the side of the pier just as lights came on in the maintenance offices. Seconds later a string of sailors raced out of their sideboard offices and raced aboard the sub. By their actions, they weren't fortifying against or engaging intruders as no one carried a weapon. The SEAL Team leader mouthed, "Emergency departure?"

A pair of metal doors—not unlike the blast doors at NORAD only several magnitudes thinner—opened above and behind them. The SEALs were on full alert, ready to engage a flanking force. The incongruous sight of a bright green and white gilded subway car rolled out of the tunnel and came to a stop a bus-length away from the old airplane. An old man exited the subway car and walked down the pier to the submarine. His shuffling gait suggested he was likely aged or injured and was moving as fast as arthritic or damaged legs could possibly carry him. The SEALs watched with fascination as sailors stopped and bowed until the old man had passed them.

SEALs exchanged looks. *The dude was important.*

More pictures were snapped by two SEALs. One SEAL directed two others to follow the subway tracks and find out what lay behind the bank vault-like French doors. They were not going anywhere fast until someone lowered the underwater fence.

The tunnel was dark; night vision goggles with an external IR source were essential. Both SEALs reached up to their helmets and clicked on the tiny infrared flashlights that flooded the tunnel with photons. With the artificial illumination they saw a uniform tube arcing to the left into oblivion. In the green haze of the NVGs the tunnel was unlike anything they had ever seen before. It was tiled with differently shaded and shaped tiles from rail to rail, up one wall and down the other with intricate mosaics portraying seafaring scenes of *dhows* and submarines and other sailing vessels at sea and in ports. Some of the depictions were strangely obscured by adjacently-placed similarly-colored tiles. They looked like a color-blind test of similarly-colored bubbles with numbers imbedded. Only those with color vision could discern the true image. It was a little disorienting for both men.

They took up a defensive posture on either side of the rails while avoiding the deadly electrified inner third rail. The men looked for surveillance cameras and strained their ears for the sound of anything as they made their way around the bend. After an anxious walk of several hundred yards, a landing came into view. The SEALs peered through telephoto rifle scope of their M-4 carbines to determine what lay ahead.

They saw a pair of external security cameras, one pointed at the doorway of a grand entrance and the other covered the landing approach. Muffled fire from their silenced rifles obliterated the cameras; their blue laser sights darted from door to tunnel and back to the door atop the landing. When no one poured through the door, the SEALs nodded toward the target and moved with the silence of a cheetah stalking its prey. Once on the landing, one U.S. Navy SEAL used his dive knife to jimmy the lock and open the locked door.

There were lights on deep inside the room. And women. Dozens of women in flimsy, sheer, transparent tops and bottoms reminiscent of the genie who lived in a bottle on an old television show. They exchanged looks and figured they had stumbled into the old man's harem. Time to retreat.

One of the women closest to the landing turned suddenly and saw the men in the shadows. She approached barefooted in her diaphanous pastel coverings; her breasts and her pubic area were visible. Red laser dots fell between her breasts, but she continued to approach. She gripped her hands tightly as if she were praying and covered her chest. She had never seen anything like the frogmen. The girl discerned from the frogmen's actions and body language they were not supposed to be in the room. Her eyes pleading mercy, she asked, "Are you here to save us?"

English? The men were stunned; one waved the girl to come closer. "Anyone bad here?"

She shook her head once. Her eyes were wide open with excitement.

"What's your name?"

"Celeste Germaine...from Abilene, Texas."

The men exchanged glances as the tunnel behind them suddenly lit up and a rush of air filled the room. They heard the unmistakable sound and felt the pressure wave of an approaching subway car barreling through the tunnel. Floodlights illuminated the landing platform and chased the SEALs further inside the room of near naked women. Celeste, newly freed from the locked room, debated whether to run, but one SEAL dragged her back into the room with him. He motioned for her to be silent.

. . . . .

Hunter picked up the subtly-ringing telephone in the subway car. Compere said, "According to this board the other car stopped at the terminus. What I think is the location of the sub pen."

Hunter replied, "Copy" and turned to McGee. "He's trying to get away. In the sub. That's first glance. There's the yacht in the basin, too."

McGee nodded. "Too foggy for the yacht. My vote goes to the submarine. A sub crew is always ready for action. Fog is no issue. They operate in the blind every day. Let me say, a normal sub crew. There's nothing normal about this operation." He scanned the inside of the carriage and the outside walls of the tunnel taking in the stunning artwork portrayed in bas relief and mosaic. As the subway car sped through the tunnel, sensors near the tracks detected the movement of a car and triggered dozens of relays to flood the tunnel with lights as the car moved forward. The same sensors shut off the lamps behind them.

Hunter asked McGee, "How do you stop a sub?"

"With another sub. Don't you watch movies? U-571?"

"I'm not into boats. Airplanes," said Hunter.

"No shit, Sherlock." McGee grinned at him for the first time in hours. "I say we stop short of where he stopped. I don't want these crazy stroboscopic tunnel lights to give away our position."

Hunter agreed and handed the telephone receiver to McGee. He said, "Campy, can you stop us short of the end?"

"Can do—coming up soon. Be advised there appears to be an outlet or a landing near there. I have no sense of proportion at this board so the terminus and the landing could be close or a couple of miles away. But you are coming up on the last...I don't know what to call it...*a detent*...or a landing in a few minutes. Or less."

"We'll stop when you stop us."

"Roger. Standby. I'm decelerating your car. Hope I don't overshoot the target."

McGee hung up the telephone. He looked at Hunter and the other SEAL and said, "Let's see what this asshole is up to. I'll be pissed if he has already gotten underway."

Lights continued to illuminate the tunnel as the car traveled down the rails. They had passed dozens of landing platforms adorned with tiles, mosaics, inset bas relief figures. And doors. Huge intricately carved doors—usually French doors. Some of the artwork reminded the men of the more wealthy mosques they had seen in their travels in the Middle East.

As the car decelerated, McGee said, "We have to plan for what we expect to find at the end. Soldiers. Sailors. Dogs."

"Not dogs," offered Hunter, frowning.

The two retired SEALs said with a grin, "Probably not."

．　．　．　．　．

Inside the harem room, the two U.S. Navy SEAL frogmen spun around and took up positions on either side of the open door leading out to the landing platform. A subway car as gilded and as ostentatious as the one that stopped in the submarine pen came to a stop at the platform. Lights inside the subway car illuminated the passengers—a normal sized man in Western-style clothing, a man in black coveralls, and the largest black man the two SEALs had ever seen. Only they had seen that build, that superstructure before. As the three men stepped from the subway car and out onto the platform the lead U.S. Navy SEAL inside the room called, "Hey, Bullfrog!"

McGee, Hunter, and the other former SEAL froze. Trapped out in the open, Hunter believed his luck had run out.

McGee lowered his weapon and the two SEALs in wetsuits moved from the room to greet the newcomers. For a moment Hunter could not believe his eyes. The SEALs, current and former, shook hands and rapidly exchanged what they knew and found. The active duty U.S. Navy SEALs named Naylor and Williamson took an instant dislike to Hunter in his bloodied black flight suit, carrying his flying helmet. *Who the hell is this guy?* McGee could read their minds and said, "Spook. SAP. We're chasing an old dude that came down this way. Did you see him?"

Naylor said, "We did. He's probably aboard the sub by now. Underground pen a few hundred yards down the tracks. We were to check it out and get back to the boat, but they raised a barrier and we can't get our SDV back out to sea...."

The young barefoot lady from Texas ran to the men on the landing. She jumped on tippy-toes bouncing with excitement and quietly exclaimed, "You're Americans! You have to save us!" Hunter and McGee instinctively swung their weapons at the nearly nude girl, but she would not be denied. "You have to save us! *We need help!*" With no open arms to run into, she stopped, clasped her hands and started to weep.

Hunter flipped his M-4 over his back, stepped forward, and took the girl's trembling hands. He asked her, "Are there any guards?"

She shook her head with increasing excitement. "They're not here! They come for...for us much earlier. It's too late for them to be here now."

"How many of you are there?" Hunter looked at her pleading eyes as the other men looked through her transparent coverings and then at each other. *That girl is naked.... What the....*

"A couple of hundred. I think, ah, there's a girl....um, from, at least one from each country." Hunter closed his eyes for a long second. He turned to McGee and said, "You have to stop the old guy. Whatever it takes. I'll think of something to get them out of here."

"*No!* Bullshit! Bullshit! Are you crazy?!" roared McGee in his radio announcer voice. It boomed and reverberated around the landing and tunnel at a level that wasn't safe. McGee could care less. The fire in his eyes said unequivocally, *No!*

It was like being a mule in a hailstorm. Hunter just took McGee's invective and vitriol and let it roll off his back. He didn't shout, but his voice was strong. "I think I know how to do it. You get the old man; I don't know a thing about subs and you do. I'll get them...I'll get them...out, *on top.*" Hunter hadn't entirely convinced himself he could accomplish the impossible task that lay before him, but he had an idea.

McGee wasn't having any of it and nixed the notion. "We are not going to split up, Maverick. I'm not leaving you. I am sympathetic. But they have a problem we cannot fix. And neither can you." As soon as he said, "It's not our problem" McGee began to feel ashamed. He put his hands on his head and tried to scrape out the poisonous thoughts and replace them with *Of course someone has to save these girls….*

"Go get the old man. If I fail to find a way out, I'll call you." Hunter insisted, "I cannot leave…*them.* We need to move!"

Hunter thought McGee was going to explode and hit him on top of the head to put him out of his misery. Maybe toss his unconscious carcass on the subway car and send it back. McGee's massive head shook violently; he knew leaving Hunter was wrong and could be fatal. But there was still a mission to complete. Hunter had completed his, now McGee needed to complete his.

Bill McGee had saved Hunter once before from a Muslim madman, and now here he was willing to go back into a completely undefined situation based on the hysterical ramblings of some chick who claimed she was from Texas. His SEAL training kicked into overdrive. It stunk of a set up to keep them on the landing or in the area until reinforcements arrived. *Bullshit!* McGee turned to the girl and demanded, "How did you get here?"

"I was drugged. I remember being at a roller skating rink—in Abilene—and the next thing I remember I'm in one of those metal boxy things that go on ships."

"A shipping container?" asked one of the SEALs in a frog suit.

She nodded. "Everyone in here has a similar story, they wake up in a *shipping container,* or they wake up on some kind of boat. Mostly." Thoughts of again being molested and raped bubbled up like a volcano erupting. She shouted, "But what they do to us, to those girls….*please don't leave me.* Don't leave us! Don't leave us! Don't leave us! *You're Americans. Save us!*"

"Bill, go get that old bastard! I'll take care of this," directed Hunter. He pinched off a golf-ball-sized of *plastique* and transferred the rest of the C-4, along with all of his remaining detonators save one to a defeated McGee. Hunter grabbed the girl's hand and they ran inside the harem room leaving McGee furious. He was distracted by Hunter's actions and was immediately indifferent to the challenges that lay ahead.

"That dude's gonna die happy," uttered the lead U.S. Navy SEAL, Naylor. McGee, still reeling from being dismissed, turned toward the exit of the tunnel and walked off spitting mad. *It's impossible, Maverick. You're a dead man and you don't even know it yet.*

CHAPTER FORTY-ONE

0200 July 24, 2014
Dubai

The enormity of the challenge hit him square in the face when he saw hundreds of eyes staring back at him. Some wore transparent *abayas*, some with *hijabs* and some without. As he walked through the testosterone-free zone, he didn't see a single woman or girl disguised as a mound of laundry. Their only coverings were the gauze-like two-piece I-Dream-of-Genie ensembles that did little to mask areolae or pubis.

Hunter asked Celeste if there was anything that resembled a way out, like an emergency exit. "Are there any other doors? Anything that looks like doors?" he asked. He looked into her eyes. He was all business.

"No…no…. There is something like a door in the kitchen, big. Locked." She gestured something big and round.

"Show me." He re-gripped his helmet and followed the barefoot girl. They ran through the middle of the expansive area; it was like running through a warehouse of women of different colors and heights. Women and girls *and children* were everywhere. They were clearly stunned and afraid of the strange man in black. Some unconsciously covered their private parts with their hands or crossed their arms across their chests as he approached. The children, mainly black children, just stood in silence as the white man ran past them.

Hunter could barely comprehend what he saw as he passed mounds of garishly colored pillows and acres of curtains suspended from the ceiling. The warehouse-sized space was largely supported by columns.

Once he was free of the distraction of children and young girls, Hunter noticed the inside of the structure was adorned with the same tilework as the tunnels, but with fewer bas relief figures or raised three-dimensional calligraphy. More utilitarian than luxury. Some of the concrete walls were rough abstract, in the style of the *Citius, Altius, Fortius* murals at the metro station in Montreal, Quebec. The closer he scrutinized some of the other murals he saw that they were pornographic; panels depicting sexual acts and positions as if they had been modeled after the pages in the *Kama Sutra*. A billboard-sized how-to manual for a sex slave. Nasty bits and all. Then it struck him; it was just a functional waypoint in the women's lives, like the lyrics in *Hotel California*. *They can check out, but they can never leave.*

Hunter asked, "What did you mean, it's too late for the guards?"

Celeste Germaine watched where she was running. She said, "Once they take the girls...." She put her hand to her mouth and continued, "...we don't see them again. Once they leave...we don't ever see the girls again." Terror was still embedded in her eyes as they approached the far end of the structure.

Something bad happened in the building; Hunter didn't want to know the particulars. At least, not yet.

He ran harder as he followed the barefooted youngster who could run like the wind. Perfumes, oils, and incense hung in the air like levels of atmosphere. They plowed through them all, stirring up a nasty concoction of odors more like unguents than the exotic sticky scent of rare spices that he had first encountered.

Celeste burst through a stainless steel door and stopped in an industrial kitchen. There was a roaring sound not unlike what you hear standing on the landing at the top of Niagara Falls staring into the abyss of the mist and pulverized water. Hunter watched as the color drained from her face. The woman stared at the food preparation area as if evil was hiding among the food processors and the Hobart meat grinder. She stared at a large drain and turned away as if repelled by the area.

Hunter thought, *Something bad had happened here. I can smell it. Evil.* He was on alert. He looked around for evidence of what could make a young woman think this was some bad juju area but finding nothing obvious, he pushed ahead.

He had seen the schematics. There had to be a way out. He assessed the rest of the space and looked for exhaust vents and dumbwaiters or anything that resembled a way out. Celeste had recovered from her sudden encounter with stainless steel tables, industrial power tools, and a drain and pointed to a large reinforced stainless steel door found in the rear of most commercial kitchens. The refrigerator was the size of a four-car garage and filled with bulk food stuffs. He scanned the walls until he found another stainless steel door on the far wall. With a lock. A huge lock. He didn't think he could destroy it with the silenced M-4. He removed the small ball of *plastique* from his pocket, jammed a pencil-like detonator into the white ball, and spun the timer for ten seconds. Hunter grabbed the girl from Texas, pulled her outside the refer to a safe area, and covered her body with his. The shackle was obliterated; the concussion was deafening. Celeste held her ringing ears.

Hunter tried to open the freed door but it wouldn't budge. The fraction of movement he felt in his hand suggested the door wasn't locked or braced but was immobile, as the Qantas aircraft door had been. The subtle movement suggested the door was likely wedged. *Just in case someone had opened the lock.* His fingers frantically searched up and around the edges of the door looking for a secondary locking device. Finding nothing, he dropped to the floor and felt under the door. His fingers bumped into something solid; a simple wedge had been cleverly placed and hidden under the door to prevent its unauthorized opening. When Hunter pulled his knife out of its leg scabbard, Celeste Germaine—arms across her chest to keep warm—jumped back. He slid the blade under the door and dislodged the impediment. The steel door suddenly flew open. The pressure built-up behind it knocked Hunter over onto his back. He found the source of the roaring, but there was no water.

Millions of insects carcasses spilled inside and flew around the inside of the refrigerator like debris inside an Iowa tornado. Celeste jumped at the sight of beetle casings and scorpion parts. She ran out of the cooler squealing like a child in a Halloween haunted house. Hunter stuck his head inside the space; the wind above his head howled with a decreasing roar. The rushing wind pushed him around a bit as the moving air found the path of least resistance. It filled the refrigerator with the neutral aroma of salt and sea. He filled his lungs with fresh air and knew he was getting close. The first step of a spiral staircase rose above him, but all above it was blackness. He held the M-4 close to his body and ran back into the kitchen to get his helmet. The girl from Texas followed him as she continually dusted bug parts off her flimsy clothing.

Ok, I might be able to get them out but then what do I do with them? As his feet pounded the concrete floor he thought of an old Arab proverb, "The eagle that chases two rabbits catches neither." The odds of UAE authorities rounding up hundreds of newly freed kidnapped women, girls, and children were nearly impossible. If he could get them to the surface the worst thing that could happen to them—and him—would be that very few of them would likely be caught again.

As Hunter donned his helmet he told Celeste, "Tell them to get their shoes on; we're getting out of here!"

The girl from Texas stood still, unmoving except for a gentle shaking of her head. "We have no shoes. They took them from us."

He barked at her incredulously. "No one has shoes?" *Maybe an eagle can catch two rabbits if they cannot run. They must have shoes! We don't have time to find shoes!*

She continued to shake her head and worried that the lack of shoes would somehow negate their escape. She said, "But...but...I...I know where they are. There's another room, an old door, an old part of this place. It isn't far from here."

"Lead on. We don't have much time."

They ran through a warren of curtains and pillows and stunned women until they came to an ancient ornate door. She tried the glass doorknob, but it wouldn't turn. Hunter shot the mechanism with the silenced M-4 and kicked the door in. Light from the living area spilled inside. It was one of the most bizarre things Hunter had ever seen. Old concrete walls, sloppy layers of motar and stacked brick, but no light fixtures. But shoes, sandals, slippers, sneakers, and moccasins were heaped in a pile to the ceiling of the room. The smell of old feet and decaying leather assaulted his senses. Hunter fiddled in his flight suit for a flashlight and scanned the spectacle. "Tell them to get their shoes and line up outside the kitchen. We're leaving."

Celeste spirits were buoyed when she spied her blue Nike tennis shoes inside the room, grabbed them from the pile, and then raced back into the crowd of anxious women and squealing girls. Hunter shone the powerful torch into the room. As the beam moved quickly around the mound of footwear, an odd pair of boots caught his eye. They were sitting on the only shelf in the room along with other unique and strange shoes, like those that bound the feet of Chinese women at the turn of the century. There was also a pair of carved wooden clogs from Holland.

In the brilliant white light, the boots were unlike any other shoe in the room. They would have stood tall, boots that covered the calf, with gussets and doublers, but they were folded over, cracked at the bend. A dozen eyelets and a half-dozen hooks at the top. The short leather stacked heels were delaminating. The laces were fuzzy from age.

Then women rushed past him into the room, gently pushing him aside as they scrambled for the newest shoes in the pile. *Their shoes.* He realized that the pile of shoes could represent tens of thousands of women who were no longer hidden away and used for whatever deviant purpose. Hunter shook the thought from his mind as he watched the women, girls, and children organize themselves into an efficient line of shoe finders who then quickly left the room to allow the next person to discover an old friend. It was like Christmas morning in a hurry.

He had now been pushed closer to the old boots by the throng of women. The boots triggered an old memory. He had seen something like them before at the National Museum of the U.S. Air Force, the compression boots of WWI and WWII pilots. Hunter reached for them, knowing that no one running into the shoe room would be looking for that particular pair of shoes. *Those are just too old....* Dusty and brittle under his fingers, he brought the dried out boots out into the light amid countless women on the floor lacing up sneakers or sliding on slippers and sandals. Once shod, they raced for the kitchen. The word traveled quickly; how, he could not fathom. He recognized a few native tongues but the vast majority of sounds coming from the women's lips were indistinguishable. The African children made no sounds and held each other close. They had never before seen a white man like Hunter.

As the last of the women left the shoe room, he moved toward the kitchen with Celeste Germaine in tow. He carried the boots with him and he curiously fingered the collar of one of them. A string of letters were embossed within. An initial. A last name. He stopped suddenly. Celeste bumped into him and snapped him out of his reverie. He unzipped his flight suit and slipped the boots inside. He was dumbfounded and strained to speak the words, "What do you...call this place?"

The girl from Texas looked around for an answer and re-gripped his hand. "They call it the zoo, we call it the Devil's Hole."

He was speechless. He shook his head all the way as they ran to the refrigerator.

. . . . .

McGee continued to fume. "I'm just going to kill him when I see him." *SEALs do not split up unless it's a dire do-or-die circumstance. And the dumbass did it for some chick he didn't know and...and...who knows how the hell she got there. That's probably the last time I'll ever see him. His stupidity, his death will be his own damn fault! Damn Marines; can't tell them a damn thing!*

But of course Hunter had to do it. Someone had to do it! Screw that old dude! McGee's ire lasted for a fraction of a minute more. He and his fellow SEALs were known across Special Operations Command to willingly giving their own life in order to save a shipmate. The girls were Hunter's problem now. He had more pressing things to consider. Like finding the old man.

The U.S. Navy frogman leading the group back to the pier raised a fist to indicate *Stop*! As they crept forward to the massive blast doors, Naylor whispered to McGee what he knew of the layout and of the men of the submarine. He pointed out the office spaces obscured by the red lighting. McGee keyed on the words "*no weapons.*"

McGee assessed the scene and whispered, "Andy, you've accomplished your mission. You need to get out of here. I think the barrier is down; looks like they are ready to cast off."

The men didn't shake hands as they departed quietly. SEALs Naylor and Williamson slipped into the water near the floatplane and joined up with the rest of their team. Once they buckled on their scuba tanks, fins, and diving mask, the six SEALs set off for their SDV.

McGee indicated to Boroff, "Follow me." They raced along the wall for concealment and cover until they approached the well-lit area of the submarine. Just as one sailor removed and tossed a guyline onto the pier then turned to an open hatch, McGee sprinted down the pier, laser-tagged the sailor with the silenced M-4 and shot him in the middle of his back. He leaped off the pier and onto the deck of the submarine. McGee flipped the dead sailor into the water like he was a ragdoll. In seconds, McGee disappeared into the belly of the sub.

Two minutes later McGee emerged from the same hatch he had entered. A muffled explosion from within shook the boat. Smoke drifted from the open hatch. That was when Boroff saw McGee carrying a human head by its hair before he dropped it over the side of the submarine.

·   ·   ·   ·   ·

Hunter energized his night vision goggles and IR torch, then cautiously moved up the spiral staircase to a landing platform. He surveyed the area around him and above looking for anything that resembled a way to get out or a boobytrap. Above him was a four-by-eight sheet of press-locked steel bar grating typically used to dissipate the build-up of air from a speeding subway car. He shook it, but it didn't move. It easily weighed several hundred pounds. He tried to budge it with his back; his quadriceps strained under the load that would not move. It was more than he could push; much heavier than he could budge He looked for another answer. On either side of the rectangular ventilation shaft there were arms, levers, and springs, and those mechanisms were bolted to the grate, suggesting the grate was attached to a counterweight system and could be opened in an emergency. There were no visible combination locks or deadbolts or latches. He just had to find the key. He regretted giving McGee his last bit of C-4. His sense of urgency pushed him to find the solution to rescue the damsels three or four stories below him and to save himself. With no observable locking mechanism visible, he tried one last thing. Counterintuition.

He reached up, grabbed the grate, and *pulled*. The grate moved and groaned. It was stiff from years of not being exercised or lubricated. Hunter let go and the grate slowly swung open ninety degrees. He shouted down the stairs, "Celeste! Let's go, let's go." He looked over the edge to freedom and saw only fog. Pea soup-thick fog. Then the staircase and landing vibrated under his feet as the women began climbing the spiral staircase in the pitch black ventilation shaft.

·   ·   ·   ·   ·

McGee and Boroff jogged to the platform and entered the harem room to find it abandoned and silent. McGee shook his head in amazement. *That's impossible!* They turned and reentered the subway car. In seconds the two men were speeding back through the subway system.

After several quiet minutes, Boroff asked, "You okay?"

McGee nodded and bit off his preferred sarcastic answer. He was reflective of what he had seen and done in the submarine. He said, "I took care of the crew. The old man was there. Asshole came after me with a dagger."

"Last thing he ever did."

McGee looked up and nodded.

"Been quite a night."

"That it has. May you live during interesting times." McGee allowed the scene in the control room of the submarine to enter his thoughts. His eyes darted around as if he could see the young men again. *Unarmed. With their backs toward him. Just like parishioners in a church, staring at the old man in front of them. Never knew what hit them even as they fell.* Then that left the old dude; the man who might have been the captain. Or the owner of the boat. *Didn't check his ID card when I shot him.* Those sailors in the maneuvering room sitting behind steering wheels were shocked to see a maniac with a weapon aboard their boat. He shot every stunned submariner like they were tin cans on a fence rail. *The old man never moved, never flinched.* Whoever he was, he was just livid as he withdrew his dagger from his chest scabbard. *Came after me spitting mad! Shot him in the knees; took his knife away from him.* He begged in English. *I cut off his head with his own blade. I always wanted to do that…just once, as payback for the men and women and children massacred…murdered… mutilated. All in the name of Allah. Well, asshole, Allah was not so Akbar today!*

McGee removed the tiny glasses from his face and dug out crud from the corners of his eyes. *I don't even know who it was that I killed. Maybe one day I'll find out. Or maybe not. Not going to matter. I won't lose any sleep. Allahu Akbar, asshole.*

· · · · ·

Duncan Hunter couldn't pull the two or three hundred women along any faster than a crawl. Hand-in-hand the snake of humans inched along in the black sticky fog. The ground was uneven and rocky. *They needed their shoes; hope that decision doesn't come back to haunt me.* His ubiquitous BlackBerry was fired up; a Global Positioning System application had his location overlaid onto a satellite map. The primary target of his quest, according to the GPS, should be a few hundred yards ahead. He turned to look over his shoulder at the line of girls who quickly vanished in the thick fog. With his very next step he smashed into a chain link fence, bounced off, and fell. He shushed the women who erupted in a flutter, but the focus of his shushing was the little Texas girl who had been holding his hand with a death grip. It was a time to be quiet; she wanted to talk and celebrate her freedom. But they still had a very long way to go. The line of women and girls had placed their trust in the man with the strange black clothes and helmet. Freedom wasn't theirs yet, but as long as they were moving toward some imaginary goal they were happy. When the line stopped, their hearts sank.

Hunter sprang to his feet; he drew out the big bowie knife and cut the flimsy metal using the heavy sawblade teeth that made up the spine. Twisting and bending the metal in strategic places he opened a hole for him to pass through. Celeste Germaine was astonished by everything he did. With a tug on her hand, Celeste stepped through the hole in the fence and the line of women and girls started forward again. Relief rippled down the line.

He was close now. A few more plodding steps and he felt the transition from sand and hardscrabble to concrete. The GPS indicated he was in a parking lot. If it was accurate, then his ultimate target lay a hundred yards ahead. If it was there. If it wasn't he would try to get the girls to the beach and wait for the fog to dissipate.

After five, long, agonizing minutes he reached out for the shade differential and tried to touch the side of a boat, but it was still too far away due to the dock bumpers and fenders. From the satellite photos he knew a ship had been there. *If I'm in the right place this should be the only boat along the quay. Now how do I get aboard this thing?* Hunter found the raised edge of the pier with his toe.

Decisions. He had never before been on a yacht. Things were going too easy, but with the fog no one in their right mind would be traveling or boating or trying to lead a few hundred women across a thousand yards of gravel to safety.

When he bumped into one of the pier's bollards with a heavy rope ascending into the fog, he knew there was a ship attached to the rope and he ascertained in which direction it was pointed. Duncan Hunter pulled

Celeste Germaine close. He put his face into her hair and whispered into her ear. "Do not move, I'll be right back. Got it?" He felt her nod her acknowledgement as her hair rustled against his face. He let go of her hand and put his prized Colt Python in her other hand. "You know how to use this?" He switched on the laser sights.

She nodded vigorously, wide-eyed. She whispered, "Yes, sir. I was on the ROTC pistol team." The revolver was almost as big as she was.

Hunter patted her shoulder and winked at her. With one hand on the silenced M-4 he gingerly walked along the dock, keeping the pier and elevated edge in sight until he found what he was looking for. A gangplank. And a door. He reversed course and ran back to get the girls. He spoke with Celeste and gave her directions, then dragged her and her friends along the pier.

Once Hunter and Celeste had passed the threshold of the yacht's pier-side door, the young woman leaned forward and rushed inside pulling whoever was holding onto her hand. She directed traffic, and pointed the Colt revolver straight up and with her other hand, motioned the women to run up and through the halls of the ship. *Go! Go! Go!* The sense of urgency was conveyed through touch; gripping and pulling. The increased tempo of shuffling feet telegraphed to the ones behind to hurry. Some bunched up, but they quickly understood the message of torsion and tension, and they ran.

Hunter turned opposite and climbed stairs two-at-a-time, up and aft to where he thought the bridge should be. When he crashed through a heavy teakwood door and found himself inside the bridge no one was more surprised than the two men in starched white uniforms. He placed the laser dot of the M-4 on the chest of the sailor with scrambled eggs and bars on his epaulets and said, "I don't want to kill you, but if you screw with me I will. *Capiche?*"

In flawless English, the first officer recovered from the shock of the intrusion and said, "Fully. Where do you want to go, *Cowboy?*"

Hunter almost shot the man for his insubordinate tone but decided he needed him alive. "For the moment I'm going to let you live. As soon as all my friends are aboard, I want you to back this thing out of here. I'll tell you where we're going. No bullshit and you will not be harmed."

The officer of the ship turned to the sailor behind the center console and said, "Assist the gentleman's friends aboard, cast off, and make the ship ready. Secure the hatches. Come right back."

Hunter placed the red laser dot on the sailor's chest. "Just to warn you, if you try anything stupid, my friend at the base of the stairwell will shoot your ass. She is a crack shot. Do not piss her off. I will kill both of you if you fuck with me, understand?"

The sailor nodded and Hunter hissed, "You have exactly sixty seconds to cast off and get back here. Otherwise he's dead, and then I'm coming after you."

The first officer nodded toward the bow.

The sailor cast a wary eye at Hunter and his black carbine and said, "Aye, aye, sir."

A minute passed when the sailor returned and announced, "Bow lines free. I must free the stern. I'll need more time."

Hunter waved the M-4. "Two minutes. Go!" Hunter peppered the first officer with questions.

A small crew of four was aboard the ship; first officer, helmsman, engine mechanic, and a purser. No one else was aboard the royal yacht and no one was expected. Hunter learned the captain was likely in his hotel room in Abu Dhabi with a friend.

The sailor returned on time, breathless. "We're free. I do not believe all are aboard, sir. Dockside hatch is unsecure."

Hunter barked, "Help them aboard and secure the hatch, and get back up here. You contact the rest of the crew to make ready to shove off."

Five agonizing minutes passed. Hunter was about to shoot the first officer and check on the sailor's taskings when the man returned to the helm and announced, "All aboard. All secure, sir." He did not like the weapon being pointed at him.

The first officer said, "Take the helm. All reverse, quarter thrust. Slowly. Radar and GPS up."

Hunter said, "We are in no hurry."

"I don't want to run into anything."

"That's a good idea. What's your name and where are you from?"

"Eric Boyington. Corpus Christi." The first officer offered a feeble smile. "Stealing the emir's yacht is likely a death sentence. He has friends in very high places. I don't see how you can get away with this."

"He can always get a new boat. I like this boat. In fact, I like it so much, I think I'll keep it."

"You cannot be serious."

"I am as serious as a heart attack, *Eric*. And if you do a good job as the captain and don't piss me off, I won't shoot your ass or throw you overboard." *That's two.* Hunter lowered the M-4 and withdrew the silenced Kimber. It was a better weapon in close quarters than the rifle. And it terrified the sailors on the bridge.

Eric Boyington knew it was time to show a little respect. The unarmed first officer pondered the alternatives Hunter suggested. He replied, "Sir, I will take you anywhere you want to go."

"When we get free of the Palm, point this thing to Kuwait."

"Aye, aye, sir. Do you have a name?"

"Sir, is fine. Drive the boat and don't piss me off."

Boyington nodded as the helmsman steered the yacht.

CHAPTER FORTY-TWO

2000 July 28, 2014
Arlington National Cemetery

A ten-man detail from Marine Barracks, 8th and I, stood at attention at the gravesite waiting for the arrival of their fallen brother in arms. The Marines wore dress blues with white covers and gloves. No media covered the event; there was no family to mourn the dead. Two men in black business suits stood at the gravesite and monitored the ceremony.

The "President's Own" Marine Corps band in their finest red and gold trimmed uniforms led the procession, followed by a color guard and a platoon of Marines with weapons carried at "shoulder arms." A U.S. Navy chaplain with heavy gold stripes on his sleeves followed at a discrete distance.

The procession slowly climbed the hill. The coffin was drawn by six horses on the wheels of a caisson. It was enveloped in the flag of his country. A drummer marked time until the funeral caisson stopped.

A casket team of Marines gently moved the coffin to the gravesite. The chaplain read the service for the dead. Three volleys of seven were fired. A single bugler played Taps. Six Marines took positions to lift the American Flag off the casket, the blue field with stars was at the head and over the left shoulder of the deceased. The flag was folded into the symbolic tri-cornered shape. A properly proportioned flag can fold 13 times on the triangles, representing the 13 original colonies. A properly folded flag is emblematic of the tri-cornered hat worn by the Patriots of the American Revolution. When folded and presented, no red or white stripe were evident, only the blue field with stars.

A Marine Corps colonel presented the flag to Director Greg Lynche. "On behalf of the President of the United States, the Commandant of the Marine Corps, and a grateful nation, please accept this flag as a symbol of our appreciation for your loved one's service to Country and Corps."

Lynche received and cradled the flag. He said, "Thank you." A minute later, all of the uniformed men and women had departed and the two men were left alone. Lynche turned and said, "There is no time for grief. Thank you for coming, sir."

President Hernandez said, "Such is a military funeral. I'll see you in the office." They shook hands and walked to their limousines in silence.

A burial crew lowered the remains of Duncan Hunter into the ground.

．　．　．　．　．

For his brave reporting on international terrorism the host of the most watched show on cable television thanked his guest. Demetrius Eastwood wore his trademark multi-pocketed cargo pants and white denim, open-collared shirt. The network special had begun with a warning that viewer discretion was advised because the show contained scenes that some viewers could find disturbing. Ten minutes into the discussion, the host again warned his viewership that they could find the following material very disturbing. After a few seconds of on-camera silence, a picture popped up from behind him on a huge flat-panel monitor. Seven severed heads were arranged in a circle and rested atop what appeared to be a conference table.

The photograph stunned the camera crew, the producer, and the prime time audience to their core. Most viewers across America turned away from the instantaneous shock to their senses. After the initial shock and despair of seeing such a gruesome scene, something that most people had only read about in the newspaper or heard on the radio, the cable viewers began to peek at the image like a voyeur stumbling upon a bloody crime scene. They looked past the horrific and ghastly image. None of sullen and sunken faces were recognizable to those viewers who now couldn't take their eyes off of the disturbing image.

Eastwood somberly provided, "Sean, UAE counterterrorism authorities confirmed the veracity of the photograph. It was taken on the 154th floor of the Burj Khalifa in the corporate offices of a little known international conglomerate called R-O-C. The initial indication is that this ROC has been one of, if not the prime sponsor of Islamic-based terrorism throughout the globe. And the men on the table were likely the chief culprits in funding terrorist groups."

"Do the UAE authorities have any idea who these men were, or who could have done this? To these men? Do we know who took the picture?"

Eastwood said, "Who they are hasn't been released. Some counterterrorism experts have suggested they are some of the 'hidden' emirs of the Emirates. Possibly brothers or uncles of the official royal family of emirs who wished to remain out of the public eye. That maybe this ROC was something of a secret society. We know so little at this stage of our investigation. We do know it wasn't a drone attack, although there appears to have been a small explosion on the floor. A number of window panes were blown out suggesting whatever explosive charge used was small. It wasn't a hand grenade. Whatever it was, counterterrorism authorities are calling it, 'Precise.' I would say, 'Surgical.' On scene investigators claimed the 154th floor was one of the safest places on earth. They suggest that someone likely interrupted a board meeting—the only rationale for these men to be in the conference room of this conglomerate. By the looks of the photo, someone put them out of business."

"Permanently," uttered the amazed television host.

"My UAE contact suggested they couldn't see how any human could enter the floor from the outside; it's simply too tall a building for someone to scale, and the elevator system was secured. Somehow, someone apparently used enough explosive material to get in and not damage the building. A small drone may have been able to gain entry, but there are no answers currently as to how or why this happened." The photograph was taken down and the cameraman focused on the host and visitor. Eastwood continued, "The UAE has no suspects other than the possibility of Batman or Spiderman. No one is saying how the floor was entered or how many were involved in the…."

The host interjected, "*Message?* It seems to me whoever, uh, posed those heads was sending a message." The network host became more serious and wanted better answers.

The photograph didn't appear to be digitally enhanced and Eastwood had staked his reputation on the veracity of it. The broadcaster had a sympathetic ear for the old Marine, having worked with him on numerous projects in Iraq and Afghanistan. They had run through what would be asked and in what direction the host wanted to take the conversation before they went on the air.

Eastwood smiled. "Sean, maybe someone is fighting back. Maybe they are sending a message that we are not going to take it anymore. An eye for an eye. Whatever evil you consider will be met with—not with an equal opposing, but with an overpowering force."

The TV host raised his hands to encourage Eastwood to continue.

"This was a different level of…*mutilation*. My contact at the CIA and Special Operations Command disavowed any knowledge of the incident and indicated they do not comment on any operations. I can tell you, Sean, I've been with men and women of the Armed Forces and the Intelligence Community. This is not something they would do or even consider. This…this…is far *different*."

"Could it have been CIA?" asked the TV host.

"No; they have rules too. This is well outside what the Agency would do or allow."

Intrigued by the off-script analysis, the host asked, "So if it wasn't Special Forces or the CIA, who do you think would do something like this?"

Eastwood had read the name "Duncan Hunter" on the list of the dead from the Qantas aircraft. He had spoken to him, had actually done his friend a tremendous favor by telling a host and her panel of experts that the problem with the aircraft was electrical, not terrorism. He turned to the camera and said, "If the Islamic State or al-Qaeda doesn't claim responsibility, then someone who is angry, someone who has lost much, someone who is not going to stand by and take it anymore. Someone capable of fighting back." He tried to remain sanguine but failed spectacularly by smiling.

The host had his own agenda and was too preoccupied to notice the old Marine's words and body language. He became more animated, flailing about with his arms and hands. "Brits? SAS? Royal Marines? How about the Russians?"

"I cannot see it. The British are too proper and the Russians…well, like ISIS or al-Qaeda, they too are at war with the West. Again, this is not their style. It is something the Islamic State has done in the past, but they haven't been known to have the kind of reachback into the heart of the UAE. ISIS uses a quiet remote strip of desert. They mug for the camera in hoods. No, this one is different."

The television host nodded. He liked the direction of the discussion. But it was time to move to another issue. He asked, "Can you tell our viewers what else you have uncovered in your investigation?"

"Sean, there have been several stunning revelations and events surrounding, as you like to call the '*message*,' that occurred during or shortly after the assault on the Burj Khalifa. This was from four days ago. The Pentagon divulged that almost three hundred women, girls, and children were rescued in the Persian Gulf on the same night that that picture was believed to have been taken. Four days ago the FBI began to interview several American women who were recovered. They had been kidnapped and held as sex slaves. They had been missing anywhere from weeks to years. British Intelligence is also interviewing women who had been taken from across the British Empire; from England, Scotland, Australia...."

"Three hundred women?"

Eastwood nodded. "Girls and children. From across the globe. The initial evidence points to hundreds of mosques, some in the United States and Europe, that were likely involved in the kidnapping and transportation of these women to the UAE. Some were kidnapped here, from the heartland of America. We've just learned of one brave young woman from Texas who is the only one of the freed women currently talking. She claimed that 'she and the others were saved by an American. A handsome man in a black helmet and bloody black coveralls.'"

The host smirked and said, "That's very interesting. We'll have much more on this developing story, but first we need to take a profit timeout—this ain't no NPR. We pay our bills."

"Sean, I'd like to ask a quick favor."

"Anything for you, Colonel. Thirty seconds til we're back on air."

"I'd like to honor the passing of a friend of mine, as you say, a great American. He was a passenger on the Qantas aircraft that's been in the news recently. Marine Corps Captain Duncan Hunter was buried at Arlington National Cemetery. He was an amazing gentleman and a true American hero."

• • • • •

President Hernandez, CIA Director Lynche, and the Director of the National Counter Terrorism Center, Nazy Cunningham looked at one another at Eastwood's mention of a man in a black helmet and what they knew to be a black flightsuit. The Oval Office was stone cold quiet. Then the President pointed at the television and said, "Nice touch, Greg."

"That should definitely get them off his back."

Nazy smoothed her hands over her buttocks before she touched the sofa to ensure her fire-engine red chiffon maxi-dress wouldn't get unnecessarily wrinkled. The President and Director Lynche sat down and only glanced at her covered legs before turning their eyes back to the screen.

Nazy Cunningham was proud and cold and frightened. She only had heard from Duncan via a text message, which she had not shared with her boss.

Director Lynche had heard from Hunter. A full-color photograph rested inside his CIA-embossed notebook.

. . . . .

Vertical green lights illuminated on the camera to indicate the men were "back on the air." Somber small talk about the dead Marine's burial passed and was replaced by Eastwood's spontaneous and incongruous smile. He too had been rescued by a man in a black helmet and a black flight suit, or what he knew to be *flying coveralls*. The scene of Duncan Hunter and Bill McGee dispatching terrorists on a hijacked jet in the middle of Africa came flooding back to him. Eastwood wasn't an emotional man but he could feel his emotions rising inside and changed the subject.

"*An American in a black helmet and black coveralls?*" The host crossed his arms as if to telegraph, *That's impossible or unbelievable.* His skepticism was palpable. "And the CIA and the Pentagon disavow all knowledge?"

Eastwood nodded. "The photograph was sent to me by a counterterrorism source from the UAE, and I turned it over to DOD. Then I was given exclusive access by the Pentagon and the Department of Justice to conduct my investigation. I've met with a sex trafficking task force that is run out of the FBI's National Crime Information Center.

They have taken the lead on interviewing as many of the rescued English-speaking women as possible. Investigators at the Pentagon and the FBI are being tight-lipped. This is a fast moving situation, and they have provided a little insight, off the record, of course."

"Of course."

Eastwood continued, "I'll have a special report on the sex trafficking and my interview with the brave young woman from Texas. Also, with the cooperation from the UAE government, the FBI and MI-6 are investigating the connection—the possibility of a network—between the company R-O-C, headquartered out of Dubai, and radical mosques across the U. S and Europe."

"Islamic cultural centers across America and Europe? Where did this information come from? FBI?" The television host smirked.

Eastwood continued, "Sean, there's the Multinational Syndicate of Investigative Journalists (MSIJ), a global non-profit network of investigative journalists in more than 60 countries, including the U.S., which collaborate on these types of stories or stories that have been spiked by politically leaning editors. One particular group cooperates with leading news organizations worldwide to investigate—to the extent that they can—questionable conglomerates, shell companies, and offshore holdings, as well as their connections with terrorist organizations and political parties. As you know, a shell company is a fictitious legal entity that has no active business operations but allows people to hold and move cash around under a corporate name. For years, the journalists of the MSIJ have been discovering and tracing transactions—money—from companies like the ROC to the owners of these shell companies. The surprise was that the vast majority of these ROC-related shell companies, at least on paper, lead directly to the most radical mosques in the U.S. and Europe. After the penetration of the Burj Khalifa, the MSIJ released the files that they had on this ROC and exposed some of their hidden financial dealings with terrorist groups."

"MI5 and MI6 are doing the same in England, and Interpol is investigating possible connections in Europe. Other nations are conducting raids on mosques and madrassas. On the surface, it appears this R-O-C could have been the head of a network funding mosques, funding everything: sabotage, murder, sex slaves, kidnapping, precious metals, blood diamonds—there was nothing they weren't into. Even elephant ivory and rhinoceros horns. The FBI thinks this is how they likely recruited jihadis, through these radical mosques. It also appears this ROC had their own personal security force made up of former special operations forces from the Middle East. So some credit goes to this American, whoever he may be, the one in the black helmet and black coveralls, for blowing the cover of not only this significant sex trade operation, but this international conglomerate. As a consequence, the government of UAE has seized their assets. The Pentagon and the FBI have also reported that the funding of international terrorism has taken a big hit."

"You have one more bit of information...."

"Sean, this case gets more interesting by the day. Intelligence sources reported an American computer scientist was found in the basement of the Burj Khalifa—his throat was cut clear through to his spine. Apparently there was a computer glitch with the security system as there was no video of any of the suspicious activity on any of the floors or in the elevators. UAE Intelligence services are investigating—they are trying to blame the Israelis. Another man was found dead in his room at the Armani Hotel in the Burj Khalifa. Very little is known of him, investigators haven't released his name, and the investigation continues."

The host reached across the table and shook Eastwood's hand and said, "Great job, Colonel. Welcome back. We look forward to your line of specials. Maybe next time we can get an update on the whereabouts of former President Mazibuike and how he helped a designated terrorist organization, the Muslim Brotherhood, infiltrate the U.S. government."

"My pleasure Sean, thank you for having me."

The scene transitioned into a male enhancement commercial with a sultry female model.

· · · · ·

The President muted the television. Nazy Cunningham's eyes rocketed to his. Lynche avoided looking at her as he slipped the photograph from his notebook to President Hernandez. He looked at the single head for long seconds. Then nodded toward the television monitor, and said, "You think Duncan did...*that?*"

"Sir, who else could it be? He was the only one on the floor. He used his little jetpack—the weather wasn't conducive for flying the *Wraith*."

Nazy was aghast that Lynche would suggest such a thing. She covered her mouth as her world started spinning out of control. *Duncan did not do that!*

The President said, "That doesn't sound like him."

All thoughts of eliminating the former president had been pushed into some subbasement of the White House. If the CIA Director brought it up, the President would be happy to follow along. But for the present, seven severed heads held all their attention. The President returned the photograph of the former president to Lynche. Nazy Cunningham was not offered to see the picture. President repeated, "That doesn't sound like him."

Nazy offered, "The CIA will leak that it was the Islamic State."

The President turned to Nazy and asked, "Is he back?" Nazy's eyes turned to her boss for an answer.

Lynche shook his head gently. "Enroute from Jordan. I plan to dispatch Nazy to debrief him. He got to the Embassy in Amman and filed an abbreviated report stating he was safe, uninjured, and that he completed his mission. No other specifics except that photograph. Mission complete. I'm not real happy with him right now."

The implication from the CIA Director was that Hunter had gone on a killing spree and only presented a single trophy head.

"Greg, he didn't do that," reiterated the President. The scene was horrible, but Nazy knew her husband didn't do that either. "Men like Duncan have an inviolable inner code. He would never betray his friends or his country. He doesn't exploit the weak. Look at what he did with those women. He didn't do that."

Nazy nodded her agreement.

Lynche ignored them. "I've worried about his mental state. That maybe this type of flying is too stressful. Even though killing these master terrorists likely doesn't affect him, he's been targeted time and time again. Colombia, Jordan, at his ranch. I've pulled him off the program. I'm putting him out to pasture."

The assertion caught Nazy off guard. The President said, "Greg, let's not be rash. Am I correct—he hasn't been debriefed, and we still do not have a capability to replace him?"

"No, sir. The technology is getting better." Lynche wasn't budging from his decision.

"But not the footprint," said Nazy Cunningham. It wasn't a question. There wasn't another program like the *Wraith*. The only way the YO-3A airplane could have a smaller footprint would be to turn it into an origami airplane and toss it out of the back of a cargo aircraft where it would magically unfold and just fly away.

The President asked, "But not the footprint?"

Lynche yielded and nodded, "But not the footprint."

Nazy was quiet as the men discussed Hunter's future, and what the President wanted to see from Hunter. "We cannot afford to just let him go. Duncan is a lone avenger who stands up to evil. He represents the true American. And he has a beautiful mind."

Lynche wanted to dispute the President with the image of the seven unknown troubadours' heads on a table still fresh in his mind. He found a way.

"Sir, no disrespect, he butchered seven men—maybe eight—because he thought they were targeting him. He snapped."

President Hernandez looked back to the black television monitor. He looked at Nazy and said, "I know that wasn't him." She concurred with her eyes.

"If it wasn't him, then who was it?" asked Lynche.

President Hernandez' cold eyes stared at his Director of Central Intelligence for a long time. It was uncomfortable for Lynche. It was uncomfortable for Nazy. Lynche thought the next words out of the Chief Executive's mouth were going to be, "You're fired."

But those words didn't slip out. Lynche found some that might work. He mewled, "I suppose before we get crazy we need to give Duncan the benefit of doubt. We need to debrief Duncan before we get …uh, a little carried away. Pack your bags, Nazy. I want a full debrief when he arrives."

The President asked, "He's not coming here?"

Lynche said, "He'll probably go to his new safe space. I'm not sure when or where he will turn up."

Nazy recalled the text message from Duncan and offered, "I know."

CHAPTER FORTY-THREE

2200 August 4, 2014
Jackson Hole, Wyoming

Duncan Hunter used the remote control to shut off the television and then turned to watch Nazy Cunningham stroll from the bathroom to the kitchen. Her ass-length hair looked as though it had been caught in a cyclone. It was only like that after hours of romping in bed. She closed the refrigerator door and padded to the sofa; her pendulous breasts swayed with every step. She carried bottled water and wore only a smile. As she got closer he noticed the perspiration that covered her torso and legs as if she had stepped from a sauna. She was a beautiful mess. She opened the bottle and offered it to Duncan who politely refused.

"*Ladies first.*" After she drained half of the bottle, Duncan finished it off and opened the blanket he was wrapped in. Her nipples were erect and hard from the blast of cold air from the cooler as she accepted the invitation and snuggled in close. They kissed tenderly. As a consequence of their intimate marathon, their lips were raw and numb. Duncan inhaled through Nazy's mouth, and she collapsed in a heap on top of him. Typical afterplay for the near-newlyweds.

As their lips slowly and deliberately uncoupled, she slipped down his torso to find the comfortable spot under his arm; the one where her breasts weren't crushed and her arm wouldn't be in the way. After a few quiet minutes she cooed, "Did I miss anything?"

Duncan said, "Only one of those ubiquitous Viagra commercials."

Mutilation. The pain from his lips wasn't enough to distract him. The word bounced around his cranium with repugnant depravity. For almost a week the media had been wild with the news of seven unknown men from the United Arab Emirates who had been decapitated by the growing terrorist group, the Islamic State. Demetrius Eastwood had been on several talk shows to discuss the photograph of the men and how terrorism groups were responding, now that one of their prime

430

benefactors was apparently out of business.

Hunter had seen snippets of the Eastwood report while passing through the British Airways Lounge at London's Heathrow. It was gruesome, and the media lapped it up. He had immediately texted Nazy and Lynche, "That's not my work." Then he texted Nazy he would meet her where they wed.

He asked her to get some more water. She took the circuitous route to the kitchen through the bathroom. It was a big new house and getting around was still like exploring the multiple paths of a crop maze.

When she returned with the water, she climbed back under the blanket and arched her back sensually as she reached down to squeeze him. She was surprised that he was still a little sticky. She wanted to go back to bed and avoid the upcoming discussion. In her best sexy Liverpool she said, "You don't have any problem with that, Mister Hunter."

"I don't know, *Miss* Cunningham," he said playfully pulling her close with warm hands. "I think you have worn it out. It might even be broken. *Kaput.*"

"I'm a little tender too, but I never get tired of kissing you. I can't get enough of you. In case you couldn't tell, I missed you very much." *And I am so grateful you're still alive!*

Hours earlier as she stepped from the jet, she had trembled with anticipation. Their times together over the previous year had been too few, so infrequent. But this time Nazy couldn't contain her glee. Not only was Duncan alive, but he wasn't damaged. Not like the last time. For Duncan, the reunion was all about getting reacquainted with his wife, the woman of his dreams. For Nazy, it was all about sex. Sex with Duncan. She hadn't slept the night before and hadn't slept on the airplane either. She preferred thinking about her naked husband. He could please her like no other; the unbridled pleasure and passion moved her to her core. "*Ladies first.*" He was always along for the ride.

He kissed the top of her head and said, "I missed you, too, Baby." Another squeeze of his arms and she settled in for the moment.

She spoke to his chest, not daring to look at him. Suddenly lugubrious she said, "It was so hard to watch you go. I didn't know if I would see you again." After a minute she whispered, "Greg…we…still don't know how…you did *it.*"

It. Two insignificant letters, a thousand meanings. With the preliminaries over, with a completely trashed and soaked bed, they could debrief. She raised up and turned to see if the neon green Growler was still working, still flashing. Once satisfied that it was, she returned to her safe and happy place in Duncan's arms, her leg between his like he was a body pillow, her fingers barely touching the side of his face. She would normally fall asleep in his arms after their lovemaking, but she wanted…no, she *needed* answers. Answers were essential. DCI Lynche demanded them. She had a report to file.

He understood and expected it. On a mission of such magnitude, Greg Lynche would usually have insisted on debriefing Hunter himself in his office. He wouldn't have allowed her to come to where he was hiding. But obviously a new protocol had been established, and it didn't portend well. Something had changed. Hunter had a good idea why he wasn't called to Washington D.C. *If I saw that television show, I'd be livid at me too.*

Lynche had good reason to believe that Hunter had willingly crossed the demarcation line of what was permissible and rational, and that he had purposely ignored the protocols and plunged into the realm of the impermissible and irrational. The President and Lynche had given Hunter free rein to hunt his quarry as he saw fit and dispatch them as the conditions permitted. That usually meant he would kill the primary target and other targets of opportunity from the air. A big-bore bullet from the silent aircraft would tear through even the best of body armor. If the situation permitted, he would kill them all, all of the radical terrorists in the vicinity, and if there were any adjunct martyrs among the dead, he would let Allah sort them out. If he was on the ground, two quick hollow-points to the cranium and cremation of the body was the unstated, yet preferred method. However, decapitation was an excessive use of force. *Taboo.* Mutilation was the purview of the madman. Operationally, both took longer to perform than the microseconds needed to put bullets into a terrorist's brain. Two shots ensured death. Mutilation regaled death.

Those that cut off the heads of their enemies did so with a flourish, a perverse celebration of evil for vanquishing the enemy. With every decapitation, a message was clearly communicated. A new terrorist group, the Islamic State, was becoming the benchmark for communicating terrorism with weekly killings in the most depraved and gruesome manner imaginable. Mass decapitations were their specialty. Cruelty Incorporated. They recorded the events as if they were a ceremony, a graduation exercise for the degenerate, and when Al-Jazeera didn't broadcast the killings, ISIS posted their murderous videos on social media.

Lynche's CIA didn't have sufficient on-the-ground intelligence assets to send Hunter after their leaders from the air, and it pissed off the DCI. But that situation was improving. There would be another time for the *Wraith* to engage the deviant and depraved leaders of the Islamic State. The intelligence analysts confirmed the IS wasn't a flash in the pan; they were growing and expanding into other countries. With every day, they became more gruesome.

Hunter's most recent mission was uncharted territory, heretofore, only an anarchist from the political left would ever consider killing an American President. When a president left office he wasn't prey; he was a revered statesmen. The liberal Lynche wrung his hands raw worrying about the fallout. The unintended consequences. If the man had simply vanished after being exposed as a fraud, that would have been considered a positive political outcome. The Director of the CIA worried that if the information ever got out that the U.S. government, a Republican administration, hunted down and killed their former president, the man derided as 3M, that irrespective of his assumed Muslim and Communist leanings he would become, at the very least, a martyr. Martyrdom for Maxim Mohammad Mazibuike was to be avoided, and the President and the DCI had put their trust in Hunter to ensure there would be no body to mourn, no martyr to worship. Martyrdom had been the last thing on Hunter's mind when he had drawn the Bowie knife from its scabbard and finished his work.

Hunter and Nazy held each other quietly. The only sound in the house was the crackling logs in the fireplace. He gently stroked her back to comfort her, she responded by stroking his unshaven face and snuggling closer. It was like that between them since their injuries. Touches and pressure at appropriate times and places communicated their reassurance that they were there solely for each other.

After minutes of quiet, he told her the essentials. No details. Words came out in bullets. Some made sense; others would need amplification.

Nazy could fill in the gaps with her imagination or questions later. He needed to be allowed to speak freely, unencumbered by feelings or shame.

Hunter felt her become tense, but he tightened his embrace to reassure her. In *sotto voce*, "The fog was worse than expected. I couldn't use the airplane. Used the jetpack. A little *plastique* was necessary to get inside." He whispered, "Rothwell's *nurse* was on the floor. He was the first. He had been injured from the blast and shot at me but missed." Nazy and Lynche had surmised the rest of Hunter's actions after learning the particulars from the investigators in the UAE and the reporter, Eastwood, who had splashed pictures of the mayhem on the top floor of the Burj Khalifa.

He wouldn't say how infuriated, enraged, *primitive* he felt when he came face to face with…*him*. That he was ashamed—*Christians don't cut off the heads of their enemies*—that's what *they* do.

It wasn't part of the original plan. Hunter was just going to shoot everyone in the room from the comfort of his airplane, if he had positively identified Mazibuike. But the issue of martyrdom could not be solved with a bullet through the sternum. There would still be a body. The coastal fog and the availability of the jetpack had changed the concept of operations while complicating the solution.

After flying through the blown-out window and standing in the conference room with debris flying all around as he stood in his all-black flight suit and helmet, Hunter was all-business. *They put a fatwa on my ass and tried to kill me. On my ranch and in a jet. They tried to kill Nazy. They even cut off my hand.*

He would never admit to Nazy or Lynche that he was pleased with himself for the first time since starting the special access program—*this time it had become personal.* The other times, it was just work. This time it was revenge. Hunter stared off toward the vaulted wooden ceiling.

She didn't have a need to know all of *it.* For a few seconds, he had become the basest of animals; he had hunted down his prey, *the prize*, and proudly displayed his trophy. A photograph to capture the moment. *See what you get when you screw with me?* But who would ever see it; the evidence that he had completed the mission? Lynche wouldn't like the vulgarity of it, the crassness or the depravity, but it was proof of mission accomplishment. Now he was distracted by Eastwood and his picture of seven severed heads. Hunter photographed only one.

Who the hell did that?

Nazy felt his heart racing wildly. She tried to distract him by pressing closer to him. She asked, "And the, ahh, *girls?*" The application of pressure to his most sensitive pressure points calmed him immediately. He was glad for the momentary distraction.

More bullet answers described the escape from the underground prison. Then a continuous stream of consciousness. "They were in a room. Huge...underground...almost the size of a *warehouse.* From your engineering drawings I surmised there had to be a way out. I found it; backdoor of a refrigerator—it was easily five times the size of the one I used to clean when I was a kid working for a Shakey's Pizza Parlor. Got them out. GPS to the yacht. Got them aboard. I used my Agency distress codeword. Asked the ship's captain to contact the National Command Authority for approval, for assistance. I told the captain, 'I have two-three hundred sex slaves from a prison; I need some help.' He gave me 'permission to come aboard.' The hardest thing I did was not shoot the guy driving the yacht."

Nazy told him about the FBI Special Agent who sounded the alarm and told the CIA that some entity was killing Duncan Hunters. She was also the head of a domestic task force for missing women. "That agent found you in her database; you found some of her missing girls in the UAE."

"That's crazy."

"She knew you." Then she remembered, "She knew *us.*" He tried to move to look Nazy in the eye, but Nazy wasn't having any of that. He relented and searched his memory. He came up empty. Nazy lazily said, "She was at the Naval War College with you. Hunter Louise Papp."

"Kind of rings a bell. I think she was in the junior class. If I recall correctly, she was a pretty girl."

She frowned as if she knew he was being purposely obtuse. "She's beautiful. She saw us enter the restaurant in Newport."

He smiled as he chortled. "The Red Parrot. White Rolls. White dress. Red heels. Your cinnamon perfume." He would always remember *that night. Her hair was unbound, long wavy hair spilled across her shoulders coquettishly and hid part of her face as if she were embarrassed. Rock hard nipples strained against the little white turtleneck dress that hugged every curve. Legs wrapped in misty black nylons. Crimson enameled nails. Her exotic perfume. That was no Muslim girl in that outfit!* There were some things you never want to blot from your memory. He filled his lungs, straining for a hint of that spice. All he could smell was the residue of their lovemaking. Hunter continued, "That night there could have been three hundred semi-naked girls at the entrance to the Red Parrot and I wouldn't have noticed."

She moved into him sensually as if she were trying to arouse him again. Then the outburst, "They were almost naked? No one said anything about that."

"Once we were aboard the emir's yacht, the girls raided the closets of the bedrooms to cover themselves. Shirts, shorts, whatever they could find. Then on the aircraft carrier, the captain called for the ship's population to bring uniform items and flight suits. They had shoes...." Again there was an immediate shift in Duncan's demeanor. Another powerful memory. She wondered if it was Post Traumatic Stress Disorder, if he was reliving a previous catastrophic event. She moved closer to him to convey her concern and compassion.

"What is it, Duncan?" She got up on her elbow to look at him. While he gathered his thoughts, she reached over for a water bottle. She held the base and he twisted the cap. Teamwork.

"Whoever held those girls had confiscated their shoes and put them in a huge room, almost as if they were collecting... *trophies.* Tens of thousands of shoes but...I saw a pair of old leather flying boots. I think Amelia Earhart's name was embossed in the collar. *A. Earhart.*"

Nazy's eyes went wide. "The woman who tried to fly around the world? She went missing July second, 1937."

Hunter was stunned. "How would you know that?"

She told him of the Yazhov archive. It was still highly classified never to be shared with the public. "Nikolai Ivanovich Yazhov was the head of the Soviet secret police and the All Union Communist Party under Joseph Stalin. Apparently Yazhov took a lover, a teenage daughter, we believe, of a former aristocrat. Her writings suggest that she was *his* sex slave. He regaled this woman—Rani—in his work. He tried to impress her with his position and power. He thought she should be grateful he had saved her from the ravages of the Bolsheviks. Somehow she acquired scraps of paper and wrote down everything he said. He was a braggart. The part that would be of interest to you was that Stalin was jealous of the West's growing aviation power and the flying records they were setting. Stalin directed the Soviet air force and navy leaders to stop Amelia Earhart."

He was stunned and confused, but he wasn't surprised. "Wow! How did they do that?"

"Rani's writings did not say. She asked Yazhov, 'How will you know if you're successful? It will be in the papers,' was all he said."

"And it was," murmured Hunter.

"In another archive we have from that era, however, contained several Soviet submarine radio dispatches. A Soviet Union sub was known to be operating in that area of the Pacific at the time her airplane went missing. All we have is their report that their mission was accomplished."

"What did they do, spoof a DF signal? Direction finding." Nazy still had trouble with acronyms and appreciated Duncan explaining them to her when he was on one of his rolls.

It wasn't a simple yes or no answer. Nazy provided some background. "The American Navy built a runway and positioned fuel, oil and fresh water on Howland Island. And, as I recall, a direction finding radio beacon."

"So commies *spoofed the signal* and drew her off course?"

"Apparently. The satellite system that found the underground city, what Greg called the Valley of the Kings, was programmed to look for an airplane within five hundred miles from this Howland island. They found...."

"A Lockheed Electra...."

She nodded. "At least something that looks like a Lockheed Electra...about three hundred miles south of the island. In two hundred feet of water. But we still don't know what happened to her."

"Somehow she ended up in the UAE before it was the UAE. Probably got picked up by a passing Muslim dhow or trading vessel."

"Or maybe another submarine?"

Hunter looked at Nazy curiously then continued, "Probably became a sex slave since her boots were near those other women's shoes. I don't like to think she died at the hands of a seagoing Bedouin or was traded for her good looks. It's better to think that she was just lost at sea."

Nazy didn't want to hear any more about the missing aviatrix, or her boots, or women being held as sex slaves. The topic suddenly depressed her. But she had more information to share. He would reciprocate. "There's more." She talked of the Hindenburg airship, of sympathetic communists stealing plans, the unmanned airplane that brought it down, and the widespread conspiracy of sympathetic communists who had stolen every aircraft and engine schematic from every airplane and engine manufacturer from the U.S., Britain, and France for fifty years.

"I don't remember seeing anything in the air as the Hindenburg set up to dock." Hunter frowned.

"According to Rani, Yazhov bragged that he was the brains behind the effort, and fellow communists in the United States facilitated it all. This was before the OSS and the CIA. Naval Intelligence had some of the intel on the movement of everyone's submarines, but no one monitored the security requirements of the aviation industry."

Hunter agreed. "Security wasn't a high priority then. So, basically, there were communist sympathizers that worked their way into aircraft and engine manufacturing plants, conducted espionage and stole everything they could, just like there are radical Islamic sympathizers today who have worked their way into and around airports, conducting espionage and stealing the secrets of airport security and commercial aircraft operations. Yesterday's commies are today's radical Islamists who hijack airplanes and blow up airports. Communists and fascists attacked the weakest links of the aviation industry for seventy years. And now the Islamists are doing it; instead of building aircraft they are trying to destroy them. And airports."

"That's some insight, Mister Hunter."

"Not really. Stalin was infatuated with aviation. If he had a hand in bringing down Amelia and the Hindenburg, maybe he had a hand in bringing down some of the PanAm Clippers too. Flying boats. I seem to recall a couple of the Boeing flying boats crashing short of their destinations in the Pacific. Roughly the same time. 1936, 1937."

Nazy shook her head in disgust.

"And, I'll bet whoever was behind that red diaper ROC group was just as infatuated with airplanes as Uncle Joe Stalin was. They wanted something they could not achieve, and when they couldn't buy or steal it, they punished those that said no. Maybe one day we'll find out what this ROC's connection was to aviation. To that submarine. To those boots. I know there's something there. They have to be connected. All vectors point to the ROC. Must be."

Nazy smiled at him, more amused than impressed.

Hunter asked, "Did this Rani say why she did it?"

"We surmise she might have been able to use the information to gain or trade for her freedom. Maybe she thought she could gain her freedom by blowing Yazhov's cover as Stalin's intel chief. Everyone hated him."

As Nazy spoke, Hunter recalled the theme of one of his graduate school lessons. A billionaire Emirate sheik, the CEO of a Sharjah airline, had openly wanted the French-Anglo Concordes for his airline. When Airbus refused, a Concorde crashed under mysterious circumstances. The French blamed an American airline and ignored the fact that Muslim mechanics were the last people to have fueled and touched the outside of the aircraft. Then Hunter had an insight. *What are the chances the CEO was the old guy at the head of the table who got away?*

Nazy moved to distract him and get him to shift positions. When he was finally on his back where she wanted him and she was astride him, she settled down. He was cognizant that their genitals were aligned for action but it would be a long while before even suggestions of intimacy could resurrect the dead. The final phase of the debrief was in play and their minds were on work and not pleasure.

"Greg came up with the idea that the upstart Islamic State bit the hand that fed them and were responsible for the killings at the Burj Khalifa. Decapitation is their MO. Articles were placed in Islamic newspapers, all of it free publicity. They haven't denied it."

"I'll bet he's pleased with himself." Hunter had returned to the revelation that there were seven heads on a table and that his wife and Lynche had thought he had done the dirty deed, maybe even sent the photograph to Eastwood.

"He *is* the master spy." She smiled at him. "I'm still learning. Before he came up with that solution, he was positively livid. He didn't want to talk with you and wanted me to bring back your badge. I was to tell you that your contract was cancelled." She paused to find the right words, but there was no way to sugarcoat the tip of a turd. "He said, just as he was getting over what you did in Iran, you do this. He couldn't trust you anymore."

Hunter's heart sank lower than the sofa he was on. He suddenly had the attention span of a goldfish. *I didn't do it. But who the hell did?*

CHAPTER FORTY-FOUR

2200 August 4, 2014
Jackson Hole, Wyoming

Duncan Hunter lowered his eyes in shame, as a puppy would when scolded for messing on the floor. Lynche had every right to be angry with him and to boot him from the program, but not over this. His method of dispatch of the former president was impromptu, mercurial; it would never have been approved. They weren't called special access programs for fun; you were supposed to do what was required to complete the mission and get out without anyone knowing you had been there. You had to find a way of disposing of the body of high value targets. From the air, that was largely impossible. A successful mission meant no celebrating at the end of a touchdown, no spiking the ball, and absolutely no parading the faces of dead master terrorists. At the American Embassy in Amman, he had transmitted the picture of the head of 3M to Lynche under the rubric—*DCI Eyes Only*.

Nazy continued. "The President called for a formal debrief. I hadn't been back in DC for more than a few hours when Greg and I were summoned to the White House. President Hernandez handed Greg a spreadsheet. He said, 'Thanks to Captain Hunter and his airplane, we've eliminated the top forty men on this list. Then Greg added, 'Not only did Captain Hunter and the team find the former president, but apparently they found the mythical and theoretical *Number One*.' A man they knew that had to exist. The ultimate decision maker. He probably fancied himself as the head of the *caliphate*. The President announced that it was likely the unnamed man at the very top of his Disposition Matrix was likely this *Number One. The One*. The man McGee found in the submarine. Time will tell who he really was. We'll have to find out in the papers when he doesn't show up for some event and people start asking questions. Or maybe not. The festivities stopped when Eastwood's report splashed on the television."

440

Hunter thought, *Like airplanes over the Pacific. An airline CEO with an infatuation for supersonic transports. Airplanes.*

Nazy remembered the rest of the conversation and paused to ensure she got it right. "The President also said that one of his predecessors had turned loose the greatest Islamic charismatic radical, that the United States had him in a box for years and let him out. He started the war between Islam and Western civilization."

"Khomeini?"

She nodded. "The President said the de-westernization of Islamic countries began with the return of the Ayatollah to Iran, that the President let the genie out of the bottle. He said, 'Knowing what I know now, if it was another time, I would have had Khomeini on the Matrix. At the very top. I would have sent Duncan to rid the world of that cancer. But the world is what it is today. So Greg, unless you have a new set of candidates, other than those of the Islamic State—which I propose to bomb back to the Stone Age—I propose we terminate *Noble Savage* and let Captain Hunter get on with his life. All generals have to hang up their uniforms sometime. It's time for Duncan to hang up his flight suit. What he's accomplished is extraordinary, and I know it has taken its toll on him, and you. It has me. You two have been the best of friends. Loyal to the nth degree. I cannot imagine the level of stress we placed on Duncan. Greg said the stress was so great that he had to stop. That flying alone, at night, in a single engine airplane over the most hostile of territories. It cannot be done for any length of time without damaging the mind. He said you singlehandedly scrubbed the Earth of the worst that radical Islamists could produce.'"

Hunter smiled his goofy smile and shook his head slowly in embarrassment.

Nazy continued, "He said to Greg, 'You and I know during these last few operations he operated well outside the box, a box of expectations and protocols with which we are comfortable. You also know I have much admiration for men like Duncan, men who fight evil. Whether their choice of ends and means be right or wrong, I'm not going to judge. Results matter. Everything he has done for our Nation has had a positive effect. It's time to let him go. He's taken care of the people of the United States of America and now we need to take care of him.'"

Hunter was quietly shocked. He would have bet one of his

Gulfstreams that, if he were going to be canned by anyone, it would have been the Director of Central Intelligence. He asked, incredulously, "The President let me go?"

Nazy ignored the question and continued. "The President asked about Kelly...."

"*What?* The *President* is interested in...."

"You shouldn't be surprised. Greg and the President discussed your replacement. President Hernandez asked Greg to set her on a path where she can be most effective for the Agency. Greg said he would, and she will take your place on *Weedbusters.*"

A bit relieved, Hunter said, "Well, that not kinetic." *Killing opium poppies is different than blowing a hole in terrorists.*

"Exactly. But someone of your experience and stature doesn't need to be doing that anymore. The President said to find you some other work. Something at the *doctoral level.*"

What does that mean? Hunter chortled inside and said, "What kind of work?" He was afraid of the answer.

"Greg said, 'Duncan's going to be the next Chief of Air Branch. He can play with airplanes and robots and help the Agency move ISR aviation into the 21st century.'"

"*What?*" *The best job in aviation? Seriously?* Suddenly he smiled like a naked lottery winner playing with hundred dollar bills in the middle of a room.

"In my bag, your green badge was upgraded to blue. You're a civil servant again."

"Don't I get a vote?"

"According to the President and the DCI, apparently not. Unless you want to go to Oxford. Get a PhD. Then the President pointed to me and said, 'As for Nazy, she needs some time off.' I took it to mean I would accompany you to Oxford. If you wanted to do that." She rubbed her breasts against his chest to telegraph her approval.

He was reeling from being moved from the special access programs to a leadership position in the CIA. And then, off to *Oxford?*

"What? Seriously? Send me to school? And you? Time off? We could hang out at the King's Arms Pub? What do you think of that?" *We were supposed to go to Bora Bora! Bikinis—white crocheted seashell things. Sand between our toes. Or Banff. Snow bunny. Skiing. Hot chocolates around the fire. But that was years ago. There was always work. Or there was another terrorist to find and kill.*

"I haven't used hardly any leave. There's always something needing my attention. Keeping me close to the office."

Hunter thought, *Yeah, away from me.*

Tired of the debrief and the discussion. He pulled her close. "I think I need your attention." He stroked her back until both of his hands were on her buttocks. He indelicately squeezed her firm callipygian ass. The action was only teasing; he was still dead from the waist down, but his mind shifted into overdrive. He debated whether to change the subject. The question he wanted answered was, *Who in hell got onto the floor after me? How was that even possible?*

She poked his chest with a heavily lacquered green-pearl nail. "Don't try to start something you cannot finish."

He finally realized her nails matched her eyes. Being poked playfully momentarily snapped him out of his ruminations of who could have finished what he had started with the former president. *Who else was on the floor? How did I miss them?* Then, it struck him; someone had to have an intel officer monitoring and controlling the security cameras in the hotel, as well as someone who managed the elevators. *Did they see something...anything?* Then it struck him. *Did one of our Agency guys let the cat out of the bag, inform someone what we were doing?*

There was something more to the meaning behind that photograph, and he needed time to think it through. He changed the subject. "So you are on leave? I guess I'm on leave too. What am I; some GS-oh my God? Like you."

"I think you're working for free. Doesn't Greg and the Agency pay for your jet fuel? Haven't you heard the term quid pro quo?" She broke out in a huge smile.

"You have a point." His smile reflected a new line of embarrassment. A U.S. Government "gold card" for fuel was priceless. It would have been impossible to operate his aircraft if he had to feed two Gulfstream business jets on his own dime. He noticed he was beginning to sound like a whinny liberal, so he changed the topic into something more benign.

"Well, Theresa will be thrilled to fix your breakfast," he sputtered. At the mention of Theresa Yazzie, the sweet overbearing and insanely loyal housekeeper, Nazy was suddenly distracted by the other woman in

Duncan's life.

She asked, "How are Carlos and Theresa doing? I cannot believe you got them to come to Wyoming."

"After that guy nearly killed me at the ranch, I told them I had bought a house. When I thought I was officially dead in the Philippines, that my cover had been completely blown, I asked them if they were interested in continuing on up here. I'm not sure of Carlos, but I'm fairly certain Theresa was ready to go. I don't think he put up much of a fight. All the furniture came with the house, and she didn't have to do much to set it up for...*us*."

"This house is... breathtaking. I've never seen anything like it."

"It's six thousand square feet of log cabin—a *lodge*—on a hundred wild acres, with a guesthouse and a separate home for the Yazzies. It was called Split Rail or Split something; I renamed it the Split-S Ranch. Tomorrow if you like, we'll take a walk along the Snake River. See the Grand Tetons in all of their glory."

Her smile preceded, "That sounds like fun. I'll tell you what Greg has me doing now."

"Tell me now."

"Really? Now? It's...*work*." He encouraged her with a thin smile and a hug. She had seen that faraway look before when he had something complex on his mind. She asked, "What are you thinking?"

His eyes rolled around the tops of his sockets.

"This Rani. What's her story?"

Nazy hesitated in answering. The diversion into an old Russian woman was strange, at least on the surface. No one at the Agency had asked about "her story." The focus of her papers by the analysts had been the verbal history and boastings of the man she lived with. Nazy had often wondered about the woman, who she was, where she came from, how she came to be the apparent lover of Nikolai Ivanovich Yazhov, Stalin's head of Internal Affairs. Yazhov's history was fairly well-known; there wasn't much on the unknown Rani.

"There is virtually nothing. We think we have triangulated her age, roughly. She never mentioned how old she was, only that Yazhov had told her she was very special."

"From my Naval War College classes, I recall that Yazhov had an evil, mean, repellent personality, that he was a cruel man. He set fire to cats' tails, skinned squirrels alive...and there was a rumor he had been present...." Duncan filled his lungs and exhaled, "When the Romanovs were executed."

Nazy gasped and blinked wildly. She tried to do the mental math. She remembered a conversation from the old KGB colonel, Boris Nastakovich. The Tsar Nickolas wouldn't allow Vladimir Lenin to acquire the royal family's and other Russian aristocrats' priceless artwork and treasures. Nickolas II had moved them to France under the cover of darkness by train. Lenin was furious to learn the riches of Russia's most wealthy had been moved to Paris to be stored at the Louvre. Lenin punished Nickolas Romanov in the most horrific way possible. The tsarina and the princesses were brutally raped by the Bolsheviks. After that horrific night it was rumored that the Grand Duchess Anastasia Nikolaevna of Russia, the youngest daughter of Tsar Nicholas II, the last sovereign of Imperial Russia, might have escaped the family execution.

"I know what you're thinking, Duncan."

"Isn't Rani 'queen' in Russian? Who names their little girl queen?"

"Yes, but.... We have very little on Rani. We don't know; we'll never know."

"It's an interesting...*thought*. There's been a lot of discussion on sex slaves. You know there are no coincidences in intelligence work."

Nazy nodded, lost in thought at the possibilities, the probabilities. She shook her head absentmindedly. "Her papers are all we have and they don't provide any hints. You don't want to think Amelia Earhart died as a sex slave, and I don't want to think Rani could have been stolen from her family by Yazhov. Some men can be so cruel."

Hunter pinched his lips; he was ready to move on. "I don't want to talk about work anymore. May I change the subject?"

Nazy jumped ahead of him and asked, "Weren't you supposed to get another airplane? And a car?"

"Bill took delivery of both just yesterday. The new airplane is in the hangar in Texas. The Aston Martin is in the shop in Fredericksburg. I can't wait to see them."

She said, "Bill obviously made it back to Sharjah in one piece. Greg debriefed him. Bill told him you completed *Broken Lance* and that he had "cut off the head of the snake," whatever that meant. He was worried about you. He's back in Texas?"

"He is. I texted him. Since I am supposedly dead, I turned the ownership of the garage over to the troops. Bill is managing everything else. I thought since I was effectively retired, my new permanent hideout would be here. He shot one across my bow when he said, 'No more trips for me.' Bill hasn't anything else to prove. He'll be ok being retired and running the training center."

"That will be hard to believe. Men like that just cannot walk away from...*it*."

"I would agree. But I have to tell you, he wasn't very happy with me, leaving me in the belly of that underground city. I know he was certain I was going to die trying to get those girls out of that hole.... He thought I was making the biggest mistake of my life." Hunter inhaled at the recent memory and dismissed the unfortunate cross words they had exchanged. But McGee had a few surprises to deliver once he knew Hunter was alive and well in the U.S. "Bill said he found a Nazi floatplane in the submarine pen. I was going to ask the president, if I was going to debrief with him, if I could have a crack at that airplane. But our favorite DCI is not talking to me and would likely tell me to pound sand."

"Duncan, I'll see what I can do. He won't yell at me."

"He stopped yelling at me...*temporarily* when I got him a ride in a *Blue Angels* F-18. Speaking of which, Bill, he, ah, also got a ride in a jet this week. They had the airshow at the airbase in Del Rio. I may not have told you, but I was supposed to go. I even went through the pressure chamber trainer, but I knew I really wasn't able to go. And now that I'm dead officially, I couldn't go. I had set it up that if I weren't able to fly in the back seat of that F-16, that amazing good deal rolled over to Captain Bill McGee, former U.S. Navy SEAL extraordinaire. So whatever was between us was wiped clean with a little demonstration of afterburner and excessive applications of G. Even if it was the Thunderbirds and not his beloved Navy Blue Angels, Bill got the ride of his life. It all worked out. I'm sure he's happy with me now. *Happy, happy, happy.*"

Nazy nodded and grinned at her smiling husband. *I know, you can only be mad at Duncan for so long.*

She looked down on her husband. A thin grin broke across his face. Her little devious smile made him apprehensive. She was holding something back; he could tell. After a few quiet minutes, neither had the temerity to break the silence.

He knew she had something else to say; she would spit it out in her own time. Hunter keyed off the word *spit* and was reminded of a saying, *If you're going to play ball, sometimes you have to learn to spit tobacco juice.* It wasn't a great time, but now was as good as any.

He whispered, "Will they martyr him?"

She matched his tone and volume. "Only if the world finds out about it."

"How could they not?"

"I don't suppose there was much left of him to identify. Greg pressured the UAE's intelligence service to not investigate the incident, return his remains, and to keep their mouth shut. The sex trafficking operation had to have touched everyone important in the country. It is a huge international issue and reflects poorly on the UAE. He's giving them the opportunity to do what is right; keep their mouth shut and stop their sex trade in its tracks. They lost their submarine. 3M's remains were turned over to the U.S. Embassy."

Nazy didn't say the former president's remains were also incinerated and his ashes were dumped into an embassy toilet.

A quiet minute passed between them. She considered his concerns of the former president achieving martyrdom through the backdoor; he considered the direction the CIA Director had taken to squash the issue. The world didn't have a need to know in what manner the former president's body was disposed.

He couldn't look at her. He struggled with what to say. Finally he whispered, "Nazy, I didn't do it. The seven amigos. Greg can polygraph me for a month!"

She cocked her head in confusion. It took a few seconds for his words to mean something. She shook her head gently, trying to shake the notions away that *he did one* but he didn't do the others. "I know. Greg is coming around."

He was uneasy talking about any part of the mission. He could easily speak to Lynche or McGee or another man, but the topic was borderline taboo between husband and wife. He struggled with the wording until he said, "I tossed him out the window. That's all I did. Someone else arranged those guys like a house of horrors roulette wheel." He shook his head. "*That wasn't me.*"

She believed him and kissed him, long and hard. Raw lips be

damned. Her relief gushed from her mouth and her body tried to keep up. Suddenly aware that there was an unresolved issue, Nazy asked, "Then, who did...*that*?"

"That's the problem. I don't know. Or why."

"You have to tell Greg. He thinks you, and I quote, 'wandered off the reservation and lost your mind.' Unquote. I sort of know what that means, but not really."

He smiled and said, "It's a cowboys and Indians reference. Before I left Heathrow, I sent him a quick text message."

"He doesn't believe you." Nazy shook her head imperceptibly.

"I haven't lied to him ever. Not going to start with this. Maybe it's better if it came from you. If he hasn't figured it out, tell him there's a problem. If I talked to him, I'd remind him that they let Rothwell's nurse get away in Amman. Maybe that was an oversight since I was in the hospital. But *the nurse* was one of the seven. There were at least two others on the floor below. Likely guards. Maybe it's related."

Nazy collapsed on his chest, buoyed by the news that her husband and lover wasn't a drooling mutilating maniac with PTSD. She felt relief that Duncan was, in fact, the man who she thought he was. He had done what he was supposed to do. His last mission involved the indelicate work of finding and killing the worst possible spy, one who didn't have to be subject to polygraphs and background investigations but had direct access to America's most valuable secrets. Hunter was a loving, serious, and dedicated patriot who had found and dispatched the enemies of America. He loved her without bounds. Rocked by all of the disparate information, she felt she was comfortable enough to push all talk of the former president into a tiny box never to be opened again. In doing so, the debrief was nearly complete. There was only two questions and two more items to discuss.

He could feel her tense up. He countered by pulling her tight when she asked, "Will they find us here?"

He stared up at the ceiling of the great log house. "I don't think so, Baby. The place is in Carlos' and Theresa's name. Document searches won't help someone looking for me. And officially, I'm dead. So I doubt it. I'm not going to worry. Now with you at your place in Bethesda, that's not good. I think you need to move. If you still want to work we'll have to find you a nice new place."

For a long time she considered the implications of what he said. Being out in the wilds of Wyoming was not something she had ever considered. Maybe Jackson would grow on her. She was ready to move on; another topic. They were going to get emotional.

"Why did the Sky Link jet happen?"

It was hard to shrug laying down with a women laying on top of you, but Hunter tried. "Probably a proof of concept. Random. Found Allah. Discovered he had a way to hurt America. Shopped it to jihadis. No one would ever suspect anyone in the UAE was so involved."

The thought of hundreds of innocent people being callously murdered upset her. *Intel is a nasty business. You're dealing with the worst of the worst.* She whispered as if she couldn't believe what she had heard. "That is unconscionable. Evil. That's why I left Islam."

"I knew it was the computer dude when I saw him in his little suit. When I saw those guys racing for the elevator I was so pissed that I couldn't stop them. After 3M, I wanted to find them and stomp them into the ground like a stain."

She saved the best for last. Her chest heaved as she moved her head like a lioness stretching; a cascade of her mane fell across both of their faces. A wall of black strands blocked his view. He moved her locks away gently until he saw her smiling, conspiratorially. He smiled back, curiously. He repositioned his hands to surround her and pull her close.

"Well, I think I have something that might make *you*...I don't know if 'happy' is the right word. As far as I'm concerned, the debrief is over."

His naked supermodel of a wife was straddling him on the sofa and she thought she had something *else* that could make him happy? It was incongruous and inconceivable that anything, over and above what filled his hands and what lay on top of him could put a bigger smile on his face.

"Before I left the Oval Office, the President didn't quite know who to thank for the gift *of a yacht*...." She accusingly and playfully touched his nose with her finger. "Apparently it was donated to America by one of the...ah, *good* emirs of the UAE. I understand the old Presidential yacht hasn't been used in years...."

"That would be the *Sequoia*." He smiled like a goofball.

She wouldn't be distracted by his command of trivia. "The Navy is sailing it back to Washington. It will likely go to the Naval Academy."

The thought of hundreds of Midshipmen crawling over a captured Muslim potentate's yacht made him smile. *From the Halls of Montezuma to the Shores of Tripoli....* "Spoils of war?" Hunter wondered what happened to the cavalier first officer Eric Boyington of Corpus Christi. Did he jump ship or return to the U.S. as part of the ship's crew? The bastard Boyington was lucky he hadn't pressed his luck and gotten shot. Blood would have ruined the carpet on the bridge.

Hunter was suddenly reflective and said, "Getting them out of that hole was very, ah, I think the right word is *fulfilling*. And getting those girls off that yacht and onto the carrier...." He paused and exhaled, trying to find the right words to covey what he had seen and heard. "Baby, once they realized they were safe, they started singing and crying and celebrating their freedom. It was very powerful. I got emotional. Witnessing that spark of freedom was like an electric religious experience. Not something I will ever forget."

Tears ran down Nazy's cheeks. She placed her head on Hunter's chest and worked to recover and calm down. Several quiet minutes passed as the emotional highs ebbed and dissolved like sand castles at high tide. "The President is pressuring the UAE for answers and actions...greater human rights. Western nations are howling in their disgust...." She composed herself after a quiet tearful minute.

When Duncan kissed the top of her head and hugged her, she continued, "Also, the President informed our favorite Director that the Queen of England...wished...to confer... *knighthood upon you....*" This was the moment she had been waiting for. She grinned, nodded, and let the news sink in the old Marine's head.

Hunter was stunned speechless. He mashed his lips; he crushed one brow and closed an eye in the ultimate question: "*What?*"

"It's a honorary knighthood, of course. For rescuing British Airways and the Qantas airliners, and all of the passengers and crew. That you've made important contributions to...." She was so proud of him she began to tear. She cried softly, like rain on a window pane.

"*What...how...?*" He was mumbling. She kissed him.

Once they both recovered, Nazy wiped her tears away and continued. "President Hernandez said the Australian Prime Minister informed the Queen that an American had rescued the Qantas aircraft, otherwise it and all of its passengers would have been lost. She called the President to thank him personally on behalf of all Englishmen and Australians. The President told her, 'Your Majesty, it's the same man that interrupted the hijacking of one of your British Airways flight several years earlier.' Then she asked if you were also responsible for rescuing 'those girls.' The President blew your cover and said that you did. And the ones in Nigeria and Somalia. He told Greg, 'She can keep a secret.' So she wants to knight you as soon as possible."

"Are you serious? Does that come with a fancy title, some land or something? Family crest? I know those princes drive Aston Martins." He wasn't smiling, just confused. That confusion translated to Nazy who expected glee and gratitude. When she received neither she wasn't impressed with his penchant for flippancy

"No, silly. You're not a Brit, and it's an honorary knighthood. It's like getting a ribbon for perfect attendance. Only better. *Sir* Paul McCartney got a medal."

"So, I'm *still* Billy Ray Joe Bob Average?"

Pulling the covers over her shoulders she said, "There is nothing average about you. But I'll call you 'Sir Duncan' from now on if that will make you feel better." Her condescension was playful, teasing. She slid down his chest a few inches and yawned.

Hunter tried to mimic her accent and cadence. He failed miserably. "Then can you be my little Dame Nazy? Dame of Jackson Hole just doesn't sound...*proper* for a woman of your status and station. It may not matter. You know how I turn to mush and get turned on by...a little *British* accent." He smiled as he yawned. Dying flames in the fireplace reflected in her pupils.

For the briefest of moments, Nazy and Duncan locked eyes. There was no movement except the rising and falling of the blanket as they breathed. She smiled, snuggled into his arms, and closed her eyes. He wrapped his arms around her. Then he said, "You definitely know how to do a debrief. All questions answered?"

She nodded and repositioned her arms and legs to a more comfortable position.

He lifted his head to whisper directly into her ear, "I love you."

She moaned, "You too, Baby" and then fell asleep.

Hunter lay there for several minutes listening to the logs in the fireplace crackle and pop until he too, drifted off.

CHAPTER FORTY-FIVE

1200 August 11, 2014
CIA Headquarters

"I have never seen him in the building before. He was introduced only as 'the pilot.' He first showed up in a commercial pilot's uniform. He was older, what you would expect of a, um, transoceanic airline pilot. Fit; in profile, flat belly, big chest. Graying temples. I'd say he reminded me of Steve McQueen had he lived to be sixty. Seventy."

The Director of the National Clandestine Service asked Duane House, the other man in the room, "You?"

"Confident. Decisive. He was like a chessmaster—he was several steps ahead of us. He knew what had to happen next. He called for an IR beacon on the patio. We didn't bring one. The SEALs had one."

"The SEALs?" asked NCS Director Castaño.

Computer specialist Bob Marsh said, "Arrived from a different source. We came in through nonofficial channels. No Embassy. Private jet through Great Britain. As directed, we pretended to be part of the crew for the CTC Director's photo shoot."

"Who were those guys? How many and what did they do?" Castaño was now more interested in the SEALs than anything else.

"Retired, I'm sure. And I'm sure the huge black dude was Bill McGee. I had only heard about him. I know he had a couple of tours at Headquarters. You cannot miss him. He's huge. There are no senior black dudes like that in the SEALs."

"The Black Ghost," said the other man, Marsh. "Four total."

"Maybe. But the pilot was the real black ghost. Popped out of nowhere, out of the fog with the damndest thing I'd ever seen." Duane House was excited to relay what information had been building up in his head since their operation in Dubai was shut down.

The NCS Director was confused. "What?"

"It was obviously a jetpack, like from that old James Bond movie.

The exact same shape but more modernized, bigger and maybe streamlined, but it was black. All black.... I thought it had to be from S&T."

Duane House added, "It wasn't just *black*, it was coated with something. It was very strange—it played tricks with your eyes. All you could make out was the outline. There wasn't any definition of anything else except the harness. Every piece of metal was... *black*."

Castaño was incredulous. "It was just...*black?*" He waved scarred hands to beg for more clarity.

"Yes. It seemed to suck...no, kill all the light. I tried to photograph it and even tried to shine a light on it, and the light just disappeared, like if you tried to shine a flashlight to the moon. Even three inches away—nothing. Nothing but the blackest black hole in the shape of a jetpack. Weird. I had never seen anything like it."

"I managed the elevators and the security cameras," offered Bob Marsh.

Duane House said, "The Agency guy, Saldaná, took care of all the comms and the pilot gave him a laptop computer. I took care of the hotel registry as well helped managed the hotel's security cameras during the initial phase and contact phase of the op."

The men explained the operation, from the moment the unnamed men and the CIA women left the room up until the time they departed the hotel and arrived at the U.S. Embassy. Standard special activities operation with covered players.

House said, "I only knew the CTC Director...."

"Cunningham," said the NCS Director.

"Yes, sir. But I didn't know her redheaded sidekick. She didn't offer her name; I didn't offer mine. I thought she was NCS too by her actions. The other man, Saldaná, didn't like to speak. I asked him if he knew her, but he shook his head. He didn't know her either."

"Did Cunningham or the redhead seem to know the pilot or the SEALs?"

"The redhead, not really. Maybe. It wasn't readily apparent the pilot and Cunningham knew each other. As did McGee. For the sixty seconds we were in the same room, what I saw was that they were all business. But it is possible both women knew the men. As I expected, once the pilot arrived, Cunningham asked for privacy. We hadn't been read-in on and had no need to know the particulars of the operation other than what was expected of us. We were directed to go into the other room. The redhead herded us in the bedroom and indicated it was a private brief from Cunningham."

"She was with you?" Castaño frowned a bit, as her presence didn't make much sense. He knew her name was Kelly Horne and she was National Clandestine Service. Horne was one of his agents on temporarily assignment to the DCI's staff. And she was a pilot. *Could she have been a backup pilot for an op? Can't ask her that.*

The men nodded and looked at each other for confirmation. The NCS Director took up the rhythm and smiled. It was obvious DCI Lynche was running a closed, extremely limited-access operation. He thought, *That's my bailiwick! What the hell is that asshole doing? That had to be the smallest operational footprint possible. Why would he do that?* Then he asked, "Who was the target?"

Marsh and House were surprised and responded as if their director was unaware of who the target was. "President Mazibuike."

Castaño was stunned. For the next hour the men briefed what they had seen and said to the SEALs and the pilot. The pilot asked Marsh to disable the cameras on the 154th floor. They relayed how the old man in the elevator killed the civilian computer scientist. They reported that when the pilot returned to the hotel patio, he handed a laptop to the Agency comm guy, Freddy Saldaná. They discussed how the SEALs chased after the old man. NCS Director Castaño jumped when Marsh indicated the pilot demanded he kill all cameras in the hotel and told House to open the door of a room.

"I remember it was room 707," offered House. "Director Cunningham gave me a name and I found it in the registry. Zavian Vonnah. Never heard of a name like that. More like a rack of unusable Scrabble letters than a name."

Marsh offered, "There was a cleaning crew that took one of the elevators to one of the topmost floors."

Castaño nodded indifferently and pointed with a bony scarred finger, "Did you see the Eastwood special?"

Marsh and House nodded but offered no further discussion. Castaño raised his eyebrows at the lack of information, then asked, "Did the pilot do that? The seven sisters?" The men were confused by the "seven sisters" reference but knew the only time the number seven was an issue was when they saw the seven heads of dead terrorists on a television screen. And they were men.

Both men shrugged. House was ready for the debrief to be over. "Had to be him. His flight suit was covered in blood, as if he butchered an ox. After he landed on the patio, he told us what he wanted us to do, and then he was virtually out the door in seconds. He didn't change or clean up. I never saw him again."

"You have any idea what he did in that room? That Vonnah's room? Why he did that?"

House offered, "No, sir. We just did what we were told. When it was time to leave, we bugged out. The pilot also asked us to take his jetpack to the embassy, which we did."

NCS Director Castaño said, "Ok, thanks. If you think of anything else drop me a line that you need to meet me again. As always, absolutely no details on the email system. Understand?" Both men nodded which signaled the meeting was over. Castaño shook the two men's hands across his small conference table. They let themselves out of his office.

He stood and walked to the largest of his office windows. Hands in his pockets, he played with a few coins as he pondered the information. He whispered, "*President Mazibuike? Damn!*"

· · · · · ·

America was transfixed to the Demetrius Eastwood special, "Escape from The Devil's Hole." The retired Marine colonel strutted around in his trademark field gear—billowy white shirt, tan cargo pants, brown Merrell boots—to set up the telecast. "The sex trade was alive and well in the United Arab Emirates until our guest and almost three hundred others managed to escape the underground prison they called 'The Devil's Hole.' Celeste Germaine is her real name. Celeste is a beautiful 16-year old student at Abilene High School. A competitive shooter with the Junior ROTC. She had gone to the skating rink in Abilene, Texas in June. She remembers talking to a policeman and then waking up in a pitch-black shipping container on a ship knowing, thinking she was going to her death. Once she was let out of the container Celeste was handcuffed by her armed captors and pushed into a large building and down into what she thought was a cellar. That is when her story took a horrific and terrifying turn."

"Celeste said she will always remember that scene. There were five large men who spoke in a language she had never heard. Four girls like her were stripped of their clothes and shoes and thrown into a room. They were convinced they were about to be raped or tortured. One of the men brought in a black child, presumably from Africa, and killed the little girl in front of them. Celeste and the other women watched in horror and screamed and pleaded for their lives. Celeste stated that the men had used long knives to dismember the child while she was alive. Then they fed the girl's body parts into a meat processor. After what seemed an eternity, one of the men, covered in blood, came to Celeste and the others and said in English, "You will do exactly as we say and no harm will come to you or your family. Failure to comply and you will return to this room to be dealt with. Your families will be hunted down and killed."

"What she saw that day was just one of many horrific experiences she went through as a potential sex slave. Celeste Germaine and three hundred other children, adolescents, and women escaped when several unknown men entered the Devil's Hole. Only one remained with the women to try and save them. I met up with Celeste in her home town of Abilene for a short interview to talk about her harrowing ordeal and amazing rescue."

"I saw children die in horrible ways," she said, drinking a Coke and eating a Subway sandwich on her parent's patio. "I want to talk because people have to know what is happening to the girls who disappear, from skating rinks or while walking to the ATM. It's happening all over the world. And I want to thank the amazing man who rescued us. We...I never got to tell him 'thank you' for saving us."

She told her story of how she and "her sisters," as she called her fellow captives, arrived and lived in the underground warehouse. And how some girls were tortured and killed to coerce the women to comply with their minders. Then, the door opened and strange men entered their living area.

Eastwood could barely contain his emotions. Even the cameraman was caught up in the event. Celeste told the correspondent, "...there were others in the underground building who just wanted to leave us to die;

leave us to the bad men. I was pleading with them when a man in black...*coveralls* and a funny black helmet stepped in front of me and said he would get us out. And he did." A tidal wave of tears appeared on the girl's cheeks and she let them flow. Only after Eastwood handed her a handkerchief did she wipe her eyes and face; a huge smile and rosy cheeks emerged.

Eastwood pointed at the camera and said, "Here's your chance, Celeste. Tell him. Trust me, he'll get the message."

It was as if all her suppressed emotions were released as one giant wave of joy and comfort overtook her. Again, tears gushed from her eyes; Celeste trembled as she struggled to say, "Thank you, good Sir."

* * * * *

Bill McGee watched the Eastwood special with his family. His wife looked at him and wondered if he had been part of the rescued woman's story. He had to have been, but he would never tell. He felt horrible now that he was one of men who had turned their backs on the women in the Devil's Hole.

* * * * *

President Hernandez watched the Eastwood special. He telephoned the CEO of the network to convey his congratulations for a well-produced and uplifting story. He said, "The next time we have a State dinner, I'd like Colonel Eastwood to cover it for your network."

* * * * *

Greg Lynche also followed the network special from home. He turned to Connie, his wife, and said, "I think that asshole Eastwood knows it was Duncan who saved those women."

"That's a problem?" she asked.

He nodded and frowned. Hunter's cover had been blown by a thousand infinitesimal events.

• • • • •

Kelly Horne shut off her television with the remote. She said aloud, "That's my dad." She grinned broadly and recalled how he and Bill McGee had rescued her from a group of terrorists who had hijacked a jumbo jet. *I know it was him. Who else could it be?* She lifted a wine cooler toward the TV monitor and said, "Nice job, Dad. Again."

• • • • •

The Director of the National Clandestine Service, Steve Castaño, had been on his way out of his office when the Eastwood special began. He stood there, playing with coins in his pocket, watching the old Marine grunt until the show was over. He returned to his desk, dialed his deputy on the STU, and railed at the man over the speakerphone, "Did you see that? *Who the hell did that?*"

"He's not one of ours," oozed out of the encrypted telephone speaker.

"That's not Navy SEALs; that's not Army Delta." Castaño grew more livid by the second. In the darkness of the office, he pulled his lips into a sly grin.

"No, sir. Not our guys. Not theirs either. They are asking the same question. I determined there were some SEALs in the area that night, but they insist it wasn't them. The captain of the ship who took custody of those women isn't talking. We have a dispatch from our guy aboard the aircraft carrier that the guy who is likely responsible sent a "DCI Eyes Only" dispatch from the comm center. Then he flew off the ship in a jet. I think someone's running an op—excuse me, ran an op that should have been ours."

No shit, Sherlock! Castaño was quiet, thinking, seething. He pounded a stubby, bony, and scarred finger on the desk in exasperation.

"What did you find out on this Duncan Hunter dude that was interred at Arlington?"

A long silence presaged the response. "He was a Marine. Business guy and a college professor. And he was a pilot. He died in that Qantas jet that landed in the Philippines with dead people."

"Our guys who worked the Burj Khalifa said the dude was a pilot." Castaño thought there was an awful lot of talk about pilots.

"He received full military honors. It was truly something."

Castaño was shocked. "What are you saying?"

"Full Marine Corps Band. Silent Drill team. You'll never guess who attended the funeral."

The NCS director's mind raced to find the answer. But he was overwhelmed. "Who?"

"Just the DCI and POTUS."

Castaño rolled his eyes and said, "Let's talk about this in the morning." He disconnected and after ten minutes of reflection, walked uneasily out the door.

. . . . .

Arms akimbo, FBI Special Agent in Charge Hunter Louise Papp stood staring out of the window of her office at the National Crime Information Center. She was in a state of shock. The Attorney General was inbound via an FBI helicopter to give her the FBI Medal for Meritorious Achievement. She had received an advanced copy of the citation via the classified email system from a CIA address. The citation read, in part, "…for extraordinary, decisive, exemplary acts in the line of duty that resulted in the direct saving of life in severe jeopardy."

The Director of Central Intelligence had initiated an inter-agency commendation for Special Agent in Charge Papp's outstanding analysis and immediate notification that a deep undercover intelligence officer on a special access program was in imminent danger. Her timely warning saved the asset's life. A promotion would accompany the award.

The Director NCTC had called Papp to thank the FBI Special Agent for her remarkable and selfless efforts. She had saved the life of a CIA operative whose official cover had been blown. He had been targeted by radical Islamic elements. More than the award, Papp wanted the answer to a simple, single question. "Was it him?"

Over the encrypted telephone Nazy Cunningham said, "Louise, *officially*, you saved the life of one of our officers and many of your missing girls were rescued. Their freedom significantly damaged the underground railroad and slave trade in that part of the world. I wanted to tell you, 'thank you' for all you have done and to say best wishes."

FBI Special Agent Papp could read between the lines. Even the war correspondent Demetrius Eastwood announced Duncan Hunter had died and received a hero's burial. Hunter was now completely off the books. She exhaled audibly and said, "10-4" and hung up the telephone.

At the sound of an approaching helicopter, FBI Special Agent in Charge Hunter Louise Papp turned away from her office window, smoothed her skirt, adjusted her shirt collar, fluffed her hair, and headed out the door to meet her distinguished visitor.

. . . . .

Across America newspapers and network anchors reported, "Researchers announced they found what they believe is the missing Amelia Earhart Lockheed Electra. Divers entered the wreckage looking for human remains but only found moray eels and tropical fish. The leader of the research team indicated that the Lockheed Electra was in remarkable condition, suggesting a non-traumatic water landing. He surmised that Amelia Earhart and Fred Noonan most likely survived the landing. The hunt continues for clues to determine what happened to the missing aviators."

. . . . .

STRATCOM Commander and Captain Pamela Frappier gazed at the billboard-sized "Knowledge Board" to track the status of a French Redoubtable Class submarine under tow from the United Arab Emirates. Frappier said, "The reactor was shut down, and the submarine is heading back to France, sir."

General Magnusson pointed at the big board and asked, "Inquiring minds want to know, Frappier, was it related to the sex slavery trade the emirates were obviously engaged in? What was it, 300 women and girls from across the globe were released by…. Were they SEALs?"

"Press reports…that Eastwood Special indicated it was just one man, a man in black." She grinned at an old amusing thought. The General caught her.

"Out with it, Pam. What are you thinking that you cannot share?"

She shook her head, unable to reconcile the spontaneous juxtaposition of "SEALs" and a "man in black." She suddenly remembered. "Sir, there was this guy—all mysterious—at the Naval War College. Always wore a black power suit and always sat with the class president, an African-American SEAL, who was usually in whites. They made quite a pair."

"Sounds like Captain McGee."

"Yes, sir." She nodded and told him the other man's name. His response was unexpected. It brought a bemused smile to the general's face.

"You know him?"

"He was one of my F-4 students. More than a vague recollection. I'll have to check my logbook to see how many times I flew with him." The general chuckled at the thought, but then suddenly got very serious. With the bearing and mien of a man who is responsible for the strategic triad of the United States, the hardnose Marine Corps four-star General Magnusson exchanged nervous intimate glances with his subordinate. They had suddenly discovered a likely secret of immense importance. He removed his glasses and stuck an earpiece into his mouth; he was thinking wildly. With the delicate spectacles wavering in and out of his mouth, he waved Frappier closer and whispered. "His call sign was Maverick. Well before that Tom Cruise movie—which wasn't half bad. I was a major; he was a lieutenant. Played racquetball with all the visiting generals; he beat the crap out of all of them. The absolute best student pilot anyone had ever seen. One instructor pilot accused him of being an old Air Force pilot. I thought the same thing—he could fly that jet better than I could. Remarkable fella." He jammed the wing of his eyeglasses back into his mouth. Her turn.

"He was this retired Marine, Air Force civilian, at the war college. The resident CIA officer…I think you can say she showed a great deal of favoritism toward him. We always wondered why."

The old general grimaced as if he had been poked with a stick. "How so?"

"We had several students from the three letter agencies and this Air Force civilian got the prized assignment during the final wargaming exercise. He was Chief of Station, and the resident CIA instructor acted as the ambassador. I remember at the conclusion of the exercise he was singled out for taking the exercise scenario into a different, more real-world direction. Knocked the socks off of the battle staff and the faculty. There was talk of him becoming an instructor. Even with all of the

461

special operators in school—SEALs, Army Delta, Marine Recon, Air Force Special Ops—as well as the civilian superstars from the three-letter agencies, he just stood out. He wasn't a normal student. And everyone knew it."

"He wasn't a normal fighter pilot student either," repeated the general, nodding. Then, "If it was...*him*...." Somehow the two officers had telepathically agreed not to utter his name. "...then I think his little stunt...rescuing those girls could have the unintended effect of blowing his cover, if it hasn't already. Not good." The eyeglass wing flew back into his mouth.

"Yes, sir. That's what I was just thinking. But Colonel Eastwood said Hunter had died and was buried at Arlington."

"I saw that too and didn't believe it for a military micro-minute. My assessment is that he is a very difficult man to kill. He didn't die in an accident."

"Wow. So, it had to be him. White man in black—I think the press called them coveralls. And a black helmet with four little binoculars."

Magnusson asserted, "There's no doubt it was a black flight suit. Black flight helmet, probably a helicopter helmet with the SEAL Team's panoramic NVGs." The general knew what the man had been wearing. What the press described was definitely a pilot. *He had to be working for the CIA. That is the only scenario which makes absolute sense.*

Frappier said, "I'm thinking, in hindsight, rescuing those girls was probably...in retrospect, it had to be a suicide mission. Whoever was running that slavery operation will be gunning to find him, punish and kill him."

General Magnusson nodded and cooed, "It's him. It's obvious. And if we can figure it out it's only a matter of time before the unfriendlies figure it out too. But Eastwood's special probably threw the bad guys completely off the track. He's dead."

Captain Frappier looked on forlornly. She nodded.

"What do you think, Pam? I think we just need to never bring him or his name up again." He sucked a lungsful of air. Something else had penetrated his defenses. He scribbled a note and handed it to her.

Drinks, dinner, 1930. Green Parrot? She smiled thinly while trying to remain professional. She nodded and stepped away from the general's desk. He watched her crush the pile carpeting with her heels.

EPILOGUE

1200 August 11, 2014
London

The last group of the day, a small group of 25 visitors, shielded their eyes and gazed up at one of the United Kingdom's most recognizable landmarks, the Tower of London. The guide—Jeremy—was doughy, delightful, funny, enthusiastic and interactive as he described. "It was formerly a fortress, a prison, and the execution site of three Queens of England." The tour group was atwitter as the guide led the group through the torture exhibition. In one of the rooms he announced, "Henry the Eighth was reportedly to have said after his sixth wife passed away—are there any children here—ok, good. Henry the Eighth said, 'Pussy and religion is all I need.'" The laughter reverberated against the Tower.

Jeremy counted, recounted, and double checked that everyone was there before he moved the group along to witness the opening ceremony performed by the Yeoman Warders, better known as the Beefeaters, trooping and stomping, and clacking their heels in precision movements. After the ceremonial changing of the guard and a delicious, afternoon tea, the group of men and women perambulated at a snail's pace through the rooms of Buckingham Palace. Seemingly out of thin air, a courtier appeared and approached a man and women who were lagging behind the group despite the gentle encouragements and admonishments of the tour guide to "stay together, please." The courtier checked their blue tour badges and pulled the two pikers out of the crowd. He directed them to follow him. Jeremy and group mouthed, "Good riddance" as the annoying pair continued their vector out of the building.

· · · · ·

Duncan Hunter emerged from the changing room in a tailored black suit, red power tie, and his polished black Lucchese crocodile cowboy boots. The boots didn't elicit a frown or a shake of the head from the courtier, but did cause a hefty raised eyebrow. *Americans and their damned cowboy boots!*

Nazy Cunningham had changed into an elegant pink chiffon maxi-dress. A delicate James Avery gold cross dangled between her breasts. The courtier gave Hunter a torrent of instructions, how to walk, where to walk.

"This is not a medal ceremony. Her Majesty will receive you in the appropriate manner," he explained. He exhaled in a bit of exasperation, as if he didn't approve of the knighthood for some American. He didn't have to like it, but he had a job to do, just as his father did, and his father did in the service of the Royal Family. He continued, "Do not hurry. Do not click your heels together like a Beefeater when you approach Her Majesty. Kneel on the pillow—only one knee—and lower your head. Once you touch the pillow, at that instant you become 'a squire.' The kneeling squire shall swear an oath. Follow Her Majesty's lead. Respond accordingly. After the ceremony you will return to the changing room. I will escort you. Any questions?"

Hunter gently shook his head. He turned to gaze at the furnishings and the endless ceilings. The artwork was total, old, stunning, and breathtaking from floor to ceiling. The Throne Room at Buckingham Palace was much larger and more elegant than he could ever envision. Hunter leaned over and asked Nazy, "How do I look?" In her best husky, estuary British she leaned into his ear and whispered, "Scrumptious. I want you to remember this as you're being knighted. While the Queen will be wearing underwear, I'm not."

He winked at her. Humor and suggestive thoughts were not what he needed at this moment. His stomach was doing six-G loops and catapult launches.

With a tug and a push from the courtier, they knew it was time. Nazy was ushered to the viewing area. There was no music. At the sound of his name, Duncan Hunter turned and walked sixty-feet down the middle of the Throne Room. Not too fast, not too slow. His legs shook, but not enough for the small private audience to notice. At the end of the red Persian carpet sat the Queen of England, in full ceremonial regalia and a crown.

The Queen liked what she saw and imperceptibly nodded. *He is worthy!*

As directed, Hunter stopped in front of the Queen, knelt with one knee on the velvet pillow, and lowered his head. His emotions were running so high he gritted his teeth to stop himself from shaking.

He heard the words that reverberated in the room.

The Queen's voice was strong and unwavering. "In times of war, knights were called to arms by their lords or by the King or Queen. Knights led foot soldiers and archers into battle. They were called upon in times of great trouble. Knights were trained to be brave men, chivalrous men, honorable men. Duncan Hunter, by your most heroic of actions, saving the countless lives of perfect strangers, subjects of the British Empire, you have repeatedly demonstrated the uncommon characteristics, the unrequited bravery, the unadulterated chivalry, and the unmitigated honor of a knight. You have trained for battle and have answered the call of the needy, those in great distress, and those in great peril. Duncan Hunter, do you swear you will always defend a lady in need?"

"I swear, I will always defend a lady in need."

"Duncan Hunter, do you swear you will always speak only the truth?"

"I swear, I will always speak only the truth."

"Duncan Hunter, do you swear you will always be charitable and defend the poor and helpless, in times of great distress and great peril?"

"I swear, I will always be charitable and defend the poor and helpless, in times of great distress and great peril."

"Duncan Hunter, do you swear you will never avoid dangerous paths out of fear?"

"I swear, I will never avoid dangerous paths out of fear."

"Duncan Hunter, do you swear you will always be brave?"

"I swear, I will always be brave."

Hunter felt the gentle tap of a sword on each shoulder. The Queen boomed, "I dub thee Sir Duncan; Knight of the Order of the Garter. Rise, Sir Duncan!"

Acronyms/Abbreviations

ABO	Aviator's Breathing oxygen
ACC	Area Control Center
ACP	Automatic Colt Pistol
AGL	Above Ground Level
AK	Automatic Kalashnikov
ANVIS	Aviator Night Vision
APU	Auxiliary Power Unit
AQ	Al-Qaeda
ATLS	Automating Takeoff and Landing System
ASR	Airport Surveillance Radar
BOLO	Be On the Lookout
C	Cargo aircraft
CIA	Central Intelligence Agency
CEO	Chief Executive Officer
CFR	Crash Fire Rescue
COS	Chief of Station
CTC	Counter Terrorism Center; short for NCTC
CVR	Cockpit Voice Recorder
C-4	Composition C-4; a variety of plastic explosive
DARPA	Defense Advanced Research Projects Agency
D.C.	District of Columbia
DCI	Director of Central Intelligence
DEVGRU	Naval Special Warfare Development Group
DIP	Diplomatic Passport
DME	Distance Measuring Equipment
DO	Director of Operations
DOD	Department of Defense
DOJ	Department of Justice
DOS	Disc Operating System
ETA	Estimated Time of Arrival
F	Fighter aircraft

FARC	Fuerzas Armadas Revolucionariasde Colombia; the Revolutionary Armed Forces of Colombia
FBI	Federal Bureau of Investigation
FLIR	Forward Looking Infra-Red
FSTC	Full Spectrum Training Center
G	Gravity
G	Gulfstream aircraft
G-IVSP	Gulfstream Model 4, Special Purpose
G-550	Gulfstream Model 550
GID	General Intelligence Directorate
GOC	Global Operations Center
GPS	Global Positioning System
GS	General Schedule
H	Helicopter
HQ	Headquarters
HVT	High-Value Target
ID	Identify/Identity/Identification
IED	Improvised Explosive Device
IC	Intelligence Community
ICBM	Intercontinental Ballistic Missile
IL	Ilyushin_Design Bureau
IO	Intelligence Officer
IARPA	Intelligence Advanced Research Projects Agency
ISR	Intelligence, Surveillance, and Reconnaissance
KGB	Komitet Gosudarstvennoy Bezopasnosti; the foreign intelligence and domestic security agency of the Soviet Union
LD	Laser Designator
LIDAR	Light Detection and Ranging
MI5	Military Intelligence, Section 5; the domestic counter-intelligence and security agency of the United Kingdom
MI6	Military Intelligence, Section 6; the secret intelligence service of the United Kingdom
MO	Modus Operendi
MPH	Miles per Hour
M-4	Carbine version of the longer barreled M16
NASA	National Aeronautics and Space Administration

NATO	North Atlantic Treaty Organization
NCS	National Clandestine Service
NCTC	National Counter Terrorism Center
NE	Near East Division
NRO	National Reconnaissance Office
NSA	National Security Agency
O	Observation aircraft
ONI	Office of Naval Intelligence
OSS	Office of Strategic Services
PDB	President's Daily Brief
PhD	Doctor of Philosophy
POTUS	President of the United States
RAPCON	Radar Approach Control
ROTC	Reserve Officer Training Corps
RPM	Revolutions per Minute
SAD	Special Activities Division
SAM	Surface to Air Missile
SAP	Special Access Program
S&T	Science and Technology Directorate
SCI	Sensitive Compartmented Information
SCIF	Sensitive Compartmented Information Facility
SEAL	Sea, Air, Land
SIS	Senior Intelligence Service
SLBM	Submarine Launched Ballistic Missile
SOC	Special Operations Command
SOF	Special Operations Forces
SR	Surveillance Reconnaissance aircraft; SR-71
STRATCOM	Strategic Command
STE	Secure Terminal Equipment
SUV	Sport Utility Vehicle
SWAT	Special Weapons and Tactics
TS	Top Secret
TSA	Transportation Security Administration
TS/SCI	Top Secret/Sensitive Compartmented Information
TV	Television
10-4	Message Received, from Ten Code
10-20	What is your Location, from Ten Code

UAV	Unmanned Aerial Vehicle
U.S.	United States
U.S.S.	United States Ship
USTDA	United States Trade and Development Agency
UV	Ultra Violet
VIP	Very Important Person
V12	V-type engine with twelve cylinders
WWII	World War Two
Y	Prototype aircraft
YO-3A	Prototype Observation aircraft, model 3, series A
XKE	Jaguar E-Type
XO	Executive Officer

ACKNOWLEDGEMENTS

Without some major help this book could not have been possible. A special salute to Colonel George "Curious" Fenimore, USAF Retired, and the "recovering attorney" Rosemary Harris for their continued wisdom, guidance, and suggestions that helped turn my ramblings and ruminations into a story.

Duncan "Maverick" Hunter wishes to salute and say, "Thanks" to the American patriots Steve "Mudflap" McGrew and Chad Prather for singing *Friends in Safe Spaces* at his 4th of July picnic.

And a very special "thank you" to my editor and wife, Barbara, who was (sometimes necessarily) brutally honest with the manuscript and story, and who helped improve my thoughts and words to make me a better writer. I still need a little work. Any errors found in this novel are my responsibility and mine alone.

View other Black Rose Writing titles at www.blackrosewriting.com/books and use promo code **PRINT** to receive a **20% discount** when purchasing.

BLACK ROSE
writing™

Made in the USA
Las Vegas, NV
05 February 2024

85334003R00277